The First Cadfael Omnibus

Ellis Peters
The First Cadfael Omnibus

A MORBID TASTE FOR BONES
ONE CORPSE TOO MANY
MONK'S-HOOD

Futura

A Futura BOOK

First published in Great Britain in 1990 by Futura Publications
A division of Macdonald & Co (Publishers) Ltd
London & Sydney

A MORBID TASTE FOR BONES first published by Macmillan in 1977 and by Futura
in paperback in 1984
ONE CORPSE TOO MANY first published by Macmillan in 1979 and by Futura in
paperback in 1984
MONK'S-HOOD first published by Macmillan in 1980 and by Futura in paperback in
1984

Reprinted 1990

Typeset by Selectmove Ltd., London
Reproduced, printed and bound in Great Britain by
The Guernsey Press Co. Ltd, Guernsey, Channel Islands.

ISBN 0 7088 4922 9

Futura Publications
A Division of
Macdonald & Co (Publishers) Ltd
Orbit House
1 New Fetter Lane
London EC4A 1AR

A member of Maxwell Macmillan Pergamon Publishing Corporation

Contents

A MORBID TASTE FOR BONES

Chapter One

N THE fine, bright morning in early May when the whole sensational affair of the Gwytherin relics may properly be considered to have begun, Brother Cadfael had been up long before Prime, pricking out cabbage seedlings before the day was aired, and his thoughts were all on birth, growth and fertility, not at all on graves and reliquaries and violent deaths, whether of saints, sinners or ordinary decent, fallible men like himself. Nothing troubled his peace but the necessity to take himself indoors for Mass, and the succeeding half-hour of chapter, which was always liable to stray over by an extra ten minutes. He grudged the time from his more congenial labours out here among the vegetables, but there was no evading his duty. He had, after all, chosen this cloistered life with his eyes open, he could not complain even of those parts of it he found unattractive, when the whole suited him very well, and gave him the kind of satisfaction he felt now, as he straightened his back and looked about him.

He doubted if there was a finer Benedictine garden in the whole kingdom, or one better supplied with herbs both good for spicing meats, and also invaluable as medicine. The main orchards and lands of the Shrewsbury abbey of Saint Peter and Saint Paul lay on the northern side of the road, outside the monastic enclave, but here, in the enclosed garden within the walls, close to the abbot's fish-ponds and the brook that worked the abbey mill, Brother Cadfael ruled unchallenged. The herbarium in particular was his kingdom, for he had built it up gradually through fifteen years of labour, and added to it many exotic plants of his own careful raising, collected in a roving youth that had taken him as far afield as Venice, and Cyprus and the Holy Land. For Brother Cadfael had come late to the monastic life, like a battered ship settling at last for a quiet harbour. He was well aware that in the first years of his vows the novices and lay servants had been wont to point him out to one another with awed whisperings.

'See that brother working in the garden there? The thickset fellow who rolls from one leg to the other like a sailor? You wouldn't think to look at him, would you, that he went on crusade when he was young? He was with Godfrey de Bouillon at Antioch, when the Saracens surrendered it. And he took to the seas as a captain when the king of Jerusalem ruled all the coast of the Holy Land, and served against the corsairs ten years! Hard to believe it now, eh?'

Brother Cadfael himself found nothing strange in his wide-ranging career, and had forgotten nothing and regretted nothing. He saw no contradiction in the delight he had taken in battle and adventure, and the keen pleasure he now found in quietude. Spiced, to be truthful, with more than a little mischief when he could get it, as he liked his victuals well-flavoured, but quietude all the same, a ship becalmed and enjoying it. And probably the youngsters who eyed him with such curiosity also whispered that in a life such as he had led there must have been some encounters with women, and not all purely chivalrous, and what sort of grounding was that for the conventual life?

They were right about the women. Quite apart from Richildis, who had not unnaturally tired of waiting for his return after ten years, and married a solid yeoman with good prospects in the shire, and no intention of flying off to the wars, he remembered other ladies, in more lands than one, with whom he had enjoyed encounters pleasurable to both parties, and no harm to either. Bianca, drawing water at the stone well-head in Venice – the Greek boat-girl Arianna – Mariam, the Saracen widow who sold spices and fruit in Antioch, and who found him man enough to replace for a while the man she had lost. The light encounters and the grave, not one of them had left any hard feelings behind. He counted that as achievement enough, and having known them was part of the harmonious balance that made him content now with this harboured, contemplative life, and gave him patience and insight to bear with these cloistered, simple souls who had put on the Benedictine habit as a life's profession, while for him it was a timely retirement. When you have done everything else, perfecting a conventual herb-garden is a fine and satisfying thing to do. He could not conceive of coming to this stasis having done nothing else whatever.

Five minutes more, and he must go and wash his hands and repair to the church for Mass. He used the respite to walk the length of his pale-flowered, fragrant inner kingdom, where Brother John and Brother Columbanus, two youngsters barely a year tonsured, were busy weeding and edge-trimming. Glossy and dim, oiled and furry, the leaves tendered every possible variation on green. The flowers were mostly shy, small, almost furtive, in soft, sidelong colours, lilacs and shadowy blues and diminutive yellows, for they were the unimportant and unwanted part, but for ensuring seed to follow. Rue, sage, rosemary, gilvers, gromwell, ginger, mint, thyme, columbine, herb of grace, savoury, mustard, every manner of herb grew here, fennel, tansy, basil and dill, parsley, chervil and marjoram. He had taught the uses even of the unfamiliar to all his assistants, and made plain their dangers, too, for the benefit of herbs is in their right proportion, and over-dosage can be worse than the disease. Small of habit, modest of tint, close-growing and shy, his herbs called attention to themselves only by their disseminated sweetness as the sun rose on them. But behind their shrinking ranks rose others taller and more clamorous, banks of peonies grown for their spiced seeds, and lofty, pale-leaved, budding poppies, as yet barely showing the white or purple-black petals through their close armour. They stood as tall as a short man, and their home was the eastern part of the middle sea, and from that far place Cadfael had brought their ancestors in the seed long ago, and raised and cross-bred them in his own garden, before ever he brought the perfected progeny here with him to make medicines against pain, the chief enemy of man. Pain, and the absence of sleep, which is the most beneficent remedy for pain.

The two young men, with habits kilted to the knee, were just straightening their backs and dusting the soil from their hands, as well aware as he of the hour. Brother Columbanus would not for the world have let slip one grain of his duties, or countenanced such a backsliding in any of his fellows. A very comely, well-made, upstanding young fellow he was, with

11

a round, formidable, Norman head, as he came from a formidable, aristocratic Norman family, a younger son despatched to make his way in the monastic ranks as next-best to inheriting land. He had stiff, upstanding yellow hair and full blue eyes, and his modest demeanour and withdrawn pallor tended to obscure the muscular force of his build. Not a very comfortable colleague, Brother Columbanus, for in spite of his admirable bodily equipment he had some while since proved that he had a mental structure of alarming sensitivity, and was liable to fits of emotional stress, crises of conscience, and apocalyptic visions far removed from the implications of his solid skull. But he was young and idealistic, he had time to get over his self-torments. Brother Cadfael had worked with him for some months, and had every hope for him. He was willing, energetic, and almost too eager to please. Possibly he felt his debt to his aristocratic house too nearly, and feared a failure that would reflect on his kin. You cannot be of high Norman blood, and not excel! Brother Cadfael felt for any such victims as found themselves in this trap, coming, as he did, of antique Welsh stock without superhuman pretensions. So he tolerated Brother Columbanus with equanimity, and doctored his occasional excesses philosophically. The juice of the paynim poppies had quieted Columbanus more than once when his religious fervour prostrated him.

Well, at any rate there was no nonsense of that kind with the other one! Brother John was as plain and practical as his name, a square young man with a snub nose and an untamable ring of wiry russet curls round his tonsure. He was always hungry, and his chief interest in all things that grew in gardens was whether they were eatable, and of agreeable flavour. Come autumn he would certainly find a way of working his passage into the orchards. Just now he was content to help Brother Cadfael prick out early lettuces, and wait for the soft fruits to come into season. He was a handsome, lusty, good-natured soul, who seemed to have blundered into this enclosed life by some incomprehensible error, and not yet to have realised that he had come to the wrong place. Brother Cadfael detected a lively sense of mischief the fellow to his own, but never yet given its head in a wider world, and confidently expected that some day this particular red-crested bird would certainly fly. Meantime, he got his entertainment wherever it offered, and found it sometimes in unexpected places.

'I must be in good time,' he said, unkilting his gown and dusting his hands cheerfully on his seat. 'I'm reader this week.'

So he was, Cadfael recalled, and however dull the passages they chose for him in the refectory, and innocuous the saints and martyrs he would have to celebrate at chapter. John would contrive to imbue them with drama and gusto from his own sources. Give him the beheading of Saint John the Baptist, and he would shake the foundations.

'You read for the glory of God and the saints, brother,' Columbanus reminded him, with loving reproof and somewhat offensive humility, 'not for your own!' Which showed either how little he knew about it, or how false he could be, one or the other.

'The blessed thought is ever in my mind,' said Brother John with irrepressible zest, and winked at Cadfael behind his colleague's back, and set off enthusiastically along the aisles of shrubs towards the abbot's gate and the great court. They followed him more demurely, the slender, fair, agile youth and the squat, barrel-chested, bandy-legged veteran of fifty-seven. Was I ever, wondered Cadfael, rolling with his powerful seaman's gait beside the other's long, supple strides, as young and earnest as this? It cost him an effort to recall that Columbanus was actually fully twenty-five, and the sprig of a sophisticated and ambitious house. Whose fortunes, surely, were not founded wholly on piety?

This third Mass of the day was non-parochial and brief, and after it the Benedictine brothers of the abbey of Shrewsbury filed in procession from the choir into the chapter-house, and made their way to their stalls in due order, Abbot Heribert leading. The abbot was old, of mild nature and pliant, a gentle grey ascetic very wishful of peace and harmony around him. His figure was unimpressive, though his face was beguiling in its anxious sweetness. Novices and pupils were easy in his presence, when they could reach it, which was by no means always easy, for the extremely impressive figure of Prior Robert was liable to loom between.

Prior Robert Pennant, of mixed Welsh and English blood, was more than six feet tall, attenuated and graceful, silver-grey of hair at fifty, blanched and beautiful of visage, with long, aristocratic features and lofty marble brow. There was no man in the midland shires would look more splendid in a mitre, superhuman in height and authority, and there was no man in England better aware of it, or more determined to prove it at the earliest opportunity. His very motions, sweeping across the chapter-house to his stall, understudied the pontificate.

13

After him came Brother Richard the sub-prior, his antithesis, large, ungainly, amiable and benevolent, of a good mind, but mentally lazy. Doubtful if he would ever become prior when Robert achieved his end, with so many ambitious and industrious younger men eyeing the prospect of advancement, and willing to go to a great deal of trouble to secure it.

After Richard came all the other brothers in their hierarchies. Brother Benedict the sacristan, Brother Anselm the precentor, Brother Matthew the cellarer, Brother Dennis the hospitaller, Brother Edmund the infirmarer, Brother Oswald the almoner, Brother Jerome, the prior's clerk, and Brother Paul, master of the novices, followed by the commonalty of the convent, and a very flourishing number they made. Among the last of them Brother Cadfael rolled to his own chosen corner, well to the rear and poorly lit, half-concealed behind one of the stone pillars. Since he held no troublesome parchment office, he was unlikely to be called upon to speak in chapter upon the various businesses of the house, and when the matter in hand was dull into the bargain it was his habit to employ the time to good account by sleeping, which from long usage he could do bolt upright and undetected in his shadowy corner. He had a sixth sense which alerted him at need, and brought him awake instantly and plausibly. He had even been known to answer a question pat, when it was certain he had been asleep when it was put to him

On this particular May morning he remained awake long enough to enjoy Brother John's extraction of the last improbable ounce of drama from the life of some obscure saint whose day fell on the morrow, but when the cellarer began to expound a complicated matter of a legacy partly to the altar of Our Lady, partly to the infirmary, he composed himself to slumber. After all, he knew that most of the remaining time, once a couple of minor malefactors had been dealt with, would be given to Prior Robert's campaign to secure the relics and patronage of a powerful saint for the monastery. For the past few months very little else had been discussed. The prior had had it on his mind, in fact, ever since the Cluniac house of Wenlock had rediscovered, with great pride and jubilation, the tomb of their original foundress, Saint Milburga, and installed her bones triumphantly on their altar. An alien priory, only a few miles distant, with its own miracle-working saint, and the great Benedictine house of Shrewsbury as empty of relics as a plundered almsbox! It was more than Prior Robert could stomach. He had been scouring

14

the borderlands for a spare saint now for a year or more, looking hopefully towards Wales, where it was well known that holy men and women had been common as mushrooms in autumn in the past, and as little regarded. Brother Cadfael had no wish to hear the latest of his complaints and urgings. He slept.

The heat of the sun rebounded from honed facets of pale, baked rock, scorching his face, as the floating arid dust burned his throat. From where he crouched with his fellows in cover he could see the long crest of the wall, and the steel-capped heads of the guards on the turrets glittering in the fierce light. A landscape carved out of reddish stone and fire, all deep gullies and sheer cliffs, with never a cool green leaf to temper it, and before him the object of all his journeyings, the holy city of Jerusalem, crowned with towers and domes within its white walls. The dust of battle hung in the air, dimming the clarity of battlement and gate, and the hoarse shouting and clashing of armour filled his ears. He was waiting for the trumpet to sound the final assault, and keeping well in cover while he waited, for he had learned to respect the range of the short, curly Saracen bow. He saw the banners surge forward out of hiding, streaming on the burning wind. He saw the flash of the raised trumpet, and braced himself for the blare.

The sound that brought him leaping wide-awake out of his dream was loud enough and stirring enough, but not the brazen blast of a trumpet, nor was he launched from his stillness towards the triumphant storming of Jerusalem. He was back in his stall in the dark corner of the chapter-house, and starting to his feet as alertly as the rest, and with the same consternation and alarm. And the shriek that had awakened him was just subsiding into a series of rending moans and broken cries that might have been of extreme pain or extreme ecstasy. In the open space in the centre of the chapter-house Brother Columbanus lay on his face, threshing and jerking like a landed fish, beating his forehead and his palms against the flagstones, kicking and flailing with long, pale legs bared to the knee by his contortions, and barking out of him those extraordinary sounds of shattering physical excitement, while the nearest of the brothers hovered in helpless shock, and Prior Robert with lifted hands exhorted and exclaimed.

Brother Cadfael and Brother Edmund, the infirmarer, reached the victim together, kneeled over him one on either side, and restrained him from battering his brains out against the stones of the floor, or dislocating his joints in his flailings.

15

'Falling sickness!' said Brother Edmund tersely, and wedged the thick cord of Columbanus' girdle between his teeth, and a fold of his habit with it, to prevent him from biting his tongue.

Brother Cadfael was less certain of the diagnosis, for these were not the grunting, helpless noises of an epileptic in an attack, but such as might be expected from a hysterical woman in a frenzy. But at least the treatment stopped half the noise, and even appeared to diminish the vigour of the convulsions, though they resumed again as soon as the restraining grip on him was loosed.

'Poor young man!' fluttered Abbot Heribert, hovering in the background. 'So sudden, so cruel an affliction! Handle him gently! Carry him to the infirmary. We must pray for his restoration.'

Chapter broke up in some disorder. With the help of Brother John, and certain others of a practical turn of mind, they got Brother Columbanus securely but comfortably swathed in a sheet, confining arms and legs so that he could do himself no injury, wedged his teeth apart with a wooden spit instead of the cloth, on which he might have gagged and choked, and carried him on a shutter to the infirmary, where they got him into bed, and secured him there with bandages round breast and thighs. He moaned and gurgled and heaved still, but with weakening force, and when they had managed to get a draught of Brother Cadfael's poppy-juice into him his moans subsided into pitiful mutterings, and the violence of his struggles against his confinement grew feebler.

'Take good care of him,' said Prior Robert, frowning anxiously over the young man's bed. 'I think someone should be constantly by to watch over him, in case the fit comes again. You have your other sick men to attend to, you cannot sit by his side day and night. Brother Jerome, I put this sufferer in your charge, and excuse you from all other duties while he needs you.'

'Willingly,' said Brother Jerome, 'and prayerfully!' He was Prior Robert's closest associate and most devoted hanger-on, and an inevitable choice whenever Robert required strict obedience and meticulous reporting, as might well be the case where a brother of the house succumbed to what might elsewhere be whispered abroad as a fit of madness.

'Stay with him in particular during the night,' said the prior, 'for in the night a man's resistance falters, and his bodily evils may rise against him. If he sleeps peacefully, you may rest also, but remain close, in case he needs you.'

16

'He'll sleep within the hour,' said Cadfael confidently, 'and may pass into natural sleep well before night. God willing, he may put this off before morning.'

For his part, he thought Brother Columbanus lacked sufficient work for both mind and body, and took his revenge for his deprivation in these excesses, half-wilful, half-involuntary, and both to be pitied and censured. But he retained enough caution to reserve a doubt with every conviction. He was not sure he knew any of his adopted brothers well enough to judge with certainty. Well, Brother John – yes, perhaps! But inside the conventual life or outside, cheerful, blunt, extrovert Brother Johns are few and far between.

Brother Jerome appeared at chapter next morning with an exalted countenance, and the air of one bursting with momentous news. At Abbot Heribert's mild reproof for leaving his patient without permission, he folded his hands meekly and bowed his head, but lost none of his rapt assurance.

'Father, I am sent here by another duty, that seemed to me even mere urgent. I have left Brother Columbanus sleeping, though not peacefully, for even his sleep is tormented. But two lay-brothers are watching by him. If I have done wrong, I will abide it humbly.'

'Our brother is no better?' asked the abbot anxiously.

'He is still deeply troubled, and when he wakes he raves. But, Father, this is my errand! There is a sure hope for him! In the night I have been miraculously visited. I have come to tell you what divine mercy has instructed me. Father, in the small hours I fell into a doze beside Brother Columbanus' bed, and had a marvellously sweet dream.'

By this time he had everyone's attention, even Brother Cadfael was wide awake. 'What, another of them?' whispered Brother John wickedly into his ear. 'The plague's spreading!'

'Father, it seemed to me that the wall of the room opened, and a great light shone in, and through the light and radiating the light there came in a most beautiful young virgin, and stood beside our brother's bed, and spoke to me. She told me that her name was Winifred, and that in Wales there is a holy spring, that rose to the light where she suffered martyrdom. And she said that if Brother Columbanus bathed in the water of that well, he would surely be healed, and restored at once to his senses. Then she uttered a blessing upon our house, and vanished in a great light, and I awoke.'

17

Through the murmur of excitement that went round the chapter-house, Prior Robert's voice rose in reverent triumph: 'Father Abbot, we are being guided! Our quest for a saint has drawn to us this sign of favour, in token that we should persevere.'

'Winifred!' said the abbot doubtfully. 'I do not recall clearly the story of this saint and martyr. There are so many of them in Wales. Certainly we ought to send Brother Columbanus to her holy spring, it would be ingratitude to neglect so clear an omen. But exactly where is it to be found?'

Prior Robert looked round for the few Welshmen among the brothers, passed somewhat hurriedly over Brother Cadfael, who had never been one of his favourites, perhaps by reason of a certain spark in his eye, as well as his notoriously worldly past, and lit gladly upon old Brother Rhys, who was virtually senile but doctrinally safe, and had the capacious if capricious memory of the very old. 'Brother, can you tell us the history of this saint, and where her well is to be found?'

The old man was slow to realise that he had become the centre of attention. He was shrunken like a bird, and toothless, and used to a tolerant oblivion. He began hesitantly, but warmed to the work as he found all eyes upon him.

'Saint Winifred, you say, Father? Everybody knows of Saint Winifred. You'll find her spring by the name they gave the place, Holywell, it's no great way in from Chester. But she's not there. You won't find her grave at Holywell.'

'Tell us about her,' coaxed Prior Robert, almost fawning in his eagerness. 'Tell us all her story.'

'Saint Winifred,' declaimed the old man, beginning to enjoy his hour of glory, 'was the only child of a knight named Tevyth, who lived in those parts when the princes were yet heathens. But this knight and all his household were converted by Saint Beuno, and made him a church there, and gave him house-room. The girl was devoted even above her parents, and pledged herself to a virgin life, hearing Mass every day. But one Sunday it happened that she was sick, and stayed at home when all the rest of the household went to church. And there came to the door the prince of those parts. Cradoc, son of the king, who had fallen in love with her at a distance. For this girl was very beautiful. *Very* beautiful!' gloated Brother Rhys, and licked his lips loudly. Prior Robert visibly recoiled, but refrained from stopping the flow by reproof. 'He pleaded that he was hot and parched from hunting,' said Brother Rhys darkly, 'and asked

18

for a drink of water, and the girl let him in and gave him to drink. Then,' he shrilled, hunching himself in his voluminous habit and springing erect with a vigour nobody present would have credited, 'he pressed his suit upon her, and grappled her in his arms. *Thus!*' The effort was almost too much for him, and moreover, the prior was eyeing him in alarm; he subsided with dignity. 'The faithful virgin put him off with soft words, and escaping into another room, climbed from a window and fled towards the church. But finding that she had eluded him, Prince Cradoc took horse and rode after, and overtaking her just within sight of the church, and dreading that she would reveal his infamy, struck off her head with his sword.'

He paused for the murmur of horror, pity and indignation, and got it, with a flurry of prayerfully-folded hands, and a tribute of round eyes.

'Then thus piteously she came by her death and beatitude?' intoned Brother Jerome enthusiastically.

'Not a bit of it!' snapped Brother Rhys. He had never liked Brother Jerome. 'Saint Beuno and the congregation were coming out of the church, and saw what had passed. The saint drew a terrible curse upon the murderer, who at once sank to the ground, and began to melt like wax in fire, until all his body had sunk away into the grass. Then Saint Beuno fitted the head of the virgin onto her neck, and the flesh grew together, and she stood up alive, and the holy fountain sprang up on the spot where she arose.'

They waited, spellbound, and he let them wait. He had lost interest after the death.

'And afterwards?' insinuated Prior Robert. 'What did the saint do with her restored life?'

'She went on a pilgrimage to Rome,' said Brother Rhys indifferently, 'and she attended at a great synod of saints, and was appointed to be prioress over a community of virgin sisters at Gwytherin, by Llanrwst. And there she lived many years, and did many miracles in her lifetime. If it should be called her lifetime? She was once dead already. When she died a second time, that was where it befell.' He felt nothing concerning this residue of life, he offered it with a shrug. The girl had had her chance with Prince Cradoc, and let it slip, obviously her natural bent was to be prioress of a nest of virgins, and there was nothing more to be told about her.

'And she is buried there at Gwytherin?' persisted the prior. 'And her miracles continued after death?'

'So I have heard. But it's a long time,' said the old man, 'since I've heard her name mentioned. And longer since I was in those parts.'

Prior Robert stood in the circle of sunlight that filtered between the pillars of the chapter-house, drawn to his full imposing height, and turned a radiant face and commanding eyes upon Abbot Heribert.

'Father, does it not seem to you that our reverent search for a patron of great power and sanctity is being divinely guided? This gentle saint has visited us in person, in Brother Jerome's dream, and beckoned us to bring our afflicted brother to her for healing. Shall we not hope, also, that she will again show us the next step? If she does indeed receive our prayers and restore Brother Columbanus to health of body and mind, may we not be encouraged to hope that she will come in person and dwell among us? That we may humbly beg the church's sanction to take up her blessed relics and house them fittingly here in Shrewsbury? To the great glory and lustre of our house!'

'And of Prior Robert!' whispered Brother John in Cadfael's ear.

'It certainly seems that she has shown us singular favour,' admitted Abbot Heribert.

'Then, Father, have I your leave to send Brother Columbanus with a safe escort to Holywell? This very day?'

'Do so,' said the abbot, 'with the prayers of us all, and may he return as Saint Winifred's own messenger, hale and grateful.'

The deranged man, still wandering in mind and communing with himself in incoherent ravings, was led away out of the gatehouse on the first stage of his journey immediately after the midday meal, mounted on a mule, with a high, cradling saddle to give him some security from falling, in case the violent fit took him again, and with Brother Jerome and a brawny lay-brother one on either side, to support him at need. Columbanus looked about him with wide, pathetic, childlike eyes, and seemed to know nobody, though he went submissively and trustfully where he was led.

'I could have done with a nice little trip into Wales,' said Brother John wistfully, looking after them as they rounded the corner and vanished towards the bridge over the Severn. 'But I probably shouldn't have seen the right visions. Jerome will do the job better.'

'Boy,' said Brother Cadfael tolerantly, 'you become more of an unbeliever every day.'

'Not a bit of it! I'm as willing to believe in the girl's sanctity and miracles as any man. We know the saints have power to help and bless, and I'll believe they have the goodwill, too. But when it's Prior Robert's faithful hound who has the dream, you're asking me to believe in *his* sanctity, not hers! And in any case, isn't her favour glory enough? I don't see why they should want to dig up the poor lady's dust. It seems like charnel-house business to me, not church business. And you think exactly the same,' he said firmly, and stared out his elder, eye to eye.

'When I want to hear my echo,' said Brother Cadfael, 'I will at least speak first. Come on, now, and get that bottom strip of ground dug, there are kale plants waiting to go in.'

The delegation to Holywell was gone five days, and came home towards evening in a fine shower of rain and a grand glow of grace, chanting prayers as the three entered the courtyard. In the midst rode Brother Columbanus, erect and graceful and jubilant, if that word could be used for one so humble in his gladness. His face was bright and clear, his eyes full of wonder and intelligence. No man ever looked less mad, or less likely to be subject to the falling sickness. He went straight to the church and gave thanks and praise to God and Saint Winifred on his knees, and from the altar all three went dutifully to report to the abbot, prior and sub-prior, in the abbot's lodging.

'Father,' said Brother Columbanus, eager and joyous, 'I have no skill to tell what has befallen me, for I know less than these who have cared for me in my delirium. All I know is that I was taken on this journey like a man in an ill dream, and went where I was taken, not knowing how to fend for myself, or what I ought to do. And suddenly I was like a man awakened out of that nightmare to a bright morning and a world of spring, and I was standing naked in the grass beside a well, and these good brothers were pouring water over me that healed as it touched. I knew myself and them, and only marvelled where I might be, and how I came there. Which they willingly told me. And then we went, all, and many people of that place with us, to sing Mass in a little church that stands close by the well. Now I know that I owe my recovery to the intervention of Saint Winifred, and I praise and worship her from my heart, as I do God who caused her to take pity on me. The rest these brothers will tell.'

21

The lay-brother was large, taciturn, weary – having done all the work throughout – and by this time somewhat bored with the whole business. He made the appropriate exclamations where needed, but left the narrative in the able hands of Brother Jerome, who told all with zest. How they had brought their patient to the village of Holywell, and asked the inhabitants for directions and aid, and been shown where the saint had risen living after her martyrdom, in the silver fountain that still sprang in the same spot, furnished now with a stone basin to hold its sacred flow. There they had led the rambling Columbanus, stripped him of habit, shirt and drawers, and poured the sacred water over him, and instantly he had stood erect and lifted his hands in prayer, and given thanks for a mind restored. Afterwards he had asked them in wonder how he came there, and what had happened to him, and had been greatly chastened and exalted at his humbling and his deliverance, and most grateful to his patroness, by whose guidance he had been made whole.

'And, Father, the people there told us that the saint is indeed buried at Gwytherin, where she died after her ministry, and that the place where her body is laid has done many miracles. But they say that her tomb, after so long, is neglected and little thought of, and it may well be that she longs for a better recognition, and to be installed in some place where pilgrims may come, where she may be revered as is her due, and have room to enlarge her grace and blessing to reach more people in need.'

'You are inspired, having been present at this miracle,' said Prior Robert, tall and splendid with faith rewarded, 'and you speak out what I have felt in listening to you. Surely Saint Winifred is calling us to her rescue as she came to the rescue of Brother Columbanus. Many have need of her goodness as he had, and know nothing of her. In our hands she would be exalted as she deserves, and those who need her grace would know where to come and seek it. I pray that we may mount that expedition of faith to which she summons us. Father Abbot, give me your leave to petition the church, and bring this blessed lady home to rest here among us, and be our proudest boast. For I believe it is her will and her command.'

'In the name of God,' said Abbot Heribert devoutly, 'I approve that project, and pray the blessing of heaven upon it!'

'He had it all planned beforehand,' said Brother John over the bed of mint, between envy and scorn. 'That was all a show, all

22

that wonder and amazement, and asking who Saint Winifred was, and where to find her. He knew it all along. He'd already picked her out from those he's discovered neglected in Wales, and decided she was the one most likely to be available, as well as the one to shed most lustre on him. But it had to come out into the open by miraculous means. There'll be another prodigy whenever he needs his way smoothed for him, until he gets the girl here safely installed in the church, to his glory. It's a great enterprise, he means to climb high on the strength of it. So he starts out with a vision, and a prodigious healing, and divine grace leading his footsteps. It's as plain as the nose on your face.'

'And are you saying,' asked Brother Cadfael mildly, 'that Brother Columbanus is in the plot as well as Brother Jerome, and that falling fit of his was a fake, too? I should have to be very sure of my reward in heaven before I volunteered to break the paving with my forehead, even to provide Prior Robert with a miracle.'

Brother John considered seriously, frowning. 'No, that I don't say. We all know our meek white lamb is liable to the horrors over a penance scamped, and ecstasies over a vigil or a fast, and pouring ice-cold water over him at Holywell would be the very treatment to jolt him back into his right wits. We could just as well have tossed him in the fish-pond here! But of course *he*'d believe what they told him, and credit it all to the saint. Catch him missing such a chance! No, I wouldn't say he was a party to it – not knowingly. But he gave them the opportunity for a splendid demonstration of grace. You notice it was Jerome who was set to take care of him overnight! It takes only one man to be favoured with a vision, but it has to be the right man.' He rolled a sprig of the young green leaves sadly between his palms, and the fragrance distilled richly on the early morning air. 'And it will be the right men who'll accompany Prior Robert into Wales,' he said with sour certainty. 'You'll see!'

No doubt about it, this young man was hankering after a glimpse of the world again, and a breath of air from outside the walls. Brother Cadfael pondered, not only with sympathy for his young assistant, but also with some pleasurable stirrings of his own. So momentous an event in the otherwise even course of monastic life ought not be missed. Besides the undoubted possibilities of mischief!

'True!' he said thoughtfully. 'Perhaps we ought to take some steps to leaven the lump. Wales should not be left with the notion that Jerome is the best Shrewsbury can muster, that's very true.'

'You have about as much chance of being invited as I,' said Brother John with his customary bluntness. 'Jerome is sure of his place, Prior Robert must have his right hand with him. And Columbanus, fool innocent, was the instrument of grace, and could be made to serve the same turn again. Brother Sub-Prior they have to take along, for form's sake. Surely we could think up some way of getting a foot in the door? They can't move for a few days yet, the carpenters and carvers are working hard on this splendid reliquary coffin they're going to take with them for the lady, but it will take them a while to finish it. Get your wits to work, brother! There isn't anything you couldn't do, if you've a mind! Prior or no prior!'

'Well, well, did I say you had no faith?' wondered Brother Cadfael, charmed and disarmed. 'I might worm my own way in, there could be ways, but how am I to recommend a graceless rogue like you? What are you good at, to be taken along on such an errand?'

'I'm a good hand with mules,' said Brother John hopefully, 'and you don't think Prior Robert intends to go on foot, I suppose? Or to do the grooming and feeding and watering himself? Or the mucking-out? They'll need *somebody* to do the hard work and wait on them. Why not me?'

It was, indeed, something nobody as yet seemed to have thought of. And why take a lay-brother, if there was a cloister-brother, with a sweet voice in the Mass, willing to do the sweating into the bargain? And the boy deserved his outing, since he was willing to earn it the hard way. Besides, he might be useful before the end. If not to Prior Robert, to Brother Cadfael.

'We'll see,' he said, and with that drove his mutinous protégé back to the work in hand. But after dinner, in the somnolent half-hour of sleep for the elders and play for the novices, he sought out Abbot Heribert in his study.

'Father Abbot, it is on my mind that we are undertaking this pilgrimage to Gwytherin without full consideration. First we must send to the bishop of Bangor, in whose see Gwytherin lies, for without his approval the matter cannot proceed. Now it is not essential to have a speaker fluent in Welsh there, since the bishop is obviously conversant with Latin. But not every parish priest in Wales has that tongue, and it is vital to be able to speak freely with the priest at Gwytherin, should the bishop sanction our quest. But most of all, the see of Bangor is wholly within the sovereignty of the king of Gwynedd, and surely his goodwill and permission are as essential as those of the church. The princes of Gwynedd speak only Welsh, though they have learned clerks. Father Prior, certainly, has a smattering of Welsh, but. . . .'

'That is very true,' said Abbot Heribert, easily dismayed. 'It is but a smattering. And the king's agreement is all-important. Brother Cadfael, Welsh is your first, best language, and has no mysteries for you. Could you . . . ? The garden, I am aware. . . . But with your aid there would be no problem.'

'In the garden,' said Brother Cadfael, 'everything is well forward, and can manage without me ten days or more, and take no hurt. I should be glad indeed to be the interpreter, and lend my skills also in Gwytherin.'

'Then so be it!' sighed the abbot in heartfelt relief. 'Go with Prior Robert, and be our voice to the Welsh people. I shall sanction your errand myself, and you will have my authority.'

He was old and human and gentle, full of experience, short on ambition, self-righteousness and resolution. There could have been two ways of approaching him concerning Brother John, Cadfael took the more honest and simple way.

'Father, there is a young brother concerning whose vocation I have doubts, but concerning whose goodness I have none. He is close to me, and I would that he might find his true way, for if he finds it he will not forsake it. But it may not be with us. I beg that I may take him with me, as our hewer of wood and drawer of water in this enterprise, to allow him time to consider.'

Abbot Heribert looked faintly dismayed and apprehensive, but not unsympathetic. Perhaps he remembered long-ago days when his own vocation had suffered periods of storm.

'I should be sorry,' he said, 'to refuse a choice to any man who may be better fitted to serve God elsewhere. Which of us can say he has never looked over his shoulder? You have not,' he questioned delicately, approaching the aspect that really daunted him, though with a cautiously dauntless face, 'broached this matter to Prior Robert?'

'No, Father,' said Brother Cadfael virtuously. 'I thought it wrong to charge him with so small a responsibility, when he already carries one so great.'

'Very proper!' agreed the abbot heartily. 'It would be ill-done to distract his mind from his great purpose at this stage. I should say no word to him of the reason for adding this young man to the party. Prior Robert in his own unshaken certainty is apt to take an austere view of any man who looks back, once having set his hand to the plough.'

'Yet, Father, we were not all cut out to be ploughmen. Some could be more useful labouring in other ways.'

'True!' said the abbot, and warily smiled, pondering the recurring but often forgotten riddle of Brother Cadfael himself. 'I have often wondered, I confess. . . . But never mind! Very well, tell me this young brother's name, and you shall have him.'

Chapter Two

RIOR ROBERT'S fine, frosty face momentarily registered displeasure and suspicion when he heard how his delegation was to be augmented. Brother Cadfael's gnarled, guileless-eyed self-sufficiency caused him discomfort without a word amiss or a glance out of place, as though his dignity were somehow under siege. Of Brother John he knew no particular evil, but the redness of his hair, the exuberance of his health and high spirits, the very way he put live blood back into old martyrdoms with his extravagant gusto in the reading, were all offensive in themselves, and jarred on the prior's aesthetic sensibilities. However, since Abbot Heribert had innocently decreed that they should join the party, and since there was no denying that a fluent Welsh speaker might become an urgent necessity at some stage, Prior Robert accepted the fiat without demur, and made the best of it.

They set out as soon as the fine reliquary for the saint's bones was ready, polished oak ornamented with silver, to serve as a proof what honours awaited Winifred in her new shrine. In the third week of May they came to Bangor, and told their story to Bishop David, who was sympathetic, and readily gave his consent to the proposed translation, subject only to the agreement of Prince Owain, who was regent of Gwynedd owing to the illness of the old king, his father. They ran the prince to

27

earth at Aber, and found him equally obliging, for he not only gave the desired approval, but sent his one English-speaking clerk and chaplain to show them the best and quickest way to Gwytherin, and commend them and their errand to the parish priest there. Thus episcopally and royally blessed, Prior Robert led his party on the last stage of their journey, a little too easily convinced that his progress was being divinely smoothed, and would be so to its triumphant end.

They turned aside from the Conway valley at Llanrwst, climbing away from the river into forested hill country. Beyond the watershed they crossed the Elwy where it is young and small, and moved steadily south-eastwards through thick woods, over another ridge of high land, to descend once again into the upland valley of a little river, that provided some marshy water-meadows along its banks, and a narrow band of tilled fields, sloping and sturdy but protected by the forests, above these lush pastures. The wooded ridge on either hand ran in oblique folds, richly green, hiding the scattered house-steads. The fields were already planted, and here and there orchards flowered. Beiow them, where the woods drew back to leave an amphitheatre of green, there was a small stone church, white-washed and shimmering, and a little wooden house beside it.

'You see the goal of your pilgrimage,' said the chaplain Urien. He was a compact, neat, well-shaven personage, hand-somely dressed and mounted, more of an ambassador than a clerk.

'That is Gwytherin?' asked Prior Robert.

'It is the church and priest's house of Gwytherin. The parish stretches for several miles along the river valley, and a mile or more from the Cledwen on either bank. We do not congregate in villages as you English do. Land good for hunting is plentiful, but good for tillage meagre. Every man lives where best suits him for working his fields and conserving his game.'

'It is a very fair place,' said the sub-prior, and meant it, for the fold on fold of well-treed hills beyond the river made a pattern of spring beauty in a hundred different greens, and the water-meadows were strung like a necklace of emeralds along the fringes of a necklace of silver and lapis-lazuli.

'Good to look at, hard to work,' said Urien practically. 'See there's an ox-team on the far side trying to break a new strip, now all the rest are planted. Watch the beasts strain at it, and you'll know how the higher ground weighs.'

28

Across the river, some way below them and a great way off, the snaky curve of the furrows already won patterned the slope between cultivated fields and leaning trees, a dark brown writing upon the hillside, and on the higher furrow, as yet uncompleted, the oxen leaned into their yokes and heaved, and the ploughman behind them clung and dragged at the heavy share. Before the leading pair a man walked backwards, arms gently waving and beckoning, his goad only a wand, flourished for magic, not for its sting, his high, pure calls carried aloft on the air, cajoling and praising. Towards him the beasts leaned willingly, following his cries with all their might. The new-turned soil, greyish-brown and sluggish, heaved moist and fresh to light after the share.

'A harsh country,' said Urien, as one assessing, not complaining, and set his horse moving downhill towards the church. 'Come, I'll hand you over to Father Huw, and see you well-received.'

They followed him by a green path that wound out of the hills, and soon lost its view of the valley between scattered, flowering trees. A wooden house or two showed among the woods, surrounded by small garden plots, and again vanished.

'Did you see?' said Brother John in Cadfael's ear, pacing beside the sumpter mule. 'Did you see how the beasts laboured towards that fellow not to escape the goad, only to go where he willed, only to please him? And such labour! That I should like to learn!'

'It's labour for man as well as beast,' said Brother Cadfael.

'But for free goodwill! They wanted to go with him, to do what he wanted them to do. Brother, could devoted disciples do more? Do you tell me he takes no delight in what he does?'

'No man nor God who sees his faithful delight to serve him,' said Brother Cadfael patiently and carefully, 'but he knows delight. Hush, now, we're barely here, there'll be time to look round us.'

They were down in the little arena of grass and vegetable plots, clear of the trees. The stone church with its tiny turret and tinier bell visible within shone blindingly white, bluish-white against all the lush green. And out of the cabbage-patch, freshly planted, in the lee of the wooden cabin, rose a small, square man in a brown sackcloth gown hoisted to the knees, thick brown legs sturdy under him, and a thicket of curly brown hair and beard half-concealing a brown, broad, wondering face round two large, dark-blue eyes. He came out hastily, scrubbing his hands on his skirts. At close quarters his eyes were larger, bluer and more astonished than ever, and as timid as the mild eyes of a doe.

'Good-day to you, Father Huw,' said Urien, reining in before him, 'I've brought you distinguished guests from England, upon important church business, and with the blessing of prince and bishop.'

When they had ridden into the clearing the priest had certainly been the only man in sight, but by the time Urien had ended his greeting a score of silent, sudden figures had appeared from nowhere, and made a wary and curious half-circle about their pastor. By the distracted look in Father Huw's eyes he was busy reckoning up in some alarm how many of these strangers his modest hut could fittingly house, and where to bestow the rest of them, and how much food there was in his larder to make a meal for so many, and where he could best commandeer whatever extra was needed. But no question of not extending a welcome. Guests were sacrosanct, and must not even be questioned on the proposed length of their stay, however ruinous.

'My poor household is at the reverend fathers' disposal,' he said, 'and whatever powers I have to serve them, also. You come fresh from Aber?'

'From Aber,' said Urien, 'from Prince Owain, and I must rejoin him there tonight. I am only the herald for these Benedictine brothers, who come on a holy errand, and when I have explained their case to you, then I leave them in your hands.' He presented them by name, Prior Robert first. 'And have no fear when I have left, for Brother Cadfael here is a man of Gwynedd himself, and speaks Welsh as well as you do.'

Huw's look of harassed apprehension was immediately eased, but in case he should be in any doubt, Cadfael favoured him with a rapid brotherly greeting in the promised language, which gratifyingly produced the identical look of slight distrust and insecurity in Prior Robert's normally assured grey eyes.

'You are welcome to this poor house you honour,' said Huw, and ran a quick eye over the horses and mules and their loads, and without hesitation called a couple of names over his shoulder. A shaggy-headed elder and a sunburned boy of about ten came forward readily in answer. 'Ianto, help the good brother water the beasts, and put them in the little paddock to graze, until we see how best to stable them. Edwin, run and tell Marared we have guests, and help her bring water and wine.'

They ran to do his bidding, and several of the others who had gathered, brown, bare-legged men, slender dark women and half-naked children, drew nearer, conferred softly among themselves, and the women slipped away to their own cooking-fires and bake-ovens to bring whatever they could to contribute to Gwytherin's hospitality.

'While it's so fine and mild,' said Huw, standing aside to wave them into the little enclosure of his garden, 'it may please you best to sit in the orchard. I have benches and table there. Through the summer I live out of doors. Time enough to go within and light fires when the days draw in and the nights grow cold.'

His holding was tiny and his living poor enough, but he took good care of his fruit-trees and was a diligent gardener, Brother Cadfael noted with approval. And for one who seemed, unlike many of the parish priests of the Celtic persuasion, to be celibate, and happily so, he had the bare little house and grounds in very neat order, and could produce from his own store, or his parishioners' shared stock, clean wooden trenchers and good bread to put on them, and plain but presentable drinking-horns for his raw red wine. He performed all the ceremonies due from a host with humble dignity. The boy Edwin returned with a lively old woman, Huw's neighbour, bringing food and drink. And all the while that the visitors sat there in the sun, various of the people of Gwytherin, scattered though the parish might be, found occasion to walk past the wattle fence of the orchard and examine the party carefully, though without seeming to do so. It was not every day, or every year, indeed, that they had so momentous a visitation. Every soul in the parish would know before evening not only that monks from Shrewsbury were guests at Huw's house, but also how many they were, what they looked like, what fine horses and handsome mules they had, and most probably what they had come for, into the bargain. But the eyeing and the listening were done with perfect courtesy and discretion.

'And now, since Master Urien has to return to Aber,' said Huw, when they had eaten and were sitting at ease, 'it might be well if he would tell me in what particular I can serve the brothers of Shrewsbury, so that he may be assured we understand each other before he leaves us. And whatever is in my competence I will surely do.'

Urien told the story as he had heard it, and Prior Robert elaborated at such length that Brother John, growing bored and

31

restless, let his eyes stray to take stock of the occasional figures that passed along the fence, with alert ears and shy but sharp eyes. His interest and curiosity were somewhat less discreet than theirs. And there were some very handsome girls among them! The one passing now, for instance, her step graceful and slow – she knew she was watched! – and her hair a great, heavy braid over her shoulder, the colour of polished oak, a light, silken brown, even with silvery dashes in it like the grain of oak. . . .

'And the bishop has given his consent to your proposal?' asked Huw, after a long minute of silence, and in a voice that suggested wonder and doubt.

'Both bishop and prince have sanctioned it.' Prior Robert was uneasy at the very hint of a hitch at this stage. 'The omens have surely not misled us? Saint Winifred is here? She lived out her restored life here, and is buried in this place?'

Huw owned that it was so, with so curious an intonation of caution and reluctance that Cadfael decided he was trying to recall exactly where the lady was to be found, and wondering in what state her grave would be discovered, after all this time since last he had so much as thought of it.

'She is here, in this cemetery?' The little whitewashed church gleamed provocatively in the sunshine.

'No, not here.' Some relief this time, he did not have to reveal her whereabouts immediately. 'This church is new since her time. Her grave is in the old burial-ground of the wooden church on the hill, a mile or more from here. It is long disused. Yes, certainly the omens favour your plans, and beyond question the saint is here in Gwytherin. But. . . .'

'But?' said Prior Robert with displeasure. 'Both prince and bishop have given us their blessing, and commended our cause to you. Moreover, we have heard, and they have agreed, that the saint in her stay here among you has been much neglected, and may well wish to be received where greater honour will be paid to her.'

'In my church,' said Huw humbly, 'I have never heard that the saints desired honour for themselves, but rather to honour God rightly. So I do not presume to know what Saint Winifred's will may be in this matter. That you and your house should desire to honour *her* rightly, that is another matter, and very proper. But. . . this blessed virgin lived out her miraculously restored life in this place, and no other. Here she died for the second time, and here is buried, and even if my people have

32

neglected her, being human and faulty, yet they always knew that she was here among them, and at a pinch they could rely on her, and for a Welsh saint I think that counts for much. Prince and bishop – both of whom I reverence as I ought – may not altogether understand how my flock will feel, if their holiest girl is to be dug up out of her grave and taken away into England. It may matter little to the crown and the crozier, a saint is a saint wherever her relics rest. But I tell you plainly, the people of Gwytherin are not going to like it at all!'

Brother Cadfael, stirred to an atavistic fervour of Welshness by this homely eloquence, snatched the initiative from Urien at this point, and translated with the large declamation of the bards.

In full spate, he turned his eyes away from the distracting faces, to light upon one even more distracting. The girl with the light-oak sheen on her hair was again passing the fence, and had been so charmed by what she heard, and the vehemence of its delivery, that for a moment she forgot to keep moving, and stood there at gaze, apple-blossom face radiant and rose-leaf lips laughing. And with the same fascination with which she gazed at Cadfael, Brother John gazed at her. Cadfael observed both, and was dazzled. But the next moment she caught herself up in hasty alarm, and blushed beautifully, and swept away out of sight. Brother John was still gaping long after she had vanished.

'It is hardly important, surely?' said Prior Robert with ominous mildness. 'Your bishop and your prince have made their views plain. The parishioners need not be consulted.'

That, too, Cadfael interpreted, Urien choosing to remain neutral and mute.

'Impossible!' said Huw firmly, knowing himself on secure ground. 'In such a grave matter affecting the whole parish, nothing can be done without calling together the assembly of the free men, and putting the case to them fully and publicly. Doubtless the will of prince and bishop will prevail, but even so, these must be put to the people before they can say yes or no to them. I shall call such an assembly tomorrow. Your case can only be vindicated absolutely by public acceptance.'

'He says truly,' said Urien, holding the prior's austere and half affronted eyes. 'You will do well to get the goodwill of Gwytherin, however many blessings you already have. They respect their bishop, and are very content with their king and his sons, I doubt if you need grudge the delay.'

Prior Robert accepted both the warning and the reassurance, and felt the need of a period of quietude in which to review his strategy and prepare his persuasions. When Urien rose to take his leave, his errand punctiliously completed, the prior also rose, half a head taller than the tallest there, and folded his long white hands in submissive resignation.

'We have yet two hours or more to Vespers,' he said, eyeing the angle of the sun. 'I should like to withdraw into your church and spend some while in meditation, and prayer for right guidance. Brother Cadfael, you had better remain with Father Huw, and help him in any arrangements he needs to make, and you, Brother John, bestow the horses as he directs, and see them cared for. The rest will join me in intercession, that we may conduct this enterprise rightly.'

He swept away, elongated and silvery and majestic, and had to stoop his head to enter under the low round arch of the church door. Brother Richard, Brother Jerome, Brother Columbanus vanished within on his heels. Not all the time they were together there would be spent in prayer. They would be considering what arguments would be most likely to carry the day with Father Huw's free assembly, or what oblique ecclesiastical threats daunt them into submission.

Brother John looked after the lofty silver head until it stooped with accurate dignity just low enough to pass under the stone, and let out something between a sigh and an arrested gurgle of laughter, as though he had been praying for a miscalculation. What with the journey, and the exercise, and the outdoor living, he looked ruddier and healthier and more athletic than ever.

'I've been hoping all this while for a chance to get my leg over that dapple-grey,' he said. 'Richard rides him like a badly-balanced woolsack. I hope Father Huw's stabling is a mile or more away.'

Father Huw's plans for them, it seemed, involved two of the nearer and more prosperous members of his flock, but even so, in the scattered Welsh way, their houses were dispersed in valley and forest.

'I shall give up my own house to the prior and sub-prior, of course,' he said, 'and sleep in the loft above my cow. For the beasts, my grazing here is too small, and I have no stable, but Bened the smith has a good paddock above the water-meadows, and stabling with a loft, if this young brother will not mind being lodged the better part of a mile from his fellows. And for you and your two companions, Brother Cadfael, there is open house

34

half a mile from here through the woods, with Cadwallon, who has one of the biggest holding in these parts.'

Brother Cadfael considered the prospect of being housed with Jerome and Columbanus, and found it unattractive. 'Since I am the only one among us who has fluent Welsh,' he said diplomatically, 'I should remain close to Prior Robert's side. With your goodwill, Huw, I'll share your loft above the cow-byre, and be very comfortable there.'

'If that's your wish,' said Huw simply, 'I shall be glad of your company. And now I must set this young man on his way to the smithy.'

'And I,' said Cadfael, 'if you don't need me along with you – and yonder boy will make himself understood in whatever language, or none! – will go a piece of the way back with Urien. If I can pick up an acquaintance or so among your flock, so much the better, for I like the look of them and their valley.'

Brother John came out from the tiny paddock leading the two tall horses, the mules following on leading reins. Huw's eyes glowed almost as bright as John's, caressing the smooth lines of neck and shoulder.

'How long it is,' he said wistfully, 'since I was on a good horse!'

'Come on, then, Father,' urged Brother John, understanding the look if not the words, 'up with you! Here's a hand, if you fancy the roan. Lead the way in style!' And he cupped a palm for the priest's lifted foot, and hoisted him, dazed and enchanted, into the saddle. Up himself on the grey, he fell in alongside, ready if the older man should need a steadying hand, but the brown knees gripped happily. He had not forgotten how. 'Bravely!' said John, hugely laughing. 'We shall get on famously together, and end up in a race!'

Urien, checking his girth, watched them ride away out of the gentle bowl of the clearing. 'There go two happy men,' he said thoughtfully.

'More and more I wonder,' said Cadfael, 'how that youngster ever came to commit himself to the monastic life.'

'Or you, for instance?' said Urien, with his toe in the stirrup. 'Come, if you want to view the ground, we'll take the valley way a piece, before I leave you for the hills.'

They parted at the crest of the ridge, among the trees but where a fold of the ground showed them the ox-team still doggedly labouring at a second strip, continuing the line of the first, above the richer valley land. Two such strips in one day was prodigious work.

'Your prior will be wise,' said Urien, taking his leave, 'to take a lesson from yonder young fellow. Leading and coaxing pays better than driving in these parts. But I need not tell you – a man as Welsh as myself.'

Cadfael watched him ride away gently along the cleared track until he vanished among the trees. Then he turned back towards Gwytherin, but went steeply downhill towards the river, and at the edge of the forest stood in green shadow under an oak tree, gazing across the sunlit meadows and the silver thread of river to where the team heaved and strained along the last furrow. Here there was no great distance between them, and he could see clearly the gloss of sweat on the pelts of the oxen, and the heavy curl of the soil as it heeled back from the share. The ploughman was dark, squat and powerful, with a salting of grey in his shaggy locks, but the ox-caller was tall and slender, and the curling hair that tossed on his neck and clung to his moist brow was as fair as flax. He managed his backward walking without a glance behind, feeling his way light-footed and gracefully, as if he had eyes in the back of his heels. His voice was hoarse and tired with long use now, but still clear and merry, more effective than any goad, as he cajoled his weary beasts along the final furrow, calling and luring and praising, telling them they had done marvels, and should get their rest and their meed for it, that in moments now they would be going home, that he was proud of them and loved them, as if he had been talking to Christian souls. And the beasts heaved and leaned, throwing their weight into the yokes and keeping their eyes upon him, and plainly would do anything in their power to please him. When the plough curved to the end and halted, and the steaming oxen stood with lowered heads, the young man came and flung an arm over the neck of the near leader, and scrubbed with brisk knuckles in the curly hair on the other's brow, and Cadfael said aloud: 'Bravely! But, my friend, how did you stray into Wales?'

Something small, round and hard dropped rustling through the leaves above him, and hit him neatly in the middle of his weather-beaten tonsure. He clapped a hand to his crown, and said something unbecoming his habit. But it was only one of last year's oak-balls, dried out by a winter's weathering to the hardness of a pebble. He looked up into the foliage above his head, already thick and turning rich green from its early gold, and it seemed to him that the tremor of leaves where there was no wind required more explanation than the accidental fall of one small remnant of a dead year. It stilled very quickly, and even its stillness, by contrast, seemed too careful and aware. Cadfael removed himself a few yards, as if about to walk on, and doubled round again behind the next barrier of bushes to see if the bait had been taken.

A small bare foot, slightly stained with moss and bark, reached down out of the branches to a toe-hold on the trunk. Its fellow, stretched at the end of a long, slim leg, swung clear, as the boy prepared to drop. Brother Cadfael, fascinated, suddenly averted his eyes in haste, and turned his back, but he was smiling, and he did not, after all, withdraw, but circled his screen of bushes and reappeared innocently in view of the bird that had just flown down out of its nest. No boy, as he had first supposed, but a girl, and a most personable girl, too, now standing decorously in the grass with her skirts nobly disposed round her, and even the small bare feet concealed.

They stood looking at each other with candid curiosity, neither at all abashed. She might have been eighteen or nineteen years old, possibly younger, for there was a certain erect assurance about her that gave her the dignity of maturity even when newly dropped out of an oak tree. And for all her bare feet and mane of unbraided dark hair, she was no villein girl. Everything about her said clearly that she knew her worth. Her gown was of fine homespun wool, dyed a soft blue, and had embroidery at neck and sleeves. No question but she was a beauty. Her face was oval and firm of feature, the hair that fell in wild waves about her shoulders was almost black, but black with a tint of dark and brilliant red in it where the light caught, and the large, black-lashed eyes that considered Brother Cadfael with such frank interest were of almost the same colour, dark as damsons, bright as the sparkles of mica in the river pebbles.

'You are one of the monks from Shrewsbury,' she said with certainty. And to his astonishment she said it in fluent and easy English.

'I am,' said Cadfael. 'But how did you come to know all about us so soon? I think you were not among those who made it their business to walk along Huw's garden fence while we were talking. There was one very fine girl, I remember, but not a black lass like you.'

She smiled. She had an enchanting smile, sudden and radiant. 'Oh, that would be Annest. But everybody in Gwytherin knows by now all about you, and what you've come for. Father Huw is right, you know,' she warned seriously, 'we shan't like it at all. Why do you want to take Saint Winifred away? When she's been here so long, and nobody ever paid any attention to her before? It doesn't seem neighbourly or honest to me.'

It was an excellent choice of words, he thought, and marvelled how a Welsh girl came by it, for she was using English as if she had been born to it, or come to it for love.

'I question the propriety of it myself, to be truthful,' he agreed ruefully. 'When Father Huw spoke up for his parish, I confess I found myself inclining to his side of the argument.'

That made her look at him more sharply and carefully than before, frowning over some sudden doubt or suspicion in her own mind. Whoever had informed her had certainly witnessed all that went on in Father Huw's garden. She hesitated a moment, pondering, and then launched at him unexpectedly in Welsh: 'You must be the one who speaks our language, the one who translated what Father Huw said.' It seemed to trouble her more than was reasonable. 'You do know Welsh! You understand me now.'

'Why, I'm as Welsh as you, child,' he admitted mildly, 'and only a Benedictine in my middle years, and I haven't forgotten my mother-tongue yet, I hope. But I marvel how you've come to speak English as well as I do myself, here in the heart of Rhos.'

'Oh, no,' she said defensively, 'I've only learned a very little. I tried to use it for you, because I thought you *were* English. How was I to know you'd be just *that* one?' Now why should his being bilingual cause her uneasiness? he wondered. And why was she casting so many rapid, furtive glances aside towards the river, brightly glimpsed through the trees? Where, as he saw in a glance just as swift as hers, the tall, fair youngster who was no Welshman, and was certainly the finest ox-caller in Gwynedd, had broken away from his placidly-drinking team, and was wading the river thigh-deep towards this particular tall oak, in a flurry of sparkling spray. The girl had been ensconced in this very tree, whence, no doubt, she had a very good view of the ploughing. And came down as soon as it was finished! 'I'm shy of my English,' she said, pleading and vulnerable. 'Don't tell anyone!'

She was wishing him away from here, and demanding his discretion at the same time. His presence, he gathered, was inconvenient.

'I've known the same trouble myself,' he said comfortably, 'when first I tried getting my tongue round English. I'll never call your efforts into question. And now I'd better be on my way back to our lodgings, or I shall be late for Vespers.'

'God go with you, then, Father,' she said, radiant and relieved.

'And with you, my child.'

He withdrew by a carefully chosen route that evaded any risk of bumping into the fair young man. And she watched him go for a long moment, before she turned eagerly to meet the ox-caller as he came splashing through the shallows and climbed the bank. Cadfael thought that she was perfectly aware how much he had observed and understood, and was pleased by his reticence. Pleased and reassured. A Welsh girl of status, with embroidery along the hems of her gown, had good need to go softly if she was meeting an outlander, a man landless and rootless here in a clan society, where to be without place in a kinship was to be without the means of living. And yet a very pleasing, comely young man, good at his work and feeling for his beasts. Cadfael looked back, when he was sure the bushes covered him, and saw the two of them draw together, still and glad, not touching, almost shy of each other. He did not look back again.

Now what I really need here, he thought as he walked back towards the church of Gwytherin, is a good, congenial acquaintance, someone who knows every man, woman and child in the parish, without having to carry the burden of their souls. A sound drinking companion with good sense is what I need.

Chapter Three

E FOUND not one of what he wanted, but three at one stroke, after Compline that evening, when he walked back with Brother John in the twilight to the smithy and croft at the edge of the valley fields. Prior Robert and Brother Richard had already withdrawn for the night into Huw's house, Jerome and Columbanus were on their way through the woods to Cadwallon's holding, and who was to question whether Brother Cadfael had also gone to his pallet in the priest's loft, or was footloose among the gossips of Gwytherin? The lodging arrangements were working out admirably. He had never felt less inclined for sleep at this soft evening hour, nor was anyone going to rouse them at midnight here for Matins. Brother John was delighted to introduce him into the smith's household, and Father Huw favoured the acquaintance for his own reasons. It was well that others besides himself should speak for the people of the parish, and Bened the smith was a highly respected man, like all of his craft, and his words would carry weight.

There were three men sitting on the bench outside Bened's door when they arrived, and the mead was going round as fast as the talk. All heads went up alertly at the sound of their steps approaching, and a momentary silence marked the solidarity of the local inhabitants. But Brother John seemed already to have made himself welcome, and Cadfael cast them a greeting in Welsh, like a fisherman casting a line, and was accepted with something warmer than the strict courtesy the English would have found. Annest with the light-brown, sunflecked hair had spread word of his Welshness far and wide. Another bench was pulled up, and the drinking-horns continued their circling in a wider ring. Over the river the light was fading gradually, the dimness green with the colours of meadow and forest, and threaded through with the string of silver water.

Bened was a thickset, muscular man of middle years, bearded and brown. Of his two companions the younger was recognisable as the ploughman who had followed the ox-team that day, and no wonder he was dry after such labour. And the third was a grey-headed elder with a long, smoothly-trimmed beard and fine, sinewy hands, in an ample homespun gown that had seen better days, perhaps on another wearer. He bore himself as one entitled to respect, and got it.

'Padrig, here, is a good poet and a fine harpist,' said Bened, 'and Gwytherin is lucky to have him staying a while among us, in Rhisiart's hall. That's away beyond Cadwallon's place, in a forest clearing, but Rhisiart has land over this way, too, both sides the river. He's the biggest landowner in these parts. There are not many here entitled to keep a harp, or maybe we'd be honoured with more visits from travelling bards like Padrig. I have a little harp myself – I have that privilege – but Rhisiart's is a fine one, and kept in use, too. I've heard his girl play on it sometimes.'

'Women cannot be bards,' said Padrig with tolerant scorn. 'But she knows how to keep it tuned, and well looked after, that I will say. And her father's a patron of the arts, and a generous, open-handed one. No bard goes away disappointed from his hall, and none ever leaves without being pressed to stay. A good household!'

'And this is Cai, Rhisiart's ploughman. No doubt you saw the team cutting new land, when you came over the ridge today.'

'I did, and admired the work,' said Cadfael heartily. 'I never saw better. A good team you had there, and a good caller, too.'

'The best,' said Cai without hesitation. 'I've worked with a good many in my time, but never known one with the way Engelard has with the beasts. They'd die for him. And as good a hand with all cattle, calving or sick or what you will. Rhisiart would be a sorry man if ever he lost him. Ay, we did a good day's work today.'

'You'll have heard from Father Huw,' said Cadfael, 'that all the free men are called to the church tomorrow after Mass, to hear what our prior is proposing. No doubt we shall see Rhisiart there.'

'See and hear him,' said Cai, and grinned. 'He speaks his mind. An open-hearted, open-natured man, with a temper soon up and soon down, and never a grudge in him, but try and move him when his mind's made up, and you're leaning on Snowdon.'

'Well, a man can but hold fast to what he believes right, and even the opponent he baulks should value him for that. And have his sons no interest in the harp, that they leave it to their sister?'

'He has no sons,' said Bened. 'His wife is dead, and he never would take another, and there's only this one girl to follow him.'

'And no male heir anywhere in his kinship? It's rare for a daughter to inherit.'

'Not a man on his side the family at all,' said Cai, 'and a pity it is. The only near kin is her mother's brother, and he has no claim, and is old into the bargain. The greatest match anywhere in this valley, is Sioned, and young men after her like bees. But God willing, she'll be a contented wife with a son on her knee long before Rhisiart goes to his fathers.'

'A grandson by a good man, and what could any lord want more,' said Padrig, and emptied the jug of mead and passed the horn along. 'Understand me, I'm not a Gwytherin man myself, and have no right to give a voice one way or the other. But if I may say a word my friends won't say for themselves – you having your duty to your prior as Cai has to his lord, or I to my art and my patrons – don't look for any easy passage, and don't take offence if your way is blocked. Nothing personal to you! But where the free men of Wales see no fair dealing, they won't call it by fair names, and they won't stand aside.'

'I should be sorry if they did,' said Cadfael. 'For my part, the ending I want is the fair ending, leaving no man with a just grievance. And what of the other lords we can expect to see there? Of Cadwallon we've heard, two of our brothers are enjoying his hospitality. And his lands are neighbour to Rhisiart's?'

'It's a fair piece beyond to Rhisiart's hall, on through the forest. But they're neighbours, boundary to boundary, yes, and friends from youth. A peaceable man, Cadwallon, he likes his comfort and his hunting. His way would be to say yes to what ever bishop and prince commend, but then, his way normally is also to say yes to Rhisiart. For that matter,' owned Bened, tilting the last drop from the horn. 'I know no more than you what either of them will have to say in this matter. For all I know they'll accept your omens and bless your errand. If the free voice goes with your prior, then Saint Winifred goes home with you, and that's the end of it.'

It was the end of the mead, too, for that night.

'Bide the night here,' said Bened to Padrig when the guests rose to walk home, 'and we'll have a little music before you leave tomorrow. My small harp needs to be played, I've kept it in fettle for you.'

'Why, so I will, since you're so kind,' said Padrig, and weaved his way gently into the house with his host. And Cai and Brother Cadfael, taking their leave, set off companionably shoulder to shoulder, to make their way back to Father Huw's house, and thence in courtesy a measure of the way through the woods towards Rhisiart's hall before they parted.

'I would not say more nor plainer,' said Cai confidingly, 'while Bened was present, nor in front of Padrig, for that matter, though he's a good fellow – so are they both! – but a traveller, not a native. This Sioned, Rhisiart's girl. . . . The truth is, Bened would like to be a suitor for her himself, and a good, solid man he is, and a girl might well do worse. But a widower, poor soul, and years older than the lass, and a poor chance he has. But you haven't seen the girl!'

Brother Cadfael was beginning to suspect that he had indeed seen the girl, and seen more than any here had ever been allowed to see. But he said nothing.

'A girl like a squirrel! As swift, as sudden, as black and as red! If she had nothing, they'd still be coming from miles around, and she will have lands any man might covet even if she squinted! And there's poor Bened, keeping his own counsel and feeding on his own silence, and still hoping. After all, a smith is respected in any company. And give him his due, it isn't her heritage he covets. It's the girl herself. If you'd seen her, you'd know. In any case,' said Cai, sighing gustily for his friend, 'her father has a favourite for son-in-law already, and has had all along. Cadwallon's lad has been in and out of Rhisiart's hall, and made free with Rhisiart's servants and hawks and horses, ever since he could run, and grown up with the girl. And he's sole heir to the neighbouring holding, and what could suit either

43

father better? They've had it made up between them for years. And the children seem ideally matched, they know each other through and through, like brother and sister.'

'I doubt if I'd say that made for an ideal match,' said Brother Cadfael honestly.

'So Sioned seems to think, too,' said Cai drily. 'So far she's resisted all pressures to accept this lad Peredur. And mind you, he's a very gay, lively, well-looking young fellow, spoiled as you please, being the only one, but show me a girl round here who wouldn't run if he lifted his finger – all but this girl! Oh, she likes him well enough, but that's all. She won't hear of marriage yet, she's still playing the heartfree child.'

'And Rhisiart bears with her?' asked Cadfael delicately.

'You don't know him, either. He dotes on her, and well he may, and she reveres him, and well *she* may, and where does that get any of us? He won't force her choice. He never misses a chance to urge how suitable Peredur is, and she never denies it. He hopes, if he bides his time, she'll come round.'

'And will she?' asked Brother Cadfael, responding to something in the ploughman's voice. His own was midler than milk.

'No accounting,' said Cai slowly, 'for what goes on in a girl's head. She may have other plans of her own. A bold, brave one she is, clever and patient at getting her own way. But what that may be, do I know? Do you? Does any man?'

'There may be one man who does,' said Brother Cadfael with guileful disinterest.

If Cai had not risen to that bait, Cadfael would have let well alone then, for it was no business of his to give away the girl's secrets, when he had stumbled upon them himself only by chance. But he was no way surprised when the ploughman drew meaningfully close against his arm, and jabbed a significant elbow into his ribs. A man who had worked closely with the young ox-caller as he had must surely have noted a few obvious things by now. This afternoon's purposeful bee-line across the meadows and through the water to a certain well-grown oak would be enough in itself for a sharp man. And as for keeping his mouth shut about it, it was pretty plain that his sympathies were with his work-mate.

'Brother Cadfael, you wouldn't be a talking man, not out of turn, and you're not tied to one side or the other in any of our little disputes here. No reason *you* shouldn't know. Between you and me, she *has* got a man in her eye, and one that wants her worse than Bened does, and has even less chance of ever getting her. You remember we were talking of my fellow on the team, Engelard? A good man with cattle, worth plenty to his lord, and Rhisiart knows it and values him fairly on it. But the lad's an *alltud* – an outlander!'

'Saxon?' asked Cadfael.

'The fair hair. Yes, you saw him today. The length and slenderness of him too. Yes, he's a Cheshire man from the borders of Maelor, on the run from the bailiffs of Earl Ranulf of Chester. Oh, not for murder or banditry or any such! But the lad was simply the most outrageous deer-poacher in the earldom. He's a master with the short bow, and always stalked them afoot and alone. And the bailiff was after his blood. Nothing for him to do, when he was cornered on the borders, but run for it into Gwynedd. And he daren't go back, not yet, and you know what it means for a foreigner to want to make a living in Wales.'

Cadfael knew indeed. In a country where every native-born man had and knew his assured place in a clan kinship, and the basis of all relationships was establishment on the land, whether as free lord or villein partner in a village community, the man from outside, owning no land here, fitting into no place, was deprived of the very basis of living. His only means of establishing himself was by getting some overlord to make compact with him, give him house-room and a stake in the land, and employ him for whatever skills he could offer. For three generations this bargain between them was revocable at any time, and the outlander might leave at the fair price of dividing his chattels equally with the lord who had given him the means of acquiring them.

'I do know. So Rhisiart took this young man into his service and set him up in a croft?'

'He did. Two years ago now, a little more. And neither of them has had any call to regret it. Rhisiart's a fair-minded master, and gives credit where it's due. But however much he respects and values him, can you see a Welsh lord ever letting his only daughter go to an *alltud?*'

'Never!' agreed Cadfael positively. 'No chance of it! It would be against all his laws and customs and conscience. His own kinship would never forgive it.'

'True as I'm breathing!' sighed Cai ruefully. 'But you try telling that to a proud, stubborn young fellow like Engelard, who has his own laws and rights from another place, where his father's lord of a good manor, and carries every bit as much weight in his feudal fashion as Rhisiart does here.'

45

'Do you tell me he's actually spoken for her to her father?' demanded Cadfael, astonished and admiring.

'He has, and got the answer you might expect. No malice at all, but no hope, either. Yes, and stood his ground and argued his case just the same. And comes back to the subject every chance that offers, to remind Rhisiart he hasn't given up, and never will. I tell you what, those two are two of a kind, both hot-tempered, both obstinate, but both as open and honest as you'll find anywhere, and they've a great respect for each other that somehow keeps them from bearing malice or letting this thing break them apart. But every time this comes up, the sparks fly. Rhisiart clouted Engelard once, when he pushed him too hard, and the lad came within an ace of clouting back. What would the answer to that have been? I never knew it happen with an *alltud,* but if a slave strikes a free man he stands to lose the hand that did it. But he stopped himself in time, though I don't think it was fear that stopped him – he knew he was in the wrong. And what did Rhisiart do, not half an hour later, but fling back and ask his pardon! Said he was an insolent, unreasonable, unWelsh rascal, but he should not have struck him. There's a battle going on all the time between those two and neither of them can get any peace, but let any man say a word against Rhisiart in Engelard's hearing, and he'll get it back down his throat with a fist behind it. And if one of the servants ever called down Engelard, thinking to curry favour with Rhisiart, he'd soon get told that the *alltud's* an honest man and a good worker, worth ten of the likes of his backbiters. So it goes! And I can see no good end to it.'

'And the girl?' said Cadfael. 'What does she say to all this?'

'Very little, and very softly. Maybe at first she did argue and plead, but if so it was privately with her father alone. Now she's biding her time, and keeping them from each other's throat as best she can.'

And meeting her lover at the oak tree, thought Cadfael, or any one of a dozen other private places, wherever his work takes him. So that's how she learned her English, all through those two years while the Saxon boy was busy learning Welsh from her, and that's why, though she was willing to pass the time of day in his own language with a visiting monk, she was concerned about having betrayed her accomplishment to a Welsh-speaking stranger, who might innocently blurt it abroad locally. She'd hardly want to let slip how often she's been meeting Engelard in secret, if she's biding her time, and

46

keeping father and lover from each other's throat till she can get her own way with them. And who's to say which of the three will give way first, where all look immovable?

'It seems you've your own troubles here in Gwytherin, let alone what we've brought with us,' he said, when he parted from Cai.

'God resolves all given time,' said Cai philosophically and trudged away into the darkness. And Cadfael returned along the path with the uncomfortable feeling that God, nevertheless, required a little help from men, and what he mostly got was hindrance.

All the free men of Gwytherin came to the meeting next day, and their womenfolk and all the villein community came to the Mass beforehand. Father Huw named the chief among them softly to Brother Cadfael as they made their appearance. He had seldom had such a congregation.

'Here is Rhisiart, with his daughter and his steward, and the girl's waiting-woman.'

Rhisiart was a big, bluff, hearty-looking man of about fifty, high-coloured and dark-haired, with a short, grizzled beard, and bold features that could be merry or choleric, fierce or jovial, but were far too expressive ever to be secretive or mean. His stride was long and impetuous, and his smile quick in response when he was greeted. His dress hardly distinguished him from any of the other free landholders who came thronging into the church, being plain as any, but of good homespun cloth. To judge from his bright face, he came without prejudice, willing to listen, and for all his thwarted family plans, he looked an expansively happy man, proud and fond of his daughter.

As for the girl, she followed at his heels modestly, with poised head and serene eyes. She had shoes on for this occasion, and her hair was brushed and braided into a burnished dark coil on her neck, and covered with a linen coif, but there was no mistaking her. This was the urchin of the oak tree, and the greatest heiress and most desirable prize in marriage in all this country-side.

The steward was an older man, grey-headed and balding, with a soft, good-humoured face. 'He is Rhisiart's kinsman by marriage,' whispered Huw, 'his wife's elder brother.'

'And the other girl is Sioned's tirewoman?' No need to name her, he already knew her name. Dimpled and smiling, Annest followed her friend with demure little steps into the church, and the sun stroked all the bright, silvery grain in the sheaf of her pale hair. 'She is the smith's niece,' said Father Huw helpfully. 'A good girl, she visits him often since he buried his wife, and bakes for him.'

'Bened's niece?' Brother John pricked his ears, and looked after the shapely waist and glowing hair with fascinated eyes, no doubt hoping there would be a baking day before they had to leave Gwytherin. The lodging arrangements had certainly been inspired, though whether by an angel or an imp remained to be seen.

'Lower your eyes, brother,' said Jerome chidingly. 'It is not seemly to look so straightly upon women.'

'And how did he know there were women passing,' whispered Brother John rebelliously, 'if his own eyes were so dutifully lowered?'

Brother Columbanus, at least, was standing as prescribed in the presence of females, with pale hands prayerfully folded, and lofty eyelids lowered, his gaze upon the grass.

'And here comes Cadwallon now,' said Father Huw. 'These good brothers already know him, of course. And his lady. And his son Peredur.'

So this young man, loping after his parents with the long, springy gait of a yearling roebuck, was the chosen husband for Sioned, the lad she liked well enough, and had known familiarly all her life, but was in no way inclined to marry. It occured to Cadfael that he had never asked how the groom felt about the situation, but it needed only a glimpse of Peredur's face when he caught sight of Sioned to settle the matter. Here was a tangle. The girl might have worn out in mere liking all her inclination to love, but the boy certainly had not. At sight of her his face paled, and his eyes took fire.

The parents were ordinary enough, comfortable people grown plump from placid living, and expecting things to go smoothly still as they always had. Cadwallon had a round, fleshy, smiling face, and his wife was fat, fair and querulous. The boy cast back to some more perilous ancestor. The spring of his step was a joy to watch. He was not above middle height, but so well-proportioned that he looked tall. His dark hair was cut short, and curled crisply all over his head. His chin was shaven clean, and all the bones of his face were as bold and elegant as his colouring was vivid, with russet brushings of sun on high cheek-bones, and a red, audacious, self-willed mouth. Such a young person might well find it hard to bear that another, and an alien at that, should be preferred to him. He proclaimed in his every movement and glance that everything and everyone in his life had responded subserviently to his charm, until now.

At the right moment, when the church was full, Prior Robert, tall and imposing and carefully groomed, swept in through the tiny sacristy and took his place, and all the Shrewsbury brothers fell into line and followed on his heels. The Mass began.

In the deliberations of the free assembly of the parish, of course, the women had no part. Neither had the villeins, though they had their indirect influence through those of their friends who were free. So while the free men lingered after the Mass, the rest dispersed, moving away with slow dignity, and not too far, just far enough to be discreetly out of sight and earshot, but handy to detect what was passing by instinct, and confirm it as soon as the meeting broke up.

The free men gathered in the open before the church. The sun was already high, for it was little more than an hour to noon. Father Huw stood up before the assembly, and gave them the gist of the matter, as it had been presented to him. He was the father of this flock, and he owed his people truth, but he also owed his church fealty. He told them what bishop and prince had answered to the request from Shrewsbury, reverently presented, and with many proofs. Which proofs he left to Robert to deliver.

The prior had never looked holier or more surely headed for sainthood himself. He had always a sense of occasion, and beyond a doubt it had been his idea to hold the meeting here in the open, where the sun could gild and illuminate his otherworldly beauty. It was Cadfael's detached opinion that he did himself more than justice, by being less overbearing than might have been expected. Usually he overdid things, this time he got it right, or as right as something only equivocally right in itself can be got.

'They're not happy!' whispered Brother John in Cadfael's ear, himself sounding far from sad about it. There were times when even Brother John could be humanly smug. And indeed, those Welsh faces ranged round them were singularly lacking in enthusiasm for all these English miracles performed by a Welsh saint. Robert at his best was not exactly carrying his audience.

They swayed and murmured, and eyed one another, and again turned as one man to eye him.

'If Owain ap Griffith wills it, and the bishop gives his blessing, too,' began Cadwallon hesitantly, 'as loyal sons of the church, and true men of Gwynedd, we can hardly. . .'

'Both prince and bishop have blessed our errand,' said the prior loftily.

'But the girl is here, in Gwytherin,' said Rhisiart abruptly. He had the voice that might have been expected from him, large, melodious and deep, a voice that sang what it felt, and waited for thought afterwards, to find that the thought had been there already in the feeling. 'Ours, not Bishop David's! Not Owain ap Griffith's! She lived out her life here, and never said word about wanting to leave us. Am I to believe easily that she wants to leave us now, after so long? Why has she never told us? Why?'

'She has made it clear to us,' said the prior, 'by many manifestations, as I have told you.'

'But never a word to *us*,' cried Rhisiart, roused. 'Do you call that courtesy? Are we to believe that, of a virgin who chose to make her home here among us?'

They were with him, his assurance had fired their smouldering reluctance. They cried out from a dozen directions at once that Saint Winifred belonged to Gwytherin, and to no other place.

'Do you dare tell me,' said Prior Robert, high and clear, 'that you have visited her? That you have committed your prayers to her? That you have invoked the aid of this blessed virgin, and given her the honour that is her due? Do you know of any reason why she should desire to remain here among you? Have you not neglected even her grave?'

'And if we have,' said Rhisiart with blithe conviction, 'do you suppose the girl wonders at it? You have not lived here among us. She did. You are English, she was Welsh, she knew us, and was never so moved against us that she withdrew or complained. We know she is there, no need to exclaim or make any great outcry. If we have needs, she knows it, and never asks that we should come with prayers and tears, knocking our knees on the ground before her. If she grudged a few brambles and weeds, she would have found a means to tell us. Us, not some distant Benedictine house in England!'

Throats were opening joyfully, shouting where they had muttered. The man was a poet and a preacher, match for any Englishman. Brother Cadfael let loose his bardic blood, and rejoiced silently. Not even because it was Prior Robert

50

recoiling into marble rage under Welsh siege. Only because it was a Welsh voice that cried battle.

'And do you deny,' thundered Robert, stretching his ascetic length to its loftiest, 'the truth of those omens and miracles I have declared to you, the beckoning that led us here?'

'No!' said Rhisiart roundly. 'I never doubted you believed and had experienced these portents. But portents can arise, miracles can be delivered, either from angels or devils. If these are from heaven, why have we not been instructed? The little saint is here, not in England. She owes us the courtesy of kinsmen. Dare you say she is turned traitor? Is there not a church in Wales, a Celtic church such as she served? What did she know of yours? I do not believe she would speak to you and not to us. You have been deceived by devils! Winifred never said a word!'

A dozen voices took up the challenge, hallooing applause for their most articulate spokesman, who had put his finger on the very pulse of their resentment. Even the very system of bishoprics galled the devout adherents of the old, saintly Celtic church, that had no worldly trappings, courted no thrones, but rather withdrew from the world into the blessed solitude of thought and prayer. The murmur became a subdued rumbling, a thunder, a roar. Prior Robert, none too wisely, raised his commanding voice to shout them down.

'She said no word to you, for you had left her forgotten and unhonoured. She has turned to us for recognition, when she could get none from you.'

'That is not true,' said Rhisiart, 'though you in your ignorance may believe it. The saint is a good Welshwoman, and knows her countrymen. We are not quick in respect to rank or riches, we do not doff and bow and scrape when any man flaunts himself before us. We are blunt and familiar even in praise. What we value we value in the heart, and this Welsh girl knows it. She would never leave her own unfurnished, even if we have neglected to trim her grave. It is the spirit that leans to us, and is felt by us as guardian and kin. But these bones you come hunting are also hers. Not ours, not yours! Until she tells us she wills to have them moved, here they stay. We should be damned else!'

It was the bitterest blow of Prior Robert's life to know that he had met his match and overmatch in eloquence and argument, here in a half-barbaric Welsh landholder, no great lord, but a mere squireling elevated among his inferiors to a status he barely rated, at least in Norman eyes. It was the difference between them that Robert thought in hierarchies, and Rhisiart thought in blood-ties, high and low of one mind and in one kinship, and not a man among them aware of inferiority, only of his due place in a united family.

The thunder was one voice now, demanding and assured, but it was one man who had called it into being. Prior Robert, well aware that a single adversary confronted him, subdued his angry tones, and opted for the wisdom of the dove, and the subtlety of single combat. He raised his long, elegant arms, from which the wide sleeves of his habit fell free, and smiled on the assembly, turning the smile at its most compelling and fatherly upon Rhisiart.

'Come, Brother Cadfael, say this for me to the lord Rhisiart, that it is all too easy for us, who have the same devotion at heart, to disagree about the means. It is better to speak quietly, man to man, and avoid the deformation of anger. Lord Rhisiart, I beg you to come apart with me, and let us debate this matter in quietude, and then you shall have liberty to speak out what you will. And having had my say fairly with you, I will say no word further to challenge what you have to impart to your people.'

'That is fair and generous,' said Rhisiart promptly to this offer, and stood forward with ingenuous pleasure from the crowd, which parted to let him through.

'We will not take even the shadow of dissension into the church,' said Prior Robert. 'Will you come with us into Father Huw's house?' All those bright, sullen, roused eyes followed them in through the low doorway, and clung there to wait for them to come forth again. Not a man of the Welsh moved from his place. They trusted the voice that had spoken for them hitherto to speak for them still.

In the small, wood-scented room, dark after the brightness of the day outside, Prior Robert faced his opponent with a calm and reasonable face.

'You have spoken well,' he said, 'and I commend your faith, and the high value you set on the saint, for so do we value her highly. And at her own wish, for so we believe, we have come here, solely to serve her. Both church and state are with us, and you know better than I the duty a nobleman of Wales owes to both. But I would not willingly leave Gwytherin with a sense of grievance, for I do know that by Saint Winifred's departure Gwytherin's loss is great. That we own, and I would wish to make due reparation.'

'Reparation to Gwytherin?' repeated Rhisiart, when this was translated to him. 'I do not understand how. . . .'

'And to you,' said Robert softly and matter-of-factly, 'if you will withdraw your opposition, for then I feel sure all your fellows will do the same, and sensibly accept what bishop and prince decree.'

It occurred to Cadfael as he interpreted this, even before the prior began the slow, significant motion of one long hand into the breast of his habit, that Robert was about to make the most disastrous miscalculation of his life. But Rhisiart's face remained dubious and aloof, quite without understanding, as the prior drew from his bosom a soft leather bag drawn up with a cord at the neck, and laid it on the table, pushing it gently across until it rested against Rhisiart's right hand. Its progress over the rough boards gave out a small chinking sound. Rhisiart eyed it suspiciously, and lifted uncomprehending eyes to stare at the prior. 'I don't understand you. What is this?'

'It is yours,' said Robert, 'if you will persuade the parish to agree to give up the saint.'

Too late he felt the unbelieving coldness in the air, and sensed the terrible error he had made. Hastily he did his best to recover some of the ground lost. 'To be used as you think best for Gwytherin – a great sum. . . .' It was useless. Cadfael let it lie in silence.

'Money!' said Rhisiart in the most extraordinary of tones, at once curious, derisory and revolted. He knew about money, of course, and even understood its use, but as an aberration in human relations. In the rural parts of Wales, which indeed were almost all of Wales, it was hardly used at all, and hardly needed. Provision was made in the code for all necessary exchange of goods and services, nobody was so poor as to be without the means of living, and beggars were unknown. The kinship took care of its helpless members, and every house was open as of right. The minted coins that had seeped in through the marches were a pointless eccentricity. Only after a moment of scornful wonder did it occur to Rhisiart that in this case they were also a mortal insult. He snatched away his hand from the affronting touch, and the blood surged into his face darkly red, suffusing even the whites of his eyes.

'Money? You dare offer to *buy* our saint? To buy *me?* I was in two minds about you, and about what I ought to do, but now, by God, I know what to think! You had your omens. Now I have mine!'

'You mistake me!' cried the prior, stumbling after his blunder and seeing it outdistance him at every breath. 'One cannot buy what is holy, I am only offering a gift to Gwytherin, in gratitude and compensation for their sacrifice – '

'Mine, you said it was,' Rhisiart reminded him, glowing copper bright with dignified rage. 'Mine, if I *persuaded* . . .! Not a gift! A bribe! This foolish stuff you hoard about you more dearly far than your reputations, don't you think you can use it to buy *my* conscience. I know now that I was right to doubt you. You have said your say, now I will say mine to those people without, as you promised me I should, without hindrance.'

'No, wait!' The prior was in such agitation that he actually reached out a hand and caught his opponent by the sleeve. 'Do nothing in haste! You have mistaken my meaning indeed, and if I was wrong even to offer an alms to Gwytherin, I am sorry for it. But do not call it – '

Rhisiart withdrew himself angrily from the detaining clasp, and cut off the protest curtly, wheeling on Cadfael. 'Tell him he need not be afraid. I should be ashamed to tell my people that a prior of Shrewsbury tried to corrupt me with a bribe. I don't deal in that kind of warfare. But where I stand – that they shall know, and you, too.' And he strode out from them, and Father Huw put out a warning hand to prevent any of them from attempting to impede or follow him.

'Not now! He is hot now. Tomorrow something may be done to approach him, but not now. You must let him say what he will.'

'Then at least let's put in an appearance,' said the prior, magnificently picking up what pieces he could of the ruin he had created; and he swept out into the sunlight and took his stand close to the door of the church, with all his fellow-monks dutifully following on his heels, and stood with erect head and calmly folded hands, in full view, while Rhisiart thundered his declaration to the assembled people of Gwytherin.

'I have listened to what these men from Shrewsbury have had to say to me, and I have made my judgement accordingly, and now I deliver it to you. I say that so far from changing my views, I am confirmed a thousand times that I was right to oppose the sacrilege they desire. I say that Saint Winifred's place is here among us, where she has always belonged, and that it would be mortal sin to let her be taken away to a strange place, where not even the prayers would be in a tongue she knows, where foreigners not worthy to draw near her would be her only company. I pledge my opposition to the death, against any attempt to move her bones, and I urge upon you the same duty. And now this conference is ended.'

So he said, and so it was. There could be no possible way of prolonging it. The prior was forced to stand with marble face and quiet hands while Rhisiart strode away towards the forest path, and all the assembly, in awed and purposeful silence, melted away mysteriously in all directions after his departure, so that within minutes all that green, trodden arena was empty.

Chapter Four

OU SHOULD have told me what you intended,' said Father Huw, timidly reproachful. 'I could have told you it was folly, the worst possible. What attraction do you think money has for a man like Rhisiart? Even if he was for sale, and he is not, you would have had to find other means to purchase him. I thought you had taken his measure, and were proposing to plead to him the sorry plight of English pilgrims, who have no powerful saints of their own, and are sadly in need of such a protectress. He would have listened to something that entreated of his generosity.'

'I am come with the blessing of church and sovereign,' said the prior fiercely, though the repetition was beginning to pall even on him. 'I cannot be repudiated at the will of a local squire. Has my order no rights here in Wales?'

'Very few,' said Cadfael bluntly. 'My people have a natural reverence, but it leans towards the hermitage, not the cloister.'

The heated conference went on until Vespers, and poisoned even Vespers with its bitterness, for there Prior Robert preached a fearful sermon detailing all the omens that Winifred desired above all things to remove to the sanctity of Shrewsbury, and issuing her prophetic denunciation against all who stood in the way of her translation. Terrible would be her wrath visited on those who dared resist her will. Thus Prior Robert approached the necessary reconciliation with Rhisiart.

And though Cadfael in translating toned down the threat as much as he dared, there were some among the congregation who understood enough English to get the full drift of it. He knew by their closed, mute faces. Now they would go away to spread the word to those who had not been present, until everyone in Gwytherin knew that the prior had bidden them remember what befell Prince Cradoc, whose very flesh watered away into the ground like rain, so that he vanished utterly as to the body expunged out of the world, as to the soul, the fearful imagination dared not guess. So also it might happen to those who dared offend against Winifred now.

Father Huw, harried and anxious, cast about him as honestly as he could for a way of pleasing everybody. It took him most of the evening to get the prior to listen, but from sheer exhaustion a calm had to set in at last.

'Rhisiart is not an impious man – '

'Not impious!' fluted Brother Jerome, appealing to heaven with uplifted eyes. 'Men have been excommunicated for less!'

'Then men have been excommunicated for no evil at all,' said Huw sturdily, 'and truly I think they sometimes have. No, I say he is a decent, devout man, open-handed and fair, and had a right to resent it when he was misunderstood and affronted. If he is ever to withdraw his opposition, it must be you, Father Prior, who make the first approach to him, and upon a different footing. Not in person first, I would not ask or advise it. But if I were to go to him, perhaps with Brother Cadfael here, who is known to be a good Welshman himself, and ask him to forget all that has been said and done, and come with an open mind to begin the discussion over again, I think he would not refuse. Moreover, the very act of seeking him out would disarm him, for he has a generous heart. I don't say he would necessarily change his mind – it would depend on how he is handled this time – but I do say he would listen.'

'Far be it from me,' said Prior Robert loftily, 'to pass over any means of saving a soul from perdition. I wish the man no ill, if he tempers his offences. It is not a humiliation to stoop to deliver a sinner.'

'O wondrous clemency!' intoned Brother Jerome. 'Saintly generosity towards the ill-doer!'

Brother John flashed a narrow, glittering glance, and shifted one foot uneasily, as if restraining an impulse to kick. Father Huw, desperate to preserve his stock of goodwill with prince, bishop, prior and people alike, cast him a warning look, and resumed hurriedly: 'I will go to Rhisiart tonight, and ask him to dine here at my house tomorrow. Then if we can come to terms between us, another assembly can be called, so that all may know there is peace.'

'Very well!' said the prior, after consideration. In that way he need never actually admit any guilt on his part, or apologise for any act of his, nor need he enquire too closely what Huw might have to say on his behalf. 'Very well, do so, and I hope you may succeed.'

'It would be a mark of your status, and the importance of this gesture,' suggested Cadfael with an earnest face, 'if your messengers went mounted. It's not yet dark, and the horses would be the better for exercise.'

'True,' said the prior, mildly gratified. 'It would be in keeping with our dignity and lend weight to our errand. Very well, let Brother John bring the horses.'

'Now that's what I call a friend!' said Brother John heartily, when they were all three in the saddle, and safely away into the early dusk under the trees, Father Huw and John on the two tall horses, Brother Cadfael on the best of the mules. 'Ten more minutes, and I should have earned myself a penance that would have lasted a month or more, and now here we are in the best company around, on a decent errand, and enjoying the quiet of the evening.'

'Did I ever say word of your coming with us?' said Cadfael slyly. 'I said the horses would add lustre to the embassage, I never went so far as to say *you* would add any.'

'I go with the horses. Did you ever hear of an ambassador riding without a groom? I'll keep well out of the way while you confer, and play the dutiful servant. And by the by, Bened will be doing his drinking up there at the hall tonight. They go the rounds, and it's Cai's turn.'

'And how did you learn so much,' wondered Cadfael, 'without a word of Welsh?'

'Oh, they knock their meaning into me somehow, and I into them. Besides, I have several words of Welsh already, and if we're held up here for a while I shall soon learn a great many more, if I can get my tongue round them. I could learn the smith's art, too. I lent him a hand at the forge this morning.'

'You're honoured. In Wales not everyone can be a smith.'

Huw indicated the fence that had begun to run alongside them on the right. 'Cadwallon's holding. We have a mile of forest to go yet to Rhisiart's hall.'

It was still no more than dusk when they emerged into a large clearing, with ploughed and planted strips surrounding a long stockade fence. The smell of wood-smoke drifted on the air, and glimmer of torches lit the open doorway of the hall. Stables and barns and folds clung to the inner side of the fence, and men and women moved briskly about the evening business of a considerable household.

'Well, well!' said the voice of Cai the ploughman, from a bench under the eaves of one of the byres. 'So you've found your way by nose to where the mead is tonight, Brother Cadfael.' And he moved up obligingly to make room, shoulder to shoulder with Bened. 'Padrig's making music within, and from all I hear it may well be war music, but he'll be with us presently. Sit yourself down, and welcome. Nobody looks on you as the enemy.'

There was a third with them already, a long man seated in deeper shadow, his legs stretched well out before him at ease, and his hair showing as a primrose pallor even in the dimness. The young outlander, Engelard, willingly gathered up his long limbs and also moved to share the bench. He had a quick, open smile vivid with white teeth.

'We've come expressly to halt the war,' said Brother Cadfael as they dismounted, and a groom of the household came running to take their bridles. 'Father Huw has the peace in hand, I'm only an assessor to see fair play. And, sadly, we'll be expected back with an answer as soon as we've spoken with your lord. But if you'll take charge of Brother John while we deal, he'll be grateful. He can speak English with Engelard, a man should practise his own tongue when he can.'

But Brother John, it appeared, had at that moment completely lost the use of his tongue in any language, for he stood at gaze, and let the reins be taken from his hands like a man in a dream. Nor was he looking at Engelard, but towards the open doorway of the hall, from which a girl's figure had issued, and was crossing gaily towards the drinkers under the eaves, a large jug carried in both hands. The lively brown eyes flickered over the visitors, took in Cadfael and the priest with easy friendliness, and opened wide upon Brother John, standing like a very lifelike statue, all thorny russet hair, weather-burned cheeks and wild, admiring eyes. Cadfael

59

looked where Annest's eyes were looking, and approved a very upstanding, ruggedly-built, ingenuous, comely young fellow, maybe two or three years older than the girl. The Benedictine habit, kilted to the knee for riding and forgotten now, looked as much like a working Welsh tunic as made no matter, and the tonsure, however well a man (or a girl!) knew it was there, was invisible behind the burning bush of curls.

'Thirsty people you are, then!' said Annest, still with one eye upon Brother John, and set down her pitcher on the bench beside Cai, and with a flick of her skirts and a wave of her light-brown mane, sat down beside it, and accepted the horn Bened offered her. Brother John stood mute and enchanted.

'Come on, then, lad,' said Bened, and made a place for him between himself and Cai, only one remove from where the girl sat delicately sipping. And Brother John, like a man walking in his sleep, though perhaps with rather more zestful purpose, strode forward towards the seat reserved for him.

'Well, well!' said Cadfael silently to himself, and left the insoluble to the solver of all problems, and with Father Huw moved on into the hall.

'I will come,' said Rhisiart, shut into a small chamber apart with his visitors. 'Of course I will come. No man should refuse another his say. No man can be sure he will not belie himself and do himself less than justice, and God forbid I should refuse anyone his second chance. I've often spoken in haste myself, and been sorry after, and said so, as your prior has said so now.' He had not, of course, nor had Huw claimed, in so many words, that he had. Rather he had expressed his own shame and regret, but if Rhisiart attributed these to Prior Robert, Huw was desperate enough to let him continue in the delusion. 'But I tell you this, I expect little from this meeting. The gap between us is too wide. To you I can say what I have not said to any who were not there, because I am ashamed. The man offered me money. He says now he offered it to Gwytherin, but how is that possible? Am I Gwytherin? I am a man like other men, I fill my place as best I can, but remain one only. No, he offered the purse to me, to take back my voice against him. To persuade my own people to go along with his wishes. I accept his desire to talk to me again, to bring me to see this matter as he sees it. But I cannot forget that he saw it as something he could buy with money. If he wishes to change me, that must change, and be shown to be changed. As for his threats, for threats they are, and I approve you for reporting them faithfully, they move me not at all. My reverence for our little saint is the equal of his or any man's. Do you think she does not know it?'

'I am sure she does,' said Father Huw.

'And if all they want is to honour and adore her rightly, why can they not do so here, where she lies? Even dress her grave, if that is what disturbs them, that we've let it run wild?'

'A good question,' said Brother Cadfael. 'I have asked it myself. The sleep of saints should be more sacred and immune even than the sleep of ordinary men.'

Rhisiart looked him over with those fine, challenging eyes, a shade or two lighter than his daughter's, and smiled. 'Howbeit, I will come, and my thanks for all your trouble. At the hour of noon, or a little after, I will come to your dinner, and I will listen faithfully to whatever may be said to me.'

There was a good laughter echoing from end to end of the bench under the eaves, and it was tempting to join the drinkers, at least for one quick cup, as Cai demanded. Bened had got up to replenish his horn from the pitcher, and Brother John, silent and flushed but glowingly happy, sat with no barrier between him and the girl, their sleeves all but touching when she leaned curiously closer, her hair dropping a stray lock against his shoulder.

'Well, how have you sped?' asked Cai, pouring mead for them. 'Will he come and talk terms with your prior?'

'He'll come,' said Cadfael. 'Whether he'll talk terms I doubt. He was greatly affronted. But he'll come to dine, and that's something.'

'The whole parish will know it before ever you get back to the parsonage,' said Cai. 'News runs faster than the wind in these parts, and after this morning they're all building on Rhisiart. I tell you, if he changed his tune and said amen, so would they. Not for want of their own doubts and waverings, but because they trust him. He took a stand, and they know he won't leave it but for good reason. Sweeten him, and you'll get your way.'

'Not my way.' said Cadfael. 'I never could see why a man can't reverence his favourite saint without wanting to fondle her bones, but there's great rivalry for such relics among the abbeys these days. A good mead, this, Cai.'

'Our Annest here brewed it,' said Bened, with tolerant pride in his niece, and clapped a hand fondly on her shoulder. 'And only one of her skills! She'll be a treasure for some man when she weds, but a sad loss to me.'

'I might bring you a good smith to work with you,' said the girl, dimpling. 'Where's the loss then?'

It was deep dusk, and with all the longing they felt to linger, they had to be away. Huw was fidgety, thinking of Prior Robert's rising impatience, his tall figure pacing the garden and looking out for the first glimpse of his messengers returning. 'We should be off. We shall be looked for. Come, brother, make your farewells.'

Brother John rose reluctantly but dutifully. The groom was leading the horses forward, an arm under each arching neck. With composed face but glowing eyes Brother John said his general goodnight and blessing. In careful but resounding Welsh!

The echo swept the riders away towards the gate on a wave of laughter and goodwill, in which the girl's light voice soared gaily, and Engelard's hearty English 'God go with you!' balanced tongues.

'And who taught you that between evening and dark?' asked Brother Cadfael with interest, as they entered the deep green twilight under the trees. 'Bened or Cai?'

'Neither,' said Brother John, contentedly pondering a deep private satisfaction.

Small use asking how she had managed it, she having no English and he no Welsh, to determine what the phrase was she was drumming into him. There was a kind of language at work here that made short shrift of interpreters.

'Well, you can fairly claim the day hasn't been wasted,' owned Cadfael generously, 'if something's been learned. And have you made any other discoveries to add to that?'

'Yes,' said Brother John, placidly glowing. 'The day after tomorrow is baking-day at Bened's.'

'You may rest and sleep, Father Prior,' said Huw, fronting the tall, pale forehead gallantly with his low, brown one. 'Rhisiart has said he will come, and he will listen. He was gracious and reasonable. Tomorrow at noon or soon after he will be here.'

Prior Robert certainly loosed a cautious, suppressed sigh of relief. But he required more before they could all go away and sleep. Richard loomed at his shoulder, large, benign and anxious.

'And is he sensible of the wrong-mindedness of his resist-ance? Will he withdraw his opposition?'

In the dimness where the candle-light barely reached, Broth-ers Jerome and Columbanus trembled and hoped, for while doubt remained they had not been permitted to remove to their rest at Cadwallon's house. Anxious eyes appealed. Reflecting the light.

Father Huw hedged, wanting his own sleep. 'He offers friendly interest and faithful consideration. I asked no more.'

Brother Cadfael said bluntly: 'You will need to be persuasive, and sincere. *He* is sincere. I am no way convinced that he can be lightly persuaded.' He was tired of nursing wounded vanities, he spoke out what was in his mind. 'Father Prior, you made your mistake with him this morning. You will need a change of heart, *his or yours,* to undo that damage.'

Prior Robert made his dispositions as soon as Mass was over next morning, and with some care.

'Only Brother Sub-Prior and I, with Father Huw, and Brother Cadfael as interpreter, will sit at table together. You, Brother John, will make yourself useful to the cooks, and do whatever is needed, and you may also see to Father Huw's cattle and chickens. And you two, Brother Jerome, Brother Columbanus, I have a special mission for you. Since we are about Saint Winifred's business, I would have you go and spend the hours while we deliberate in vigil and prayer, imploring her aid to bring the obdurate to reason, and our errand to a success-ful conclusion. Not in the church here, but in her own chapel in the old graveyard where she is buried. Take your food and your measure of wine with you, and go there now. The boy Edwin will show you the way. If we prevail upon Rhisiart, as with her aid I trust we may, I will send to release you. But continue your intercessions until I do send word.'

They scattered dutifully, John, cheerfully enough, to tend the fire for Marared, and fetch and carry as she directed. The old woman, long widowed and her own sons grown, preened herself at having a strapping young fellow to keep her company, and Cadfael reflected that John might well be favoured with the best bits before the meal ever came to table. As for Jerome and Columbanus, he saw them set out with the boy, bread and meat wrapped in napkins in the breasts of their habits, and Columbanus carrying the flask with their ration of wine, and a small bottle of spring water for himself.

63

'It is very little to offer,' he said meekly, 'but I will touch nothing but water until our cause has prevailed.'

'More fool he,' said Brother John blithely, 'for he may well be swearing off wine for life!'

It was a fine spring morning, but capricious as May can be. Prior Robert and his attendants sat in the orchard until they were driven indoors by a sharp and sparkling shower that lasted almost half an hour. It was then approaching noon, the time when Rhisiart should join them. He would have a wet walk by the short path through the forest. Or perhaps he had waited for the sun's return at Cadwallon's house, which was on his way. Making allowances for that, they thought little of it when another half-hour passed, and he did not put in an appearance. But when he was an hour late for the meeting, and still no sign of him, Prior Robert's face grew both grim and cautiously triumphant.

'He has heard the warning I issued against his sin, and he fears to come and face me,' he said.

'He had heard the warning, indeed,' said Father Huw heavily, 'but I saw no signs of fear in him. He spoke very firmly and calmly. And he is a man of his word. I don't understand this, it is not like him.'

'We will eat, but frugally,' said the prior, 'and give him every chance of keeping his promise, if something has happened to delay him. So it may, to any man. We will wait until it is time to prepare for Vespers.'

'I'll walk as far as Cadwallon's house,' offered Brother Richard, 'for the way is all one to that point, and see if I can meet with him, or get word if he's on his way.'

He was gone more than an hour and a half, and came back alone. 'I went beyond, some way along the ride, but saw no sign of him. On my way back I asked at Cadwallon's gate, but no one had seen him pass. I feared he might have walked by the short path while I was taking the other road.'

'We'll wait for him until Vespers, and no longer,' said the prior, and by then his voice was growing grimly confident, for now he did not expect the guest to come, and the enemy would have put himself in the wrong, to Prior Robert's great gain. Until Vespers, therefore, they waited, five hours after the appointed time. The people of Gwytherin could hardly say Rhisiart had been written off too hastily.

'So it ends,' said the prior, rising and shaking out his skirts like one shaking off a doubt or an incubus. 'He has turned tail, and his opposition will carry no weight now with any man. Let us go!'

The sunlight was still bright but slanting over the green bowl where the church stood, and a number of people were gathering for the service. And out of the deeper green shadow where the forest path began, came, not Rhisiart, but his daughter, sailing gallantly out into the sunlight in a green gown, with her wild hair tamed and braided, and a linen coif over it, Sioned in her church-going person, with Peredur on her heels, his hand possessively cupping her elbow, though she paid little heed to that attention. She saw them issuing in a silent procession from Huw's gate, and her eyes went from person to person, lingering on Cadfael who came last, and again looking back with a small frown, as though one face was missing from the expected company.

'Where is my father?' she asked, her wide eyes surprised but not yet troubled. 'Is he not still here with you? Have I missed him? I rode as far as Cadwallon's house, and he was on foot, so if he has left more than an hour ago he may well be home by now. I came to bear him company to church and go back with him afterwards.'

Prior Robert looked down at her in some wonder, the first flickering uneasiness twitching his nostrils. 'What is she saying? Do you tell me that the lord Rhisiart set out to come to our meeting?'

'Of course!' said Sioned, amazed. 'He had said he would.'

'But he did not come,' said Robert. 'We've waited for him since noon, and we've seen no sign of him. Brother Sub-Prior went a part of the way to see if he could meet with him, but in vain. He has not been here.'

She caught the meaning of that without Cadfael's services. Her eyes flashed from face to face, distrustful and ready for anger. 'Are you telling me truth? Or have you hidden him away under lock and key until you can get Winifred out of her grave and away to Shrewsbury? He was all that stood in your way. And you have threatened him!'

Peredur closed his fingers anxiously on her arm, and drew her against his side. 'Hush, you must not say such things. These brothers would not lie to you.'

'At what hour,' asked Cadfael, 'did your father set out this morning?'

65

She looked at him, and was a little reassured. The ring of silent onlookers drew nearer, listening attentively, ready to take her part if she needed an army.

'A good hour before noon. He was going first to the fields in the clearing, so he would be coming here by the shortest way, cutting through a quarter of a mile of forest to the usual path. He had plenty of time to be here before noon. As far as the clearing Engelard would be with him, he was going beyond, to the byres over the hill. There are two cows there ready to drop their calves.'

'We are telling you truly, child,' said Father Huw, his voice as grave and anxious as her own, 'we waited for him, and he never came.'

'What can have happened to him? Where can he be?'

'He will have crossed with us and gone home,' urged Peredur, hovering unhappily at her shoulder. 'We'll ride back, we shall surely find him there before us.'

'No! Why should he turn back, and never come to the dinner? And if he did, why so late? He would have been home long before I dressed my hair and set out to meet him, if he had changed his mind. And besides, he never would.'

'I think,' said Father Huw, 'that my whole parish has some interest in this matter, and we had better put off everything else, even the services of the church, until we have found Rhisiart and assured ourselves that all's well with him. Truly this may be no more than a tangle of mistiming and misunderstanding, but let's resolve it first, and wonder about it afterwards. There are enough of us here. Let's send out in parties along all the roads he may have taken, and Sioned shall show us where she thinks his short cut from the upland fields would bring him to the path. He could not well meet with any dangerous beasts in these woods, but he may have had a fall, an injury that has halted or slowed him. Father Prior, will you join with us?'

'With all my heart,' said Prior Robert, 'and so will we all.'

The less active among them were sent along the open ride, with orders to scatter on either side and comb the surroundings as they went, while the more athletic took the narrow footpath beyond Cadwallon's stockade. The woods here were not yet close-set, there was thick, springy grass under the trees, and no dense undergrowth. They spread out into a half-circle, moving along within a few paces of one another, Sioned pressing purposefully forward up the path with set lips and fixed eyes, Peredur with every evidence of desperate affection following close and murmuring agitated urgings into her unheeding ears. Whether he believed in his own reassurances or not, out of all question he was a young man fathoms deep in love, and ready to do anything to serve and protect Sioned, while she saw in him nothing but the boy from the next holding, and tiresome at that.

They were perhaps half a mile beyond Cadwallon's enclosure when Father Huw suddenly plucked at Brother Cadfael's sleeve.

'We have forgotten Brother Jerome and Brother Columbanus! The hill of the chapel is off to the right here, no great way. Ask Prior Robert, should we not send and call them to join us?'

'I had indeed forgotten,' admitted the prior. 'Yes, by all means send someone. Best one of your parishioners, they all know the way.'

One of the young men swerved aside obediently between the trees, and ran. The slow-moving scythe swept on into deeper forest.

'About here,' said Sioned, halting, 'he would have come down from the clearing. If we go obliquely to the right here, and spread out as before, we shall be covering his likely way.'

The ground rose, the trees grew closer, the undergrowth thicker. They began to thread the encroaching bushes, having to part company by a few yards, losing sight momentarily of their neighbours. They had gone thus only a short way when Bened the smith, crashing through bushes at Brother Cadfael's left hand, uttered a great shout of discovery and dismay, and everyone in the wavering line halted and shook to the sound.

Cadfael turned towards the cry, thrusting through thorn-branches, and came out in a narrow oval of grass surrounded every way with thick bushes, through which a used track no wider than a man's shoulders clove, the long way of the oval. Just where he must have brushed through into the clear space, Rhisiart lay on his back, his right hip hollowing the grass under him, shoulders flattened to the ground and arms spread wide. His legs were drawn up under him with bent knees, the left leg crossed over the right. His short, defiant beard pointed at the sky. So, and at the very same slanting angle, did the feathered flight of the arrow that jutted out from under the cage of his ribs.

Chapter Five

ROM BOTH sides they gathered, drawn to the smith's call, breaking through bushes like the running of a startled herd of deer, and halting appalled round the oval where the body lay. Cadfael went on his knees, and looked for any sign of breath within the drawn-back lips, any pulse in the stretched throat or rise and fall of the pierced breast, but there was none. And for that first moment he was the only one who moved within the open space of grass, and what he did was done in strange, too-intense silence, as though everyone round him held his breath.

Then everything broke out at once in noise and motion. Sioned clawed through the screening circle and saw her father's body, and uttered a great shriek that was more of fury even than of grief, and flung herself forward. Peredur caught her by the wrist and pulled her round into his arms, one hand cupped behind her head to press her face into his shoulder, but she shrieked again, and struck out at him with all her strength, and breaking loose, hurled herself to her knees facing Cadfael, and reached out to embrace her father's body. Cadfael leaned across to ward her off, his hand braced into the grass under Rhisiart's right armpit.

'No! Touch nothing! Not yet! Let him alone, he has things to tell us!'

By some intuitive quickness of mind that had not deserted her even at this moment, she obeyed the tone first, and awakened to the words immediately after. Her eyes questioned him, widening, and slowly she sat back in the grass, and drew her hands together in her lap. Her lips shaped the words after him silently: '– things to tell us!' She looked from his face into the face of the dead man. She knew he was dead. She also knew that the dead speak, often in thunder. And she came of proud Welsh stock to which the blood-feud is sacred, a duty transcending even grief.

When those following gathered closer, and one reached to touch, it was she who spread her arm protectively over the body, and said with authority: 'No! Let him be!'

Cadfael had drawn back his arm, and for a moment wondered what troubled him about the palm he had lifted from the grass beside Rhisiart's breast. Then he knew. Where he knelt the grass was perceptibly damp from the morning's sharp shower, he could feel the cling of the habit when he shifted his knee. Yet under the outflung right arm the grass was dry, his hand rose from it with no hint of moisture, no scent of rain. He touched again, ran his fingers up and down alongside Rhisiart's right flank. He was down to the knee before he felt the dampness and stirred the green fragrance. He felt outwards, the width of the body, to find the same signs. Strange! Very strange! His mind recorded and forbore to wonder then, because there were other things to be observed, and all manner of dangers were falling in upon all manner of people.

The tall shape looming at his back, motionless and chill, could be none other than Prior Robert, and Prior Robert in a curious state of exalted shock, nearer to Brother Columbanus' ecstatic fit than he had ever been before or would ever be again. The high, strained voice asked, over the shuddering quietness of Sioned's tearless sob: 'He is dead?'

'Dead,' said Cadfael flatly, and looked into Sioned's wide, dry eyes and held them, promising something as yet undefined. Whatever it was, she understood it and was appeased, for he was Welsh, too, he knew about the blood-feud. And she was the only heir, the only close kin, of a murdered man. She had a task far above sorrow.

The prior's voice soared suddenly, awed and exalted. 'Behold the saint's vengeance! Did I not say her wrath would be wreaked upon all those who stood in the way of her desire? Tell them what I am saying! Tell them to look well at the fulfilment of my prophecy, and let all other obdurate hearts take warning. Saint Winifred has shown her power and her displeasure.'

There was hardly any need for translation, they had the sense of it already. A dozen of those standing close shrank warily away, a dozen voices muttered hurried submission. Not for worlds would they stand in the saint's way.

'The impious man reaps what he sows,' declaimed Robert. 'Rhisiart had his warning, and did not heed it.'

The most timorous were on their knees by then, cowed and horrified. It was not as if Saint Winifred had meant very much to them, until someone else wanted her, and Rhisiart stated a prior claim on behalf of the parish. And Rhisiart was dead by violence, struck down improbably in his own forests.

Sioned's eyes held Cadfael's, above her father's pierced heart. She was a gallant girl, she said never a word, though she had words building up in her ripe for saying, spitting, rather, into Prior Robert's pallid, aristocratic, alabaster face. It was not she who suddenly spoke out. It was Peredur.

'I don't believe it!' He had a fine, clear, vehement voice that rang under the branches. 'What, a gentle virgin saint, to take such vengeance on a good man? Yes, a good man, however mistaken! If she had been so pitiless as to want to slay – and I do not believe it of her! – what need would she have of arrows and bows? Fire from heaven would have done her will just as well, and shown her power better. You are looking at a murdered man, Father Prior. A man's hand fitted that arrow, a man's hand drew the bow, and for a man's reason. There must have been others who had a grudge against Rhisiart, others whose plans he was obstructing, besides Saint Winifred. Why blame this killing on her?'

This forthright Welsh sense Cadfael translated into English for Robert's benefit, who had caught the dissenting tone of it, but not the content. 'And the young man's right. This arrow never was shot from heaven. Look at the angle of it, up from under his ribs into the heart. Out of the earth, rather! A man with a short bow, on his knee among the bushes? True, the ground slopes, he may even have been lower than Rhisiart, but even so. . . .'

'Avenging saints may make use of earthly instruments,' said Robert overbearingly.

'The instrument would still be a murderer,' said Cadfael.

'There is law in Wales, too. We shall need to send word to the prince's bailiff.'

Bened had stood all this time darkly gazing, at the body, at the very slight ooze of blood round the wound, at the jutting shaft with its trimmed feathers. Slowly he said: 'I know this arrow. I know its owner, or at least the man whose mark it bears. Where young men are living close together in a household, they mark their own with a distinctive sign, so that there can be no argument. See the tip of the feathering on one side, dyed blue.' It was as he said, and at the mention of it several there drew breath hard, knowing the mark as well as he knew it.

'It's Engelard's,' said Bened outright, and three or four hushed voices bore him out.

Sioned raised her stricken face, shocked into a false, frozen calm that suddenly melted and crumbled into dread and anger. Rhisiart was dead, there was nothing she could do now for him but mourn and wait, but Engelard was alive and vulnerable, and an outlander, with no kinship to speak for him. She rose abruptly, slender and straight, turning her fierce eyes from face to face all round the circle.

'Engelard is the most trustworthy of all my father's men, and would cut off his own drawing hand rather than loose against my father's life. Who dares say this is his work?'

'I don't say so,' said Bened reasonably. 'I do say this is marked as his arrow. He is the best shot with the short bow in all this countryside.'

'And everybody in Gwytherin knows,' spoke up a voice from among the Welshmen, not accusing, only pointing out facts, 'that he has quarrelled often and fiercely with Rhisiart, over a certain matter at issue between them.'

'Over me,' said Sioned harshly. 'Say what you mean! I, of all people, know the truth best. Better than you all! Yes, they have had high words many times, on this one matter, and only this, and would have had more, but for all that, these two have understood each other, and neither one of them would ever have done the other harm. Do you think the prize fought over does not get to know the risks to herself and both the combatants? Fight they did, but they thought more highly of each other than either did of any of you, and with good reason.'

'Yet who can say,' said Peredur in a low voice, 'how far a man may step aside even from his own nature, for love?'

She turned and looked at him with measuring scorn. 'I thought you were his friend!'

'So I am his friend,' said Peredur, paling but steadfast. 'I said what I believe of myself, no less than of him.'

'What is this matter of one Engelard?' demanded Prior Robert, left behind in this exchange. 'Tell me what they are saying.' And when Cadfael had done so, as tersely as possible: 'It would seem that at least this young man must be asked to account for his movements this day,' decreed Robert, appropriating an authority to which he had no direct right here. 'It may be that others have been with him, and can vouch for him. But if not. . . .'

'He set out this morning with your father,' said Huw, distressfully eyeing the girl's fixed and defiant face. 'You told us so. They went together as far as the cleared fields. Then your father turned to make his way down to us, and Engelard was to go a mile beyond, to the byres where the cows were in calf. We must send out and ask if any man has seen your father since he parted from Engelard. Is there any who can speak to that?'

There was a silence. The numbers gathered about them were growing steadily. Some of the slower searchers from the open ride had made their way up here without news of their own, to find the matter thus terribly resolved. Others, hearing rumours of the missing man, had followed from the village. Father Huw's messenger came up behind with Brother Columbanus and Brother Jerome from the chapel. But no one spoke up to say he had seen Rhisiart that day. Nor did any volunteer word of having encountered Engelard.

'He must be questioned,' said Prior Robert, 'and if his answers are not satisfactory, he must be held and handed over to the bailiff. For it's clear from what has been said that this man certainly had a motive for wishing to remove Rhisiart from his path.'

'Motive?' blazed Sioned, burning up abruptly as a dark and quiet fire suddenly spurts flame. Instinctively she recoiled into Welsh, though she had already revealed how well she could follow what was said around her in English, and the chief reason for her reticence concerning her knowledge had been cruelly removed. 'Not so strong a motive as *you* had, Father Prior! Every soul in this parish knows what store you set upon getting Saint Winifred away from us, what glory it will be to your abbey, and above all, to you. And who stood in your way but my father? *Yours*, not the saint's! Show me a better reason for wanting him dead! Did any ever wish to lift hand against him, all these years! Until *you* came here with your quest for Winifred's relics? Engelard's disagreement with my father was constant and understood, yours was new and urgent. Our need could wait, we're young. Yours could not wait. And who knew better than you at what hour my father would be coming through the forest to Gwytherin? Or that he would not change his mind?'

Father Huw spread a horrified hand to hush her long before this, but she would not be hushed. 'Child, child, you must not make such dreadful accusations against the reverend prior, it is mortal sin.'

'I state facts, and let them speak,' snapped Sioned. 'Where's the offence in that? Prior Robert may point out the facts that suit him, I show you the others, those that do not suit him. My father was the sole obstacle in his path, and my father has been removed.'

'Child, I tell you every soul in this valley knew that your father was coming to my house, and the hour of his coming, and many would know all the possible ways, far better than any of these good brethren from Shrewsbury. The occasion might well suit another grudge. And you must know that Prior Robert has been with me, and with Brother Richard and Brother Cadfael here, ever since morning Mass.' And Father Huw turned in agitated supplication to Robert, wringing his hands. 'Father Prior, I beg you, do not hold it against the girl that she speaks so wildly. She is in great grief – a father lost. . . . You cannot wonder if she turns on us all.'

'I say no word of blame,' said the prior, though coldly. 'I gather she is casting doubts upon myself and my companions, but doubtless you have answered her. Tell the young woman, in my name, that both you and others here can witness for my own person, for all this day I have been within your sight.'

Grateful for at least one certainty, Huw turned to repeat as much to Sioned yet again, but she blazed back with biting promptness and force, forgetting all restraints in the need to confront Robert face to face, without the tedious intervention of interpreters. 'So you may have been, Father Prior,' she flashed in plain English. 'In any case I don't see *you* as likely to make a good bowman. But a man who would try to buy my father's compliance would be willing and able to buy some more pliable person to do even this work for him. You still had your purse! Rhisiart spurned it!'

'Take care!' thundered Robert, galled beyond the limits of his arduous patience. 'You put your soul in peril! I have borne with you thus far, making allowances for your grief, but go no further along this road!'

They were staring upon each other like adversaries in the lists before the baton falls, he very tall and rigid and chill as ice, she slight and ferocious and very handsome, her coif long ago lost among the bushes, and her sheaves of black hair loose on her shoulders. And at that moment, before she could spit further fire, or he threaten more imminent damnation, they all heard voices approaching from higher up among the woods, a man's voice and a girl's in quick, concerned exchanges, and coming rapidly nearer with a light threshing of branches, as though they had caught the raised tones and threatening sounds of many people gathered here improbably deep in the forest, and were hurrying to discover what was happening.

The two antagonists heard them, and their concentration on each other was shaken and disrupted. Sioned knew them, and a fleeting shadow of fear and desperation passed over her face. She glanced round wildly, but there was no help. A girl's arm parted the bushes above the oval where they stood, and Annest stepped through, and stood in astonishment, gazing round at the inexplicable gathering before her.

It was the narrowness of the track – no more than the shadow of a deer-path in the grass – and the abruptness with which she had halted that gave Sioned her one chance. She took it valiantly. 'Go back home, Annest,' she said loudly. 'I am coming with company. Go and prepare for guests, quickly, you'll have little time.' Her voice was high and urgent. Annest had not yet lowered her eyes to the ground, and grass and shadows veiled Rhisiart's body.

The effort was wasted. Another hand, large and gentle, was laid on Annest's shoulder while she hesitated, and moved her aside. 'The company sounds somewhat loud and angry,' said a man's voice, high and clear, 'so, with your leave, Sioned, we'll all go together.'

Engelard put the girl aside between his hands, as familiarly and serenely as a brother might have done, and stepped past her into the clearing.

He had eyes for no one but Sioned, he walked towards her with the straight gait of a proprietor, and as he came he took in her stiff erectness, and fixed face of fire and ice and despair, and his own face mirrored everything he saw in her. His brows drew together, his smile, taut and formidable to begin with, vanished utterly, his eyes burned bluer than cornflowers. He passed by Prior Robert as though he had not even been there, or not alive, a stock, a dead tree by the path. He put out his hands, and Sioned laid her hands in them, and for an instant closed her eyes. There was no frowning him away now, he was here in the midst, quite

74

without defences. The circle, not all inimical but all hampering, was closing round him.

He had her by the hands when he saw Rhisiart's body.

The shock went into him as abruptly as the arrow must have gone into Rhisiart, stopping him instantly. Cadfael had him well in view, and saw his lips part and whisper soundlessly: 'Christ aid!' What followed was most eloquent. The Saxon youth moved with loving slowness, shutting both Sioned's hands in one of his, and with his freed right hand stroked softly over her hair, down temple and cheek and chin and throat, all with such mastered passion that she was soothed, as he meant, while he had barely stopped shaking from the shock.

He folded an arm about her, holding her close against his side, and slowly looked all round the circle of watching faces, and slowly down at the body of his lord. His face was bleakly angry.

'Who did this?'

He looked round, seeking the one who by rights should be spokesman, hesitating between Prior Robert, who arrogated to himself authority wherever he came, and Father Huw, who was known and trusted here. He repeated his demand in English, but neither of them answered him, and for a long moment neither did anyone else. Then Sioned said, with clear, deliberate warning: 'There are some here are saying that *you* did.'

'I?' he cried, astonished and scornful rather than alarmed, and turned sharply to search her face, which was intent and urgent.

Her lips shaped silently: 'Run! They're blaming you!'

It was all she could do, and he understood, for they had such a link between them that meanings could be exchanged in silence, in a look. He measured with a quick glance the number of his possible enemies, and the spaces between them, but he did not move. 'Who accuses me?' he said. 'And on what ground? It seems to me I might rather question all of you, whom I find standing here about my lord's dead body, while I have been all day out with the cows, beyond Bryn. When I got home Annest was anxious because Sioned had not returned, and the sheep boy told her there was no service at Vespers at the church. We came out to look for you, and found you by the noise you were making among you. And I ask you again, and I will know before ever I give up: *Who did this?*'

'We are all asking that,' said Father Huw. 'Son, there's no man here has accused you. But there are things that give us the right to question you, and a man with nothing on his conscience won't be ashamed or afraid to answer. Have you yet looked carefully at the arrow that struck Rhisiart down? Then look at it now!'

Frowning, Engelard drew a step nearer, and looked indeed, earnestly and bitterly at the dead man, only afterwards at the arrow. He saw the flutter of deep blue, and gasped.

'This is one of mine!' He looked up with wild suspicion at them all. 'Either that, or someone has copied my mark. But no, this is mine, I know the trim, I fletched it new only a week or so ago.'

'He owns it his?' demanded Robert, following as best as he could. 'He admits it?'

'Admit?' flashed Engelard in English. 'What is there to admit? I *say* it! How it was brought here, who loosed it, I know no more than you do, but I know the shaft for mine. God's teeth!' he cried furiously, 'do you think if I had any hand in this villainy I should leave my mark flaunting in the wound? Am I fool as well as outlander? And do you think I would do anything to harm Rhisiart? The man who stood my friend and gave me the means of living here when I'd poached myself out of Cheshire?'

'He refused to consider you as a suitor for his daughter,' Bened said almost reluctantly, 'whatever good he did for you otherwise.'

'So he did, and according to his lights, rightly so. And I know it, knowing as much as I've learned of Wales, and even if I did smart under it, I knew he had reason and custom on his side. Never has he done anything I could complain of as unfair to me. He stood much arrogance and impatience from me, come to that. There isn't a man in Gwynedd I like and respect more. I'd as soon have cut my own throat as injured Rhisiart.'

'He knew and knows it,' said Sioned, 'and so do I.'

'Yet the arrow is yours,' said Huw unhappily. 'And as for reclaiming or disguising it, it may well have been that speedy flight after such an act would be more important.'

'If I had planned such an act,' said Engelard, 'though God forbid I should ever have to imagine a thing so vile, I could as easily have done what some devil has done now to me, and used another man's shaft.'

'But, son, it would be more in keeping with your nature,' the priest pursued sadly, 'to commit such a deed without planning, having with you only your own bow and arrows. Another approach, another quarrel, a sudden wild rage! No one supposes this was plotted beforehand.'

'I had no bow with me all this day. I was busy with the cattle, what should I want with a bow?'

76

'It will be for the royal bailiff to enquire into all possible matters concerning this case,' said Prior Robert, resolutely reclaiming the dominance among them. 'What should be asked at once of this young man is where he has been all this day, what doing, and in whose company.'

'In no man's company. The byres behind Bryn are in a lonely place, good pasture but apart from the used roads. Two cows dropped their calves today, one around noon, the second not before late afternoon, and that was a hard birth, and gave me trouble. But the young things are there alive and on their legs now, to testify to what I've been doing.'

'You left Rhisiart at his fields along the way?'

'I did, and went straight on to my own work. And have not seen him again until now.'

'And did you speak with any man, there at the byres? Can anyone testify as to where you were, at any time during the day?' No one was likely to try and wrest the initiative from Robert now. Engelard looked around him quickly, measuring chances. Annest came forward silently, and took her stand beside Sioned. Brother John's roused, anxious eyes followed her progress, and approved the loyalty which had no other way of expressing itself.

'Engelard did not come home until half an hour ago,' she said stoutly.

'Child,' said Father Huw wretchedly, 'where he was not does not in any way confirm where he says he was. Two calves may be delivered far more quickly than he claims, how can we know, who were not there? He had time to slip back here and do this thing, and be back with his cattle and never noticed. Unless we can find someone who testifies to having seen him elsewhere, at whatever time this deed may have been done, then I fear we should hold Engelard in safe-keeping until the prince's bailiff can take over the charge for us.'

The men of Gwytherin hovered, murmuring, some convinced, many angry, for Rhisiart had been very well liked, some hesitant, but granting that the outlander ought to be held until his innocence was established or his guilt proved. They shifted and closed, and their murmur became one of consent.

'It is fair,' said Bened, and the growl of assent answered him.

'One lone Englishman with his back to the wall,' whispered Brother John indignantly in Cadfael's ear, 'and what chance will he have, with nobody to bear out what he says?

77

And plain truth, for certain! Does he act or speak like a murderer?'

Peredur had stood like a stock all this while, hardly taking his eyes from Engelard's face but to gaze earnestly and unhappily at Sioned. As Prior Robert levelled an imperious arm at Engelard, and the whole assembly closed in slowly in obedience, braced to lay hands on him, Peredur drew a little further back at the edge of the trees, and Cadfael saw him catch Sioned's eyes, flash her a wild, wide-eyed look, and jerk his head as though beckoning. Out of her exhaustion and misery she roused a brief, answering blaze, and leaned to whisper rapidly in Engelard's ear.

'Do your duty, all of you,' commanded Robert, 'to your laws and your prince and your church, and lay hold of this man!'

There was one instant of stillness, and then they closed in all together, the only gap in their ranks where Peredur still hung back. Engelard made a long lead from Sioned's side, as though he would break for the thickest screen of bushes, and then, instead, caught up a dead, fallen bough that lay in the grass, and whirled it about him in a flailing circle, laying two unwary elders flat, and sending others reeling back out of range. Before they could reassemble, he had changed direction, leaped over one of the fallen, and was clean through the midst of them, arming off the only one who almost got a grip on him, and made straight for the gap Peredur had left in their ranks. Father Huw's voice, uplifted in vexed agitation, called on Peredur to halt him, and Peredur sprang to intercept his flight. How it happened was never quite clear, though Brother Cadfael had a rough idea, but at the very moment when his outstretched hand almost brushed Engelard's sleeve, Peredur stepped upon a rotten branch in the turf, that snapped under his foot and rolled, tossing him flat on his face, half-blinded among the bushes. And winded, possibly, for certainly he made no move to pick himself up until Engelard was past him and away.

Even then it was not quite over, for the nearest pursuers on either side, seeing how the hunt had turned, had also begun to run like hares, on courses converging with the fugitive's at the very edge of the clearing. From the left came a long-legged villein of Cadwallon's, with a stride like a greyhound, and from the right Brother John, his habit flying, his sandalled feet pounding the earth mightily. It was perhaps the first time Brother John had ever enjoyed Prior Robert's whole-hearted approval. It was certainly the last.

There was no one left in the race but these three, and fleet though Engelard was, it seemed that the long-legged fellow would collide with him before he could finally vanish. All three were hurtling together for a shattering collision, or so it seemed. The villein stretched out arms as formidably long as his legs. So, on the other side, did Brother John. A great hand closed on a thin fold of Engelard's tunic from one side. Brother John bounded exuberantly in from the other. The prior sighed relief, expecting the prisoner to be enfolded in a double embrace. And Brother John, diving, caught Cadwallon's villein round the knees and brought him crashing to the ground, and Engelard, plucking his tunic out of the enemy's grasp, leaped into the bushes and vanished in a receding susurration of branches, until silence and stillness closed over the path of his withdrawal.

Half the hunt, out of excitement rather than any real enmity, streamed away into the forest after the quarry, but half-heartedly now. They had little chance of capturing him. Probably they had no great desire to do anything of the kind, though once put to it, hounds must follow a scent. The real drama remained behind in the clearing. There, at least, justice had one clear culprit to enjoy.

Brother John unwound his arms from his victim's knees, sat up in the grass, fended off placidly a feeble blow the villein aimed at him, and said in robust but incomprehensible English: 'Ah, let well alone, lad! What did he ever do to you? But faith, I'm sorry I had to fetch you down so heavily. If you think you're hard-done-to, take comfort! I'm likely to pay dearer than you.'

He looked round him complacently enough as he clambered to his feet and dusted off the debris of leaves and twigs that clung to his habit. There stood Prior Robert, not yet unfrozen from the shock of incredulous disillusionment, tall and stiff and grey, a Norman lordling debating terrible penalties for treason. But there, also, stood Sioned, tired, distraught, worn out with passion, but with a small, reviving glow in her eyes, and there was Annest at her elbow, an arm protectively round her waist, but her flower-face turned towards John. Not much use Robert thundering and lightning, while she so smiled and blossomed, beaming her gratitude and admiration.

Brother Richard and Brother Jerome loomed like messengers of doom, one at either elbow. 'Brother John, you are summoned. You are in gross offence.'

He went with them resignedly. For all the threatening thunder-bolts he had never felt freer in his life. And having

79

now nothing to lose but his own self-respect, he was sturdily determined not to sacrifice that.

'Unfaithful and unworthy brother,' hissed Prior Robert, towering in terrible indignation, 'what have you done? Do not deny what we have all witnessed. You have not merely connived at the escape of a felon, you have frustrated the attempt of a loyal servant to arrest him. You felled that good man deliberately, to let Engelard go free. Traitor against church and law, you have put yourself beyond the pale. If there is anything you can say in your defence, say it now.'

'I thought the lad was being harried beyond reason, on very suspect suspicion,' said Brother John boldly. 'I've talked with Engelard, I've got my own view of him, a decent, open soul, who'd never do violence to any man by stealth, let alone Rhisiart, whom he liked and valued high. I don't believe he has any part in this death, and what's more, I think he'll not go far until he knows who had, and God help the murderer then! So I gave him his chance, and good luck to him!'

The two girls, their heads close together in women's solidarity, interpreted the tone for themselves, if they lacked the words, and glowed in silent applause. Prior Robert was helpless, though he did not know it. Brother Cadfael knew it very well.

'Shameless!' thundered Robert, bristling until even his suave purity showed knife-edged with affront. 'You are condemned out of your own mouth, and a disgrace to our order. I have no jurisdiction here as regards Welsh law. The prince's bailiff must resolve this crime that cries for vengeance here. But where my own subordinates are concerned, and where they have infringed the law of this land where we are guests, there two disciplines threaten you, Brother John. As to the sovereignty of Gwynedd, I cannot speak. As to my own discipline, I can and do. You are set far beyond mere ecclesiastical penance. I consign you to close imprisonment until I can confer with the secular authority here, and I refuse to you, meanwhile, all the comforts and consolations of the church.' He looked about him and took thought, brooding. Father Huw hovered miserably, lost in this ocean of complaints and accusations. 'Brother Cadfael, ask Father Huw where there is a safe prison, where he can be held.'

This was more than Brother John had bargained for, and though he repented of nothing, like a practical man he did begin to look round to weigh up the chances of evading the consequences. He eyed the gaps in the ring as Engelard had

80

done, braced his sturdy feet well apart, and flexed his shoulders experimentally, as though he had thoughts of elbowing Brother Richard smartly in the belly, kicking the legs from under Jerome, and making a dash for freedom. He stopped himself just in time when he heard Cadfael report sedately: 'Father Huw suggests there is only one place secure enough. If Sioned is willing to allow her holding to be used, a prisoner could be safe enough there.'

At this point Brother John unaccountably lost interest in immediate escape.

'My house is at Prior Robert's disposal,' said Sioned in Welsh, with appropriate coldness, but very promptly. She had herself well in hand, she made no more lapses into English. 'There are storehouses and stables, if you wish to use them. I promise I shall not go near the prisoner, or hold the key to his prison myself. Father Prior may choose his guard from among my people as he sees fit. My household shall provide him his living, but even that charge I shall give to someone else. If I undertook it myself I fear my impartiality might be doubted, after what has happened.'

A good girl, Cadfael thought, translating this for Robert's benefit rather less than for John's. Clever enough to step resolutely round any actual lies even when she was thus wrung by one disaster after another, and generous enough to think for the wants and wishes of others. The someone else who would be charged with seeing Brother John decently housed and fed was standing cheek to cheek with her mistress as she spoke, fair head against dark head. A formidable pair! But they might not have found this unexpected and promising path open to them but for the innocence of celibate parish priests.

'That may be the best plan,' said Prior Robert, chilly but courteous, 'and I thank you for your dutiful offer, daughter. Keep him straitly, see he has what he needs for life, but no more. He is in great peril of his soul, his body may somewhat atone. If you permit, we will go before and bestow him securely, and let your uncle know what has happened, so that he may send down to you to bring you home. I will not intrude longer in a house of mourning.'

'I will show you the way,' said Annest, stepping demurely from Sioned's side.

'Hold him fast!' warned the prior, as they massed to follow her uphill through the woods. Though he might have seen for himself, had he looked closely, that the culprit's resignation had mellowed into something very like complacency, and he stepped

81

out as briskly as his guards, a good deal more intent on keeping Annest's slender waist and lithe shoulders in sight than on any opportunity for escape.

Well, thought Cadfael, letting them go without him, and turning to meet Sioned's steady gaze, God sort all! As doubtless he is doing, now as ever!

The men of Gwytherin cut young branches and made a green litter to carry Rhisiart's body home. Under the corpse, when they lifted it, there was much more blood than about the frontal wound, though the point of the arrow barely broke through skin and clothing. Cadfael would have liked to examine tunic and wound more closely, but forbore because Sioned was there beside him, stiffly erect in her stony grief, and nothing, no word or act that was not hieratic and ceremonial, was permissible then in her presence. Moreover, soon all the servants of Rhisiart's household came down in force to bring their lord home, while the steward waited at the gate with bards and mourning women to welcome him back for the last time, and this was no longer an enquiry into guilt, but the first celebration of a great funeral rite, in which probing would have been indecent. No hope of enquiring further tonight. Even Prior Robert had acknowledged that he must remove himself and his fellows reverently from a mourning community in which they had no rights.

When it was time to raise the litter and its burden, now stretched out decently with his twisted legs drawn out straight and his hands laid quietly at his sides, Sioned looked round for one more to whom she meant to confide a share in this honourable load. She did not find him.

'Where is Peredur? What became of him?'

No one had seen him go, but he was gone. No one had had attention to spare for him after Brother John had completed what Peredur had begun. He had slipped away without a word, as though he had done something to be ashamed of, something for which he might expect blame rather than thanks. Sioned was a little hurt, even in her greater hurt, at his desertion.

'I thought he would have wanted to help me bring my father home. He was a favourite with him, and fond of him. From a little boy he was in and out of our house like his own.'

'He maybe doubted his welcome,' said Cadfael, 'after saying a word that displeased you concerning Engelard.'

'And doing a thing afterwards that more than wiped that out?' she said, but for his ears only. No need to say outright before

82

everyone what she knew very well, that Peredur had contrived a way out for her lover. 'No, I don't understand why he should slink away without a word, like this.' But she said no more then, only begged him with a look to walk with her as she fell in behind the litter. They went some distance in silence. Then she asked, without looking aside at him: 'Did my father yet tell you those things he had to tell?'

'Some,' said Cadfael. 'Not all.'

'Is there anything I should do, or not do? I need to know. We must make him seemly tonight.' By the morrow he would be stiff, and she knew it. 'If you need anything from me, tell me now.'

'Keep me the clothes he's wearing, when you take them off him, and take note for me where they're damp from this morning's rain, and where they're dry. If you notice anything strange, remember it. Tomorrow, as soon as I can, I'll come to you.'

'I must know the truth,' she said. 'You know why.'

'Yes, I know. But tonight sing to him and drink to him, and never doubt but he'll hear the singing.'

'Yes,' she said, and loosed a great, renewing sigh. 'You are a good man. I'm glad you're here. You do not believe it was Engelard.'

'I'm as good as certain it was not. First and best, it isn't in him. Lads like Engelard hit out in a passion, but with their fists, not with weapons. Second, if it had been in his scope, he'd have made a better job of it. You saw the angle of the arrow. Engelard, I judge, is the breadth of three fingers taller than your father. How could he shoot an arrow under a man's rib-cage who is shorter than he, even from lower ground? Even if he kneeled or crouched in the undergrowth in ambush, I doubt if it could be done. And why should it ever be tried? No, this is folly. And to say that the best shot in all these parts could not put his shaft clean through his man, at any distance there where he could see him? Not more than fifty yards clear in any direction. Worse folly still, why should a good bowman choose such a blind tangled place? They have not looked at the ground, or they could not put forward such foolishness. But first and last and best, that young man of yours is too open and honest to kill by stealth, even a man he hated. And he did not hate Rhisiart. You need not tell me, I know it.'

Much of what he had said might well have been hurtful to her, but none of it was. She went with him every step of that way,

83

and flushed and warmed into her proper, vulnerable girlhood at hearing her lover thus accepted.

'You've said no word in wonder,' she said, 'that I have not been more troubled over what has become of Engelard, and where he is gone to earth now.'

'No,' said Cadfael, and smiled. 'You know where he is, and how to get in touch with him whenever you need. I think you two have two or three places better for secrecy than your oak tree, and in one of them Engelard is resting now, or soon will be. You seem to think he'll be safe enough. Tell me nothing, unless you need a messenger, or help.'

'You can be my messenger, if you will, to another,' she said. They were emerging from the forest at the edge of Rhisiart's home fields, and Prior Robert stood tall and grim and non-committal aside from their path, his companions discreetly disposed behind him, his hands, features, and the angle of his gently bowed head all disposed to convey respect for death and compassion for the bereaved without actually owning to forgiveness of the dead. His prisoner was safely lodged, he was waiting only to collect the last stray from his flock, and make an appropriately impressive exit. 'Tell Peredur I missed him from among those my father would have liked to carry him home. Tell him what he did was generous, and I am grateful. I am sorry he should ever have doubted it.'

They were approaching the gate, and Uncle Meurice, the steward, came out to meet them with his kindly, soft-lined face quaking and shapeless with shock and distress.

'And come tomorrow,' said Sioned on an almost soundless breath, and walked away from him alone, and entered the gateway after her father's body.

Chapter Six

IONED'S MESSAGE might not have been delivered so soon, for it would not have been any easy matter to run aside at Cadwallon's house, without a word of request or excuse to Prior Robert; but in the dimness of the woods, a little above the holding, Cadfael caught a glimpse of a figure withdrawing from them, with evident intent, some fifty yards into cover, and knew it for Peredur. He had not expected to be followed, for he went only far enough to be secure from actual encounter on the path, and there sat down moodily on a fallen trunk, his back against a young tree that leaned with him, and kicked one foot in the litter of last year's leaves. Cadfael asked no permission, but went after him.

Peredur looked up at the sound of other feet rustling the beech-mast, and rose as if he would have removed further to avoid speech, but then gave up the thought, and stood mute and unwelcoming, but resigned.

'I have a word to you,' said Brother Cadfael mildly, 'from Sioned. She bade me tell you that she missed you when she would gladly have asked you to lend a shoulder for her father's bier. She sends you word that what you did was generous, and she is grateful.'

Peredur stirred his feet uneasily, and drew a little back into deeper shadow.

'There were plenty of her own people there,' he said, after a pause that seemed awkward rather than sullen. 'She had no need of me.'

'Oh, there were hands enough, and shoulders enough,' agreed Cadfael, 'nevertheless, she missed you. It seems to me that she looks upon you as one having a forward place among her own people. You have been like a brother to her from children, and she could well do with a brother now.'

The stiffness of Peredur's young body was palpable even in the green dusk, a constraint that crippled even his tongue. He got out, with a bitter spurt of laughter: 'It was not her brother I wanted to be.'

'No, that I understand. Yet you behaved like one, towards her and towards Engelard, when it came to the testing.'

What was meant to comfort and compliment appeared, instead, to hurt. Peredur shrank still deeper into his morose stillness. 'So she feels she has a debt to me, and wants to pay it, but not for my sake. She does not want *me*.'

'Well,' said Cadfael equably, 'I have delivered her message, and if you'll go to her she'll convince you, as I cannot. There was another would have wanted you there, if he could have spoken.'

'Oh, hush!' said Peredur, and jerked his head aside with a motion of sudden pain. 'Don't say more. . . .'

'No, pardon me, I know this is a grief to you, as well as to her. She said so. "He was a favourite with him," she said, "and fond of him –"'

The boy gave a sharp gasp, and turning with blundering haste, walked away rapidly through the trees, deeper into the wood, and left Brother Cadfael to return very thoughtfully to his companions, with the feel of that unbearably tender spot still wincing under his probing finger.

'You and I,' said Bened, when Cadfael walked down to the smithy after Compline, 'must do our drinking alone tonight, my friend. Huw has not yet come down from Rhisiart's hall, and Padrig will be busy singing the dead man till the small hours. Well that he was there at this time. A man's all the better for being sung to his grave by a fine poet and harpist, and it's a great thing for his children to remember. And Cai – Cai we shan't be seeing down here much for a while, not until the bailiff comes to take his prisoner off his hands.'

'You mean Brother John has *Cai* for his gaoler?' asked Cadfael, enlightened.

'He volunteered for the job. I fancy that girl of mine ran and prompted him, but he wouldn't need much prodding. Between them, Brother John will be lying snug enough for a day or two. You need not worry about him.'

'Nothing was further from my mind,' said Cadfael. 'And it's Cai who keeps the key on him?'

'You may be sure. And what with Prince Owain being away in the south, as I hear he is, I doubt if sheriff or bailiff will have much time to spare for a small matter of insubordination in Gwytherin.' Bened sighed heavily over his horn, filled this time with coarse red wine. 'It grieves me now that ever I spoke up and called attention to the blue on the feathers, at least in front of the lass. But someone would have said it. And it's truth that now, with only her Uncle Meurice as guardian, she could have got her own way. She twists him round her finger, he wouldn't have stood in her road. But now I misdoubt me, no man would be such a fool as to leave his private mark on a dead man for all to see. Not unless he was disturbed and had to take to his heels. All it needed was the corner clipping, how long does that take if you've a knife on you? No, it's hard to understand. And yet it could be so!'

By his deep gloom there was more on Bened's mind than that. Somewhere within, he was in abysmal doubt whether he had not spoken up in the hope of having a better chance with Sioned himself if his most favoured rival was removed. He shook his head sadly. 'I was glad when he broke clear as he did, but I'll be satisfied if he makes his way back to Cheshire after this alarm. And yet it's hard to think of him as a murderer.'

'We might give our minds to that, if you're willing,' said Cadfael, 'for you know the people of these parts better than I do. Let's own it, the girl's suspicion, that she spoke out to Prior Robert's face, will be what many a one here is thinking, whether he says it or not. Here are we come into the place and starting a great contention, chiefly with this one lord – no need to argue who's in the right – and there he stands as the one obstacle to what we've come for, and suddenly he's dead, murdered. What's more natural than to point the finger at us, all of us?'

'It's blasphemy even to consider such a charge against such reverend brothers,' said Bened, shocked.

'Kings and abbots are also men, and can fall to temptation. So how do we all stand in regard to this day's doings? All six of us were together or close within sight of one another until after Mass. Then Prior Robert, Brother Richard and I were with Father Huw, first in the orchard, and when it rained, half an hour before noon, in the house. None of the four of us could have gone into the forest. Brother John, too, was about the house and holding, Marared can vouch for him as well as we. The only one who left, before we all came forth for Vespers and set off to search for Rhisiart, was Brother Richard, who offered to go and see if he could meet with him or get word of him, and was gone perhaps an hour and a half, and came back empty-handed. From an hour after noon he was gone, and into the forest, too, for what it's worth, and makes no claim to have spoken with anyone until he enquired at Cadwallon's gate on his way back, which would be nearing half past two. I must speak with the gate-keeper, and see if he bears that out. Two of us are left, but not unaccounted for. Brother Jerome and Brother Columbanus were sent off to keep a vigil together at Saint Winifred's chapel, to pray for a peaceful agreement. We all saw them set off together, and they'd be in the chapel and on their knees long before ever Rhisiart came down towards the path. And there they stayed until Father Huw's messenger went to fetch them to join us. Each of them is warranty for the other.'

'I said so,' said Bened, reassured. 'Holy men do not do murder.'

'Man,' said Cadfael earnestly, 'there are as holy persons outside orders as ever there are in, and not to trifle with truth, as good men out of the Christian church as most I've met within it. In the Holy Land I've know Saracens I'd trust before the common run of the crusaders, men honourable, generous and courteous, who would have scorned to haggle and jostle for place and trade as some of our allies did. Meet every man as you find him, for we're all made the same under habit or robe or rags. Some better made than others, and some better cared for, but on the same pattern all. But there it is. As far as I can see, only one of us, Brother Richard, had any chance at all to be in the neighbourhood when Rhisiart was killed, and of all of us he makes the least likely murderer. So we're forced to look if the ground is not wide open for others, and Saint Winifred only an opportunity and an excuse. Had Rhisiart any enemies around Gwytherin? Some who might never have moved against him if we had not blown up this storm and put the temptation in their way?'

Bened considered gravely, nursing his wine. 'I wouldn't say there's a man anywhere who has not someone to wish him ill, but it's a far cry from that to murder. Time was when Father Huw himself came up against Rhisiart over a patch of land both claimed, and tempers ran high, but they settled it the proper way, by witness from the neighbours, and there's been no malice after. And there have been lawsuits – did you ever hear of a Welsh landholder without one or two lawsuits in hand? One with Rhys ap Cynan over a disputed boundary, one over some beasts that strayed. Nothing to make lasting bad blood. We thrive on suits at law. One thing's true, with the interest you've roused here, every soul for miles around knew that Rhisiart was due at Father Huw's parsonage at noon. No limit at all, there, on who might have decided to waylay him on the road.'

That was as far as they could get. The field was wide, wide enough still to include Engelard, however persuaded Cadfael might be that he was incapable of such an act. Wide enough to enfold even neighbours like Cadwallon, villeins from the village, servants of the household.

But not, surely, thought Brother Cadfael, making his way back to Huw's loft in the green and fragrant dark, not that strange young man who had been a favourite of Rhisiart, and fond of him, and in and out of his house like a son from childhood? The young man who had said of Engelard, and of himself, that a man might step far aside even from his own nature, for love, and then, presumably for love, had opened a way for Engelard to escape, as Cadfael had seen for himself. And who was now avoiding Sioned's gratitude and affection, either because it was not love, and love was the only thing he wanted from her, or for some darker reason. When he flung away in silence into the forest he had had the look of one pursued by a demon. But surely not *that* demon? So far from furthering his chances, Rhisiart's death robbed him of his most staunch ally, who had waited patiently and urged constantly, to bring his daughter to the desired match in the end. No, whichever way a man looked at him, Peredur remained mysterious and disturbing.

Father Huw did not come back from Rhisiart's house that night. Brother Cadfael lay alone in the loft, and mindful that Brother John was locked up somewhere in Sioned's barns, and there was no one to prepare food, got up in good time and went to do it himself, and then set off to Bened's paddock to see to the horses, who were also left without a groom. It suited him better to be out and working in the fresh morning than cooped up with Prior Robert, but he was obliged to return in time for chapter, which the prior had decreed should be held daily as at home, however brief the business they had to transact here.

They met in the orchard, the five of them, Prior Robert presiding in as solemn dignity as ever. Brother Richard read out the saints to be celebrated that day and the following day. Brother Jerome composed his wiry person into his usual shape of sycophantic reverence, and made all the appropriate responses. But it seemed to Cadfael that Brother Columbanus looked unusually withdrawn and troubled, his full blue eyes veiled. The contrast between his athletic build and fine, autocratic head, and his meek and anxious devoutness of feature and bearing, was always confusing to the observer, but that morning his extreme preoccupation with some inward crisis of real or imagined sin made it painful to look at him. Brother Cadfael sighed, expecting another falling fit like the one that had launched them all on this quest. Who knew what this badly-balanced half-saint, half-idiot would do next?

'Here we have but one business in hand,' said Prior Robert firmly, 'and we shall pursue it as in duty bound. I mean to press more resolutely than ever for our right to take up the relics of the saint, and remove them to Shrewsbury. But we must admit, at this moment, that we have not so far been successful in carrying the people with us. I had great hopes yesterday that all would be resolved. We made very reverent preparation to deserve success. . . .'

At this point he was interrupted by an audible sob from Brother Columbanus, that drew all eyes to that young man. Trembling and meek, he rose from his place and stood with lowered eyes and folded hands before Robert.

'Father Prior, alas, *mea culpa*! I am to blame! I have been unfaithful, and I desire to make confession. I came to chapter determined to cleanse my bosom and ask penance, for my backsliding is the cause of our continued distresses. May I speak?'

I knew there was something brewing, thought Brother Cadfael, resigned and disgusted. But at least without rolling on the ground and biting the grass, this time!

'Speak out,' said the prior, not unkindly. 'You have never sought to make light of your failings, I do not think you need fear our too harsh condemnation. You have been commonly your own sternest judge.' So he had, but that, well handled, can be one way of evading and forestalling the judgments of others.

Brother Columbanus sank to his knees in the orchard turf. And very comely and aristocratic he looked, Cadfael admitted, again admiring with surprise the compact grace and strength of his body, and the supple flow of his movements.

'Father, you sent me with Brother Jerome, yesterday, to keep vigil in the chapel, and pray earnestly for a good outcome, in amity and peace. Father, we came there in good time, before eleven, as I judge, and having eaten our meal, we went in and took our places, for there are prayer-desks within, and the altar is kept clean and well-tended. Oh, Father, my will to keep vigil was good, but the flesh was weak. I had not been half an hour kneeling in prayer, when I fell asleep on my arms on the desk, to my endless shame. It is no excuse that I have slept badly and thought much since we came here. Prayer should fix and purify the mind. I slept, and our cause was weakened. I must have slept all the afternoon, for the next thing I remember is Brother Jerome shaking me by the shoulder and telling me there was a messenger calling us to go with him.'

He caught his breath, and a frantic tear rolled down his cheek, circling the bold, rounded Norman bone. 'Oh, do not look askance at Brother Jerome, for he surely never knew I had been sleeping, and there is no blame at all to him for not observing and reporting my sin. I awoke as he touched me, and arose and went with him. He thought me as earnest in prayer as he, and knew no wrong.'

Nobody, probably, had thought of looking askance at Brother Jerome until then, but Cadfael was probably the quickest and most alert, and the only one who caught the curious expression of apprehension, fading rapidly into complacency, that passed over Brother Jerome's normally controlled countenance. Jerome had not been pursuing the same studies as Cadfael, or he would have been far from complacent. For Brother Columbanus in his self-absorbed innocence had just removed all certainty that Jerome had spent the previous noon and afternoon motionless in Saint Winifred's chapel, praying for a happy solution. His only guarantor had been fast asleep throughout. He could have sauntered out and gone anywhere he chose.

'Son,' said Prior Robert, in an indulgent voice he would certainly never have used to Brother John, 'your fault is human, and frailty is in our nature. And you redeem your own error, in defending your brother. Why did you not tell us of this yesterday?'

'Father, how could I? There was no opportunity, before we learned of Rhisiart's death. Thus burdened, how could I burden you further at that time? I kept it for this chapter, the right place for erring brothers to receive their penance, and make their abasement. As I do abase myself, as all unworthy the vocation I chose. Speak out sentence on me, for I desire penance.'

The prior was opening his lips to give judgment, patiently enough, for such devout submission and awareness of guilt disarmed him, when they were distracted by the clap of the wooden bar of the garden gate, and there was Father Huw himself advancing across the grass towards them, hair and beard even more disordered than usual, and his eyes heavy and tired with sleeplessness, but his face resolved and calm.

'Father Prior,' he said, halting before them, 'I have just come from holding council with Cadwallon, and Rhys, and Meurice, and all the men of substance in my parish. It was the best opportunity, though I'm sad indeed about the cause. They all came to the mourning for Rhisiart. Every man there knew how he had been struck down, and how such a fate was prophesied. . . .'

'God forbid,' said Prior Robert hastily, 'that I should threaten any man's death. I said that Saint Winifred would be revenged in her own time on the man who stood in the way and did her offence. I never said a word of killing.'

'But when he was dead you did claim that this was the saint's vengeance. Every man there heard it, and most believed. I took this chance of conferring with them again in the matter. They do not wish to do anything that is against the will of heaven, nor to give offence to the Benedictine order and the abbey of Shrewsbury. They do not think it right or wise, after what has happened, even to put any man, woman or child of Gwytherin in peril. I am commissioned, Father Prior, to tell you that they withdraw all opposition to your plans. The relics of Saint Winifred are yours to take away with you.'

Prior Robert drew a great breath of triumph and joy, and whatever will he might have had to deal even the lightest punishment left him in an instant. It was everything he had hoped for. Brother Columbanus, still kneeling, cast up his eyes radiantly towards heaven and clasped his hands in gratitude, and somehow contrived to look as though he had brought about this desired consummation himself, the deprivation caused by his unfaithfulness compensated in full by this reward of his penitence. Brother Jerome, just as determined to impress prior and priest with his devotion, threw up his hands and uttered a reverent Latin invocation of praise to God and the saints.

'I am certain,' said Prior Robert magnanimously, 'that the people of Gwytherin never wished to offend, and that they have done wisely and rightly now. I am glad, for them as for my abbey, that we may complete our work here and take our leave in amity with you all. And for your part in bringing about this good ending, Father Huw, we are all grateful. You have done well for your parish and your people.'

'I am bound to tell you,' said Huw honestly, 'that they are not at all happy at losing the saint. But none of them will hinder what you wish. If you so will, we will take you to the burial place today.'

'We will go in procession after the next Mass,' said the prior, unwonted animation lighting up his severe countenance now that he had his own way, 'and not touch food until we have knelt at Saint Winifred's altar and given thanks.' His eyes lit upon Brother Columbanus, patiently kneeling and gazing upon him with doglike eyes, still insistent upon having his sin recognised. Robert looked faintly surprised for a moment, as if he had forgotten the young man's existence. 'Rise, brother, and take heart, for you see that there is forgiveness in the air. You shall not be deprived of your share in the delight of visiting the virgin saint and paying honour to her.'

'And my penance?' insisted the incorrigible penitent. There was a good deal of iron in Brother Columbanus' meekness.

'For penance you shall undertake the menial duties that fell to Brother John, and serve your fellows and their beasts until we return home. But your part in the glory of this day you shall have, and help to bear the reliquary in which the saint's bones are to rest. We'll carry it with us, and set it up before the altar. Every move we make I would have the virgin approve plainly, in all men's sight.'

'And will you break the ground today?' asked Father Huw wearily. No doubt he would be glad to have the whole episode over and forgotten, and be rid of them all, so that Gwytherin could settle again to its age-old business, though short of one good man.

'No,' said Prior Robert after due thought. 'I wish to show forth at every stage our willingness to be guided, and the truth of what we have claimed, that our mission was inspired by Saint

93

Winifred herself. I decree that there shall be three nights of vigil and prayer before the chapel altar, before ever we break the sod, to confirm to all that what we are doing is indeed right and blessed. We are six here, if you will join us, Father Huw. Two by two we will watch nightlong in the chapel, and pray to be guided rightly.'

They took up the silver-inlaid coffin made in implicit faith in Shrewsbury, and carried it in procession up through the woods, past Cadwallon's house, taking the right-hand path that led them obliquely away from the scene of Rhisiart's death, until they came to a small clearing on a hillside, ringed round on three sides by tall, thick clumps of hawthorn, then in snowy bloom. The chapel was of wood, dark with age, small and shadowy within, a tiny bell-turret without a bell leaning over the doorway. Round it the old graveyard lay spread like billowing green skirts, thick with herbs and brambles and tall grasses. By the time they reached this place they had a silent and ever-growing company of local inhabitants following them, curious, submissive, wary. There was no way of telling whether they still felt resentment. Their eyes were steady, observant and opaque, determined to miss nothing and give nothing away.

At the sagging wooden gate that still hung where the path entered, Prior Robert halted, and made the sign of the cross with large, grave gestures. 'Wait here!' he said, when Huw would have led him forward. 'Let us see if prayer can guide my feet, for I have prayed. You shall not show me the saint's grave. I will show it to you, if she will be my aid.'

Obediently they stood and watched his tall figure advance with measured steps, as if he felt his way, the skirts of his habit sweeping through the tangles of grass and flowers. Without hesitation and without haste he made his way to a little, overgrown mound aligned with the east end of the chapel, and sank to his knees at its head.

'Saint Winifred lies here,' he said.

Cadfael thought about it every step of the way, as he went up through the woods that afternoon to Rhisiart's hall. A man could count on Prior Robert to be impressive, but that little miracle had been a master-stroke. The breathless hush, the rippling outbreak of comment and wonder and awe among the men of Gwytherin were with him still. No question but the remotest villein hut and the poorest free holding in the parish would be buzzing with the news by now. The monks of Shrewsbury were vindicated. The saint had taken their prior by the hand and led him to her grave. No, the man had never before been to that place, nor had the grave been marked in any way, by a belated attempt to cut the brambles from it, for instance. It was as it had always been, and yet he had known it from all the rest.

No use at all pointing out, to a crowd swayed by emotion, that if Prior Robert had not previously been to the chapel, Brothers Jerome and Columbanus, his most faithful adherents, had, only the previous day, and with the boy Edwin to guide them, and what more probable than that one of them should have asked the child the whereabouts of the lady they had come all this way to find?

And now, with this triumph already establishing his claim, Robert had given himself three whole days and nights of delay, in which other, similar prodigies might well confirm his ascendancy. A very bold step, but then, Robert was a bold and resourceful man, quite capable of gambling his chances of providing further miracles against any risk of contrary chance refuting him. He meant to leave Gwytherin with what he had come for, but to leave it, if not fully reconciled, then permanently cowed. No scuttling away in haste with his prize of bones, as though still in terror of being thwarted.

But he could not have killed Rhisiart, thought Cadfael with certainty. That I know. Could he have gone so far as to procure . . .? He considered the possibility honestly, and discarded it. Robert he endured, disliked, and in a fashion admired. At Brother John's age he would have detested him, but Cadfael was old, experienced and grown tolerant.

He came to the gatehouse of Rhisiart's holding, a wattle hut shored into a corner of the palisade fence. The man knew him again from yesterday, and let him in freely. Cai came across the enclosed court to meet him, grinning. All grins here were somewhat soured and chastened now, but a spark of inward mischief survived.

'Have you come to rescue your mate?' asked Cai. 'I doubt he wouldn't thank you, he's lying snug, and feeding like a fighting cock, and no threats of the bailiff yet. *She's* said never a word, you may be sure, and Father Huw would be in no hurry. I reckon we've a couple of days yet, unless your prior makes it his business, where it's none. And if he does, we have boys out will give us plenty of notice before any horseman reaches the gate. Brother John's in good hands.'

It was Engelard's fellow-worker speaking, the man who knew him as well as any in this place. Clearly Brother John had established himself with his gaoler, and Cai's mission was rather to keep the threatening world from him, than to keep him from sallying forth into the world. When the key was needed for the right purpose, it would be provided.

'Take care for your own head,' said Cadfael, though without much anxiety. They knew what they were doing. 'Your prince may have a lawyer's mind, and want to keep in with the Benedictines along the border.'

'Ah, never fret! An escaped felon can be nobody's fault. And everybody's quarry and nobody's prize! Have you never hunted zealously in all the wrong places for something you desired not to find?'

'Say no more,' said Cadfael, 'or I shall have to stop my ears. And tell the lad I never even asked after him, for I know there's no need.'

'Would you be wishing to have a gossip with him?' offered Cai generously. 'He's lodged over yonder in a nice little stable that's clean and empty, and he gets his meals princely, I tell you!'

'Tell me nothing, for I might be asked,' said Cadfael. 'A blind eye and a deaf ear can be useful sometimes. I'll be glad to spend a while with you presently, but now I'm bound to *her*. We have business together.'

Sioned was not in the hall, but in the small chamber curtained off at its end, Rhisiart's private room. And Rhisiart was private there with his daughter, stretched out straight and still on draped furs, on a trestle table, with a white linen sheet covering him. The girl sat beside him, waiting, very formally attired, very grave, her hair austerely braided about her head. She looked older, and taller, now that she was the lady-lord of this holding. But she rose to meet Brother Cadfael with the bright, sad, eager smile of a child sure now of counsel and guidance.

'I looked for you earlier. No matter, I'm glad you're here. I have his clothes for you. I did not fold them; if I had, the damp would have spread evenly through, and now, though they may have dried off, I think you'll still feel a difference.' She brought them, chausses, tunic and shirt, and he took them from her one by one and felt at the cloth testingly. 'I see,' she said, 'that you already known where to feel.'

Rhisiart's hose, though partly covered by the tunic he had worn, were still damp at the back of the thighs and legs, but in front dry, though the damp had spread round through the

96

threads to narrow the dry part to a few inches. His tunic was moist all down the back to the hem, the full width of his shoulders still shaped in a dark patch spread wings, but all the breast of it, round the dark-rimmed slit the arrow had made, was quite dry. The shirt, though less definitely, showed the same pattern. The fronts of the sleeves were dry, the backs damp. Where the exit wound pierced his back, shirt and tunic were soaked in blood now drying and encrusted.

'You remember,' said Cadfael, 'just how he lay when we found him?'

'I shall remember it my life long,' said Sioned. 'From the hips up flat on his back, but his right hip turned into the grass, and his legs twisted, the left over the right, like. . . .' She hesitated, frowning, feeling for her own half-glimpsed meaning, and found it. 'Like a man who has been lying on his face, and heaves himself over in his sleep on to his back, and sleeps again at once.'

'Or,' said Cadfael, 'like a man who has been taken by the left shoulder, as he lay on his face, and heaved over on to his back. After he was well asleep!'

She gazed at him steadily, with eyes hollow and dark like wounds. 'Tell me all your thoughts. I need to know. I must know.'

'First, then,' said Brother Cadfael, 'I call attention to the place where this thing happened. A close-set, thicketed place, with plenty of bushes for cover, but not more than fifty paces clear view in any direction. Is that an archer's ground? I think not. Even if he wished the body to be left in woodlands where it might lie undiscovered for hours he could have found a hundred places more favourable to him. An expert bowman does not need to get close to his quarry, he needs room to draw on a target he can hold in view long enough for a steady aim.'

'Yes,' said Sioned. 'Even if it could be believed of him that he would kill, that rules out Engelard.'

'Not only Engelard, any good bowman, and if someone so incompetent as to need so close a shot tried it, I doubt if he could succeed. I do not like this arrow, it has no place here, and yet here it is. It has one clear purpose, to cast the guilt on Engelard. But I cannot get it out of my head that it has some other purpose, too.'

'To kill!' said Sioned, burning darkly.

'Even that I question, mad though it may seem. See the angle at which it enters and leaves. And then see how the blood is all at the back, and not where the shaft entered. And remember all we have said and noted about his clothes, how they were wet behind, though he lay on his back. And how you yourself said it was the attitude of a man who had heaved himself over from lying on his face. And one more thing I found out yesterday, as I kneeled beside him. Under him the thick grass was wet. But all down by his right side, shoulder to hip and body-wide, it was bone-dry. There was a brisk shower yesterday morning, half an hour of rain. When that rain began, your father was lying on his face, already dead. How else could that patch of grass have remained dry, but sheltered by his body?'

'And then,' said Sioned low but clearly, 'as you say, he was taken by his left shoulder and heaved over on to his back. When he was well asleep. Deep asleep!'

'So it looks to me!'

'But the arrow entered his breast,' she said. 'How, then, could he fall on his face?'

'That we have to find out. Also why he bled behind, and not in front. But lie on his face he did, and that from before the rain began until after it ceased, or the grass beneath him could not have been dry. From half an hour before noon, when the first drops fell, until some minutes past noon, when the sun came out again. Sioned, may I, with all reverence, look closely again now at his body?'

'I know no greater reverence anyone can pay to a murdered man,' she said fiercely, 'than to seek out by all possible means and avenge him on his murder. Yes, handle him if you must. I'll help you. No one else! At least,' she said with a pale and bitter smile, 'you and I are not afraid to touch him, in case he bleeds in accusation against us.'

Cadfael was sharply arrested in the act of drawing down the sheet that covered Rhisiart's body, as though what she had said had put a new and promising idea into his head. 'True! There are not many who do not believe in that trial. Would you say everyone here holds by it?'

'Don't your people believe it? Don't you?' She was astonished. Her eyes rounded like a child's

'My cloister-brothers. . . . Yes, I dare say all or most believe in it. I? Child, I've seen too many slaughtered men handled over and over after a battle by those who finish them off, and never known one of them gush fresh blood, once the life was out of him. But what I believe or don't believe is not to the point. What the murderer believes well may be. No, you have endured enough. Leave him now to me.'

Nevertheless, she did not turn her eyes away, as Cadfael drew off the covering sheet. She must have anticipated the need to examine the body further, for as yet she had left him naked, unshrouded. Washed clean of blood, Rhisiart lay composed and at rest, a thick, powerful trunk brown to the waist, whiter below. The wound under his ribs, an erect slit, now showed ugly and torn, with frayed, bluish lips, though they had done their best to smooth the lacerated flesh together.

'I must turn him,' said Cadfael. 'I need to see the other wound.'

She did not hesitate, but with the tenderness of a mother rather than a daughter she slipped an arm under her father's shoulders, and with her free hand flattened under him from the other side, raised the stiffened corpse until he lay on his right side, his face cradled in the hollow of her arm. Cadfael steadied the stretched-out legs, and leaned to peer closely at the wound high on the left side of the back.

'You would have trouble pulling out the shaft. You had to withdraw it frontally.'

'Yes.' She shook for a moment, for that had been the worst of the ordeal. 'The tip barely broke the skin behind, we had no chance to cut it off. Shame to mangle him so, but what could we do? And yet all that blood!'

The steel point had indeed done little more than puncture the skin, leaving a small, blackened spot, dried blood with a bluish bruise round it. But there was a further mark there, thin and clear and faint. From the black spot the brown line of another upright slit extended, a little longer above the arrow-mark than below, its length in all about as great as the width of Cadfael's thumb-joint, and a faint stain of bruising extending it slightly at either end, beyond where the skin was broken. All that blood – though in fact it was not so very much, though it took Rhisiart's life away with it – had drained out of this thin slit, and not from the wound in his breast, though that now glared, and this lay closed and secret.

'I have done,' said Cadfael gently, and helped her to lay her father at peace again. When they had smoothed even the thick mane of his hair, they covered him again reverently. Then Cadfael told her exactly what he had seen. She watched him with great eyes, and thought for some moments in silence. Then she said: 'I did see this mark you speak of. I could not account for it. If you can, tell me.'

'It was there his life-blood came out,' said Cadfael. 'And not by the puncture the arrow certainly made, but by a prior wound. A wound made, as I judge, by a long dagger, and a very thin and sharp one, no common working knife. Once it was withdrawn, the wound was nearly closed. Yet the blade passed clean through him. For it was possible, afterwards, to trace and turn that same thrust backwards upon itself, and very accurately, too. What we took for the exit wound is no exit wound at all, but an entry wound. The arrow was driven in from the front after he was dead, to hide the fact that he was stabbed in the back. That was why the ambush took place in thick undergrowth, in a tangled place. That was why he fell on his face, and why, afterwards, he was turned on his back. And why the upward course of the arrow is so improbable. It never was shot from any bow. To *thrust* in an arrow is hard work, it was made to get its power from flight. I think the way was opened first with a dagger.'

'The same that struck him down from behind,' she said, white and translucent as flame.

'It would seem so. Then the arrow was inserted after. Even so he could not make it penetrate further. I mistrusted that shot from the first. Engelard could have put a shaft through a couple of oak boards and clean away at that distance. So could any archer worth his pay. But to thrust it in with your hands – no, it was a strong, lusty arm that made even this crude job of it. And at least he got the line right. A good eye, a sensitive hand.'

'A devil's heart,' said Sioned, 'and Engelard's arrow! Someone who knew where to find them, and knew Engelard would not be there to prevent.' But for all her intolerable burdens, she was still thinking clearly. 'I have a question yet. Why did this murderer leave it so long between killing and disguising his kill? My father was dead before ever the rain came. You have shown it clearly. But he was not turned on his back to receive Engelard's arrow until after the rain had stopped. More than half an hour. Why? Was his murderer startled away by someone passing close? Did he wait in the bushes to be sure Rhisiart was dead before he dared touch him? Or did he only think of this devilish trick later, and have to go and fetch the shaft for his purpose? Why so long?'

'That,' said Cadfael honestly, 'I do not know.'

'What do we know? That whoever it was wished to pin this thing upon Engelard. Was that the whole cause? Was my father just a disposable thing, to get rid of Engelard? Bait to trap another man? Or did someone want my father disposed of, and only afterwards realise how easy, how convenient, to dispose of Engelard, too?'

'I know no more than you,' said Cadfael, himself shaken. And he thought, and wished he had not, of that young man fretting his feet tormentedly among the leaves, and flinching from Sioned's trust as from a death-wound. 'Perhaps whoever it was did the deed, and slipped away, and then paused to think, and saw how easy it might be to point the act away from himself, and went back to do it. All we are sure of is this, and, child, thank God for it. Engelard has been set up as a sacrificial victim, and is clear of all taint. Keep that at heart, and wait.'

'And whether we discover the real murderer or not, if ever it should be needful you will speak out for Engelard?'

'That I will, with all my heart. But for now, say nothing of this to anyone, for *we* are still here, the troublers of Gwytherin's peace, and never think that I have set us apart as immaculate. Until we know the guilty, we do not know the innocent.'

'I take back nothing,' said Sioned firmly, 'of what I said concerning your prior.'

'Nevertheless, he could not have done it. He was not out of my sight.'

'No, that I accept. But he buys men, and he is utterly set upon getting his saint, and now, as I understand, he has his will. It is a cause. And never forget, Welshmen, as well as Englishmen, may be for sale. I pray not many. But a few.'

'I don't forget,' said Cadfael.

'Who is he? *Who?* He knows my father's movements. He knows where to lay hands on Engelard's arrows. He wants God knows what from my father's death, but certainly he wants to pin murder on Engelard. Brother Cadfael, who can this man be?'

'That, God willing,' he said, 'you and I between us will find out. But as at this moment, I cannot judge nor guess, I am utterly astray. What was done I see, but why, or by whom, I know no more than you. But you have reminded me how the dead are known to rebel against the touch of those who struck them down, and as Rhisiart has told us much, so he may yet tell us all.

He told her, then, of the three nights of prayer and vigil Prior Robert had decreed, and how all the monks and Father Huw, by turns, would share the duty. But he did not tell her how Columbanus, in his single-minded innocence and his concern for his own conscience, had added one more to those who had had the opportunity to lie in wait for her father in the forest.

101

Nor did he admit to her, and hardly to himself, that what they had discovered here lent a sinister meaning to Columbanus' revelation. Jerome out hunting his man with bow and arrow was a most unlikely conception, but Jerome creeping up behind a man's back in thick cover, with a sharp dagger in hand. . . .

Cadfael put the thought behind him, but it did not go far. There was a certain credibility about it that he did not like at all.

'Tonight and for two nights following, two of us will be keeping watch in the chapel from after Compline in the evening until Prime in the morning. All six of us can be drawn into the same trial, and not one can feel himself singled out. After that, we'll see. Now this,' said Brother Cadfael, 'is what you must do. . . .'

Chapter Seven

FTER COMPLINE, in the soft evening light, with
the slanting sunset filtering through young viridian
leaves, they went up, all six together, to the wooden
chapel and the solitary graveyard, to bring their first
pair of pilgrims to the vigil. And there, advancing to meet them
in the clearing before the gate, came another procession, eight
of Rhisiart's household officers and servants, winding down out
of the woods with their lord's bier upon their shoulders, and
their lord's daughter, now herself their lord, walking erect and
dignified before them, dressed in a dark gown and draped with
a grey veil, under which her long hair lay loose in mourning.
Her face was calm and fixed, her eyes looked far. She could
have daunted any man, even an abbot, Prior Robert baulked
at sight of her. Cadfael was proud of her.

So far from checking at sight of Robert, she gave a slight
spring of hope and purpose to her step, and came on without
pause. Face to face with him at three paces distance, she halted
and stood so still and quiet that he might have mistaken this for
submission, if he had been fool enough. But he was not a fool,
and he gazed and measured silently, seeing a woman, a mere
girl, who had come to match him, though not yet recognising
her as his match.

'Brother Cadfael,' she said, without taking her eyes from
Robert's face, 'stand by me now and make my words plain to

the reverend prior, for I have a prayer to him for my father's sake.'

Rhisiart was there at her back, not coffined, only swathed and shrouded in white linen, every line of body and face standing clear under the tight wrappings, in a cradle of leafy branches, carried on a wooden bier. All those dark, secret Welsh eyes of the men who bore him glowed like little lamps about a catafalque, betraying nothing, seeing everything. And the girl was so young, and so solitary. Prior Robert, even in his assured situation, was uneasy. He may even have been moved.

'Make your prayer, daughter,' he said.

'I have heard that you intend to watch three nights in reverence to Saint Winifred, before you take her hence with you. I ask that for the ease of my father's soul, if he has offended against her, which was never his intent, he may be allowed to lie those three nights before her altar, in the care of those who keep watch. I ask that they will spare one prayer for forgiveness and rest to his soul, one only, in a long night of prayer. Is that too much to ask?'

'It is a fair asking,' said Robert, 'from a loyal daughter.' And after all, he came of a noble family, and knew how to value the ties of blood and birth, and he was not all falsity.

'I hope for a sign of grace,' said Sioned, 'all the more if you approve me.'

There was no way that such a request could do anything but add lustre and glory to his reputation. His opponent's heiress and only child came asking his countenance and patronage. He was more than gratified, he was charmed. He gave his consent graciously, aware of more pairs of Gwytherin eyes watching him than belonged to Rhisiart's bearers. Scattered though the households were, apart from the villein community that farmed as one family, the woods were full of eyes now wherever the strangers went. A pity they had not kept as close a watch on Rhisiart when he was man alive!

They installed his green bier on the trestles before the altar, beside the reliquary that awaited Saint Winifred's bones. The altar was small and plain, the bier almost dwarfed it, and the light that came in through the narrow east window barely illuminated the scene even by morning sunlight. Prior Robert had brought altar-cloths in the chest, and with these the trestles were draped. There the party from Rhisiart's hall left their lord lying in state, and quietly withdrew on the way home.

'In the morning,' said Sioned, before she went with them, 'I shall come to say my thanks to those who have asked grace for my father during the night. And so I shall do each morning, before we bury him.'

She made the reverence due to Prior Robert, and went away without another word, without so much as a glance at Brother Cadfael, drawing the veil close round her face.

So far, so good! Robert's vanity and self-interest, if not his compunction, had assured her of her chance, it remained to be seen what would come of it. The order of their watches had been decreed by Robert himself, in consultation with no one but Father Huw, who wished to be the first to spend the night opening his heart to the saint's influence, if she pleased to make her presence known. His partner was Brother Jerome, of whose obsequious attendance the prior occasionally grew weary, and Cadfael was thankful for the accidental choice that suited him best. That first morning, at least, no one would know what to expect. After that the rest would have due warning, but surely no way of evading the issue.

In the morning, when they went to the chapel, it was to find a fair number of the inhabitants of Gwytherin already gathered there, though unobtrusively, lurking in the edges of the woods and under the fragrant shadow of the hawthorn hedges. Only when the prior and his companions entered the chapel did the villagers emerge silently from cover and gather close, and the first of them to draw near was Sioned, with Annest at her elbow. Way was opened for the two girls, and the people of Gwytherin closed in after them, filling the doorway of the chapel and blocking off the early light, so that only the candles on the altar cast a pale glow over the bier where the dead man lay.

Father Huw got up from his knees somewhat creakily, leaning on the solid wood of the desk till he could get his old legs straightened and working again. From the other desk beside him Jerome rose briskly and supply. Cadfael thought suspiciously of devout watchkeepers who fell asleep as comfortably as possible on their folded arms, but at the moment that was of no importance. He would hardly have expected heaven to open and rain down roses of forgiveness at Jerome's request, in any case.

'A quiet watch,' said Huw, 'and all most calm I was not visited by any great experience, but such hardly fall to humble parish priests. We have prayed, child, and I trust we have been heard.'

'I am grateful,' said Sioned. 'And before you go, will you do one more kindness for me and mine? As you have all been sufferers in this trouble and dissension, will you show your own will to mercy? You have prayed for him, now I ask you to lay your hand, each of you, upon my father's heart, in token of reassurance and forgiveness.'

The people of Gwytherin, still as trees in the doorway, but live as trees, too, and all eyes as a tree is all leaves, made never a sound, and missed never a move.

'Gladly!' said Father Huw, and stepped to the bier and laid his rough hand gently on the stilled heart, and by the wagging of his beard his lips were again moving in silent intercession. All eyes turned upon Brother Jerome, for Brother Jerome was hesitating.

He did not look greatly disturbed, but he did look evasive. The face he turned upon Sioned was benevolent and sweet, and having bestowed on her the obligatory glance of compassion, he modestly lowered his eyes before her as was prescribed, and turned to look trustfully at Prior Robert.

'Father Huw holds the cure of this parish, and is subject to one discipline, but I to another. The lord Rhisiart surely carried out his religious duties faithfully, and I feel with him. But he died by violence, unconfessed and unshriven, and such a death leaves the health of his soul in doubt. I am not fit to pronounce in this case. I have prayed, but blessing is not for me to dispense without authority. If Prior Robert feels it is justified, and gives me leave, I will gladly do as I am asked.'

Along this devious path Cadfael followed him with some amazement and considerable doubt. If the prior had himself authorised the death, and sent his creature out to accomplish it, Jerome could not have turned the threat back on his superior more neatly. On the other hand, knowing Jerome, this could as well be his way of flattering and courting, at this opportunity as at every other. And if Robert graciously gave his leave, did he suppose that would protect him, as having plainly handed on the guilt and the threat where they truly belonged, and leave him free to touch his victim with impunity? It would have mattered less if Cadfael had firmly believed that the murdered bleed when the murderer touches, but what he believed was very different, simply that the belief was general among most people, and could drive the guilty, when cornered, to terror and confession. That very terror and stress might even produce some small effusion of blood, though

106

he doubted it. He was beginning to think that Jerome doubted it, too.

The watching eyes had changed their quarry, and hung heavily upon the prior. He frowned, and considered gravely for some moments, before he gave judgment. 'You may do what she wishes, with a good conscience. She is asking only for forgiveness, which is every man's to give, not for absolution.'

And Brother Jerome, gratefully acknowledging the instruction, stepped readily to the bier, and laid his hand upon the swathed heart without a tremor. No spurt of red showed through the shroud to accuse him. Complacently he followed Prior Robert out of the chapel, the others falling in behind, and the silent, staring people fell back from the doorway and let them pass.

And where, thought Cadfael, following, does that leave us? Is he quite hardy about the ordeal, not believing in it at all, or does he feel he has passed the guilt to the guilty, whatever his own part in it, and is therefore out of danger? Or had he no part in it at all, and was all this to no purpose? He is quite narrow enough to refuse the girl a kindness, unless he could turn it to his own credit and advantage.

Well, we shall see tomorrow, reasoned Cadfael, what Robert will do when he's asked for his own forgiveness, instead of being generous with another man's.

However, things did not turn out quite as he had expected. Prior Robert had certainly elected to take that night's watch himself, along with Brother Richard. But as the two were on their way to the chapel, and passing by Cadwallon's holding, the prior was hailed by the gateman, and Cadwallon himself came hastening out to intercept him, with a burly, handsomely dressed Welshman in a short riding tunic at his heels.

The first Cadfael knew of it was when the prior came striding back into Huw's garden with the stranger beside him, just at the hour when he should have been sinking to his knees in the sombre chapel with its tiny lights, to keep nightlong company with his dead man, in a confrontation which might yet produce fruitful evidence. But here he was, just in time to prevent Cadfael from slipping away to Bened's smithy to exchange the news of the day, and share a cup of wine. And plainly not seriously displeased at having his night's vigil disrupted, either.

'Brother Cadfael, we have a visitor, and I shall require your services. This is Griffith ap Rhys, Prince Owain's bailiff in Rhos. Cadwallon sent to him concerning the death of the lord Rhisiart, and I must make my own statement to him, and discuss what is to be done. He will be enquiring of all those who may have witness to deliver, but now he requires that I shall render my account first. I have had to send Brother Richard on to the chapel without me.'

Jerome and Columbanus had been about to set out for their own beds in Cadwallon's house, but they lingered dutifully at hearing this. 'I will go in your place, Father Prior.' offered Jerome devotedly, certain he would be refused.

'No, you have had one sleepless night.' (Had he? In that dim interior there was no being sure, even if Father Huw had been a suspicious man. And Jerome was not the kind to wear himself out needlessly.) 'You must get your rest.'

'I would gladly take your place, Father Prior,' offered Columbanus just as ardently.

'You have your turn tomorrow. Beware, brother, of taking too much to yourself, of arrogance in the guise of humility. No Brother Richard will keep the vigil alone tonight. You may wait, both, until you have given your witness as to what you did and saw the day before yesterday, and then leave us, and get your proper sleep.'

That was a long and tedious session, and greatly fretted Brother Cadfael, who was obliged to fall back on his own conception of truth, not, indeed, by translating falsely, but by adding his own view of those things that had happened in the forest by Rhisiart's body. He did not suppress anything Robert said, but he severed plain fact from supposition, the thing observed from the conclusion leaped to, on his own authority. Who was there with Welsh enough to challenge him, except Griffith ap Rhys himself? And that experienced and sceptical officer soon proved himself not only a quick and agile listener, but a very shrewd dissector of feelings and motives, too. He was, after all, Welsh to the bone, and Welsh bones were at the heart of this tangle. By the time he had dealt with Columbanus and Jerome, those two faithful watchers of whom one had turned out to be a treasonous sleeper-on-duty (though neither they nor Prior Robert saw fit to mention that lapse!), Cadfael was beginning to feel he could rely on the good sense of the prince's bailiff, and need not have gone to so much trouble to suppress most of what he himself knew and was about. Better so, though, he decided finally, for what he most needed now was time, and a day or two saved by sending Griffith all round the parish after evidence might see the satisfactory conclusion of his own enquiries. Official justice does not dig deep, but regards what comes readily to the surface, and draws conclusions accordingly. A nagging doubt now and then is the price it pays for speedy order and a quiet land. But Cadfael was not prepared to let the nagging doubt occur in the person of either Engelard or Brother John. No, better go his own way to the end, and have a finished case to present to bailiff and prince.

So there was nothing at all for Sioned to do, when she came, the next morning, but to ask Brother Richard, that large, lazy, kindly man who willed peace and harmony all round him, for his personal pity towards her father, and his benediction in the laying on of hands. Which he gave willingly and guilelessly, and departed still in ignorance of what he had done, and what he had been absolved from doing.

'I missed you,' said Bened, briefly visited between Mass and dinner. 'Padrig came down for a while, we were talking over the old days, when Rhisiart was younger. Padrig's been coming here a good many years now. He knows us all. He asked after you.'

'Tell him we'll share a cup one of these day, here or there. And say I'm about Rhisiart's business, if that's any comfort.'

'We're getting used to you.' said Bened, stooping to his fire, where a sinewy boy was bending into the bellows. 'You should stay, there'd be a place for you.'

'I've got my place,' said Cadfael. 'Never fret about me, I chose the cowl with both eyes open. I knew what I did.'

'There are some I can't reconcile with you,' said Bened, with the iron in hand for the shoe that waited.

'Ah, priors and brothers come and go, as mixed as the rest of men, but the cloister remains. Now, there are some who did lose their way, I grant you,' said Cadfael, 'mostly young things who mistook a girl's "no" for the end of the world. Some of them might make very useful craftsmen, if ever they broke free. Always supposing they were free men, and could get entry to, say, the smith's mystery. . . .'

'He has a good arm and wrist on him, that one,' said Bened reflectively, 'and knows how to jump and do as he's bid when the man bidding knows his business. That's half the craft. If he hasn't let Rhisiart's killer loose on the world, then there isn't an outlander would be more welcome here. But that I don't yet know, though the poor girl up yonder may think she does. How if she's wrong? Do *you* know?'

'Not yet,' owned Cadfael. 'But give us time and we shall know.'

On this third day of Brother John's nominal captivity he found himself more closely confined. The word had gone round that the bailiff was in the parish and asking questions everywhere concerning the circumstances of Rhisiart's death, and it was known that he had had a lengthy session with the prior at Father Huw's parsonage, and must certainly have been urged and admonished as to his duty to take action also in the matter of Brother John's crime. Not that John had any complaints as to his lodging, his food or his company; he had seldom been so completely content. But for two days, with brief intervals when caution had seemed advisable, he had been out from dawn to dusk about the holding, lending a hand with the cattle, replenishing the wood-pile, fetching and carrying, planting out in the vegetable garden, and had had neither time nor inclination to worry about his situation. Now that he was hustled out of sight, and sat idle in the stable, the realities fretted even John, and the want of Welsh, or of Brother Cadfael to supply the want, was a frustration no longer so easy to bear. He did not know what Cadfael and Sioned were up to, he did not know what was happening to Saint Winifred, or to Prior Robert and his fellows, and above all he did not know where Engelard was, or how he was to be extricated from the tangle of suspicion roused against him. Since his instinctive gesture of solidarity, John took a proprietorial interest in Engelard, and wanted him safe, vindicated, and happy with his Sioned.

But Sioned, true to her word, did not come near him, and there was no one else in the holding who could talk to him freely. Simple things could be conveyed, but there was no way of communicating to him everything he wanted and needed to know. There was he, willing but useless, wondering and fretting how his friends were faring, and quite unable to do anything to aid them.

Annest brought his dinner, and sat by him while he ate, and the same want of words troubled her. It was all very well teaching him simple words and phrases in Welsh by touching the thing she meant, but how to set about pouring out to him, as she would have liked, all that was happening at the chapel, and what the village was saying and thinking? The helplessness of talking at all made their meetings almost silent, but sometimes they did speak aloud, he in English, she in Welsh, saying things because they could not be contained, things that would be understood by the other only in some future day, though the tone might convey at least the sense of friendship, like a kind of restrained caress. Thus they conducted two little monologues which yet were an exchange and a comfort.

Sometimes, though they did not know it, they were even answering each other's questions.

'I wonder who she was,' said Annest, soft and hesitant, 'that one who drove you to take the cowl? Sioned and I, we can't help wondering how a lad like you ever came to do it.' Now if he had known Welsh, she could never have said that to him.

'How did I ever come to think that Margery such a beauty!' marvelled John. 'And take it so hard when she turned me down? But I'd never really seen beauty then – I'd never seen *you*!'

'She did us all a bad turn,' said Annest, sighing, 'whoever she was, driving you into that habit for life!'

'Dear God,' said John, 'to think I might have married her! At least she did me that much of a favour, with her "no". There's only the matter of a cowl between you and me, not a wife.' And that was the first moment when he had entertained the dazzling idea that escape from his vows might be possible at all. The thought caused him to turn his head and look with even closer and more ardent attention at the fair face so close to his. She had smooth, rounded, apple-blossom cheeks, and delicate, sun-glossed bones, and eyes like brook-water in the sun over bright pebbles, glittering, polished, crystal-clear.

'Do you still fret after her?' wondered Annest in a whisper. 'A conceited ninny who hadn't the wit to know a good man when she saw one?' For he was indeed a very well-grown, handy, handsome, good-humoured young fellow, with his long, sturdy legs and his big, deft hands, and his bush of russet curls, and the girl who thought herself too good for him must have been the world's fool. 'I hate her!' said Annest, leaning unwarily towards him.

The lips that tantalised him with soft utterances he could not understand were only a little way from his own. He resorted in desperation to a kind of sign-language that needed no interpreter. He hadn't kissed a girl since Margery, the draper's daughter, who threw him over when her father became bailiff of Shrewsbury, but it seemed he hadn't forgotten how. And Annest melted into his arms, where she fitted a great deal better than his too-hasty vows had ever fitted him.

'Oh, Annest!' gasped Brother John, who had never in his life felt less like a brother, 'I think I love you!'

Brother Cadfael and Brother Columbanus walked up through the woodland together, to keep the third night of prayer. The evening was mild and still but overcast, and under the trees the light grew dusky green. Until the last moment it had remained a possibility that Prior Robert, having missed his chosen night of duty, might elect to be present on this last occasion, but he had said no word, and to tell the truth, Cadfael was beginning to wonder if that long session with the bailiff had really been necessary at all, or whether the prior had welcomed it as an alternative to keeping the night-watch and facing Sioned with her request in the morning. Not necessarily a proof of any guilt on his part, beyond the guilt of still wishing to refuse grace to Rhisiart, without actually having to do so face to face with his daughter. For whatever virtues might be found in Prior Robert, humility was not one, nor magnanimity. He was invariably sure of his own rightness, and where it was challenged he was not a forgiving man.

'In this quest and this vigil, brother,' said Columbanus, his long young steps keeping easy pace with Cadfael's seaman's roll, 'we are greatly privileged. The history of our abbey will record our names, and brothers in the generations to come will envy us.'

'I have already heard,' said Cadfael drily, 'that Prior Robert is proposing to write a life of Saint Winifred, and complete it with the story of this translation to Shrewsbury. You think he'll record the names of *all* his companions?' Yours, however, he thought, he well might mention, as the afflicted brother who first fell sick and was sent to Holywell to be cured. And Jerome's, who had the dream that took you there. But mine, I feel sure, will remain a silence, and so much the better!

'I have a fault to atone for,' recalled Columbanus devoutly, 'having betrayed my trust once in this same chapel, I, who most of all should have been faithful.' They were at the decrepit gate, the tangle of the graveyard before them, threaded by a narrow path just discernible through the long grass. 'I feel a holy air reaching out to me,' said the young man, quivering, his face uplifted and pale. 'I am drawn into a light. I believe we are approaching a wonder, a miracle of grace. Such mercy to me, who fell asleep in betrayal of her service!' And he led the way to the open door, his stride lengthening in eagerness, his hands

112

extended as if to clasp a mistress rather than make obeisance before a saint. Cadfael followed morosely but resignedly, used to these uncomfortable ardours, but not looking forward to being confined in so small a chapel with them overnight. He had thinking as well as praying to do, and Columbanus was not conducive to either activity.

Inside the chapel the air was heavy with the scent of old wood, and the spices and incense of the draperies on which the reliquary lay, and the faint, aromatic aura of years of dust and partial disuse. A small oil-lamp burned with a dark yellow flame on the altar, and Cadfael went forward and lit the two altar candles from it, and set them one on either side. Through the narrow east window the fragrance of the falling may-blossom breathed freshness on a very light breeze, causing the flames to flicker for a few minutes. Their faint, dancing radiance glanced from every near surface, but did not reach the corners of the roof, or fix the walls in place. They were in a narrow cavern of brown, wood-scented darkness, with a dim focus of light before them, that shone on an empty coffin and an uncoffined body, and just showed them the rough outlines of the two prayer-desks drawn up side by side at a little distance from the catafalque. Rhisiart lay nearer to them, the black and silver bulk of the reliquary like a low wall shading him from the altar lights.

Brother Columbanus bowed humbly low to the altar, and took his place at the desk on the right. Brother Cadfael settled solidly at the one on the left, and with practised movements sought and found the best place for his knees. Stillness came down on them gently. He composed himself for a long watch, and said his prayer for Rhisiart, not the first he had said for him. Great darkness and constant, feeble light, the slow flowing of time from far beyond his conception to far beyond his power to follow, the solitude about him and the troubled and peopled world within, all these settled into their perpetual pattern, a steady rhythm as perfect as sleep. He thought no more of Columbanus, he forgot that Columbanus existed. He prayed as he breathed, forming no words and making no specific request, only holding in his heart, like broken birds in cupped hands, all those people who were in stress or in grief because of this little saint, for if he suffered like this for their sake, how much more must she feel for them?

The candles would last the night, and by instinct he traced time by the rate at which they dwindled, and knew when it was near to midnight.

He was thinking of Sioned, to whom he had nothing but himself to offer in the morning, this pietistic innocent being essentially nothing, and Cadfael himself by no means enough, when he heard the faintest and strangest of sounds issuing from the prie-dieu on his right, where Columbanus leaned in total absorption. Not now with face hidden on his linked hands, but uplifted and strained upwards into what light could reach him, and faint though it was, it conjured his sharp profile into primrose pallor. His eyes were wide open and staring beyond the chapel wall, and his lips open and curved in ecstasy, and singing, a mere thread of Latin chant in praise of virginity. It was barely audible, yet clear as in a dream. And before Cadfael was fully aware of what he heard, he saw the young man thrust himself upwards, holding by the desk, and stand upright before the altar. The chant ceased. Suddenly he reared himself erect to his tallest, drawing back his head as though he would see through the roof into a spring night full of stars, and spreading out his arms on either side like a man stretched on a cross. He gave a great, wordless cry, seemingly both of pain and triumph, and fell forward full-length on the earthen floor, crashing to the ground stiffly, arms still outspread, body stretched to the very toes, and lay still, his forehead against the trailing fringe of the altar-cloth that spilled from beneath Rhisiart's body.

Cadfael got up in a hurry and went to him, torn between anxiety and alarm on one hand, and disgusted resignation on the other. Exactly what was to be expected of the idiot, he thought with exasperation, even as he was on his knees feeling at the prone brow, and adjusting a fold of the altar drapery under it to ease the position of nose and mouth, turning the young man's head to one side so that he could breathe freely. I should have recognised the signs! Never an opportunity but he can produce a devotional fit or a mystic ecstasy to order. One of these days he'll be drawn into that light of his, and never come back. Yet I've noticed he can fall flat on his face without hurting himself, and go into pious convulsions over his visions or his sins without ever hurling himself against anything sharp or hard, or even biting his tongue. The same sort of providence that takes care of drunken men looks out for Columbanus in his throes. And he reflected at the back of his mind, and tartly, that there ought somewhere to be a moral in that, lumping all excesses together.

No convulsions this time, at any rate. He had simply seen whatever he had seen, or thought he had seen, and fallen down before it in this destroying rapture. Cadfael shook him by the shoulder gently, and then more sharply, but he was rigid and unresponsive. His forehead was cool and smooth, his features, very dimly seen, yet looked serene, composed, if anything, in a gentle and joyful peace. But for the rigidity of body and limbs, and that unnatural attitude as though he lay stretched on a cross, he might have been asleep. All Cadfael had been able to do by way of easing him was to turn his head so that he lay on his right cheek, pillowed on the draperies. When he tried to bend the right arm and turn the young man more comfortably on his side, the joints resisted him, so he let well alone.

And now, he thought, what am I supposed to do? Abandon my watch and go down and fetch the prior with help for him? What could they do for him that I cannot do here? If I can't rouse him, then neither could they. He'll come out of it when the right time comes, and not before. He's done himself no injury, his breathing is steady and deep. His heart beats strongly and regularly, he has no fever. Why interfere with a man's peculiar pleasures, if they're doing him no harm? It isn't cold here, and he can have one of these altar-cloths for blanket, a fancy that ought to please him. No, we came to watch out the night together, and so we will, I here on my knees as is due, and he wherever he may be at this moment in his dreams.

He covered Columbanus, adjusted the cloths to cushion his head, and went back to his own prie-dieu. But whatever this visitation had done for Columbanus, it had shattered all possibility of thought or concentration for Cadfael. The more he tried to focus his mind, whether upon his duty of prayer and meditation, or the urgent need to consider where Sioned stood now, and what more could be done, the more was he drawn to look again at the prone body, and listen again to make sure it still breathed as evenly as ever. What should have been a profitable night hung heavy upon him, wasted as worship, useless as thought, as long and dreary and tedious a night as he had ever passed.

The first dove-grey softening of the darkness came as a blessing, bringing release at least within sight. The narrow space of sky seen through the altar window changed from grey to pale, clear green, from green to saffron, from saffron to gold, a cloudless morning, the first sunray piercing through the slit and falling on the altar, the reliquary, the shrouded body, and then striking like a golden sword across the chapel, leaving Columbanus in darkness. Still he lay rigid,

115

yet breathing deeply and softly, and no touch or word could reach him.

He was in the same condition when Prior Robert came with his fellows, and Sioned with Annest in attendance, and all the people from the village and the nearby holdings, silent and watchful as before, to see the end of this three-night vigil.

Sioned was the first to enter, and the dimness within, after the brightness without, made her blind for a moment, so that she halted in the doorway until her eyes should grow accustomed to the change. Prior Robert was close behind her when she saw the soles of Brother Columbanus' sandals upturned before her, just touched by the sunray from the window, while the rest of him lay still in shadow. Her eyes widened in wonder and horror, and before Cadfael could rise and turn to reassure her she had uttered a sharp cry: 'What is it? Is he dead?'

The prior put her aside quickly, and strode past her, and was brought up short with his foot on the hem of Columbanus' habit.

'What happened here? Columbanus! Brother!' He stooped and laid his hand upon a rigid shoulder. Columbanus slept and dreamed on, unmoved and unmoving. 'Brother Cadfael, what does this mean? What has befallen him?'

'He is not dead,' said Cadfael, putting first things first, 'nor do I think he is in any danger. He breathes like a man peacefully sleeping. His colour is good, he is cool to the touch, and has no injury. Simply, at midnight he suddenly stood up before the altar, and spread out his arms and fell forward thus in trance. He has lain all night like this, but without distress or agitation.'

'You should have called us to his aid,' said the prior, shaken and dismayed.

'I had also a duty,' said Cadfael shortly, 'to remain here and keep the vigil I was sent to keep. And what could have been done for him more than I have done, in giving him a pillow for his head and a cover against the chill of the night? Nor, I think, would he have been grateful if we had carried him away before the appointed time. Now he has kept his own watch faithfully, and if we cannot rouse him we may bear him away to his bed, without doing violence to his sense of duty.'

'There is something in that,' said Brother Richard earnestly, 'for you know that Brother Columbanus has several times been visited and favoured by visions, and it might have been a great wrong to take him away from the very place where such blessings befell him. An offence, perhaps, against the saint herself,

116

if she was pleased to reveal herself to him. And if that is so, then he will awake when the time is right that he should, and it might do him great harm to try and hasten the hour.'

'It is true,' said the prior, a little reassured, 'that he seems at peace, and has a good colour, and no sign of trouble or pain. This is most strange. Is it possible that this young brother will be the occasion of another such prodigy as when his affliction first drew us to Saint Winifred?'

'He was the instrument of grace once,' said Richard, 'and may be so again. We had better carry him down to his bed at Cadwallon's house, and keep him quiet and warm, and wait. Or had we not better take him to Father Huw's parsonage, so that he may be close to the church? It may be that his first need will be to give thanks.'

With a heavy altar-cloth and their girdles they made a sling in which to carry Columbanus, lifting him from the floor, stiff as a branch, even his extended arms still rigid. They laid him on his back in their improvised litter, and he suffered whatever they did to him, and made no sound or sign. A few of the watching natives, moved and awed by the spectacle, came forward to lend a hand in carrying him down through the forest to Huw's house. Cadfael let them go. He turned to look at Sioned, as she was looking at him, with dubious and speculative eyes.

'Well, I, at least,' he said, 'am in my right senses, and can and will do what you have not asked of me.' And he stepped to Rhisiart's side, and laid his hand upon the dead man's heart, and signed his forehead with a cross.

She walked beside him as they followed the slow procession down towards the village.

'What more can we do? If you know of anything, only tell me. We have not been favoured so far. And today is to be his burial.'

'I know it,' said Cadfael, and brooded. 'As for this affair in the night, I'm torn two ways. I should think it possible it was all planned, to reinforce our cause with another miracle, but for two things. To me Prior Robert's amazement and concern, however I look at them, seem to be true and not false. And Columbanus has shown these strange properties before, and the way they overtake him is violent and perilous, and it's hard to believe he is feigning. A tumbler at a fair, making his living by playing the devil with his own body, could not outdo Columbanus when the fit comes on him. I am not able to judge. I think there are some who live on a knife-edge in the soul, and

117

at times are driven to hurl themselves into the air, at the mercy of heaven or hell which way to fall.'

'All I know,' said Sioned, burning darkly red like a slow torch, 'is that my father whom I loved is murdered, and I want justice on the murderer, and I do not want a blood price. There is no price I will accept for Rhisiart's blood.'

'I know, I know!' said Cadfael. 'I am as Welsh as you. But keep a door open to pity, as who knows when you or I may need it! And have you spoken with Engelard? And is all well with him?'

She quivered and flushed and softened beside him, like a frost-blighted flower miraculously revived by a southern wind. But she did not answer. There was no need.

'Ah, you'll live!' said Brother Cadfael, satisfied. 'As he'd want you to. Even if he did set his face against, like a proper Welsh lord. You'd have got your way in the end, you were right about that. And listen, I have thought of two things you should yet do. We must try whatever we can. Don't go home now. Let Annest take you to Bened's smithy to rest, and the both of you come to Mass. Who knows what we may learn once our half-fledged saint regains his senses? And then, also, when you bury your father, make certain Peredur comes with *his* father. He might try to avoid else, if he's eluded you this far, but if you ask him, he cannot refuse. I am still in more minds than one, and none of them very clear, concerning Master Peredur.'

Chapter Eight

T WAS the little brazen bell ringing for Mass that penetrated Brother Columbanus' enchanted sleep at last. It could not be said that it awoke him, rather it caused him to open his closed eyes, quiver through all his frozen members, flex his stiff arms, and press his re-quickened hands together over his breast. Otherwise his face did not change, nor did he seem to be aware of those who were gathered anxiously about the bed on which he lay. They might not have been there at all. All Brother Columbanus responded to was the bell, the first call to worship. He stirred and sat up. He rose from the bed, and stood firmly on his feet. He looked radiant, but still private and apart.

'He is preparing to take his usual place with us,' said the prior, moved and awed. 'Let us go, and make no attempt yet to rouse him. When he has given thanks he'll come back to us, and speak out what he has experienced.'

And he led the way to the church, and as he had supposed. Columbanus fell into his usual place as the youngest in the attendant brotherhood now that John was disgraced, and followed modestly, and modestly took part in the service, still like a man in a dream.

The church was full as it would hold, and there were more people clustered outside the doorway. The word had gone

119

round already that something strange and wonderful had happened at Saint Winifred's chapel, and revelations might very well follow at Mass.

Not until the end did any further change occur in the condition of Brother Columbanus. But when the prior, slowly and expectantly, as one turning a key and almost confident of entry, took the first step towards the doorway, suddenly Columbanus gave a great start, and uttered a soft cry, staring wonderingly about him at all these known faces. His own visage came to life, smiling. He put out a hand as if to arrest the prior's departure, and said in a high voice: 'Oh, Father, I have been so blessed. I have known such bliss! How did I come here, when I know I was elsewhere, and translated out of night's darkness into so glorious a light? And surely this is again the world I left! A fair world enough, but I have been in a fairer, far beyond any deserts of mine. Oh, if I could but tell you!'

Every eye was upon him, and every ear stretched to catch his least word. Not a soul left the church, rather those without crowded in closer.

'Son,' said Prior Robert, with unwontedly respectful kindness, 'you are here among your brothers, engaged in the worship of God, and there is nothing to fear and nothing to regret, for the visitation granted you was surely meant to inspire and arm you to go fearless through an imperfect world, in the hope of a perfect world hereafter. You were keeping night watch with Brother Cadfael at Saint Winifred's chapel – do you remember that? In the night something befell you that drew your spirit for a time away from us, out of the body, but left that body unharmed and at rest like a child asleep. We brought you back here still absent from us in the spirit, but now you are here with us again, and all is well. You have been greatly privileged.'

'Oh, greatly, far more than you know,' sang Columbanus, glowing like a pale lantern. 'I am the messenger of such goodness, I am the instrument of reconciliation and peace. Oh, Father. . . . Father Huw . . . brothers . . . let me speak out here before all, for what I am bidden to tell concerns all.'

Nothing, thought Cadfael, could have stopped him, so plainly did his heavenly embassage override any objection mere prior or priest might muster. And Robert was proving surprisingly compliant in accepting this transfer of authority. Either he already knew that the voice from heaven was about to say something entirely favourable to his plans and conducive to his glory, or else he was truly impressed, and inclining heart and ear to listen as devoutly as any man there present.

'Speak freely, brother,' he said, 'let us share your joy.'

'Father, at the hour of midnight as I knelt before the altar I heard a sweet voice crying my name, and I arose and went forward to obey the call. What happened to my body then I do not know, you tell me it was lying as if asleep when you came. But it seemed to me that as I stepped towards the altar there was suddenly a soft, golden light all about it, and there rose up, floating in the midst of the light, a most beautiful virgin, who moved in a miraculous shower of white petals, and distilled most sweet odours from her robe and from her long hair. And this gracious being spoke to me, and told me that her name was Winifred, and that she was come to approve our enterprise, and also to forgive all those who out of mistaken loyalty and reverence had opposed it hitherto. And then, oh, marvellous goodness! – she laid her hand on Rhisiart's breast, as his daughter has begged us to do in token of our mere personal forgiveness, but she in divine absolution, and with such perfection of grace, I cannot describe it.'

'Oh, son,' said Prior Robert in rapture, riding over the quivering murmurs that crossed the church like ripples on a pool, 'you tell a greater wonder than we dared hope. Even the lost saved!'

'It is so! And, Father, there is more! When she laid her hand on him, she bade me speak out to all men in this place, both native and stranger, and make known her merciful will. And it is this: "where my bones shall be taken out of the earth," she said, "there will be an open grave provided. What I relinquish, I may bestow. In this grave," said Winifred, "let Rhisiart be buried, that his rest may be assured, and my power made manifest."'

'What could I do,' said Sioned, 'but thank him for his good offices, when he brought divine reassurance for my father's weal? And yet it outrages me, I would rather have stood up and said that I am not and never have been in the least doubt that my father is in blessedness this moment, for he was a good man who never did a mean wrong to anyone. And certainly it's kind of Saint Winifred to offer him the lodging she's leaving, and graciously forgive him, but – forgiveness for what? Absolution for what? She might rather have praised him while she was about it, and said outright that he was justified, not forgiven.'

121

'Yet a very ambassadorial message,' admitted Cadfael appreciatively, 'calculated to get us what we came for, assuage the people of Gwytherin, make peace all round – '

'And to placate me, and cause me to give up the pursuit of my father's murderer,' said Sioned, 'burying the deed along with the victim. Except that I will not rest until I know.'

' – and shed reflected glory upon Prior Robert, I was going to say. And I wish I knew which mind conceived the idea!'

They had met for a few hurried minutes at Bened's smithy, where Cadfael had gone to borrow mattock and spade for the holy work now to be undertaken. Even a few of the men of Gwytherin had come forward and asked to have a share in breaking the sacred earth, for though they were still reluctant to lose their saint, if it was her will to leave them they had no wish to cross her. Prodigious things were happening, and they intended to be in receipt of her approval and blessing rather than run the risk of encountering her arrows.

'It seems to me most of the glory is falling, rather, on Brother Columbanus of late,' said Sioned shrewdly. 'And the prior took it meekly, and never made any attempt to filch it back from him. That's the one thing that makes me believe he may be honest.'

She had said something that caused Cadfael to pause and look attentively at her, scrubbing dubiously at his nose. 'You may well be right. And certainly this story is bound to go back to Shrewsbury with us, and spread through all our sister houses, when we come home with our triumph. Yes, Columbanus will certainly have made himself a great name for holiness and divine favour in the order.'

'They say an ambitious man can make a grand career in the cloister,' she said. 'Maybe he's busy laying the foundations, a great step up towards being prior himself when Robert becomes abbot. Or even abbot, when Robert supposes *he's* about to become abbot! For it's not *his* name they'll be buzzing round the shires as the visionary the saints use to make their wants known.'

'That,' agreed Cadfael, 'may not even have dawned on Robert yet, but when the awe of the occasion passes it will. And he's the one who's pledged to write a life of the saint, and complete it with the account of this pilgrimage. Columbanus may very well end up as an anonymous brother who happened to be charged with a message to the prior from his patroness. Chroniclers can edit names out as easily as visionaries can noise them abroad. But I grant you, this lad comes of a thrusting

Norman family that doesn't put even its younger sons into the Benedictine habit to spend their lives doing menial work like gardening.'

'And we're no further forward,' said Sioned bitterly.

'No. But we have not finished yet.'

'But as I see it, this is devised to be an ending, to close this whole episode in general amity, as if everything was resolved. But everything is *not* resolved! Somewhere in this land there is a man who stabbed my father in the back, and we're all being asked to draw a veil over that and lose sight of it in the great treaty of peace. But I want that man found, and Engelard vindicated, and my father avenged, and I won't rest, or let anyone else rest, until I get what I want. And now tell me what I am to do.'

'What I've already told you,' said Cadfael. 'Have all your household party and friends gathered at the chapel to watch the grave opened, and make sure that Peredur attends.'

'I've already sent Annest to beg him to come,' said Sioned. 'And then? What have I to say or do to Peredur?'

'That silver cross you wear round your neck,' said Cadfael. 'Are you willing to part with it in exchange for one step ahead towards what you want to know?'

'That and all the rest of the valuables I own. You know it.'

'Then this,' said Cadfael, 'is what you will do . . .'

With prayers and psalms they carried their tools up to the tangled graveyard by the chapel, trimmed back the brambles and wild flowers and long grass from the little mound of Winifred's grave, and reverently broke the sod. By turns they laboured, all taking a share in the work for the merit to be acquired. And most of Gwytherin gathered round the place in the course of the day, all work left at a standstill in the fields and crofts, to watch the end of this contention. For Sioned had spoken truly. She and all her household servants were there among the rest, in mourning and massed to bring out Rhisiart's body for burial when the time came, but this funeral party had become, for the time being, no more than a side-issue, an incident in the story of Saint Winifred, and a closed incident at that.

Cadwallon was there, Uncle Meurice was there, and Bened, and all the other neighbours. And there at his father's elbow, withdrawn and brooding, stood young Peredur, by the look of him wishing himself a hundred leagues away. His thick dark brows were drawn together as though his head ached, and whenever his brown eyes wandered, it was never towards Sioned. He had crept here reluctantly at her express asking, but he could not or would not face her. The bold red mouth was chilled and pale from the tension with which it was tightened against his teeth. He watched the dark pit deepen in the grass, and breathed hard and deep, like a man containing pain. A far cry from the spoiled boy with the long, light step and the audacious smile, who so plainly had taken it for granted that the world was his for the wooing. Peredur's demons were at him within.

The ground was moist but light, not hard to work, but the grave was deep. Gradually the diggers sank to the shoulders in the pit, and by mid-afternoon Brother Cadfael, shortest of the party, had almost disappeared from view when he took his final turn in the depths. No one dared to doubt openly if they were in the right place, but some must have been wondering. Cadfael, for no good reason that he could see, had no doubts at all. The girl was here. She had lived many years as an abbess after her brief martyrdom and miraculous restoration, yet he thought of her as that devout, green girl, in romantic love with celibacy and holiness, who had fled from Prince Cradoc's advances as from the devil himself. By some perverse severance of the heart in two he could feel both for her and for the desperate lover, so roughly molten out of the flesh and presumably exterminated in the spirit. Did anyone ever pray for him? He was in greater need than Winifred. In the end, perhaps the only prayers he ever benefited by were Winifred's prayers. She was Welsh, and capable of detachment and subtlety. She might well have put in a word for him, to reassemble his liquefied person and congeal it again into the shape of a man. A chastened man, doubtless, but still the same shape as before. Even a saint may take pleasure, in retrospect, in having been once desired.

The spade grated on something in the dark, friable soil, something neither loam nor stone. Cadfael checked his stroke instantly and its suggestion of age, frailty and crumbling dryness. He let the blade lie, and stooped to scoop away with his hands the cool, odorous, gentle earth that hid the obstruction from him. Dark soil peeled away under his fingers from a slender, pale, delicate thing, the gentle dove-grey of pre-dawn, but freckled with pitted points of black. He drew out an arm-bone, scarcely more than child size, and stroked away the clinging earth. Islands of the same soft colouring showed below, grouped loosely together. He did not want to break

124

any of them. He hoisted the spade and tossed it out of the pit.

'She is here. We have found her. Softly, now, leave her to me.'

Faces peered in upon him. Prior Robert gleamed in silvery agitation, thirsting to plunge in and dredge up the prize in person, but deterred by the clinging darkness of the soil and the whiteness of his hands. Brother Columbanus at the brink towered and glittered, his exalted visage turned, not towards the depths where this fragile virgin substance lay at rest, but rather to the heavens from which her diffused spiritual essence had addressed him. He displayed, no doubt of it, an aura of distinct proprietorship that dwarfed both prior and sub-prior, and shone with its full radiance upon all those who watched from the distance. Brother Columbanus meant to be, was, and knew that he was, memorable in this memorable hour.

Brother Cadfael kneeled. It may even have been a significant omen that at this moment he alone was kneeling. He judged that he was at the feet of the skeleton. She had been there some centuries, but the earth had dealt kindly, she might well be whole, or virtually whole. He had not wanted her disturbed at all, but now he wanted her disturbed as little as might be, and delved carefully with scooping palms and probing, stroking finger-tips to uncover the whole slender length of her without damage. She must have been a little above medium height, but willowy as a seventeen-year-old girl. Tenderly he stroked the earth away from round her. He found the skull, and leaned on stretched arms, fingering the eye-sockets clear, marvelling at the narrow elegance of the cheek-bones, and the generosity of the dome. She had beauty and fineness in her death. He leaned over her like a shield, and grieved.

'Let me down a linen sheet,' he said, 'and some bands to raise it smoothly. She shall not come out of here bone by bone, but whole woman as she went in.'

They handed a cloth down to him, and he spread it beside the slight skeleton, and with infinite care eased her free of the loosed soil, and edged her by inches into the shroud of linen, laying the disturbed arm-bone in its proper place. With bands of cloth slung under her she was drawn up into the light of day, and laid tenderly in the grass at the side of her grave.

'We must wash away the soil-marks from her bones,' said Prior Robert, gazing in reverent awe upon the prize he had gone to such trouble to gain, 'and wrap them afresh.'

125

'They are dry and frail and brittle,' warned Cadfael impatiently. 'If she is robbed of this Welsh earth she may very well crumble to Welsh earth herself in your hands. And if you keep her here in the air and the sun too long, she may fall to dust in any case. If you are wise, Father Prior, you'll wrap her well as she lies, and get her into the reliquary and seal her from the air as tight as you can, as quickly as you can.'

That was good sense, and the prior acted on it, even if he did not much relish being told what to do so brusquely. With hasty but exultant prayers they brought the resplendent coffin out to the lady, to avoid moving her more than they must, and with repeated swathings of linen bound her little bones carefully together, and laid her in the coffin. The brothers who made it had realised the need for perfect sealing to preserve the treasure, and taken great pains to make the lid fit down close as a skin, and line the interior with lead. Before Saint Winifred was carried back into the chapel for the thanksgiving Mass the lid was closed upon her, the catches secured, and at the end of the service the prior's seals were added to make all fast. They had her imprisoned, to be carried away into the alien land that desired her patronage. All the Welsh who could crowd into the chapel or cling close enough to the doorway to catch glimpses of the proceedings kept a silence uncannily perfect, their eyes following every move, secret eyes that expressed no resentment, but by their very attention, fixed and unwavering, implied an unreconciled opposition they were afraid to speak aloud.

'Now that this sacred duty is done,' said Father Huw, at once relieved and saddened, 'it is time to attend to the other duty which the saint herself has laid upon us, and bury Rhisiart honourably, with full absolution, in the grave she has bequeathed to him. And I call to mind, in the hearing of all, how great a blessing is thus bestowed, and how notable an honour.' It was as near as he would go to speaking out his own view of Rhisiart, and in this, at least, he had the sympathy of every Welshman there present.

That burial service was brief, and after it six of Rhisiart's oldest and most trusted servants took up the bier of branches, a little wilted now but still green, and carried it out to the graveside. The same slings which had lifted Saint Winifred waited to lower Rhisiart into the same bed.

Sioned stood beside her uncle, and looked all round her at the circle of her friends and neighbours, and unclasped the silver

126

cross from her neck. She had so placed herself that Cadwallon and Peredur were close at her right hand, and it was simple and natural to turn towards them. Peredur had hung back throughout, never looking at her but when he was sure she was looking away, and when she swung round upon him suddenly he had no way of avoiding.

'One last gift I want to give to my father. And I would like you, Peredur, to be the one to give it. You have been like a son to him. Will you lay this cross on his breast, where the murderer's arrow pierced him? I want it to be buried with him. It is my farewell to him here, let it be yours, too.'

Peredur stood dumbstruck and aghast, staring from her still and challenging face to the little thing she held out to him, in front of so many witnesses, all of whom knew him, all of whom were known to him. She had spoken clearly, to be heard by all. Every eye was on him, and all recorded, though without understanding, the slow draining of blood from his face, and his horror-stricken stare. He could not refuse what she asked. He could not do it without touching the dead man, touching the very place where death had struck him.

His hand came out with aching reluctance, and took the cross from her. To leave her thus extending it in vain was more than he could stand. He did not look at it, but only desperately at her, and in her face the testing calm had blanched into incredulous dismay, for now she believed she knew everything, and it was worse than anything she had imagined. But as he could not escape from the trap she had laid for him, neither could she release him. It was sprung, and now he had to fight his way out of it as best he could. They were already wondering why he made no move, and whispering together in concern at his hanging back.

He made a great effort, drawing himself together with a frantic briskness that lasted only a moment. He took a few irresolute steps towards the bier and the grave, and then baulked like a frightened horse, and halted again, and that was worse, for now he stood alone in the middle of the circle of witnesses, and could go neither forward nor back. Cadfael saw sweat break in great beads on his forehead and lip.

'Come, son,' said Father Huw kindly, the last to suspect evil, 'don't keep the dead waiting, and don't grieve too much for them, for that would be sin. I know, as Sioned has said, he was like another father to you, and you share her loss. So do we all.'

127

Peredur stood quivering at Sioned's name, and at the word 'father', and tried to go forward, and could not move. His feet would not take him one step nearer to the swathed form that lay by the open grave. The light of the sun on him, the weight of all eyes, bore him down. He fell on his knees suddenly, the cross still clutched in one hand, the other spread to hide his face.

'He cannot!' he cried hoarsely from behind the shielding palm.

'He cannot accuse me! I am not guilty of murder! What I did was done when Rhisiart was already dead!'

A great, gasping sigh passed like a sudden wind around the clearing and over the tangled grave, and subsided into a vast silence. It was a long minute before Father Huw broke it, for this was his sheep, not Prior Robert's, a child of his flock, and hitherto a child of grace, now stricken into wild self-accusation of some terrible sin not yet explained, but to do with violent death.

'Son Peredur,' said Father Huw firmly, 'you have not been charged with any ill-doing by any other but yourself. We are waiting only for you to do what Sioned has asked of you, for her asking was a grace. Therefore do her bidding, or speak out why you will not, and speak plainly.'

Peredur heard, and ceased to tremble. A little while he kneeled and gathered his shattered composure about him doggedly, like a cloak. Then he uncovered his face, which was pale, despairing but eased, no longer in combat with truth but consenting to it. He was a young man of courage. He got to his feet and faced them squarely.

'Father, I come to confession by constraint, and not gladly, and I am as ashamed of that as of what I have to confess. But it is not murder. I did not kill Rhisiart. I found him dead.'

'At what hour?' asked Brother Cadfael, wholly without right, but nobody questioned the interruption.

'I went out after the rain stopped. You remember it rained.' They remembered. They had good reason. 'It would be a little after noon. I was going up to the pasture our side of Bryn, and I found him lying on his face in that place where afterwards we all saw him. He was dead then, I swear it! And I was grieved, but also I was tempted, for there was nothing in this world I could do for Rhisiart, but I saw a way. . . .' Peredur swallowed and sighed, bracing his forehead against his fate, and went on. 'I saw a means of ridding myself of a rival. Of the favoured rival. Rhisiart had refused his daughter to Engelard, but Sioned had

128

not refused him, and well I knew there was no hope for me, however her father urged her, while Engelard was there between us. Men might easily believe that Engelard should kill Rhisiart, if – if there was some proof. . . .'

'But *you* did not believe it,' said Cadfael, so softly that hardly anyone noticed the interruption, it was accepted and answered without thought.

'No!' said Peredur almost scornfully. 'I knew him, he never would!'

'Yet you were willing he should be taken and accused. It was all one to you if it was death that removed him out of your way, so he was removed.'

'No!' said Peredur again, smouldering but aware that he was justly lashed. 'No, not that! I thought he would run, take himself away again into England, and leave us alone, Sioned and me. I never wished him worse than that. I thought, with him gone, in the end Sioned would do what her father had wished, and marry me. I could wait! I could wait! I would have waited years. . . .'

He did not say, but there were two there, at least, who knew, and remembered in his favour, that he had opened the way for Engelard to break out of the ring that penned him in, and deliberately let him pass, just as Brother John, with a better conscience, had frustrated the pursuit.

Brother Cadfael said sternly: 'But you went so far as to steal one of this unfortunate young man's arrows, to make sure all eyes turned on him.'

'I did not steal it, though no less discredit to me that I used it as I did. I was out with Engelard after game, not a week earlier, with Rhisiart's permission. When we retrieved our arrows, I took one of his by error among mine. I had it with me then.'

Peredur's shoulders had straightened, his head was up, his hands, the right still holding Sioned's cross, hung gently and resignedly at his sides. His face was pale but calm. He had got the worst of it off his back, after what he had borne alone these last days confession and penance were balm.

'Let me tell the whole of it, all the thing I did, that has made me a monster in my own eyes ever since. I will not make it less than it was, and it was hideous. Rhisiart was stabbed in the back, and the dagger withdrawn and gone. I turned him over on his back, and I turned that wound back to front, and I tell you, my hands burn now, but I did it. He was dead, he suffered nothing. I pierced my own flesh, not his. I could tell the line of the wound, for the dagger had gone right through him, though the breast wound was small. I took my own dagger, and opened the way for Engelard's arrow to follow, and I thrust it through and left it standing in him for witness. And I have not had one quiet moment, night or day,' said Peredur, not asking pity, rather grateful that now his silence was broken and his infamy known, and nothing more to hide, 'since I did this small, vile thing, and now I am glad it's out, whatever becomes of me. And at least grant me this, I did not make my trap in such a way as to accuse Engelard of shooting a man in the back! I knew him! I lived almost side by side with him since he came here a fugitive, we were of an age, we could match each other. I have liked him, hunted with him, fought with him, been jealous of him, even hated him because he was loved where I was not. Love makes men do terrible things,' said Peredur, not pleading, marvelling, 'even to their friends.'

He had created, all unconsciously, a tremendous hush all about him, of awe at his blasphemy, of startled pity for his desolation, of chastened wonder at their own misconceivings. The truth fell like thunder, subduing them all. Rhisiart had not been shot down with an arrow, but felled from behind at close quarters, out of thick cover, a coward's killing. Not saints, but men, deal in that kind of treachery.

Father Huw broke the silence. In his own province, where no alien dignitaries dared intrude, he grew taller and more secure in his gentle, neighbourly authority. And great violence had been done to what he knew to be right, and great requital was due from the sinner, and great compassion due to him.

'Son Peredur,' he said, 'you stand in dire sin, and cannot be excused. Such violation of the image of God, such misuse of a clean affection – for such I know you had with Rhisiart – and such malice towards an innocent man – for such you proclaimed Engelard – cannot go unpunished.'

'God forbid,' said Peredur humbly, 'that I should escape any part of what is due. I want it! I cannot live with myself if I have only this present self to live with!'

'Child, if you mean that, then give yourself into my hands, to be delivered up both to secular and religious justice. As to the law, I shall speak with the prince's bailiff. As to the penance due before God, that is for me as your confessor, and I require that you shall wait my considered judgment.'

'So I will, Father,' said Peredur. 'I want no unearned pardon. I take penance willingly.'

130

'Then you need not despair of grace. Go home now, and remain withindoors until I send for you.'

'I will be obedient to you in all things. But I have one prayer before I go.' He turned slowly and faced Sioned. She was standing quite still where the awful dread had fallen upon her, her hands clutched to her cheeks, her eyes fixed in fascination and pain upon the boy who had grown up as her playfellow. But the rigidity had ebbed out of her, for though he called himself a monster, he was not, after all, the monster she had briefly thought him. 'May I now do what you asked of me? I am not afraid now. He was a fair man always. He won't accuse me of more than my due.'

He was both asking her pardon and saying his farewell to any hope he had still cherished of winning her, for now that was irrevocably over. And the strange thing was that now he could approach her, even after so great an offence, without constraint, almost without jealousy. Nor did her face express any great heat or bitterness against him. It was thoughtful and intent.

'Yes,' she said, 'I still wish it.' If he had spoken the whole truth, and she was persuaded that he had, it was well that he should take his appeal to Rhisiart, in a form every man there would acknowledge. In otherworldly justice the body would clear him of the evil he had not committed, now that confession was made of what he had.

Peredur went forward steadily enough now, sank to his knees beside Rhisiart's body, and laid first his hand, and then Sioned's cross, upon the heart he had pierced, and no gush of blood sprang at his touch. And if there was one thing certain, it was that here was a man who did believe. He hesitated a moment, still kneeling, and then, feeling a need rather to give thanks for this acceptance than to make any late and unfitting display of affection, stooped and kissed the right hand that lay quiet over the left on Rhisiart's breast, their clasped shape showing through the close shroud. That done, he rose and went firmly away by the downhill path towards his father's house. The people parted to let him through in a great silence, and Cadwallon, starting out of a trance of unbelieving misery, lurched forward in haste and went trotting after his son.

Chapter Nine

HE EVENING was drawing in by the time they had buried Rhisiart, and it was too late for Prior Robert and his companions to take their prize and leave at once for home, even if it had been a seemly thing to do, after all that had happened. Some ceremony was due to the community the saint was leaving, and the houses that had offered hospitality freely even to those who came to rob them.

'We will stay this night over, and sing Vespers and Compline in the church with you, and give due thanks,' said the prior. 'And after Compline one of us will again watch the night through with Saint Winifred, as is only proper. And should the prince's bailiff require that we stay longer, we will do as he asks. For there is still the matter of Brother John, who stands in contempt of the law, to our disgrace.'

'At present,' said Father Huw deprecatingly, 'the bailiff is giving his attention to the case of Rhisiart's murder. For though we have suffered many revelations in that matter, you see that we are no nearer knowing who is guilty. What we have seen to-day is one man who certainly is innocent of the crime, whatever his other sins may be.'

'I fear,' said Prior Robert with unwonted humility, 'that without ill intent we have caused you great grief and trouble here, and for that I am sorry. And greatly sorry for the parents of that sinful young man, who are suffering, I think, far worse than he, and without blame.'

'I am going to them now,' said Huw. 'Will you go on ahead, Father Prior, and sing Vespers for me? For I may be delayed some time. I must do what I can for this troubled household.'

The people of Gwytherin had begun to drift away silently by many paths, vanishing into the woods to spread the news of the day's happening to the far corners of the parish. In the long grass of the graveyard, trampled now by many feet, the dark, raw shape of Rhisiart's grave made a great scar, and two of his men were filling in the earth over him. It was finished. Sioned turned towards the gate, and all the rest of her people followed.

Cadfael fell in beside her as the subdued, straggling procession made its way home towards the village.

'Well,' he said resignedly, 'it was worth trying. And we can't say it got us nothing. At least we know now who committed the lesser crime, if we're very little nearer knowing who committed the greater. And we know why there were two, for they made no sense, being one and the same. And at any rate, we have shaken the devil off that boy's back. Are you quite revolted at what he did? As *he* is?'

'Strangely,' said Sioned. 'I don't believe I am. I was too sick with horror, that short time while I thought him the murderer. After that, it was simple relief that he was not. He has never gone short of anything he wanted, you see, until he wanted me.'

'It was a real wanting,' said Brother Cadfael, remembering long-past hungers of his own. 'I doubt if he'll ever quite get over it, though I'm pretty sure he'll make a sound marriage, and get handsome children like himself, and be very fairly content. He grew up today, she won't be disappointed, whoever she may be. But she'll never be Sioned.'

Her tired, woeful, discouraged face had softened and warmed, and suddenly she was smiling beside him, faintly but reassuringly. 'You are a good man. You have a way of reconciling people. But no need! Do you think I did not see how he dragged himself painfully to this afternoon's business, and has gone striding away with his head up to embrace his punishment? I might really have loved him a little, if there had been no Engelard. But only a little! He may do better than that.'

'You are a fine girl,' said Brother Cadfael heartily. 'If I had met you when I was thirty years younger, I should have made Engelard sweat for his prize. Peredur should be thankful even

133

for such a sister. But we're no nearer knowing what we want and need to know.'

'And have we any more shafts left to loose?' she asked ruefully. 'Any more snares to set? At least we've freed the poor soul we caught in the last one.'

He was silent, glumly thinking.

'And tomorrow,' she said sadly, 'Prior Robert will take his saint and all his brothers, and you with them, and set out for home, and I shall be left with nobody to turn to here. Father Huw is as near a saint himself, in his small, confused way, as ever Winifred was, but no use to me. And Uncle Meurice is a gentle creature who knows about running a manor, but nothing about anything else, and wants no trouble and no exertion. And Engelard must go on hiding, as well you know. Peredur's plot against him is quite empty now, we all know it. But does that prove he did not kill my father, after a raging quarrel?'

'In the back?' said Cadfael, unguardedly indignant.

She smiled. 'All that proves is that you know him! Not everyone does. Some will be saying at this moment, perhaps, after all . . . that Peredur may have been right without even knowing it.'

He thought about it and was dismayed, for no question but she was right. What, indeed, did it prove if another man had wished to burden him with the guilt? Certainly not that the guilt was *not* his. Brother Cadfael confronted his own voluntarily assumed responsibility, and braced himself to cope with it.

'There is also Brother John to be considered,' said Sioned. It may well be that Annest, walking behind, had prodded her.

'I have not forgotten Brother John,' agreed Cadfael.

'But I think the bailiff well may have done. He would shut his eyes or look the other way, if Brother John left for Shrewsbury with the rest of you. He has troubles enough here, what does he want with alien trouble?'

'And if Brother John should seem to him to have left for Shrewsbury, he would be satisfied? And ask no questions about one more outlander taken up by a patron here?'

'I always knew you were quick,' said Sioned, brown and bright and animated, almost herself again. 'But would Prior Robert pursue him still, when he hears he's gone from custody? I don't see him as a forgiving man.'

'No, nor he is, but how would he set about it? The Benedictine order has no real hold in Wales. No, I think he'd let it ride, now he has what he came for. I'm more concerned for Engelard. Give me this one more night, child, and do this for me! Send your people home, and stay the night over with Annest at Bened's croft, and if God aids me with some new thought – for never forget God is far more deeply offended even than you or I by this great wrong! – I'll come to you there.'

'We'll do that,' said Sioned. 'And you'll surely come.'

They had slowed to let the cortège move well ahead of them, so that they could talk freely. They were approaching the gatehouse of Cadwallon's holding, and Prior Robert and his companions were far in front and had passed by the gate, bent upon singing Vespers in good time. Father Huw, issuing forth in haste and agitation in search of help, seemed relieved rather than dismayed to find only Cadfael within call. The presence of Sioned checked him to a decent walk and a measured tone, but did nothing to subdue the effect of his erected hair and frantic mien.

'Brother Cadfael, will you spare some minutes for this afflicted household? You have some skills with medicines, you may be able to advise. . . .'

'His mother!' whispered Sioned in immediate reassurance. 'She weeps herself into a frenzy at everything that crosses her. I knew this would set her off. Poor Peredur, he has his penance already! Shall I come?'

'Better not,' he said as softly, and moved to meet Father Huw. Sioned was, after all, the innocent cause of Peredur's fall from grace, she would probably be the last person calculated to calm his mother's anguish. And Sioned understood him so, and went on, and left the matter to him, so calmly that it was clear she expected no tragic results from the present uproar. She had known Cadwallon's wife all her life, no doubt she had learned to treat her ups and downs as philosophically as Cadfael did Brother Columbanus' ecstasies and excesses. He never really hurt himself in his throes, either!

'Dame Branwen is in such a taking,' fluttered Father Huw distractedly, steering Cadfael in haste towards the open door of the hall. 'I fear for her wits. I've seen her upset before, and hard enough to pacify, but now, her only child, and such a shock. . . . Really, she may do herself an injury if we cannot quiet her.'

Dame Branwen was indeed audible before they even entered the small room where husband and son were trying to soothe her, against a tide of vociferous weeping and lamentation that all but deafened them. The lady, fat and fair and outwardly fashioned only for comfortable, shallow placidity, half-sat, half-lay on a couch, throwing her substantial person about in extravagant distress, now covering her silly, fond face, now throwing her arms abroad in sweeping gestures of desolation and despair, but never for one moment ceasing to bellow her sorrow and shame. The tears that flowed freely down her round cheeks and the shattering sobs that racked her hardly seemed to impede the flow of words that poured out of her like heavy rain.

Cadwallon on one side and Peredur on the other stroked and patted and comforted in vain. As often as the father tried to assert himself she turned on him with wild reproaches, crying that he had no faith in his own son, or he could never have believed such a terrible thing of him, that the boy was bewitched, under some spell that forced false confession out of him, that he ought to have stood up for him before everybody and prevented the tale from being accepted so lightly, for somewhere there was witch-craft in it. As often as Peredur tried to convince her he had told truth, that he was willing to make amends, and she must accept his word, she rounded on him with fresh outbursts of tears, screaming that her own son had brought dreadful disgrace upon himself and her, that she wondered he dare come near her, that she would never be able to lift up her head again, that he was a monster. . . .

As for poor Father Huw, when he tried to assert his spiritual authority and order her to submit to the force of truth and accept her son's act with humility, as Peredur himself had done in making full confession and offering full submission, she cried out that she had been a God-fearing and law-abiding woman all her life, and done everything to bring up her child in the same way, and she could not now accept his guilt as reflecting upon her.

'Mother,' said Peredur, haggard and sweating worse than when he faced Rhisiart's body, 'nobody blames you, and nobody will. What I did I did, and it's I who must abide the consequence, not you. There isn't a woman in Gwytherin won't feel for you.'

At that she let out a great wail of grief, and flung her arms about him, and swore that he should not suffer any grim penalties, that he was her own boy, and she would protect him. And when he extricated himself with fading patience, she screamed that he meant to kill her, the unfeeling wretch, and went off into peals of ear-piercing, sobbing laughter.

Brother Cadfael took Peredur firmly by the sleeve, and hauled him away to the back of the room. 'Show a little sense, lad, and take yourself out of her sight, you're fuel to her fire. If nobody marked her at all she'd have stopped long ago, but now she's got herself into this state she's past doing that of her own accord. Did our two brothers stop in here, do you know, or go on with the prior?'

Peredur was shaking and tired out, but responded hopefully to this matter-of-fact treatment. 'They've not been here, or I should have seen them. They must have gone on to the church.'

Naturally, neither Columbanus nor Jerome would dream of absenting himself from Vespers on such a momentous day.

'Never mind, you can show me where they lodge. Columbanus brought some of my poppy syrup with him, in case of need, the phial should be there with his scrip, he'd hardly have it on him. And as far as I know, he's had no occasion to use it, his cantrips here in Wales have been of a quieter kind. We can find a use for it now.'

'What does it do?' asked Peredur, wide-eyed.

'It soothes the passions and kills pain – either of the body or the spirit.'

'I could use some of that myself,' said Peredur with a wry smile, and led the way out to one of the small huts that lined the stockade. The guests from Shrewsbury had been given the best lodging the house afforded, with two low brychans, and a small chest, with a rush lamp for light. Their few necessaries occupied almost no space, but each had a leather scrip to hold them, and both of these dangled from a nail in the timber wall. Brother Cadfael opened first one, and then the other, and in the second found what he was seeking.

He drew it out and held it up to the light, a small phial of greenish glass. Even before he saw the line of the liquid in it, its light weight had caused him to check and wonder. Instead of being full to the stopper with the thick, sweet syrup, the bottle was three-quarters empty.

Brother Cadfael stood stock-still for a moment with the phial in his hand, staring at it in silence. Certainly Columbanus might at some time have felt the need to forestall some threatening spiritual disturbance but Cadfael could recall no occasion when he had said any word to that effect, or shown any sign of the rosy, reassuring calm the poppies could bring. There was enough gone from the bottle to restore serenity three times over, enough to put a man to sleep for hours. And now that he came to think back, there had been at least one occasion when a man had slept away hours of the day, instead of keeping the watch he was set to keep. The day of Rhisiart's death Columbanus had failed

137

of his duty, and confessed as much with heartfelt penitence. Columbanus, who had the syrup in his possession, and knew its use. . . .

'What must we do?' asked Peredur, uneasy in the silence. 'If it tastes unpleasant you'll have trouble getting her to drink it.'

'It tastes sweet.' But there was not very much of it left, a little reinforcement with something else soothing and pleasant might be necessary. 'Go and get a cup of strong wine, and we'll see how that goes down.'

They had taken with them a measure of wine that day, he remembered, the ration for two of them, when they set off for the chapel. Columbanus had drawn and carried it. And a bottle of water for himself, since he had made an act of piety of renouncing wine until their mission was accomplished. Jerome had done well, getting a double ration.

Brother Cadfael stirred himself out of his furious thoughts to deal with the immediate need. Peredur hurried to do his bidding, but brought mead instead of wine.

'She's more likely to drink it down before she thinks to be obstinate, for she likes it better. And it's stronger.'

'Good!' said Cadfael. 'It will hide the syrup better. And now, go somewhere quiet, and harden your heart and stop your ears and stay out of her sight, for it's the best thing you can do for her, and God knows the best for yourself, after such a day. And leave agonising too much over your sins, black as they are, there isn't a confessor in the land who hasn't heard worse and never turned a hair. It's a kind of arrogance to be so certain you're past redemption.'

The sweet, cloying drink swirled in the cup, the syrup unwinding into it in a long spiral that slowly melted and vanished. Peredur with shadowy eyes watched and was silent.

After a moment he said, very low: 'It's strange! I never could have done so shabbily by anyone I hated.'

'Not strange at all,' said Cadfael bluntly, stirring his potion. 'When harried, we go as far as we dare, and with those we're sure of we dare go very far, knowing where forgiveness is certain.'

Peredur bit his lip until it was biddable. '*Is* it certain?'

'As tomorrow's daylight, child! And now be off out of my way, and stop asking fool questions. Father Huw will have no time for you today, there's more important business waiting.'

Peredur went like a docile child, startled and comforted, and wherever he hid himself, he did it effectively, for Cadfael saw no more of him that evening. He was a good lad at heart, and this wild lunge of his into envy and meanness had brought him up short against an image of himself that he did not like at all. Whatever prayers Huw set him by way of penance were likely to hit heaven with the irresistible fervour of thunderbolts, and whatever hard labour he was given, the result was likely to stand solid as oak and last for ever.

Cadfael took his draught, and went back to where Dame Branwen was still heaving and quivering with uncontrollable sobs, by this time in genuine distress, exhausted by her efforts but unable to end them. He took advantage of her sheer weariness to present the cup to her as soon as he reached her side, and with abrupt authority that acted on her before she could muster the fibre of stubbornness.

'Drink this!' And automatically she drank it, half of it going down out of pure surprise, the second half because the first had taught her how dry and sore her throat was from all its exertions, and how smooth was the texture and how sweet the taste of this brew. The very act of swallowing it broke the frightening rhythm of the huge sighs that had convulsed her almost worse than the sobbing. Father Huw had time to mop his brow with a fold of his sleeve before she was able to resume her complaints. Even then, by comparison with what had gone before, they sounded half-hearted.

'We women, we mothers, we sacrifice our lives to bringing up children, and when they're grown they reward us by bringing disgrace upon us. What did I ever do to deserve this?'

'He'll do you credit yet,' said Cadfael cheerfully. 'Stand by him in his penance, but never try to excuse his sin, and he'll think the better of you for it.'

That went by her like the wind sighing at the time, though she may have remembered it later. Her voice declined gradually from its injured self-justification, dwindled into a half-dreamy monologue of grief, and took on at length a tone of warm and drowsy complacency, before it lapsed into silence. Cadwallon breathed deep and cautiously, and eyed his advisers.

'I should call her women and get her to bed,' said Cadfael. 'She'll sleep the night through, and it'll do her nothing but good.' And you more good still, he thought but did not say. 'Let your son rest, too, and never say another word about his trouble but by the way, like any other daily business, unless he speaks up first. Father Huw will take care of him faithfully.'

'I will,' said Huw. 'He's worth our efforts.'

139

Dame Branwen went amiably where she was led, and the house was wonderfully quiet. Cadfael and Huw went out together, pursued as far as the gate by Cadwallon's distracted gratitude. When they were well away from the holding, at the end of the stockade, the quietness of the dusk came down on them softly, a cloud descending delicately upon a cloud.

'In time for supper, if not for Vespers,' said Huw wearily. 'What should we have done without you, Brother Cadfael? I have no skill at all with women, they confuse me utterly. I marvel how you have learned to deal with them so ably, you, a cloistered brother.'

Cadfael thought of Bianca, and Arianna, and Mariam and all the others, some known so briefly, all so well.

'Both men and women partake of the same human nature, Huw. We both bleed when we're wounded. That's a poor, silly woman, true, but we can show plenty of poor, silly men. There are women as strong as any of us, and as able.' He was thinking of Mariam – or was it of Sioned? You go to supper, Huw, and hold me excused, and if I can be with you before Compline, I will. I have some business first at Bened's smithy.'

The empty phial swung heavily in the pocket in his right sleeve, reminding him. His mind was still busy with the implications. Before ever he reached Bened's croft he had it clear in his mind what must be done, but was no nearer knowing how to set about it.

Cai was with Bened on the bench under the eaves, with a jug of rough wine between them. They were not talking, only waiting for him to appear, and there could be no reason for that, but that Sioned had told them positively that he would.

'A fine tangle it turns out,' said Bened, shaking his grizzled head. 'And now you'll be off and leave us holding it. No blame to you, you have to go where your duty is. But what are we to do about Rhisiart when you're gone? There's more than half this parish thinks your Benedictines have killed him, and the lesser half thinks some enemy here has taken the chance to blame you, and get clean away into cover. We were a peaceful community until you came, nobody looked for murder among us.'

'God knows we never meant to bring it,' said Cadfael. 'But there's still tonight before we go, and I haven't shot my last bolt yet. I must speak with Sioned. We've things to do, and not much time for doing them.'

'Drink one cup with us before you go in to her,' insisted Cai. 'That takes no time at all, and is a powerful aid to thought.'

They were seated all together, three simple, honest men, and the wine notably lower in the jug, when someone turned in at the gate, light feet came running in great haste along the path, and suddenly there was Annest confronting them, skirts flying and settling about her like wings folding, her breath short and laboured, and excitement and consternation in her face. And ready to be indignant at the very sight of them sitting peacefully drinking wine.

'You'd better stir yourselves,' she said, panting and sparkling. 'I've been along to Father Huw's house to see what's going on there – Marared and Edwin between them have been keeping an eye open for us. Do you know who's there taking supper with the Benedictines? Griffith ap Rhys, the bailiff! And do you know where he's bound, afterwards? Up to our house, to take Brother John to prison!'

They were on their feet fast enough at this news, though Bened dared to question it. 'He can't be there! The last I heard of him he was at the mill.'

'And that was this morning, and I tell you now he's eating and drinking with Prior Robert and the rest. I've seen him with my own eyes, so don't tell me he can't be there. And here I find you sitting on your hams drinking, as thought we had all the time in the world!'

'But *why* in such a hurry tonight?' persisted Bened. 'Did the prior send for him, because he's wanting to be away tomorrow?'

'The devil was in it! He came to Vespers just by way of compliment to Father Huw, and who should he find celebrating instead but Prior Robert, and the prior seized on it as just the chance he wanted, and has hung on to him and persuaded him Brother John must be taken in charge tonight, for he can't leave without knowing he's safely in the hands of the law. He says the bailiff should deal with him for the secular offence of hindering the arrest of a criminal, and when he's served his penalty he's to be sent back to Shrewsbury to answer for his defiance of discipline, or else the prior will send an escort to fetch him. And what could the bailiff do but fall in with it, when it was put to him like that? And here you sit – !'

'All right, girl, all right,' said Cai placatingly. 'I'm off this minute, and Brother John will be out of there and away to a safe place before ever the bailiff gets near us. I'll take one of your ponies, Bened. . . .'

'Saddle another for me,' said Annest with determination. 'I'm coming with you.'

Cai went off at a jogtrot to the paddock, and Annest, drawing breath more easily now that the worst was told, drank off the wine he had left in his cup, and heaved a huge, resolute sigh.

'We'd better be out of here fast, for that young brother who looks after the horses now will be coming down after supper to get them. The prior means to be there to see John safe bound. "There's time yet before Compline," he said. He was complaining of wanting you, too, to interpret for him, they were managing lamely with only Latin between them. Dear God, what a day it's been!'

And what a night, thought Cadfael, it's still likely to be. 'What else was going on there?' he asked. 'Did you hear anything that might give me a light? For heavens knows I need one!'

'They were debating which one of them should watch the night through at the chapel. And that same young fair one, the one who has visions, up and prayed it might be him. He said he'd been unfaithful to his watch once, and longed still to make amends. And the prior said he might. That much I understood myself. All the prior's thinking about seems to be making all the trouble he can for John,' said Annest resentfully, 'or I should think he might have sent somebody else instead. That young brother – what is it you call him?'

'Columbanus,' said Brother Cadfael.

'That's him, Columbanus! He begins to put on airs as if he *owned* Saint Winifred. I don't want her to go away at all, but at least it was the prior who first thought of it, and now if there's a halo for anybody it's shifted to this other fellow's head.'

She did not know it, but she had indeed given Cadfael a light, and with every word she said it burned more steadily. 'So he's to be the one who watches the night through before the altar – and alone, is he?'

'So I heard.' Cai was coming with the ponies, at a gay trot out of the meadow. Annest rose eagerly and kilted her gown, knotting her girdle tightly about the broad pleat she drew up over her hips. 'Brother Cadfael, you don't think it wrong of me to love John? Or of him to love me? I don't care about the rest of them, but I should be sorry if *you* thought we were doing something wicked.'

142

Cai had not bothered with a saddle for himself, but had provided one for her. Quite simply and naturally Brother Cadfael cupped his hands for her foot, to give her a lift on to the pony's broad back, and the fresh scent of her linen and the smooth coolness of her ankle against his wrists as she mounted made one of the best moments of that interminably long and chaotic day. 'As long as I may live, girl,' he said, 'I doubt if I shall ever know two creatures with less wickedness between them. He made a mistake, and there should be provision for everybody to make one fresh start. I don't think he's making any mistake this time.'

He watched her ride away, setting an uphill pace to which Cai adopted himself goodhumouredly. They had a fair start, it would be ten minutes or more yet before Columbanus came to fetch the horses, and even then he had to take them back to the parsonage. It might be well to put in an appearance and go with Robert dutifully to interpret his fulminations, too, in which case there was need of haste, for he had now a great deal to say to Sioned, and this night's moves must be planned thoroughly. He withdrew into the croft as soon as Annest and Cai were out of sight, and Sioned came out of the shadows eagerly to meet him.

'I expected Annest to be here before you. She went to find out what's happening at Father Huw's. I thought best to stay out of sight. If people think I'm away home, so much the better. You haven't seen Annest?'

'I have, and heard all her news,' said Cadfael, and told her what was in the wind, and where Annest was gone. 'Never fear for John, they'll be there well ahead of any pursuit. We have other business, and no time to waste, for I shall be expected to ride with the prior, and it's as well I should be there to see fair play. If we manage our business as well as I fancy Cai and Annest will manage theirs, before morning we may know what we want to know.'

'You've found out something,' she said with certainty. 'You are changed. You are sure!'

He told her briefly all that had happened at Cadwallon's house, how he had brooded upon it without enlightenment as to how it was to be used, and how Annest in innocence had shown him. Then he told her what he required of her.

'I know you can speak English, you must use it tonight. This may be a more dangerous trap than any we've laid before, but I shall be close by. And you may call in Engelard, too, if he'll

143

promise to stay close in cover. But, child, if you have any doubts or fears, if you'd rather let be, and have me try some other way, say so now, and so be it.'

'No,' she said, 'no doubts and no fears. I can do anything. I dare do anything.'

'Then sit down with me, and learn your part well, for we haven't long. And while we plan, can I ask you to bring me some bread and a morsel of cheese? For I've missed my supper.'

Prior Robert and Brother Richard rode into Rhisiart's yard with the prince's bailiff between them, his two henchmen and Brother Cadfael close behind, at about half past seven, in a mild twilight, with all the unhurried ceremony of the law, rather as if Griffith ap Rhys held his commission from Saint Benedict, and not from Owain Gwynedd. The bailiff was, in fact, more than a little vexed at this unfortunate encounter, which had left him no alternative but to comply with Robert's demands. An offence against Welsh law was alleged, and had been reported to him, and he was obliged to investigate it, where, considering the circumstances, he would much have preferred to pack all the Benedictine delegation back to Shrewsbury, and let them sort out their own grudges there, without bothering a busy man who had plenty of more important things on his mind. Unhappily Cadwallon's villein, the long-legged fellow who had been brought down by Brother John, had given vociferous evidence in support of the accusation, or it would have been easier to ignore it.

There was no one on duty at the gate, which was strange, and as they rode in, a number of people seemed to be running hither and thither in a distracted way, as if something unforeseen had happened, and confused and conflicting orders were being given from several authorities at once. No groom ran to attend to them, either. Prior Robert was displeased. Griffith ap Rhys was mildly and alertly interested. When someone did take notice of them, it was a very handsome young person in a green gown, who came running with her skirts gathered in her hands, and her light-brown hair slipping out of its glossy coil to her shoulders.

'Oh, sirs, you must excuse us this neglect, we've been so disturbed! The gate-keeper was called away to help, and all the grooms are hunting. . . . But I'm ashamed to let our troubles cast a shadow over our hospitality. My lady's resting, and can't be disturbed, but I'm at your service. Will it please you light down? Shall I have lodgings made ready?'

'We don't propose to stay,' said Griffith ap Rhys, already suspecting this artless goodwill, and approving the way she radiated it. 'We came to relieve you of a certain young malefactor you've had in hold here. But it seems you've suffered some further calamity, and we should be sorry to add to your troubles, or disturb your lady, after the grievous day she's endured.'

'Madam,' said Prior Robert, civilly but officiously, 'you are addressing the prince's bailiff of Rhos, and I am the prior of Shrewsbury abbey. You have a brother of that abbey in confinement here, the royal bailiff is come to relieve you of his care.'

All of which Cadfael duly and solemnly translated for Annest's benefit, his face as guileless as hers.

'Oh, sir!' She opened her eyes wide and curtseyed deeply to Griffith and cursorily to the prior, separating her own from the alien. 'It's true we had such a brother here a prisoner. . . .'

'Had?' said Robert sharply, for once detecting the change of tense.

'Had?' said Griffith thoughtfully.

'He's gone, sir! You see what confusion he's left behind. This evening, when his keeper took him his supper, this brother struck him down with a board torn loose from the manger in his prison, and dropped the bolt on him and slipped away. It was some time before we knew. He must have climbed the wall, you see it is not so high. We have men out now looking for him in the woods, and searching everywhere here within. But I fear he's clean gone!'

Cai made his entrance at the perfect time, issuing from one of the barns with shaky steps, his head wreathed in a white cloth lightly dabbled with red.

'The poor man, the villain broke his head for him! It was some time before he could drag himself to the door and hammer on it, and make himself heard. There's no knowing how far the fellow may have got by now. But the whole household is out hunting for him.'

The bailiff, as in duty bound, questioned Cai, but gently and briefly, questioned all the other servants, who ran to make themselves, useful and succeeded only in being magnificently confusing. And Prior Robert, burning with vengeful zeal, would have pressed them more strenuously but for the bailiff's presence and obvious prior right, and the brevity of the time at his disposal if he was to get back for Compline. In any case, it was quite clear that Brother John was indeed over the wall and clean gone. Most willingly they showed the place where he had been confined, and the manger from which he had ripped the board, and the board itself, artistically spattered at one end with spots of Cai's gore, though it may, of course, have been pigment borrowed from the butcher.

'It seems your young man has given us all the slip,' said Griffith, with admirable serenity for a man of law who has lost a malefactor. 'There's nothing more to be done here. They could hardly expect such violence from a Benedictine brother, it's no blame to them.'

With considerable pleasure Cadfael translated that neat little stab. It kindled a spark in the speaking eyes of the young person in green, and Griffith did not miss it. But to challenge it would have been folly. The clear brown eyes would have opened wide enough and deep enough to drown a man in their innocence. 'We'd best leave them in peace to mend their broken mangers and broken heads,' said Griffith, 'and look elsewhere for our fugitive.'

'The wretch compounds his offences,' said Robert, furious. 'But I cannot allow his villainy to disrupt my mission. I must set out for home tomorrow, and leave his capture to you.'

'You may trust me to deal properly with him,' said Griffith drily, 'when he is found.' If he laid the slightest of emphasis on the 'when', no one appeared to remark it but Cadfael and Annest. By this time Annest was quite satisfied that she liked this princely official, and could trust him to behave like a reasonable man who is not looking for trouble, or trying to make it for others as harmless as himself.

'And you will restore him to our house when he has purged his offences under Welsh law?'

'When he has done so,' said Griffith, decidedly with some stress this time on the 'when', 'you shall certainly have him back.'

With that Prior Robert had to be content, though his Norman spirit burned at being deprived of its rightful victim. And on the ride back he was by no means placated by Griffith's tales of the large numbers of fugitive outlaws who had found no difficulty in living wild in these forests, and even made friends among the country people, and been accepted into families, and even into respectability at last. It galled his orderly mind to think of insubordination mellowing with time and being tolerated and condoned. He was in no very Christian mood when he swept into Father Huw's church, only just in time for Compline.

They were all there but Brother John, the remaining five

146

brethren from Shrewsbury and a good number of the people of Gwytherin, to witness the last flowering of Brother Columbanus' devotional gift of ecstasy, now dedicated entirely to Saint Winifred, his personal patroness who had healed him of madness, favoured him with her true presence in a dream, and made known her will through him in the matter of Rhisiart's burial. For at the end of Compline, rising to go to his self-chosen vigil, Columbanus turned to the altar, raised his arms in a sweeping gesture, and prayed aloud in a high, clear voice that the virgin martyr would deign to visit him once more in his holy solitude, in the silence of the night, and reveal to him again the inexpressible bliss from which he had returned so reluctantly to this imperfect world. And more, that this time, if she found him worthy of translation out of the body, she would take him up living into that world of light. Humbly he submitted his will to endure here below, and do his duty in the estate assigned him, but rapturously he sent his desire soaring to the timber roof, to be uplifted out of the flesh, transported through death without dying, if he was counted ready for the assumption.

Everyone present heard, and trembled at such virtue. Everyone but Brother Cadfael, who was past trembling at the arrogance of man, and whose mind, in any case, was busy and anxious with other, though related, matters.

Chapter Ten

rother Columbanus entered the small, dark, wood-scented chapel heavy with the odours of centuries, and closed the door gently behind him, without latching it. There were no candles lighted, tonight, only the small oil-lamp upon the altar, that burned with a tall, unwavering flame from its floating wick. That slender, single turret of light cast still shadows all around, and being almost on a level with the bier of Saint Winifred, braced on trestles before it, made of it a black coffin shape, only touched here and there with sparkles of reflected silver.

Beyond the capsule of soft golden light all was darkness, per-fumed with age and dust. There was a second entrance, from the minute sacristy that was no more than a porch beside the altar, but no draught from that or any source caused the lamp-flame to waver even for an instant. There might have been no storms of air or spirit, no winds, no breath of living creature, to disturb the stillness.

Brother Columbanus made his obeisance to the altar, briefly and almost curtly. There was no one to see, he had come alone, and neither seen nor heard any sign of another living soul in the graveyard or the woods around. He moved the second prayer-desk aside, and set the chosen one squarely in the centre of the chapel, facing the bier. His behaviour was markedly more practical and moderate than when there were people by to see him, but did not otherwise greatly differ. He had come to watch out the night on his knees, and he was prepared to do so, but there was no need to labour his effects until morning, when his fellows would come to take Saint Winifred in reverent procession on the first stage of her journey. Columbanus padded the prie-dieu for his knees with the bunched skirts of his habit, and made himself as comfortable as possible with his gowned arms broadly folded as a pillow for his head. The umber darkness was scented and heavy with the warmth of wood, and the night outside was not cold. Once he had shut out the tiny, erect tower of light and the few bright surfaces from which it was reflected, the drowsiness he was inviting came stealing over him in long, lulling waves until it washed over his head, and he slept.

It seemed, after the fashion of sleep, no time at all before he was startled awake, but in fact it was more than three hours, and midnight was approaching, when his slumbers began to be strangely troubled with a persistent dream that someone, a woman, was calling him by name low and clearly, and over and over and over again: 'Columbanus. . . . Columbanus . . .' with inexhaustible and relentless patience. And he was visited, even in sleep, by a sensation that this woman had all the time in the world, and was willing to go on calling for ever, while for him there was no time left at all, but he must awake and be rid of her.

He started up suddenly, stiff to the ends of fingers and toes, ears stretched and eyes staring wildly, but there was the enclosing capsule of mild darkness all about him as before, and the reliquary dark, too, darker than before, or so it seemed, as if the flame of the lamp, though steady, had subsided, and was now more than half hidden behind the coffin. He had forgotten to check the oil. Yet he knew it had been fully supplied when last he left it, after Rhisiart's burial, and that was only a matter of hours ago.

It seemed that of all his senses, hearing had been the last to return to him, for now he was aware, with a cold crawling of fear along his skin, that the voice of his dream was still with him, and had been with him all along, emerging from dream into reality without a break. Very soft, very low, very deliberate, not a whisper, but the clear thread of a voice, at once distant and near, insisting unmistakably: 'Columbanus . . . Columbanus . . . Columbanus, what have you done?'

Out of the reliquary the voice came, out of the light that was dwindling even as he stared in terror and unbelief.

149

'Columbanus, Columbanus, my false servant, who blasphemes against my will and murders my champions, what will you say in your defence to Winifred? Do you think you can deceive me as you deceive your prior and your brothers?'

Without haste, without heat, the voice issued forth from the darkening apse of the altar, so small, so terrible, echoing eerily out of its sacred cave.

'You who claim to be my worshipper, you have played me false like the vile Cradoc, do you think you will escape his end? I never wished to leave my resting-place here in Gwytherin. Who told you otherwise but your own devil of ambition? I laid my hand upon a good man, and sent him out to be my champion, and this day he has been buried here, a martyr for my sake. The sin is recorded in heaven, there is no hiding-place for you. Why,' demanded the voice, cold, peremptory and menacing in its stillness, 'have you killed my servant Rhisiart?'

He tried to rise from his knees, and it was as if they were nailed to the wood of the prie-dieu. He tried to find a voice, and only a dry croaking came out of his stiff throat. She could not be there, there was no one there! But the saints go where they please, and reveal themselves to whom they please, and sometimes terribly. His cold fingers clutched at the desk, and felt nothing. His tongue, like an unplaned splinter of wood, tore the roof of his mouth when he fought to make it speak.

'There is no hope for you but in confession, Columbanus, murderer! Speak! Confess!'

'No!' croaked Columbanus, forcing out words in frantic haste. 'I never touched Rhisiart! I was here in your chapel, holy virgin, all that afternoon, how could I have harmed him? I sinned against you, I was faithless, I slept. . . . I own it! Don't lay a greater guilt on me. . . .'

'It was not you who slept,' breathed the voice, a tone higher, a shade more fiercely, 'liar that you are! Who carried the wine? Who poisoned the wine, causing even the innocent to sin? Brother Jerome slept, not you! *You* went out into the forest and waited for Rhisiart, and struck him down.'

'No . . . no, I swear it!' Shaking and sweating, he clawed at the desk before him, and could get no leverage with his palsied hands to prise himself to his feet and fly from her. How can you fly from beings who are everywhere and see everything? For nothing mortal could possibly know what this being knew. 'No, it's all wrong, I am misjudged! I was asleep here when Father Huw's messenger came for us. Jerome shook me awake. . . . The messenger is witness. . . .'

'The messenger never passed the doorway. Brother Jerome was already stirring out of his poisoned sleep, and went to meet him. As for you, you feigned and lied, as you feign and lie now. Who was it brought the poppy syrup? Who was it knew its use? You were pretending sleep, you lied even in confessing to sleep, and Jerome, as weak as you are wicked, was glad enough to think you could not accuse him, not even seeing that you were indeed accusing him of worse, of *your* act, of *your* slaying! He did not know you lied, and could not charge you with it. But *I* know, and I do charge you! And my vengeance loosed upon Cradoc may also be loosed upon you, if you lie to me but once more!'

'No!' he shrieked, and covered his face as though she dazzled him with lightnings, though only a thin, small, terrible sound threatened him. 'No, spare! I am not lying! Blessed virgin, I have been your true servant . . . I have tried to do your will . . . I know nothing of this! I never harmed Rhisiart! I never gave poisoned wine to Jerome!'

'Fool!' said the voice in a sudden loud cry. 'Do you think you can deceive *me? Then what is this?'*

There was a sudden silvery flash in the air before him, and something fell and smashed with a shivering of glass on the floor just in front of the desk, spattering his knees with sharp fragments and infinitesimal, sticky drops, and at the same instant the flame of the lamp died utterly, and black darkness fell.

Shivering and sick with fear, Columbanus groped forward along the earth floor, and slivers of glass crushed and stabbed under his palms, drawing blood. He lifted one hand to his face, whimpering, and smelled the sweet, cloying scent of the poppy syrup, and knew that he was kneeling among the fragments of the phial he had left safe in his scrip at Cadwallon's house.

It was no more than a minute before the total darkness eased, and there beyond the bier and the altar the small, oblong shape of the window formed in comparative light, a deep, clear sky, moonless but starlit. Shapes within the chapel again loomed very dimly, giving space to his sickening terror. There was a figure standing motionless between him and the bier.

It took a little while for his eyes to accustom themselves to the dimness, and assemble out of it this shadowy, erect pallor, a woman lost in obscurity from the waist down, but head and shoulders feebly illuminated by the starlight from the altar window. He had not seen her come, he had heard nothing. She had appeared while he was dragging his torn palm over the shards of glass, and moaning as if at the derisory pain. A slender, still form swathed from head to foot closely in white, Winifred in her grave clothes, long since dust, a thin veil covering her face and head, and her arm outstretched and pointing at him.

He shrank back before her, scuffling abjectly backwards along the floor, making feeble gestures with his hands to fend off the very sight of her. Frantic tears burst out of his eyes, and frantic words from his lips.

'It was for you! It was for you and for my abbey! I did it for the glory of our house! I believed I had warranty—from you and from heaven! He stood in the way of God's will! He would not let you go. I meant only rightly when I did what I did!'

'Speak plainly,' said the voice, sharp with command, 'and say out what you did.'

'I gave the syrup to Jerome—in his wine— and when he was asleep I stole out to the forest path, and waited for Rhisiart. I followed him. I struck him down. . . . Oh, sweet Saint Winifred, don't let me be damned for striking down the enemy who stood in the way of blessedness. . . .'

'Struck in the back!' said the pale figure, and a sudden cold gust of air swept over her and shuddered in her draperies, and surging across the chapel, blew upon Columbanus and chilled him to the bone. As if she had touched him! And she was surely a pace nearer, though he had not seen her move. 'Struck in the back, as mean cowards and traitors do! Own it! Say it all!'

'In the back!' babbled Columbanus, scrambling back from her like a broken animal, until his shoulders came up against the wall, and he could retreat no farther. 'I own it. I confess it all! Oh, merciful saint, you know all, and I cannot hide from you! Have pity on me! Don't destroy me! It was all for you, I did it for you!'

'You did it for yourself,' charged the voice, colder than ice and burning like ice. 'You who would be master of whatever order you enter, you with your ambitions and stratagems, you setting out wilfully to draw to yourself all the glory of possessing me, to work your way into the centre of all achievements, to show as the favourite of heaven, the paragon of piety, to elbow Brother Richard out of his succession to your prior, and if you could, the prior out of his succession to your abbot. You with your thirst to become the youngest head under a mitre in this or any land!

152

I know you, and I know your kind. There is no way too ruthless for you, provided it leads to power.'

'No, no!' he panted, bracing himself back against the wall, for certainly she was advancing upon him, and now in bitter, quiet fury, jetting menace from her outstretched finger-tips. 'It was all for you, only for you! I believed I was doing your will!'

'My will to evil?' the voice rose into a piercing cry, sharp as a dagger. 'My will to murder?'

She had taken one step too many. Columbanus broke in frenzied fear, clawed himself upright by the wall, and struck out with both hands, beating at her blindly to fend her off from touching, and uttering thin, babbling cries as he flailed about him. His left hand caught in her draperies and dragged the veil from her face and head. Dark hair fell round her shoulders. His fingers made contact with the curve of a smooth, cool cheek, cool, but not cold, smooth with the graceful curves of firm young flesh, where in his sick horror he had expected to plunge his hand into the bony hollows of a skull.

He uttered a scream that began in frantic terror and ended in soaring triumph. The hand that had shrunk from contact turned suddenly to grasp hold, knotting strong fingers in the dark tangle of hair. He was very quick, Columbanus. It took him no more than the intake of a breath to know he had a flesh-and-blood woman at the end of his arm, and scarcely longer to know who she must be, and what she had done to him, with this intolerable trap in which she had caught him. And barely another breath to consider that she was here alone, and to all appearances had set her trap alone, and if she survived he was lost, and if she did not survive, if she vanished—there was plenty left of the night!—he was safe, and still in command of all this expedition, and inheritor of all its glory.

It was his misfortune that Sioned was almost as quick in the uptake as he. In a darkness in which vision hardly helped or hindered, she heard the great, indrawn breath that released him from the fear of hell and heaven together, and felt the wave of animal anger that came out from him like a foul scent, almost as sickening as the odour of his fear. She sprang back from it by instinct, and repeated the lunge of intent, dragging herself out of his grasp at the price of a few strands of hair. But his clawing hand, cheated, loosed the fragments and caught again at the linen sheet that draped her, and that would not tear so easily. She swung round to her left, to put as much distance as she could between her body and his right hand, but she saw him lunge into the breast of his habit, and saw the brief, sullen flash of the steel as he whipped it out and followed her swing, hacking into dimness. The same dagger, she thought, swooping beneath its first blind stab, that killed my father.

Somewhere a door had opened fully on the night, for the wind blew through the chapel suddenly, and sandalled feet thudded in with the night air, a thickset, powerful body driving the draught before it. A loud voice thundered warning. Brother Cadfael erupted into the chapel from the sacristy like a bolt from a crossbow, and drove at full speed into the struggle.

Columbanus was in the act of striking a second time, and with his left hand firmly clutching the linen sheet wound about Sioned's body. But she was whirling round away from him to unloose those same folds that held her, and the blow that was meant for her heart only grazed painfully down her left forearm. Then his grip released her, and she fell back against the wall, and Columbanus was gone, hurtling out at the door in full flight, and Brother Cadfael was embracing her with strong, sustaining arms, and upbraiding her with a furious, bracing voice, while he held her in a bear's hug, and felt at her as tenderly and fervently as a mother.

'For God's sake, fool daughter, why did you get within his reach? I *told* you, keep the bier between you and him . . . !'

'Get after him,' shouted Sioned wrathfully, 'do you want him clean away? I'm sound enough, go get *him*! He killed my father!'

They headed for the door together, but Cadfael was out of it first. The girl was strong, vigorous and vengeful, a Welshwoman to the heart, barely grazed, he knew the kind. The wind of action blew her, she felt no pain and was aware of no effusion of blood, blood she wanted, and with justification. She was close on his heels as he rolled like a thunderbolt down the narrow path through the graveyard towards the gate. The night was huge, velvet, sewn with stars, their veiled and delicate light barely casting shadows. All that quiet space received and smothered the sound of their passage, and smoothed the stillness of the night over it.

Out of the bushes beyond the graveyard wall a man's figure started, tall, slender and swift, leaping to block the gateway. Columbanus saw him, and baulked for a moment, but Cadfael was running hard behind him, and the next instant the fugitive made up his mind and rushed on, straight at the shadow that moved to intercept him. Hard on Cadfael's

154

heels, Sioned suddenly shrieked: 'Take care, Engelard! He has a dagger!'

Engelard heard her, and swerved to the right at the very moment of collision, so that the stroke meant for his heart only ripped a fluttering ribbon of cloth from his sleeve. Columbanus would have bored his way past at speed, and run for the cover of the woods, but Engelard's long left arm swept round hard into the back of his neck, sending him off-balance for a moment, though he kept his feet, and Engelard's right fist got a tight grip on the flying cowl, and twisted. Half-strangled, Columbanus whirled again and struck out with the knife, and this time Engelard was ready for the flash, and took the thrusting wrist neatly in his left hand. They swayed and wrestled together, feet braced in the grass, and they were very fairly matched if both had been armed. That unbalance was soon amended. Engelard twisted at the wrist he held, ignoring the clawing of Columbanus' free hand at his throat, and the numbed fingers opened at last and let the dagger fall. Both lunged for it, but Engelard scooped it up and flung it contemptuously aside into the bushes, and grappled his opponent with his bare hands. The fight was all but over. Columbanus hung panting and gasping, both arms pinned, looking wildly round for a means of escape and finding none.

'Is this the man?' demanded Engelard.

Sioned said: 'Yes. He has owned to it.'

Engelard looked beyond his prisoner then for the first time, and saw her standing in the soft starlight that was becoming to their accustomed eyes almost as clear as day. He saw her dishevelled and bruised and gazing with great, shocked eyes, her left arm gashed and bleeding freely, though the cut was shallow. He saw smears of her blood dabbling the white sheet in which she was swathed. By starlight there is little or no colour to be seen, but everything that Engelard saw at that moment was blood-red. This was the man who had murdered in coward's fashion Engelard's well-liked lord and good friend—whatever their differences!—and now he had tried to kill the daughter as he had killed the father.

'You dared, you dared touch her!' blazed Engelard in towering rage. 'You worthless cloister rat!' And he took Columbanus by the throat and hoisted him bodily from the ground, shook him like the rat he had called him, cracked him in the air like a poisonous snake, and when he had done with him, flung him down at his feet in the grass.

'Get up!' he growled, standing over the wreckage. 'Get up now, and I'll give you time to rest and breathe, and then you can fight a man to the death, without a dagger in your hand, instead of writhing through the undergrowth and stabbing him in the back, or carving up a defenceless girl. Take your time, I can wait to kill you till you've got your breath.'

Sioned flew to him, breast to breast, and held him fast in her arms, pressing him back. 'No! Don't touch him again! I don't want the law to have any hold on *you*, even the slenderest.'

'He tried to kill you—you're hurt. . . .'

'No! It's nothing . . . only a cut. It bleeds, but it's nothing!'

His rage subsided slowly, shaking him. He folded his arms round her and held her to him, and with a disdainful but restrained jab of a toe urged his prostrate enemy again: 'Get up! I won't touch you. The law can have you, and welcome!'

Columbanus did not move, not by so much as the flicker of an eyelid or the twitching of a finger. All three of them stood peering down at him in sudden silence, aware how utterly still he was, and how rare such stillness is among living things.

'He's foxing,' said Engelard scornfully, 'for fear of worse, and by way of getting himself pitied. I've heard he's a master at that.'

Those who feign sleep and hear themselves talked of, usually betray themselves by some exaggeration of innocence. Columbanus lay in a stillness that was perfectly detached and indifferent.

Brother Cadfael knelt down beside him, shook him by the shoulder gently, and sat back with a sharp sigh at the broken movement of the head. He put a hand inside the breast of the habit, and stooped to the parted lips and wide nostrils. Then he took the head between his hands, and gently turned and tilted it. It rolled back, as he released it, into a position so improbable that they knew the worst even before Cadfael said, quite practically: 'You'd have waited a long time for him to get his breath back, my friend. You don't know your own strength! His neck is broken. He's dead.'

Sobered and shocked, they stood dumbly staring down at what they had hardly yet recognised for disaster. They saw a regrettable accident which neither of them had ever intended, but which was, after all, a kind of justice. But Cadfael saw a scandal that could yet wreck their young lives, and others, too, for without Columbanus alive, and forced by two respected witnesses to repeat his confession, how strong was all their proof against him? Cadfael sat back on his heels, and thought. It was startling to realise, now that the unmoved silence of the night came down on them again, how all this violence and passion had passed with very little noise, and no other witnesses. He listened, and no stirring of foot or wing troubled the quiet. They were far enough away from any dwelling, not a soul had been disturbed. That, at least, was time gained.

'He can't be dead,' said Engelard doubtfully. 'I barely handled him at all. Nobody dies as easily as that!'

'This one did. And now what's to be done? I hadn't bargained for this.' He said it not complainingly, but as one pointing out that further urgent planning would now be necessary, and they had better keep their minds flexible.

'Why, what can be done?' To Engelard it was simple, though troublesome. 'We shall have to call up Father Huw and your prior, and tell them exactly what's happened. What else can we do? I'm sorry to have killed the fellow, I never meant to, but I can't say I feel any *guilt* about it.' Nor did he expect any blame. The truth was always the best way. Cadfael felt a reluctant affection for such innocence. The world was going to damage it sooner or later, but one undeserved accusation had so far failed even to bruise it, he still trusted men to be reasonable. Cadfael doubted if Sioned was so sure. Her silence was anxious and foreboding. And her grazed arm was still oozing blood. First things first, and they might as well be sensibly occupied while he thought.

'Here, make yourself useful! Help me get this carrion back into the chapel, out of sight. And, Sioned, find his dagger, we can't leave that lying about to bear witness. Then let's get that arm of yours washed and bound up. There's a stream at the back of the hawthorn hedge, and of linen we've plenty.'

They had absolute faith in him, and did his bidding without question, though Engelard, once he had assured himself that Sioned was not gravely hurt, and had himself carefully and deftly bandaged her scratch, returned to his dogged opinion that their best course was to tell the whole story, which could hardly cast infamy upon anyone but Columbanus. Cadfael busied himself with flint and tinder until he had candles lighted, and the lamp refilled, from which he himself had drained a judicious quantity of oil before Sioned took her place under the draperies of the saint's catafalque.

157

'You think,' he said at length, 'that because you've done nothing wrong, and we've all of us banded together to expose a wrong, that the whole world will be of the same opinion, and honestly come out and say so. Child, I know better! The only proof we have of Columbanus' guilt is his confession, which both of us here heard. Or rather, the only proof we had, for we no longer have even that. Alive, we two could have forced the truth out of him a second time. Dead, he's never going to give us that satisfaction. And without that, our position is vulnerable enough. Make no mistake, if we accuse him, if this fearful scandal breaks, to smirch the abbey of Shrewsbury, and all the force of the Benedictine order, backed here by the bishop and the prince, take my word for it, all the forces of authority will band together to avert the disaster, and nobody, much less a friendless outlander, will be allowed to stand in the way. They simply can't afford to have their acquisition of Saint Winifred called in question and brought to disrepute. Rather than that, they'll call this an outlaw killing by a desperate man, a fugitive already, wanted for another crime, and trying to escape both together. A pity,' he said, 'I ever suggested that Sioned should call you in to wait in reserve, in case we had trouble. But none of this is your fault, and I won't have you branded with it. I made the plot, and I must unravel it. But give up all idea of going straight to Father Huw, or the bailiff, or anyone else, with the true story. Far better use the rest of this night to rearrange matters to better advantage. Justice can be arrived at by more routes than one.'

'They wouldn't dare doubt Sioned's word,' said Engelard stoutly.

'Fool boy, they'd say that Sioned, for love's sake, might go as far aside from her proper nature as Peredur did. And as for me, my influence is small enough, and I am not interested in protecting only myself, but as many of those in this coil as I can reach. Even my prior, who is arrogant and rigid, and to tell the truth, sometimes rather stupid, but not a murderer and not a liar. And my order, which has not deserved Columbanus. Hush, now, and let me think! And while I do, you can be clearing away the remains of the syrup bottle. This chapel must be as neat and quiet tomorrow as before we ever brought our troubles into it.'

Obediently they went about removing the traces of the night's alarms, and let him alone until he should have found them a way through the tangle.

'And I wonder, now,' he said at length, 'what made you improve on all the speeches I made for you, and put such fiery words into Saint Winifred's mouth? What put it into your head to say that you'd never wanted to leave Gwytherin, and did not want it now? That Rhisiart was not merely a decent, honest man, but your chosen champion?'

She turned and looked at him in astonishment and wonder. 'Did I say that?'

'You did, and very well you delivered it, too. And very proper and apt it sounded, but I think we never rehearsed it so. Where did you get the words?'

'I don't know,' said Sioned, puzzled. 'I don't remember what I did say. The words seemed to come freely of themselves, I only let them flow.'

'It may be,' said Engelard, 'that the saint was taking her chance when it offered. All these strangers having visions and ecstasies, and interpreting them to suit themselves, yet nobody ever really asked Saint Winifred what *she* wanted. They all claimed they knew better than she did.'

'Out of the mouths of innocents!' said Cadfael to himself, and pondered the road that was gradually opening before his mind's eye. Of all the people who ought to be left happy with the outcome, Saint Winifred should surely come first. Aim, he thought, at making everybody happy, and if that'a within reach, why stir up any kind of unpleasantness? Take Columbanus, for instance! Only a few hours ago at Compline he prayed aloud before us all that if the virgin deemed him worthy, he might be taken up out of this world this very night, translated instantly out of the body. Well, that was one who got his wish! Maybe he'd have withdrawn his request if he'd known it was going to be taken up so literally, for its purpose was rather to reflect incomparable holiness upon him while he was still alive to enjoy it. But saints have a right to suppose that their devotees mean what they say, and bestow gifts accordingly. And if the saint has really spoken through Sioned, he thought—and who am I to question it?—if she really wants to stay here in her own village, which is a reasonable enough wish, well, the plot where she used to sleep has been newly turned today, no one will notice anything if it's turned again tonight.

'I believe,' said Sioned, watching him with the first faint smile, wan but trusting, 'you're beginning to see your way.'

'I believe,' said Cadfael, 'I'm beginning to see *our* way, which is more to the point. Sioned, I have something for you to do, and you need not hurry, we have work to do here while you're away. Take that sheet of yours, and go and spread it under the may trees in the hedge, where they're beginning to shed, but not yet brown. Shake the bushes and bring us a whole cloud of petals. The last time she visited him, it was with wondrous sweet odours and a shower of white flowers. Bring the one, and we shall have the other.'

Confidently, understanding nothing as yet, she took the linen sheet from which she had unwound herself as from a shroud, and went to do his bidding.

'Give me the dagger,' said Cadfael briskly when she was gone. He wiped the blade on the veil Columbanus had torn from Sioned's head, and moved the candles so that they shone upon the great red seals that closed Winifred's reliquary. 'Thank God he didn't bleed,' he said. 'His habit and clothes are unmarked. Strip him!'

And he fingered the first seal, nodded satisfaction at its fatness and the thinness and sharpness of the dagger, and thrust the tip of the blade into the flame of the lamp.

Long before daylight they were ready. They walked down all three together from the chapel towards the village, and separated at the edge of the wood, where the shortest path turned off uphill towards Rhisiart's holding.

Sioned carried with her the blood-stained sheet and veil, and the fragments of glass they had buried in the forest. A good thing the servants who had filled in Rhisiart's grave had left their spades on the scene, meaning to tidy the mound next day. That had saved a journey to borrow without leave, and a good hour of time.

'There'll be no scandal,' said Cadfael, when they halted at the place where the paths divided. 'No scandal, and no accusations. I think you may take him home with you, but keep him out of sight until we're gone. There'll be peace when we're gone. And you needn't fear that the prince or his bailiff will ever proceed further against Engelard, any more than against John. I'll speak a word in Peredur's ear. Peredur will speak it into the bailiff's ear, the bailiff will speak it into Owain Gwynedd's ear—Father Huw we'll leave out of it, no need to burden his conscience, the good, simple man. And if the monks of Shrewsbury are happy, and the people of Gwytherin are happy—for they'll hear the whisper fast enough—why should anyone want to upset such a satisfactory state of affairs, by speaking the word aloud? A wise prince—and Owain Gwynedd seems to me very wise—will let well alone.'

'All Gwytherin,' said Sioned, and shivered a little at the thought, 'will be there in the morning to watch you take the reliquary away.'

'So much the better, we want all the witnesses we can have, all the emotion, all the wonder. I am a great sinner,' said Cadfael philosophically, 'but I feel no weight. Does the end justify the means, I wonder?'

'One thing I know,' she said. 'My father can rest now, and that he owes to you. And I owe you that and more. When I first came down to you out of the tree—you remember?—I thought you would be like other monks, and not want to look at me.'

'Child, I should have to be out of my wits, not to want to look at you. I've looked so attentively, I shall remember you all my life. But your love, my children, and how you manage it with that I can't help you.'

'No need,' said Engelard. 'I am an outlander, with a proper agreement. That agreement can be dissolved by consent, and I can be a free man by dividing all my goods equally with my lord, and now Sioned *is* my lord.'

'And then there can no man prevent,' said Sioned, 'if I choose to endow him with half *my* goods, as is only fair. Uncle Meurice won't stand in our way. And it won't even be hard for him to justify. To marry an heiress to an outlander servant is one thing, to marry her to a free man and heir to a manor, even if it's in England and can't be claimed for a while, is quite another.'

'Especially,' said Cadfael, 'when you already know he's the best hand with cattle in the four cantrefs.'

It seemed that those two, at any rate, were satisfied. And Rhisiart in his honoured grave would not grudge them their happiness. He had not been a grudging man.

Engelard, no talker, said his thanks plainly and briefly when they parted. Sioned turned back impulsively, flung her arms round Cadfael's neck, and kissed him. It was their farewell, for he had thought it best to advise them not to show themselves at the chapel again. It was a wry touch that she smelled so heady and sweet with flowering may, and left so saintly a fragrance in his arms when she was gone.

*

161

On his way down to the parsonage Cadfael made a detour to the mill-pond, and dropped Columbanus' dagger into the deepest of the dark water. What a good thing, he thought, making for the bed he would occupy for no more than an hour or so before Prime, that the brothers who made the reliquary were such meticulous craftsmen, and insisted on lining it with lead!

Chapter Eleven

RIOR ROBERT arose and went to the first service of the day in so great content with his success that he had almost forgotten about the escape of Brother John, and even when he remembered that one unsatisfactory particular, he merely put it away in the back of his mind, as something that must and would be dealt with faithfully in good time, but need not cloud the splendour of this occasion. And it was indeed a clear, radiant morning, very bright and still, when they came from the church and turned towards the old graveyard and the chapel, and all the congregation fell in their heels and followed, and along the way others appeared silently from every path, and joined the procession, until it was like some memorable pilgrimage. They came to Cadwallon's gatehouse, and Cadwallon came out to join them, and Peredur, who had hung back in strict obedience to his orders to remain at home until his penance was appointed, was kindly bidden forth by Father Huw, and even smiled upon, though as saint to sinner, by Prior Robert. Dame Branwen, if not still asleep, was no doubt recuperating after her vapours. Her menfolk were not likely to be very pressing in their invitations to her to go with them, and perhaps she was still punishing them by withdrawing herself. Either way, they were relieved of her presence.

The order of procession having only a loose form, brothers and villagers could mingle, and greet, and change partners as they willed. It was a communal celebration. And that was strange, considering the contention that had threatened it for some days. Gwytherin was playing it very cautiously now, intent on seeing everything and giving nothing away.

Peredur made his way to Cadfael's side, and remained there thankfully, though silently. Cadfael asked after his mother, and the young man coloured and frowned, and then smiled guiltily like a child, and said that she was very well, a little dreamy still, but placid and amiable.

'You can do Gwytherin and me a good service, if you will,' said Brother Cadfael, and confided to his ear the word he had in mind to pass on to Griffith ap Rhys.

'So that's the way it is!' said Peredur, forgetting altogether about his own unforgivable sins. His eyes opened wide. He whistled softly. 'And that's the way you want it left?'

'That's the way it is, and that's they way I want it left. Who loses? And everyone gains. We, you, Rhisiart, Saint Winifred – Saint Winifred most of all. And Sioned and Engelard, of course,' said Cadfael firmly, probing the penitent to the heart.

'Yes . . . I'm glad for them!' said Peredur, a shade too vehemently. His head was bent, and his eyelids lowered. He was not yet as glad as all that, but he was trying. The will was there. 'Given a year or two longer, nobody's going to remember about the deer Engelard took. In the end he'll be able to go back and forth to Cheshire if he pleases, and he'll have lands when his father dies. And once he's no longer reckoned outlaw and felon he'll have no more troubles. I'll get your word to Griffith ap Rhys this very day. He's over the river at his cousin David's but Father Huw will give me indulgence if it's to go voluntarily to the law.' He smiled wryly. 'Very apt that I should be your man! I can unload my own sins at the same time, while I'm confiding to him what everyone must know but no one must say aloud.'

'Good!' said Brother Cadfael, contented. 'The bailiff will do the rest. A word to the prince, and that's the whole business settled.'

They had come to the place where the most direct path from Rhisiart's holding joined with their road. And there came half the household from above, Padrig the bard nursing his little portable harp, perhaps bound for some other house after this leave-taking, Cai the ploughman still with an impressive bandage round his quite intact head, an artistic lurch to his gait, and a shameless gleam in his one exposed eye. No Sioned, no Engelard, no Annest, no John. Brother Cadfael, though he himself had given the orders, felt a sudden grievous deprivation.

Now they were approaching the little clearing, the woodlands fell back from them on either side, the narrow field of wild grass opened, and then the stone-built wall, green from head to foot, of the old graveyard. Small, shrunken, black, a huddled shape too tall for its base, the chapel of Saint Winifred loomed, and at its eastern end the raw, dark oblong of Rhisiart's grave scarred the lush spring green of the grass.

Prior Robert halted at the gate, and turned to face the following multitude with a benign and almost affectionate countenance, and through Cadfael addressed them thus:

'Father Huw, and good people of Gwytherin, we came here with every good intent, led, as we believed and still believe, by divine guidance, desiring to honour Saint Winifred as she had instructed us, not at all to deprive you of a treasure, rather to allow its beams to shine upon many more people as well as you. That our mission should have brought grief to any is great grief to us. That we are now of one mind, and you are willing to let us take the saint's relics away with us to a wider glory, is relief and joy. Now you are assured that we meant no evil, but only good, and that what we are doing is done reverently.'

A murmur began at one end of the crescent of watchers, and rolled gently round to the other extreme, a murmur of acquiescence, almost of complacency.

'And you do not grudge us the possession of this precious thing we are taking with us? You do believe that we are doing justly, that we take only what has been committed to us?'

He could not have chosen his words better, thought Brother Cadfael, astonished and gratified, if he had known everything – or if I had written this address for him. Now if there comes an equally well-worded answer, I'll believe in a miracle of my own.

The crowd heaved, and gave forth the sturdy form of Bened, as solid and respectable and fit to be spokesman for his parish as any man in Gwytherin, barring, perhaps, Father Huw, who here stood in the equivocal position of having a foot in both camps, and therefore wisely kept silence.

'Father Prior,' said Bened gruffly, 'there's not a man among us now grudges you the relics within there on the altar. We do believe they are yours to take, and you take them with our consent home to Shrewsbury, where by all the omens they rightly belong.'

165

It was altogether too good. It might bring a blush of pleasure, even mingled with a trace of shame, to Prior Robert's cheek, but it caused Cadfael to run a long, considering glance round all those serene, secretive, smiling faces, all those wide, honest, opaque eyes. Nobody fidgeted, nobody muttered, nobody, even at the back, sniggered. Cai gazed with simple admiration from his one visible eye. Padrig beamed benevolent bardic satisfaction upon this total reconciliation.

They knew already! Whether through some discreet whisper started on its rounds by Sioned, or by some earth-rooted intuition of their own, the people of Gwytherin knew, in essence if not in detail, everything there was to be known. And not a word aloud, not a word out of place, until the strangers were gone.

'Come, then,' said Prior Robert, deeply gratified, 'let us release Brother Columbanus from his vigil, and take Saint Winifred on the first stage of her journey home.' And he turned, very tall, very regal, very silvery-fine, and paced majestically to the door of the chapel, with most of Gwytherin crowding into the graveyard after him. With a long, white, aristocratic hand he thrust the door wide and stood in the doorway.

'Brother Columbanus, we are here. Your watch is over.'

He took just two paces into the interior, his eyes finding it dim after the brilliance outside, in spite of the clear light pouring in through the small east window. Then the dark-brown, wood-scented walls came clear to him, and every detail of the scene within emerged from dimness into comparative light, and then into a light so acute and blinding that he halted where he stood, awed and marvelling.

There was a heavy, haunting sweetness that filled all the air within, and the opening of the door had let in a small morning wind that stirred it in great waves of fragrance. Both candles burned steadily upon the altar, the small oil-lamp between them. The prie-dieu stood centrally before the bier, but there was no one kneeling there. Over altar and reliquary a snowdrift of white petals lay, as though a miraculous wind had carried them in its arms across two fields from the hawthorn hedge, without spilling one flower on the way, and breathed them in here through the altar window. The snowy sweetness carried as far as the prie-dieu, and sprinkled both it and the crumpled, empty garments that lay discarded there.

'Columbanus . . .! What is this? He is not here!'

Brother Richard came to the prior's left shoulder, Brother Jerome to the right, Bened and Cadwallon and Cai and others

166

crowded in after them and flowed round on either side to line the dark walls and stare at the marvel, nostrils widening to the drowning sweetness. No one ventured to advance beyond where the prior stood, until he himself went slowly forward, and leaned to look more closely at all that was left of Brother Columbanus.

The black Benedictine habit lay where he had been kneeling, skirts spread behind, body fallen together in folds, sleeves spread like wings on either side, bent at the elbow as though the arms that had left them had still ended in hands pressed together in prayer. Within the cowl an edge of white showed.

'Look!' whispered Brother Richard in awe. 'His shirt is still within the habit, and look! – his sandals!' They were under the hem of the habit, neatly together, soles upturned, as the feet had left them. And on the book-rest of the prie-dieu, laid where his prayerful hands had rested, was a single knot of flowering may.

'Father Prior, all his clothes are here, shirt and drawers and all, one within another as he would wear them. As though – as though he had been lifted out of them and left them lying, as a snake discards its old skin and emerges bright in a new. . . .'

'This is most marvellous,' said Prior Robert. 'How shall we understand it, and not sin?'

'Father, may we take up these garments? If there is trace or mark on them . . . .'

There was none, Brother Cadfael was certain of that. Columbanus had not bled, his habit was not torn, nor even soiled. He had fallen only in thick spring grass, bursting irresistibly through the dead grass of last autumn.

'Father, it is as I said, as though he has been lifted out of these garments quite softly, and let them fall, not needing them any more. Oh, Father, we are in the presence of a great wonder! I am afraid!' said Brother Richard, meaning the wonderful, blissful fear of what is holy. He had seldom spoken with such eloquence, or been so moved.

'I do recall now,' said the prior, shaken and chastened (and that was no harm!), 'the prayer he made last night at Compline. How he cried out to be taken up living out of this world, for pure ecstasy, if the virgin saint found him fit for such favour and bliss. Is it possible that he was in such a state of grace as to be found worthy?'

'Father, shall we search? Here, and without? Into the woods?'

'To what end?' said the prior simply. 'Would he be running naked in the night? A sane man? And even if he ran mad, and shed the clothes he wore, would they be thus discarded, fold within fold as he kneeled, here in such pure order? It is not possible to put off garments thus. No, he is gone far beyond these forests, far out of this world. He has been marvellously favoured, and his most demanding prayers heard. Let us say a Mass here for Brother Columbanus, before we take up the blessed lady who has made him her herald, and go to make known this miracle of faith.'

There was no knowing, Prior Robert being the man he was, at what stage his awareness of the use to be made of this marvel thrust his genuine faith and wonder and emotion into the back of his mind, and set him manipulating events to get the utmost glory out of them. There was no inconsistency in such behaviour. He was quite certain that Brother Columbanus had been taken up living out of this world, just as he had wished. But that being so, it was not only his opportunity, but his duty, to make the utmost use of the exemplary favour to glorify the abbey of Saint Peter and Saint Paul of Shrewsbury, and not only his duty, but his pleasure, to make use of the same to shed a halo round the head of Prior Robert, who had originated this quest. And so he did. He said Mass with absolute conviction, in the cloud of white flowers, the huddle of discarded garments at his feet. Almost certainly he would also inform Griffith ap Rhys, through Father Huw, of all that had befallen, and ask him to keep an alert eye open in case any relevant information surfaced after the brothers from Shrewsbury were gone. Brother Prior was the product of his faith and his birth, his training for sanctity and for arbitrary rule, and could shake off neither.

The people of Gwytherin, silent and observant, crowded in to fill the space available, made no sound, expressed no opinion. Their presence and silence passed for endorsement. What they really thought they kept to themselves.

'Now,' said Prior Robert, moved almost to tears, 'let us take up this blessed burden, and praise God for the weight we carry.'

And he moved forward to offer his own delicate hands and frail shoulder, first of the devout.

That was Brother Cadfael's worst moment, for it was the one thing he had overlooked. But Bened, unwontedly quick at the right moment, called aloud: 'Shall Gwytherin be backward, now peace is made?' and rolled forward with less stateliness

168

and greater speed, and had a solid shoulder under the head end of the reliquary before the prior was able to reach it, and half a dozen of the smith's own powerful but stocky build took up the challenge with enthusiasm. Apart from Cadfael, the only monk of Shrewsbury who got a corner hoisted into his neck was Jerome, being of much the same height, and his was the sole voice that cried out in astonishment at the weight, and sagged under it until Bened shifted nearer and hefted most of the load from him.

'Your pardon, Father Prior! But who would have thought those slender little bones could weigh so heavily?'

Cadfael spoke up in hasty interpretation 'We are surrounded here by miracles, both small and great. Truly did Father Prior say that we thank God for the weight we carry. Is not this evidence of singular grace, that heaven has caused the weight of her worthiness to be so signally demonstrated?'

In his present state, at once humbled and exalted, Prior Robert apparently did not find the logic of this nearly as peculiar as did Brother Cadfael himself. He would have accepted and embraced anything that added to his own triumph. So it was on sturdy Gwytherin shoulders that the reliquary and its contents were hoisted out of the chapel and borne in procession down to the parsonage, with such brisk enthusiasm that it almost seemed the parish could hardly wait to get rid of them. It was Gwytherin men who fetched the horses and mules, and rigged a little cart, spread with cloths, on which the precious casket could be drawn home. Once installed on this vehicle, which, after all, cost little in materials or labour, given the smith's benevolent interest, the casket need not be unloaded until it reached Shrewsbury. Nobody wanted anything untoward to happen to it on the way, such as Brother Jerome crumpling under his end, and starting the joints by dropping it.

'But you we'll miss,' said Cai regretfully, busy with the harness. 'Padrig has a song in praise of Rhisiart you'd have liked to hear, and one more companionable drinking night would have been pleasant. But the lad sends you his thanks and his godspeed. He's only in hiding until the pack of you have gone. And Sioned told me to tell you from him, look out for your pear trees, for the winter moth's playing the devil with some of ours here.'

'He's a good helper in a garden,' Cadfael confirmed judicially. 'A shade heavy-handed, but he shifts the rough digging faster than any novice I ever had under me. I shall miss him, too. God knows what I shall get in his place.'

'A light hand's no good with iron,' said Bened, standing back to admire the banded wheels he had contributed to the cart. 'Deft, yes! Not light. I tell you what, Cadfael! I'll see you in Shrewsbury yet. For years I've had a fancy to make a great pilgrimage across England some day and get to Walsingham. I reckon Shrewsbury would be just about on my way.'

At the last, when all was ready and Prior Robert mounted, Cai said in Cadfael's ear: 'When you're up the hill, where you saw us ploughing that day, cast a look the other way. There's a place where the woods fall away, and an open hillock just before they close again. We'll be there, a fair gathering of us. And that's for you.'

Brother Cadfael, without shame, for he had been up and busy all night and was very tired, annexed the gentler and cleverer of the two mules, a steady pad that would follow where the horses led, and step delicately on any ground. It had a high, supporting saddle, and he had not lost the trick of riding through his knees, even when asleep. The larger and heavier beast was harnessed to draw the cart, but the carriage was narrow yet stable, rode well even on a forest floor, and Jerome, no great weight, could still ride, either on the mule's back or the shafts and yoke. In any case, why trouble too much about the comfort of Jerome, who had concocted that vision of Saint Winifred in the first place, almost certainly knowing that the prior's searches in Wales had cast up this particular virgin as one most desirable, and most available? Jerome would have been courting Columbanus just as assiduously, if he had survived to oust Robert.

The cortège set forth ceremoniously, half of Gwytherin there to watch it go, and sigh immense relief when it was gone, Father Huw blessed the departing guests. Peredur, almost certainly, was away across the river, planting the good seed in the bailiff's mind. He deserved that his errand should be counted to his own credit. Genuine sinners are plentiful, but genuine penitents are rare. Peredur had done a detestable thing, but remained a very likeable young man. Cadfael had no serious fears for his future, once he was over Sioned. There were other girls, after all. Not many her match, but some not so very far behind.

Brother Cadfael settled himself well down in the saddle, and shook his bridle to let the mule know it might conduct him where it would. Very gently he dozed. It could not yet be called sleep. He was aware of the shifting light and shadow under the trees,

170

and the fresh cool air, and movement under him, and a sense of something completed. Or almost completed, for this was only the first stage of the way home.

He roused when they came to the high ridge above the river valley. There was no team ploughing down there now, all the ploughing, even the breaking of new ground, was done. He turned his head towards the wooden uplands on his right, and waited for the opening vista between the trees. It was brief and narrow, a sweep of grass soaring to a gentle crest beyond which the trees loomed close and dark. There were a number of people clustered there on the rounded hillock, most of Sioned's household, far enough removed to be nameless to anyone who knew them less well than he. A cloud of dark hair beside a cap of flaxen, Cai's flaunting bandage shoved back like a hat unseated in a hot noon, a light brown head clasped close against a red thorn-hedge that looked very like Brother John's abandoned tonsure. Padrig, too, not yet off on his wanderings. They were all waving and smiling, and Cadfael returned the salute with enthusiasm. Then the ambulant procession crossed the narrow opening, and the woods took away all.

Brother Cadfael, well content, subsided into his saddle comfortably, and fell asleep.

Overnight they halted at Penmachno, in the shelter of the church, where there was hospitality for travellers. Brother Cadfael, without apology to any, withdrew himself as soon as he had seen to his mule, and continued his overdue sleep in the loft above the stables. He was roused after midnight by Brother Jerome in delirious excitement.

'Brother, a great wonder!' bleated Jerome, ecstatic. 'There came a traveller here in great pain from a malignant illness, and made such outcry that all of us in the hostel were robbed of sleep. And Prior Robert took a few of the petals we saved from the chapel, and floated them in holy water, and gave them to this poor soul to drink, and afterwards we carried him out into the yard and let him kiss the foot of the reliquary. And instantly he was eased of his pain, and before we laid him in his bed again he was asleep. He feels nothing, he slumbers like a child! Oh, brother, we are the means of astonishing grace!'

'Ought it to astonish you so much?' demanded Brother Cadfael censoriously, malicious half out of vexation at being awakened, and half in self-defence, for he was considerably more taken aback than he would admit. 'If you had any faith in what we have brought from Gwytherin, you should not be amazed that it accomplishes wonders along the way.'

But by the same token, he thought honestly, after Jerome had left him to seek out a more appreciative audience, *I* should! I do believe I begin to grasp the nature of miracles! For would it be a miracle, if there was any reason for it? Miracles have nothing to do with reason. Miracles contradict reason, overturn reason, make game of reason, they strike clean across mere human deserts, and deliver and save where they will. If they made sense, they would not be miracles. And he was comforted and entertained, and fell asleep again readily, feeling that all was well with a world he had always known to be peculiar and perverse.

Minor prodigies, most of them trivial, some derisory, trailed after them all the way to Shrewsbury, though how many of the crutches discarded had been necessary, and how many, even of those that were, had to be resumed shortly afterwards, how many of the speech impediments had been in the will rather than in the tongue, how many feeble tendons in the mind rather than in the legs, it was difficult to judge, not even counting all the sensation-seekers who were bound to bandage an eye or come over suddenly paralytic in order to be in with the latest cult. It all made for a great reputation that not only kept pace with them, but rushed ahead, and was already bringing in awestruck patronage in gifts and legacies to the abbey of Saint Peter and Saint Paul, in the hope of having dubious sins prayed away by a grateful saint.

When they reached the outskirts of Shrewsbury, crowds of people came out to meet them, and accompany the procession as far as the boundary church of Saint Giles, where the reliquary was to await the great day of the saint's translation to the abbey church. This could hardly take place without the blessing of the bishop, and due notice to all churches and religious houses, to add to the glory accruing. It was no surprise to Brother Cadfael that when the day came it should come with grey skies and squally rain, to leave room for another little miracle. For though it rained heavily on all the surrounding fields and countryside, not a drop fell on the procession, as they carried Saint Winifred's casket at last to its final resting-place on the altar of the abbey church, where the miracle-seekers immediately betook themselves in great numbers, and mostly came away satisfied.

In full chapter Prior Robert gave his account of his mission to Abbot Heribert. 'Father, to my grief I must own it, we have come back only four, who went out from Shrewsbury six brethren together. And we return without both the glory and the blemish of our house, but bringing with us the treasure we set out to gain.'

On almost all of which counts he was in error, but since no one was ever likely to tell him so, there was no harm done. Brother Cadfael dozed gently behind his pillar through the awed encomiums on Brother Columbanus, out of whom they would certainly have wished to make a new saint, but for the sad fact that they supposed all his relics but his discarded clothes to be for ever withdrawn from reach. Letting the devout voices slip out of his consciousness, Cadfael congratulated himself on having made as many people as possible happy, and drifted into a dream of a hot knife-blade slicing deftly through the thick wax of a seal without ever disturbing device. It was a long time since he had exercised some of his more questionable skills, he was glad to be confirmed in believing that he had forgotten none of them, and that every one had a meritorious use in the end.

Chapter Twelve

IT WAS more than two years later, and the middle of a bright June afternoon, when Brother Cadfael, crossing the great court from the fish-ponds, saw among the travellers arriving at the gate a certain thickset, foursquare, powerful figure that he knew. Bened, the smith of Gwytherin, a little rounder in the belly and a little greyer in the hair, had found the time ripe for realising an old ambition, and was on his way in a pilgrim's gown to the shrine of Our Lady of Walsingham.

'If I'd put it off much longer,' he confided, when they were private together with a bottle of wine in a corner of the herb-garden, 'I should have grown too old to relish the journey. And what was there to keep me now with a good lad ready and able to take over the smithy while I'm gone? He took to it like a duck to water. Oh, yes, they've been man and wife eighteen months now, and as happy as larks. Annest always knew her own mind, and this time I will say she's made no mistake.'

'And have they a child yet?' asked Brother Cadfael, imagining a bold, sturdy boy-baby with a bush of red hair, rubbed away by his pillow in an infant tonsure.

'Not yet, but there's one on the way. By the time I get back he'll be with us.'

'And Annest is well?'

'Blossoming like a rose.'

174

'And Sioned and Engelard? They had no troubles after we were gone?'

'None, Bless you! Griffith ap Rhys let it be known that all was well, and should be let well alone. They're married, and snug, and I'm to bring you their warmest greetings, and to tell you they have a fine son – three months old, I reckon he'd be now – dark and Welsh like his mother. And they've named him Cadfael.'

'Well, well!' said Brother Cadfael, absurdly gratified. 'The best way to get the sweet out of children and escape the bitter is to have them by proxy. But I hope they'll never find anything but sweet in their youngster. There'll be a Bened yet, in one household or the other.'

Bened the pilgrim shook his head, but without any deep regret, and reached for the bottle. 'There was a time when I'd hoped. . . . But it would never have done. I was an old fool ever to think of it, and it's better this way. And Cai's well, and sends you remembrances, and says drink down one cup for him.'

They drank many more than one before it was time for Vespers. 'And you'll see me again at chapter tomorrow,' said Bened, as they walked back to the great court, 'for I'm charged with greetings from Father Huw to Prior Robert and Abbot Heribert, and I'll need you to be my interpreter.'

'Father Huw must be the one person in Gwytherin, I suppose, who doesn't know the truth by this time,' said Cadfael, with some compunction. 'But it wouldn't have been fair to lay such a load on his conscience. Better to let him keep his innocence.'

'His innocence is safe enough,' said Bened, 'for he's never said word to bring it in question, but for all that I wouldn't be too sure that he doesn't know. There's a lot of merit in silence.'

The next morning at chapter he delivered his messages of goodwill and commendation to the monastery in general, and the members of Prior Robert's mission in particular, from the parish of Saint Winifred's ministry to the alter of her glorification. Abbot Heribert questioned him amiably about the chapel and the graveyard which he himself had never seen, and to which, as he said, the abbey owed its most distinguished patroness and most precious relics.

'And we trust,' he said gently, 'that in our great gain you have not suffered equally great deprivation, for what was never our intent.'

'No, Father Abbot,' Bened reassured him heartily, 'you need have no regrets upon that score. For I must tell you that at the place of Saint Winifred's grave wonderful things are happening. More people come there for help than ever before. There have been marvellous cures.'

Prior Robert stiffened in his place, and his austere face turned bluish-white and pinched with incredulous resentment.

'Even now, when the saint is here on our altar, and all the devout come to pray to her here? Ah, but small things – the residue of grace. . . .'

'No, Father Prior, great things! Women in mortal labour with cross-births have been brought there and laid on the grave from which she was taken, where we buried Rhisiart, and their children have been soothed into the world whole and perfect, with no harm to the mothers. A man blind for years came and bathed his eyes in a distillation of her may-blossoms, and threw away his stick and went home seeing. A young man whose leg-bone had been broken and knitted awry came in pain, and set his teeth and danced before her, and as he danced the pain left him, and his bones straightened. I cannot tell you half the wonders we have seen in Gwytherin these last two years.'

Prior Robert's livid countenance was taking on a shade of green, and under his careful eyelids his eyes sparkled emerald jealousy. How dare that obscure village, bereft of its saint, outdo the small prodigies of rain that held off from falling, and superficial wounds that healed with commendable but hardly miraculous speed, and even the slightly suspicious numbers of lame who brought their crutches and left them before the altar, and walked away unsupported?

'There was a child of three who went into a fit,' pursued Bened with gusto, 'stiff as a board in his mother's arms, and stopped breathing, and she ran with him all the way from the far fields, fording the river, and carried him to Winifred's grave, and laid him down in the grass there dead. And when he touched the chill of the earth, he breathed and cried out, and she picked him up living, and took him home joyfully, and he is live and well to this day.'

'What, even the dead raised?' croaked Prior Robert, almost speechless with envy.

'Father Prior,' said Brother Cadfael soothingly, 'surely this is but another proof, the strongest possible, of the surpassing merit and potency of Saint Winifred. Even the soil that once held her bones works wonders, and every wonder must redound to the credit and glory of that place which houses the very body that blessed the earth that still blesses others.'

And Abbot Heribert, oblivious of the chagrin that was consuming his prior, benignly agreed that it was so, and that universal grace, whether it manifested itself in Wales, or England, or the Holy Land, or wheresoever, was to be hailed with universal gratitude.

'Was that innocence or mischief?' demanded Cadfael, when he saw Bened off from the gatehouse afterwards.

'Work it out for yourself! The great thing is, Cadfael, it was truth! These things happened, and are happening yet.'

Brother Cadfael stood looking after him as he took the road towards Lilleshall, until the stocky figure with its long, easy strides dwindled to child-size, and vanished at the curve of the wall. Then he turned back towards his garden, where a new young novice, barely sixteen and homesick, was waiting earnestly for his orders, having finished planting out lettuces to follow in succession. A silent lad as yet. Maybe once he had taken Brother Cadfael's measure his tongue would begin to wag, and then there'd be no stopping it. He knew nothing, but was quick to learn, and though he was still near enough to childhood to attract any available moist soil to his own person, things grew for him. On the whole, Cadfael was well content.

I don't see, he thought, reviewing the whole business again from this peaceful distance, how I could have done much better. The little Welsh saint's back where she always wanted to be, bless her, and showing her pleasure by taking good care of her own, it seems. And we've got what belonged to us in the first place, all we have a right to, and probably all we deserve, too, and by and large it seems to be thought satisfactory. Evidently the body of a calculating murderer does almost as well as the real thing, given faith enough. Almost, but never quite! Knowing what they all know by now, those good people up there in Gwytherin may well look forward to great things. And if a little of their thanks and gratitude rubs off on Rhisiart, well, why not? He earned it, and it's a sign she's made him welcome. She may even be glad of his company. He's no threat to her virginity now, and if he is trespassing, that's no fault of his. His bed-fellow won't grudge him a leaf or two from her garland!

ONE CORPSE TOO MANY

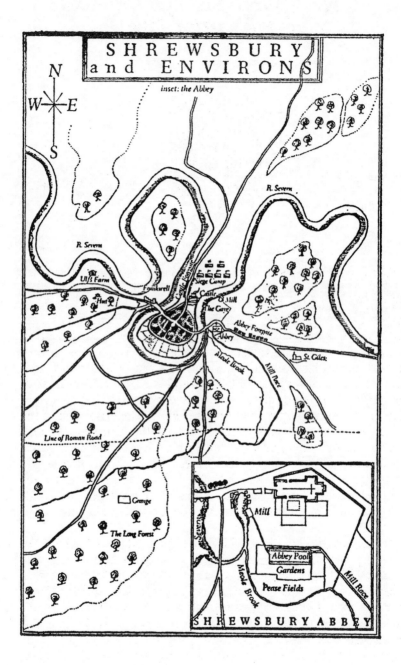

SHREWSBURY and ENVIRONS

inset: the Abbey

N
W E
S

R. Severn

R. Severn

R. Severn

Ulf's Farm

Frankwell

Siege Camp

Hut

Castle

Mill

The Gaye

Abbey Foregate

Abbey

Meole Brook

Mill Race

St. Giles

Line of Roman Road

Grange

The Long Forest

Mill

Abbey Pool

Gardens

Pease Fields

Meole Brook

Mill Race

SHREWSBURY ABBEY

Chapter One

ROTHER CADFAEL was working in the small kitchen garden by the abbot's fish-ponds when the boy was first brought to him. It was hot August noon, and if he had had his proper quota of helpers they would all have been snoring in the shade at this hour, instead of sweating in the sun; but one of his regular assistants, not yet out of his novitiate, had thought better of the monastic vocation and taken himself off to join his elder brother in arms on King Stephen's side, in the civil war for the crown of England, and the other had taken fright at the approach of the royal army because his family were of the Empress Maud's faction, and their manor in Cheshire seemed a far safer place to be than Shrewsbury under siege. Cadfael was left to do everything alone, but he had in his time laboured under far hotter suns than this, and was doggedly determined not to let his domain run wild, whether the outside world fell into chaos or no.

In this early summer of 1138 the fratricidal strife, hitherto somewhat desultory, was already two years old, but never before had it approached Shrewsbury so closely. Now its threat hung over castle and town like the shadow of death. But for all that, Brother Cadfael's mind was firmly upon life and growth, rather than destruction and war, and certainly he had no suspicion that another manner of killing, simple murder, furtive and unlicensed even in these anarchic times, was soon to disrupt the calm of his chosen life.

August should not, in normal circumstances, have been one of his busiest times in the gardens, but there was more than enough for one man to do properly, and the only relief they had to offer him was Brother Athanasius, who was deaf, half-senile, and not to be relied upon to know a useful herb from a weed, and the offer had been firmly declined. Better by far manage alone. There was a bed to be prepared for planting out late cabbages for succession, and fresh seed to be sown for the kind that can weather the winter, as well as pease to be gathered, and the dead, dried haulms of the early crop to be cleared away for fodder and litter. And in his wooden work-shed in the herbarium, his own particular pride, he had half a dozen preparations working in glass vessels and mortars on the shelves, all of them needing attention at least once a day, besides the herb wines that bubbled busily on their own at this stage. It was high harvest time among the herbs, and all the medicines for the winter demanding his care.

However, he was not the man to let any part of his kingdom slip out of his control, however wastefully the royal cousins Stephen and Maud contended for the throne of England outside the abbey walls. If he lifted his head from digging compost into the cabbage bed he could see the sluggish plumes of smoke hanging over the abbey roofs and the town and castle beyond, and smell the acrid residue of yesterday's fires. That shadow and stink had hung like a pall over Shrewsbury for almost a month, while King Stephen stamped and raged in his camp beyond the Castle Foregate, the one dry-foot way into the town unless he could get possession of the bridges, and William FitzAlan within the fortress held on grimly, keeping an anxious eye on his dwindling supplies, and left the thundering of defiance to his incorrigible uncle, Arnulf of Hesdin, who had never learned to temper valour with discretion. The townspeople kept their heads low, locked their doors, shuttered their shops, or, if they could, made off westwards into Wales, to old, friendly enemies less to be feared than Stephen. It suited the Welsh very well that Englishmen should fear Englishmen – if either Maud or Stephen could be regarded as English! – and let Wales alone, and they would not grudge a helping hand to the fleeing casualties, provided the war went on merrily.

Cadfael straightened his back and mopped the sweat from a tonsured scalp burned to the colour of a ripe hazel-nut; and there was Brother Oswald the almoner bustling along the path towards him, with skirts flapping, and propelling before him by the shoulder a box of about sixteen, in the coarse brown cotte and short summer hose of the countryside, barelegged but very decently shod in leather, and altogether looking carefully scrubbed and neat for a special occasion. The boy went where he was directed, and kept his eyes lowered with nervous meekness. Another family taking care to put its children out of reach of being pressed for either side, thought Cadfael, and small blame to them.

'Brother Cadfael, I think you have need of a helper, and here is a youngster who says he's not afraid of hard work. A good woman of the town has brought him in to the porter, and asked that he be taken and taught as a lay servant. Her nephew from Hencot, she says, and his parents dead. There's a year's endowment with him. Prior Robert has given leave to take him, and there's room in the boys' dortoir. He'll attend school with the novices, but he'll not take vows unless he himself comes to wish it. What do you say, will you have him?'

Cadfael looked the boy over with interest, but said yes without hesitation, glad enough to be offered someone young, able-bodied and willing. The lad was slenderly built, but vigorous and firm on his feet, and moved with a spring. He looked up warily from under a cropped tangle of brown curls, and his eyes were long-lashed and darkly blue, very shrewd and bright. He was behaving himself meekly and decorously, but he did not look intimidated.

'Very heartily I'll have you,' said Cadfael, 'if you'll take to this outdoor work with me. And what's your name, boy?'

'Godric, sir,' said the young thing, in a small, gruff voice, appraising Cadfael just as earnestly as he was being appraised.

'Good, then, Godric, you and I will get on well enough. And first, if you will, walk around the gardens here with me and see what we have in hand, and get used to being within these walls. Strange enough I daresay you'll find it, but safer than in the town yonder, which I make no doubt is why your good aunt brought you here.'

The blue, bright eyes flashed him one glance and were veiled again.

'See you come to Vespers with Brother Cadfael,' the almoner instructed, 'and Brother Paul, the master of the novices, will show you your bed, and tell you your duties after supper. Pay attention to what Brother Cadfael tells you, and be obedient to him as you should.'

'Yes, sir,' said the boy virtuously. Under the meek accents a small bubble of laughter seemed to be trying, though vainly, to burst. When Brother Oswald hurried away, the blue eyes watched him out of sight, and then turned their intent gaze upon Cadfael. A demure, oval face, with a wide, firm mouth shaped properly for laughter, but quick to revert to a very sombre gravity. Even for those meant to be light-hearted, these were grave times.

'Come, see what manner of labour you're taking on yourself,' said Cadfael cheerfully, and downed his spade to take his new boy round the enclosed garden, showing him the vegetables, the herbs that made the noon air heady and drunken with fragrance, the fish ponds and the beds of pease that ran down almost to the brook. The early field was already dried and flaxen in the sun, all its harvest gathered, even the later-sown hung heavy and full in pod.

'These we should gather today and tomorrow. In this heat they'll pass their best in a day. And these spent ones have to be cleared. You can begin that for me. Don't pull them up, take the sickle and cut them off low to the ground, and the roots we plough in, they're good food for the soil.' He was talking in an easy, good-humoured flow, to pass off peacefully whatever residue of regret and strangeness there might be in this abrupt change. 'How old are you, Godric?'

'Seventeen,' said the husky voice beside him. He was on the small side for seventeen; let him try his hand at digging later on, the ground Cadfael was working was heavy to till. 'I can work hard,' said the boy, almost as though he had guessed at the thought, and resented it. 'I don't know much, but I can do whatever you tell me.'

'So you shall, then, and you can begin with the pease. Stack the dry stuff aside here, and it goes to provide stable litter. And the roots go back to the ground.'

'Like humankind,' said Godric unexpectedly.

'Yes, like humankind.' Too many were going back to the earth prematurely now in this fratricidal war. He saw the boy turn his head, almost involuntarily, and look across the abbey grounds and roofs to where the battered towers of the castle loomed in their pall of smoke. 'Have you kin within there, child?' asked Cadfael gently.

'No!' said the boy, too quickly. 'But I can't but think of them. They're saying in the town it can't last long – that it may fall tomorrow. And surely they've done only rightly! Before

King Henry died he made his barons acknowledge the Empress Maud as his heir, and they all swore fealty. She was his only living child, she *should* be queen. And yet when her cousin, Count Stephen, seized the throne and had himself crowned, all too many of them took it meekly and forgot their oaths. That can't be right. And it can't be wrong to stand by the empress faithfully. How can they excuse changing sides? How can they justify Count Stephen's claim?'

'Justify may not be the apt word, but there are those among the lords, more by far than take the opposite view, who would say, better a man for overlord than a woman. And if a man, why, Stephen was as near as any to the throne. He is King William's grandchild, just as Maud is.'

'But not son to the last king. And in any case, through his mother, who was a woman like Maud, so where's the difference?' The young voice had emerged from its guarded undertone, and rang clear and vehement. 'But the real difference was that Count Stephen rushed here and took what he wanted, while the empress was far away in Normandy, thinking no evil. And now that half the barons have recollected their oaths and declared for her, after all, it's late, and what's to come of it but bloodshed and deaths? It begins here, in Shrewsbury, and this won't be the end.'

'Child,' said Cadfael mildly, 'are you not trusting me to extremes?'

The boy, who had picked up the sickle and was swinging it in a capable, testing hand, turned and looked at him with blue eyes suddenly wide open and unguarded. 'Well, so I do,' he said.

'And so you may, for that matter. But keep your lips locked among others. We are in the battlefield here, as sure as in the town, our gates never being closed to any. All manner of men rub shoulders here, and in rough times some may try to buy favour with carrying tales. Some may even be collectors of such tales for their living. Your thoughts are safe in your head, best keep them there.'

The boy drew back a little, and hung his head. Possibly he felt himself reproved. Possibly not! 'I'll pay you trust for trust,' said Cadfael. 'In my measure there's little to choose between two such monarchs, but much to be said for keeping a man's fealty and word. And now let me see you hard at work, and when I've finished my cabbage patch I'll come and help you.'

He watched the boy set to work, which he did with immense

185

vigour. The coarse tunic was cut very full, turning a lissome body into a bundle of cloth tied at the waist; possibly he had got it from some older and larger relative after the best of the wear was out of it. My friend, thought Cadfael, in this heat you won't keep up that pace very long, and then we shall see!

By the time he joined his assistant in the rustling field of bleached pea-stems, the boy was red in the face, and sweating, and puffing audibly with the strokes of the sickle, but had not relaxed his efforts. Cadfael swept an armful of cut haulms to the edge of the field, and said earnestly: 'No need to make a penance of it, lad. Strip off to the waist and be comfortable.' And he slid his own frock, already kilted to the knee, down from powerful brown shoulders, and let the folds hang at his middle.

The effect was complex, but by no means decisive. The boy checked momentarily in his stroke, said: 'I'm well enough as I am!' with admirable composure, but several tones above the gruff, young-mannish level of his earlier utterances, and went on resolutely with his labours, at the same time as a distant wave of red arose from his collar to engulf his slender neck and the curve of his cheek. Did that necessarily mean what it seemed to mean? He might have lied about his age, his voice might be but newly broken and still unstable. And perhaps he wore no shirt beneath the cotte, and was ashamed to reveal his lacks to a new acquaintance. Ah, well, there were other tests. Better make sure at once. If what Cadfael suspected was true, the matter was going to require very serious thought.

'There's that heron that robs our hatcheries, again!' he cried suddenly, pointing across the Meole brook, where the unsuspecting bird waded, just folding immense wings. 'Toss a stone across at him, boy, you're nearer than I!' The heron was an innocent stranger, but if Cadfael was right he was unlikely to come to any harm.

Godric stared, clawed up a sizeable stone, and heaved it heartily. His arm swung far back, swung forward with his slight weight willingly behind it, and hurled the stone under-arm across the brook and into the shallows, with a splash that sent the heron soaring, certainly, but several feet from where he had been standing.

'Well, well!' said Cadfael silently, and settled down to do some hard thinking.

In his siege camp, deployed across the entire land approach to the Castle Foregate, between broad coils of the river Severn,

King Stephen fretted, fumed and feasted, celebrating the few loyal Salopians – loyal to him, that is! – who came to offer him aid, and planning his revenge upon the many disloyal who absented themselves.

He was a big, noisy, handsome, simple-minded man, very fair in colouring, very comely in countenance, and at this stage in his fortunes totally bewildered by the contention between his natural good nature and his smarting sense of injury. He was said to be slow-witted, but when his Uncle Henry had died and left no heir but a daughter, and she handicapped by an Angevin husband and far away in France, no matter how slavishly her father's vassals had bowed to his will and accepted her as queen, Stephen for once in his life had moved with admirable speed and precision, and surprised his potential subjects into accepting him at his own valuation before they even had time to consider their own interests, much less remember reluctant vows. So why had such a successful coup abruptly turned sour? He would never understand. Why had half of his more influential subjects, apparently stunned into immobility for a time, revived into revolt now? Conscience? Dislike of the king imposed upon them? Superstitious dread of King Henry and his influence with God?

Forced to take the opposition seriously and resort to arms, Stephen had opened in the way that came naturally to him, striking hard where he must, but holding the door cheerfully open for penitents to come in. And what had been the result? He had spared, and they had taken advantage and despised him for it. He had invited submission without penalty, as he moved north against the rebel holds, and the local baronage had held off from him with contempt. Well, tomorrow's dawn attack should settle the fate of the Shrewsbury garrison, and make an example once for all. If these midlanders would not come peacefully and loyally at his invitation, they should come scurrying like rats to save their own skins. As for Arnulf of Hesdin ... The obscenities and defiances he had hurled from the towers of Shrewsbury should be regretted bitterly, if briefly.

The king was conferring in his tent in the meads in the late afternoon, with Gilbert Prestcote, his chief aide and sheriff-designate of Salop, and Willem Ten Heyt, the captain of his Flemish mercenaries. It was about the time that Brother Cadfael and the boy Godric were washing their hands and tidying their clothing to go to Vespers. The failure of the local

gentry to bring in their own levies to his support had caused
Stephen to lean heavily upon his Flemings, who in
consequence were very well hated, both as aliens and as
impervious professionals, who would as soon burn down a
village as get drunk, and were not at all averse to doing both
together. Ten Heyt was a huge, well-favoured man with
reddish-fair hair and long moustaches, barely thirty years old
but a veteran in warfare. Prestcote was a quiet, laconic knight
past fifty, experienced and formidable in battle, cautious in
counsel, not a man to go to extremes, but even he was arguing
for severity.

'Your Grace has tried generosity, and it has been
shamelessly exploited to your loss. It's time to strike terror.'

'First,' said Stephen drily, 'to take castle and town.'

'That your Grace may consider as done. What we have
mounted for the morning will get you into Shrewsbury. Then,
if they survive the assault, your Grace may do what you will
with FitzAlan, and Adeney, and Hesdin, and the commons of
the garrison are no great matter, but even there you may be
well advised to consider an example.'

The king would have been content enough then with his
revenge on those three who led the resistance here. William
FitzAlan owed his office as sheriff of Salop to Stephen, and yet
had declared and held the castle for his rival. Fulke Adeney,
the greatest of FitzAlan's vassal lords, had connived at the
treason and supported his overlord wholeheartedly. And
Hesdin had condemned himself over and over out of his own
arrogant mouth. The rest were pawns, expendable but of no
importance.

'They are noising it abroad in the town, as I've heard,' said
Prestcote, 'that FitzAlan had already sent his wife and children
away before we closed the way north out of the town. But
Adeney also has a child, a daughter. She's said to be still within
the walls. They got the women out of the castle early.'
Prestcote was a man of the shire himself, and knew the local
baronage at least by name and repute. 'Adeney's girl was
betrothed from a child to Robert Beringar's son, of Maesbury,
by Oswestry. They had lands neighbouring in those parts. I
mention it because this is the man who is asking audience of
you now, Hugh Beringar of Maesbury. Use him as you find,
your Grace, but until today I would have said he was
FitzAlan's man, and your enemy. Have him in and judge for
yourself. If he's changed his coat, well and good, he has men

enough at his command to be useful, but I would not let him in too easily.'

The officer of the guard had entered the pavilion, and stood waiting to be invited to speak; Adam Courcelle was one of Prestcote's chief tenants and his right-hand man, a tested soldier at thirty years old.

'Your Grace has another visitor,' he said, when the king turned to acknowledge his presence. 'A lady. Will you see her first? She has no lodging here as yet, and in view of the hour ... She gives her name as Aline Siward, and says that her father, whom she has only recently buried, was always your man.'

'Time presses,' said the king. 'Let them both come, and the lady shall have first word.'

Courcelle led her by the hand into the royal presence, with every mark of deference and admiration, and she was indeed well worth any man's attention. She was slender and shy, and surely no older than eighteen, and the austerity of her mourning, the white cap and wimple from which a few strands of gold hair crept out to frame her cheeks, only served to make her look younger still, and more touching. She had a child's proud, shy dignity. Great eyes the colour of dark irises widened wonderingly upon the king's large comeliness as she made her reverence.

'Madam,' said Stephen, reaching a hand to her, 'I am sorry indeed for your loss, of which I have this minute heard. If my protection can in any way serve you, command me.'

'Your Grace is very kind,' said the girl in a soft, awed voice. 'I am now an orphan, and the only one of my house left to bring you the duty and fealty we owe. I am doing what my father would have wished, and but for his illness and death he would have come himself, or I would have come earlier. Until your Grace came to Shrewsbury we had no opportunity to render you the keys of the two castles we hold. As I do now!'

Her maid, a self-possessed young woman a good ten years older than her mistress, had followed into the tent and stood withdrawn. She came forward now to hand the keys to Aline, who laid them formally in the king's hands.

'We can raise for your Grace five knights, and more than forty men-at-arms, but at this time I have left all to supply the garrisons at home, since they may be of more use to your Grace so.' She named her properties and her castellans. It was like hearing a child recite a lesson learned by heart, but her dignity and gravity were those of a general in the field. 'There

189

is one more thing I should say plainly, and to my much sorrow. I have a brother, who should have been the one to perform this duty and service.' Her voice shook slightly, and gallantly recovered. 'When your Grace assumed the crown, my brother Giles took the part of the Empress Maud, and after an open quarrel with my father, left home to join her party. I do not know where he is now, though we have heard rumours that he made his way to her in France. I could not leave your Grace in ignorance of the dissension that grieves me as it must you. I hope you will not therefore refuse what I can bring, but use it freely, as my father would have wished, and as I wish.'

She heaved a great sigh, as if she had thrown off a weight. The king was enchanted. He drew her by the hand and kissed her heartily on the cheek. To judge by the look on his face, Courcelle was envying him the opportunity.

'God forbid, child,' said the king, 'that I should add any morsel to your sorrows, or fail to lift what I may of them. With all my heart I take your fealty, as dear to me as that of earl or baron, and thank you for your pains taken to help me. And now show me what I can do to serve you, for there can be no fit lodging for you here in a military camp, and I hear you have made no provision as yet for yourself. It will soon be evening.'

'I had thought,' she said timidly, 'that I might lodge in the abbey guest house, if we can get a boat to put us across the river.'

'Certainly you shall have safe escort over the river, and our request to the abbot to give you one of the grace houses belonging to the abbey, where you may be private but protected, until we can spare a safe escort to see you to your home.' He looked about him for a ready messenger, and could not well miss Adam Courcelle's glowing eagerness. The young man had bright chestnut hair, and eyes of the same burning brown, and knew that he stood well with his king. 'Adam, will you conduct Mistress Siward, and see her safely installed?'

'With all my heart, your Grace,' said Courcelle fervently, and offered an ardent hand to the lady.

Hugh Beringar watched the girl pass by, her hand submissive in the broad brown hand that clasped it, her eyes cast down, her small, gentle face with its disproportionately large and noble brow tired and sad now that she had done her errand faithfully. From outside the royal tent he had heard every word. She looked now as if she might melt into tears at any moment, like a little girl after a formal ordeal, a child-bride dressed up to advertise her riches or her lineage, and then as briskly dismissed to the nursery when the transaction was assured. The king's officer walked delicately beside her, like a conqueror conquered, and no wonder.

'Come, the lord king waits,' said the guttural voice of Willem Ten Heyt in his ear, and he turned and ducked his head beneath the awning of the tent. The comparative dimness within veiled the large, fair presence of the king.

'I am here, my liege,' said Hugh Beringar, and made his obeisance. 'Hugh Beringar of Maesbury, at your Grace's service with all that I hold. My muster is not great, six knights and some fifty men-at-arms, but half of them bowmen, and skilled. And all are yours.'

'Your name, Master Beringar, is known to us,' said the king drily. 'Your establishment also. That it was devoted to our cause was not so well known. As I have heard of you, you have been an associate of FitzAlan and Adeney, our traitors, until very recently. And even this change of heart comes rather belatedly. I have been some four weeks in these parts, without word from you.'

'Your Grace,' said Beringar, without haste to excuse himself or apparent discomfort at his cool reception, 'I grew up from a child regarding these men whom you understandably name your traitors, as my peers and friends, and in friendship have never found them wanting. Your Grace is too fair-minded a man not to admit that for one like me, who has not so far sworn fealty to any, the choice of a path at this moment may require a deal of thought, if it is to be made once for all. That King Henry's daughter has a reasonable claim is surely beyond question, I cannot call a man traitor for choosing that cause, though I may blame him for breaking his oath to you. As for me, I came into my lands only some months ago, and I have so far sworn fealty to none. I have taken my time in choosing where I will serve. I am here. Those who flock to you without thought may fall away from you just as lightly.'

'And you will not?' said the king sceptically. He was studying this bold and possibly over-fluent young man with critical attention. A lightweight, not above the middle height and slenderly built, but of balanced and assured movement; he might well make up in speed and agility what he lacked in bulk and reach. Perhaps two or three years past twenty, black-avised, with thin, alert features and thick, quirky dark brows. An unchancy fellow, because there was no guessing from his face what went on behind the deep-set eyes. His forthright speech might be honest, or it might be calculated. He looked quite subtle enough to have weighed up his sovereign and reasoned that boldness might not be displeasing.

'And I will not,' he said firmly. 'But that need not pass on my word. It can be put to the proof hereafter. I am on your Grace's probation.'

'You have not brought your force with you?'

'Three men only are with me. It would have been folly to leave a good castle unmanned or half-manned, and small service to you to ask that you feed fifty more without due provision for the increase. Your Grace has only to tell me where you would have me serve, and it shall be done.'

'Not so fast,' said Stephen. 'Others may also have need of time and thought before they embrace you, young man. You were close and in confidence with FitzAlan, some time ago.'

'I was. I still have nothing against him but that he has chosen one way, and I the other.'

'And as I hear, you are betrothed to Fulke Adeney's daughter.'

'I hardly know whether to say to that: I am! or: I was! The times have altered a great many plans previously made, for others as well as for me. As at this time, I do not know where the girl is, or whether the bargain still holds.'

'There are said to be no women now in the castle,' said the king, eyeing him closely. 'FitzAlan's family may well be clean away, perhaps out of the country by now. But Adeney's daughter is thought to be in hiding in the town. It would not be displeasing to me,' he said with soft emphasis, 'to have so valuable a lady in safe-keeping – in case even my plans should need to be altered. You were of her father's party, you must know the places likely to be sheltering her now. When the way is clear, you, of all people, should be able to find her.'

The young man gazed back at him with an inscrutable face, in which shrewd black eyes signalled understanding, but nothing more, neither consent nor resistance, no admission at all that he knew he was being set a task on which acceptance and favour might well depend. His face was bland and his voice guileless as he said: 'That is my intent, your Grace. I came from Maesbury with that also in mind.'

'Well,' said Stephen, warily content, 'you may remain in attendance against the town's fall, but we have no immediate

192

work for you here. Should I have occasion to call you, where will you be found?'

'If they have room,' said Beringar, 'at the abbey guest house.'

The boy Godric stood through Vespers among the pupils and the novices, far back among the small fry of the house, and close to the laity, such as lived here outside the walls on the hither bank of the river, and could still reach this refuge. He looked, as Brother Cadfael reflected when he turned his head to look for the child, very small and rather forlorn, and his face, bright and impudent enough in the herbarium, had grown very solemn indeed here in church. Night was looming, his first night in this abode. Ah well, his affairs were being taken in hand more consolingly than he supposed, and the ordeal he was bracing himself to master need not confront him at all, if things went right, and at all events not tonight. Brother Paul, the master of the novices, had several other youngsters to look after, and was glad to have one taken firmly off his hands.

Cadfael reclaimed his protégé after supper, at which meal he was glad to see that Godric ate heartily. Evidently the boy was of a mettle to fight back against whatever fears and qualms possessed him, and had the good sense to fortify himself with the things of the flesh for the struggles of the spirit. Even more reassuringly, he looked up with relief and recognition when Cadfael laid a hand on his shoulder as they left the refectory.

'Come, we're free until Compline, and it's cool out in the gardens. No need to stay inside here, unless you wish.'

The boy Godric did not wish, he was happy to escape into the summer evening. They went down at leisure towards the fish ponds and the herbarium, and the boy skipped at Cadfael's side, and burst into a gay whistling, abruptly broken off.

'He said the master of the novices would want me, after supper. Is it really proper for me to come with you, like this?'

'All approved and blessed, child, don't be afraid. I've spoken with Brother Paul, we have his good word. You are my boy, and I am responsible for you.' They had entered the walled garden, and were suddenly engulfed and drowned in all those sun-drenched fragrances, rosemary, thyme, fennel, dill, sage, lavender, a whole world of secret sweetness. The heat of the sun lingered, heady with scent, even into the cool of the evening. Over their heads swifts wheeled and screamed in ecstasy.

They had arrived at the wooden shed, its oiled timbers radiated warmth towards them. Cadfael opened the door. 'This is your sleeping-place, Godric.'

There was a low bench-bed neatly arrayed at the end of the room. The boy stared, and quaked under Cadfael's hand.

'I have all these medicines brewing here, and some of them need tending regularly, some very early, they'd spoil if no one minded them. I'll show you all you have to do, it's not so heavy a task. And here you have your bed, and here a grid you may open for fresh air.' The boy had stopped shaking, the dark blue eyes were large and measuring, and fixed implacably upon Cadfael. There seemed to be a smile pending, but there was also a certain aura of offended pride. Cadfael turned to the door, and showed the heavy bar that guarded it within, and the impossibility of opening it from without, once that was dropped into its socket. 'You may shut out the world and me until you're ready to come out to us.'

The boy Godric, who was not a boy at all, was staring now in direct accusation, half-offended, half-radiant, wholly relieved.

'How did you know?' she demanded, jutting a belligerent chin.

'How were you going to manage in the dortoir?' responded Brother Cadfael mildly.

'I would have managed. Boys are not so clever, I could have cozened them. Under a wall like this,' she said, hoisting handfuls of her ample tunic, 'all bodies look the same, and men are blind and stupid.' She laughed then, viewing Cadfael's placid competence, and suddenly she was all woman, and startlingly pretty in her gaiety and relief. 'Oh, not *you*! How *did* you know? I tried so hard, I thought I could pass all trials. Where did I go wrong?'

'You did very well,' said Cadfael soothingly. 'But, child, I was forty years about the world, and from end to end of it, before I took the cowl and came to my green, sweet ending here. Where did you go wrong? Don't take it amiss, take it as sound advice from an ally, if I answer you. When you came to argument, and meant it with all your heart, you let your voice soar. And never a crack in it, mind you, to cover the change. That can be learned, I'll show you when we have leisure. And then, when I bade you strip and be easy – ah, never blush, child, I was all but certain then! – of course you put me off. And last, when I got you to toss a stone across the brook, you did it like a girl, under-arm, with a round swing. When did you ever see a boy throw like that? Don't let anyone else trick you into such another throw, not until you master the art. It betrays you at once.'

He stood patiently silent then, for she had dropped on to the bed, and sat with her head in her hands, and first she began to laugh, and then to cry, and then both together; and all the while he let her alone, for she was no more out of control than a man tossed between gain and loss, and manfully balancing his books. Now he could believe she was seventeen, a budding woman, and a fine one, too.

When she was ready, she wiped her eyes on the back of her hand, and looked up alertly, smiling like sunlight through a rainbow. 'And did you mean it?' she said. 'That you're responsible for me? I *said* I trusted you to extremes!'

'Daughter dear,' said Cadfael patiently, 'what should I do with you now but serve you as best I can, and see you safe out of here to wherever you would be?'

'And you don't even know who I am,' she said, marvelling. 'Who is trusting too far now?'

'What difference should it make to me, child, what your name may be? A lass left forlorn here to weather out this storm and be restored to her own people – is not that enough? What you want to tell, you'll tell, and I need no more.'

'I think I want to tell you everything,' said the girl simply, looking up at him with eyes wide and candid as the sky. 'My father is either in Shrewsbury castle this minute with his death hanging over him, or out of it and running for his life with William FitzAlan for the empress's lands in Normandy, with hue and cry ready to be loosed after him any moment. I'm a burden to anyone who befriends me now, and likely to be a hunted hostage as soon as I'm missed from where I should be. Even to you, Brother Cadfael, I could be dangerous. I'm daughter to FitzAlan's chief ally and friend. My name is Godith Adeney.'

Lame Osbern, who had been born with both legs withered, and scuttled around at unbelievable speed on hands provided with wooden pattens, dragging his shrivelled knees behind him on a little wheeled trolley, was the humblest of the king's camp-followers. Normally he had his pitch by the castle gates in the town, but he had forsaken in time a spot now so dangerous, and transferred his hopeful allegiance to the edge of the siege camp, as near as he was allowed to get to the main

195

guard, where the great went in and out. The king was notoriously open-handed, except towards his enemies-at-arms, and the pickings were good. The chief military officers, perhaps, were too preoccupied to waste thought or alms on a beggar, but some of those who came belatedly seeking favour, having decided which way fortune was tending, were apt to give to the poor as a kind of sop to God for luck, and the common bowmen and even the Flemings, when off-duty and merry, tossed Osbern a few coppers, or the scraps from their mess.

He had his little wagon backed well into the lee of a clump of half-grown trees, close to the guard-post, where he might come in for a crust of bread or a drink, and could enjoy the glow of the field-fire at night. Even summer nights can strike chill after the heat of the August day, when you have only a few rags to cover you, and the fire was doubly welcome. They kept it partially turfed, to subdue the glow, but left themselves light enough to scrutinise any who came late.

It was close to midnight when Osbern stirred out of an uneasy sleep, and straining his ears for the reason, caught the rustling of the bushes behind and to his left, towards the Castle Foregate but well aside from the open road. Someone was approaching from the direction of the town, and certainly not from the main gates, but roundabout in cover from along the riverside. Osbern knew the town like his own callused palm. Either this was a scout returning from reconnaissance – but why keep up this stealth right into the camp? – or else someone had crept out of town or castle by the only other way through the wall on this side, the water-port that led down to the river.

A dark figure, visible rather as movement than matter in a moonless night, slid out from the bushes and made at a crouching, silent scurry for the guard-post. At the sentry's challenge he halted immediately, and stood frozen but eager, and Osbern saw the faint outline of a slight, willowy body, wrapped closely in a black cloak, so that only a gleam of pale face showed. The voice that answered the challenge was young, high-pitched, tormentedly afraid and desperately urgent.

'I beg audience – I am not armed! Take me to your officer. I have something to tell – to the king's advantage ...'

They hauled him in and went over him roughly to ensure he bore no weapons; and whatever was said between them did not reach Osbern's ears, but the upshot of it was that he had his

196

will. They led him within the camp, and there he vanished from view.

Osbern did not doze again, the cold of the small hours was gnawing through his rags. Such a cloak as that, he thought, shivering, I wish the good God would send me! Yet even the owner of so fine a garment had been shaking, the quavering voice had betrayed his fear, but also his avid hope. A curious incident, but of no profit to a poor beggar. Not, that is, until he saw the same figure emerge from the shadowy alleys of the camp and halt once more at the gate. His step was lighter and longer now, his bearing less furtive and fearful. He bore some token from the authorities that was enough to let him out again as he had entered, unharmed and unmolested. Osbern heard a few words pass: 'I am to go back, there must be no suspicion ... I have my orders!'

Ah, now, in pure thankfulness for some alleviating mercy, he might be disposed to give. Osbern wheeled himself forward hurriedly into the man's path, and extended a pleading hand.

'For God's love, master! If he has been gracious to you, be gracious to the poor!'

He caught a glimpse of a pale face much eased, heard long breaths of relief and hope. A flicker of firelight caught the elaborate shape of a metal clasp that fastened the cloak at the throat. Out of the muffling folds a hand emerged, and dropped a coin into the extended palm. 'Say some prayers for me tomorrow,' said a low, breathless whisper, and the stranger flitted away as he had come, and vanished into the trees before Osbern had done blessing him for his alms.

Before dawn Osbern was roused again from fitful sleep, to withdraw himself hastily into the bushes out of all men's way. For it was still only the promise of a clear dawn, but the royal camp was astir, so quietly and in such practical order that he felt rather than heard the mustering of men, the ordering of ranks, the checking of weapons. The air of the morning seemed to shake to the tramping of regiments, while barely a sound could be heard. From curve to curve of Severn, across the neck of land that afforded the only dry approach to the town, the steady murmur of activity rippled, awesome and exhilarating, as King Stephen's army turned out and formed its divisions for the final assault of Shrewsbury castle.

197

Chapter Two

ONG BEFORE noon it was all over, the gates fired with brushwood and battered down, the baileys cleared one by one, the last defiant bowman hunted down from the walls and towers, smoke heavy and thick like a pall over fortress and town. In the streets not a human creature or even a dog stirred. At the first assault every man had gone to earth with wife and family and beasts behind locked and barred doors, and crouched listening with stretched ears to the thunder and clash and yelling of battle. It lasted only a short while. The garrison had reached exhaustion, ill-supplied, thinned by desertions as long as there was any possibility of escape. Everyone had been certain the next determined attack must carry the town. The merchants of Shrewsbury waited with held breath for the inevitable looting, and heaved sighs of relief when it was called to heel peremptorily by the king himself – not because he grudged his Flemings their booty, but because he wanted them close about his person. Even a king is vulnerable, and this had been an enemy town, and was still unpacified. Moreover, his urgent business was with the garrison of the castle, and in particular with FitzAlan, and Adeney, and Arnulf of Hesdin.

Stephen stalked through the smoky, bloody, steel-littered bailey into the hall, and despatched Courcelle and Ten Heyt and their men with express orders to isolate the ring leaders and bring them before him. Prestcote he kept at his side; the keys were in the new lieutenant's hands, and provisions for the royal garrison were already in consideration.

'In the end,' said Prestcote critically, 'it has cost your Grace fairly low. In losses, certainly. In money – the delay was costly, but the castle is intact. Some repairs to the walls – new gates ... This is a stronghold you need never lose again, I count it worth the time it took to win it.'

'We shall see,' said Stephen grimly, thinking of Arnulf of Hesdin bellowing his lordly insults from the towers. As though he courted death!

Courcelle came in, his helmet off and his chestnut hair blazing. A promising officer, alert, immensely strong in personal combat, commanding with his men: Stephen approved him. 'Well, Adam. Are they run to earth? Surely FitzAlan is not hiding somewhere among the barns, like a craven servant?'

'No, your Grace, by no means!' said Courcelle ruefully. 'We have combed this fortress from roof to dungeons, I promise you we have missed nothing. But FitzAlan is clean gone! Give us time, and we'll find for you the day, the hour, the route they took, their plans ...'

'*They*?' blazed Stephen, catching at the plural.

'Adeney is away with him. Not a doubt of it, they're loose. Sorry I am to bring your Grace such news, but truth is truth.' And give him his due, he had the guts to utter such truths. 'Hesdin,' he said, 'we have. He is here without. Wounded, but not gravely, nothing but scratched. I put him in irons for safety, but I think he is hardly in such heart as when he lorded it within here, and your Grace was well outside.'

'Bring him in,' ordered the king, enraged afresh to find he had let two of his chief enemies slip through his fingers.

Arnulf of Hesdin came in limping heavily, and dragging chains at wrist and ankle; a big, florid man nearing sixty, soiled with dust, smoke and blood. Two of the Flemings thrust him to his knees before the king. His face was fixed and fearful, but defiant still.

'What, are you tamed?' exulted the king. 'Where's your insolence now? You had plenty to say for yourself only a day or two ago, are you silenced? Or have you the wit to talk another language now?'

'Your Grace,' said Hesdin, grating out words evidently hateful to him, 'you are the victor, and I am at your mercy, and at your feet, and I have fought you fair, and I look to be treated honourably now. I am a nobleman of England and of

France. You have need of money, and I am worth an earl's ransom, and I can pay it.'

'Too late to speak me fair, you who were loud-mouthed and foul-mouthed when there were walls between us. I swore to have your life then, and have it I will. An earl's ransom cannot buy it back. Shall I quote you my price? Where is FitzAlan? Where is Adeney? Tell me in short order where I may lay hands on those two, and better pray that I succeed, and I may – *may!* – consider letting you keep your miserable life.'

Hesdin reared his head and stared the king in the eyes. 'I find your price too high,' he said. 'Only one thing I'll tell you concerning my comrades, they did not run from you until all was already lost. And live or die, that's all you'll get from me. Go hunt your own noble game!'

'We shall see!' flared the king, infuriated. 'We shall see whether we get no more from you! Have him away, Adam, give him to Ten Heyt, and see what can be done with him. Hesdin, you have until two of the clock to tell us everything you know concerning their flight, or else I hang you from the battlements. Take him away!'

They dragged him out still on his knees. Stephen sat fuming and gnawing his knuckles. 'Is it true, you think, Prestcote, the one thing he did say? That they fled only when the fight was already lost? Then they may well be still in the town. How could they break through? Not by the Foregate, clean through our ranks. And the first companies within were sped straight for the two bridges. Somewhere in this island of a town they must be hiding. Find them!'

'They could not have reached the bridges,' said Prestcote positively. 'There's only one other way out, and that's by the water-gate to the river. I doubt if they could have swum Severn there without being seen, I am sure they had no boat. Most likely they are in hiding somewhere in the town.'

'Scour it! Find them! No looting until I have them safe in hold. Search everywhere, but find them.'

While Ten Heyt and his Flemings rounded up the prisoners taken in arms, and disposed the new garrison under Prestcote's orders, Courcelle and others with their companies pressed on through the town, confirmed the security of the two bridges, and set about searching every house and shop within the walls. The king, his conquest assured, returned to his camp with his own bodyguard, and waited grimly for news of his two fugitives. It was past two o'clock when Courcelle reported back to him.

'Your Grace,' he said bluntly, 'there is no better word than failure to bring you. We have searched every street, every officer and merchant of the town has been questioned, all premises ransacked. It is not such a great town, and unless by some miracle I do not see how they can well have got outside the walls unseen. But we have not found them, neither FitzAlan nor Adeney, nor trace nor word of them. In case they've swum the river and got clear beyond the Abbey Foregate, I've sent out a fast patrol that way, but I doubt if we shall hear of them now. And Hesdin is obdurate still. Not a word to be got from him, and Ten Heyt has done his best, short of killing too soon. We shall get nothing from him. He knows the penalty. Threats will do nothing.'

'He shall have what he was promised,' said Stephen grimly. 'And the rest? How many were taken of the garrison?'

'Apart from Hesdin, ninety-three in arms.' Courcelle watched the handsome, frowning face; bitterly angry and frustrated as the king was, he was unlikely to keep his grudges hot too long. They had been telling him for weeks that it was a fault in him to forgive too readily. 'Your Grace, clemency now would be taken for weakness,' said Courcelle emphatically.

'Hang them!' said Stephen, jerking out sentence harshly before he wavered.

'All?'

'All! And at once. Have them all out of the world before tomorrow.'

They gave the grisly work to the Flemings to do. It was what mercenaries were for, and it kept them busy all that day, and out of the houses of the town, which otherwise would have been pillaged of everything of value. The interlude, dreadful as it was, gave the guilds and the reeve and the bailiffs time to muster a hasty delegation of loyalty to the king, and obtain at least a grim and sceptical motion of grace. He might not believe in their sudden devotion, but he could appreciate its urgency.

Prestcote deployed his new garrison and made all orderly in the castle below, while Ten Heyt and his companies despatched the old garrison wholesale from the battlements. Arnulf of Hesdin was the first to die. The second was a young squire who had had a minor command under him; he was in a state of frenzied dread, and was hauled to his death yelling and protesting that he had been promised his life. The Flemings who handled him spoke little English, and were highly diverted by his pleadings, until the noose cut them off short.

Adam Courcelle confessed himself only too glad to get away from the slaughter, and pursue his searches to the very edges of the town, and across the bridges into the suburbs. But he found no trace of William FitzAlan or Fulke Adeney.

From the morning's early alarm to the night's continuing slaughter, a chill hush of horror hung over the abbey of St Peter and St Paul. Rumours flew thick as bees in swarm, no one knew what was really happening, but everyone knew that it would be terrible. The brothers doggedly pursued their chosen régime, service after service, chapter and Mass and the hours of work, because life could only be sustained by refusing to let it be disrupted, by war, catastrophe or death. To the Mass after chapter came Aline Siward with her maid Constance, pale and anxious and heroically composed; and perhaps as a result, Hugh Beringar also attended, for he had observed the lady passing from the house she had been given in the Foregate, close to the abbey's main mill. During the service he paid rather more attention to the troubled, childish profile beneath the white mourning wimple than to the words of the celebrant.

Her small hands were devoutly folded, her resolute, vulnerable lips moved silently, praying piteously for all those dying and being hurt while she kneeled here. The girl Constance watched her closely and jealously, a protective presence, but could not drive the war away from her.

Beringar followed at a distance until she re-entered her house. He did not seek to overtake her, nor attempt as yet to speak to her. When she had vanished, he left his henchmen behind, and went out along the Foregate to the end of the bridge. The section that drew up was still lifted, sealing in the town, but the clamour and shrieking of battle was already subsiding to his right, where the castle loomed in its smoky halo beyond the river. He would still have to wait before he could carry out his promised search for his affianced bride. Within the hour, if he had read the signs aright, the bridge should be down, and open. Meantime, he went at leisure to take his midday meal. There was no hurry.

Rumours flew in the guest house, as everywhere else. Those who had business of unimpeachable honesty elsewhere were all seeking to pack their bags and leave. The consensus of opinion was that the castle had certainly fallen, and the cost would run very high. King Stephen's writ had better be respected henceforth, for he was here, and victorious, and the Empress Maud, however legitimate her claim, was far away in Normandy, and unlikely to provide any adequate protection. There were whispers, also, that FitzAlan and Adeney, at the last moment, had broken out of the trap and were away. For which many breathed thanks, though silently.

When Beringar went out again, the bridge was down, the way open, and King Stephen's sentries manning the passage. They were strict in scrutinising his credentials, but passed him within respectfully when they were satisfied. Stephen must have given orders concerning him. He crossed, and entered at the guarded but open gate in the wall. The street rose steeply, the island town sat high. Beringar knew it well, and knew where he was bound. At the summit of the hill the row of the butchers' stalls and houses levelled out, silent and deserted.

Edric Flesher's shop was the finest of the row, but it was shuttered and still like all the rest. Hardly a head looked out, and even then only briefly and fearfully, and was withdrawn as abruptly behind barred doors. By the look of the street, they had not so far been ravaged. Beringar thudded at the shut door, and when he heard furtive stirrings within, lifted his voice: 'Open to me, Hugh Beringar! Edric – Petronilla – Let me in, I'm alone!'

He had half expected that the door would remain sealed like a tomb, and those within silent, and he would not have blamed them; but, instead, the door was flung wide, and there was Petronilla beaming and opening her arms to him as if to a saviour. She was getting old, but still plump, succulent and kindly, the most wholesome thing he had seen in this siege town so far. Her grey hair was tight and neat under its white cap, and her twinkling grey eyes bright and intelligent as ever, welcoming him in.

'Master Hugh – to see a known and trusted face here now!' Beringar was instantly sure that she did not quite trust him! 'Come in, and welcome! Edric, here's Hugh – Hugh Beringar!' And there was her husband, prompt to her call, large and rubicund and competent, the master of his craft in this town, and a councillor.

They drew him within, and closed the door firmly, as he noted and approved. Beringar said what a lover should say, without preamble: 'Where is Godith? I came to look for her, to provide

203

for her. Where has he hidden her?'

It seemed they were too intent on making sure the shutters were fast, and listening for hostile footsteps outside, to pay immediate attention to what he was saying. And too ready with questions of their own to answer his questions.

'Are you hunted?' asked Edric anxiously. 'Do you need a place to hide?'

And: 'Were you in the garrison?' demanded Petronilla, and patted him concernedly in search of wounds. As though she had been his nurse once, instead of Godith's, and seen him every day of his life instead of twice or thrice since the childhood betrothal. A little too much solicitude! And a neat, brief breathing-space while they considered how much or how little to tell him!

'They've been hunting here already,' said Edric. 'I doubt if they'll come again, they had the place to pieces after the sheriff and the Lord Fulke. You're welcome to a shelter here if you need it. Are they close on your heels?'

He was sure by that time that they knew he had never been inside the castle, nor committed in any way to FitzAlan's stand. This clever, trusted old servant and her husband had been deep in Adeney's confidence, they knew very well who had held with him, and who had held aloof.

'No, it's not that, I'm in no danger and no need. I came only to look for Godith. They're saying he left it too late to send her away with FitzAlan's family. Where can I find her?'

'Did someone send you here to look for her? asked Edric.

'No, no, none ... But where else would he place her? Who is there to be trusted like her nurse? Of course I came first to you! Never tell me she was not here!'

'She was here,' said Petronilla. 'Until a week ago we had her. But she's gone, Hugh, you're too late. He sent two knights to fetch her away, and not even we were told where she was bound. What we don't know we can't be made to tell, he said. But it's my belief they got her away out of the town in good time, and she's far off by now, and safe, pray God!' No doubt about the fervency of that prayer, she would fight and die for her nurseling. And lie for her, too, if need be!

'But for God's sake, friends, can you not help me to her at all? I'm her intended husband. I'm responsible for her if her father is dead, as by now, for all I know, he may well be ...'

That got him something for his trouble, at any rate, if it was no more than the flicker of a glance passing between them, before they exclaimed their 'God forbid!' in unison. They knew very well, by the frenzied search, that FitzAlan and Adeney had been neither killed nor taken. They could not yet be sure that they were clean away and safe, but they were staking their lives and loyalty on it. So now he knew he would get nothing more from them, he, the renegade. Not, at any rate, by this direct means.

'Sorry I am, lad,' said Edric Flesher weightily, 'to have no better comfort for you, but so it is. Take heart that at least no enemy has laid hand on her, and we pray none ever will.' Which could well be taken, reflected Beringar whimsically, as a thrust at me.

'Then I must away, and try what I can discover elsewhere,' he said dejectedly. 'I'll not put you in further peril. Open, Petronilla, and look if the street's empty for me.' Which she did, nothing loth, and reported it as empty as a beggar's palm. Beringar clasped Edric's hand, and leaned and kissed Edric's wife, and was rewarded and avenged by a vivid, guilty blush.

'Pray for her,' he said, asking one thing at least they would not grudge him, and slipped through the half-open door, and heard it closed firmly behind him. Not too loudly, since he was supposed to be affecting stealth, but still audibly, he tramped with hasty steps along the street as far as the corner of the house. Then, whirling, he skipped back silently on his toes to lay an ear to the shutter.

'Hunting for his bride!' Petronilla was saying scornfully. 'Yes, and a fair price he'd pay for her, too, and she a certain decoy for her father's return, if not for FitzAlan's! He has his way to make with Stephen now, and my girl's his best weapon.'

'Maybe we're too hard on him,' responded Edric mildly. 'Who's to say he doesn't truly want to see the girl safe? But I grant you we dared take no chances. Let him do his own hunting.'

'Thank God,' she said fiercely, 'he can't well know I've hid my lamb away in the one place where no sane man will look for her!' And she chuckled at the word 'man'. 'There'll be a time to get her out of there later, when all the hue and cry's forgotten. Now I pray her father's miles from here and riding hard. And that those two lads in Frankwell will have a lucky run westward with the sheriff's treasury tonight. May they all come safe to Normandy, and be serviceable to the empress, bless her!'

'Hush, love!' said Edric chidingly. 'Even behind locked doors ...'

They had moved away into an inner room; a door closed between. Hugh Beringar abandoned his listening-post and walked demurely away down the long, curving hill to the town gate and the bridge, whistling softly and contentedly as he went.

He had got more even that he had bargained for. So they were hoping to smuggle out FitzAlan's treasury, as well as his person, and this very night, westward into Wales! And had had the forethought to stow it away meantime, against this desperate contingency, outside the walls of the town, somewhere in the suburb of Frankwell. No gates to pass, no bridges to cross. As for Godith – he had a shrewd idea now where to look for her. With the girl *and* the money, he reflected, a man could buy the favour of far less corruptible men than King Stephen!

Godith was in the herbarium workshop, obstinately stirring, diluting and mixing as she had been shown, an hour before Vespers, with her heart in anguished suspense, and her mind in a twilight between hope and despair. Her face was grubby from smearing away tears with a hand still soiled from the garden, and her eyes were rimmed with the washed hollows and grimed uplands of her grief and tension. Two tears escaped from her angry efforts at damming them, while both hands were occupied, and fell into a brew which should not have been weakened. Godith swore, an oath she had learned in the mews, long ago, when the falconers were suffering from a careless and impudent apprentice who had been her close friend.

'Rather say a blessing with them,' said Brother Cadfael's voice behind her shoulder, gently and easily. 'That's likely to be the finest tisane for the eyes I ever brewed. Never doubt God was watching.' She had turned her dirty, dogged, appealing face to him in silence, finding encouragement in the very tone of his voice. 'I've been to the gate house, and the mill, and the bridge. Such ill news as there is, is ill indeed, and presently we'll go pray for the souls of those quitting this world. But all of us quit it at last, by whatever way, that's not the worst of evils. And there is some news not all evil. From all I can hear this side Severn, and at the bridge itself – there's an archer among the guard there was with me in the Holy Land – your father and FitzAlan are neither dead, wounded nor captive, and all search of the town has failed to find them.

They're clear away, Godric, my lad. I doubt if Stephen for all his hunting will lay hand on them now. And now you may tend to that wine you're watering, and practise your young manhood until we can get you safely out of here after your sire.'

Just for a moment she rained tears like the spring thaw, and then she glinted radiance like the spring sun. There was so much to grieve over, and so much to celebrate, she did not know which to do first, and essayed both together, like April. But her age was April, and the hopeful sunshine won.

'Brother Cadfael,' she said when she was calm, 'I wish my father could have known you. And yet you are not of his persuasion, are you?'

'Child dear,' said Cadfael comfortably, 'my monarch is neither Stephen nor Maud, and in all my life and all my fighting I've fought for only one king. But I value devotion and fidelity, and doubt if it matters whether the object falls short. What you do and what you are is what matters. Your loyalty is as sacred as mine. Now wash your face and bathe your eyes, and you can sleep for half an hour before Vespers – but no, you're too young to have the gift!'

She had not the gift that comes with age, but she had the exhaustion that comes of youthful stress, and she fell asleep on her bench-bed within seconds, drugged with the syrup of relief. He awoke her in time to cross the close for Vespers. She walked beside him discreetly, her shock of clipped curls combed forward on her brow to hide her still reddened eyes.

Driven to piety by shock and terror, all the inhabitants of the guest house were also converging on the church, among them Hugh Beringar; not, perhaps, a victim of fear, but drawn by the delicate bait of Aline Siward, who came hastening from her house by the mill with lowered eyes and heavy heart. Beringar had, none the less, a quick eye for whatever else of interest might be going on round about him. He saw the two oddly contrasted figures coming in from the gardens, the squat, solid, powerful middle-aged monk with the outdoor tan and the rolling, seaman's gait, with his hand protectively upon the shoulder of a slip of a boy in a cotte surely inherited from an older and larger kinsman, a barelegged, striding youth squinting warily through a bush of brown hair. Beringar looked, and considered; he smiled, but so inwardly that on his long, mobile mouth the smile hardly showed.

Godith controlled both her face and her pace, and gave no

sign of recognition. In the church she strolled away to join her fellow-pupils, and even exchange a few nudges and grins with them. If he was still watching, let him wonder, doubt, change his mind. He had not seen her for more than five years. Whatever his speculations, he could not be sure. Nor was he watching this part of the church, she noted; his eyes were on the unknown lady in mourning most of the time. Godith began to breathe more easily, and even allowed herself to examine her affianced bridegroom almost as attentively as he was observing Aline Siward. When last seen, he had been a coltish boy of eighteen, all elbows and knees, not yet in full command of his body. Now he had a cat's assured and contemptuous grace, and a cool, aloof way with him. A presentable enough fellow, she owned critically, but no longer of interest to her, or possessed of any rights in her. Circumstances alter fortunes. She was relieved to see that he did not look in her direction again.

All the same, she told Brother Cadfael about it, as soon as they were alone together in the garden after supper, and her evening lesson with the boys was over. Cadfael took it gravely.

'So that's the fellow you were to marry! He came here straight from the king's camp, and has certainly joined the king's party, though according to Brother Dennis, who collects all the gossip that's going among his guests, he's on sufferance as yet, and has to prove himself before he'll get a command.' He scrubbed thoughtfully at his blunt, brown nose, and pondered. 'Did it seem to you that he recognised you? Or even looked over-hard at you, as if you reminded him of someone known?'

'I thought at first he did give me a hard glance, as though he might be wondering. But then he never looked my way again, or showed any interest. No, I think I was mistaken. He doesn't know me. I've changed in five years, and in this guise ... In another year,' said Godith, astonished and almost alarmed at the thought, 'we should have been married.'

'I don't like it!' said Cadfael, brooding. 'We shall have to keep you well out of his sight. If he wins his way in with the king, maybe he'll leave here with him in a week or so. Until then, keep far from the guest house or the stables, or the gate house, or anywhere he may be. Never let him set eyes on you if you can avoid.'

'I know!' said Godith, shaken and grave. 'If he does find me he may turn me to account for his own advancement. I do know! Even if my father had reached shipboard, he would come back and surrender himself, if I were threatened. And then he would die, as all those poor souls over there have died ...' She could not bear to turn her head to look towards the towers of the castle, hideously ornamented. They were dying there still, though she did not know it; the work went on well into the hours of darkness. 'I will avoid him, like the plague,' she said fervently, 'and pray that he'll leave soon.'

Abbot Heribert was an old, tired and peace-loving man, and disillusionment with the ugly tendencies of the time, combined with the vigour and ambition of his prior, Robert, had disposed him to withdraw from the world ever deeper into his own private consolations of the spirit. Moreover, he knew he was in disfavour with the king, like all those who had been slow to rally to him with vociferous support. But confronted with an unmistakable duty, however monstrous, the abbot could still muster courage enough to rise to the occasion. There were ninety-four dead or dying men being disposed of like animals, and every one had a soul, and a right to proper burial, whatever his crimes and errors. The Benedictines of the abbey were the natural protectors of those rights, and Heribert did not intend King Stephen's felons to be shovelled haphazard and nameless into an unmarked grave. All the same, he shrank from the horror of the task, and looked about him for someone more accomplished in these hard matters of warfare and bloodshed than himself, to lend support. And the obvious person was Brother Cadfael, who had crossed the world in the first Crusade, and afterwards spent ten years as a sea captain about the coasts of the Holy Land, where fighting hardly ever ceased.

After Compline, Abbot Heribert sent for Cadfael to his private parlour.

'Brother, I am going – now, this night – to ask King Stephen for his leave and authority to give Christian burial to all those slaughtered prisoners. If he consents, tomorrow we must take up their poor bodies, and prepare them decently for the grave. There will be some who can be claimed by their own families, the rest we shall bury honourably with the rites due to them. Brother, you have yourself been a soldier. Will you – if I speed with the king – will you take charge of this work?'

'Not gladly, but with all my heart, for all that,' said Brother Cadfael, 'yes, Father, I will.'

Chapter Three

ES, I will,' said Godith, 'if that's how I can best be useful to you. Yes, I will go to my morning lesson and my evening lesson, eat my dinner without a word or a look to anyone, and then make myself scarce and shut myself up here among the potions. Yes, and drop the bar on the door, if need be, and wait until I hear your voice before I open again. Of course I'll do as you bid. But for all that, I wish I could go with you. These are my father's people and my people, I wish I could have some small part in doing them these last services.'

'Even if it were safe for you to venture there,' said Cadfael firmly, 'and it is not, I would not let you go. The ugliness that man can do to man might cast a shadow between you and the certainty of the justice and mercy God can do to him hereafter. It takes half a lifetime to reach the spot where eternity is always visible, and the crude injustice of the hour shrivels out of sight. You'll come to it when the time's right. No, you stay here and keep well out of Hugh Beringar's way.'

He had even thought of recruiting that young man into his working-party of able-bodied and devoutly inclined helpers, to make sure that he spent the day away from anywhere Godith might be. Whether in a bid to acquire merit for their own souls, out of secret partisan sympathy with the dead men's cause, or to search anxiously for friends or kin, three of the travellers in the guest house had volunteered their aid, and it might have been possible, with such an example, to inveigle others, even

Beringar, into feeling obliged to follow suit. But it seemed that the young man was already out and away on horseback, perhaps dancing hopeful attendance on the king; a newcomer seeking office can't afford to let his face be forgotten. He had also ridden out the previous evening, as soon as Vespers was over, so said the lay brothers in the stables. His three men-at-arms were here, idling their day away with nothing to do once the horses were groomed, fed and exercised, but they saw no reason why they should involve themselves in an activity certainly unpleasant, and possibly displeasing to the king. Cadfael could not blame them. He had a muster of twenty, brothers, lay brothers and the three benevolent travellers, when they set out across the bridge and through the streets of the town to the castle.

Probably King Stephen had been glad enough to have a service offered voluntarily which he might otherwise have had to impose by order. Someone had to bury the dead, or the new garrison would be the first to suffer, and in an enclosed fortress in a tightly walled town disease can fester and multiply fearfully. All the same, the king would perhaps never forgive Abbot Heribert for the implied reproach, and the reminder of his Christian duty. Howbeit, the old man had brought back the needful authority; Cadfael's party was passed through the gates without question, and Cadfael himself admitted to Prestcote's presence.

'Your lordship will have had orders about us,' he said briskly. 'We are here to take charge of the dead, and I require clean and adequate space where they may be decently laid until we take them away for burial. If we may draw water from the well, that's all besides that we need ask. Linen we have brought with us.'

'The inner ward has been left empty,' said Prestcote indifferently. 'There is room there, and there are boards you may use if you need them.'

'The king has also granted that such of these unfortunates as were men of this town, and have families or neighbours here, can be claimed and taken away for private burial. Will you have that cried through the town, when I am satisfied that all is ready? And give them free passage in and out?'

'If there are any bold enough to come,' said Prestcote drily, 'they may have their kin and welcome. The sooner all this carrion is removed, the better shall I be pleased.'

'Very well! Then what have you done with them?' For the

211

walls and towers had been denuded before dawn of their sudden crop of sorry fruit. The Flemings must have worked half the night to put the evidence out of sight, which was surely not their idea, but might well be Prestcote's. He had approved these deaths, he did not therefore have to take pleasure in them, and he was an old soldier of strict and orderly habits, who liked a clean garrison.

'We cut them down, when they were all dead, and dropped them over the parapet into the green ditch under the wall. Go out by the Foregate, and between the towers and the road you'll find them.'

Cadfael inspected the small ward offered him, and it was at least clean and private, and had room for all. He led his party out through the gate into the town wall, and down into the deep, dry ditch beneath the towers. Long, fruiting grasses and low bushes partially hid what on closer approach looked like a battlefield. The dead lay piled deep at one spot close under the wall, and were sprawled and scattered like broken toys for yards on either side. Cadfael and his helpers tucked up their gowns and went to work in pairs, without word spoken, disentangling the knotted skein of bodies, carrying away first the most accessible, lifting apart those shattered into boneless embraces by their fall from above. The sun climbed high, and the heat was reflected upon them from the stone of the walls. The three pious travellers shed their cottes. In the deep hollow the air grew heavy and stifling, and they sweated and laboured for breath, but never flagged.

'Pay close attention always,' said Cadfael warningly, 'in case some poor soul still breathes. They were in haste, they may have cut someone down early. And in this depth of cushioning below, a man could survive even the fall.'

But the Flemings, for all their hurry, had been thorough. There was no live man salvaged out of that massacre.

They had started work early, but it was approaching noon by the time they had all the dead laid out in the ward, and were beginning the work of washing and composing the bodies as becomingly as possible, straightening broken limbs, closing and weighting eyelids, even brushing tangled hair into order, and binding fallen jaws, so that the dead face might be no horror to some unfortunate parent or wife who had loved it in life. Before he would go to Prestcote and ask for the promised proclamation to be made, Cadfael walked the range of his salvaged children, and checked that they were as presentable as they could well be made. And as he paced, he counted. At the end he frowned, and stood to consider, then went back and counted again. And that done, he began a much closer scrutiny of all those he had not himself handled, drawing down the linen wrappings that covered the worst ravages. When he rose from the last of them, his face was grim, and he marched away in search of Prestcote without a word to any.

'How many,' demanded Cadfael, 'did you say you despatched at the king's order?'

'Ninety-four,' said Prestcote, puzzled and impatient.

'Either you did not count,' said Cadfael, 'or you miscounted. There are ninety-five here.'

'Ninety-four or ninety-five,' said Prestcote, exasperated, 'one more or less, what does it matter? Traitors all, and condemned, am I to tear my hair because the number does not tally?'

'Not you, perhaps,' said Cadfael simply, 'but God will require an accounting. Ninety-four, including Arnulf of Hesdin, you had orders to slay. Justified or not, that at least was ordered, you had your sanction, the thing is registered and understood. Any accounting for those comes later and in another court. But the ninety-fifth is not in the reckoning, no king authorised his removal out of this world, no castellan had orders to kill him, never was he accused or convicted of rebellion, treason or any other crime, and the man who destroyed him is guilty of murder.'

'God's wounds!' exploded Prestcote violently. 'An officer in the heat of fighting miscounts by one, and you would make a *coram rege* case out of it! He was omitted in the count delivered, but he was taken in arms and hanged like the rest, and no more than his deserts. He rebelled like the rest, he is hanged like the rest, and that's an end of it. In God's name, man, what do you want me to do?'

'It would be well,' said Cadfael flatly, 'if you would come and look at him, to begin with. For he is *not* like the rest. He was not hanged like the rest, his hands were not bound like the rest – he is in no way comparable, though someone took it for granted we would all see and think as you, and omit to count. I am telling you, my lord Prestcote, there is a murdered man among your executed men, a leaf hidden in your forest. And if you regret that my eyes found him, do you think God had not seen him long before? And supposing you could silence me, do you think God will keep silence?'

Prestcote had stopped pacing by that time, and stood staring very intently. 'You are in good earnest,' he said, shaken. 'How could there be a man there dead in some other way? Are you sure of what you say?'

'I am sure. Come and see! He is there because some felon put him there, to pass for one among the many, and arouse no curiosity, and start no questions.'

'Then he would need to know that the many would be there.'

'Most of this town and all this garrison would know that, by nightfall. This was a deed of night. Come and see!'

And Prestcote went with him, and showed every sign of consternation and concern. But so would a guilty man, and who was better placed to know all a guilty man needed to know, to protect himself? Still, he kneeled with Cadfael beside the body that was different, there in the confines of the ward, between high walls, with the odour of death just spreading its first insidious pall over them.

A young man, this. No armour on him, but naturally the rest had been stripped of theirs, mail and plate being valuable. But his dress was such as to suggest that he had worn neither mail nor leather, he was clad in lightweight, dark cloth, but booted, the manner of dress a man would wear for a journey in summer weather, to ride light, be warm enough by night, and shed the short cotte to be cool enough by day. He looked about twenty-five years old, no more, reddish brown in colouring and round and comely of face, if the eye could make allowance for the congestion of strangulation, now partially smoothed out by Cadfael's experienced fingers. The bulge and stare of the eyes was covered, but the lids stood large.

'He died strangled,' said Prestcote, relieved to see the signs.

'He did, but not by a rope. And not with hands bound, like these others. Look!' Cadfael drew down the folds of the capuchon from the round young throat, and showed the sharp, cruel line that seemed to sever head from body. 'You see the thinness of this cord that took his life? No man ever dangled from such a noose. It runs level round his neck, and is fine as fishing line. It may well have been fishing line. You see the edges of this furrow in his flesh, discoloured, and shiny? The cord that killed him was waxed, to bite smooth and deep. And you see this pit here behind?' He raised the lifeless head gently on his arm, and showed, close to the knotted cord of the spine, a single, deep, bruised hollow, with a speck of black blood at its heart. 'The mark of one end of a wooden peg, a hand-hold

214

to twist when the cord was round the victim's throat. Stranglers use such waxed cords, with two hand-holds at the ends – killers by stealth, highway birds of prey. Given strength of hand and wrist, it is a very easy way of seeing your enemies out of this world. And do you see, my lord, how his neck, where the thong bites, is lacerated and beaded with dried blood? Now see here, both hands – Look at his nails, black at the tips with his own blood. He clawed at the cord that was killing him. His hands were free. Did you hang any whose hands were not tied?'

'No!' Prestcote was so fascinated by the details he could not deny that the answer escaped him involuntarily. It would have been futile to snatch it back. He looked up at Brother Cadfael across the unknown young man's body, and his face sharpened and hardened into hostility. 'There is nothing to be gained,' he said deliberately, 'by making public so wild a tale. Bury your dead and be content. Let the rest be!'

'You have not considered,' said Cadfael mildly, 'that as yet there is no one who can put a name or a badge to this boy. He may as well be an envoy of the king as an enemy. Better treat him fairly, and keep your peace with both God and man. Also,' he said, in a tone even more cloistrally innocent, 'you may raise doubts of your own integrity if you meddle with truth. If I were you, I would report this faithfully, and send out that proclamation to the townsfolk at once, for we are ready. Then, if any can claim this young man, you have delivered your soul. And if not, then clearly you have done all man can do to right a wrong. And your duty ends there.'

Prestcote eyed him darkly for some moments, and then rose abruptly from his knees. 'I will send out the word,' he said, and stalked away into the hall.

The news was cried through the town, and word sent formally to the abbey, so that the same announcement might be made at the guest house there. Hugh Beringar, riding in from the east on his return from the king's camp, having forded the river at an island downstream, heard the proclamation at the gate house of the abbey, and saw among those anxiously listening the slight figure of Aline Siward, who had come out from her house to hear the news. For the first time he saw her with head uncovered. Her hair was the light, bright gold he had imagined it would be, and shed a few curling strands on either side her oval face. The long lashes shadowing her eyes were many shades darker, a rich bronze. She stood listening intently, gnawed a doubtful lip, and knotted her small hands together. She looked hesitant, and burdened, and very young.

Beringar dismounted only a few paces from her, as if he had by mere chance chosen that spot in order to be still and hear to the end what Prior Robert was saying.

' – and his Grace the king gives free warranty to any who may wish, to come and claim their kin, if there be any such among the executed, and give them burial in their own place and at their own charge. Also, since there is one in particular whose identity is not known, he desires that all who come may view him, and if they can, name him. All which may be done without fear of penalty or disfavour.'

Not everyone would take that at its face value, but she did. What was troubling her was not fear of any consequences to herself, but a desperate feeling that she ought to make this dolorous pilgrimage, while equally earnestly she shrank from the horrors she might have to see. She had, Beringar remembered, a brother who had defied his father and run off to join the empress's adherents; and though she had heard rumours that he might have reached France, she had no means of knowing if they were true. Now she was struggling to escape the conviction that wherever there were garrisons of her brother's faction fallen victims of this civil war, she ought to go and assure herself that he was not among them. She had the most innocent and eloquent of faces, her every thought shone through.

'Madam,' said Beringar, very softly and respectfully, 'if there is any way I can be of service to you, I beg you command me.'

She turned to look at him, and smiled, for she had seen him in church, and knew him to be a guest here like herself, and stress had turned Shrewsbury into a town where people behaved to one another either as loyal neighbours or potential informers, and of the latter attitude she was incapable. Nevertheless, he saw fit to establish his credentials. 'You will remember I came to offer the king my troth when you did. My name is Hugh Beringar of Maesbury. It would give me pleasure to serve you. And it seemed to me that you were finding cause for perplexity and distress in what we have just heard. If there is any errand I can do for you, I will, gladly.'

'I do remember you,' said Aline, 'and I take your offer very kindly, but this is something only I can do, if it must be done.

216

No one else here would know my brother's face. To tell the truth, I was hesitating ... But there will be women from the town, I know, going there with certain knowledge to find their sons. If they can do it, so can I.'

'But you have no good reason,' he said, 'to suppose that your brother may be among these unfortunates.'

'None, except that I don't know *where* he is, and I do know he embraced the empress's cause. It would be better, wouldn't it, to be sure? Not to miss any possibility? As often as I do not find him dead, I may hope to see him again alive.'

'Was he very dear to you?' asked Beringar gently.

She hesitated to answer that, taking it very gravely. 'No, I never knew him as sister should know brother. Giles was always for his own friends and his own way, and five years my elder. By the time I was eleven or twelve he was for ever away from home, and came back only to quarrel with my father. But he is the only brother I have, and *I* have not disinherited him. And they're saying there's one there more than they counted, and unknown.'

'It will not be Giles,' he said firmly.

'But if it were? Then he needs his name, and his sister to do what's right.' She had made up her mind. 'I must go.'

'I think you should not. But I am sure you should not go alone.' He thought ruefully that her answer to that would be that she had her maid to accompany her, but instead she said at once: 'I will not take Constance into such a scene! She has no kin there, and why should she have to suffer it as well as I?'

'Then, if you will have me, I will go with you.'

He doubted if she had any artifice in her; certainly at this pass she showed none. Her anxious face brightened joyfully, she looked at him with the most ingenuous astonishment, hope and gratitude. But she still hesitated. 'That is kind indeed, but I can't let you do it. Why should you be subjected to such pain, just because I have a duty?'

'Oh, come now!' he said indulgently, sure of himself and of her. 'I shall not have a moment's peace if you refuse me and go alone. But if you tell me I shall only be adding to your distress by insisting, then I'll be silent and obey you. On no other condition.'

It was more than she could do. Her lips quivered. 'No – it would be a lie. I am not very brave!' she said sadly. 'I shall be grateful indeed.'

He had what he had wanted; he made the most of it. Why

ride, when the walk through the town could be made to last so much longer, and provide so much more opportunity to get to know her better? Hugh Beringar sent his horse to the stables, and set out with Aline along the highway and over the bridge into Shrewsbury.

Brother Cadfael was standing guard over his murdered man in a corner of the inner ward, beside the archway, where every citizen who came in search of child or kinsman must pass close, and could be questioned. But all he got so far was mute shaking of heads and glances half-pitying, half-relieved. No one knew the young man. And how could he expect great concern from these poor souls who came looking, every one, for some known face, and barely saw the rest?

Prestcote had made good his word, there was no tally kept of those who came, and no hindrance placed in their way, or question asked of them. He wanted his castle rid of its grim reminders as quickly as possible. The guard, under Adam Courcelle, had orders to remain unobtrusive, even to help if that would get the unwelcome guests off the premises by nightfall.

Cadfael had persuaded every man of the guard to view his unknown, but none of them could identify him. Courcelle had frowned down at the body long and sombrely, and shaken his head.

'I never saw him before, to my knowledge. What can there possibly have been about a mere young squire like this, to make someone hate him enough to kill?'

'There can be murders without hate,' said Cadfael grimly. 'Footpads and forest robbers take their victims as they come, without any feeling of liking or disliking.'

'Why, what can such a youth have had to make him worth killing for gain?'

'Friend,' said Cadfael, 'there are those in the world would kill for the few coins a beggar has begged during the day. When they see kings cut down more than ninety in one sweep, whose fault was only to be in arms on the other side, is it much wonder rogues take that for justification? Or at least for licence!' He saw the colour burn high in Courcelle's face, and a momentary spark of anger in his eye, but the young man made no protest. 'Oh, I know you had your orders, and no choice but to obey them. I have been a soldier in my time, and borne the same discipline, and done things I would be glad now to think I had not done. That's one reason I've accepted, in the end, another discipline.'

'I doubt,' said Courcelle drily, 'if I shall ever come to that.'

'So would I have doubted it, then. But here I am, and would not change again to your calling. Well, we do the best we can with our lives!' And the worst, he thought, viewing the long lines of motionless forms laid out along the ward, with other men's lives, if we have power.

There were some gaps in the silent ranks by then. Some dozen or so had been claimed by parents and wives. Soon there would be piteous little hand-carts pushed up the slope to the gate, and brothers and neighbours lifting limp bodies to carry them away. More of the townspeople were still coming timidly in through the archway, women with shawls drawn close over their heads and faces half-hidden, gaunt old men trudging resignedly to look for their sons. No wonder Courcelle, whose duties could hardly have encompassed this sort of guard before, looked almost as unhappy as the mourners.

He was frowning down at the ground in morose thought when Aline came into view in the archway, her hand drawn protectively through Hugh Beringar's arm. Her face was white and taut, her eyes very wide and her lips stiffly set, and her fingers clutched at her escort's sleeve as drowning men clutch at floating twigs, but she kept her head up and her step steady and firm. Beringar matched his pace attentively to hers, made no effort to divert her eyes from the sorry spectacle in the ward, and cast only few and brief, but very intent, side-glances at her pale countenance. It would certainly have been a tactical error, Cadfael thought critically, to attempt the kind of protective ardour that claims possession; young and ingenuous and tender as she might be, this was a proud patrician girl of old blood, not to be trifled with if once that blood was up. If she had come here on her own family business, like these poor, prowling citizens, she would not thank any man to try and take it out of her hands. She might, none the less, be deeply thankful for his considerate and reticent presence.

Courcelle looked up, almost as though he had felt a breath of unease moving before them, and saw the pair emerge into the sunlight in the ward, cruel afternoon sunlight that spared no detail. His head jerked up and caught the light, his bright hair burning up like a furze fire. 'Christ God!' he said in a hissing undertone, and went plunging to intercept them on the threshold.

'Aline! – Madam, should you be here? This is no place for you, so desolate a spectacle. I marvel,' he said furiously to Beringar, 'that you should bring her here, to face a scene so harrowing.'

'He did not bring me,' said Aline quickly. 'It was I insisted on coming. Since he could not prevent me, he has been kind enough to come with me.'

'Then, dear lady, you were foolish to impose such a penance on yourself,' said Courcelle fiercely. 'Why, how can you have business here? Surely there's none here belonging to you.'

'I pray you may be right,' she said. Her eyes, huge in the white face, ranged in fearful fascination over the shrouded ranks at her feet, and visibly the first horror and revulsion changed gradually into appalled human pity. 'But I must know! Like all these others! I have only one way of being certain, and it's no worse for me than for them. You know I have a brother – you were there when I told the king …'

'But he cannot be here. You said he was fled to Normandy.'

'I said it was rumoured so – but how can I be sure? He *may* have won to France, he may have joined some company of the empress's men nearer home, how can I tell? I must see for myself whether he chose Shrewsbury or not.'

'But surely the garrison here were known. Your name is very unlikely to have been among them.'

'The sheriff's proclamation,' said Beringar mildly, speaking up for the first time in this encounter, 'mentioned that there was one here, at least, who was not known. One more, apparently, than the expected tally.'

'You must let me see for myself,' said Aline, gently and firmly, 'or how can I have any peace?'

Courcelle had no right to prevent, however it grieved and enraged him. And at least this particular corpse was close at hand, and could bring her nothing but reassurance. 'He lies here,' he said, and turned her towards the corner where Brother Cadfael stood. She gazed, and was surprised into the faint brightness of a smile, a genuine smile though it faded soon.

'I think I should know you. I've seen you about the abbey, you are Brother Cadfael, the herbalist.'

'That is my name,' said Cadfael. 'Though why you should have learned it I hardly know.'

'I was asking the porter about you,' she owned, flushing. 'I saw you at Vespers and Compline, and – Forgive me, brother, if I have trespassed, but you had such an air – as though you had lived adventures before you came to the cloister. He told me you were in the Crusade – with Godfrey of Bouillon at the siege of Jerusalem! I have only dreamed of such service ... Oh!' She had lowered her eyes from his face, half abashed by her own ardour, and seen the young, dead face exposed at his feet. She gazed and gazed, in controlled silence. The face was not offensive, rather its congestion had subsided; the unknown lay youthful and almost comely.

'This is a most Christian service you are doing now,' said Aline, low-voiced, 'for all these here. This is the unexpected one? The one more than was counted?'

'This is he.' Cadfael stooped and drew down the linen to show the good but simple clothing, the absence of anything warlike about the young man. 'But for the dagger, which every man wears when he travels, he was unarmed.'

She looked up sharply. Over her shoulder Beringar was gazing down with frowning concentration at the rounded face that must have been cheerful and merry in life. 'Are you saying,' asked Aline, 'that he was not in the fight here? Not captured with the garrison?'

'So it seems to me. You don't know him?'

'No.' She looked down with pure, impersonal compassion. 'So young! It's great pity! I wish I could tell you his name, but I never saw him before.'

'Master Beringar?'

'No. A stranger to me.' Beringar was still staring down very sombrely at the dead. They were almost of an age, surely no more than a year between them. Every man burying his twin sees his own burial.

Courcelle, hovering solicitously, laid a hand on the girl's arm, and said persuasively: 'Come now, you've done your errand, you should quit this sad place at once, it is not for you. You see your fears were groundless, your brother is not here.'

'No,' said Aline, 'this is not he, but for all that he *may* – How can I be sure unless I see them all?' She put off the urging touch, but very gently. 'I've ventured this far, and how is it worse for me than for any of these others?' She looked round appealingly. 'Brother Cadfael, this is your charge now. You know I must ease my mind. Will you come with me?'

'Very willingly,' said Cadfael, and led the way without more words, for words were not going to dissuade her, and he thought her right not to be dissuaded. The two young men followed side by side, neither willing to give the other pre-cedence. Aline looked down at every exposed face, wrung but resolute.

'He was twenty-four years old – not very like me, his hair was darker ... Oh, here are all too many no older than he!'

They had traversed more than half of the dolorous passage when suddenly she caught at Cadfael's arm, and froze where she stood. She made no outcry, she had breath only for a soft moan, audible as a word only to Cadfael, who was nearest. 'Giles!' she said again more strongly, and what colour she had drained from her face and left her almost translucent, staring down at a face once imperious, wilful and handsome. She sank to her knees, stooping to study the dead face close, and then she uttered the only cry she ever made over her brother, and that very brief and private, and swooped breast to breast with him, gathering the body into her arms. The mass of her hair slipped out of its coils and spilled gold over them both.

Brother Cadfael, who was experienced enough to let her alone until she seemed to need comfort for her grief instead of decent reticence, would have waited quietly, but he was hur-riedly thrust aside, and Adam Courcelle fell on his knees beside her, and took her beneath the arms to lift her against his shoulder. The shock of discovery seemed to have shaken him fully as deeply as it had Aline, his face was stricken and dismayed, his voice an appalled stammer.

'Madam! – Aline – Dear God, is this indeed your brother? If I'd known ... if I'd known, I'd have saved him for you ... Whatever the cost, I would have delivered him ... God forgive me!'

She lifted a tearless face from the curtain of her yellow hair, and looked at him with wonder and compunction, seeing him so shattered. 'Oh, hush! How can this be any fault of yours? You could not know. You did only what you were ordered to do. And how could you have saved one, and let the rest die?'

'Then truly this *is* your brother?'

'Yes,' she said, gazing down at the dead youth with a face now drained even of shock and grief. 'This is Giles.' Now she knew the worst, and now she had only to do what was needful, what fell to her for want of father and brothers. She crouched motionless in Courcelle's arm, earnestly regarding the dead face. Cadfael, watching, was glad he had managed to mould some form back into features once handsome, but in death fallen into a total collapse of terror. At least she was not viewing that hardly human disintegration.

Presently she heaved a short, sharp sigh, and made to rise, and Hugh Beringar, who had shown admirably judicious restraint throughout, reached a hand to her on the other side, and lifted her to her feet. She was mistress of herself as perhaps she had never been before, never having had to meet such a test until now. What was required of her she could and would do.

'Brother Cadfael, I do thank you for all you have done, not only for Giles and me, but for all these. Now, if you permit, I will take my brother's burial into my charge, as is only fitting.'

Close and anxious at her shoulder, still deeply shaken, Courcelle asked: 'Where would you have him conveyed? My men shall carry him there for you, and be at your orders as long as you need them. I wish I might attend you myself, but I must not leave my guard.'

'You are very kind,' she said, quite composed now. 'My mother's family has a tomb at St Alkmund's church, here in the town. Father Elias knows me. I shall be grateful for help in taking my brother there, but I need not keep your men from their duties longer. All the rest I will do.' Her face had grown intent and practical, she had work to do, all manner of things to take into account, the need for speed, the summer heat, the provision of all the materials proper to decent preparation for the grave. She made her dispositions with authority.

'Messire Beringar, you have been kind, and I do value it, but now I must stay to see to my family's rites. There is no need to sadden all the rest of your day, I shall be safe enough.'

'I came with you,' said Hugh Beringar, 'and I shall not return without you.' The very way to talk to her now, without argument, without outward show of sympathy. She accepted his resolve simply, and turned to her duty. Two of the guards brought a narrow litter, and lifted Giles Siward's body into it, and she herself steadied and straightened the lolling head.

At the last moment Courcelle, frowning down distressfully at the corpse, said abruptly: 'Wait! I have remembered – I believe there is something here that must have belonged to him.'

He went hastily through the archway and across the outer ward to the guard-towers, and in a few moments came back carrying over his arm a black cloak. 'This was among the gear they left behind in the guardroom at the end. I think it must have been his – this clasp at the neck has the same design, see, as the buckle of his belt.'

It was true enough, there was the same dragon of eternity, tail in mouth, lavishly worked in bronze. 'I noticed it only now. That cannot be by chance. Let me at least restore him this.' He spread out the cloak and draped it gently over the litter, covering the dead face. When he looked up, it was into Aline's eyes, and for the first time they regarded him through a sheen of tears.

'That was very kindly done,' she said in a low voice, and gave him her hand. 'I shall not forget it.'

Cadfael went back to his vigil by the unknown, and continued his questioning, but it brought no useful response. In the coming night all these dead remaining must be taken on carts down the Wyle and out to the abbey; this hot summer would not permit further delay. At dawn Abbot Heribert would consecrate a new piece of ground at the edge of the abbey enclosure, for a mass grave. But this unknown, never condemned, never charged with any crime, whose dead body cried aloud for justice, should not be buried among the executed, nor should there be any rest until he could go to his grave under his own rightful name, and with all the individual honours due to him.

In the house of Father Elias, priest of St Alkmund's church, Giles Siward was reverently stripped, washed, composed and shrouded, all by his sister's hands, the good father assisting. Hugh Beringar stood by to fetch and carry for them, but did not enter the room where they worked. She wanted no one else, she was quite sufficient to the task laid on her, and if she was robbed of any part of it now she would feel deprivation and resentment, not gratitude. But when all was done, and her brother laid ready for rest before the altar of the church, she was suddenly weary to death, and glad enough of Beringar's almost silent company and ready arm back to her house by the mill.

On the following morning Giles Siward was interred with all due ceremony in the tomb of his maternal grandfather in the church of St Alkmund, and the monks of the abbey of St Peter and St Paul buried with due rites all the sixty-six soldiers of the defeated garrison still remaining in their charge.

Chapter Four

 LINE BROUGHT back with her the cotte and hose her brother had worn, and the cloak that had covered him, and herself carefully brushed and folded them. The shirt no one should ever wear again, she would burn it and forget; but these stout garments of good cloth must not go to waste, in a world where so many went half-naked and cold. She took the neat bundle, and went in at the abbey gate house, and finding the whole courtyard deserted, crossed to the ponds and the gardens in search of Brother Cadfael. She did not find him. The digging out of a grave large enough to hold sixty-six victims, and the sheer repetitive labour of laying them in it, takes longer than the opening of a stone tomb to make room for one more kinsman. The brothers were hard at work until past two o'clock, even with every man assisting.

But if Cadfael was not there, his garden-boy was, industriously clipping off flower-heads dead in the heat, and cutting leaves and stems of blossoming savory to hang up in bunches for drying. All the end of the hut, under the eaves, was festooned with drying herbs. The diligent boy worked barefoot and dusty from the powdery soil, and a smear of green coloured one cheek. At the sound of approaching footsteps he looked round, and came out in haste from among his plants, in a great wave of fragrance, which clung about him and distilled from the folds of his coarse tunic like the miraculous sweetness conferred upon some otherwise unimpressive-looking saint. The hurried swipe of a hand over his tangle of hair only served to smear the other cheek and half his forehead.

'I was looking,' said Aline, almost apologetically, 'for Brother Cadfael. You must be the boy called Godric, who works for him.'

'Yes, my lady,' said Godith gruffly. 'Brother Cadfael is still busy, they are not finished yet.' She had wanted to attend, but he would not let her; the less she was seen in full daylight, the better.

'Oh!' said Aline, abashed. 'Of course, I should have known. Then may I leave my message with you? It is only – I've brought these, my brother's clothes. He no longer needs them, and they are still good, someone could be glad of them. Will you ask Brother Cadfael to dispose of them somewhere they can do good? However he thinks best.'

Godith had scrubbed grubby hands down the skirts of her cotte before extending them to take the bundle. She stood suddenly very still, eyeing the other girl and clutching the dead man's clothes, so startled and shaken that she forgot for a moment to keep her voice low. 'No longer needs ... You had a brother in there, in the castle? Oh, I am sorry! Very sorry!'

Aline looked down at her own hands, empty and rather lost now that even this last small duty was done. 'Yes. One of many,' she said. 'He made his choice. I was taught to think it the wrong one, but at least he stood by it to the end. My father might have been angry with him, but he would not have had to be ashamed.'

'I am sorry!' Godith hugged the folded garments to her breast and could find no better words. 'I'll deliver your message to Brother Cadfael as soon as he comes. And he would want me to give you his thanks for your most feeling charity, until he can do it for himself.'

'And give him this purse, too. It is for Masses for them all. But especially a Mass for the one who should not have been there – the one nobody knows.'

Godith stared in bewilderment and wonder. 'Is there one like that? One who did not belong? I didn't know!' She had seen Cadfael for only a few hurried moments when he came home late and weary, and he had had no time to tell her anything. All she knew was that the remaining dead had been brought to the abbey for burial; this mysterious mention of one who had no place in the common tragedy was new to her.

'So he said. There were ninety-five where there should have been only ninety-four, and one did not seem to have been in arms. Brother Cadfael was asking all who came, to look and see if they knew him, but I think no one has yet put a name to him.'

'And where, then, is he now?' asked Godith, marvelling.

'That I don't know. Though they must have brought him here to the abbey. Somehow I don't think Brother Cadfael will let him be put into the earth with all the rest, and he nameless and unaccounted for. You must know his ways better than I. Have you worked with him long?'

'No, a very short time,' said Godith, 'but I do begin to know him.' She was growing a little uneasy, thus innocently studied at close quarters by those clear iris eyes. A woman might be more dangerous to her secret than a man. She cast a glance back towards the beds of herbs where she had been working.

'Yes,' said Aline, taking the allusion, 'I must not keep you from your proper work.'

Godith watched her withdraw, almost regretting that she dared not prolong this encounter with another girl in this sanctuary of men. She laid the bundle of clothing on her bed in the hut, and went back to work, waiting in some disquiet for Cadfael to come; and even when he did appear he was tired, and still burdened with business.

'I'm sent for to the king's camp. It seems his sheriff has thought best to let him know what sort of unexpected hare I've started, and he wants an accounting from me. But I'm forgetting,' he said, passing a hard palm over cheeks stiff with weariness, 'I've had no time to talk to you at all, you've heard nothing of all that –'

'Ah, but I have,' said Godith. 'Aline Siward was here looking for you. She brought these, see, for you to give as alms, wherever you think best. They were her brother's. She told me. And this money is for Masses – she said especially a Mass for this one man more than was looked for. Now tell me, what is this mystery?'

It was pleasant to sit quietly for a while and let things slide, and therefore he relaxed and sat down with her, and told her. She listened intently, and when he was done she asked at once: 'And where is he now, this stranger nobody knows?'

'He is in the church, on a bier before the altar. I want all who come to services to pass by him, in the hope that someone must know him, and give him a name. We can't keep him beyond

227

tomorrow,' he said fretfully, 'the season is too hot. But if we must bury him unknown, I intend it to be where he can as easily be taken up again, and to keep his clothes and a drawing of his face, until we discover the poor lad.'

'And you truly believe,' she questioned, awed, 'that he was murdered? And then cast in among the king's victims, to hide the crime away for ever?'

'Child, I've told you! He was taken from behind, with a strangler's cord ready prepared for the deed. And it was done in the same night that the others died and were flung over into the ditch. What better opportunity could a murderer have? Among so many, who was to count, and separate, and demand answers? He had been dead much the same time as some of those others. It should have been a certain cover.'

'But it was not!' she said, vengefully glowing. 'Because *you* came. Who else would have cared to be so particular among ninety-five dead men? Who else would have stood out alone for the rights of a man not condemned – killed without vestige of law? Oh, Brother Cadfael, you have made me as irreconcilable as you are on this. Here am I, and have not seen this man. Let the king wait a little while! Let me go and see! Or go with me, if you must, but let me look at him.'

Cadfael considered and got to his feet, groaning a little at the effort. He was not so young as he once had been, and he had had a hard day and night. 'Come, then, have your will, who am I to shut you out where I invite others in? It should be quiet enough there now, but keep close to me. Oh, girl, dear, I must also be about getting you safe out of here as soon as I may.'

'Are you so eager to get rid of me?' she said, offended. 'And just when I'm getting to know sage from marjoram! What would you do without me?'

'Why, train some novice I can expect to keep longer than a few weeks. And speaking of herbs,' said Cadfael, drawing out a little leather bag from the breast of his habit, and shaking out a six-inch sprig of sun-dried herbage, a thin, square stem studded at intervals with pairs of spreading leaves, with tiny brown balls set in the joints of them, 'do you know what this one is?'

She peered at it curiously, having learned much in a few days. 'No. We don't grow it here. But I might know it if I saw it growing fresh.'

'It's goose-grass – cleavers it's also called. A queer, creeping thing that grows little hooks to hold fast, even on these tiny

228

seeds you see here. And you see it's broken in the middle of this straight stem?'

She saw, and was curiously subdued. There was something here beyond her vision; the thing was a wisp of brown, bleached and dry, but indeed folded sharply in the midst by a thin fracture. 'What is it? Where did you find it?'

'Caught into the furrow in this poor lad's throat,' he said, so gently that she could take it in without shock, 'broken here by the ligament that strangled him. And it's last year's crop, not new. The stuff is growing richly at this season, seeding wild everywhere, this was in fodder, or litter, grass cut last autumn and dried out. Never turn against the herb, it's sovereign for healing green wounds that are stubborn to knit. All the things of the wild have their proper uses, only misuse makes them evil.' He put the small slip of dryness away carefully in his bosom, and laid an arm about her shoulders. 'Come, then, let's go and look at this youngster, you and I together.'

It was mid-afternoon, the time of work for the brothers, play for the boys and the novices, once their limited tasks were done. They came down to the church without meeting any but a few half-grown boys at play, and entered the cool dimness within.

The mysterious young man from the castle ditch lay austerely shrouded on his bier in the choir end of the nave, his head and face uncovered. Dim but pure light fell upon him; it needed only a few minutes to get accustomed to the soft interior glow in this summer afternoon, and he shone clear to view. Godith stood beside him and gazed in silence. They were alone there, but for him, and they could speak, in low voices. But when Cadfael asked softly: 'Do you know him?' he was already sure of the answer.

A fine thread of a whisper beside him said: 'Yes.'

'Come!' He led her out as softly as they had come. In the sunlight he heard her draw breath very deep and long. She made no other comment until they were secure together in the herbarium, in the drowning summer sweetness, sitting in the shade of the hut.

'Well, who is he, this young fellow who troubles both you and me?'

'His name,' she said, very low and wonderingly, 'is Nicholas Faintree. I've known him, by fits and starts, since I was twelve years old. He is a squire of FitzAlan's, from one of his northern manors, he's ridden courier for his lord several times in the last few years. He would not be much known in Shrewsbury, no. If he was waylaid and murdered here, he must have been on his lord's business. But FitzAlan's business was almost finished in these parts.' She hugged her head between her hands, and thought passionately. 'There are some in Shrewsbury could have named him for you, you know, if they had had reason to come looking for men of their own. I know of some who may be able to tell you what he was doing here that day and that night. If you can be sure no ill will come to them?'

'Never by me,' said Cadfael, 'that I promise.'

'There's my nurse, the one who brought me here and called me her nephew. Petronilla served my family all her grown life, until she married late, too late for children of her own, and she married a good friend to FitzAlan's house and ours, Edric Flesher, the chief of the butchers' guild in town. The two of them were close in all the plans when FitzAlan declared for the Empress Maud. If you go to them from me,' she said confidently, 'they'll tell you anything they know. You'll know the shop, it has the sign of the boar's head, in the butchers' row.'

Cadfael scrubbed thoughtfully at his nose. 'If I borrow the abbot's mule, I can make better speed, and spare my legs, too. There'll be no keeping the king waiting, but on the way back I can halt at the shop. Give me some token, to show you trust me, and they can do as much without fear.'

'Petronilla can read, and knows my hand. I'll write you a line to her, if you'll lend me a little leaf of vellum, a mere corner will do.' She was alight with ardour, as intent as he. 'He was a merry person, Nicholas, he never did harm to anyone, that I know, and he was never out of temper. He laughed a great deal ... But if you tell the king he was of the opposite party, he won't care to pursue the murderer, will he? He'll call it a just fate, and bid you leave well alone.'

'I shall tell the king,' said Cadfael, 'that we have a man plainly murdered, and the method and time we know, but not the place or the reason. I will also tell him that we have a name for him – it's a modest name enough, it can mean nothing to Stephen. As at this moment there's no more to tell, for I know no more. And even if the king should shrug it off and bid me let things lie, I shall not do it. By my means or God's means, or the both of us together, Nicholas Faintree shall have justice before I let this matter rest.'

Having the loan of the abbot's own mule, Brother Cadfael took with him in this errand the good cloth garments Aline had entrusted to him. It was his way to carry out at once whatever tasks fell him, rather than put them off until the morrow, and there were beggars enough on his way through the town. The hose he gave to an elderly man with eyes whitened over with thick cauls, who sat with stick beside him and palm extended in the shade of the town gate. He looked of a suitable figure, and was in much-patched and threadbare nethers that would certainly fall apart very soon. The good brown cotte went to a frail creature no more than twenty years old who begged at the high cross, a poor feeble-wit with hanging lip and a palsied shake, who had a tiny old woman holding him by the hand and caring for him jealously. Her shrill blessings followed Cadfael down towards the castle gate. The cloak he still had folded before him when he came to the guard-post of the king's camp, and saw Lame Osbern's little wooden trolley tucked into the bole of a tree close by, and marked the useless, withered legs, and the hands callused and muscular from dragging all that dead weight about by force. His wooden pattens lay beside him in the grass. Seeing a frocked monk approaching on a good riding mule, Osbern seized them and propelled himself forward into Cadfael's path. And it was wonderful how fast he could move, over short distances and with intervals for rest, but all the same so immobilised a creature, half his body inert, must suffer cold in even the milder nights, and in the winter terribly.

'Good brother,' coaxed Osbern, 'spare an alms for a poor cripple, and God will reward you!'

'So I will, friend,' said Cadfael, 'and better than a small coin, too. And you may say a prayer for a gentle lady who sends it to you by my hand.' And he unfolded from the saddle before him, and dropped into the startled, malformed hands, Giles Siward's cloak.

'You did right to report truly what you found,' said the king consideringly. 'Small wonder that my castellan did not make the same discovery, he had his hands full. You say this man was taken from behind by stealth, with a strangler's cord? It's a footpad's way, and foul. And above all, to cast his victim in among my executed enemies to cover the crime – that I will not bear! How dared he make me and my officers his accomplices! That I count an affront to the crown, and for that alone I would wish the felon taken and judged. And the young man's name – Faintree, you said?'

'Nicholas Faintree. So I was told by one who came and saw him, where we had laid him in the church. He comes from a family in the north of the county. But that is all I know of him.'

'It is possible,' reflected the king hopefully, 'that he had ridden to Shrewsbury to seek service with us. Several such young men from north of the county have joined us here.'

'It is possible,' agreed Cadfael gravely; for all things are possible, and men do turn their coats.

'And to be cut off by some forest thief for what he carried – it happens! I wish I could say our roads are safe, but in this new anarchy, God knows, I dare not claim it. Well, you may pursue such enquiries as can be made into this matter, if that's your wish, and call upon my sheriff to do justice if the murderer can be found. He knows my will. I do not like being made use of to shield so mean a crime.'

And that was truth, and the heart of the matter for him, and perhaps it would not have changed his attitude, thought Cadfael, even if he had known that Faintree was FitzAlan's squire and courier, even if it were proved, as so far it certainly was not, that he was on FitzAlan's rebellious business when he died. By all the signs, there would be plenty of killing in Stephen's realm in the near future, and he would not lose his sleep over most of it, but to have a killer-by-stealth creeping for cover into his shadow, that he would take as a deadly insult to himself, and avenge accordingly. Energy and lethargy, generosity and spite, shrewd action and incomprehensible inaction, would always alternate and startle in King Stephen. But somewhere within that tall, comely, simple-minded person there was a grain of nobility hidden.

'I accept and value your Grace's support,' said Brother Cadfael truthfully, 'and I will do my best to see justice done. A man cannot lay down and abandon the duty God has placed in his hands. Of this young man I know only his name, and the appearance of his person, which is open and innocent, and that he was accused of no crime, and no man has complained of wrong by him, and he is dead unjustly. I think this as unpleasing to your Grace as ever it can be to me. If I can right it, so I will.'

At the sign of the boar's head in the butchers' row he was received with the common wary civility any citizen would show to a monk of the abbey. Petronilla, rounded and comfortable and grey, bade him in and would have offered all the small attentions that provide a wall between suspicious people, if he had not at once given her the worn and much-used leaf of vellum on which Godith had, somewhat cautiously and laboriously, inscribed her trust in the messenger, and her name. Petronilla peered and flushed with pleasure, and looked up at this elderly, solid, homely brown monk through blissful tears.

'The lamb, she's managing well, then, my girl? And you taking good care of her! Here she says it, I know that scrawl, I learned to write with her. I had her almost from birth, the darling, and she the only one, more's the pity, she should have had brothers and sisters. It was why I wanted to do everything with her, even the letters, to be by her whatever she needed. Sit down, brother, sit down and tell me of her, if she's well, if she needs anything I can send her by you. Oh, and, brother, how are we to get her safely away? Can she stay with you, if it runs to weeks?'

When Cadfael could wedge a word or two into the flow he told her how her nurseling was faring, and how he would see to it that she continued to fare. It had not occurred to him until then what a way the girl had of taking hold of hearts, without at all designing it. By the time Edric Flesher came in from a cautious skirmish through the town, to see how the land lay, Cadfael was firmly established in Petronilla's favour, and vouched for as a friend to be trusted.

Edric settled his solid bulk into a broad chair, and said with a gusty breath of cautious relief: 'Tomorrow I'll open the shop. We're fortunate! Ask me, he rues the vengeance he took for those he failed to capture. He's called off all pillage here, and for once he's enforcing it. If only his claims were just, and he had more spine in his body, I think I'd be for him. And to look like a hero, and be none, that's hard on a man.' He gathered his great legs under him, and looked at his wife, and then, longer, at Cadfael. 'She says you have the girl's good word, and that's enough. Name your need, and if we have it, it's yours.'

'For the girl,' said Cadfael briskly, 'I will keep her safe as long as need be, and when the right chance offers, I'll get her away to where she should be. For my need, yes, there you may help me. We have in the abbey church, and we shall bury there tomorrow, a young man you may know, murdered on the night after the castle fell, the night the prisoners were hanged and thrown into the ditch. But he was killed elsewhere, and thrown among the rest to have him away into the ground unquestioned. I can tell you how he died, and when. I cannot tell you where, or why, or who did this thing. But Godith tells me that his name is Nicholas Faintree, and he was a squire of FitzAlan.'

All this he let fall between them in so many words, and heard and felt their silence. Certainly there were things they knew, and equally certainly this death they had not known, and it struck at them like a mortal blow.

'One more thing I may tell you,' he said. 'I intend to have the truth out into the open concerning this thing, and see him avenged. And more, I have the king's word to pursue the murderer. He likes the deed no more than I like it.'

After a long moment Edric asked: 'There was only one, dead after this fashion? No second?'

'Should there have been? Is not one enough?'

'There were two,' said Edric harshly. 'Two who set out together upon the same errand. How did this death come to light? It seems you are the only man who knows.'

Brother Cadfael sat back and told them all, without haste. If he had missed Vespers, so be it. He valued and respected his duties, but if they clashed, he knew which way he must go. Godith would not stir from her safe solitude without him, not until her evening schooling.

'Now,' he said, 'you had better tell me. I have Godith to protect, and Faintree to avenge, and I mean to do both as best I can.'

The two of them exchanged glances, and understood each other. It was the man who took up the tale.

'A week before the castle and the town fell, with FitzAlan's family already away, and our plans made to place the girl with your abbey in hiding, FitzAlan also took thought for the end, if he died. He never ran until they broke in at the gates, you know that? By the skin of his teeth he got away, swam the river with Adeney at his shoulder, and got clear. God be thanked! But the day before the end he made provision for whether he lived or died. His whole treasury had been left with us here, he wanted it to reach the empress if he were slain. That day we moved it out into Frankwell, to a garden I hold there, so that there need be no bridge to pass if we had to convey it away at short notice. And we fixed a signal. If any of his party came with a certain token – a trifle it was, a drawing, but private to us who knew – they should be shown where the treasury was, provided with horses, all they might need, and put over there to pick up the valuables and make their break by night.'

'And so it was done?' said Cadfael.

'On the morning of the fall. It came so early, and in such force, we'd left it all but too late. Two of them came. We sent them over the bridge to wait for night. What could they have done by daylight?'

'Tell me more. What time did these two come to you that morning, what had they to say, how did they get their orders? How many may have known what was toward? How many would have known the way they would take? When did you last see them both alive?'

'They came just at dawn. We could hear the din by then, the assault had begun. They had the parchment leaf that was the signal, the head of a saint drawn in ink. They said there had been a council the night before, and FitzAlan had said then he would have them go the following day, whatever happened and whether he lived or no, get the treasury away safe to the empress, for her use in defending her right.'

'Then all who were at that council would know those two would be on the road the following night, as soon as it was dark enough. Would they also know the road? Did they know where the treasury was hidden?'

'No, where we had put it, beyond that it was in Frankwell, no one had been told. Only FitzAlan and I knew that. Those two squires had to come to me.'

'Then any who had ill designs on the treasury, even if they knew the time of its removal, could not go and get it for themselves, they could only waylay it on the road. If all those officers close to FitzAlan knew that it was to be taken westward into Wales from Frankwell, there'd be no doubt about the road. For the first mile and more there is but one, by reason of the coils of the river on either side.'

'You are thinking that one of those who knew thought to get the gold for himself, by murder?' said Edric. 'One of FitzAlan's own men? I cannot believe it! And surely all, or most, stayed to the end, and died. Two men riding by night could well be waylaid by pure chance, by men living wild in the forest …'

'Within a mile of the town walls? Don't forget, whoever killed this lad did so close enough to Shrewsbury castle to have ample time and means to take his body and toss it among all those others in the ditch, long before the night was over.

Knowing very well that all those others would be there. Well, so they came, they showed their credentials, they told you the plan had been made the previous evening, come what might. But what came, came earlier and more fiercely than anyone had expected, and all done in haste. Then what? You went with them over to Frankwell?'

'I did. I have a garden and a barn there, where they and their horses lay in hiding until dark. The valuables were packed into two pairs of saddle-bags – one horse with his rider and that load would have been overdone – in a cavity in a dry well on my land there. I saw them safe under cover, and left them there about nine in the morning.'

'And at what time would they venture to start?'

'Not until full dark. And do you truly tell me Faintree was murdered, soon after they set out?'

'Past doubt he was. Had it been done miles away, he would have been disposed of some other way. This was planned, and ingenious. But not ingenious enough. You knew Faintree well – or so Godith gave me to think. Who was the other? Did you also know him?'

Heavily and slowly, Edric said 'No!' It seemed to me that Nicholas knew him well enough, they were familiar together like good comrades, but Nicholas was one open to any new friend. I had never seen this lad before. He was from another of FitzAlan's northern manors. He gave his name as Torold Blund.'

They had told him all they knew, and something more than had been said in words. Edric's brooding frown spoke for him. The young man they knew and trusted was dead, the one they did not know vanished, and with him FitzAlan's valuables, plate and coin and jewellery, intended for the empress's coffers. Enough to tempt any man. The murderer clearly knew all he needed to know in order to get possession of that hoard; and who could have known half so well as the second courier himself? Another might certainly waylay the prize on the road. Torold Blund need not even have waited for that. Those two had been in hiding together all that day in Edric's barn. It was possible that Nicholas Faintree had never left it until he was dead, draped over a horse for the short ride back to the castle ditch, before two horses with one rider set out westward into Wales.

'There was one more thing happened that day,' said Petronilla, as Cadfael rose to take his leave. 'About two of the clock, after the king's men had manned both bridges and dropped the draw-bridge, *he* came – Hugh Beringar, he that was betrothed to my girl from years back – making pretence to be all concern for her, and asking where he could find her. Tell him? No, what do you take me for? I told him she'd been taken away a good week before the town fell, and we were not told where, but I thought she was far away by now, and safe out of Stephen's country. Right well we knew he must have come to us with Stephen's authority, or he would never have been let through so soon. He'd been to the king's camp before ever he came hunting for my Godith, and it's not for love he's searching for her. She's worth a fat commission, as bait for her father, if not for FitzAlan himself. Don't let my lamb get within his sight, for I hear he's living in the abbey now.'

'And he was here that very afternoon?' pressed Cadfael, concerned. 'Yes, yes, I'll take good care to keep her away from him, I've seen that danger. But there could not have been any mention when he came here, could there, of Faintree's mission? Nothing to make him prick his ears? He's very quick, and very private! No – no, I ask your pardon, I know you'd never let out word. Ah, well, my thanks for your help, and you shall know if I make progress.'

He was at the door when Petronilla said grievingly at his shoulder: 'And he seemed such a fine young lad, this Torold Blund! How can a body tell what lies behind the decent, ordinary face?'

'Torold Blund!' said Godith, testing the name slow syllable by syllable. 'That's a Saxon name. There are plenty of them up there in the northern manors, good blood and old. But I don't know him. I think I can never have seen him. And Nicholas was on good, close terms with him? Nicholas was easy, but not stupid, and they sound much of an age, he must have known him well. And yet ...'

'Yes,' said Cadfael, 'I know! And yet! Girl dear, I am too tired to think any more. I'm going to Compline, and then to my bed, and so should you. And tomorrow ...'

'Tomorrow,' she said, rising to the touch of his hand, 'we shall bury Nicholas. *We!* He was in some measure my friend, and I shall be there.'

'So you shall, my heart,' said Cadfael, yawning, and led her away in his arm to celebrate, with gratitude and grief and hope, the ending of the day.

Chapter Five

ICHOLAS FAINTREE was laid, with due honours, under a stone in the transept of the abbey church, an exceptional privilege. He was but one, after so many, and his singleness was matter for celebration, besides the fact that there was room within rather than without, and the labour involved was less. Abbot Heribert was increasingly disillusioned and depressed with all the affairs of this world, and welcomed a solitary guest who was not a symbol of civil war, but the victim of personal malice and ferocity. Against all the probabilities, in due course Nicholas might find himself a saint. He was mysterious, feloniously slain, young, to all appearances clean of heart and life, innocent of evil, the stuff of which martyrs are made.

Aline Siward was present at the funeral service, and had brought with her, intentionally or otherwise, Hugh Beringar. That young man made Cadfael increasingly uneasy. True, he was making no inimical move, nor showing any great diligence in his search for his affianced bride, if, indeed, he was in search of her at all. But there was something daunting in the very ease and impudence of his carriage, the small, sardonic turn of his lip, and the guileless clarity of the black eyes when they happened to encounter Cadfael's. No doubt about it, thought Cadfael, I shall be happier when I've got the girl safely away from here, but in the meantime at least I can move her away from anywhere he's likely to be.

The main orchards and vegetable gardens of the abbey were

not within the precinct, but across the main road, stretched along the rich level beside the river, called the Gaye; and at the far end of this fertile reach there was a slightly higher field of corn. It lay almost opposite the castle, and no great distance from the king's siege camp, and had suffered some damage during the siege; and though what remained had been ripe for cutting for almost a week, it had been too dangerous to attempt to get it in. Now that all was quiet, they were in haste to salvage a crop that could not be spared, and all hands possible were mustered to do the work in one day. The second of the abbey's mills was at the end of the field, and because of the same dangers had been abandoned for the season, just when it was beginning to be needed, and had suffered damage which would keep it out of use until repairs could be undertaken.

'You go with the reapers,' said Cadfael to Godith. 'My thumbs prick, and rightly or wrongly, I'd rather have you out of the enclave, if only for a day.'

'Without you?' said Godith, surprised.

'I must stay here and keep an eye on things. If anything threatens, I'll be with you as fast as legs can go. But you'll be well enough, no one is going to have leisure to look hard at you until that corn is in the barns. But stay by Brother Athanasius, he's as blind as a mole, he wouldn't know a stag from a hind. And take care how you swing a sickle, and don't come back short of a foot!'

She went off quite happily among the crowd of reapers in the end, glad of an outing and a change of scene. She was not afraid. Not afraid enough, Cadfael considered censoriously, but then, she had an old fool here to do the fearing for her, just as she'd once had an old nurse, protective as a hen with one chick. He watched them out of the gate house and over the road towards the Gaye, and went back with a relieved sigh to his own labours in the inner gardens. He had not been long on his knees, weeding, when a cool, light voice behind him, almost as quiet as the steps he had not heard in the grass, said: 'So this is where you spend your more peaceful hours. A far cry and a pleasant change from harvesting dead men.'

Brother Cadfael finished the last corner of the bed of mint before he turned to acknowledge the presence of Hugh Beringar. 'A pleasant change, right enough. Let's hope we've finished with that kind of crop, here in Shrewsbury.'

'And you found a name for your stranger in the end. How was that? No one in the town seemed to know him.'

239

'All questions get their answers,' said Brother Cadfael sententiously, 'if you wait long enough.'

'And all searches are bound to find? But of course,' said Beringar, smiling, 'you did not say how long is long enough. If a man found at eighty what he was searching for at twenty, he might prove a shade ungrateful.'

'He might well have stopped wanting it long before that,' said Brother Cadfael drily, 'which is in itself an answer to any want. Is there anything you are looking for here in the herbarium, that I can help you to, or are you curious to learn about these simples of mine?'

'No,' owned Beringar, his smile deepening, 'I would hardly say it was any simplicity I came to study.' He pinched off a sprig of mint, crushed it between his fingers, and set it first to his nose and then closed fine white teeth upon its savour. 'And what should such as I be looking for here? I may have *caused* a few ills in my time, I'm no hand at healing them. They tell me, Brother Cadfael, you have had a wide-ranging career before you came into the cloister. Don't you find it unbearably dull here, after such battles, with no enemy left to fight?'

'I am not finding it at all dull, these days,' said Cadfael, plucking out willowherb from among the thyme. 'And as for enemies, the devil makes his way in everywhere, even into cloister, and church, and herbarium.'

Beringar threw his head back and laughed aloud, until the short black hair danced on his forehead. 'Vainly, if he comes looking for mischief where you are! But he'd hardly expect to blunt his horns against an old crusader here! I take the hint!'

But all the time, though he scarcely seemed to turn his head or pay much attention to anything round him, his black eyes were missing nothing, and his ears were at stretch while he laughed and jested. By this time he knew that the well-spoken and well-favoured boy of whom Aline had innocently spoken was not going to make his appearance, and more, that Brother Cadfael did not care if he poked his nose into every corner of the garden, sniffed at ever drying herb and peered at every potion in the hut, for they would tell him nothing. The bench-bed was stripped of its blanket, and laden with a large mortar and a gently bubbling jar of wine. There was no trace of Godith anywhere to be found. The boy was simply a boy like the rest, and no doubt slept in the dortoir with the rest.

'Well, I'll leave you to your cleansing labours,' said Beringar, 'and stop hampering your meditations with my prattle. Or have you work for me to do?'

'The king has none?' said Cadfael solicitously.

Another ungrudging laugh acknowledged the thrust. 'Not yet, not yet, but that will come. Such talent he cannot afford to hold off suspiciously for ever. Though to be sure, he did lay one testing task upon me, and I seem to be making very little progress in that.' He plucked another tip of mint, and bruised and bit it with pleasure. 'Brother Cadfael, it seems to me that you are the most practical man of hand and brain here. Supposing I should have need of your help, you would not refuse it without due thought – would you?'

Brother Cadfael straightened up, with some creaking of back muscles, to give him a long, considering look. 'I hope,' he said cautiously, 'I never do anything without due thought – even if the thought sometimes has to shift its feet pretty briskly to keep up with the deed.'

'So I supposed,' said Beringar, sweet-voiced and smiling. 'I'll bear that in mind as a promise.' And he made a small, graceful obeisance, and walked away at leisure to the courtyard.

The reapers came back in time for Vespers, sun-reddened, weary and sweat-stained, but with the corn all cut and stacked for carrying. After supper Godith slipped out of the refectory in haste, and came to pluck at Cadfael's sleeve.

'Brother Cadfael, you must come! Something vital!' He felt the quivering excitement of her hand, and the quiet intensity of her whispering voice. 'There's time before Compline – come back to the field with me.'

'What is it?' he asked as softly, for they were within earshot of a dozen people if they had spoken aloud, and she was not the woman to fuss over nothing. 'What has happened to you? What have you left down there that's so urgent?'

'A man! A wounded man! He's been in the river, he was hunted into it upstream and came down with the current. I dared not stay to question, but I know he's in need. And hungry! He's been there a night and a day ...'

'How did you find him? You alone? No one else knows?'

'No one else.' She gripped Cadfael's sleeve more tightly, and her whisper grew gruff with shyness. 'It was a long day ... I went aside, and had to go far aside, into the bushes near the mill. Nobody saw ...'

'Surely, child! I know!' Please God all the boys, her

241

contemporaries, were kept hard at it, and never noticed such daintiness. Brother Athanasius would not have noticed a thunderclap right behind him. 'He was there in the bushes? And is still?'

'Yes. I gave him the bread and meat I had with me, and told him I'd come back when I could. His clothes have dried on him – there's blood on his sleeve ... But I think he'll do well, if *you* take care of him. We could hide him in the mill – no one goes there yet.' She had thought of all the essentials, she was towing him towards his hut in the herb garden, not directly towards the gate house. Medicines, linen, food, they would need all these.

'Of what age,' asked Cadfael, more easily now they were well away from listeners, 'is this wounded man of yours?'

'A boy,' she said on a soft breath. 'Hardly older than I am. And hunted! He thinks *I* am a boy, of course. I gave him the water from my bottle, and he called me Ganymede ...'

Well, well, thought Cadfael, bustling before her into the hut, a young man of some learning, it seems! 'Then, Ganymede,' he said, bundling a roll of linen, a blanket and a pot of salve into her arms, 'stow these about you, while I fill this little vial and put some vittles together. Wait here a few minutes for me, and we'll be off. And on the way you can tell me everything about this young fellow you've discovered, for once across the road no one is going to hear us.'

And on the way she did indeed pour out in her relief and eagerness what she could not have said so freely by daylight. It was not yet dark, but a fine neutral twilight in which they saw each other clear but without colours.

'The bushes there are thick. I heard him stir and groan, and I went to look. He looks like a young gentleman of family, someone's squire. Yes, he talked to me, but – but told me nothing, it was like talking to a wilful child. So weak, and blood on his shoulder and arm, and making little jests ... But he trusted me enough to know I wouldn't betray him.' She skipped beside Cadfael through the tall stubble into which the abbey sheep would soon be turned to graze, and to fertilise the field with their droppings. 'I gave him what I had, and told him to lie still, and I would bring help as soon as it grew dusk.'

'Now we're near, do you lead the way. You he'll know.'

There was already starlight before the sun was gone, a lovely August light that would still last them, their eyes being accustomed, an hour or more, while veiling them from other eyes. Godith withdrew from Cadfael's clasp the hand that had clung like a child's through the stubble, and waded forward into the low, loose thicket of bushes. On their left hand, within a few yards of them, the river ran, dark and still, only the thrusting sound of its current like a low throb shaking the silence, and an occasional gleam of silver showing where its eddies swirled.

'Hush! It's me – Ganymede! And a friend to us both!'

In the sheltered dimness a darker form stirred, and raised into sight a pale oval of face and a tangled head of hair almost as pale. A hand was braced into the grass to thrust the half-seen stranger up from the ground. No broken bones there, thought Cadfael with satisfaction. The hard-drawn breath signalled stiffness and pain, but nothing mortal. A young, muted voice said: 'Good lad! Friends I surely need ...'

Cadfael kneeled beside him and lent him a shoulder to lean against. 'First, before we move you, where's the damage? Nothing out of joint – by the look of you, nothing broken.' His hands were busy about the young man's body and limbs, he grunted cautious content.

'Nothing but gashes,' muttered the boy laboriously, and gasped at a shrewd touch. 'I lost enough blood to betray me, but into the river ... And half-drowned ... they must think wholly ...' He relaxed with a great sigh, feeling how confidently he was handled.

'Food and wine will put the blood back into you, in time. Can you rise and go?'

'Yes,' said his patient grimly, and all but brought his careful supporters down with him, proving it.

'No, let be, we can do better for you than that. Hold fast by me, and turn behind me. Now, your arms round my neck ...'

He was long, but a light weight. Cadfael stooped forward, hooked his thick arms round slim, muscular thighs, and shrugged the weight securely into balance on his solid back. The dank scent of the river water still hung about the young man's clothing. 'I'm too great a load,' he fretted feebly. 'I could have walked ...'

'You'll do as you're bid, and no argument. Godric, go before, and see there's no one in sight.'

It was only a short way to the shadow of the mill. Its bulk loomed dark against the still lambent sky, the great round of the undershot wheel showing gaps here and there like breaks in a set of teeth. Godith heaved open the leaning door, and felt her way before them into gloom. Through narrow cracks in the floorboards on the left side she caught fleeting, spun gleams of the river water hurrying beneath. Even in this hot, dry season, lower than it had been for some years, the Severn flowed fast and still.

'There'll be dry sacks in plenty piled somewhere by the landward wall,' puffed Cadfael at her back. 'Feel your way along and find them.' There was also a dusty, rustling layer of last harvest's chaff under their feet, sending up fine powder to tickle their noses. Godith groped her way to the corner, and spread sacks there in a thick, comfortable mattress, with two folded close for a pillow. 'Now take this long-legged heron of yours under the armpits, and help me ease him down ... There, as good a bed as mine in the dortoir! Now close the door, before I make light to see him by.'

He had brought a good end of candle with him, and a handful of the dry chaff spread on a millstone made excellent tinder for the spark he struck. When his candle was burning steadily he ground it into place on the flickering chaff, quenching the fire that might have blown and spread, and anchoring his light on a safe candlestick, as the wax first softened and then congealed again. 'Now let's look at you!'

The young man lay back gratefully and heaved a huge sigh, meekly abandoning the responsibility for himself. Out of a soiled and weary face, eyes irrepressibly lively gazed up at them, of some light, bright colour not then identifiable. He had a large, generous mouth, drawn with exhaustion but wryly smiling, and the tangle of hair matted and stained from the river would be as fair as corn-stalks when it was clean. 'One of them ripped your shoulder for you, I see,' said Cadfael, hands busy unfastening and drawing off the dark cotte encrusted down one sleeve with dried blood. 'Now the shirt – you'll be needing new clothes, my friend, before you leave this hostelry.'

'I'll have trouble paying my shot,' said the boy, valiantly grinning, and ended the grin with a sharp indrawn breath as the sleeve was detached painfully from his wound.

'Our charges are low. For a straight story you can buy such hospitality as we're offering. Godric, lad, I need water, and river water's better than none. See if you can find anything in this place to carry it in.'

She found the sound half of a large pitcher among the debris under the wheel, left by some customer after its handle and lip had got broken, scrubbed it out industriously with the skirt of her cotte, and went obediently to bring water, he hoped safely. The flow of the river here would be fresher than the leat, and occupy her longer on the journey, while Cadfael undid the boy's belt, and stripped off his shoes and hose, shaking out the blanket to spread over his nakedness. There was a long but not deep gash, he judged from a sword-cut, down the right thigh, a variety of bruises showing bluish on his fair skin, and most strangely, a thin, broken graze on the left side of his neck, and another curiously like it on the outer side of his right wrist. Mere healed, dark lines, these, older by a day or two than his wounds. 'No question,' mused Cadfael aloud, 'but you've been living an interesting life lately.'

'Lucky to keep it,' murmured the boy, half-asleep in his new ease.

'Who was hunting you?'

'The king's men – who else?'

'And still will be?'

'Surely. But in a few days I'll be fit to relieve you of the burden of me ...'

'Never mind that now. Turn a little to me – so! Let's get this thigh bound up, it's clean enough, it's knitting already. This will sting.' It did, the youth stiffened and gasped a little, but made no complaint. Cadfael had the wound bound and under the blanket by the time Godith came with the pitcher of water. For want of a handle she had to use two hands to carry it.

'Now we'll see to this shoulder. This is where you lost so much blood. An arrow did this!' It was an oblique cut sliced through the outer part of his left arm just below the shoulder, bone-deep, leaving an ugly flap of flesh gaping. Cadfael began to sponge away the encrustations of blood from it, and press it firmly together beneath a pad of linen soaked in one of his herbal salves. 'This will need help to knit clean,' he said, busy rolling his bandage tightly round the arm. 'There, now you should eat, but not too much, you're over-weary to make the best use of it. Here's meat and cheese and bread, and keep some by you for morning, you may well be ravenous when you wake.'

'If there's water left,' besought the young man meekly, 'I should like to wash my hands and face. I'm foul!'

Godith knelt beside him, moistened a piece of linen in the pitcher, and instead of putting it into his hand, very earnestly and thoroughly did it for him, putting back the matted hair

245

from his forehead, which was wide and candid, even teasing out some of the knots with solicitous fingers. After the first surprise he lay quietly and submissively under her ministering touch, but his eyes, cleansed of the soiled shadows, watched her face as she bent over him, and grew larger and larger in respectful wonder. And all this while she had hardly said a word.

The young man was almost too worn out to eat at all, and flagged very soon. He lay for a few moments with lids drooping, peering at his rescuers in silent thought. Then he said, his tongue stumbling sleepily: 'I owe you a name, after all you've done for me ...'

'Tomorrow,' said Cadfael firmly. 'You're in the best case to sleep sound, and here I believe you may. Now drink this down – it helps keep wounds from festering, and eases the heart.' It was a strong cordial of his own brewing, he tucked away the empty vial in his gown. 'And here's a little flask of wine to bear you company if you wake. In the morning I'll be with you early.'

'We!' said Godith, low but firmly.

'Wait, one more thing!' Cadfael had remembered it at the last moment. 'You've no weapon on you – yet I think you did wear a sword.'

'I shed it,' mumbled the boy drowsily, 'in the river. I had too much weight to keep afloat – and they were shooting. It was in the water I got this clout ... I had the wit to go down, I hope they believe I stayed down ... God knows it was touch and go!'

'Yes, well, tomorrow will do. And we must find you a weapon. Now, good night!'

He was asleep before ever they put out the candle, and drew the door closed. They walked wordlessly through the rustling stubble for some minutes, the sky over them an arch of dark and vivid blue paling at the edges into a fringe of sea-green. Godith asked abruptly: 'Brother Cadfael, who was Ganymede?'

'A beautiful youth who was cup-bearer to Jove, and much loved by him.'

'Oh!' said Godith, uncertain whether to be delighted or rueful, this success being wholly due to her boyishness.

'But some say that it's also another name for Hebe,' said Cadfael.

'Oh! And who is Hebe?'

'Cup-bearer to Jove, and much loved by him – but a beautiful maiden.'

'Ah!' said Godith profoundly. And as they reached the road and crossed towards the abbey, she said seriously: 'You know who he must be, don't you?'

'Jove? The most god-like of all the pagan gods ...'

'*He!*' she said severely, and caught and shook Brother Cadfael's arm in her solemnity. 'A Saxon name, and Saxon hair, and on the run from the king's men ... He's Torold Blund, who set out with Nicholas to save FitzAlan's treasury for the empress. And of course he had nothing to do with poor Nicholas's death. I don't believe he ever did a shabby thing in his whole life!'

'That,' said Cadfael, 'I hesitate to say of any man, least of all myself. But I give you my word, child, this one most shabby thing he certainly did not do. You may sleep in peace!'

It was nothing out of the ordinary for Brother Cadfael, that devoted gardener and apothecary, to rise long before it was necessary for Prime, and have an hour's work done before he joined his brothers at the first service; so no one thought anything of it when he dressed and went out early on that particular morning, and no one even knew that he also roused his boy, as he had promised. They went out with more medicaments and food, and a cotte and hose that Brother Cadfael had filched from the charity offerings that came in to the almoner. Godith had taken away with her the young man's bloodstained shirt, which was of fine linen and not to be wasted, had washed it before she slept, and mended it on rising, where the arrow-head had sliced the threads asunder. On such a warm August night, spread out carefully on the bushes in the garden, it had dried well.

Their patient was sitting up in his bed of sacks, munching bread with appetite, and seemed to have total trust in them, for he made no move to seek cover when the door began to open. He had draped his torn and stained cotte round his shoulders, but for the rest was naked under his blanket, and the bared, smooth chest and narrow flanks were elegantly formed. Body and eyes still showed blue bruises, but he was certainly much restored after one long night of rest.

'Now,' said Cadfael with satisfaction, 'you may talk as much as you like, my friend, while I dress this wound of yours. The leg will do very well until we have more time, but this shoulder is a tricky thing. Godric, see to him on the other side while I uncover it, it may well stick. You steady bandage and arm while I unbind. Now, sir ...' And he added, for fair exchange: 'They call me Brother Cadfael, I'm as Welsh as Dewi Sant, and

247

I've been about the world, as you may have guessed. And this boy of mine is Godric, as you've heard, and brought me to you. Trust us both, or neither.'

'I trust both,' said the boy. He had more colour this morning, or it was the flush of dawn reflected, his eyes were bright and hazel, more green than brown. 'I owe you more than trust can pay, but show me more I can do, and I'll do it. My name is Torold Blund, I come from a hamlet by Oswestry, and I'm FitzAlan's man from head to foot.' The bandage stuck then, and Godith felt him flinch, and locked the fold until she could ease it free by delicate touches. 'If that puts you in peril,' said Torold, suppressing the pain, 'I do believe I'm fit to go, and go I will. I would not for the world shrug off my danger upon you.'

'You'll go when you're let,' said Godith, and for revenge snatched off the last fold of bandage, but very circumspectly, and holding the anointed pad in place. 'And it won't be today.'

'Hush, let him talk, time's short,' said Cadfael. 'Go to it, lad. We're not in the business of selling Maud's men to Stephen, or Stephen's men to Maud. How did you come here in this pass?'

Torold took a deep breath, and talked to some purpose. 'I came to the castle here with Nicholas Faintree, who was also FitzAlan's man, from the next manor to my father's, we joined the garrison only a week before it fell. The evening before the assault there was a council – we were not there, we were small fry – and they resolved to get the FitzAlan treasury away the very next day for the use of the empress, not knowing then it would be the last day. Nicholas and I were told off to be the messengers because we were new to Shrewsbury, and not known, and might get through well enough where others senior to us might be known and cut down at sight. The goods – they were not too bulky, thank God, not much plate, more coin, and most of all in jewellery – were hidden somewhere no one knew but our lord and his agent who had them in guard. We had to ride to him when the word was given, take them from where he would show us, and get clear by night for Wales. FitzAlan had an accord with Owain Gwynedd – not that he's for either party here, he's for Wales, but civil war here suits him well, and he and FitzAlan are friends. Before it was well dawn they attacked, and it was plain we could not hold. So we were sent off on our errand – it was to a shop in the town ...' He wavered, uneasy at giving any clue.

'I know,' said Cadfael, wiping away the exudation of the

248

night from the shoulder wound, and anointing a new pad. 'It was Edric Flesher, who himself has told me his part in it. You were taken out to his barn in Frankwell, and the treasury laid up with you to wait for the cover of night. Go on!'

The young man, watching the dressing of his own hurts without emotion, went on obediently: 'We rode as soon as it was dark. From there clear of the suburb and into trees is only a short way. There's a herdsman's hut there in the piece where the track is in woodland, though only along the edge, the fields still close. We were on this stretch when Nick's horse fell lame. I lighted down to see, for he went very badly, and he had picked up a caltrop, and was cut to the bone.'

'Caltrops?' said Brother Cadfael, startled. 'On such a forest path, away from any field of battle?' For those unobtrusive martial cruelties, made in such a shape as to be scattered under the hooves of cavalry, and leaving always one crippling spike upturned, surely had no part to play on a narrow forest ride.

'Caltrops,' said Torold positively. 'I don't speak simply from the wound, the thing was there embedded, I know, I wrenched it out. But the poor beast was foundered, he could go, but not far, and not loaded. There's a farm I know of very close there, I thought I could get a fresh horse in exchange for Nick's, a poor exchange, but what could we do? We did not even unload, but Nick lighted down, to ease the poor creature of his weight, and said he would wait there in the hut for me. And I went, and I got a mount from the farm – it's off to the right, heading west as we were, the man's name is Ulf, he's distant kin to me on my mother's side – and rode back, with Nick's half the load on this new nag.

'I came up towards the hut,' he said, stiffening at the recollection, 'and I thought he would be looking out for me, ready to mount, and he was not. I don't know why that made me so uneasy. Not a breath stirring, and for all I was cautious, I knew I could be heard by any man truly listening. And he never showed face or called out word. So I never went too near. I drew off, and reined forward a little way, and made a single tether of the horses, to be off as fast as might be. One knot to undo, and with a single pluck. And then I went to the hut.'

'It was full dark then?' asked Cadfael, rolling bandage.

'Full dark, but I could see, having been out in it. Inside it was black as pitch. The door stood half open to the wall. I went inside stretching my ears, and not a murmur. But in the middle of the hut I fell over him. Over Nick! If I hadn't I might not be here to tell as much,' said Torold grimly, and cast a sudden uneasy glance at his Ganymede, so plainly some years his junior, and attending him with such sedulous devotion. 'This is not good hearing.' His eyes appealed eloquently to Cadfael over Godith's shoulder.

'You'd best go on freely,' said Cadfael with sympathy. 'He's deeper in this than you think, and will have your blood and mine if we dare try to banish him. No part of this matter of Shrewsbury has been good hearing, but something may be saved. Tell your part, we'll tell ours.'

Godith, all eyes, ears and serviceable hands, wisely said nothing at all.

'He was dead,' said Torold starkly. 'I fell on him, mouth to mouth, there was no breath in him. I held him, reaching forward to save myself as I fell, I had him in my arms and he was like an armful of rags. And then I heard the dry fodder rustle behind me, and started round, because there was no wind to stir it, and I was frightened ...'

'Small blame!' said Cadfael, smoothing a fresh pad soaked in his herbal salve against the moist wound. 'You had good reason. Trouble no more for your friend, he is with God surely. We buried him yesterday within the abbey. He has a prince's tomb. You, I think, escaped the like very narrowly, when his murderer lunged from behind the door.'

'So I think, too,' said the boy, and drew in hissing breath at the bite of Cadfael's dressing. 'There he must have been. The grass warned me when he made his assay. I don't know how it is, every man throws up his right arm to ward off blows from his head, and so did I. His cord went round my wrist as well as my throat. I was not clever or a hero, I lashed out in fright and jerked it out of his hands. It brought him down on top of me in the dark. I know only too well,' he said, defensively, 'that you may not believe me.'

'There are things that go to confirm you. Spare to be so wary of your friends. So you were man to man, at least, better odds than before. How did you escape him?'

'More by luck than valour,' said Torold ruefully. 'We were rolling about in the hay, wrestling and trying for each other's throat, everything by feel and nothing by sight, and neither of us could get space or time to draw, for I don't know how long, but I suppose it was no more than minutes. What ended it was that there must have been an old manger there against the wall, half fallen to pieces, and I banged my head against one of the boards lying loose in the hay. I hit him with it, two-handed, and he dropped. I doubt I did him any lasting damage, but it knocked him witless long enough for me to run, and run I did, and loosed both the horses, and made off westward like a hunted hare. I still had work to do, and there was no one but me left to do it, or I might have stayed to try and even the account for Nick. Or I might not,' owned Torold with scowling honesty. 'I doubt I was even thinking about FitzAlan's errand then, though I'm thinking of it now, and have been ever since. I ran for my life. I was afraid he might have had others lying in ambush to come to his aid. All I wanted was out of there as fast as my legs would go.'

'No need to make a penance of it,' said Cadfael mildly, securing his bandage. 'Sound sense is something to be glad of, not ashamed. But my friend, it's taken you two full days, by your own account, to get to much the same spot you started from. I take it, by that, the king has allies pretty thick between here and Wales, at least by the roads.'

'Thick as bees in swarm! I got well forward by the more northerly road, and all but ran my head into a patrol where there was no passing. They were stopping everything that moved, what chance had I with two horses and a load of valuables? I had to draw off into the woods, and by that time it was getting light, there was nothing to be done but lie up until dark again and try the southerly road. And that was no better, they had loose companies ranging the countryside by then. I thought I might make my way through by keeping off the roads and close to the curve of the river, but it was another night lost. I lay up in a copse on the hill all day Thursday, and tried again by night, and that was when they winded me, four or five of them, and I had to run for it, with only one way to run, down towards the river. They had me penned, I couldn't get out of the trap. I took the saddle-bags from both horses, and turned the beasts loose, and started them off at a panic gallop, hoping they'd crash through and lead the pursuit away from me, but there was one of the fellows too near, he saw the trick, and made for me instead. He gave me this slash in the thigh, and his yell brought the others running. There was only one thing to do. I took to the water, saddle-bags and all. I'm a strong swimmer, but with that weight it was hard work to stay afloat, and let the current bring me downstream. That's when they started shooting. Dark as it was, they'd been out in it long

251

enough to have fair vision, and there's always light from the water when there's something moving in it. So I got this shoulder wound, and had the sense to go under and stay under as long as I had breath. Severn's fast, even in summer water it carried me down well. They followed along the bank for a while, and loosed one or two more arrows, but then I think they were sure I was under for good. I worked my way towards the bank as soon as it seemed safe, to get a foot to ground and draw breath here and there, but I stayed in the water. I knew the bridge would be manned, I dared not drag myself ashore until I was well past. It was high time by then. I remember crawling into the bushes, but not much else, except rousing just enough to be afraid to stir when your people came reaping. And then Godric here found me. And that's the truth of it,' he ended firmly, and looked Cadfael unblinkingly in the eye.

'But not the whole truth,' said Cadfael, placidly enough. 'Godric found no saddle-bags along with you.' He eyed the young face that fronted him steadily, lips firmly closed, and smiled. 'No, never fret, we won't question you. You are the sole custodian of FitzAlan's treasury, and what you've done with it, and how, God knows, you ever managed to do anything sensible with it in your condition, that's your affair. You haven't the air of a courier who has failed in his mission, I'll say that for you. And for your better peace, all the talk in the town is that FitzAlan and Adeney were not taken, but broke out of the ring and are got clean away. Now we have to leave you alone here until afternoon, we have duties, too. But one of us, or both, will come and see how you're faring then. And here's food and drink, and clothes I hope will fit you well enough to pass. But lie quiet for today, you're not your own man yet, however wholeheartedly you may be FitzAlan's.'

Godith laid the washed and mended shirt on top of the folded garments, and was following Cadfael to the door when the look on Torold's face halted her, half uneasy, half triumphant. His eyes grew round with amazement as he stared at the crisp, clean linen, and the fine stitches of the long mend where the blood-stained gash had been. A soft whistle of admiration saluted the wonder.

'Holy Mary! Who did this? Do you keep an expert seamstress within the abbey walls? Or did you pray for a miracle?'

'That? That's Godric's work,' said Cadfael, not altogether innocently, and walked out into the early sunshine, leaving

252

Godith flushed to the ears. 'We learn more skills in the cloister than merely cutting wheat and brewing cordials,' she said loftily, and fled after Cadfael.

But she was grave enough on the way back, going over in her mind Torold's story, and reflecting how easily he might have died before ever she met him; not merely once, in the murderer's cord, nor the second time from King Stephen's roaming companies, but in the river, or from his wounds in the bushes. It seemed to her that divine grace was taking care of him, and had provided her as the instrument. There remained lingering anxieties.

'Brother Cadfael, you do believe him?'

'I believe him. What he could not tell truth about, he would not lie about, either. Why, what's on your mind still?'

'Only that before I saw him I said – I was afraid the companion who rode with Nicholas was far the most likely to be tempted to kill him. How simple it would have been! But you said yesterday, you *did* say, he did not do it. Are you quite sure? How do you know?'

'Nothing simpler, girl dear! The mark of the strangler's cord is on his neck and on his wrist. Did you not understand those thin scars? He was meant to go after his friend out of this world. No, you need have no fear on that score, what he told us is truth. But there may be things he could not tell us, things we ought to discover, for Nicholas Faintree's sake. Godith, this afternoon, when you've seen to the lotions and wines, you may leave the garden and go and keep him company if you please, and I'll come there as soon as I can. There are things I must look into, over there on the Frankwell side of Shrewsbury.'

Chapter Six

 ROM THE Frankwell end of the western bridge, the
suburb outside the walls and over the river, the road
set off due west, climbing steadily, leaving behind
the gardens that fringed the settlement. At first it
was but a single road mounting the hill that rose high above
Severn, then shortly it branched into two, of which the more
southerly soon branched again, three spread fingers pointing
into Wales. But Cadfael took the road Nicholas and Torold
had taken on the night after the castle fell, the most northerly
of the three.

He had thought of calling on Edric Flesher in the town, and
giving him the news that one, at least, of the two young
couriers had survived and preserved his charge, but then he
had decided against it. As yet Torold was by no means safe,
and until he was well away, the fewer people who knew of his
whereabouts the better, the less likely was word of him to slip
out in the wrong place, where his enemies might overhear.
There would be time later to share any good news with Edric
and Petronilla.

The road entered the thick woodland of which Torold had
spoken, and narrowed into a grassy track, within the trees but
keeping close to the edge, where cultivated fields showed
between the trunks. And there, withdrawn a little deeper into
the woods, lay the hut, low and roughly timbered. From this
place it would be a simple matter to carry a dead body on
horseback as far as the castle ditch. The river, as everywhere

here, meandered in intricate coils, and would have to be crossed in order to reach the place where the dead had been flung, but there was a place opposite the castle on this side where a central island made the stream fordable even on foot in such a dry season, once the castle itself was taken. The distance was small, the night had been long enough. Then somewhere off to the right lay Ulf's holding, where Torold had got his exchange of horses. Cadfael turned off in that direction, and found the croft not a quarter of a mile from the track.

Ulf was busy gleaning after carrying his corn, and not at first disposed to be talkative to an unknown monk, but the mention of Torold's name, and the clear intimation that here was someone Torold had trusted, loosened his tongue.

'Yes, he did come with a lamed horse, and I did let him have the best of mine in exchange. I was the gainer, though, even so, for the beast he left with me came from FitzAlan's stables. He's still lame, but healing. Would you see him? His fine gear is well hidden, it would mark him out for stolen or worse if it was seen.'

Even without his noble harness the horse, a tall roan, showed suspiciously fine for a working farmer to possess, and undoubtedly he was still lame of one fore-foot. Ulf showed him the wound.

'Torold said a caltrop did this,' mused Cadfael. 'Strange place to find such.'

'Yet a caltrop it was, for I have it, and several more like it that I went and combed out of the grass there next day. My beasts cross there, I wanted no more of them lamed. Someone seeded a dozen yards of the path at its narrowest there. To halt them by the hut, what else?'

'Someone who knew in advance what they were about and the road they'd take, and gave himself plenty of time to lay his trap, and wait in ambush for them to spring it.'

'The king had got wind of the matter somehow,' Ulf opined darkly, 'and sent some of his men secretly to get hold of whatever they were carrying. He's desperate for money – as bad as the other side.'

Nevertheless, thought Cadfael, as he walked back to the hut in the woods, for all that I can see, this was no party sent out by the king, but one man's enterprise for his own private gain. If he had indeed been the king's emissary he would have had a company with him. It was not King Stephen's coffers that were to have profited, if all had gone according to plan.

To sum up, then, it was proven there had indeed been a third here that night. Over and over Torold was cleared of blame. The caltrops were real, a trail of them had been laid to ensure laming one or other of the horses, and so far the stratagem had succeeded, perhaps even better than expected, since it had severed the two companions, leaving the murderer free to deal with one first, and then lie in wait for the other.

Cadfael did not at once go into the hut; the surroundings equally interested him. Somewhere here, well clear of the hut itself, Torold had regarded the pricking of his thumbs, and tethered the horses forward on the road, ready for flight. And somewhere here, too, probably withdrawn deeper into cover, the third man had also had a horse in waiting. It should still be possible to find their traces. It had not rained since that night, nor was it likely that many men had roamed these woods since. All the inhabitants of Shrewsbury were still keeping close under their own roof-trees unless forced to go abroad, and the king's patrols rode in the open, where they could ride fast.

It took him a little while, but he found both places. The solitary horse had been hobbled and left to graze, and by the signs he had been a fine creature, for the hoof-marks he had left in a patch of softer ground, a hollow of dried mud where water habitually lay after rain, and had left a smooth silt, showed large and well shod. The spot where two had waited together was well to westward of the hut, and in thick cover. A low branch showed the peeled scar where the tether had been pulled clear in haste, and two distinguishable sets of prints could be discerned where the grass thinned to bare ground.

Cadfael went into the hut. He had broad daylight to aid him, and with the door set wide there was ample light even within. The murderer had waited here for his victim, he must have left his traces.

The remains of the winter fodder, mown along the sunlit fringes of the woods, had been left here against the return of autumn, originally in a neat stack against the rear wall, but now a stormy sea of grass was spread and tossed over the entire earthen floor, as though a gale had played havoc within. The decrepit manger from which Torold had plucked his loose plank was there, drunkenly leaning. The dry grass was well laced with small herbs now rustling and dead but still fragrant, and there was a liberal admixture of hooky, clinging goose-grass in it. That reminded him not only of the shred of stem dragged deep into Nick Faintree's throat by the ligature

256

that killed him, but also of Torold's ugly shoulder wound. He needed goose-grass to make a dressing for it, he would look along the fringe of the fields, it must be plentiful here. God's even-handed justice, that called attention to one friend's murder with a dry stem of last year's crop, might well, by the same token, design to soothe and heal the other friend's injuries by the gift of this year's.

Meantime, the hut yielded little, except the evident chaos of a hand-to-hand struggle waged within it. But in the rough timbers behind the door there were a few roving threads of deep blue woollen cloth, rather pile than thread. Someone had certainly lain in hiding there, the door drawn close to his body. There was also one clot of dried clover that bore a smaller clot of blood. But Cadfael raked and combed in vain among the rustling fodder in search of the strangler's weapon. Either the murderer had found it again and taken it away with him, or else it lay deeply entangled in some corner, evading search. Cadfael worked his way backwards on hands and knees from the manger to the doorway, and was about to give up, and prise himself up from his knees, when the hand on which he supported his weight bore down on something hard and sharp, and winced from the contact in surprise. Something was driven half into the earth floor under the thinning layers of hay, like another caltrop planted here for inquisitive monks to encounter to their grief and injury. He sat back on his heels, and carefully brushed aside the rustling grasses, until he could get a hand to the hidden thing and prise it loose. It came away into his hand readily, filling his palm, hard, encrusted and chill. He lifted it to the invading sunlight in the doorway behind him, and it glittered with pinpoints of yellow, a miniature sun.

Brother Cadfael rose from his knees and took it into the full daylight of afternoon to see what he had found. It was a large, rough-cut gem stone, as big as a crab-apple, a deep-yellow topaz still gripped and half-enclosed by an eagle's talon of silver-gilt. The claw was complete, finely shaped, but broken off at the stem, below the stone it clutched. This was the tip of some excellent setting in silver, perhaps the end of a brooch-pin – no, too large for that. The apex of a dagger-hilt? If so, a noble dagger, no common working knife. Beneath that jagged tip would have been the rounded hand-grip, and on the cross-piece, perhaps, some smaller topaz stones to match this master-stone. Broken off thus, it lay in his hand a sullen, faceted ball of gold.

One man had threshed and clawed here in his death-throes, two others had rolled and flailed in mortal combat; any one of the three, with a thrusting hip and the weight of a convulsed body, could have bored this hilt into the hard-packed earth of the floor, and snapped off the crown-stone thus at its most fragile point, and never realised the loss.

Brother Cadfael put it away carefully in the scrip at his girdle, and went to look for his goose-grass. In the thick herbage at the edge of the trees, where the sun reached in, he found sprawling, angular mats of it, filled his scrip, and set off for home with dozens of the little hooked seeds clinging in his skirts.

Godith slipped away as soon as all the brothers had dispersed to their afternoon work, and made her way by circumspect deviations to the mill at the end of the Gaye. She had taken with her some ripe plums from the orchard, the half of a small loaf of new bread, and a fresh flask of Cadfael's wine. The patient had rapidly developed a healthy appetite, and it was her pleasure to enjoy his enjoyment of food and drink, as though she had a proprietorial interest in him by reason of having found him in need.

He was sitting on his bed of sacks, fully dressed, his back against the warm timbers of the wall, his long legs stretched out comfortably before him with ankles crossed. The cotte and hose fitted reasonably well, perhaps a little short in the sleeves. He looked surprisingly lively, though still rather greyish in the face, and careful in his movements because of the lingering aches and pains from his wounds. She was not best pleased to see that he had struggled into the cotte, and said so.

'You should keep that shoulder easy, there was no need to force it into a sleeve yet. If you don't rest it, it won't heal.'

'I'm very well,' he said abstractedly. 'And I must bear whatever discomfort there may be, if I'm to get on my way soon. It will knit well enough, I dare say.' His mind was not on his own ills, he was frowning thoughtfully over other matters. 'Godric, I had no time to question, this morning, but – your Brother Cadfael said Nick's buried, and in the abbey. Is that truth?' He was not so much doubting their word as marvelling how it had come about. 'How did they ever find him?'

'That was Brother Cadfael's own doing,' said Godith. She sat down beside him and told him. 'There was one more than there should have been, and Brother Cadfael would not rest until he had found the one who was different, and since then he has not let anyone else rest. The king knows there was murder done, and has said it should be avenged. If anyone can get justice for your friend, Brother Cadfael is the man.'

'So whoever it was, there in the hut, it seems I did him little harm, only dimmed his wits for a matter of minutes. I was afraid of it. He was fit enough and cunning enough to get rid of his dead man before morning.'

'But not clever enough to deceive Brother Cadfael. Every individual soul must be accounted for. Now at least Nicholas has had all the rites of the church in his own clean name, and has a noble tomb.'

'I'm glad,' said Torold, 'to know he was not left there to rot unhonoured, or put into the ground nameless among all the rest, though they were our comrades, too, and not deserving of such a death. If we had stayed, we should have suffered the same fate. If they caught me, I might suffer it yet. And yet King Stephen approves the hunt for the murderer who did his work for him! What a mad world!'

Godith thought so, too; but for all that, there was a difference, a sort of logic in it, that the king should accept the onus of the ninety-four whose deaths he had decreed, but utterly reject the guilt for the ninety-fifth, killed treacherously and without his sanction.

'He despised the manner of the killing, and he resented being made an accomplice in it. And no one is going to capture you,' she said firmly, and hoisted the plums out of the breast of her cotte, and tumbled them between them on the blanket. 'Here's a taste of something sweeter than bread. Try them!'

They sat companionably eating, and slipping the stones through a chink in the floorboards into the river below. 'I still have a task laid on me,' said Torold at length, soberly, 'and now I'm alone to see it done. And heaven knows, Godric, what I should have done without you and Brother Cadfael, and sad I shall be to set off and leave you behind, with small chance of seeing you again. Never shall I forget what you've done for me. But go I must, as soon as I'm fit and can get clear. It will be better for you when I'm gone, you'll be safer so.'

'Who is safe? Where?' said Godith, biting into another ripe purple plum. 'There is no safe place.'

'There are degrees in danger, at any rate. And I have work to do, and I'm fit to get on with it now.'

She turned and gave him a long, roused look. Never until

that moment had she looked far enough ahead to confront the idea of his departure. He was something she had only newly discovered, and here he was, unless she was mistaking his meaning, threatening to take himself off, out of her hands and out of her life. Well, she had an ally in Brother Cadfael. With the authority of her master she said sternly: 'If you're thinking you're going to set off anywhere until you're fully healed, then think again, and smartly, too. You'll stay here until you're given leave to go, and that won't be today, or tomorrow, you can make up your mind to that!'

Torold gaped at her in startled and delighted amusement, laid his head back against the rough timber of the wall, and laughed aloud. 'You sound like my mother, the time I had a bad fall at the quintain. And dearly I love you, but so I did her, and I still went my own way. I'm fit and strong and able, Godric, and I'm under orders that came before your orders. I must go. In my place, you'd have been out of here before now, as fierce as you are.'

'I would not,' she said furiously, 'I have more sense. What use would you be, on the run from here, without even a weapon, without a horse – you turned your horses loose, remember, to baffle the pursuit, you told us so! How far would you get? And how grateful would FitzAlan be for your folly? Not that we need go into it,' she said loftily, 'seeing you're not fit even to walk out of here as far as the river. You'd be carried back on Brother Cadfael's shoulders, just as you came here the first time.'

'Oh, would I so, Godric, my little cousin?' Torold's eyes were sparkling mischief. He had forgotten for the moment all his graver cares, amused and nettled by the impudence of this urchin, vehemently threatening him with humiliation and failure. 'Do I look to you so feeble?'

'As a starving cat,' she said, and plunged a plum-stone between the boards with a vicious snap. 'A ten-year-old could lay you on your back!'

'You think so, do you?' Torold rolled sideways and took her about the middle in his good arm. 'I'll show you, Master Godric, whether I'm fit or no! He was laughing for pure pleasure, feeling his muscles stretch and exult again in a sudden, sweet bout of horseplay with a trusted familiar, who needed taking down a little for everyone's good. He reached his wounded arm to pin the boy down by the shoulders. The arrogant imp had uttered only one muffled squeak as he was tipped on his back. 'One hand of mine can more than deal with you, my lovely lad!' crowed Torold, withdrawing half his weight, and flattening his left palm firmly in the breast of the over-ample cotte, to demonstrate.

He recoiled, stricken and enlightened, just as Godith got breath enough to swear at him, and strike out furiously with her right hand, catching him a salutary box on the ear. They fell apart in a huge, ominous silence, and sat up among the rumpled sacks with a yard or more between them.

The silence and stillness lasted long. It was a full minute before they so much as tilted cautious heads and looked sidewise at each other. Her profile, warily emerging from anger into guilty sympathy, was delicate and pert and utterly feminine, he must have been weak and sick indeed, or he would surely have known. The soft, gruff voice was only an ambiguous charm, a natural deceit. Torold scrubbed thoughtfully at his stinging ear, and asked at last, very carefully: 'Why didn't you tell me? I never meant to offend you, but how was I to know?'

'There was no need for you to know,' snapped Godith, still ruffled, 'if you'd had the sense to do as you're bid, or the courtesy to treat your friends gently.'

'But you goaded me! Good God,' protested Torold, 'it was only the rough play I'd have used on a young brother of my own, and you asked for it.' He demanded suddenly: 'Does Brother Cadfael know?'

'Of course he does! Brother Cadfael at least can tell a hart from a hind.'

There fell a second and longer silence, full of resentment, curiosity and caution, while they continued to study each other through lowered lashes, she furtively eyeing the sleeve that covered his wound, in case a telltale smear of blood should break through, he surveying again the delicate curves of her face, the jut of lip and lowering of brows that warned him she was still offended.

Two small, wary voices uttered together, grudgingly: 'Did I hurt you?'

They began to laugh at the same instant, suddenly aware of their own absurdity. The illusion of estrangement vanished utterly; they fell into each other's arms helpless with laughter, and nothing was left to complicate their relationship but the slightly exaggerated gentleness with which they touched each other.

261

'But you shouldn't have used that arm so,' she reproached at last, as they disentangled themselves and sat back, eased and content. 'You could have started it open again, it's a bad gash.'

'Oh, no, there's no damage. But you – I wouldn't for the world have vexed you.' And he asked, quite simply, and certain of his right to be told: 'Who are you? And how did you ever come into such a coil as this?'

She turned her head and looked at him long and earnestly; there would never again be anything with which she would hesitate to trust him.

'They left it too late,' she said, 'to send me away out of Shrewsbury before the town fell. This was a desperate throw, turning me into an abbey servant, but I was sure I could carry it off. And I did, with everyone but Brother Cadfael. *You* were taken in, weren't you? I'm a fugitive of your party, Torold, we're two of a kind. I'm Godith Adeney.'

'Truly?' He beamed at her, round-eyed with wonder and delight. 'You're Fulke Adeney's daughter? Praise God! We were anxious for you! Nick especially, for he knew you ... I never saw you till now, but I, too ...' He stooped his fair head and lightly kissed the small, none too clean hand that had just picked up the last of the plums. 'Mistress Godith, I am your servant to command! This is splendid! If I'd known, I'd have told you better than half a tale.'

'Tell me now,' said Godith, and generously split the plum in half, and sent the stone whirling down into the Severn. The riper half she presented to his open mouth, effectively closing it for a moment. 'And then,' she said, 'I'll tell you my side of it, and we shall have a useful whole.'

Brother Cadfael did not go straight to the mill on his return, but halted to check that his workshop was in order, and to pound up his goose-grass in a mortar, and prepare a smooth green salve from it. Then he went to join his young charges, careful to circle into the shadow of the mill from the opposite direction, and to keep an eye open for any observer. Time was marching all too swiftly, within an hour he and Godith would have to go back for Vespers.

They had both known his step; when he entered they were sitting side by side with backs propped against the wall, watching the doorway with rapt, expectant smiles. They had a certain serene, aloof air about them, as though they inhabited a world immune from common contacts or common cares, but generously accessible to him. He had only to look at them, and he knew they had no more secrets; they were so rashly and candidly man and woman together that there was no need even to ask anything. Though they were both waiting expectantly to tell him!

'Brother Cadfael ...' Godith began, distantly radiant.

'First things first,' said Cadfael briskly. 'Help him out of cotte and shirt, and start unwinding the bandage until it sticks – as it will, my friend, you're not out of the wood yet. Then wait, and I'll ease it off.'

There was no disconcerting or chastening them. The girl was up in a moment, easing the seam of the cotte away from Torold's wound, loosening the ties of his shirt to slip it down from his shoulder, gently freeing the end of the linen bandage and beginning to roll it up. The boy inclined this way and that to help, and never took his eyes from Godith's face, as she seldom took hers from his absorbed countenance, and only to concentrate upon his needs.

'Well, well!' thought Cadfael philosophically. 'It seems Hugh Beringar will seek his promised bride to little purpose – if, indeed, he really is seeking her?'

'Well, youngster,' he said aloud, 'you're a credit to me and to yourself, as clean-healing flesh as ever I saw. This slice of you that somebody tried to sever will stay with you lifelong, after all, and the arm will even serve you to hold a bow in a month or so. But you'll have the scar as long as you live. Now hold steady, this may burn, but trust me, it's the best salve you could have for green wounds. Torn muscles hurt as they knit, but knit they will.'

'It doesn't hurt,' said Torold in a dream. 'Brother Cadfael ...'

'Hold your tongue until we have you all bound up trim. Then you can talk your hearts out, the both of you.'

And talk they did, as soon as Torold was helped back into his shirt, and the cotte draped over his shoulders. Each of them took up the thread from the other, as though handed it in a fixed and formal ceremony, like a favour in a dance. Even their voices had grown somehow alike, as if they matched tones without understanding that they did it. They had not the least idea, as yet, that they were in love. The innocents believed they were involved in a partisan comradeship, which was but the lesser half of what had happened to them in his absence.

'So I have told Torold all about myself,' said Godith, 'and he has told me the only thing he did not tell us before. And now he wants to tell you.'

Torold picked up the tendered thread willingly. 'I have FitzAlan's treasury safely hidden,' he said simply. 'I had it in two pairs of linked saddle-bags, and I kept it afloat, too, all down the river, though I had to shed sword and sword-belt and dagger and all to lighten the load. I fetched up under the first arch of the stone bridge. You'll know it as well as I. That first pier spreads, there used to be a boat-mill moored under it, some time ago, and the mooring chain is still there, bolted to a ring in the stone. A man can hold on there and get his breath, and so I did. And I hauled up the chain and hooked my saddle-bags on to it, and let them down under the water, out of sight. Then I left them there, and drifted on down here just about alive, to where Godith found me.' He found no difficulty in speaking of her as Godith; the name had a jubilant sound in his mouth. 'And there all that gold is dangling in the Severn still, I hope and believe, until I can reclaim it and get it away to its rightful owner. Thank God he's alive to benefit by it.' A last qualm shook him suddenly and severely. 'There's been no word of anyone finding it?' he questioned anxiously. 'We should know if they had?'

'We should know, never doubt it! No, no one's hooked any such fish. Why should anyone look for it there? But getting it out again undetected may not be so easy. We three must put our wits together,' said Cadfael, 'and see what we can do between us. And while you two have been swearing your alliance, let me tell you what I've been doing.'

He made it brief enough. 'I found all as you told it. The traces of your horses are there, and of your enemy's, too. One horse only. This was a thief bent on his own enrichment, no zealot trying to fill the king's coffers. He had seeded the path for you liberally with caltrops, your kinsman collected several of them next day, for the sake of his own cattle. The signs of your struggle within the hut are plain enough. And pressed into the earth floor I found this.' He produced it from his scrip, a lump of deep yellow roughly faceted, and clenched in the broken silver-gilt claw. Torold took it from him and examined it curiously, but without apparent recognition.

'Broken off from a hilt, would you think?'

'Not from yours, then?'

'Mine?' Torold laughed. 'Where would a poor squire with his way to make get hold of so fine a weapon as this must have

264

been? No, mine was a plain old sword my grandsire wore before me, and a dagger to match, in a heavy hide sheath. If it had been light as this, I'd have tried to keep it. No, this is none of mine.'

'Nor Faintree's, either?'

Torold shook his head decidedly. 'If he had any such, I should have known. Nick and I are of the same condition, and friends three years and more.' He looked up intently into Brother Cadfael's face. 'Now I remember a very small thing that may have meaning, after all. When I broke free and left the other fellow dazed, I trod on something under the hay where we'd been struggling, a small, hard thing that almost threw me. I think it could well have been this. It was *his*? Yes, it must have been his! Snapped off against the ground as we rolled.'

'His, almost certainly, and the only thing we have to lead us to him,' said Cadfael, taking back the stone and hiding it again from view in his pouch. 'No man would willingly discard so fine a thing because one stone was broken from it. Whoever owned it still has it, and will get it repaired when he dare. If we can find the dagger, we shall have found the murderer.'

'I wish,' said Torold fiercely, 'I could both go and stay! I should be glad to be the one to avenge Nick, he was a good friend to me. But my part is to obey my orders, and get FitzAlan's goods safely over to him in France. And,' he said, regarding Cadfael steadily, 'to take with me also Fulke Adeney's daughter, and deliver her safe to her father. If you will trust her to me.'

'And help us,' added Godith with immense confidence.

'Trust her to you – I might,' said Cadfael mildly. 'And help you both I surely will, as best I can. A very simple matter! All I have to do – and mark you, she has the assurance to demand it of me! – is to conjure you two good horses out of the empty air, where even poor hacks are gold, retrieve your hidden treasure for you, and see you well clear of the town, westward into Wales. Just a trifle! Harder things are done daily by the saints ...'

He had reached this point when he stiffened suddenly, and spread a warning hand to enjoin silence. Listening with ears stretched, he caught for a second time the soft sound of a foot moving warily in the edge of the rustling stubble, close to the open door.

'What is it?' asked Godith in a soundless whisper, her eyes immense in alarm.

'Nothing!' said Cadfael as softly. 'My ears playing tricks.'

And aloud he said: 'Well, you and I must be getting back for Vespers. Come! It wouldn't do to be late.'

Torold accepted his silent orders, and let them go without a word from him. If someone had indeed been listening ... But he had heard nothing, and it seemed to him that even Cadfael was not sure. Why alarm Godith? Brother Cadfael was her best protector here, and once within the abbey walls she would again be in sanctuary. As for Torold, he was his own responsibility, though he would have been happier if he had had a sword!

Brother Cadfael reached down into the capacious waist of his habit, and drew out a long poniard in a rubbed and worn leather scabbard. Silently he put it into Torold's hands. The young man took it, marvelling, staring as reverently as at a first small miracle, so apt was the answer to his thought. He had it by the sheath, the cross of the hilt before his face, and was still gazing in wonder as they went out from him into the evening, and drew the door closed after them. Cadfael took the memory of that look with him into the fresh, saffron air of sunset. He himself must once have worn the same rapt expression, contemplating the same uplifted hilt. When he had taken the Cross, long ago, his vow had been made on that hilt, and the dagger had gone with him to Jerusalem, and roved the eastern seas with him for ten years. Even when he gave up his sword along with the things of this world, and surrendered all pride of possessions, he had kept the poniard. Just as well to part with it at last, to someone who had need of it and would not disgrace it.

He looked about him very cautiously as they rounded the corner of the mill and crossed the race. His hearing was sharp as a wild creature's, and he had heard no whisper or rustle from outside until the last few moments of their talk together, nor could he now be certain that what he had heard was a human foot, it might well have been a small animal slipping through the stubble. All the same, he must take thought for what might happen if they really had been spied upon. Surely, at the worst, only the last few exchanges could have been overheard, though those were revealing enough. Had the treasure been mentioned? Yes, he himself had said that all that was required of him was to obtain two horses, retrieve the treasure, and see them safely headed for Wales. Had anything been said then of *where* the treasure was hidden? No, that had been much earlier. But the listener, if listener there had been, could well have learned that a hunted fugitive of FitzAlan's party was in hiding there, and worse, that Adeney's daughter was being sheltered in the abbey.

This was getting too warm for comfort. Best get them away as soon as the boy was fit to ride. But if this evening passed, and the night, and no move was made to betray them, he would suspect he had been fretting over nothing. There was no one in sight here but a solitary boy fishing, absorbed and distant on the river bank.

'What was it?' asked Godith, meek and attentive beside him. 'Something made you uneasy, I know.'

'Nothing to worry your head about,' said Cadfael. 'I was mistaken. Everything is as it should be.'

From the corner of his eye, at that moment, he caught the sudden movement down towards the river, beyond the clump of bushes where she had found Torold. Out of the meagre cover a slight, agile body unfolded and stood erect, stretching lazily, and drifted at an oblique angle towards the path on which they walked, his course converging with theirs. Hugh Beringar, his stride nicely calculated to look accidental and yet bring him athwart their path at the right moment, showed them a placid and amiable face, recognising Cadfael with pleasure, accepting his attendant boy with benevolence.

'A very fair evening, brother! You're bound for Vespers? So am I. We may walk together?'

'Very gladly,' said Cadfael heartily. He tapped Godith on the shoulder, and handed her the small sacking bundle that held his herbs and dressings. 'Run ahead, Godric, and put these away for me, and come down to Vespers with the rest of the boys. You'll save my legs, and have time to give a stir to that lotion I have been brewing. Go on, child, run!'

And Godith clasped the bundle and ran, taking good care to run like an athletic boy, rattling one hand along the tall stubble, and whistling as she went, glad enough to put herself out of that young man's sight. Her own eyes and mind were full of another young man.

'A most biddable lad you have,' said Hugh Beringar benignly, watching her race ahead.

'A good boy,' said Cadfael placidly, matching him step for step across the field blanched to the colour of cream. 'He has a year's endowment with us, but I doubt if he'll take the cowl. But he'll have learned his letters, and figuring, and a deal about herbs and medicines, it will stand him in good stead. You're at leisure today, my lord?'

'Not so much at leisure,' said Hugh Beringar with equal
serenity, 'as in need of your skills and knowledge. I tried your
garden first, and not finding you there, thought you might have
business today over here in the main gardens and orchard. But
for want of a sight of you anywhere, I sat down to enjoy the
evening sunshine, here by the river. I knew you'd come to
Vespers, but never realised you had fields beyond here. Is all
the corn brought in now?'

'All that we have here. The sheep will be grazing the stubble
very shortly. What was it you wanted of me, my lord? If I may
serve you in accord with my duty, be sure I will.'

'Yesterday morning, Brother Cadfael, I asked you if you
would give any request of mine fair consideration, and you told
me you give fair consideration to all that you do. And I believe
it. I had in mind what was then no more than a rumoured
threat, now it's a real one. I have reason to know that King
Stephen is already making plans to move on, and means to
make sure of his supplies and his mounts. The siege of
Shrewsbury has cost him plenty, and he now has more mouths
to feed and more men to mount. It's not generally known, or
too many would be taking thought to evade it, as I am,' owned
Beringar blithely, 'but he's about to issue orders to have every
homestead in the town searched, and a tithe of all fodder and
provisions in store commandeered for the army's use. And all –
mark that, *all* – the good horses to be found, no matter who
owns them, that are not already in army or garrison service.
The abbey stables will not be exempt.'

This Cadfael did not like at all. It came far too pat, a shrewd
thrust at his own need of horses, and most ominous indication
that Hugh Beringar, who had this information in advance of
the general citizens, might also be as well informed of what
went on in other quarters. Nothing this young man said or did
would ever be quite what it seemed, but whatever game he
played would always be his own game. The less said in reply, at
this stage, the better. Two could play their own games, and
both, possibly, benefit. Let him first say out what he wanted,
even if what he said would have to be scrutinised from all
angles, and subjected to every known test.

'That will be bad news to Brother Prior,' said Cadfael
mildly.

'It's bad news to me,' said Beringar ruefully. 'For I have four
horses in those same abbey stables, and while I might have a

268

claim to retain them all for myself and my men, once the king has given me his commission, I can't make any such claim at this moment with security. It might be allowed, it might not. And to be open with you, I have no intention of letting my two best horses be drafted for the king's army. I want them out of here and in some private place, where they can escape Prestcote's foraging parties, until this flurry is over.'

'Only two?' said Cadfael innocently. 'Why not all?'

'Oh, come, I know you have more cunning than that. Would I be here without horses at all? If they found none of mine, they'd be hunting for all, and small chance I'd have left for royal favour. But let them take the two nags, and they won't question further. Two I can afford. Brother Cadfael, it takes no more than a few days in this place to know that you are the man to take any enterprise in hand, however rough and however risky.' His voice was brisk and bland, even hearty, he seemed to intend no double meanings. 'The lord abbot turns to you when he's faced with an ordeal beyond his powers. I turn to you for practical help. You know all this countryside. Is there a place of safety where my horses can lie up for a few days, until this round-up is over?'

So improbable a proposal Cadfael had not looked for, but it came as manna from heaven. Nor did he hesitate long over taking advantage of it for his own ends. Even if lives had not depended on the provision of those two horses, he was well aware that Beringar was making use of him without scruple, and he need have no scruples about doing as much in return. It went a little beyond that, even, for he had a shrewd suspicion that at this moment Beringar knew far too much of what was going on in his, Cadfael's, mind, and had no objection whatever to any guesses Cadfael might be making as to what was going on in his, Beringar's. Each of us, he thought, has a hold of sorts upon the other, and each of us has a reasonable insight into the other's methods, if not motives. It will be a fair fight. And yet this debonair being might very well be the murderer of Nicholas Faintree. That would be a very different duel, with no quarter asked or offered. In the meantime, make the most of what might or might not be quite accidental circumstances.

'Yes,' said Cadfael, 'I do know of such a place.'

Beringar did not even ask him where, or question his judgement as to whether it would be remote enough and secret enough to be secure. 'Show me the way tonight,' he said outright, and smiled into Cadfael's face. 'It's tonight or never, the order will be made public tomorrow. If you and I can make the return journey on foot before morning, ride with me. Rather you than any!'

Cadfael considered ways and means; there was no need to consider what his answer would be.

'Better get your horses out after Vespers then, out to St Giles. I'll join you there when Compline is over, it will be getting dark then. It wouldn't do for me to be seen riding out with you, but you may exercise your own horses in the evening as the fit takes you.'

'Good!' said Beringar with satisfaction. 'Where is this place? Have we to cross the river anywhere?'

'No, nor even the brook. It's an old grange the abbey used to maintain in the Long Forest, out beyond Pulley. Since the times grew so unchancy we've withdrawn all our sheep and cattle from there, but keep two lay brothers still in the house. No one will look for horses there, they know it's all but abandoned. And the lay brothers will credit what I say.'

'And St Giles is on our way?' It was a chapel of the abbey, away at the eastern end of the Foregate.

'It is. We'll go south to Sutton, and then bear west and into the forest. You'll have three miles or more to walk back by the shorter way. Without horses we may save a mile or so.'

'I think my legs will hold me up for that distance,' said Beringar demurely. 'After Compline, then, at St Giles.' And without any further word or question he left Cadfael's side, lengthening his easy stride to gain ground; for Aline Siward was just emerging from the doorway of her house and turning towards the abbey gateway on her way to church. Before she had gone many yards Beringar was at her elbow; she raised her head and smiled confidingly into his face. A creature quite without guile, but by no means without proper pride or shrewd sense, and she opened like a flower at sight of this young man devious as a serpent, whatever else of good or ill might be said of him. That, thought Cadfael, watching them walk before him in animated conversation, ought to signify something in his favour? Or was it only proof of her childlike trustfulness? Blameless young women have before now been taken in by black-hearted villains, even murderers; and black-hearted villains and murderers have been deeply devoted to blameless young women, contradicting their own nature in this one perverse tenderness.

Cadfael was consoled and cheered by the sight of Godith in

270

church, nobody's fool, nudging and whispering among the boys, and flicking him one rapid, questioning blue glance, which he answered with a reassuring nod and smile. None too well-founded reassurance, but somehow he would make it good. Admirable as Aline was, Godith was the girl for him. She reminded him of Arianna, the Greek boat-girl, long ago, skirts kilted above the knee, short hair a cloud of curls, leaning on her long oar and calling across the water to him …

Ah, well! The age he had been then, young Torold had not even reached yet. These things are for the young. Meantime, tonight after Compline, at St Giles!

Chapter Seven

HE RIDE out through Sutton into the Long Forest, dense and primitive through all but the heathy summits of its fifteen square miles, was like a sudden return visit to aspects of his past, night raids and desperate ambushes once so familiar to him as to be almost tedious, but now, in this shadowy, elderly form, as near excitement as he wished to come. The horse under him was lofty and mettlesome and of high pedigree, he had not been astride such a creature for nearly twenty years, and the flattery and temptation reminded him he was mortal and fallible. Even the young man who rode beside him, accepting his directions without hesitation, reminded him of days past, when exalted and venturesome companions made all labours and privations pleasurable.

Hugh Beringar, once away from the used roads and into the trees and the night shadows, seemed to have no cares in the world, certainly no fear of any treachery on his companion's part. He chattered, even, to pass the time along the way, curious about Brother Cadfael's uncloistral past, and about the countries he had known as well as he knew this forest.

'So you lived in the world all those years, and saw so much of it, and never thought to marry? And half the world women, they say?' The light voice, seemingly idle and faintly mocking, nevertheless genuinely questioned and required an answer.

'I had thought to marry, once,' said Cadfael honestly, 'before I took the Cross, and she was a very fair woman, too, but to say truth, I forgot her in the east, and in the west she forgot me. I was away too long, she gave up waiting and married another man, small blame to her.'

'Have you ever seen her again?' asked Hugh.

'No, never. She has grandchildren by now, may they be good to her. She was a fine woman, Richildis.'

'But the east was also made up of men and women, and you a young crusader. I cannot but wonder,' said Beringar dreamily.

'So, wonder! I also wonder about you,' said Cadfael mildly. 'Do you know any human creatures who are not strangers, one to another?'

A faint gleam of light showed among the trees. The lay brothers sat up late with a reed dip, Cadfael suspected playing at dice. Why not? The tedium here must be extreme. They were bringing these decent brothers a little diversion, undoubtedly welcome.

That they were alive and alert to the slightest sound of an unexpected approach was soon proved, as both emerged ware and ready in the doorway. Brother Anselm loomed huge and muscular, like an oak of his own fifty-five years, and swung a long staff in one hand. Brother Louis, French by descent but born in England, was small and wiry and agile, and in this solitude kept a dagger by him, and knew how to use it. Both of them came forth prepared for anything, placid of face and watchful of eye; but at sight of Brother Cadfael they fell to an easy grinning.

'What, is it you, old comrade? A pleasure to see a known face, but we hardly looked for you in the middle of the night. Are you biding over until tomorrow? Where's your errand?' They looked at Beringar with measuring interest, but he left it to Cadfael to do the dealing for him here, where the abbey's writ ran with more force than the king's.

'Our errand's here, to you,' said Cadfael, lighting down. 'My lord here asks that you'll give stabling and shelter for a few days to these two beasts, and keep them out of the public eye.' No need to hide the reason from these two, who would have sympathised heartily with the owner of such horseflesh in his desire to keep it. 'They're commandeering baggage horses for the army, and that's no fit life for these fellows, they'll be held back to serve in a better fashion.'

Brother Anselm ran an appreciative eye over Beringar's mount, and an affectionate hand over the arched neck. 'A long while since the stable here had such a beauty in it! Long enough since it had any at all, barring Prior Robert's mule when he visited, and he does that very rarely now. We expect to be recalled, to tell truth, this place is too isolated and unprofitable to be kept much longer. Yes, we'll give you house-room, my fine lad, gladly, and your mate, too. All the more gladly, my lord, if you'll let me get my leg across him now and again by way of exercise.'

'I think he may carry even you without trouble,' acknowledged Beringar amiably. 'And surrender them to no one but myself or Brother Cadfael.'

'That's understood. No one will set eyes on them here.' They led the horses into the deserted stable, very content with the break in their tedious existence, and with Beringar's open-handed largesse for their services. 'Though we'd have taken them in for the pleasure of it,' said Brother Louis truthfully. 'I was groom once in Earl Robert of Gloucester's household, I love a fine horse, one with a gloss and a gait to do me credit.'

Cadfael and Hugh Beringar turned homeward together on foot. 'An hour's walking, hardly more,' said Cadfael, 'by the way I'll take you. The path's too overgrown in parts for the horses, but I know it well, it cuts off the Foregate. We have to cross the brook, well upstream from the mill, and can enter the abbey grounds from the garden side, unnoticed, if you're willing to wade.'

'I believe,' said Beringar reflectively, but with complete placidity, 'you are having a game with me. Do you mean to lose me in the woods, or drown me in the mill-race?'

'I doubt if I should succeed at either. No, this will be a most amicable walk together, you'll see. And well worth it, I trust.'

And curiously, for all each of them knew the other was making use of him, it was indeed a pleasant nocturnal journey they made, the elderly monk without personal ambitions, and the young man whose ambitions were limitless and daring. Probably Beringar was working hard at the puzzle of why Cadfael had so readily accommodated him, certainly Cadfael was just as busy trying to fathom why Beringar had ever invited him to conspire with him thus; it did not matter, it made the contest more interesting. And which of them was to win, and to get the most out of the tussle, was very much in the balance.

Keeping pace thus on the narrow forest path they were much of a height, though Cadfael was thickset and burly, and

Beringar lean and lissome and light of foot. He followed Cadfael's steps attentively, and the darkness, only faintly alleviated by starlight between the branches, seemed to bother him not at all. And lightly and freely he talked.

'The king intends to move down into Gloucester's country again, in more strength, hence this drive for men and horses. In a few more days he'll surely be moving.'

'And you go with him?' Since he was minded to be talkative, why not encourage him? Everything he said would be calculated, of course, but sooner or later even he might make a miscalculation.

'That depends on the king. Will you credit it, Brother Cadfael, the man distrusts me! Though in fact I'd liefer be put in charge of my own command here, where my lands lie. I've made myself as assiduous as I dare – to see the same face too constantly might have the worst effect, not to see it in attendance at all would be fatal. A nice question of judgment.'

'I feel,' said Cadfael, 'that a man might have considerable confidence in your judgment. Here we are at the brook, do you hear it?' There were stones there by which to cross dry-shod, though the water was low and the bed narrowed, and Beringar, having rested his eyes a few moments to assay the distance and the ground, crossed in a nicely balanced leap that served to justify Cadfael's pronouncement.

'Do you indeed?' resumed the young man, falling in beside him again as they went on. 'Have a high opinion of my judgment? Of risks and vantages only? Or, for instance, of men? – And women?'

'I can hardly question your judgment of men,' said Cadfael drily, 'since you've confided in me. If I doubted, I'd hardly be likely to own it.'

'And of women?' They were moving more freely now through open fields.

'I think they might all be well advised to beware of you. And what else is gossiped about in the king's court, besides the next campaign? There's no fresh word of FitzAlan and Adeney being sighted?

'None, nor will be now,' said Beringar readily. 'They had luck, and I'm not sorry. Where they are by now there's no knowing, but wherever it is, it's one stage on the way to France.'

There was no reason to doubt him; whatever he was about he was making his dispositions by way of truth, not lies. So the news for Godith's peace of mind was still good, and every day better, as the distance between her father and Stephen's vengeance lengthened. And now there were two excellent horses well positioned on an escape road for Godith and Torold, in the care of two stalwart brothers who would release them at Cadfael's word. The first step was accomplished. Now to recover the saddle-bags from the river, and start them on their way. Not so simple a matter, but surely not impossible.

'I see now where we are,' said Beringar, some twenty minutes later. They had cut straight across the mile of land enclosed by the brook's wanderings, and stood again on the bank; on the other side the stripped fields of pease whitened in the starlight, and beyond their smooth rise lay the gardens, and the great range of abbey buildings. 'You have a nose for country, even in the dark. Lead the way, I'll trust you for an unpitted ford, too.'

Cadfael had only to kilt his habit, having nothing but his sandals to get wet. He strode into the water at the point opposite the low roof of Godith's hut, which just showed above the trees and bushes and the containing wall of the herbarium. Beringar plunged in after him, boots and hose and all. The water was barely knee-deep, but clearly he cared not at all. And Cadfael noted how he moved, gently and steadily, hardly a ripple breaking from his steps. He had all the intuitive gifts of wild creatures, as alert by night as by day. On the abbey bank he set off instinctively round the edge of the low stubble of pease-haulms, to avoid any rustle among the dry roots soon to be dug in.

'A natural conspirator,' said Cadfael, thinking aloud; and that he could do so was proof of a strong, if inimical, bond between them.

Beringar turned on him a face suddenly lit by a wild smile. 'One knows another,' he said. They had grown used to exchanging soundless whispers, and yet making them clear to be heard. 'I've remembered one rumour that's making the rounds, that I forgot to tell you. A few days ago there was some fellow hunted into the river by night, said to be one of FitzAlan's squires. They say an archer got him behind the left shoulder, maybe through the heart. However it was, he went down, somewhere by Atcham his body may be cast up. But they caught a riderless horse, a good saddle-horse, the next day, sure to be his.'

'Do you tell me?' said Cadfael, mildly marvelling. 'You may

speak here, there'll be no one prowling in my herb-garden by night, and they're used to me rising at odd times to tend my brews here.'

'Does not your boy see to that?' asked Hugh Beringar innocently.

'A boy slipping out of the dortoir,' said Brother Cadfael, 'would soon have cause to rue it. We take better care of our children here, my lord, than you seem to think.'

'I'm glad to hear it. It's well enough for seasoned old soldiers turned monk to risk the chills of the night, but the young things ought to be protected.' His voice was sweet and smooth as honey. 'I was telling you of this odd thing about the horses ... A couple of days later, if you'll believe it, they rounded up another saddle-horse running loose, grazing up in the heathlands north of the town, still saddled. They're thinking there was a single bodyguard sent out from the castle, when the assault came, to pick up Adeney's daughter from wherever she was hidden, and escort her safely out of the ring round Shrewsbury. They think the attempt failed,' he said softly, 'when her attendant took to the river to save her. So she's still missing, and still thought to be somewhere here, close in hiding. And they'll be looking for her, Brother Cadfael – they'll be looking for her now more eagerly than ever.'

They were up at the edge of the inner gardens by then. Hugh Beringar breathed an almost silent 'Good night!' and was gone like a shadow towards the guest house.

Before he slept out the rest of the night, Brother Cadfael lay awake long enough to do some very hard thinking. And the longer he thought, the more convinced he became that someone had indeed approached the mill closely enough and silently enough to catch the last few sentences spoken within; and that the someone was Hugh Beringar, past all doubt. He had proved how softly he could move, how instinctively he adapted his movements to circumstances, he had provoked a shared expedition committing each of them to the other's discretion, and he had uttered a number of cryptic confidences calculated to arouse suspicion and alarm, and possibly precipitate unwise action – though Cadfael had no intention of giving him that last satisfaction. He did not believe the listener had been within earshot long. But the last thing Cadfael himself had said gave away plainly enough that he intended somehow to get hold of two horses, retrieve the hidden treasury, and see Torold on his way with 'her'. If Beringar had been at the door just a moment earlier, he must also have heard the girl named; but even without that he must surely have had his suspicions. Then just what game was he playing, with his own best horses, with the fugitives he could betray at any moment, yet had not so far betrayed, and with Brother Cadfael? A better and larger prize offered than merely one young man's capture, and the exploitation of a girl against whom he had no real grudge. A man like Beringar might prefer to risk all and play for all, Torold, Godith and treasure in one swoop. For himself alone, as once before, though without success? Or for the king's gain and favour? He was indeed a young man of infinite possibilities.

Cadfael thought about him for a long time before he slept, and one thing, at least, was clear. If Beringar knew now that Cadfael had as good as undertaken to recover the treasury, then from this point on he would hardly let Cadfael out of his sight, for he needed him to lead him to the spot. A little light began to dawn, faint but promising, just before sleep came. It seemed no more than a moment before the bell was rousing him with the rest for Prime.

'Today,' said Cadfael to Godith, in the garden after breakfast, 'do all as usual, go to the Mass before chapter, and then to your schooling. After dinner you should work a little in the garden, and see to the medicines, but after that you can slip away to the old mill, discreetly, mind, until Vespers. Can you dress Torold's wound without me? I may not be seen there today.'

'Surely I can,' she said blithely. 'I've seen it done, and I know the herbs now. But ... If someone, if *he*, was spying on us yesterday, how if he comes today?' She had been told of the night's expedition, briefly, and the implications at once heartened and alarmed her.

'He will not,' said Cadfael positively. 'If all goes well, wherever *I* am today, there *he* will be. That's why I want you away from me, and why you may breathe more easily away from me. And there's something I may want you and Torold to do for me, late tonight, if things go as I expect. When we come to Vespers, then I'll tell you, yes or no. If it's yes, that's all I need say, and this is what you must do ...'

She listened in glowing silence throughout, and nodded eager comprehension. 'Yes, I saw the boat, leaning against the

278

wall of the mill. Yes, I know the thicket of bushes at the beginning of the garden, close under the end of the bridge ... Yes, of course we can do it, Torold and I together!'

'Wait long enough to be sure,' cautioned Cadfael. 'And now run off to the parish Mass, and your lessons, and look as like the other boys as you can, and don't be afraid. If there should be any cause for fear, I intend to hear of it early, and I'll be with you at once.'

A part of Cadfael's thinking was rapidly proved right. He made it his business to be very active about the precincts that Sunday, attendant at every service, trotting on various errands from gate house to guest house, to the abbot's lodging, the infirmary, the gardens; and everywhere that he went, somewhere within view, unobtrusive but present, was Hugh Beringar. Never before had that young man been so constantly at church, in attendance even when Aline was not among the worshippers. Now let's see, thought Cadfael, with mild malice, whether I can lure him from the lists even when she does attend, and leave the field open for the other suitor. For Aline would certainly come to the Mass after chapter, and his last foray to the gate house had shown him Adam Courcelle, dressed for peace and piety, approaching the door of the small house where she and her maid were lodged.

It was unheard of for Cadfael to be absent from Mass, but for once he invented an errand which gave him fair excuse. His skills with medicines were known in the town, and people often asked for his help and advice. Abbot Heribert was indulgent to such requests, and lent his herbalist freely. There was a child along the Foregate towards St Giles who had been under his care from time to time for a skin infection, and though he was growing out of it gradually, and there was no great need for a visit this day, no one had the authority to contradict Cadfael when he pronounced it necessary to go.

In the gateway he met Aline Siward and Adam Courcelle entering, she slightly flushed, certainly not displeased with her escort, but perhaps a little embarrassed, the king's officer devoutly attentive and also warmly flushed, clearly in his case with pleasure. If Aline was expecting to be accosted by Beringar, as had become usual by this time, for once she was surprised. Whether relieved or disappointed there was no telling. Beringar was nowhere to be seen.

Proof positive, thought Cadfael, satisfied, and went on his

physicianly visit serenely and without haste. Beringar was discretion itself in his surveillance, he contrived not to be seen at all until Cadfael, on his way home again, met him ambling out gently for exercise on one of his remaining horses, and whistling merrily as he rode.

He saluted Cadfael gaily, as though no encounter could have been more unexpected or more delightful. 'Brother Cadfael, you astray on a Sunday morning?'

Very staidly Cadfael rehearsed his errand, and reported its satisfactory results.

'The range of your skills is admirable,' said Beringar, twinkling. 'I trust you had an undisturbed sleep after your long working day yesterday?'

'My mind was over-active for a while,' said Cadfael, 'but I slept well enough. And thus far you still have a horse to ride, I see.'

'Ah, that! I was at fault, I should have realised that even if the order was issued on a Sunday, they would not move until the sabbath was over. Tomorrow you'll see for yourself.' Unquestionably he was telling the truth, and certain of his information. 'The hunt is likely to be very thorough,' he said, and Cadfael knew he was not talking only of the horses and the provisions. 'King Stephen is a little troubled about his relations with the church and its bishops. I ought to have known he would hold back on Sunday. Just as well, it gives us a day's credit and grace. Tonight we can stay blamelessly at home in all men's sight, as the innocent should. Eh, Cadfael?' And he laughed, and leaned to clap a hand on Brother Cadfael's shoulder, and rode on, kicking his heels into his horse's side and rousing to a trot towards St Giles.

Nevertheless, when Cadfael emerged from the refectory after dinner, Beringar was visible just within the doorway of the guest-hall opposite, seemingly oblivious but well aware of everything within his field of vision. Cadfael led him harmlessly to the cloister, and sat down there in the sun, and dozed contentedly until he was sure that Godith would be well away and free from surveillance. Even when he awoke he sat for a while, to make quite sure, and to consider the implications.

No question but all his movements were being watched very narrowly, and by Beringar in person. He did not delegate such work to his men-at-arms, or to any other hired eyes, but did the duty himself, and probably took pleasure in it, too. If he was willing to surrender Aline to Courcelle, even for an hour, then maximum importance attached to what he was doing instead. I am elected, thought Cadfael, as the means to the end he desires, and that is FitzAlan's treasury. And his surveillance is going to be relentless. Very well! There's no way of evading it. The only thing to do is to make use of it.

Do not, therefore, tire out the witness too much, or alert him too soon of activities planned. He has you doing a deal of guessing, now keep him guessing.

So he betook himself to his herbarium, and worked conscientiously on all his preparations there, brewing and newly begun, all that afternoon until it was time to repair to church for Vespers. Where Beringar secreted himself he did not trouble to consider, he hoped the vigil was tedious in the extreme to a man so volatile and active.

Courcelle had either stayed – the opportunity being heaven-sent, and not to be wasted – or returned for the evening worship, he came with Aline demure and thoughtful on his arm. At sight of Brother Cadfael sallying forth from the gardens he halted, and greeted him warmly.

'A pleasure to see you in better circumstances than when last we met, brother. I hope you may have no more such duties. At least Aline and you, between you, lent some grace to what would otherwise have been a wholly ugly business. I wish I had some way of softening his Grace's mind towards your house, he still keeps a certain grudge that the lord abbot was in no hurry to come to his peace.'

'A mistake a great many others also made,' said Cadfael philosophically. 'No doubt we shall weather it.'

'I trust so. But as yet his Grace is in no mind to extend any privileges to the abbey above the other townsfolk. If I should be compelled to enforce, even within your walls, orders I'd rather see stop at the gates, I hope you'll understand that I do it reluctantly, and have no choice about it.'

He is asking pardon in advance, thought Cadfael, enlightened, for tomorrow's invasion. So it's true enough, as I supposed, and he has been given the ill work to do, and is making it clear beforehand that he dislikes the business and would evade it if he could. He may even be making rather more than he need of his repugnance, for the lady's benefit.

'If that should happen,' he said benignly, 'I'm sure every man of my order will realise that you do only what you must, like any soldier under orders. You need not fear that any odium will attach to you.'

'So I have assured Adam many times,' said Aline warmly, and flushed vividly at hearing herself call him by his Christian name. Perhaps it was for the first time. 'But he's hard to convince. No, Adam, it is true – you take to yourself blame which is not your due, as if you had killed Giles with your own hand, which you know is false. How could I even blame the Flemings? They were under orders, too. In such dreadful times as these no one can do more than choose his own road according to his conscience, and bear the consequences of his choice, whatever they may be.'

'In no times, good or bad,' said Cadfael sententiously, 'can man do more or better than that. Since I have this chance, lady, I should render you account of the alms you trusted to me, for all are bestowed, and they have benefited three poor, needy souls. For want of names, which I did not enquire, say some prayer for three worthy unfortunates who surely pray for you.'

And so she would, he reflected as he watched her enter the church on Courcelle's arm. At this crisis season of her life, bereft of kin, left mistress of a patrimony she had freely dedicated to the king's service, he judged she was perilously hesitant between the cloister and the world, and for all he had chosen the cloister in his maturity, he heartily wished her the world, if possible a more attractive world than surrounded her now, to employ and fulfil her youth.

Going in to take his place among his brothers, he met Godith making for her own corner. Her eyes questioned brightly, and he said softly: 'Yes! Do all as I told you.'

So now what mattered was to make certain that for the rest of the evening he led Beringar into pastures far apart from where Godith operated. What Cadfael did must be noted, what she did must go unseen and unsuspected. And that could not be secured by adhering faithfully to the evening routine. Supper was always a brief meal, Beringar would be sure to be somewhere within sight of the refectory when they emerged. Collations in the chapter house, the formal reading from the lives of the saints, was a part of the day that Cadfael had been known to miss on other occasions, and he did so now, leading his unobtrusive attendant first to the infirmary, where he paid a brief visit to Brother Reginald, who was old and deformed in the joints, and welcomed company, and then to the extreme end of the abbot's own garden, far away from the herbarium, and farther still from the gate house. By then Godith would be freed from her evening lesson with the novices, and might appear anywhere between the hut and the herbarium and the gates, so it was essential that Beringar should continue to concentrate on Cadfael, even if he was doing nothing more exciting than trimming the dead flowers from the abbot's roses and clove-pinks. By that stage Cadfael was checking only occasionally that the watch on his movements continued; he was quite certain that it would, and with exemplary patience. During the day it seemed almost casual, hardly expecting action, except that Cadfael was a tricky opponent, and might have decided to act precisely when it was unexpected of him. But it was after dark that things would begin to happen.

When Compline was over there was always, on fine evenings, a brief interlude of leisure in the cloister or the gardens, before the brothers went to their beds. By then it was almost fully dark, and Cadfael was satisfied that Godith was long since where she should be, and Torold beside her. But he thought it best to delay yet a while, and go to the dortoir with the rest. Whether he emerged thence by way of the night stairs into the church, or the outer staircase, someone keeping watch from across the great court, where the guest hall lay, would be able to pick up his traces without trouble.

He chose the night stairs and the open north door of the church, and slipped round the east end of the Lady Chapel and the chapter house to cross the court into the gardens. No need to look round or listen for his shadow, he knew it would be there, moving at leisure, hanging well back from him but keeping him in sight. The night was reasonably dark, but the eyes grew accustomed to it soon, and he knew how securely Beringar could move in darkness. He would expect the night-wanderer to leave by the ford, as they had returned together the previous night. Someone bound on secret business would not pass the porter on the gate, whatever his normal authority.

After he had waded the brook, Cadfael did pause to be sure Beringar was with him. The breaks in the rhythm of the water were very slight, but he caught them, and was content. Now to follow the course of the brook downstream on this side until nearing its junction with the river. There was a little footbridge there, and then it was only a step to the stone bridge that crossed into Shrewsbury. Over the road, and down the slope into the main abbey gardens, and he was already under the shadow of the first archway of the bridge, watching the faint flashes of light from the eddies where once a boat-mill had been moored. In this corner under the stone pier the bushes grew thick, such an awkward slope of ground was not worth clearing for what it would bear. Half-grown willows leaned, trailing leaves in the water, and the bushy growth under their branches would have hidden half a dozen well-screened witnesses.

The boat was there, afloat and tied up to one of the leaning branches, though it was of the light, withy-and-hide type that could be ported easily overland. This time there was good reason it should not, as it usually would, be drawn ashore and turned over in the turf. There was, Cadfael hoped, a solid bundle within it, securely tied up in one or two of the sacks from the mill. It would not have done for him to be seen to be carrying anything. Long before this, he trusted, he had been clearly seen to be empty-handed.

He stepped into the boat and loosed the mooring-rope. The sacking bundle was there, and convincingly heavy when he cautiously tested. A little above him on the slope, drawn into the edge of the bushes, he caught the slight movement of a deeper shadow as he pushed off with the long paddle into the flow under the first archway.

In the event it proved remarkably easy. No matter how keen Hugh Beringar's sight, he could not possibly discern everything that went on under the bridge, detail by detail. However sharp his hearing, it would bring him only a sound suggesting the rattling of a chain drawn up against stone, with some considerable weight on the end, the splash and trickle of water running out from something newly drawn up, and then the iron rattle of the chain descending; which was exactly what it was, except that Cadfael's hands slowed and muted the descent, to disguise the fact that the same weight was still attached, and only the bundle concealed in the boat had been sluiced in the Severn briefly, to provide the trickle of water on the stone ledge. The next part might be more risky, since he was by no means certain he had read Beringar's mind correctly. Brother Cadfael was staking his own life and those of others upon his judgment of men.

So far, however, it had gone perfectly. He paddled his light craft, warily ashore, and above him a swift-moving shadow withdrew to higher ground, and, he surmised, went to earth close to the roadway, ready to fall in behind him whichever way he took. Though he would have wagered that the way was already guessed at, and rightly. He tied up the boat again, hastily but securely; haste was a part of his disguise that night, like stealth. When he crept cautiously up to the highroad again, and loomed against the night sky for a moment in stillness, ostensibly waiting to be sure he could cross unnoticed, the watcher could hardly miss seeing that he had now a shape grossly humped by some large bundle he carried slung over his shoulder.

He crossed, rapidly and quietly, and returned by the way he had come, following the brook upstream from the river after passing the ford, and so into the fields and woods he had threaded with Beringar only one night past. The bundle he carried, mercifully, had not been loaded with the full weight it was supposed to represent, though either Torold or Godith had seen fit to give it a convincing bulk and heft. More than enough, Cadfael reflected ruefully, for an ageing monk to carry four miles or more. His nights were being relentlessly curtailed. Once these young folk were wafted away into relative safety he would sleep through Matins and Lauds, and possibly the next morning's Prime, as well, and do fitting penance for it.

Now everything was matter for guesswork. Would Beringar take it for granted where he was bound, and turn back too soon, and with some residue of suspicion, and ruin everything? No! Where Cadfael was concerned he would take nothing for granted, not until he was sure by his own observation where this load had been bestowed in safe-keeping, and satisfied that Cadfael had positively returned to his duty without it. But would he, by any chance, intercept it on the way? No, why should he? To do so would have been to burden himself with it, whereas now he had an old fool to carry it for him, to where he had his horses hidden to convey it with ease elsewhere.

Cadfael had the picture clear in his mind now, the reckoning at its worst. If Beringar had killed Nicholas Faintree in the attempt to possess himself of the treasury, then his aim now would be not only to accomplish what he had failed to do then, but also something beyond, a possibility which had been revealed to him only since that attempt. By letting Brother Cadfael stow away for him both horses and treasure at an advantageous place, he had ensured his primary objective; but in addition, if he waited for Cadfael to convey his fugitives secretly to the same spot, as he clearly intended to do, then

Beringar could remove the only witness to his former murder, and capture his once affianced bride as hostage for her father. What an enormous boon to bestow on King Stephen! His own favoured place would be assured, his crime buried for ever.

So much, of course, for the worst. But the range of possibilities was wide. For Beringar might be quite innocent of Faintree's death, but very hot on the trail of FitzAlan's valuables, now he had detected their whereabouts; and an elderly monk might be no object to his plans for his own enrichment, or, if he preferred to serve his interests in another way, his means of ingratiating himself with the king. In which case Cadfael might not long survive his depositing this infernal nuisance he carried, on shoulders already aching, at the grange where the horses were stabled. Well, thought Cadfael, rather exhilarated than oppressed, we shall see!

Once into the woods beyond the coil of the brook, he halted, and dropped the load with a huge grunt from his shoulders, and sat down on it, ostensibly to rest, actually to listen for the soft sounds of another man halting, braced, not resting. Very soft they were, but he caught them, and was happy. The young man was there, tireless, serene, a born adventurer. He saw a dark, amused, saturnine face ready for laughter. He was reasonably sure, then, how the evening would end. With a little luck – better, with God's blessing, he reproved! – he would be back in time for Matins.

There was no perceptible light in the grange when he reached it, but it needed only the rustle and stir of footsteps, and Brother Louis was out with a little pine-flare in one hand and his dagger in the other, as wide awake as at midday, and more perilous.

'God bless you, brother,' said Cadfael, easing the load gratefully from his back. He would have something to say to young Torold when next he talked to him! Someone or something other than his own shoulders could carry this the next time. 'Let me, within, and shut the door to.'

'Gaily!' said Brother Louis, and haled him within and did as he was bid.

On the way back, not a quarter of an hour later, Brother Cadfael listened carefully as he went, but he heard nothing of anyone following or accompanying him, certainly of no menace. Hugh Beringar had watched him into the grange from cover, possibly even waited for him to emerge unburdened, and then melted away into the night to which he belonged, and made his own lightsome, satisfied way home to the abbey. Cadfael abandoned all precautions and did the same. He was certain, now, where he stood. By the time the bell rang for Matins he was ready to emerge with the rest of the dortoir, and proceed devoutly down the night-stairs to give due praise in the church.

Chapter Eight

EFORE DAWN on that Monday morning in August the king's officers had deployed small parties to close every road out of Shrewsbury, while at every section within the town wall others stood ready to move methodically through the streets and search every house. There was more in the wind than the commandeering of horses and provisions, though that would certainly be done as they went, and done thoroughly.

'Everything shows that the girl must be in hiding somewhere near,' Prestcote had insisted, reporting to the king after full enquiries. 'The one horse we found turned loose is known to be from FitzAlan's stables, and this young man hunted into the Severn certainly had a companion who has not yet been run to earth. Left alone, she cannot have got far. All your advisers agree, your Grace cannot afford to let the chance of her capture slip. Adeney would certainly come back to redeem her, he has no other child. It's possible even FitzAlan could be forced to return, rather than face the shame of letting her die.'

'Die?' echoed the king, bristling ominously. 'Is it likely I'd take the girl's life? Who spoke of her dying?'

'Seen from here,' said Prestcote drily, 'it may be an absurdity to speak of any such matter, but to an anxious father waiting for better news it may seem all too possible. Of course you would do the girl no harm. No need even to harm her father if you get him into your hands, or even FitzAlan. But your Grace must consider that you should do everything possible to prevent their services from reaching the empress. It's no longer a matter of revenge for Shrewsbury, but simply of a sensible measure to conserve your own forces and cut down on your enemy's.'

'That's true enough,' admitted Stephen, without overmuch enthusiasm. His anger and hatred had simmered down into his more natural easiness of temperament, not to say laziness. 'I am not sure that I like even making such use of the girl.' He remembered that he had as good as ordered young Beringar to track down his affianced bride if he wanted to establish himself in royal favour, and the young man, though respectfully attendant since, if somewhat sporadically, had never yet produced any evidence of zeal in the search. Possibly, thought the king, he read my mind better than I did myself at the time.

'She need come by no injury, and your Grace would be saved having to contend with any forces attached to her father's standard, if not also his lord's. If you can cut off all those levies from the enemy, you will have saved yourself great labour, and a number of your men their lives. You cannot afford to neglect such a chance.'

It was sound advice, and the king knew it. Weapons are where you find them, and Adeney could sit and kick his heels in an easy imprisonment enough, once he was safe in captivity.

'Very well!' he said. 'Make your search and make it thoroughly.'

The preparations were certainly thorough. Adam Courcelle descended upon the Abbey Foregate with his own command and a company of the Flemings. And while Willem Ten Heyt went ahead and established a guard-post at St Giles, to question every rider and search every cart attempting to leave the town, and his lieutenant posted sentries along every path and by every possible crossing-place along the riverside, Courcelle took possession, civilly but brusquely, of the abbey gate house, and ordered the gates closed to all attempting to enter or leave. It was then about twenty minutes before Prime, and already daylight. There had been very little noise made, but Prior Robert from the dortoir had caught the unusual stir and disquiet from the gate house, on which the window of his own chamber looked down, and he came out in haste to see what was afoot.

Courcelle made him a reverence that deceived nobody, and asked with respect for privileges everyone knew he was empowered to take; still, the veil of courtesy did something to placate the prior's indignation.

'Sir, I am ordered by his Grace King Stephen to require of your house free and orderly entry everywhere, a tithe of your stores for his Grace's necessary provision, and such serviceable horses as are not already in the use of people in his Grace's commission. I am also commanded to search and enquire everywhere for the girl Godith, daughter of his Grace's traitor Fulke Adeney, who is thought to be still in hiding here in Shrewsbury.'

Prior Robert raised his thin, silver brows and looked down his long, aristocratic nose. 'You would hardly expect to find such a person within our precincts? I assure you there is none such in the guest house, where alone she might becomingly be found.'

'It is a formality here, I grant you,' said Courcelle, 'but I have my orders, and cannot treat one dwelling more favourably than another.'

There were lay servants listening by then, standing apart silent and wary, and one or two of the boy pupils, sleepy-eyed and scared. The master of the novices came to herd his strays back into their quarters, and stayed, instead, to listen with them.

'This should be reported at once to the abbot,' said the prior with admirable composure, and led the way at once to Abbot Heribert's lodging. Behind them, the Flemings were closing the gates and mounting a guard, before turning their practical attention to the barns and the stables.

Brother Cadfael, having for two nights running missed the first few hours of his rest, slept profoundly through all the earliest manifestations of invasion, and awoke only when the bell rang for Prime, far too late to do anything but dress in haste and go down with the rest of the brothers to the church. Only when he heard the whispers passed from man to man, and saw the closed gates, the lounging Flemings, and the subdued and huge-eyed boys, and heard the businesslike bustle and clatter of hooves from the stable-yard, did he realise that for once events had overtaken him, and snatched the initiative from his hands. For nowhere among the scared and anxious youngsters in church could he see any sign of Godith. As soon as Prime was over, and he was free to go, he hurried away to the hut in the herbarium. The door was unlatched and open, the array of drying herbs and mortars and bottles in shining order, the blankets had been removed from the bench-bed, and a basket of newly gathered lavender and one or two bottles arranged innocently along it. Of Godith there was no sign, in the hut, in the gardens, in the pease-fields along the brook, where at one side the great stack of dried haulms loomed pale as flax, waiting to be carted away to join the hay in the barns. Nor was there any trace of a large bundle wrapped in sacking and probably damp from seeping river-water, which had almost certainly spent the night under the bleached pile, or the small boat which should have been turned down upon it and carefully covered over. The boat, FitzAlan's treasury, and Godith had all vanished into thin air.

Godith had awakened somewhat before Prime, uneasily aware of the heavy responsibility that now lay upon her, and gone out without undue alarm to find out what was happening at the gate house. Though all had been done briskly and quietly, there was something about the stirring in the air and the unusual voices, lacking the decorous monastic calm of the brothers, that disturbed her mind. She was on the point of emerging from the walled garden when she saw the Flemings dismounting and closing the gates, and Courcelle advancing to meet the prior. She froze at the sound of her own name thus coolly spoken. If they were bent upon a thorough search, even here, they must surely find her. Questioned like the other boys, with all those enemy eyes upon her, she could not possibly sustain the performance. And if they found her, they might extend the search and find what she had in her charge. Besides, there was Brother Cadfael to protect, and Torold. Torold had returned faithfully to his mill once he had seen her safely home with the treasure. Last night she had almost wished he could have stayed with her, now she was glad he had the whole length of the Gaye between him and this dawn alarm, and woods not far from his back, and quick senses that would pick up the signs early, and give him due warning to vanish.

Last night had been like a gay, adventurous dream, for some reason inexpressibly sweet, holding their breath together in cover until Cadfael had led his shadow well away from the bridge, loosing the little boat, hauling up the dripping saddle-bags, swathing them in dry sacks to make another bundle the image of Cadfael's; their hands together on the chain, holding it away from the stone, muting it so that there should be no further sound, then softly paddling the short way upstream to the brook, and round to the pease-fields. Hide the boat, too, Cadfael had said, for we'll need it tomorrow night, if the chance offers. Last night's adventure had been the dream, this morning was the awakening, and she needed the boat now, this moment.

There was no hope of reaching Brother Cadfael for orders, what she guarded must be got away from here at once, and it certainly could not go out through the gates. There was no one to tell her what to do, this fell upon her shoulders now. Blessedly, the Flemings were not likely to ransack the gardens until they had looted stables and barns and stores; she had a little time in hand.

She went back quickly to the hut, folded her blankets and hid them under the bench behind a row of jars and mortars, stripped the bed and turned it into a mere shelf for more such deceits, and set the door wide open to the innocent daylight. Then she slipped away to the stack of haulms, and dragged out the boat from its hiding-place, and the sacking bundle with it. A godsend that the gentle slope of the field was so glazed with the cropped stems, and the boat so light, that it slid down effortlessly into the brook. She left it beached, and returned to drag the treasury after it, and hoist it aboard. Until last night she had never been in such a boat, but Torold had shown her how to use the paddle, and the steady flow of the brook helped her.

She already knew what she would do. There was no hope at all of escaping notice if she went downstream to the Severn; with such a search in hand, there would be watchers on the main road, on the bridge, and probably along the banks. But only a short way from her launching-place a broad channel was drawn off to the right, to the pool of the main abbey mill, where the mill-race, drawn off upstream through the abbey pool and the fish ponds, turned the wheel and emptied itself again into the pond, to return to the main stream of the brook and accompany it to the river. Just beyond the mill the three grace houses of the abbey were ranged, with little gardens down to the water, and three more like them protected the pond from open view on the other side. The house next to the mill was the one devoted to the use of Aline Siward. True, Courcelle had said he was to search for his fugitive everywhere; but if there was one place in this conventual enclosure that would receive no more than a formal visit from him, it was certainly the house where Aline was living.

What if we are on opposite sides, thought Godith, plying her paddle inexpertly but doggedly at the turn, and sailing into wider, smoother water, she can't throw me to the wolves, it isn't in her, with a face like hers! And are we on opposite sides? Are we on either side, by this time? She places everything she has at the king's disposal, and he hangs her brother! My father stakes life and lands for the empress, and I don't believe she cares what happens to him or any of his like, provided she gets her own way. I daresay Aline's brother was more to her than King Stephen will ever be, and I know I care more for my father and Torold than for the Empress Maud, and I wish the old king's son hadn't drowned when that awful ship went down, so that there'd have been no argument over who inherited, and Stephen and Maud alike could have stayed in their own manors, and left us alone!

The mill loomed on her right, but the wheel was still today, and the water of the race spilled over freely into the pond that opened beyond, with slow counter-currents flowing along the opposite bank to return to the brook. The bank here was sheer for a couple of feet, to level as much ground as possible for the narrow gardens; but if she could heave the bundle safely ashore, she thought she could drag up the boat. She caught at a naked root that jutted into the water from a leaning willow, and fastened her mooring-line to it, before she dared attempt to hoist her treasure up to the edge of the grass. It was heavy for her, but she rolled it on to the thwart, and thence manipulated it into her arms. She could just reach the level rim of turf without tilting the boat too far. The weight rested and remained stable, and Godith leaned her arms thankfully either side of it, and for the first time tears welled out of her eyes and ran down her face.

Why, she wondered rebelliously, why am I going to such trouble for this rubbish, when all I care about is Torold, and my father? And Brother Cadfael! I should be failing him if I tipped it down into the pond and left it there. He went to all sorts of pains to get it to this point, and now I have to go on with the work. And Torold cares greatly that he should carry out the task he was given. That's more than gold. It isn't this lump that matters!

She scrubbed an impatient and grubby hand over her cheeks and eyes, and set about climbing ashore, which proved tricky, for the boat tended to withdraw from under her foot to the length of its mooring; when at last she had scrambled to safety, swearing now instead of crying, she could not draw it up after

293

her, she was afraid of holing it on the jagged roots. It would have to ride here. She lay on her stomach and shortened the mooring, and made sure the knot was fast. Then she towed her detested incubus up into the shadow of the house, and hammered at the door.

It was Constance who opened it. It was barely eight o'clock, Godith realised, and it was Aline's habit to attend the Mass at ten, she might not even be out of her bed yet. But the general disquiet in the abbey had reached these retired places also, it seemed, for Aline was up and dressed, and appeared at once behind her maid's shoulder.

'What is it, Constance?' She saw Godith, soiled and tousled and breathless, leaning over a great sacking bundle on the ground, and came forward in innocent concern. 'Godric! What's the matter? Did Brother Cadfael send you? Is anything wrong?'

'You know the boy, do you, madam?' said Constance, surprised.

'I know him, he's Brother Cadfael's helper, we have talked together.' She cast one luminous glance over Godith from head to foot, took in the smudged marks of tears and the heaving bosom, and put her maid quickly aside. She knew desperation when she saw it, even when it made no abject appeal. 'Come within, come! Here, let me help you with this, whatever it may be. Now, Constance, close the door!' They were safe within, the wooden walls closed them round, the morning sun was warm and bright through an eastern window left open.

They stood looking at each other, Aline all woman in a blue gown, her golden hair loosed about her in a cloud, Godith brown and rumpled, and arrayed unbecomingly in an over-large cotte and ill-fitting hose, short hair wild, and face stained and grubby from soil, grass and sweat.

'I came to ask you for shelter,' said Godith simply. 'The king's soldiers are hunting for me. I'm worth quite a lot to them if they find me. I'm not Godric, I'm Godith. Godith Adeney, Fulke Adeney's daughter.'

Aline let her glance slide, startled and touched, from the fine-featured oval face, down the drab-clad and slender limbs. She looked again into the challenging, determined face, and a spark started and glowed in her eyes.

'You'd better come through here,' she said practically, with a glance at the open window, 'into my own sleeping-chamber, away from the road. Nobody will trouble you there – we can talk freely. Yes, bring your belongings, I'll help you with them.' FitzAlan's treasury was woman-handled between them into the inner room, where not even Courcelle, certainly not any other, would dare to go. Aline closed the door very softly. Godith sat down on a stool by the bed, and felt every sinew in her grown weak, and every stress relaxing. She leaned her head against the wall, and looked up at Aline.

'You do realise, lady, that I'm reckoned the king's enemy? I don't want to trick you into anything. You may think it your duty to give me up.'

'You're very honest,' said Aline, 'and I'm not being tricked into anything. I'm not sure even the king would think the better of me if I gave you up to him, but I'm sure God would not, and I know I should not think the better of myself. You can rest safe here. Constance and I between us will see to it that no one comes near you.'

Brother Cadfael preserved a tranquil face through Prime, and the first conventual Mass, and a greatly abbreviated chapter meeting, while mentally he was racking his brain and gnawing his knuckles over his own inexplicable complacence, which had let him sleep on while the opposing powers stole a march on him. The gates were fast shut, there was no way out there. He could not pass, and certainly by that route Godith had not passed. He had seen no soldiers on the other side of the brook, though they would certainly be watching the river bank. If Godith had taken the boat, where had she gone with it? Not upstream, for the brook was open to view for some way, and beyond that flowed through a bed too uneven and rocky to accommodate such craft. Every moment he was waiting for the outcry that would signal her capture, but every moment that passed without such an alarm was ease to him. She was no fool, and she seemed to have got away, though heaven knew where, with the treasure they were fighting to retain and speed on its way.

At chapter Abbot Heribert made a short, weary, disillusioned speech in explanation of the occupation that had descended upon them, instructed the brothers to obey whatever commands were given them by the king's officers with dignity and fortitude, and to adhere to the order of their day faithfully so far as they were permitted. To be deprived of the goods of this world should be no more than a welcome discipline to those who had aspired beyond the world. Brother

Cadfael could at least feel some complacency concerning his own particular harvest; the king was not likely to demand tithes of his herbs and remedies, though he might welcome a cask or two of wine. Then the abbot dismissed them with the injunction to go quietly about their own work until High Mass at ten.

Brother Cadfael went back to the gardens and occupied himself distractedly with such small tasks as came to hand, his mind still busy elsewhere. Godith could safely have forded the brook by broad daylight, and taken to the nearest patch of woodland, but she could not have carried the unwieldy bundle of treasure with her, it was too heavy. She had chosen rather to remove all the evidence of irregular activities here, taking away with her both the treasure and the boat. He was sure she had not gone as far as the confluence with the river, or she would have been captured before this. Every moment without the evil news provided another morsel of reassurance. But wherever she was, she needed his help.

And there was Torold, away beyond the reaped fields, in the disused mill. Had he caught the meaning of these movements in good time, and taken to the woods? Devoutly Cadfael hoped so. In the meantime there was nothing he could do but wait, and give nothing away. But oh, if this inquisition passed before the end of the day, and he could retrieve his two strays after dark, this very night he must see them away to the west. This might well be the most favourable opportunity, with the premises already scoured, the searchers tired and glad to forget their vigilance, the community totally absorbed with their grievances and comparing notes on the army's deprivations, the brothers devoted wholly to fervent prayers of thanks for an ordeal ended.

Cadfael went out to the great court in good time for Mass. There were army carts being loaded with sacks from the barns, and a great bustle of Flemings about the stables. Dismayed guests, caught here in mid-journey with horses worth commandeering, came out in great agitation to argue and plead for their beasts, but it did them no good, unless the owners could prove they were in the king's service already. Only the poor hacks were spared. One of the abbey carts was also taken, with its team, and loaded with the abbey's wheat.

Something curious was happening at the gates, Cadfael saw. The great carriage doors were closed, and guarded, but someone had had the calm temerity to knock at the wicket and ask for entry. Since it could have been one of their own, a courier from the guard-post at St Giles, or from the royal camp, the wicket was opened, and in the narrow doorway appeared the demure figure of Aline Siward, prayer-book in hand, her gold hair covered decently by the white mourning cap and wimple.

'I have permission,' she said sweetly, 'to come in to church.' And seeing that the guards who confronted her were not at home in English, she repeated it just as amiably in French. They were not disposed to admit her, and were on the point of closing the door in her face when one of their officers observed the encounter, and came in haste.

'I have permission,' repeated Aline patiently, 'from Messire Courcelle to come in to Mass. My name is Aline Siward. If you are in doubt, ask him, he will tell you.'

It seemed that she had indeed secured her privilege, for after some hurried words the wicket was opened fully, and they stood back and let her pass. She walked through the turmoil of the great court as though nothing out of the ordinary were happening there, and made for the cloister and the south door of the church. But she slowed her pace on the way, for she was aware of Brother Cadfael weaving his way between the scurrying soldiers and the lamenting travellers to cross her path just at the porch. She gave him a demure public greeting, but in the moment when they were confidingly close she said privately and low:

'Be easy, Godric is safe in my house.'

'Praise to God and you!' sighed Cadfael as softly. 'After dark I'll come for her.' And though Aline had used the boyish name, he knew by her small, secret smile that the word he had used was no surprise to her. 'The boat?' he questioned soundlessly.

'At the foot of my garden, ready.'

She went on into the church, and Cadfael, with a heart suddenly light as thistledown, went decorously to take his place among the procession of his brothers.

Torold sat in the fork of a tree at the edge of the woods east of Shrewsbury castle, eating the remains of the bread he had brought away with him, and a couple of early apples stolen from a tree at the limit of the abbey property. Looking westward across the river he could see not only the great cliff of the castle walls and towers, but further to the right, just visible between the crests of trees, the tents of the royal camp. By the numbers busy about the abbey and the town, the camp itself must be almost empty at this moment.

Torold's body was coping well enough with this sudden crisis, to his satisfaction and, if he would have admitted it, surprise. His mind was suffering more. He had not yet walked very far, or exerted himself very much, apart from climbing into this comfortable and densely leafed tree, but he was delighted with the response of his damaged muscles, and the knit of the gash in his thigh, which hardly bothered him, and the worse one in his shoulder, which had neither broken nor greatly crippled his use of his arm. But all his mind fretted and ached for Godith, the little brother so suddenly transmuted into a creature half sister, half something more. He had confidence in Brother Cadfael, of course, but it was impossible to unload all the responsibility for her on to one pair of cloistered shoulders, however wide and sustaining. Torold fumed and agonised, and yet went on eating his stolen apples. He was going to need all the sustenance he could muster.

There was a patrol moving methodically along the bank of the Severn, between him and the river, and he dared not move again until they had passed by and withdrawn from sight towards the abbey and the bridge. And how far round the outskirts of the town he would have to go, to outflank the royal cordon, was something he did not yet know.

He had awakened to the unmistakable sounds from the bridge, carried by the water, and insistent enough in their rhythm to break his sleep. Many, many men, mounted and foot, stamping out their presence and their passage upon a stone bow high above water, the combination sending echoes headlong down the river's course. The timber of the mill, the channels of water feeding it, carried the measure to his ears. He had started up and dressed instinctively, gathering everything that might betray his having been there, before he ventured out to look. He had seen the companies fan out at the end of the bridge, and waited to see no more, for this was a grimly thorough operation. He had wiped out all traces of his occupation of the mill, throwing into the river all those things he could not carry away with him, and then had slipped away across the limit of abbey land, away from the advancing patrol on the river bank, into the edge of the woodlands opposite the castle.

He did not know for whom or what this great hunt had been

launched, but he knew all too well who was likely to be taken in it, and his one aim now was to get to Godith, wherever she might be, and stand between her and danger if he could. Better still, to take her away from here, into Normandy, where she would be safe.

Along the river bank the men of the patrol separated to beat a way through the bushes where Godith had first come to him. They had already searched the abandoned mill, but thank God they would find no traces there. Now they were almost out of sight, he felt safe in swinging down cautiously from his tree and withdrawing deeper into the belt of woodland. From the bridge to St Giles the king's highway, the road to London, was built up with shops and dwellings, he must keep well clear. Was it better to go on like this, eastward, and cross the highroad somewhere beyond St Giles, or to wait and go back the way he had come, after all the tumult was over? The trouble was that he did not know when that was likely to be, and his torment for Godith was something he did not want prolonged. He would have to go beyond St Giles, in all probability, before he dared cross the highroad, and though the brook, after that, need be no obstacle the approach to the spot opposite the abbey gardens would still be perilous. He could lie up in the nearest cover and watch, and slip over into the stack of pease-haulms when the opportunity offered, and thence, if all remained quiet, into the herbarium, where he had never yet been, and the hut where Godith had slept the last seven nights in sanctuary. Yes, better go forward and make that circle. Backward meant braving the end of the bridge, and there would be soldiers there until darkness fell, and probably through the night.

It proved a tedious business, when he was longing for swift action. The sudden assault had brought out all the inhabitants in frightened and indignant unrest, and Torold had to beware of any notice in such conditions, since he was a young fellow not known here, where neighbour knew neighbour like his own kin, and any stranger was liable to be accosted and challenged out of sheer alarm. Several times he had to draw off deeper into cover, and lie still until danger passed. Those who lived close to the highway, and had suffered the first shocks, tended to slip away into any available solitude. Those who were daily tending stock or cultivating land well away from the road heard the uproar, and gravitated close enough to satisfy their curiosity about what was going on. Caught between these two tides, Torold passed a miserable day of fretting and waiting; but it brought him at last well beyond Willem Ten Heyt's tight and brutal guard-post, which by then had amassed a great quantity of goods distrained from agitated travellers, and a dozen sound horses. Here the last houses of the town ended, and fields and hamlets stretched beyond. Traffic on the road, half a mile beyond the post, was thin and easily evaded. Torold crossed, and went to earth once more in a thicket above the brook, while he viewed the lie of the land.

The brook was dual here, the mill-race having been drawn off at a weir somewhat higher upstream. He could see both silver streaks in a sunlight now declining very slightly towards the west. It must be almost time for Vespers. Surely King Stephen had finished with the abbey by now, with all Shrewsbury to ransack?

The valley here was narrow and steep, and no one had built on it, the grass being given over to sheep. Torold slid down into the cleft, easily leaping the mill-race, and picking his way over the brook from stone to stone. He began to make his way down-stream from one patch of cover to another, until about the time of Vespers he had reached the smoother meadows opposite Brother Cadfael's gleaned pease-fields. Here the ground was all too open, he had to withdraw further from the brook to find a copse to hide in while he viewed the way ahead. From here he could see the roofs of the convent buildings above the garden walls, and the loftier tower and roof of the church, but nothing of the activity within. The face that was presented to him looked placid enough, the pale slope stripped of its harvest, the stack of haulms where Godith and he had hidden boat and treasure barely nineteen hours ago, the russet wall of the enclosed garden beyond, the steep roof of a barn. He would have to wait some time for full daylight to pass, or else take a risk and run for it through the brook, and into the straw-stack beyond, when he saw his opportunity. And here there were people moving from time to time about their legitimate business, a shepherd urging his flock towards the home pasture, a woman coming home from the woods with mushrooms, two children driving geese. He might very well have strolled past all these with a greeting, and been taken for granted, but he could not be seen by any of them making a sudden dash for it through the ford and into the abbey gardens. That would have been enough to call their attention and raise an alarm, and there were sounds of unusual activity, shouts and orders and the creaking of carts and harness, still echoing distantly from beyond the gardens. Moreover, there was a man on horseback in sight on his side of the brook, some distance away downstream but drawing gradually nearer, patrolling this stretch of meadows as though he had been posted here to secure the one unwalled exit from the enclave. As probably he had, though he seemed to be taking the duty very easily, ambling his mount along the green at leisure. One man only, but one was enough. He had only to shout, or whistle shrilly on his fingers, and he could bring a dozen Flemings swarming.

Torold went to ground among the bushes, and watched him approach. A big, rawboned, powerful but unhandsome horse, dappled from cream to darkest grey, and the rider a young fellow black-haired and olive-complexioned, with a thin, assured, saturnine face and an arrogantly easy carriage in the saddle. It was this light, elegant seat of his, and the striking colouring of the horse, that caught Torold's closer attention. This was the very beast he had seen leading the patrol along the riverside at dawn, and this same man had surely lighted down from his mount and gone first into Torold's abandoned sanctuary at the mill. Then he had been attended by half a dozen footmen, and had emerged to loose them in after him, before they all mustered again and moved on. Torold was sure of this identification; he had had good reason to watch very closely, dreading that in spite of his precautions they might yet find some detail to arouse suspicion. This was the same horse, and the same man. Now he rode past upstream, apparently negligent and unobservant, but Torold knew better. There was nothing this man missed as he rode, those were lively, witty, formidable eyes that cast such seemingly languid looks about him.

But now his back was turned, and no one else moved at the moment in these evening fields. If he rode on far enough, Torold might attempt the crossing. Even if he misjudged in his haste and soaked himself, he could not possibly drown in this stream, and the night would be warm. Go he must, and find his way to Godith's bed, and somehow get some reassurance.

The king's officer rode on, oblivious, to the limit of the level ground, never turning his head. And no other creature stirred. Torold picked himself up and ran for it, across the open mead, into the brook, picking his footing by luck and instinct well enough, and out upon the pale, shaven fields on the other side. Like a mole burrowing into earth, he burrowed into the stack of haulms. In the turmoil of this day it was no surprise to find boat and bundle vanished, and he had no time to consider whether the omen was bad or good. He drew the disturbed stems about him, a stiff, creamy lace threaded by sunlight and warmth, and lay quivering, his face turned to peer through the network to where the enemy rode serenely.

And the enemy had also turned, sitting the dappled horse motionless, gazing downstream as though some pricking of his thumbs had warned him. For some minutes he remained still, as easy as before, and yet as alert; then he began the return journey, as softly as he had traced it upstream.

Torold held his breath and watched him come. He made no haste, but rode his beat in idle innocence, having nothing to do, and nothing but this repeated to and fro to pass the time here. But when he drew opposite the pease-fields he reined in, and sat gazing across the brook long and steadily, and his eyes homed in upon the loose stack of haulms, and lingered. Torold thought he saw the dark face melt into a secret smile; he even thought the raised bridle-hand made a small movement that could have been a salute. Though that was idiocy, he must have imagined it! For the horseman was moving on downstream on his patrol, gazing towards the outflow from the mill and the confluence with the river beyond. Never a glance behind.

Torold lay down under his weightless covering, burrowed his tired head into his arms, and his hips into the springy turf of the headland, and fell asleep in sheer, exhausted reaction. When he awoke it was more than half dark, and very quiet. He lay for a while listening intently, and then wormed his way out into a pallid solitude above a deserted valley, and crept furtively up the slope into the abbey gardens, moving alone among the myriad sun-warmed scents of Cadfael's herbs. He found the hut, its door hospitably open to the twilight, and peered almost fearfully into the warm silence and gloom within.

'Praise God!' said Brother Cadfael, rising from the bench to haul him briskly within. 'I thought you'd aim for here, I've been keeping an eye open for you every half-hour or so, and at last I have you. Here, sit down and ease your heart, we've come through well enough!'

Urgent and low, Torold asked the one thing that mattered: 'Where is Godith?'

Chapter Nine

ODITH, IF he had but known it, was at that moment viewing her own reflection in Aline's glass, which Constance was holding well away from her to capture more of the total image. Washed and combed and arrayed in one of Aline's gowns, brocaded in brown and gold thread, with a thin gold bandeau of Aline's round her curls, she turned this way and that to admire herself with delight at being female again, and her face was no longer that of an urchin, but of an austere young gentlewoman aware of her advantages. The soft candlelight only made her more mysterious and strange in her own eyes.

'I wish he could see me like this,' she said wistfully, forgetting that so far she had not mentioned any he except Brother Cadfael, and could not now, even to Aline, reveal anything concerning Torold's person and errand beyond his name. Concerning herself she had told almost everything, but that was the acknowledgement of a debt.

'There is a he?' asked Aline, sparkling with sympathetic curiosity. 'And he will escort you? Wherever you are going? No, I mustn't ask you anything, it would be unfair. But why shouldn't you wear the dress for him? Once away, you can as well travel as yourself as you can in boy's clothes.'

'I doubt it,' said Godith ruefully. 'Not the way we shall be travelling.'

'Then take it with you. You could put it in that great bundle of yours. I have plenty, and if you are going with nothing, then you'll need a gown for when you reach safety.'

'Oh, if you knew how you tempt me! You are kind! But I couldn't take it. And we shall have weight enough to carry, the first miles. But I do thank you, and I shall never forget.'

She had tried on, for pure pleasure, Constance assisting with relish, every dress Aline had with her, and in every one she had imagined herself confronting Torold, without warning, and studying his astonished and respectful face. And somehow, in spite of not knowing where he was or how he was faring, she had spent a blissful afternoon, unshaken by doubts. Certainly he would see her in her splendour, if not in this in other fine gowns, in jewels, with her hair, grown long again, plaited and coiled upon her head in a gold circlet like this one. Then she recalled how she had sat beside him, the two of them companionably eating plums and committing the stones to the Severn through the floorboards of the mill, and she laughed. What use would it ever be, putting on airs with Torold?

She was in the act of lifting the circlet from her head when they all heard the sudden but circumspect knocking on the outer door, and for a moment froze into wary stillness, looking at one another aghast.

'Do they mean to search here, after all?' wondered Godith in a shocked whisper. 'Have I brought you into danger?'

'No! Adam assured me I should not be disturbed, this morning, when they came.' Aline rose resolutely. 'You stay here with Constance, and bolt the door. I'll go. Can it be Brother Cadfael come for you already?'

'No, surely not yet, they'll still be on the watch.'

It had sounded the most deferential of knocks, but all the same, Godith sat very still behind the bolted door, and listened with strained attention to the snatches of voices that reached her from without. Aline had brought her visitor into the room. The voice that alternated with hers was a man's, low-pitched and ardently courteous.

'Adam Courcelle!' Constance mouthed silently, and smiled her knowing smile. 'So deep in love, he can't keep away!'

'And she – Aline?' whispered Godith curiously.

'Who knows! Not *she* – not yet!'

Godith had heard the same voice that morning, addressing the porter and the lay servants at the gate in a very different tone. But such duties can surely give no pleasure, and may well make even a decent man ill-humoured and overbearing. This devout and considerate soul enquiring tenderly after Aline's peace of mind might be his proper self.

'I hope you have not been too much put out by all this stir,' he was saying. 'There'll be no more disturbances, you may rest now.'

'I haven't been molested at all,' Aline assured him serenely. 'I have no complaint, you have been considerate indeed. But I'm sorry for those who have had goods distrained. Is the same thing happening in the town?'

'It is,' he said ruefully, 'and will go on tomorrow, but the abbey may be at peace now. We have finished here.'

'And you did not find her? The girl you had orders to search for?'

'No, we have not found her.'

'What would you say,' asked Aline deliberately, 'if I said that I was glad?'

'I should say that I would expect nothing else from you, and I honour you for it. I know you could not wish danger or pain or captivity to any creature, much less a blameless girl. I've learned so much of you, Aline.' The brief silence was charged, and when he resumed: 'Aline –' his voice sank so low that Godith could not distinguish the words. She did not want to, the tone was too intimate and urgent. But in a few moments she heard Aline say gently:

'You must not ask me to be very receptive tonight, this has been a harrowing day for so many. I can't help but feel almost as weary as they must be. And as you! Leave me to sleep long tonight, there will be a better time for talking of these matters.'

'True!' he said, resuming the soldier on duty as though he squared his shoulders to a load again. 'Forgive me, this was not the time. Most of my men are out of the gates by now, I'll follow them, and let you rest. You may hear marching and the carts rolling for a quarter of an hour or so, after that it will be quiet.'

The voices receded, towards the outer door. Godith heard it opened, and after a few exchanged and inaudible words, closed again. She heard the bolt shot, and in a few moments more Aline tapped at the bedroom door. 'You can safely open, he's gone.'

She stood in the doorway, flushed and frowning, rather in private perplexity than displeasure. 'It seems,' she said, and smiled in a way Adam Courcelle would have rejoiced to see, 'that in sheltering you I've done him no wrong. I think he's relieved at *not* finding you. They're all going. It's over. Now we have only to wait for Brother Cadfael and full darkness.'

In the hut in the herbarium Brother Cadfael fed, reassured and doctored his patient. Torold, once the first question had been answered so satisfactorily, lay down submissively on Godith's bed, and let his shoulder be dressed again, and the gash in his thigh, already healed, nevertheless be well bandaged and padded. 'For if you're to ride into Wales this night,' said Cadfael, 'we don't want any damage or delays, you could all too easily break that open again.'

'Tonight?' said Torold eagerly. 'Is it to be tonight? She and I together?'

'It is, it must, and high time, too. I don't think I could stand this sort of thing much longer,' said Cadfael, though he sounded almost complacent about it. 'Not that I've had too much of the pair of you, you understand, but all the same, I'll be relieved when you're well away towards Owain Gwynedd's country, and what's more, I'll give you a token from myself to the first Welsh you encounter. Though you already have FitzAlan's commendation to Owain, and Owain keeps his word.'

'Once mounted and started,' vowed Torold heartily, 'I'll take good care of Godith.'

'And so will she of you. I'll see she has a pot of this salve I've been using on you, and a few things she may need.'

'And she took boat and load and all with her!' mused Torold, fond and proud. 'How many girls could have kept their heads and done as well? And this other girl took her in! And brought you word of it, and so wisely! I tell you, Brother Cadfael, we breed fine women here in Salop.' He went silent for a moment, and grew thoughtful. 'Now how are we to get her out? They may have left a guard. And anyhow, I can hardly be seen to walk out at the gate house, seeing the porter will know I never walked in that way. And the boat is there, not here.'

'Hush a while,' said Cadfael, finishing off his bandage neatly, 'while I think. What about your own day? You've done well, it seems to me, and come out of it none the worse. And you must have left all open and innocent, for there's been no whisper about the old mill. You caught the wind of them soon, it seems.'

Torold told him about the whole long, dangerous and yet inexpressibly tedious day of starting and stopping, running and hiding, loitering and hurrying. 'I saw the company that combed the river bank and the mill, six armed men on foot, and an officer riding. But I'd made sure there was no sign of me left there. The officer went in first, alone, and then turned his men into it. I saw the same fellow again,' he recalled, suddenly alert to the coincidence, 'this evening, when I crossed the ford and dived into the stack. He was riding the far bank up and down, between river and mill-race, alone. I knew him by his seat in the saddle, and the horse he was riding. I'd made the crossing behind his back, and when he rode back downstream he halted right opposite, and sat and gazed straight at where I was hiding. I could have sworn he'd seen me. He seemed to be staring directly at me. And smiling! I was sure I was found out. But then he rode on. He can't have seen me, after all.'

Cadfael put away his medicines very thoughtfully. He asked mildly: 'And you knew him by his horse again? What was so notable about it?'

'The size and colour. A great, gaunt, striding beast, not beautiful but strong, and dappled clean through from creamy belly to a back and quarters all but black.'

Cadfael scrubbed at his blunt brown nose, and scratched his even browner tonsure. 'And the man?'

'A young fellow hardly older than I. Black-avised, and a light build to him. All I saw of him this morning was the clothes he wore and the way he rode, very easy on what I should guess might be a hard-mouthed brute. But I saw his face tonight. Not much flesh, and bold bones, and black eyes and brows. He whistles to himself,' said Torold, surprised at remembering this. 'Very sweetly!'

So he did! Cadfael also remembered. The horse, too, he recalled, left behind in the abbey stables when two better and less noticeable had been withdrawn. Two, their owner had said, he might be willing to sacrifice, but not all four, and not the pick of the four. Yet the cull had been made, and still he rode one of the remaining two, and doubtless the other, also, was still at his disposal. So he had lied. His position with the king was already assured, he had even been on duty in today's raiding. Very selective duty? And if so, who had selected it?

'And you thought he had seen you cross?'

'When I was safe hidden I looked, and he'd turned my way. I thought he'd seen me moving, from the corner of his eye.'

That one, thought Cadfael, has eyes all round his head, and what he misses is not worth marking. But all he said to Torold was: 'And he halted and stared across at you, and then rode on?'

'I even thought he lifted his bridle-hand a thought to me,' owned Torold, grinning at his own credulity. 'By that time I doubt I was seeing visions at every turn, I was so wild to get to Godith. But then he just turned and rode on, easy as ever. So he can't have seen me, after all.'

Cadfael pondered the implications of all this in wonder and admiration. Light was dawning as dusk fell into night. Not complete darkness yet, simply the departure of the sun, afterglow and all, leaving a faint greenish radiance along the west; not complete dawn, but a promising confirmation of the first elusive beams.

'He can't have, can he?' demanded Torold, fearful that he might have drawn danger after him all too near to Godith.

'Never a fear of it,' said Cadfael confidently. 'All's well, child, don't fret, I see my way. And now it's time for me to go to Compline. You may drop the bolt after me, and lie down here on Godith's bed and get an hour or so of sleep, for by dawn you'll be needing it. I'll come back to you as soon as service is over.'

He did, however, spare the few minutes necessary to amble through the stables, and was not surprised to note that neither the dapple-grey nor its companion, the broad-backed brown cob, was in its stall. An innocent visit to the guest hall after Compline further confirmed that Hugh Beringar was not there in the apartments for gentlefolk, nor were his three men-at-arms present among the commonalty. The porter recalled that the three retainers had gone forth soon after Beringar had ridden in from his day's duties at the end of the hunt, about the time that Vespers ended, and Beringar himself had followed, in no apparent haste, an hour or so later.

So that's how things stand, is it? thought Cadfael. He's staked his hand that it's to be tonight, and is willing to stand or fall on his wager. Well, since he's so bold and so shrewd to read my mind, let's see how good I am at reading his, and I'll stake just as boldly.

Well, then: Beringar knew from the first that his service with the king was accepted and his horses safe enough, therefore he wanted them removed for some other purpose of his own. And made a fellow-conspirator of me! Why? He could have found a refuge for himself if he'd really needed one. No, he wanted me to know just where the horses were, available and inviting. He knew I had two people to deliver out of this town and out of the king's hold, and would jump at his offer for my own ends. He offered me the bait of two horses so that I should transfer the treasury to the same place, ready for flight. And finally, he had no need to hunt for his fugitives, he had only to sit back and leave it to me to bring them to the garage as soon as I could, and then he had everything in one spot, ready to be gathered in.

It follows, therefore, that tonight he'll be waiting for us, and this time with his armed men at his back.

There were still details that baffled the mind. If Beringar had indeed turned a blind eye to Torold's hiding-place this evening, for what purpose? Granted he did not know at this moment where Godith was, and might choose to let one bird fly in order to secure its mate also. But now that Cadfael came to consider all that had passed there was no escaping the possibility, to put it no higher, that throughout, Beringar had been turning a similarly blind and sparkling eye to Godith's boyish disguise, and had had a very shrewd idea of where his missing bride was to be found. In that case, if he had known Godric was Godith, and that one of FitzAlan's men was in hiding in the old mill, then as soon as he had satisfied himself that Cadfael had recovered the treasure for him he could simply have gone in force and gathered in all three prizes, and delivered them to a presumably delighted and grateful king. If he had not done so, but chosen this furtive way, it must mean something different. As, for instance, that his intent was to secure Godith and Torold and duly hand them over for his reward, but despatch FitzAlan's gold, not back to Shrewsbury, but by his own men, or indeed in person, to his own home manor, for his own private use. In which case the horses had been moved not only to fool a simple old monk, but to transfer the treasure direct to Maesbury in complete secrecy, without having to go near Shrewsbury.

That, of course, was all supposing Beringar was not Nicholas Faintree's murderer. If he was, the plan differed in one important aspect. He would see to it that though Godith went back to bait the trap for her father, Torold Blund was taken, not alive, but dead. Dead, and therefore silent. A second murder to bury the first.

Altogether a grim prospect, thought Cadfael, surprisingly undisturbed by it. Except, of course, that it could all mean something very different. Could, and does! or my name is not Cadfael, and I'll never pick a fight with a clever young man again!

He went back to the herbarium, settled in his mind and ready for another restless night. Torold was awake and alert, quick to lift the bolt as soon as he was sure who came.

'Is it time yet? Can we get round to the house on foot?' He was on thorns until he could actually see and touch her, and know that she was safe and free, and had taken no harm.

'There are always ways. But it's neither dark enough nor quiet enough yet, so sit down and rest while you may, for you'll have a share of the weight on the way, until we get to the horses. I must go to the dortoir with the rest, and to my bed. Oh, never fret, I'll be back. Once we're in our own cells, leaving is no great problem. I'm next to the night-stairs, and the prior sleeps at the far end, and sleeps like the dead. And have you forgotten the church has a parish door, on to the Foregate? The only door not within the walls. From there to Mistress Siward's house is only a short walk, and if it passes the gate house, do you think the porter takes account of every citizen abroad somewhat late?'

'So this girl Aline could very well have gone to Mass by that door, like the rest of the laity,' Torold realised, marvelling.

'So she could, but then she would have had no chance to speak to me, and besides, she chose to exert her privilege with Courcelle, and show the Flemings she was to be reckoned with, the clever girl. Oh, you have a fine girl of your own, young Torold, and I hope you'll be good to her, but this Aline is only just stretching her powers to find out what she's worth, and what she can do, and trust me, she'll make such another as our Godith yet.'

Torold smiled in the warm darkness within the hut, sure even in his anxiety that there was but one Godric-Godith. 'You said the porter was hardly likely to pay much attention to citizens making for home late,' he reminded, 'but he may very well have a sharp eye for any such in a Benedictine habit.'

'Who said anything about Benedictine habits drifting abroad so late? *You*, young man, shall go and fetch Godith. The parish door is never closed, and with the gate house so close seldom needs to be. I'll let you out there when the time comes. Go to the last little house, beside the mill, and bring Godith and the boat down from the pond to where the water flows back into the brook, and I shall be there, waiting.'

'The third house of the three on our side,' whispered Torold, glowing even in the dark. 'I know it. I'll go!' The warmth of his gratitude and pleasure filled the hut, and set the herbal fragrances stirring headily, because it would be he, and no other, who would come to fetch Godith away, more wildly and wonderfully than in any mere runaway marriage. 'And you'll be on the abbey bank, when we come down to the brook?'

'I will so, and go nowhere without me! And now lie down for an hour, or less, and leave the latch in case you sleep too soundly, and I'll come for you when all's quiet.'

Brother Cadfael's plans worked smoothly. The day having been so rough, all men were glad to close the shutters, put out the lights, barricade themselves in from the night, and sleep. Torold was awake and waiting before Cadfael came for him. Through the gardens, through the small court between guest hall and abbot's lodging, into the cloister, and in through the south door of the church, they went together in such a silence and stillness as belonged neither to night nor day, only to this withdrawn world between services. They never exchanged a word until they were in the church, shoulder to shoulder under the great tower and pressed against the west door. Cadfael eased the huge door ajar, and listened. Peering carefully, he could see the abbey gates, closed and dark, but the wicket gallantly open. It made only a very small lancet of twilight in the night.

'All's still. Go now! I'll be at the brook.'

The boy slid through the narrow opening, and swung lightly away from the door into the middle of the roadway, as though coming from the lanes about the horse-fair. Cadfael closed the door inch by inch in silence. Without haste he withdrew as he had come, and strolled under the solitary starlight through the garden and down the field, bearing to the right along the bank of the brook until he could go no further. Then he sat down in the grass and vetches and moth-pasture of the bank to wait. The August night was warm and still, just enough breeze to rustle the bushes now and then, and make the trees sigh, and cover with slight sounds the slighter sounds made by careful and experienced men. Not that they would be followed tonight. No need! The one who might have been following was already in position at the end of the journey, and waiting for them.

Constance opened the door of the house, and was startled and silenced by the apparition of this young, secular person, instead of the monk she had expected. But Godith was there, intent and burning with impatience at her shoulder, and flew past her with a brief, wordless, almost soundless cry, into his arms and on to his heart. She was Godric again, though for him she would never now be anyone but Godith, whom he had never yet seen in her own proper person. She clung to him, and laughed, and wept, hugged, reviled, threatened him all in a breath, felt tenderly at his swathed shoulder, demanded explanations and cancelled all her demands, finally lifted to him an assuaged face in sudden silence, and waited to be kissed. Stunned and enlightened, Torold kissed her.

'You must be Torold,' said Aline from the background, so serenely that she must have known rather more about their relationship, by now, than he knew himself. 'Close the door, Constance, all's well.' She looked him over, with eyes alert to a young man's qualities by reason of certain recent experiences of her own, and thought well of him. 'I knew Brother Cadfael would send. She wanted to go back as she came this morning, but I said no. He said he would come. I didn't know he would be sending you. But Cadfael's messenger is very welcome.'

'She has told you about me?' enquired Torold, a little flushed at the thought.

'Nothing but what I needed to know. She is discretion itself, and so am I,' said Aline demurely. She, too, was flushed and glittering, but with excitement and enjoyment of her own plotting, half-regretful that her share must end here. 'If Brother Cadfael is waiting, we mustn't lose time. The farther you get by daybreak, the better. Here is the bundle Godith brought. Wait here within, until I see if everything is quiet below in the garden.'

She slipped away into the soft darkness, and stood by the edge of the pond, listening intently. She was sure they had left no guard behind, for why should they, when they had searched everywhere, and taken all they had been sent to take? Yet there might still be someone stirring in the houses opposite. But all were in darkness, she thought even the shutters were closed, in spite of the warm night, for fear some solitary Fleming should return to help himself to what he could find, under cover of the day's official looting. Even the willow leaves hung motionless here, sheltered from the faint breeze that stirred the grasses along the river bank.

'Come!' she whispered, opening the door narrowly. 'All's quiet. Follow where I step, the slope is rough.' She had even thought to change her pale gown for a dark one since afternoon, to be shadowy among the shadows. Torold hoisted

FitzAlan's treasury in its sacking shroud by the rope that secured it, and put off Godith firmly when she would have reached to share the weight with him. Surprisingly, she yielded meekly, and went before him very quickly and quietly to where the boat rode on its short mooring, half-concealed by the stooping willow branches. Aline lay down at the edge of the bank, and leaned to draw the boat in and hold it steady, for there was a two-foot hollow of undercut soil between them and the water. Very quickly and happily this hitherto cloistered and dutiful daughter was learning to be mistress of her own decisions and exploiter of her own powers.

Godith slid down into the boat, and lent both arms to steady the sacking bundle down between the thwarts. The boat was meant for only two people at most, and settled low in the water when Torold also was aboard, but it was buoyant and sturdy, and would get them as far as they needed to go, as it had done once before.

Godith leaned and embraced Aline, who was still on her knees at the edge of the grass. It was too late for spoken thanks then, but Torold kissed the small, well-tended hand held out to him, and then she loosed the end of the mooring-rope, and tossed it aboard, and the boat slipped out softly from under the bank and drifted across in the circling eddies of the outflow, back towards the brook from which the pool had been drawn. The spill from the head-race of the mill caught them and brisked their pace like a gentle push, and Torold sat with paddle idle, and let the silent flow take them out from the pond. When Godith looked back, all she could see was the shape of the willow, and the unlighted house beyond.

Brother Cadfael rose from among the long grasses as Torold paddled the boat across to the abbey shore. 'Well done!' he said in a whisper. 'And no trouble? No one stirring?'

'No trouble. Now you're the guide.'

Cadfael rocked the boat thoughtfully with one hand. 'Put Godith and the load ashore opposite, and then fetch me. I may as well go dry-shod.' And when they were all safely across to the other side of the brook, he hauled the boat out of the water into the grass, and Godith hurried to help him carry it into hiding in the nearest copse. Once in cover, they had leisure to draw breath and confer. The night was still and calm around them, and five minutes well spent here, as Cadfael said, might save them much labour thereafter.

'We may speak, but softly. And since no other eyes, I hope,

313

are to see this burden of ours until you're well away to the west, I think we might with advantage open it and split the load again. The saddle-bags will be far easier to sling on our shoulders than this single lump.'

'I can carry one pair,' said Godith, eager at his elbow.

'So you can, for a short spell, perhaps,' he said indulgently. He was busy disentangling the two pairs of linked bags from the sacks that had swathed them. They had straps comfortably broad for the shoulder, and the weights in them had been balanced in the first place for the horses. 'I had thought we might save ourselves half a mile or so by making use of the river for the first part of the way,' he said, 'but with three of us and only this hazel-shell we should founder. And it's not so far we have to go, loaded – something over three miles, perhaps.'

He shook one pair of bags into the most comfortable position over his shoulder, and Torold took the other pair on his sound side. 'I never carried goods to this value before in my life,' said Cadfael as he set off, 'and now I'm not even to see what's within.'

'Bitter stuff to me,' said Torold at his back, 'it cost Nick his life, and I'm to have no chance to avenge him.'

'You give thought to your own life and bear your own burdens,' said Cadfael. 'He will be avenged. Better you should look to the future, and leave Nick to me.'

The ways by which he led his little convoy differed from those he had used in Beringar's company. Instead of crossing the brook and making directly for the grange beyond Pulley, he bore more strongly to the west, so that by the time they were as far south as the grange they were also a good mile west of it, nearer to Wales, and in somewhat thicker forest.

'How if we should be followed?' wondered Godith.

'We shall not be followed.' He was so positive about it that she accepted the reassurance gladly, and asked nothing more. If Brother Cadfael said it, it was so. She had insisted on carrying Torold's load for half a mile or so, but he had taken it back from her at the first sign of quickening breath or faltering step.

A lace-work of sky showed paler between the branches ahead. They emerged cautiously into the edge of a broad forest ride that crossed their path on good turf at an oblique angle. Beyond it, their own track continued, a little more open to the night than up to this point.

'Now pay good heed,' said Cadfael, halting them within cover, 'for you have to find your way back without me to this spot. This ride that crosses us here is a fine, straight road the old Romans made. Eastward, here to our left, it would bring us to the Severn bridge at Atcham. Westward, to our right, it will take you two straight as an arrow for Pool and Wales, or if you find any obstacle on the way, you may bear further south at the end for the ford at Montgomery. Once you're on this, you can ride fast enough, though in parts it may be steep. Now we cross it here, and have another half-mile to go to the ford of the brook. So pay attention to the way.'

Here the path was clearly better used, horses could travel it without great difficulty. The ford, when they reached it, was wide and smooth. 'And here,' said Cadfael, 'we leave our loads. One tree among so many trees you might well lose, but one tree beside the only ford along the path, and you can't lose it.'

'Leave them?' wondered Torold. 'Why, are we not going straight to where the horses are? You said yourself we should not be followed tonight.'

'Not followed, no.' When you know where your quarry must come, and are sure of the night, you can be there waiting. 'No, waste no more time, trust me and do as I say.' And he let down his own half of the burden, and looked about him, in the dimness to which by now their eyes were accustomed, for the best and safest concealment. In the thicket of bushes close to the ford, on their right, there was a gnarled old tree, one side of it dead, and its lowest branch deep in the cover of the bushes. Cadfael slung his saddle-bags over it, and without another word Torold hoisted his own beside them, and drew back to assure himself that only those who had hidden here were likely ever to find. The full leafage covered all.

'Good lad!' said Cadfael contentedly. 'Now, from here, we bear round to the east somewhat, and this path we're on will join the more direct one I used before. For we must approach the grange from the right direction. It would never do for any curious person to suppose we'd been a mile nearer Wales.'

Unburdened now, they drew together and went after him hand in hand, trusting as children. And now that they were drawing nearer to the actual possibility of flight, they had nothing at all to say, but clung to each other and believed that things would go right.

Their path joined the direct one only some minutes walk

315

from the small clearing where the stockade of the grange rose. The sky paled as the trees fell back. There was a small rush-light burning somewhere within the house, a tiny, broken gleam showed through the pales. All round them the night hung silent and placid.

Brother Anselm opened to them, so readily that surely some aggrieved traveller from Shrewsbury must have brought word even here of the day's upheaval, and alerted him to the possibility that anyone running from worse penalties might well take warning, and get out at once. He drew them within thankfully and in haste, and peered curiously at the two young fellows at Cadfael's back, as he closed the gate.

'I thought it! My thumbs pricked. I felt it must be tonight. Things grow very rough your way, so we've heard.'

'Rough enough,' admitted Cadfael, sighing. 'I'd wish any friend well out of it. And most of all these two. Children, these good brothers have cared for your trust, and have it here safe for you. Anselm, this is Adeney's daughter, and this FitzAlan's squire. Where is Louis?'

'Saddling up,' said Brother Anselm, 'the moment he saw who came. We had it in mind the whole day that you'd have to hurry things. I've put food together, in case you came. Here's the scrip. It's ill to ride too far empty. And a flask of wine here within.'

'Good! And these few things I brought,' said Cadfael, emptying his own pouch. 'They're medicines. Godith knows how to use them.'

Godith and Torold listened and marvelled. The boy said, almost tongue-tied with wondering gratitude: 'I'll go and help with the saddling.' He drew his hand from Godith's and made for the stables, across the small untended court. This forest assart, unmanageable in such troubled times, would soon be forest again, these timber buildings, always modest enough, would moulder into the lush growth of successive summers. The Long Forest would swallow it without trace in three years, or four.

'Brother Anselm,' said Godith, running an awed glance from head to foot of the giant, 'I do thank you with all my heart, for both of us, for what you have done for us two – though I think it was really for Brother Cadfael here. He has been my master eight days now, and I understand. This and more I would do for him, if ever I might. I promise you Torold and I will never forget, and never debase what you've done for us.'

'God love you, child,' said Brother Anselm, charmed and amused, 'you talk like a holy book. What should a decent man do, when a young woman's threatened, but see her safe out of her trouble? And her young man with her!'

Brother Louis came from the stables leading the roan Beringar had ridden when first these two horses of his were brought here by night. Torold followed with the black. They shone active and ready in the faint light, excellently groomed and fed, and well rested.

'And the baggage,' said Brother Anselm significantly. 'That we have safe. For my own part I would have parted it into two, to balance it better on a beast, but I thought I had no right to open it, so it stays as you left it, in one. I should hoist it to the crupper with the lighter weight as rider, but as you think fit.'

They were away, the pair of them, to haul out the sack-bound bundle Cadfael had carried here some nights ago. It seemed there were some things they had not been told, just as there were things Torold and Godith had accepted without understanding. Anselm brought the burden from the house on his huge shoulders, and dumped it beside the saddled horses. 'I brought thongs to buckle it to the saddle.' They had indeed given some thought to this, they had fitted loops of cord to the rope bindings, and were threading their thongs into these when a blade sliced down through the plaited cords that held the latch of the gate behind them, and a clear, assured voice ordered sharply:

'Halt as you stand! Let no man move! Turn hither, all, and slowly, and keep your hands visible. For the lady's sake!'

Like men in a dream they turned as the voice commanded, staring with huge, wary eyes. The gate in the stockade stood wide open, lifted aside to the pales. In the open gateway stood Hugh Beringar, sword in hand; and over either shoulder leaned a bended long-bow, with a braced and competent eye and hand behind it; and both of them were aimed at Godith. The light was faint but steady. Those used to it here were well able to use it to shoot home.

'Admirable!' said Beringar approvingly. 'You have understood me very well. Now stay as you are, and let no man move, while my third man closes the gates behind us.'

Chapter Ten

HEY HAD all reacted according to their natures.
Brother Anselm looked round cautiously for his
cudgel, but it was out of reach, Brother Louis kept
both hands in sight, as ordered, but the right one
very near the slit seam of his gown, beneath which he kept his
dagger. Godith, first stunned into incredulous dismay, very
quickly revived into furious anger, though only the set
whiteness of her face and the glitter of her eyes betrayed it.
Brother Cadfael, with what appeared to be shocked
resignation, sat down upon the sacking bundle, so that his
skirts hid it from sight if it had not already been noted and
judged of importance. Torold, resisting the instinct to grip the
hilt of Cadfael's poniard at his belt, displayed empty hands,
stared Beringar in the eye defiantly, and took two long,
deliberate paces to place himself squarely between Godith and
the two archers. Brother Cadfael admired, and smiled
inwardly. Probably it had not occurred to the boy, in his
devoted state, that there had been ample time for both arrows
to find their target before his body intervened, had that been
the intention.

'A very touching gesture,' admitted Beringar generously,
'but hardly effective. I doubt if the lady is any happier with the
situation that way round. And since we're all sensible beings
here, there's no need for pointless heroics. For that matter,
Matthew here could put an arrow clean through the pair of you
at this distance, which would benefit nobody, not even me.

You may as well accept that for the moment I am giving the orders and calling the tune.'

And so he was. However his men had held their hands when they might have taken his order against any movement all too literally, it remained true that none of them had the slightest chance of making any effective attack upon him and changing the reckoning. There were yards of ground between, and no dagger is ever going to outreach an arrow. Torold stretched an arm behind him to draw Godith close, but she would not endure it. She pulled back sharply to free herself, and eluding the hand that would have detained her, strode forward defiantly to confront Hugh Beringar.

'What manner of tune,' she demanded, 'for me? If I'm what you want, very well, here I am, what's your will with me? I suppose I still have lands of my own, worth securing? Do you mean to stand on your rights, and marry me for them? Even if my father is dispossessed, the king might let my lands and me go to one of his new captains! Am I worth that much to you? Or is it just a matter of buying Stephen's favour, by giving me to him as bait to lure better men back into his power?'

'Neither,' said Beringar placidly. He was eyeing her braced shoulders, and roused, contemptuous face with decided appreciation. 'I admit, my dear, that I never felt so tempted to marry you before – you're greatly improved from the fat little girl I remember. But to judge by your face, you'd as soon marry the devil himself, and I have other plans, and so, I fancy, have you. No, provided everyone here acts like a sensible creature, we need not quarrel. And if it needs saying for your own comfort, Godith, I have no intention of setting the hounds on your champion's trail, either. Why should I bear malice against an honest opponent? Especially now I'm sure he finds favour in your eyes.'

He was laughing at her, and she knew it, and took warning. It was not even malicious laughter, though she found it an offence. It was triumphant, but it was also light, teasing, almost affectionate. She drew back a step; she even cast one appealing glance at Brother Cadfael, but he was sitting slumped and apparently apathetic, his eyes on the ground. She looked up again, and more attentively, at Hugh Beringar, whose black eyes dwelt upon her with dispassionate admiration.

'I do believe,' she said slowly, wondering, 'that you mean it.'

'Try me! You came here to find horses for your journey.

There they are! You may mount and ride as soon as you please, you and the young squire here. No one will follow you. No one else knows you're here, only I and my men. But you'll ride the faster and safer if you lighten your loads of all but the necessaries of life,' said Beringar sweetly. 'That bundle Brother Cadfael is so negligently sitting on, as if he thought he'd found a convenient stone – that I'll keep, by way of a memento of you, my sweet Godith, when you're gone.'

Godith had just enough self-control not to look again at Brother Cadfael when she heard this. She had enough to do keeping command of her own face, not to betray the lightning-stroke of understanding, and triumph, and laughter, and so, she knew, had Torold, a few paces behind her, and equally dazzled and enlightened. So that was why they had slung the saddle-bags on the tree by the ford, a mile to the west, a mile on their way into Wales. This prize here they could surrender with joyful hearts, but never a glimmer of joy must show through to threaten the success. And now it lay with her to perfect the coup, and Brother Cadfael was leaving it to her. It was the greatest test she had ever faced, and it was vital to her self-esteem for ever. For this man fronting her was more than she had thought him, and suddenly it seemed that giving him up was almost as generous a gesture as this gesture of his, turning her loose to her happiness with another man and another cause, only distraining the small matter of gold for his pains. For two fine horses, and a free run into Wales! And a kind of blessing, too, secular but valued.

'You mean that,' she said, not questioning, stating. 'We may go!'

'And quickly, if I dare advise. The night is not old yet, but it matures fast. And you have some way to go.'

'I have mistaken you,' she said magnanimously. 'I never knew you. You had a right to try for this prize. I hope you understand that we had also a right to fight for it. In a fair win and a fair defeat there should be no heart-burning. Agreed?'

'Agreed!' he said delightedly. 'You are an opponent after my own heart, and I think your young squire had better take you hence, before I change my mind. As long as you leave the baggage ...'

'No help for it, it's yours,' said Brother Cadfael, rising reluctantly from his seat on guard. 'You won it fairly, what else can I say?'

Beringar surveyed without disquiet the mound of sacking

presented to view. He knew very well the shape of the hump Cadfael had carried here from Severn, he had no misgivings.

'Go, then, and good speed! You have some hours of darkness yet.' And for the first time he looked at Torold, and took his time about studying him, for Torold had held his peace and let her have her head in circumstances he could not be expected to understand, and with admirable self-restraint. 'I ask your pardon, I don't know your name.'

'My name is Torold Blund, a squire of FitzAlan's.'

'I'm sorry that we never knew each other. But not sorry that we never had ado in arms, I fear I should have met my overmatch.' But he was very sunny about it, having got his way, and he was not really much in awe of Torold's longer reach and greater height. 'You take good care of your treasure, Torold, I'll take care of mine.'

Sobered and still, watching him with great eyes that still questioned, Godith said: 'Kiss me and wish me well! As I do you!'

'With all my heart!' said Beringar, and turned her face up between his hands, and kissed her soundly. The kiss lasted long, perhaps to provoke Torold, but Torold watched and was not dismayed. These could have been brother and sister saying a fond but untroubled farewell. 'Now mount, and good speed!'

She went first to Brother Cadfael, and asked his kiss also, with a frantic quiver in her voice and her face that no one else saw or heard, and that might have been of threatened tears, or of almost uncontrollable laughter, or of both together. The thanks she said to him and to the lay brothers were necessarily brief, being hampered by the same wild mixture of emotions. She had to escape quickly, before she betrayed herself. Torold went to hold her stirrup, but Brother Anselm hoisted her between his hands and set her lightly in the saddle. The stirrups were a little long for her, he bent to shorten them to her comfort, and then she saw him look up furtively and flash her a grin, and she knew that he, too, had fathomed what was going on, and shared her secret laughter. If he and his comrade had been let into the whole plot from the beginning, they might not have played their parts so convincingly; but they were very quick to pick up all the undercurrents.

Torold mounted Beringar's roan, and looked down from the saddle at the whole group within the stockade. The archers had unstrung their bows, and stood by looking on with idle interest and some amusement, while the third man opened the gate wide to let the travellers pass.

'Brother Cadfael, everything I owe to you. I shall not forget.'

'If there's anything owing,' said Cadfael comfortably, 'you can repay it to Godith. And see you mind your ways with her until you bring her safe to her father,' he added sternly. 'She's in your care as a sacred charge, beware of taking any advantage.'

Torold's smile flashed out brilliantly for an instant, and was gone; and the next moment so was Torold himself, and Godith after him, trotting out briskly through the open gate into the luminosity of the clearing, and thence into the shadowy spaces between the trees. They had but a little way to go to the wider path, and the ford of the brook, where the saddle-bags waited. Cadfael stood listening to the soft thudding of hooves in the turf, and the occasional rustling of leafy branches, until all sounds melted into the night's silence. When he stirred out of his attentive stillness, it was to find that every other soul there had been listening just as intently. They looked at one another, and for a moment had nothing to say.

'If she comes to her father a virgin,' said Beringar then, 'I'll never stake on man or woman again.'

'It's my belief,' said Cadfael drily, 'she'll come to her father a wife, and very proper, too. There are plenty of priests between here and Normandy. She'll have more trouble persuading Torold he has the right to take her, unapproved, but she'll have her own ways of convincing him.'

'You know her better than I,' said Beringar. 'I hardly knew the girl at all! A pity!' he added thoughtfully.

'Yet I think you recognised her the first time you ever saw her with me in the great court.'

'Oh, by sight, yes – I was not sure then, but within a couple of days I was. She's not so changed in looks, only fined into such a springy young fellow.' He caught Cadfael's eye, and smiled. 'Yes, I did come looking for her, but not to hand her over to any man's use. Nor that I wanted her for myself, but she was, as you said, a sacred charge upon me. I owed it to the alliance others made for us to see her into safety.'

'I trust,' said Cadfael, 'that you have done so.'

'I, too. And no hard feelings upon either side?'

'None. And no revenges. The game is over.' He sounded, he realised suddenly, appropriately subdued and resigned, but it was only the pleasant weariness of relief.

'Then you'll ride back with me to the abbey, and keep me company on the way? I have two horses here. And these lads of mine have earned their sleep, and if your good brothers will give them house-room overnight, and feed them, they may make their way back at leisure tomorrow. To sweeten their welcome, there's two flasks of wine in my saddle-bags, and a pasty. I feared we might have a longer wait, though I was sure you'd come.'

'I had a feeling,' said Brother Louis, rubbing his hands with satisfaction, 'for all the sudden alarm, that there was no real mischief in the wind tonight. And for two flasks of wine and a pasty we'll offer you beds with pleasure, and a game of tables if you've a mind for it. We get very little company here.'

One of the archers led in from the night Beringar's two remaining horses, the tall, rangy dapple-grey and the sturdy brown cob, and placidly lay brothers and men-at-arms together unloaded the food and drink, and at Beringar's orders made the unwieldy, sacking-wrapped bundle secure on the dapple's croup, well balanced and fastened with Brother Anselm's leather straps, provided with quite another end in view. 'Not that I wouldn't trust it with you on the cob,' Beringar assured Cadfael, 'but this great brute will never even notice the weight. And his rider needs a hard hand, for he has a hard mouth and a contrary will, and I'm used to him. To tell truth, I love him. I parted with two better worth keeping, but this hellion is my match, and I wouldn't change him.'

He could not better have expressed what Cadfael was thinking about him. This hellion is my match, and I wouldn't change him! He did his own spying, he gave away generously two valuable horses to discharge his debt to a bride he never really wanted, and he went to all manner of patient, devious shifts to get the girl safe and well out of his path, and lay hand upon the treasury, which was fair game, as she was not. Well, well, we live and learn in the book of our fellow-men!

They rode together, they two alone, by the same road as once before, and even more companionably than then. They went without haste, unwinding the longer way back, the way fitter for horses, the way they had first approached the grange. The night was warm, still and gentle, defying the stormy and ungentle times with its calm assertion of permanent stability.

'I am afraid,' said Hugh Beringar with compunction, 'you have missed Matins and Lauds, and the fault is mine. If I had

323

not delayed everything, you might have been back for midnight. You and I should share whatever penance is due.'

'You and I,' said Cadfael cryptically, 'share a penance already. Well, I could not wish for more stimulating company. We may compound my offence by riding at ease. It is not often a man gets such a night ride, and safely, and at peace.'

Then they were silent for some way, and thought their own thoughts, but somewhere the threads tangled, for after a while Beringar said with assurance: 'You will miss her.' It was said with brisk but genuine sympathy. He had, after all, been observing and learning for some days.

'Like a fibre gone from my heart,' owned Brother Cadfael without dismay, 'but there'll be others will fill the place. She was a good girl, and a good lad, too, if you'll grant me the fancy. Quick to study, and a hard worker. I hope she'll make as good a wife. The young man's a fair match for her. You saw he favoured one shoulder? One of the king's archers did his best to slice the round of it off him, but with Godith's care now he'll do well enough. They'll reach France.' And after a moment's thought he asked, with candid curiosity: 'What would you have done if any one of us had challenged your orders and made a fight of it?'

Hugh Beringar laughed aloud. 'I fancy I should have looked the world's fool, for of course my men knew better than to shoot. But the bow is a mighty powerful persuader, and after all, an unchancy fellow like me *might* be in earnest. Why, you never thought I'd harm the girl?'

Cadfael debated the wisdom of answering that truthfully as yet, and temporised: 'If I ever thought of it, I soon realised I was wrong. They could have killed before ever Torold stepped between. No, I soon gave up that error.'

'And it does not surprise you that I knew what you had brought to the grange, and what you came to fetch tonight?'

'No revelation of your cunning can surprise me any longer,' said Cadfael. 'I conclude that you followed me from the river the night I brought it. Also that you had procured me to help you place the horses there for a dual purpose, to encourage me to transfer the treasure from wherever it was hidden, and to make it possible for those youngsters to escape, while the gold stayed here. The right hand duelling against the left, that fits you well. Why were you so sure it would be tonight?'

'Faith, if I'd been in your shoes *I* would have got them away with all the haste I could, at this favourable time, when search had been made and failed. You would have had to be a fool to let the chance slip. And as I have found long ago, you are no fool, Brother Cadfael.'

'We have much in common,' agreed Cadfael gravely. 'But once you knew that lump you're carrying there was safe in the grange, why did you not simply remove it, and make sure of it? You could still have let the children depart without it, just as they've done now.'

'And sleep in my bed while they rode away? And never make my peace with Godith, but let her go into France believing me her enemy, and capable of such meanness? No, that I could not stomach. I have my vanity. I wanted a clean end, and no grudges. I have my curiosity, too. I wanted to see this young fellow who had taken her fancy. The treasure was safe enough until you chose to get them away, why should I be uneasy about it? And this way was far more satisfying.'

'That,' agreed Cadfael emphatically, 'it certainly was.'

They were at the edge of the forest, and the open road at Sutton, and were turning north towards St Giles, all in amicable ease, which seemed to surprise neither of them.

'This time,' said Beringar, 'we'll ride in at the gate house like orderly members of the household, even if the time is a little unusual. And if you have no objection, we may as well take this straight to your hut in the garden, and sit out the rest of the night, and see what we have here. I should like to see how Godith has been living in your care, and what skills she's been acquiring. I wonder how far they'll be by now?'

'Halfway to Pool, or beyond. Most of the way it's a good road. Yes, come and see for yourself. You went enquiring for her in the town, did you not? At Edric Flesher's. Petronilla had the worst opinion of your motives.'

'She would,' agreed Beringar, laughing. 'No one would ever have been good enough for her chick, she hated me from the start. Ah, well, you'll be able to put her mind at rest now.'

They had reached the silent Abbey Foregate, and rode between the darkened houses, the ring of hooves eerie in the stillness. A few uneasy inhabitants opened their shutters a crack to look out as they passed, but their appearance was so leisured and peaceful that no one could suspect them of harmful intent. The wary citizens went back to bed reassured. Over the high, enclosing wall the great church loomed on their left hand, and the narrow opening of the wicket showed in the dark bulk of the gate. The porter was a lay brother, a little surprised at being roused to let in two horsemen at such an hour, but satisfied, on recognising both of them, that they must have been employed on some legitimate errand, no great marvel in such troublous times. He was incurious and sleepy, and did not wait to see them cross to the stables, where they tended their horses first, as good grooms should, before repairing to the garden hut with their load.

Beringar grimaced when he hoisted it. 'You carried this on your back all that way?' he demanded with raised brows.

'I did,' said Cadfael truthfully, 'and you witnessed it.'

'Then I call that a noble effort. You would not care to shoulder it again these few paces?'

'I could not presume,' said Cadfael. 'It's in your charge now.'

'I was afraid of that!' But he was in high good humour, having fulfilled his idea of himself, made his justification in Godith's eyes, and won the prize he wanted; and he had more sinew in his slenderness than anyone would have thought, for he lifted and carried the weight lightly enough the short way to the herbarium.

'I have flint and tinder here somewhere,' said Cadfael, going first into the hut. 'Wait till I make you a light, there are breakables all round us here.' He found his box, and struck sparks into the coil of charred cloth, and lit the floating wick in his little dish of oil. The flame caught and steadied, and drew tall and still, shedding a gentle light on all the strange shapes of mortars and flasks and bottles, and the bunches of drying herbs that make the air aromatic.

'You are an alchemist,' said Beringar, impressed and charmed. 'I am not sure you are not a wizard.' He set down his load in the middle of the floor, and looked about him with interest. 'This is where she spent her nights?' He had observed the bed, still rumpled from Torold's spasmodic and unquiet sleep. 'You did this for her. You must have found her out the very first day.'

'So I did. It was not so difficult. I was a long time in the world. Will you taste my wine? It's made from pears, when the crop's good.'

'Gladly! And drink to your better success – against all opponents but Hugh Beringar.'

He was on his knees by then, unknotting the rope that bound his prize. One sack disgorged another, the second a third. It could not be said that he was feverish in his eagerness, or showed any particular greed, only a certain excited curiosity. Out of the third sack rolled a tight bundle of cloth, dark-coloured, that fell apart as it was freed from constriction, and shed two unmistakable sleeves across the earth floor. The white of a shirt showed among the tangle of dark colours, and uncurled to reveal three large, smooth stones, a coiled leather belt, a short dagger in a leather sheath. Last of all, out of the centre something hard and small and bright rolled and lay still, shedding yellow flashes as it moved, burning sullenly gold and silver when it lay still at Beringar's feet.

And that was all.

On his knees, he stared and stared, in mute incomprehension, his black brows almost elevated into his hair, his dark eyes round with astonishment and consternation. There was nothing more to be read, in a countenance for once speaking volubly, no recoil, no alarm, no guilt. He leaned forward, and with a sweep of his hand parted all those mysterious garments, spread them abroad, gaped at them, and fastened on the stones. His eyebrows danced, and came down to their normal level, his eyes blazing understanding; he cast one glittering glance at Cadfael, and then he began to laugh, a huge, genuine laughter that shook him where he kneeled, and made the bunches of herbs bob and quiver over his head. A good, open, exuberant sound it was; it made Cadfael, even at this moment, shake and laugh with him.

'And I have been commiserating with you,' gasped Beringar, wiping tears from his eyes with the back of his hand, like a child, 'all this time, while you had this in store for me! What a fool I was, to think I could out-trick you, when I almost had your measure even then.'

'Here, drink this down,' urged Cadfael, offering the beaker he had filled. 'To your own better success – with all opponents but Cadfael!'

Beringar took it, and drank heartily. 'Well, you deserve that. You have the last laugh, but at least you lent it to me a while, and I shall never enjoy a better. What was it you did? How was it done? I swear I never took my eyes from you. You *did* draw up what that young man of yours had drowned there, I heard it rise, I heard the water run from it on the stone.'

'So I did, and let it down again, but very softly. This one I had ready in the boat. The other Godith and her squire drew up as soon as you and I were well on our way.'

'And have it with them now?' asked Beringar, momentarily serious.

'They have. By now, I hope, in Wales, where Owain Gwynedd's hand will be over them.'

'So all the while you knew that I was watching and following you?'

'I knew you must, if you wanted to find your treasure. No one else could lead you to it. If you cannot shake off surveillance,' said Brother Cadfael sensibly, 'the only thing to do is make use of it.'

'That you certainly did. My treasure!' echoed Beringar, and looked it over and laughed afresh. 'Well, now I understand Godith better. In a fair win and a fair defeat, she said, there should be no heartburning! And there shall be none!' He looked again, more soberly, at the things spread before him on the earth floor, and after some frowning thought looked up just as intently at Cadfael. 'The stones and the sacks, anything to make like for like,' he said slowly, 'that I understand. But why these? What are these things to do with me?'

'You recognise none of them – I know. They are nothing to do with you, happily for you and for me. These,' said Cadfael, stooping to pick up and shake out shirt and hose and cotte, 'are the clothes Nicholas Faintree was wearing when he was strangled by night, in a hut in the woods above Frankwell, and thrown among the executed under the castle wall, to cover up the deed.'

'Your one man too many,' said Beringar, low-voiced.

'The same. Torold Blund rode with him, but they were separated when this befell. The murdered was waiting also for him, but with the second one he failed. Torold won away with his charge.'

'That part I know,' said Beringar. 'The last he said to you, and you to him, that evening in the mill, that I heard, but no more.'

He looked long at the poor relics, the dark brown hose and russet cotte, a young squire's best. He looked up at Cadfael, and eyed him steadily, very far from laughter now. 'I understand. You put these together to spring upon me when I was unprepared – when I looked for something very different. For me to see, and recoil from my own guilt. If this happened the night after the town fell, I had ridden out alone, as I recall. And I had been in the town that same afternoon, and to say all, yes, I did gather more than she bargained for from Petronilla. I knew this was in the wind, that there were two in Frankwell waiting for darkness before they rode. Though what I was listening for was a clue to Godith, and that I got, too. Yes, I see that I might well be suspect. But do I seem to you a man who would kill, and in so foul a fashion, just to secure the trash those children are carrying away with them into Wales?'

'Trash?' echoed Cadfael, mildly and thoughtfully.

'Oh, pleasant to have, and useful, I know. But once you have enough of it for your needs, the rest of it is trash. Can you eat it, wear it, ride it, keep off the rain and the cold with it, read it, play music on it, make love to it?'

'You can buy the favour of kings with it,' suggested Cadfael, but very placidly.

'I have the king's favour. He blows too many ways as his advisers persuade him, but left alone he knows a man when he finds one. And he demands unbecoming services when he's angry and vengeful, but he despises those who run too servilely to perform, and never leave him time to think better of his vindictiveness. I was with him in his camp a part of that evening, he has accepted me to hold my own castles and border for him, and raise the means and the men in my own way, which suits me very well. Yes, I would have liked, when such a chance offered, to secure FitzAlan's gold for him, but losing it is no great matter, and it was a good fight. So answer me, Cadfael, do I seem to you a man who would strangle his fellow-man from behind for money?'

'No! There were the circumstances that made it a possibility, but long ago I put that out of mind. You are no such man. You value yourself too high to value a trifle of gold above your self-esteem. I was as sure as man could well be, before I put it to the test tonight,' said Cadfael, 'that you wished Godith well out of her peril, and were nudging my elbow with the means to get her away. To try at the same time for the gold was fair dealing enough. No, you are not my man. There is not much,' he allowed consideringly, 'that I would put out of your scope, but killing by stealth is one thing I would never look for from you, now that I know you. Well, so you can't help me. There's nothing here to shake you, and nothing for you to recognise.'

'Not recognise – no, not that.' Beringar picked up the yellow topaz in its broken silver claw, and turned it thoughtfully in his hands. He rose, and held it to the lamp to examine it better. 'I never saw it before. But for all that, my thumbs prick. This, after a fashion, I think I may know. I watched with Aline while she prepared her brother's body for burial. All his things she put together and brought them, I think, to you to be given as alms, all but the shirt that was stained with his death-sweat. She spoke of something that was not there, but should have been there – a dagger that was hereditary in her family, and went always to the eldest son when he came of age. As she described it to me, I do believe this may be the great stone that tipped the hilt.' He looked up with furrowed brows. 'Where did you find this? Not on your dead man!'

'Not on him, no. But trampled into the earth floor, where Torold had rolled and struggled with the murderer. And it does not belong to any dagger of Torold's. There is only one other who can have worn it.'

'Are you saying,' demanded Beringar, aghast, 'that it was Aline's brother who slew Faintree? Has she to bear that, too?'

'You are forgetting, for once, your sense of time,' said Brother Cadfael reassuringly. 'Giles Siward was dead several hours before Nicholas Faintree was murdered. No, never fear, there's no guilt there can touch Aline. No, rather, whoever killed Nicholas Faintree had first robbed the body of Giles, and went to his ambush wearing the dagger he had contemptibly stolen.'

Beringar sat down abruptly on Godith's bed, and held his head hard between his hands. 'For God's sake, give me more wine, my mind no longer works.' And when his beaker was refilled he drank thirstily, picked up the topaz again and sat weighing it in his hand. 'Then we have some indication of the man you want. He was surely present through part, at any rate, of that grisly work done at the castle, for there, if we're right, he lifted the pretty piece of weaponry to which this thing belongs. But he left before the work ended, for it went on into the night, and by then, it seems, he was lurking in ambush on the other side Frankwell. How did he learn of their plans? May not one of those poor wretches have tried to buy his own life by betraying them? Your man was there when the killing began, but left well before the end. Prestcote was there surely, Ten Heyt and his Flemings were there and did the work, Courcelle, I hear, fled the business as soon as he could, and took to the cleaner duties of scouring the town for FitzAlan, and small blame to him.'

'Not all the Flemings,' Cadfael pointed out, 'speak English.'

'But some do. And among those ninety-four surely more than half spoke French just as well. Any one of the Flemings might have taken the dagger. A valuable piece, and a dead man has no more need of it. Cadfael, I tell you, I feel as you do about this business, such a death must not go unavenged. Don't you think, since it can't be any further grief or shame to her, I might show this thing to Aline, and make certain whether it is or is not from the hilt she knew?'

'I think,' said Cadfael, 'that you may. And after chapter we'll meet again here, if you will. If, that is, I am not so loaded with penance at chapter that I vanish from men's sight for a week.'

In the event, things turned out very differently. If his absence at Matins and Lauds had been noticed at all, it was clean forgotten before chapter, and no one, not even Prior Robert, ever cast it up at him or demanded penance. For after the former day's excitement and distress, another and more hopeful upheaval loomed. King Stephen with his new levies, his remounts and his confiscated provisions, was about to move south towards Worcester, to attempt inroads into the western stronghold of Earl Robert of Gloucester, the Empress Maud's half-brother and loyal champion. The vanguard of his army was to march the next day, and the king himself, with his personal guard, was moving today into Shrewsbury castle for two nights, to inspect and secure his defences there, before marching after the vanguard. He was well satisfied with the results of his foraging, and disposed to forget any remaining grudges, for he had invited to his table at the castle, this Tuesday evening, both Abbot Heribert and Prior Robert, and in the flurry of preparation minor sins were overlooked.

Cadfael repaired thankfully to his workshop, and lay down and slept on Godith's bed until Hugh Beringar came to wake him. Hugh had the topaz in his hand, and his face was grave and tired, but serene.

'It is hers. She took it in her hands gladly, knowing it for her own. I thought there could not be two such. Now I am going to the castle, for the king's party are already moving in there, and Ten Heyt and his Flemings will be with him. I mean to find the man, whoever he may be, who filched that dagger after Giles was dead. Then we shall know we are not far from your murderer. Cadfael, can you not get Abbot Heribert to bring you with him to the castle this evening? He must have an attendant, why not you? He turns to you willingly, if you ask, he'll jump at you. Then if I have anything to tell, you'll be close by.'

Brother Cadfael yawned, groaned and kept his eyes open

unwillingly on the young, dark face that leaned over him, a face of tight, bright lines now, fierce and bleak, a hunting face. He had won himself a formidable ally.

'A small, mild curse on you for waking me,' he said, mumbling, 'but I'll come.'

'It was your own cause,' Beringar reminded him, smiling.

'It *is* my cause. Now for the love of God, go away and let me sleep away dinner, and afternoon and all, you've cost me hours enough to shorten my life, you plague.'

Hugh Beringar laughed, though it was a muted and burdened laugh this time, marked a cross lightly on Cadfael's broad brown forehead, and left him to his rest.

Chapter Eleven

 SERVER FOR every plate was required at the king's supper. It was no problem to suggest to Abbot Heribert that the brother who had coped with the matter of the mass burial, and even talked with the king concerning the unlicensed death, should be on hand with him to be questioned at need. Prior Robert took with him his invariable toady and shadow, Brother Jerome, who would certainly be indefatigable with finger-bowl, napkin and pitcher throughout, a great deal more assiduous than Cadfael, whose mind might well be occupied elsewhere. They were old enemies, in so far as Brother Cadfael entertained enmities. He abhorred a sickly-pale tonsure.

The town was willing to put on a festival face, not so much in the king's honour as in celebration of the fact that the king was about to depart, but the effect was much the same. Edric Flesher had come down to the high street from his shop to watch the guests pass by, and Cadfael flashed him a ghost of a wink, by way of indication that they would have things to discuss later, things so satisfactory that they could well be deferred. He got a huge grin and a wave of a meaty hand in response, and knew his message had been received. Petronilla would weep for her lamb's departure, but rejoice for her safe delivery and apt escort. I must go there soon, he thought, as soon as this last duty is done.

Within the town gate Cadfael had seen the blind old man sitting almost proudly in Giles Siward's good cloth hose, holding out his palm for alms with a dignified gesture. At the high cross he saw the little old woman clasping by the hand her feeble-wit grandson with his dangling lip, and the fine brown cotte sat well on him, and gave him an air of rapt content by its very texture. Oh, Aline, you ought to give your own charity, and see what it confers, beyond food and clothing!

Where the causeway swept up from the street to the gate of the castle, the beggars who followed the king's camp had taken up new stations, hopeful and expectant, for the king's justiciar, Bishop Robert of Salisbury, had arrived to join his master, and brought a train of wealthy and important clerics with him. In the lee of the gate-house wall Lame Osbern's little trolley was drawn up, where he could beg comfortably without having to move. The worn wooden pattens he used for his callused knuckles lay tidily beside him on the trolley, on top of the folded black cloak he would not need until night fell. It was so folded that the bronze clasp at the neck showed up proudly against the black, the dragon of eternity with his tail in his mouth.

Cadfael let the others go on through the gates, and halted to say a word to the crippled man. 'Well, how have you been since last I saw you by the king's guard-post? You have a better place here.'

'I remember you,' said Osbern, looking up at him with eyes remarkably clear and innocent, in a face otherwise as misshapen as his body. 'You are the brother who brought me the cloak.'

'And has it done you good service?'

'It has, and I have prayed for the lady, as you asked. But, brother, it troubles me, too. Surely the man who wore it before me is dead. Is it so?'

'He is,' said Cadfael, 'but that should not trouble you. The lady who sent it to you is his sister, and trust me, her giving blesses the gift. Wear it, and take comfort.'

He would have walked on then, but a hasty hand caught at the skirt of his habit, and Osbern besought him pleadingly: 'But, brother, I go in dread that I bear some guilt. For I saw the man, living, with this cloak about him, hale as I ...'

'You *saw* him?' echoed Cadfael on a soundless breath, but the anxious voice had ridden over him and rushed on.

'It was in the night, and I was cold, and I thought to myself, I wish the good God would send me such a cloak to keep me warm! Brother, thought is also prayer! And no more than three days later God did indeed send me this very cloak. You dropped it into my arms! How can I be at peace? The young man gave me a groat that night, and asked me to say a prayer for him on the morrow, and so I did. But how if my first prayer made the second of none effect? How if I have prayed a man into his grave to get myself a cloak to wear?'

Cadfael stood gazing at him amazed and mute, feeling the chill of ice flow down his spine. The man was sane, clear of mind and eye, he knew very well what he was saying, and his trouble of heart was real and deep, and must be the first consideration, whatever else followed.

'Put all such thoughts out of your mind, friend,' said Cadfael firmly, 'for only the devil can have sent them. If God gave you the thing for which you wished, it was to save one morsel of good out of a great evil for which you are no way to blame. Surely your prayers for the former wearer are of aid even now to his soul. This young man was one of FitzAlan's garrison here, done to death after the castle fell, at the king's orders. You need have no fears, his death is not at your door, and no sacrifice of yours could have saved him.'

Osbern's uplifted face eased and brightened, but still he shook his head, bewildered. 'FitzAlan's man? But how could that be, when I saw him enter and leave the king's camp?'

'You saw him? You are sure? How do you know this is the same cloak?'

'Why, by this clasp at the throat. I saw it clearly in the firelight when he gave me the groat.'

He could not be mistaken, then, there surely were not two such designs exactly alike, and Cadfael himself had seen its match on the buckle of Giles Siward's sword-belt.

'When was it that you saw him?' he asked gently. 'Tell me how it befell.'

'It was the night before the assault, around midnight. I had my place then close to the guard-post for the sake of the fire, and I saw him come, not openly, but like a shadow, among the bushes. He stood when they challenged him, and asked to be taken to their officer, for he had something to tell, to the king's advantage. He kept his face hidden, but he was young. And afraid! But who was not afraid, then? They took him away within, and afterwards I saw him return, and they let him out. He said he had orders to go back, for there must be no suspicion. That was all I heard. He was in better heart then, not so frightened, so I asked him for alms, and he gave, and asked my prayers in return. Say some prayer for me tomorrow, he said – and on the morrow, you tell me, he died! This I'm sure of, when he left me he was not expecting to die.'

'No,' said Cadfael, sick with pity and grief for all poor, frightened, breakable men, 'surely he was not. None of us knows the day. But pray for him you may, and your prayers will benefit his soul. Put off all thought that ever you did him harm, it is not so. You never wished him ill, God hears the heart. Never wished him any, never did him any.'

He left Osbern reassured and comforted, but went on into the castle carrying with him the load of discomfort and depression the lame man had shed. So it always is, he thought, to relieve another you must burden yourself. And such a burden! He remembered in time that there was one more question he should have asked, the most urgent of all, and turned back to ask it.

'Do you know, friend, who was the officer of the guard, that night?'

Osbern shook his head. 'I never saw him, he never came out himself. No, brother, that I can't tell you.'

'Trouble no more,' said Cadfael. 'Now you have told it freely, and you know the cloak came to you with a blessing, not a bane. Enjoy it freely, as you deserve.'

'Father Abbot,' said Cadfael, seeking out Heribert in the courtyard, 'if you have no need of me until you come to table, there is work here I have still to do, concerning Nicholas Faintree.'

With King Stephen holding audience in the inner ward, and the great court teeming with clerics, bishops, the small nobility of the county, even an earl or so, there was no room, in any case, for the mere servitors, whose duties would begin when the feast began. The abbot had found a friend in the bishop of Salisbury, and readily dismissed Cadfael to whatever pursuit he chose. He went in search of Hugh Beringar with Osbern's story very heavy on his mind, and the last question still unanswered, though so many sad mysteries were now made plain. It was not a terrified prisoner with the rope already round his neck who had broken down and betrayed the secret of FitzAlan's plans for his treasury. No, that betrayal had taken place a day previously, when the issue of battle was still to be decided, and the thing had been done with forethought, to save a life it yet had failed to save. He came by stealth, and asked to be taken to the officer of the guard, for he had something to tell to the king's advantage! And when he left he told the guard he had orders to go back, so that there could be no suspicion, but then he was in better heart. Poor wretch, not for long!

By what means or on what pretext he had managed to get out of the castle – perhaps on pretence of reconnoitring the enemy's position? – certainly he had obeyed his instructions to return and keep all suspicion lulled. He had returned only to confront the death he had thought he was escaping.

Hugh Beringar came out and stood on the steps of the great hall, craning round him for one person among all that shifting throng. The black Benedictine habits showed here and there in strong contrast to the finery of lordlings in their best, but Cadfael was shorter than many of those about him, and saw the man he was seeking before he was himself seen. He began to weave his way towards him, and the keen black eyes sweeping the court beneath drawn brows lit upon him, and glittered. Beringar came down to take him by the arm and draw him away to a quieter place.

'Come away, come up on to the guard-walk, there'll be no one there but the sentry. How can we talk here?' And when they had mounted to the wall, he found a corner where no one could approach them without being seen, and he said, eyeing Cadfael very earnestly: 'You have news in your face. Tell it quickly, and I'll tell you mine.'

Cadfael told the story as briefly as it had been told to him, and it was understood as readily. Beringar stood leaning against the merlon of the wall as though bracing his back for a dour defence. His face was bitter with dismay.

'Her brother! No escaping it, this can have been no other. He came by night out of the castle, by stealth, hiding his face, he spoke with the king's officer, and returned as he had come. So that there might be no suspicion! Oh, I am sick!' said Beringar savagely. 'And all for nothing! His treason fell victim to one even worse. You don't know yet, Cadfael, you don't know all! But that of all people it should be *her brother*!'

'No help for it,' said Cadfael, 'it was he. In terror for his life, regretting an ill-judged alliance, he went hurrying to the besiegers to buy his life, in exchange – for what? Something of advantage to the king! That very evening they had held conference and planned the removal of FitzAlan's gold. That was how someone learned in good time of what Faintree and

Torold carried, and the way they were to go. Someone who never passed that word on, as I think, to king or any, but acted upon it himself, and for his own gain. Why else should it end as it did? The young man, so says Osbern, went back under orders, relieved and less afraid.'

'He had been promised his life,' said Beringar bitterly, 'and probably the king's favour, too, and a place about him, no wonder he went back the happier in that belief. But what was really intended was to send him back to be taken and slaughtered with the rest, to make sure he should not live to tell the tale. For listen, Cadfael, to what I got out of one of the Flemings who was in that day's murderous labour from first to last. He said that after Arnulf of Hesdin was hanged, Ten Heyt pointed out to the executioners a young man who was to be the next to go, and said the order came from above. And it was done. They found it a huge jest that he was dragged to his death incredulous, thinking at first, no doubt, they were putting up a pretence to remove him from the ranks, and then he saw it was black reality, and he screamed that they were mistaken, that he was not to die with the rest, that he had been promised his life, that they should send and ask −'

'Send and ask,' said Brother Cadfael, 'of Adam Courcelle.'

'No − I learned no name ... my man heard none. What makes you hit on that name in particular? He was not by but once, according to this man's account, he came but once to look at the bodies they had already cut down, and it was early, they would be but few. Then he went away to his work in the town, and was seen no more. Weak-stomached, they thought.'

'And the dagger? Was Giles wearing it when they strung him up?'

'He was, for my man had an eye to the thing himself, but when he was relieved for a while, and came back to get it, it was already gone.'

'Even to one with a great prize in view,' said Cadfael sadly, 'a small extra gain by the way may not come amiss.'

They looked at each other mutely for a long moment. 'But why do you say so certainly, Courcelle?'

'I am thinking,' said Cadfael, 'of the horror that fell upon him when Aline came to collect her dead, and he knew what he had done. If I had known, he said, if I had known, I would have saved him for you! No matter at what cost! God forgive me! he said, but he meant: Aline, forgive me! With all his heart he meant it then, though I would not call that repentance. And he gave back, you'll remember, the cloak. I think, truly I do think, he would then have given back also the dagger, if he had dared. But he could not, it was already broken and incomplete. I wonder,' said Cadfael, pondering, 'I wonder what he has done with it now? A man who would take it from the dead in the first place would not part with it too easily, even for a girl's sake, and yet he never dare let her set eyes on it, and he is in earnest in courting her. Would he keep it, in hiding? Or get rid of it?'

'If you are right,' said Beringar, still doubtful, 'we need it, it is our proof. And yet, Cadfael, for God's sake, how are we to deal now? God knows I can find no good to say for one who tried to purchase his own safety so, when his fellows were at their last gasp. But neither you nor I can strip this matter bare, and do so wicked an injury to so innocent and honourable a lady. It's enough that she mourns for him. Let her at least go on thinking that he held by his mistaken choice faithfully to the end, and gave his life for it – not that he died craven, bleating that he was promised grace in return for so base a betrayal. She must not know, now or ever.'

Brother Cadfael could not but agree. 'But if we accuse him, and this comes to trial, surely everything will come out. That we cannot allow, and there lies our weakness.'

'And our strength,' said Beringar fiercely, 'for neither can *he* allow it. He wants his advancement with the king, he wants offices, but he wants Aline – do you think I did not know it? Where would he stand with her if ever a breath of this reached her? No, he will be at least as anxious as we to keep the story for ever buried. Give him but fair chance to settle the quarrel out of hand, and he'll jump at it.'

'Your preoccupation,' said Cadfael gently, 'I understand, and sympathise with it. But you must also acknowledge mine. I have here another responsibility. Nicholas Faintree must not lie uneasy for want of justice.'

'Trust me, and stand ready to back me in whatever I shall do this night at the king's table,' said Hugh Beringar. 'Justice he shall have, and vengeance, too, but let it be as I shall devise.'

Cadfael went to his duty behind the abbot's chair in doubt and bewilderment, with no clear idea in his mind of what Beringar intended, and no conviction that without the broken dagger any secure case could be made against Courcelle. The Fleming had not seen him take it, what he had cried out to Aline over her brother's body, in manifest pain, was not evidence. And yet there had been vengeance and death in Hugh Beringar's face, as much for Aline Siward's sake as for Nicholas Faintree's. What mattered most in the world to him, at this moment, was that Aline should never know how her brother had disgraced his blood and his name, and in that cause Beringar would not scruple to spend not only Adam Courcelle's life, but also his own. And somehow, reflected Cadfael ruefully, I have become very much attached to that young man, and I should not like to see any ill befall him. I would rather this case went to law, even if we have to step carefully in drawing up our evidence, and leave out every word concerning Torold Blund and Godith Adeney. But for that we need, we must have, proof positive that Giles Siward's dagger passed into the possession of Adam Courcelle, and preferably the dagger itself, into the bargain, to match with the piece of it I found on the scene of the murder. Otherwise he will simply lie and lie, deny everything, say he never saw the topaz or the dagger it came from, and has nothing to answer; and from the eminence of the position he has won with the king, he will be unassailable.

There were no ladies present that night, this was strictly a political and military occasion, but the great hall had been decked out with borrowed hangings, and was bright with torches. The king was in good humour, the garrison's provisions were assured, and those who had robbed for the royal supplies had done their work well. From his place behind Heribert at the king's high table Cadfael surveyed the full hall, and estimated that some five hundred guests were present. He looked for Beringar, and found him at a lower table, in his finery, very debonair and lively in conversation, as though he had no darker preoccupation. He was master of his face; even when he glanced briefly at Courcelle there was nothing in the look to attract attention, certainly nothing to give warning of any grave purpose.

Courcelle was at the high table, though crowded to its end by the visiting dignitaries. Big, vividly coloured and handsome, accomplished in arms, in good odour with the king, how strange that such a man should feel it necessary to grasp secretly at plunder, and by such degrading means! And yet, in this chaos of civil war, was it so strange after all? Where a king's favour could be toppled with the king, where barons were changing sides according as the fortunes changed, where even earls were turning to secure their own advantage rather than that of a cause that might collapse under their feet and leave them prisoner and ruined! Courcelle was merely a sign of the times; in a few years there would be duplicates of him in every corner of the realm.

I do not like the way I see England going, thought Cadfael with anxious foreboding, and above all I do not like what is about to happen, for as surely as God sees us, Hugh Beringar is set to sally forth on to a dubious field, half-armed.

He fretted through the long meal, hardly troubled by the demands of Abbot Heribert, who was always abstemious with wine, and ate very frugally. Cadfael served and poured, proffered the finger-bowl and napkin, and waited with brooding resignation.

When the dishes were cleared away, musicians playing, and only the wine on the tables, the servitors in their turn might take their pick of what was left in the kitchens, and the cooks and scullions were already helping themselves and finding quiet corners to sit and eat. Cadfael collected a bread trencher and loaded it with broken meats, and took it out through the great court to Lame Osbern at the gate. There was a measure of wine to go with it. Why should not the poor rejoice for once at the king's cost, even if that cost was handed on down the hierarchies until it fell at last upon the poor themselves? Too often they paid, but never got their share of the rejoicing.

Cadfael was walking back to the hall when his eye fell upon a lad of about twelve, who was sitting in the torchlight on the inner side of the gate house, his back comfortably against the wall, carving his meat into small pieces with a narrow-bladed knife. Cadfael had seen him earlier, in the kitchen, gutting fish with the same knife, but he had not seen the haft of it, and would not have seen it now if the boy had not laid it down beside him on the ground while he ate.

Cadfael halted and gazed, motionless. It was no kitchen knife, but a well-made dagger, and its hilt was a slender shaft of silver, rounded to the hand, showing delicate lines of filigree-work, and glowing round the collar of the blade with small stones. The hilt ended in a twist of silver broken off short. It was hard to believe, but impossible not to believe. Perhaps thought really is prayer.

He spoke to the boy very softly and evenly; the unwitting means of justice must not be alarmed, 'Child, where did you get so fine a knife as that?'

341

The boy looked up, untroubled, and smiled. When he had gulped down the mouthful with which his cheeks were bulging, he said cheerfully: 'I found it. I didn't steal it.'

'God forbid, lad, I never thought it. Where did you find it? And have you the sheath, too?'

It was lying beside him in the shadow, he patted it proudly. 'I fished them out of the river. I had to dive, but I found them. They really are mine, father, the owner didn't want them, he threw them away. I suppose because this was broken. But it's the best knife for slitting fish I ever had.'

So he threw them away! Not, however, simply because the jewelled hilt was broken.

'You saw him throw it into the river? Where was this, and when?'

'I was fishing under the castle, and a man came down alone from the water-gate to the bank of the river, and threw it in, and went back to the castle. When he'd gone I dived in where I saw it fall, and I found it. It was early in the evening, the same night all the bodies were carried down to the abbey – a week ago, come tomorrow. It was the first day it was safe to go fishing there again.'

Yes, it fitted well. That same afternoon Aline had taken Giles away to St Alkmund's, and left Courcelle stricken and wild with unavailing regrets, and in possession of a thing that might turn Aline against him for ever, if once she set eyes on it. And he had done the only, the obvious thing, consigned it to the river, never thinking that the avenging angel, in the shape of a fisher-boy, would redeem it to confront him when most he believed himself safe.

'You did not know who this man was? What like was he? What age?' For there remained the lingering doubt; all he had to support his conviction was the memory of Courcelle's horrified face and broken voice, pleading his devotion over Giles Siward's body.

The child hoisted indifferent shoulders, unable to picture for another what he himself had seen clearly and memorably. 'Just a man. I didn't know him. Not old like you, father, but quite old.' But to him anyone of his father's generation would be old, though his father might be only a year or two past thirty.

'Would you know him if you saw him again? Could you point him out among many?'

'Of course!' said the boy almost scornfully. His eyes were young, bright, and very observant, if his tongue was none too

342

fluent, of course he would know his man again.

'Sheathe your knife, child, and bring it, and come with me,' said Cadfael with decision. 'Oh, don't fret, no one will take your treasure from you, or if later you must give it up, you shall be handsomely paid for it. All I need is for you to tell again what you have told to me, and you shan't be the loser.'

He knew, when he entered the hall with the boy beside him, a little apprehensive now but even more excited, that they came late. The music was stilled, and Hugh Beringar was on his feet and striding towards the dais on which the high table stood. They heard his voice raised, high and clear, as he mounted and stood before the king. 'Your Grace, before you depart for Worcester, there is a matter on which I beg you'll hear me and do right. I demand justice on one here in this company, who has abused his position in your confidence. He has stolen from the dead, to the shame of his nobility, and he has committed murder, to the shame of his manhood. I stand on my charges, to prove them with my body. And here is my gage!'

Against his own doubts, he had accepted Cadfael's intuition, to the length of staking his life upon it. He leaned forward, and rolled something small and bright across the table, to clang softly against the king's cup. The silence that had fallen was abrupt and profound. All round the high table heads craned to follow the flash of yellow brilliance that swayed irregularly over the board, limping on its broken setting, and then were raised to stare again at the young man who had launched it. The king picked up the topaz and turned it in his large hands, his face blank with incomprehension at first, and then wary and brooding. He, too, looked long at Hugh Beringar. Cadfael, picking his way between the lower tables, drew the puzzled boy after him and kept his eyes upon Adam Courcelle, who sat at his end of the table stiff and aware. He had command of his face, he looked no more astonished or curious than any of those about him; only the taut hand gripping his drinking-horn betrayed his consternation. Or was even that imagined, to fit in with an opinion already formed? Cadfael was no longer sure of his own judgment, a state he found distressing and infuriating.

'You have bided your time to throw your thunderbolt,' said the king at length, and looked up darkly at Beringar from the stone he was turning in his hands.

'I was loth to spoil your Grace's supper, but neither would I put off what should not be put off. Your Grace's justice is every

343

honest man's right.'

'You will need to explain much. What is this thing?'

'It is the tip of a dagger-hilt. The dagger to which it belongs is now by right the property of the lady Aline Siward, who has loyally brought all the resources of her house to your Grace's support. It was formerly in the possession of her brother Giles, who was among those who garrisoned this castle against your Grace, and have paid the price for it. I saw that it was taken from his dead body, an act not unknown among the common soldiery, but unworthy of knight or gentleman. That is the first offence. The second is murder – that murder of which your Grace was told by Brother Cadfael, of the Benedictine house here in Shrewsbury, after the count of the dead was made. Your Grace and those who carried out your orders were used as a shield for one who strangled a man from behind, as your Grace will well remember.'

'I do remember,' said the king grimly. He was torn between displeasure at having to exert himself to listen and judge, when his natural indolence had wanted only a leisurely and thoughtless feast, and a mounting curiosity as to what lay behind all this. 'What has this stone to do with that death?'

'Your Grace, Brother Cadfael is also present here, and will testify that he found the place where this murder was committed, and found there, broken off in the struggle and trodden into the ground, this stone. He will take oath, as I do, that the man who stole the dagger is the same who killed Nicholas Faintree, and that he left behind him, unnoticed, this proof of his guilt.'

Cadfael was drawing nearer by then, but they were so intent on the closed scene above that no one noticed his approach. Courcelle was sitting back, relaxed and brightly interested, in his place, but what did that mean? Doubtless he saw very well the flaw in this; no need to argue against the claim that whoever stole the dagger slew the man, since no one could trace possession to him. The thing was at the bottom of the Severn, lost for ever. The theory could be allowed to stand, the crime condemned and deplored, provided no one could furnish a name, and proof to back it. Or, on the other hand, this could far more simply be the detachment of an innocent man!

'Therefore,' said Hugh Beringar relentlessly, 'I repeat those charges I have made here before your Grace. I appeal one among us here in this hall of theft and murder, and I offer proof with my body, to uphold my claim in combat upon the body of

Adam Courcelle.'

He had turned at the end to face the man he accused, who was on his feet with a leap, startled and shaken, as well he might be. Shock burned rapidly into incredulous anger and scorn. Just so would any innocent man look, suddenly confronted with an accusation so mad as to be laughable.

'Your Grace, this is either folly or villainy! How comes my name into such a diatribe? It may well be true that a dagger was stolen from a dead man, it may even be true that the same thief slew a man, and left this behind as witness. But as for how my name comes into such a tale, I leave it to Hugh Beringar to tell – if these are not simply the lies of an envious man. When did I ever see this supposed dagger? When was it ever in my possession? Where is it now? Has any ever seen me wear such a thing? Send, my lord, and search those soldier's belongings I have here, and if such a thing is found in any ward or lodging of mine, let me know of it!'

'Wait!' said the king imperiously, and looked from one face to the other with frowning brows. 'This is indeed a matter that needs to be examined, and if these charges are made in malice there will be an account to pay. What Adam says is the nub of it. Is the monk indeed present? And does he confirm the finding of this broken ornament at the place where this killing befell? And that it came from that very dagger?'

'I brought Brother Cadfael here with me tonight,' said the abbot, and looked about for him helplessly.

'I am here, Father Abbot,' said Cadfael from below the dais, and advanced to be seen, his arm about the shoulders of the boy, now totally fascinated, all eyes and ears.

'Do you bear out what Beringar says?' demanded King Stephen. 'You found this stone where the man was slain?'

'Yes, your Grace. Trampled into the earth, where plainly there had been a struggle, and two bodies rolling upon the ground.'

'And whose word have we that it comes from a dagger once belonging to Mistress Siward's brother? Though I grant you it should be easy enough to recognise, once known.'

'The word of Lady Aline herself. It has been shown to her, and she has recognised it.'

'That is fair witness enough,' said the king, 'that whoever is the thief may well be the murderer, also. But why it should follow that either you or Beringar here suppose him to be Adam, that for my life I cannot see. There's never a thread to

345

join him to the dagger or the deed. You might as well cast round here among us, and pick on Bishop Robert of Salisbury, or any one of the squires down below there. Or prick your knife-point into a list of us with eyes closed. Where is the logic?'

'I am glad,' said Courcelle, darkly red and forcing a strained laughter, 'that your Grace puts so firm a finger on the crux of the matter. With goodwill I can go along with this good brother to condemn a mean theft and a furtive killing, but, Beringar, beware how you connect me with either, or any other honest man. Follow your thread from this stone, by all means, if thread there is, but until you can trace this dagger into my hands, be careful how you toss challenges to mortal combat about you, young man, for they may be taken up, to your great consternation.'

'My gage is now lying upon the table,' said Hugh Beringar with implacable calm. 'You have only to take it up. I have not withdrawn it.'

'My lord king,' said Cadfael, raising his voice to ride over the partisan whisperings and murmurings that were running like conflicting winds about the high table, 'it is not the case that there is no witness to connect the dagger with any person. And for proof positive that stone and dagger belong together, here is the very weapon itself. I ask your Grace to match the two with your own hands.'

He held up the dagger, and Beringar at the edge of the dais took it from him, staring like a man in a dream, and handed it in awed silence to the king. The boy's eyes followed it with possessive anxiety, Courcelle's with stricken and unbelieving horror, as if a drowned victim had risen to haunt him. Stephen looked at the thing with an eye appreciative of its workmanship, slid out the blade with rising curiosity, and fitted the topaz in its silver claw to the jagged edge of the hilt.

'No doubt but this belongs. You have all seen?' And he looked down at Cadfael. 'Where, then, did you come by this?'

'Speak up, child,' said Cadfael encouragingly, 'and tell the king what you told to me.'

The boy was rosy and shining with an excitement that had quite overridden his fear. He stood up and told his tale in a voice shrill with self-importance, but still in the simple words he had used to Cadfael, and there was no man there who could doubt he was telling the truth.

' ... and I was by the bushes at the edge of the water, and he

346

did not see me. But I saw him clearly. And as soon as he went away I dived in where it had fallen, and found it. I live by the river, I was born by it. My mother says I swam before I walked. I kept the knife, thinking no wrong, since he did not want it. And that is the very knife, my lord, and may I have it back when you are done?'

The king was diverted for a moment from the gravity of the cause that now lay in his hands, to smile at the flushed and eager child with all the good-humour and charm his nature was meant to dispense, if he had not made an ambitious and hotly contested bid for a throne, and learned the rough ways that go with such contests.

'So our fish tonight was gutted with a jewelled knife, was it, boy? Princely indeed! And it was good fish, too. Did you catch it, as well as dress it?'

Bashfully the boy said that he had helped.

'Well, you have done your part very fitly. And now, did you know this man who threw away the knife?'

'No, my lord, I don't know his name. But I know him well enough when I see him.'

'And do you see him? Here in this hall with us now?'

'Yes, my lord,' said the child readily, and pointed a finger straight at Adam Courcelle. 'That was the man.'

All eyes turned upon Courcelle, the king's most dourly and thoughtfully of all, and there was a silence that lasted no more than a long-drawn breath, but seemed to shake the foundations of the hall, and stop every heart within its walls. Then Courcelle said, with arduous and angry calm: 'Your Grace, this is utterly false. I never had the dagger, I could not well toss it into the river. I deny that ever I had the thing in my possession, or ever saw it until now.'

'Are you saying,' asked the king drily, 'that the child lies? At whose instigation? Not Beringar's – it seems to me that he was as taken aback by this witness as I myself, or you. Am I to think the Benedictine order has procured the boy to put up such a story? And for what end?'

'I am saying, your Grace, that this is a foolish error. The boy may have seen what he says he saw, and got the dagger as he claims he got it, but he is mistaken in saying he saw me. I am not the man. I deny all that has been said against me.'

'And I maintain it,' said Hugh Beringar. 'And I ask that it be put to the proof.'

The king crashed a fist upon the table so that the boards

danced, and cups rocked and spilled wine. 'There is something here to be probed, and I cannot let it pass now without probing it.' He turned again to the boy, and reined in his exasperation to ask more gently: 'Think and look carefully, now, and say again: are you certain this is the man you saw? If you have any doubt, say so. It is no sin to be mistaken. You may have seen some other man of like build or colour. But if you are sure, say that also, without fear.'

'I am sure,' said the boy, trembling but adamant. 'I know what I saw.'

The king leaned back in his great chair, and thumped his closed fists on the arms, and pondered. He looked at Hugh Beringar with grim displeasure: 'It seems you have hung a millstone round my neck, when most I need to be free and to move fast. I cannot now wipe out what has been said, I must delve deeper. Either this case goes to the long processes of court law – no, not for you nor any will I now delay my going one day beyond the morrow's morrow! I have made my plans, I cannot afford to change them.'

'There need be no delay,' said Beringar, 'if your Grace countenances trial by combat. I have appealed Adam Courcelle of murder, I repeat that charge. If he accepts, I am ready to meet him without any ceremony or preparation. Your Grace may see the outcome tomorrow, and march on the following day, freed of this burden.'

Cadfael, during these exchanges, had not taken his eyes from Courcelle's face, and marked with foreboding the signs of gradually recovered assurance. The faint sweat that had broken on his lip and brow dried, the stare of desperation cooled into calculation; he even began to smile. Since he was now cornered, and there were two ways out, one by long examination and questioning, one by simple battle, he was beginning to see in this alternative his own salvation. Cadfael could follow the measuring, narrowed glance that studied Hugh Beringar from head to foot, and understood the thoughts behind the eyes. Here was a younger man, lighter in weight, half a head shorter, much less in reach, inexperienced, over-confident, an easy victim. It should not be any problem to put him out of the world; and that done, Courcelle had nothing to fear. The judgment of heaven would have spoken, no one thereafter would point a finger at him, and Aline would be still within his reach, innocent of his dealings with her brother, and effectively separated from a too-engaging rival, without any blame to Courcelle, the wrongly accused. Oh, no, it was not so grim a situation, after all. It should work out very well.

He reached out along the table, picked up the topaz, and rolled it contemptuously back towards Beringar, to be retrieved and retained.

'Let it be so, your Grace. I accept battle, tomorrow, without formality, without need for practice. Your Grace shall march the following day.' And I with you, his confident countenance completed.

'So be it!' said the king grimly. 'Since you're bent on robbing me of one good man, between you, I suppose I may as well find and keep the better of the two. Tomorrow, then, at nine of the clock, after Mass. Not here within the wards, but in the open – the meadow outside the town gate, between road and river, will do well. Prestcote, you and Willem marshal the lists. See to it! And we'll have no horses put at risk,' he said practically. 'On foot, and with swords!'

Hugh Beringar bowed acquiescence. Courcelle said: 'Agreed!' and smiled, thinking how much longer a reach and stronger a wrist he had for sword-play.

'*A l'outrance!*' said the king with a vicious snap, and rose from the table to put an end to a sullied evening's entertainment.

Chapter Twelve

N THE way back through the streets of the town,
dark but not quite silent, somehow uneasily astir as if
rats ran in a deserted house, Hugh Beringar on his
rawboned grey drew alongside Brother Cadfael and
walked his mount for some few minutes at their foot-pace,
ignoring Brother Jerome's close proximity and attentive ears as
though they had not existed. In front, Abbot Heribert and
Prior Robert conversed in low and harried tones, concerned
for one life at stake, but unable to intervene. Two young men
at bitter enmity had declared for a death. Once both
contestants had accepted the odds, there was no retreating; he
who lost had been judged by heaven. If he survived the sword,
the gallows waited for him.

'You may call me every kind of fool,' said Beringar
accommodatingly, 'if it will give you any ease.' His voice had
still its light, teasing intonation, but Cadfael was not deceived.

'It is not for me, of all men,' he said, 'to blame, or pity – or
even regret what you have done.'

'As a monk?' asked the mild voice, the smile in it perceptible
to an attentive ear.

'As a man! Devil take you!'

'Brother Cadfael,' said Hugh heartily, 'I do love you. You
know very well you would have done the same in my place.'

'I would not! Not on the mere guess of an old fool I hardly
knew! How if I had been wrong?'

'Ah, but you were not wrong! He is the man – doubly a

murderer, for he delivered her poor coward brother to his death just as vilely as he throttled Faintree. Mind, never a word to Aline about this until all's over – one way or the other.'

'Never a word, unless she speak the first. Do you think the news is not blown abroad all through this town by now?'

'I know it is, but I pray she is deep asleep long ago, and will not go forth to hear this or any news until she goes to High Mass at ten. By which time, who knows, we may have the answer to everything.'

'And you,' said Brother Cadfael acidly, because of the pain he felt, that must have some outlet, 'will you now spend the night on your knees in vigil, and wear yourself out before ever you draw in the field?'

'I am not such a fool as all that,' said Hugh reprovingly, and shook a finger at his friend. 'For shame, Cadfael! You a monk, and cannot trust God to see right done? I shall go to bed and sleep well, and rise fresh to the trial. And now I suppose you will insist on being my deputy and advocate to heaven?'

'No,' said Cadfael grudgingly, 'I shall sleep, and get up only when the bell rings for me. Am I to have less faith than an impudent heathen like you?'

'That's my Cadfael! Still,' conceded Beringar, 'you may whisper a word or two to God on my behalf at Matins and Lauds, if you'll be so kind. If he turns a deaf ear to you, small use the rest of us wearing out our knee-bones.' And he leaned from his tall horse to lay a light hand for an instant on Cadfael's broad tonsure, like a playful benediction, and then set spurs to his horse and trotted ahead, passing the abbot with a respectful reverence, to vanish into the curving descent of the Wyle.

Brother Cadfael presented himself before the abbot immediately after Prime. It did not seem that Heribert was much surprised to see him, or to hear the request he put forward.

'Father Abbot, I stand with this young man Hugh Beringar in this cause. The probing that brought to light the evidence on which his charge rests, that was my doing. And even if he has chosen to take the cause into his own hands, refusing me any perilous part in it, I am not absolved. I pray leave to go and stand trial with him as best I may. Whether I am of help to him or not, I must be there. I cannot turn my back at this pass on my friend who has spoken for me.'

'I am much exercised in mind, also,' admitted the abbot,

sighing. 'In spite of what the king has said, I can only pray that this trial need not be pressed to the death.' And I, thought Cadfael ruefully, dare not even pray for that, since the whole object of this wager is to stop a mouth for ever. 'Tell me,' said Heribert, 'is it certain that the man Courcelle killed that poor lad we have buried in the church?'

'Father, it is certain. Only he had the dagger, only he can have left the broken part behind him. There is here a clear contest of right and wrong.'

'Go, then,' said the abbot. 'You are excused all duties until this matter is ended.' For such duels had been known to last the day long, until neither party could well see, or stand, or strike, so that in the end one or the other fell and could not rise, and simply bled to death where he lay. And if weapons were broken, they must still fight, with hands, teeth and feet, until one or the other broke and cried for quarter; though few ever did, since that meant defeat, the judgment of heaven convicting, and the gallows waiting, an even more shameful death. A bitter business, thought Cadfael, kilting his habit and going out heavily from the gate house, not worthy of being reverenced as the verdict of God. In this case there was a certain appropriateness about it, however, and the divine utterance might yet be heard in it. If, he thought, I have as much faith as he? I wonder if he did indeed sleep well! And strangely, he could believe it. His own sleep had been fitful and troubled.

Giles Siward's dagger, complete with its lopped topaz, he had brought back with him and left in his cell, promising the anxious fisher-boy either restoration or fair reward, but it was not yet time to speak to Aline in the matter. That must wait the issue of the day. If all went well, Hugh Beringar himself should restore it to her. If not – no, he would not consider any such possibility.

The trouble with me, he thought unhappily, is that I have been about the world long enough to know that God's plans for us, however infallibly good, may not take the form that we expect and demand. And I find an immense potential for rebellion in this old heart, if God, for no matter what perfect end, choose to take Hugh Beringar out of this world and leave Adam Courcelle in it.

Outside the northern gate of Shrewsbury the Castle Foregate housed a tight little suburb of houses and shops, but it ended very soon, and gave place to meadows on either side the road. The river twined serpentine coils on both sides, beyond the fields, and in the first level meadow on the left the king's marshals had drawn up a large square of clear ground, fenced in on every side by a line of Flemings with lances held crosswise, to keep back any inquisitive spectator who might encroach in his excitement, and to prevent flight by either contestant. Where the ground rose slightly, outside the square, a great chair had been placed for the king, and the space about it was kept vacant for the nobility, but on the other three sides there was already a great press of people. The word had run through Shrewsbury like the wind through leaves. The strangest thing was the quietness. Every soul about the square of lances was certainly talking, but in such hushed undertones that the sum of all those voices was no louder than the absorbed buzzing of a hive of bees in sunshine.

The slanting light of morning cast long but delicate shadows across the grass, and the sky above was thinly veiled with haze. Cadfael lingered where guards held a path clear for the procession approaching from the castle, a brightness of steel and sheen of gay colours bursting suddenly out of the dim archway of the gate. King Stephen, big, flaxen-haired, handsome, resigned now to the necessity that threatened to rob him of one of his officers, but none the better pleased for that, and not disposed to allow any concessions that would prolong the contest. To judge by his face, there would be no pauses for rest, and no limitation imposed upon the possible savagery. He wanted it over. All the knights and barons and clerics who streamed after him to his presidential chair were carrying themselves with the utmost discretion, quick to take their lead from him.

The two contestants appeared as the royal train drew aside. No shields, Cadfael noted, and no mail, only the simple protection of leather. Yes, the king wanted a quick end, none of your day-long hacking and avoiding until neither party could lift hand. On the morrow the main army would leave to follow the vanguard, no matter which of these two lay dead, and Stephen had details yet to be settled before they marched. Beringar first, the accuser, went to kneel to the king and do him reverence, and did so briskly, springing up vigorously from his knee and turning to where the ranks of lances parted to let him into the arena. He caught sight of Cadfael then, standing a little apart. In a face tight, grave and mature, still the black eyes smiled.

'I knew,' he said, 'that you would not fail me.'

'See to it,' said Cadfael morosely, 'that you do not fail me.'

'No dread,' said Hugh. 'I'm shriven white as a March lamb.'

353

His voice was even and reflective. 'I shall never be readier. And your arm will be seconding mine.'

At every stroke, thought Cadfael helplessly, and doubted that all these tranquil years since he took the cowl had really made any transformation in a spirit once turbulent, insubordinate and incorrigibly rash. He could feel his blood rising, as though it was he who must enter the lists.

Courcelle rose from his knee and followed his accuser into the square. They took station at opposite corners, and Prestcote, with his marshal's truncheon raised, stood between them and looked to the king to give the signal. A herald was crying aloud the charge, the name of the challenger, and the refutation uttered by the accused. The crowd swayed, with a sound like a great, long-drawn sigh, that rippled all round the field. Cadfael could see Hugh's face clearly, and now there was no smiling, it was bleak, intent and still, eyes fixed steadily upon his opponent.

The king surveyed the scene, and lifted his hand. The truncheon fell and Prestcote drew aside to the edge of the square as the contestants advanced to meet each other.

At first sight, the contrast was bitter. Courcelle was half as big again, half as old again, with height and reach and weight all on his side, and there was no questioning his skill and experience. His fiery colouring and towering size made Beringar look no more than a lean, lightweight boy, and though that lightness might be expected to lend him speed and agility, within seconds it was clear that Courcelle also was very fast and adroit on his feet. At the first clash of steel on steel, Cadfael felt his own arm and wrist bracing and turning the stroke, and swung aside with the very same motion Beringar made to slide out of danger; the turn brought him about, with the arch of the town gate full in view.

Out of the black hollow a girl came darting like a swallow, all swift black and white and a flying cloud of gold hair. She was running, very fleetly and purposefully, with her skirts caught up in her hands almost to the knee, and well behind her, out of breath but making what haste she could, came another young woman. Constance was wasting much of what breath she still had in calling after her mistress imploringly to stop, to come away, not to go near; but Aline made never a sound, only ran towards where two gallants of hers were newly launched on a determined attempt to kill each other. She looked neither to right nor left, but only craned to see over the heads of the crowd. Cadfael hastened to meet her, and she recognised him with a gasp, and flung herself into his arms.

'Brother Cadfael, what is this? What has he done? And you knew, you knew, and you never warned me! If Constance had not gone into town to buy flour, I should never have known ...'

'You should not be here,' said Cadfael, holding her quivering and panting on his heart. 'What can you do? I promised him not to tell you, he did not wish it. You should not look on at this.'

'But I will!' she said with passion. 'Do you think I'll go tamely away and leave him now? Only tell me,' she begged, 'is it true what they're saying – that he charged Adam with murdering that young man? And that Giles's dagger was the proof?'

'It is true,' said Cadfael. She was staring over his shoulder into the arena, where the swords clashed, and hissed and clashed again, and her amethyst eyes were immense and wild.

'And the charge – that also is true?'

'That also.'

'Oh, God!' she said, gazing in fearful fascination. 'And he is so slight ... how can he endure it? Half the other's size ... and he dared try to solve it this way! Oh, Brother Cadfael, how could you let him?'

At least now, thought Cadfael, curiously eased, I know which of those two is 'he' to her, without need of a name. I never was sure until now, and perhaps neither was she. 'If ever you succeed,' he said, 'in preventing Hugh Beringar from doing whatever he's set his mind on doing, then come to me and tell me how you managed it. Though I doubt it would work for me! He chose this way, girl, and he had his reasons, good reasons. And you and I must abide it, as he must.'

'But we are three,' she said vehemently. 'If we stand with him, we *must* give him strength. I can pray and I can watch, and I will. Bring me nearer – come with me! I must see!'

She was thrusting impetuously through towards the lances when Cadfael held her back by the arm. 'I think,' he said, 'better if *he* does not see *you*. Not now!'

Aline uttered something that sounded like a very brief and bitter laugh. 'He would not see me now,' she said, 'unless I ran between the swords, and so I would, if they'd let me – No!' She took that back instantly, with a dry sob. 'No, I would not do so to him. I know better than that. All I can do is watch, and keep silence.'

The fate of women in a world of fighting men, he thought wryly, but for all that, it is not so passive a part as it sounds. So he drew her to a slightly raised place where she could see, without disturbing, with the glittering gold sheen of her unloosed hair in the sun, the deadly concentration of Hugh Beringar. He had blood on the tip of his sword by then, though from a mere graze on Courcelle's cheek, and blood on his own left sleeve below the leather.

'He is hurt,' she said in a mourning whisper, and crammed half her small fist in her mouth to stop a cry, biting hard on her knuckles to ensure the silence she had promised.

'It's nothing,' said Cadfael sturdily. 'And he is the faster. See there, that parry! Slight he may seem, but there's steel in that wrist. What he wills to do, he'll do. And he has truth weighting his hand.'

'I love him,' said Aline in a soft, deliberate whisper, releasing her bitten hand for a moment. 'I did not know until now, but I do love him!'

'So do I, girl,' said Cadfael, 'so do I!'

They had been two full hours in the arena, with never a break for breath, and the sun was high and hot, and they suffered, but both went with relentless care, conserving their strength, and now, when their eyes met at close quarters over the braced swords, there was no personal grudge between them, only an inflexible purpose, on the one side to prove truth, on the other to disprove it, and on either side by the only means left, by killing. They had found out by then, if they had been in doubt, that for all the obvious advantages on one side, in this contest they were very evenly matched, equal in skill, almost equal in speed, the weight of truth holding a balance true between them. Both bled from minor wounds. There was blood here and there in the grass.

It was almost noon when Beringar, pressing hard, drove his opponent back with a sudden lunge, and saw his foot slip in blood-stained turf, thinned by the hot, dry summer. Courcelle, parrying, felt himself falling, and threw up his arm, and Hugh's following stroke took the sword almost out of his hand, shivered edge to edge, leaving him sprawled on one hip, and clutching only a bladeless hilt. The steel fell far aside, and lay useless.

Beringar at once drew back, leaving his foe to rise unthreatened. He rested his point against the ground, and looked towards Prestcote, who in turn was looking for guidance to the king's chair.

'Fight on!' said the king flatly. His displeasure had not abated.

Beringar leaned his point into the turf and gazed, wiping sweat from brow and lip. Courcelle raised himself slowly, looked at the useless hilt in his hand, and heaved desperate breath before hurling the thing from him in fury. Beringar looked from him to the king, frowning, and drew off two or three more paces while he considered. The king made no further move, apart from gesturing dourly that they should continue. Beringar took three rapid strides to the rim of the square, tossed his sword beneath the levelled lances, and set hand slowly to draw the dagger at his belt.

Courcelle was slow to understand, but blazed into renewed confidence when he realised the gift that was offered to him.

'Well, well!' said King Stephen under his breath. 'Who knows but I may have been mistaken in the best man, after all?'

With nothing but daggers now, they must come to grips. Length of reach is valuable, even with daggers, and the poniard that Courcelle drew from its sheath at his hip was longer than the decorative toy Hugh Beringar held. King Stephen revived into active interest, and shed his natural irritation at being forced into this encounter.

'He is mad!' moaned Aline at Cadfael's shoulder, leaning against him with lips drawn back and nostrils flaring, like any of her fighting forebears. 'He had licence to kill at leisure. Oh, he is stark mad. And I love him!'

The fearful dance continued, and the sun at its zenith shortened the shadows of the two duellists until they advanced, retreated, side-stepped on a black disc cast by their own bodies, while the full heat beat pitilessly on their heads, and within their leather harness they ran with sweat. Beringar was on the defensive now, his weapon being the shorter and lighter, and Courcelle was pressing hard, aware that he held the advantage. Only Beringar's quickness of hand and eye saved him from repeated slashes that might well have killed, and his speed and agility still enabled him at every assault to spring back out of range. But he was tiring at last; his judgment was less precise and confident, his movement less alert and steady. And Courcelle, whether he had got his second wind or simply gathered all his powers in one desperate effort, to make an end, seemed to have recovered his earlier force and fire.

357

Blood ran on Hugh's right hand, fouled his hilt and made it slippery in his palm. The tatters of Courcelle's left sleeve fluttered at the edge of his vision, a distraction that troubled his concentration. He had tried several darting attacks, and drawn blood in his turn, but length of blade and length of arm told terribly against him. Doggedly he set himself to husband his own strength, by constant retreat if necessary, until Courcelle's frenzied attacks began to flag, as they must at last.

'Oh, God!' moaned Aline almost inaudibly. 'He was too generous, he has given his life away ... The man is playing with him!'

'No man,' said Cadfael firmly, 'plays with Hugh Beringar with impunity. He is still the fresher of the two. This is a wild spurt to end it, he cannot maintain it long.'

Step by step Hugh gave back, but at each attack only so far as to elude the blade, and step by step, in a series of vehement rushes, Courcelle pursued and drove him. It seemed that he was trying to pen him into a corner of the square, where he would have to make a stand, but at the last moment the attacker's judgment flagged or Hugh's agility swung him clear of the trap, for the renewed pursuit continued along the line of lancers, Beringar unable to break out again into the centre of the arena, Courcelle unable to get through the sustained defence, or prevent this lame progress that seemed likely to end in another corner.

The Flemings stood like rocks, and let battle, like a slow tide, flow painfully along their immovable ranks. And halfway along the side of the square Courcelle suddenly drew back one long, rapid step instead of pursuing, and tossing his poniard from him in the grass, stooped with a hoarse cry of triumph, and reached beneath the levelled lances, to rise again brandishing the sword Hugh Beringar had discarded as a grace to him, more than an hour previously.

Hugh had not even realised that they had come to that very place, much less that he had been deliberately driven here for this purpose. Somewhere in the crowd he heard a woman shriek. Courcelle was in the act of straightening up, the sword in his hand, his eyes, under the broad, streaming brow half-mad with exultation. But he was still somewhat off-balance when Hugh launched himself upon him in a tigerish leap. A second later would have been too late. As the sword swung upward, he flung his whole weight against Courcelle's breast, locked his right arm, dagger and all, about his enemy's body, and caught the threatening sword-arm by the wrist in his left hand. For a moment they heaved and strained, then they went down together heavily in the turf, and rolled and wrenched in a deadlocked struggle at the feet of the indifferent guards.

Aline clenched her teeth hard against a second cry, and covered her eyes, but the next moment as resolutely uncovered them. 'No, I will see all, I must ... I will bear it! He shall not be ashamed of me! Oh, Cadfael ... oh, Cadfael ... What is happening? I can't see ...'

'Courcelle snatched the sword, but he had no time to strike. Wait, one of them is rising ...'

Two had fallen together, only one arose, and he stood half-stunned and wondering. For his enemy had fallen limp and still under him, and relaxed straining arms nervelessly into the grass; and there he lay now, open-eyed to the glare of the sun, and a slow stream of red was flowing sluggishly from under him, and forming a dark pool about him on the trampled ground.

Hugh Beringar looked from the gathering blood to the dagger he still gripped in his right hand, and shook his head in bewilderment, for he was very tired, and weak now with this abrupt and inexplicable ending, and there was barely a drop of fresh blood on his blade, and the sword lay loosely clasped still in Courcelle's right hand, innocent of his death. And yet he had his death; his life was ebbing out fast into the thick grass. So what manner of ominous miracle was this, that killed and left both weapons unstained?

Hugh stooped, and raised the inert body by the left shoulder, turning it to see where the blood issued; and there, driven deep through the leather jerkin, was the dead man's own poniard, which he had flung away to grasp at the sword. By the look of it the hilt had lodged downwards in thick grass against the solidly braced boot of one of the Flemings. Hugh's onslaught had flung the owner headlong upon his discarded blade, and their rolling, heaving struggle had driven it home.

I did not kill him, after all, thought Beringar. His own cunning killed him. And whether he was glad or sorry he was too drained to know. Cadfael would be satisfied, at least; Nicholas Faintree was avenged, he had justice in full. His murderer had been accused publicly, and publicly the charge had been justified by heaven. And his murderer was dead; that failing breath was already spent.

Beringar reached down and picked up his sword, which rose unresisting out of the convicted hand. He turned slowly, and raised it in salute to the king, and walked, limping now and dropping a few trickles of blood from stiffening cuts in hand and forearm, out of the square of lances, which opened silently to let him go free.

Two or three paces he took across the sward towards the king's chair, and Aline flew into his arms, and clasped him with a possessive fervour that shook him fully alive again. Her gold hair streamed about his shoulders and breast, she lifted to him a rapt, exultant and exhausted face, the image of his own, she called him by his name: 'Hugh … Hugh …' and fingered with aching tenderness the oozing wounds that showed in his cheek and hand and wrist.

'Why did you not tell me? Why? Why? Oh, you have made me die so many times! Now we are both alive again … Kiss me!'

He kissed her, and she remained real, passionate and unquestionably his. She continued to caress, and fret and fawn.

'Hush, love,' he said, eased and restored, 'or go on scolding, for if you turn tender to me now I'm a lost man. I can't afford to droop yet, the king's waiting. Now, if you're my true lady, lend me your arm to lean on, and come and stand by me and prop me up, like a good wife, or I may fall flat at his feet.'

'Am I your true lady?' demanded Aline, like all women wanting guarantees before witnesses.

'Surely! Too late to think better of it now, my heart!'

She was beside him, clasped firmly in his arm, when he came before the king. 'Your Grace,' said Hugh, condescending out of some exalted private place scarcely flawed by weariness and wounds, 'I trust I have proven my case against a murderer, and have your Grace's countenance and approval.'

'Your opponent,' said Stephen, 'proved your case for you, all too well.' He eyed them thoughtfully, disarmed and diverted by this unexpected apparition of entwined lovers. 'But what you have proved may also be your gain. You have robbed me, young man, of an able deputy sheriff of this shire, whatever else he may have been, and however foul a fighter. I may well take reprisal by drafting you into the vacancy you've created. Without prejudice to your own castles and your rights of garrison on our behalf. What do you say?'

'With your Grace's leave,' said Beringar, straight-faced, 'I must first take counsel with my bride.'

'Whatever is pleasing to my lord,' said Aline, equally demurely, 'is also pleasing to me.'

Well, well, thought Brother Cadfael, looking on with interest, I doubt if troth was ever plighted more publicly. They had better invite the whole of Shrewsbury to the wedding.

Brother Cadfael walked across to the guest hall before Compline, and took with him not only a pot of his goose-grass salve for Hugh Beringar's numerous minor grazes, but also Giles Siward's dagger, with its topaz finial carefully restored.

'Brother Oswald is a skilled silversmith, this is his gift and mine to your lady. Give it to her yourself. But ask her – as I know she will – to deal generously by the boy who fished it out of the river. So much you will have to tell her. For the rest, for her brother's part, yes, silence, now and always. For her he was only one of the many who chose the unlucky side, and died for it.'

Beringar took the repaired dagger in his hand, and looked at it long and sombrely. 'Yet this is not justice,' he said slowly. 'You and I between us have forced into the light the truth of one man's sins, and covered up the truth of another's.' This night, for all his gains, he was very grave and a little sad, and not only because all his wounds were stiffening, and all his misused muscles groaning at every movement. The recoil from triumph had him fixing honest eyes on the countenance of failure, the fate he had escaped. 'Is justice due only to the blameless? If he had not been so visited and tempted, he might never have found himself mired to the neck in so much infamy.'

'We deal with what is,' said Cadfael. 'Leave what might have been to eyes that can see it plain. You take what's lawfully and honourably won, and value and enjoy it. You have that right. Here you are, deputy sheriff of Salop, in royal favour, affianced to as fine a girl as heart could wish, and the one you set your mind on from the moment you saw her. Be sure I noticed! And if you're stiff and sore in every bone tomorrow – and, lad, you will be! – what's a little disciplinary pain to a young man in your high feather?'

'I wonder,' said Hugh, brightening, 'where the other two are by now.'

'Within reach of the Welsh coast, waiting for a ship to carry them coastwise round to France. They'll do well enough.' As between Stephen and Maud, Cadfael felt no allegiance; but these young creatures, though two of them held for Maud and two for Stephen, surely belonged to a future and an England delivered from the wounds of civil war, beyond this present anarchy.

'As for justice,' said Brother Cadfael thoughtfully, 'it is but half the tale.' He would say a prayer at Compline for the repose of Nicholas Faintree, a clean young man of mind and life, surely now assuaged and at rest. But he would also say a prayer for the soul of Adam Courcelle, dead in his guilt; for every untimely death, every man cut down in his vigour and strength without time for repentance and reparation, is one corpse too many. 'No need,' said Cadfael, 'for you ever to look over your shoulder, or feel any compunction. You did the work that fell to you, and did it well. God disposes all. From the highest to the lowest extreme of a man's scope, wherever justice and retribution can reach him, so can grace.'

MONK'S-HOOD

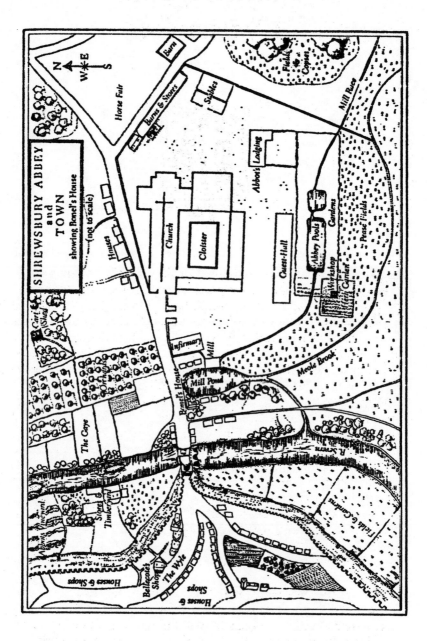

SHREWSBURY ABBEY
and
TOWN
showing Ramel's House
(not to scale)

Chapter One

N THIS particular morning at the beginning of December, in the year 1138, Brother Cadfael came to chapter in tranquillity of mind, prepared to be tolerant even towards the dull, pedestrian reading of Brother Francis, and long-winded legal haverings of Brother Benedict the sacristan. Men were variable, fallible, and to be humoured. And the year, so stormy in its earlier months, convulsed with siege and slaughter and disruptions, bade fair to end in calm and comparative plenty. The tide of civil war between King Stephen and the partisans of the Empress Maud had receded into the south-western borders, leaving Shrewsbury to recover cautiously from having backed the weaker side and paid a bloody price for it. And for all the hindrances to good husbandry, after a splendid summer the harvest had been successfully gathered in, the barns were full, the mills were busy, sheep and cattle thrived on pastures still green and lush, and the weather continued surprisingly mild, with only a hint of frost in the early mornings. No one was wilting with cold yet, no one yet was going hungry. It could not last much longer, but every day counted as blessing.

And in his own small kingdom the crop had been rich and varied, the eaves of his workshop in the garden were hung everywhere with linen bags of dried herbs, his jars of wine sat in plump, complacent rows, the shelves were thronging with bottles and pots of specifics for all the ills of winter, from snuffling colds to seized-up joints and sore and wheezing chests. It was a better world than it had looked in the spring, and an ending that improves on its beginning is always good news.

So Brother Cadfael strolled contentedly to his chosen seat in the chapter-house, conveniently retired behind one of the pillars in a dim corner, and watched with half-sleepy benevolence as his brothers of the house filed in and took their places: Abbot Heribert, old and gentle and anxious, sadly worn by the troublous year now near its ending; Prior Robert Pennant, immensely tall and patrician, ivory of face and silver of hair and brows, ever erect and stately, as if he already balanced the mitre for which he yearned. He was neither old nor frail, but an ageless and wiry fifty-one, though he contrived to look every inch a patriarch sanctified by a lifetime of holiness; he had looked much the same ten years ago, and would almost certainly change not at all in the twenty years to come. Faithful at his heels slid Brother Jerome, his clerk, reflecting Robert's pleasure or displeasure like a small, warped mirror. After them came all the other officers, sub-prior, sacristan, hospitaller, almoner, infirmarer, the custodian of the altar of St Mary, the cellarer, the precentor, and the master of the novices. Decorously they composed themselves for what bade fair to be an unremarkable day's business.

Young Brother Francis, who was afflicted with a nasal snuffle and somewhat sparse Latin, made heavy weather of reading out the list of saints and martyrs to be commemorated in prayer during the coming days, and fumbled a pious commentary on the ministry of St Andrew the Apostle, whose day was just past. Brother Benedict the sacristan contrived to make it sound only fair that he, as responsible for the upkeep of church and enclave, should have the major claim on a sum willed jointly for that purpose and to provide lights for the altar of the Lady Chapel, which was Brother Maurice's province. The precentor acknowledged the gift of a new setting for the 'Sanctus', donated by the composer's patron, but by the dubious enthusiasm with which he welcomed so generous a gift, he did not think highly of its merits, and it was unlikely to be heard often. Brother Paul, master of the novices, had a complaint against one of his pupils, suspected of levity beyond what was permitted to youth and inexperience, in that the youngster had been heard singing in the cloisters, while he was employed in copying a prayer of St Augustine, a secular song of scandalous import, purporting to be the lament of a Christian pilgrim imprisoned by the Saracens, and comforting himself by hugging to his breast the chemise given him at parting by his lover.

Brother Cadfael's mind jerked him back from incipient slumber to recognise and remember the song, beautiful and poignant. He had been in that Crusade, he knew the land, the Saracens, the haunting light and darkness of such a prison and such a pain. He saw Brother Jerome devoutly close his eyes and suffer convulsions of distress at the mention of a woman's most intimate garment. Perhaps because he had never been near enough to it to touch, thought Cadfael, still disposed to be charitable. Consternation quivered through several of the old, innocent lifelong brothers, to whom half the creation was a closed and forbidden book. Cadfael made an effort, unaccustomed at chapter and asked mildly what defence the youth had made.

'He said,' Brother Paul replied fairly 'that he learned the song from his grandfather who fought for the Cross at the taking of Jerusalem, and he found the tune so beautiful that it seemed to him holy. For the pilgrim who sang was not a monastic or a soldier but a humble person who made the long journey out of love.'

'A proper and sanctified love,' pointed out Brother Cadfael, using words not entirely natural to him, for he thought of love as a self-sanctifying force, needing no apology. 'And is there anything in the words of that song to suggest that the woman he left behind was not his wife? I remember none. And the music is worthy of noting. It is not, surely, the purpose of our order to obliterate or censure the sacrament of marriage, for those who have not a celibate vocation. I think this young man may have done nothing very wrong. Should not Brother Precentor try if he has not a gifted voice? Those who sing at their work commonly have some need to use a God-given talent.'

The precentor, startled and prompted, and none too lavishly provided with singers to be moulded, obligingly opined that he would be interested to hear the novice sing. Prior Robert knotted his austere brows, and frowned down his patrician nose; if it had rested with him, the errant youth would have been awarded a hard penance. But the master of novices was no great enthusiast for the lavish use of the discipline, and seemed content to have a good construction put on his pupil's lapse.

'It is true that he has shown as earnest and willing, Father Abbot, and has been with us but a short time. It is easy to forget oneself at moments of concentration, and his copying is careful and devoted.'

The singer got away with a light penance that would not keep him on his knees long enough to rise from them stiffly. Abbot Heribert was always inclined to be lenient, and this morning he appeared more than usually preoccupied and distracted. They were drawing near the end of the day's affairs. The abbot rose as if to put an end to the chapter.

'There are here a few documents to be sealed,' said Brother Matthew the cellarer, rustling parchments in haste, for it seemed to him that the abbot had turned absent-minded, and lost sight of this duty. 'There is the matter of the fee-farm of Hales, and the grant made by Walter Aylwin, and also the guestship agreement with Gervase Bonel and his wife, to whom we are allotting the first house beyond the mill-pond. Master Bonel wishes to move in as soon as may be, before the Christmas feast . . .'

'Yes, yes, I have not forgotten.' Abbot Heribert looked small, dignified but resigned, standing before them with a scroll of his own gripped in both hands. 'There is something I have to announce to you all. These necessary documents cannot be sealed today, for sufficient reason. It may well be that they are now beyond my competence, and I no longer have the right to conclude any agreement for this community. I have here an instruction which was delivered to me yesterday, from Westminster, from the king's court. You all know that Pope Innocent has acknowledged King Stephen's claim to the throne of this realm, and in his support has sent over a legate with full powers, Alberic, cardinal-bishop of Ostia. The cardinal proposes to hold a legatine council in London for the reform of the church, and I am summoned to attend, to account for my stewardship as abbot of this convent. The terms make clear,' said Heribert, firmly and sadly, 'that my tenure is at the disposal of the legate. We have lived through a troubled year, and been tossed between two claimants to the throne of our land. It is not a secret, and I acknowledge it, that his Grace, when he was here in the summer, held me in no great favour, since in the confusion of the times I did not see my way clear, and was slow to accept his sovereignty. Therefore I now regard my abbacy as suspended, until or unless the legatine council confirms me in office. I cannot ratify any documents or agreements in the name of our house. Whatever is now uncompleted must remain uncompleted until a firm appointment has been made. I cannot trespass on what may well be another's field.'

He had said what he had to say. He resumed his seat and folded his hands patiently, while their bewildered, dismayed murmurings gradually congealed and mounted into a boiling, bees'-hive hum of consternation. Though not everyone was horrified, as Cadfael plainly saw. Prior Robert, just as startled as the rest, and adept at maintaining a decorous front, none the less glowed brightly behind his ivory face, drawing the obvious conclusion, and Brother Jerome, quick to interpret any message from that quarter, hugged himself with glee inside the sleeves of his habit, while his face exhibited pious sympathy and pain. Not that they had anything against Heribert, except that he continued to hold an office on which impatient subordinates were casting covetous eyes. A nice old man, of course, but out of date, and far too lax. Like a king who lives too long, and positively invites assassination. But the rest of them fluttered and panicked like hens invaded by the fox, clamouring variously:

'But, Father Abbot, surely the king will restore you!'

'Oh, Father, must you go to this council?'

'We shall be left like sheep without a shepherd!'

Prior Robert, who considered himself ideally equipped to deal with the flock of St Peter himself, if need be, gave that complainant a brief, basilisk glare, but refrained from protest, indeed murmured his own commiseration and dismay.

'My duty and my vows are to the Church,' said Abbot Heribert sadly, 'and I am bound to obey the summons, as a loyal son. If it pleases the Church to confirm me in office, I shall return to take up my customary ward here. If another is appointed in my place, I shall still return among you, if I am permitted, and live out my life as a faithful brother of this house, under our new superior.'

Cadfael though he caught a brief, complacent flicker of a smile that passed over Robert's face at that. It would not greatly disconcert him to have his old superior a humble brother under his rule at last.

'But clearly,' went on Abbot Heribert with humility, 'I can no longer claim rights as abbot until the matter is settled, and these agreements must rest in abeyance until my return, or until another considers and pronounces on them. Is any one of them urgent?'

Brother Matthew shuffled his parchments and pondered, still shaken by the suddenness of the news. 'There is no reason to hurry in the matter of the Aylwin grant, he is an old friend to our order, his offer will certainly remain open as long as need be. And the Hales fee-farm will date only from Lady Day of next year, so there's time enough. But Master Bonel relies on the charter being sealed very soon. He is waiting to move his belongings into the house.'

'Remind me of the terms, if you will,' the abbot requested apologetically. 'My mind has been full of other matters, I have forgotten just what was agreed.'

'Why, he grants to us his manor of Mallilie absolutely, with his several tenants, in return for a messuage here at the abbey – the first house on the town side of the mill-pond is vacant, and the most suitable to his household – together with keep for life for himself and his wife, and for two servants also. The details are as usual in such cases. They shall have daily two monks' loaves and one servants' loaf, two gallons of conventual ale and one servants' ale, a dish of meat such as the abbey sergeants have, on meat-days, and of fish on fish-days, from the abbot's kitchen, and an intermissum whenever extra dainties are provided. These to be fetched by their manservant. They shall also have a dish of meat or fish daily for their two domestics. Master Bonel is also to have annually a robe such as the senior of the abbey officers receive, and his wife – she so prefers – shall have ten shillings yearly to provide a robe for herself as she chooses. There is also provision of ten shillings yearly for linen, shoes and firing, and livery for one horse. And at the death of either, the other to retain possession of the house and receive a moiety of all the aforesaid provisions, except that if the wife be the survivor, she need not be provided with stabling for a horse. These are the terms, and I had intended to have witnesses come hither after chapter for the ratification. The justice has a clerk waiting.'

'I fear none the less,' said the abbot heavily, 'that this also must wait. My rights are in abeyance.'

'It will greatly inconvenience Master Bonel,' said the cellarer anxiously. 'They have already prepared to remove here, and expected to do so in the next few days. The Christmas feast is coming, and they cannot well be left in discomfort.'

'Surely,' suggested Prior Robert, 'the move could be countenanced, even if the ratification must wait a while. It's highly unlikely that any abbot appointed would wish to upset this agreement.' Since it was perfectly clear that he himself was in line for the appointment, and knew himself to be in better odour with King Stephen than his superior, he spoke with easy authority. Heribert jumped at the suggestion.

'I think such a move is permissible. Yes, Brother Matthew, you may proceed, pending final sanction, which I feel sure will be forthcoming. Reassure our guest on that point, and allow him to bring his household at once. It is only right that they should feel settled and at peace for the Christmas feast. There is no other case needing attention?'

None, Father.' And he asked, subdued and thoughtful: 'When must you set forth on this journey?'

'The day after tomorrow I should leave. I ride but slowly these days, and we shall be some days on the road. In my absence, of course, Prior Robert will be in charge of all things here.'

Abbot Heribert lifted a distrait hand in blessing, and led the way out of the chapter-house. Prior Robert, sweeping after, no doubt felt himself already in charge of all things within the pale of the Benedictine abbey of St Peter and St Paul of Shrewsbury, and had every intent and expectation of continuing so to his life's end.

The brothers filed out in mourne silence, only to break out into subdued but agitated conversations as soon as they were dispersed over the great court. Heribert had been their abbot for eleven years, and an easy man to serve under, approachable, kindly, perhaps even a little too easy-going. They did not look forward to changes.

In the half-hour before High Mass at ten, Cadfael betook himself very thoughtfully to his workshop in the herb-gardens, to tend a few specifics he had brewing. The enclosure, thickly hedged and well trimmed, was beginning now to look bleached and dry with the first moderate cold, all the leaves grown elderly and lean and brown, the tenderest plants withdrawing into the warmth of the earth; but the air still bore a lingering, aromatic fragrance compounded of all the ghostly scents of summer, and inside the hut the spicy sweetness made the senses swim. Cadfael regularly took his ponderings there for privacy. He was so used to the drunken, heady air within that he barely noticed it, but at need he could distinguish every ingredient that contributed to it, and trace it to its source.

So King Stephen, after all, had not forgotten his lingering grudges, and Abbot Heribert was to be the scapegoat for Shrewsbury's offence in holding out against his claims. Yet he was not by nature a vindictive man. Perhaps it was rather that he felt a need to flatter and court the legate, since the pope had recognised him as king of England, and given him papal backing, no negligible weapon, in the contention with the Empress Maud, the rival claimant to the throne. That determined lady would certainly not give up so easily, she would be pressing

371

her case strongly in Rome, and even popes may change their allegiance. So Alberic of Ostia would be given every possible latitude in pursuing his plans for the reform of the Church, and Heribert might be but one sacrificial victim offered to his zeal on a platter.

Another curious theme intruded itself persistently into Cadfael's musings. This matter of the occasional guests of the abbey, so-called, the souls who chose to abandon the working world, sometimes in their prime, and hand over their inheritance to the abbey for a soft, shielded, inactive life in a house of retirement, with food, clothing, firing, all provided without the lifting of a finger! Did they dream of it for years while they were sweating over lambing ewes, or toiling in the harvest, or working hard at a trade? A little sub-paradise where meals dropped from the sky and there was nothing to do but bask, in the summer, and toast by the fire with mulled ale in the winter? And when they got to it, how long did the enchantment last? How soon did they sicken of doing nothing, and needing to do nothing? In a man blind, lame, sick, he could understand the act. But in those hale and busy, and used to exerting body and mind? No, that he could not understand. There must be other motives. Not all men could be deceived, or deceive themselves, into mistaking idleness for blessedness. What else could provoke such an act? Want of an heir? An urge, not yet understood, to the monastic life, without the immediate courage to go all the way? Perhaps! In a man with a wife, well advanced in years and growing aware of his end, it might be so. Many a man had taken the habit and the cowl late, after children and grandchildren and the heat of a long day. The grace house and the guest status might be a stage on the way. Or was it possible that men divested themselves of their life's work at last out of pure despite, against the world, against an unsatisfactory son, against the burden of carrying their own souls?

Brother Cadfael shut the door upon the rich horehound reek of a mixture for coughs, and went very soberly to High Mass.

Abbot Heribert departed by the London road, turning his back upon the town of Shrewsbury, in the early morning of a somewhat grey day, the first time there had been the nip of frost in the air as well as the pale sparkle in the grass. He took with him his own clerk, Brother Emmanuel, and two lay grooms who had served here longest; and he rode his own white mule. He put on a cheerful countenance as he took leave, but for

372

all that he cut a sad little figure as the four riders dwindled along the road. No horseman now, if he ever had been much of one, he used a high, cradling saddle, and sagged in it like a small sack not properly filled. Many of the brothers crowded to the gates to watch him as long as he remained in view, and their faces were apprehensive and aggrieved. Some of the boy pupils came out to join them, looking even more dismayed, for the abbot had allowed Brother Paul to conduct his schooling undisturbed, which meant very tolerantly, but with Prior Robert in charge there was no department of this house likely to go its way ungoaded, and discipline might be expected to tighten abruptly.

There was, Cadfael could not but admit, room for a little hard practicality within these walls, if the truth were told. Heribert of late had grown deeply discouraged with the world of men, and withdrawn more and more into his prayers. The siege and fall of Shrewsbury, with all the bloodshed and revenge involved, had been enough to sadden any man, though that was no excuse for abandoning the effort to defend right and oppose wrong. But there comes a time when the old grow very tired, and the load of leadership unjustly heavy to bear. And perhaps – perhaps! – Heribert would not be quite so sad as even he now supposed, if the load should be lifted from him.

Mass and chapter passed that day with unexceptionable decorum and calm, High Mass was celebrated devoutly, the duties of the day proceeded in their smooth and regular course. Robert was too sensible of his own image to rub his hands visibly, or lick his lips before witnesses. All that he did would be done according to just and pious law, with the authority of sainthood. Nevertheless, what he considered his due would be appropriated, to the last privilege.

Cadfael was accustomed to having two assistants allotted to him throughout the active part of the gardening year, for he grew other things in his walled garden besides the enclosure of herbs, though the main kitchen gardens of the abbey were outside the enclave, across the main highway and along the fields by the river, the lush level called the Gaye. The waters of Severn regularly moistened it in the flood season, and its soil was rich and bore well. Here within the walls he had made, virtually single-handed, this closed garden for the small and precious things, and in the outer levels, running down to the Meole brook that fed the mill, he grew food crops, beans and cabbages and pulse, and fields of pease. But now with the winter closing gently in, and the soil settling to its sleep like the urchins under the hedges, curled drowsily with all their prickles cushioned by straw and dead grass and leaves, he was left with just one novice to help him brew his draughts, and roll his pills, and stir his rubbing oils, and pound his poultices, to medicine not only the brothers, but many who came for help in their troubles, from the town and the Foregate, sometimes even from the scattered villages beyond. He had not been bred to this science, he had learned it by experience, by trial and study, accumulating knowledge over the years, until some preferred his ministrations to those of the acknowledged physicians.

His assistant at this time was a novice of no more than eighteen years, Brother Mark, orphaned, and a trouble to a neglectful uncle, who had sent him into the abbey at sixteen to be rid of him. He had entered tongue-tied, solitary and homesick, a waif who seemed even younger than his years, who did what he was told with apprehensive submission, as though the best to be hoped out of life was to avoid punishment. But some months of working in the garden with Cadfael had gradually loosened his tongue and put his fears to flight. He was still undersized, and slightly wary of authority, but healthy and wiry, and good at making things grow, and he was acquiring a sure and delicate touch with the making of medicines, and an eager interest in them. Mute among his fellows, he made up for it by being voluble enough in the garden workshop, and with none but Cadfael by. It was always Mark, for all his silence and withdrawal about the cloister and court, who brought all the gossip before others knew it.

He came in from an errand to the mill, an hour before Vespers, full of news.

'Do you know what Prior Robert has done? Taken up residence in the abbot's lodging! Truly! Brother Sub-prior has orders to sleep in the prior's cell in the dormitory from tonight. And Abbot Heribert barely out of the gates! I call it great presumption!'

So did Cadfael, though he felt it hardly incumbent upon him either to say so, or to let Brother Mark utter his thoughts quite so openly. 'Beware how you pass judgment on your superiors,' he said mildly, 'at least until you know how to put yourself in their place and see from their view. For all we know, Abbot Heribert may have required him to move into the lodging, as an instance of his authority while we're without an abbot. It is the place set aside for the spiritual father of this convent.'

'But Prior Robert is not that, not yet! And Abbot Heribert would have said so at chapter if he had wished it so. At least he would have told Brother Sub-prior, and no one did. I saw his face, he is as astonished as anyone, and shocked. *He* would not have taken such a liberty!'

Too true, thought Cadfael, busy pounding roots in a mortar, Brother Richard the sub-prior was the last man to presume; large, good-natured and peace-loving to the point of laziness, he never exerted himself to advance even by legitimate means. It might dawn on some of the younger and more audacious brothers shortly that they had gained an advantage in the exchange. With Richard in the prior's cell that commanded the length of the dortoir, it would be far easier for the occasional sinner to slip out by the night-stairs after the lights were out; even if the crime were detected it would probably never be reported. A blind eye is the easiest thing in the world to turn on whatever is troublesome.

'All the servants at the lodging are simmering,' said Brother Mark. 'You know how devoted they are to Abbot Heribert, and now to be made to serve someone else, before his place is truly vacant, even! Brother Henry says it's almost blasphemy. And Brother Petrus is looking blacker than thunder, and muttering into his cooking-pots something fearful. He said, once Prior Robert gets his foot in the door, it will take a dose of hemlock to get him out again when Abbot Heribert returns.'

Cadfael could well imagine it. Brother Petrus was the abbot's cook, old in his service, and a black-haired, fiery-eyed barbarian from near the Scottish border, at that, given to tempestuous and immoderate declarations, none of them to be taken too seriously; but the puzzle was where exactly to draw the line.

'Brother Petrus says many things he might do well not to say, but he never means harm, as you well know. And he's a prime cook, and will continue to feed the abbot's table nobly whoever sits at the head of it, because he can do no other.'

'But not happily,' said Brother Mark with conviction.

No question but the even course of the day had been gravely shaken; yet so well regulated was the regime within these walls that every brother, happy or not, would pursue his duties as conscientiously as ever.

'When Abbot Heribert returns, confirmed in office,' said Mark, firmly counting wishes as horses, 'Prior Robert's nose will be out of joint.' And the thought of that august organ bent aside like the misused beak of an old soldier so consoled him

375

that he found heart to laugh again, while Cadfael could not find the heart to scold him, since even for him the picture had its appeal.

Brother Edmund the infirmarer came to Cadfael's hut in the middle of the afternoon a week after Abbot Heribert's departure, to collect some medicines for his inmates. The frosts, though not yet severe, had come after such mild weather as to take more than one young brother by surprise, spreading a sneezing rheum that had to be checked by isolating the victims, most of them active youngsters who worked outdoors with the sheep. He had four of them in the infirmary, besides the few old men who now spent their days there with none but religious duties, waiting peacefully for their end.

'All the lads need is a few days in the warm, and they'll cure themselves well enough,' said Cadfael, stirring and pouring from a large flask into a smaller one, a brown mixture that smelled hot and aromatic and sweet. 'But no need to endure discomfort, even for a few days. Let them drink a dose of this, two or three times in the day and at night, as much as will fill a small spoon, and they'll be the easier for it.'

'What is in it?' asked Brother Edmund curiously. Many of Brother Cadfael's preparations he already knew, but there were constantly new developments. Sometimes he wondered if Cadfael tried them all out on himself.

'There's rosemary, and horehound, and saxifrage, mashed into a little oil pressed from flax seeds, and the body is a red wine I made from cherries and their stones. You'll find they'll do well on it, any that have the rheum in their eyes or heads, and even for the cough it serves, too.' He stoppered the large bottle carefully, and wiped the neck. 'Is there anything more you'll be wanting? For the old fellows? They must be in a taking at all these changes we're seeing. Past the three score men don't take kindly to change.'

'Not, at all events, to this change,' owned Brother Edmund ruefully. 'Heribert never knew how he was liked, until they began to feel his loss.'

'You think we have lost him?'

'I fear it's all too likely. Not that Stephen himself bears grudges too long, but what the legate wants, Stephen will let him have, to keep the pope sweet. And do you think a brisk, reforming spirit, let loose here in our realm with powers to fashion the church he wants, will find our abbot very impressive? Stephen cast the doubt, while he was still angry, but it's Alberic of Ostia who will weigh up our good little abbot, and discard him for too soft in grain,' said Brother Edmund regretfully. 'I could do with another pot of that salve of yours for bed-sores. Brother Adrian can't be much longer for this penance, poor soul.'

'It must be pain now, just shifting him for the anointing,' said Cadfael with sympathy.

'Skin and bone, mere skin and bone. Getting food down him at all is labour enough. He withers like a leaf.'

'If ever you want an extra hand to lift him, send for me, I'm here to be used. Here's what you want. I think I have it better than before, with more of Our Lady's mantle in it.'

Brother Edmund laid bottle and pot in his scrip, and considered on other needs, scouring his pointed chin between thumb and forefinger. The sudden chill that blew in through the doorway made them both turn their heads, so sharply that the young man who had opened the door a wary inch or two hung his head in instant apology and dismay.

'Close the door, lad,' said Cadfael, hunching his shoulders.

A hasty, submissive voice called: 'Pardon, brother! I'll wait your leisure.' And the door began to close upon a thin, dark, apprehensively sullen face.

'No, no,' said Cadfael with cheerful impatience, 'I never meant it so. Come into the warm, and close the door on that wicked wind. It makes the brazier smoke. Come in, I'll be with you very shortly, when Brother Infirmarer has all his needs.'

The door opened just wide enough to allow a lean young man to slide in through the aperture, which he thereupon very hastily closed, and flattened his thin person against the door in mute withdrawal, willing to be invisible and inaudible, though his eyes were wide in wonder and curiosity at the storehouse of rustling, dangling, odorous herbs that hung about the place, and the benches and shelves of pots and bottles that hoarded the summer's secret harvest.

'Ah, yes,' said Brother Edmund, recollecting, 'there was one more thing. Brother Rhys is groaning with creaks and pains in his shoulders and back. He gets about very little now, and it does pain him. I've seen it make him jerk and start. You have an oil that gave him ease before.'

'I have. Wait, now, let me find a flask to fill for you.' Cadfael hoisted from its place on a low bench a large stone bottle, and rummaged along the shelves for a smaller one of cloudy glass.

Carefully he unstoppered and poured, a viscous dark oil that gave off a strong, sharp odour. He replaced the wooden stopper firmly, bedding it in with a wisp of linen, and with another torn shred scrupulously wiped the lips of both containers, and dropped the rag into the small brazier beside which he had a stoneware pot simmering gently. 'This will answer, all the more if you get someone with good strong fingers to work it well into his joints. But keep it carefully, Edmund, never let it near your lips. Wash your hands well after using it, and make sure any other who handles it does the same. It's good for a man's outside, but bad indeed for his inside. And don't use it where there's any scratch or wound, any break in the skin, either. It's powerful stuff.'

'So perilous? What is it made from?' asked Edmund curiously, turning the bottle in his hand to see the sluggish way the oils moved against the glass.

'The ground root of monk's-hood, chiefly, in mustard oil and oil from flax seeds. It's powerfully poisonous if swallowed, a very small draught of this could kill, so keep it safe and remember to cleanse your hands well. But it works wonders for creaking old joints. He'll notice a tingling warmth when it's rubbed well in, and then the pain is dulled, and he'll be quite easy. There, is that all you need? I'll come over myself presently, and do the anointing, if you wish? I know where to find the aches, and it needs to be worked in deep.'

'I know you have iron fingers,' said Brother Edmund, mustering his load. 'You used them on me once, I thought you would break me apart, but I own I could move the better, the next day. Yes, come if you have time, he'll be glad to see you. He wanders, nowadays, there's hardly one among the young brothers he recognises, but he'll not have forgotten you.'

'He'll remember any who have the Welsh tongue,' said Cadfael simply. 'he goes back to his childhood, as old men do.'

Brother Edmund took up his bag and turned to the door. The thin young man, all eyes, slipped aside and opened it for him civilly, and again closed it upon his smiling thanks. Not such a meagre young man, after all, inches above Cadfael's square, solid bulk, and erect and supple of movement, but lean and wary, with a suggestion of wild alertness in his every motion. He had a shock of light-brown hair, unkempt from the rising wind outside, and the trimmed lines of a fair beard about lips and chin, pointing the hungry austerity of a thin, hawk-featured face. The large, bright-blue eyes, glittering with intelligence and defensive as levelled spears, turned their attention upon Cadfael, and sustained the glance unwavering, lances in rest.

'Well, friend,' said Cadfael comfortably, shifting his pot a shade further from the direct heat, 'what is it I can do for you?' And he turned and viewed the stranger candidly, from head to foot. 'I don't know you, lad,' he said placidly, 'but you're welcome. What's your need?'

'I'm sent by Mistress Bonel,' said the young man, in a voice low-pitched and pleasant to hear, if it had not been so tight and wary, 'to ask you for some kitchen-herbs she needs. Brother Hospitaller told her you would be willing to supply her when her own stocks fail. My master has today moved into a house in the Foregate, as guest of the abbey.'

'Ah, yes,' said Cadfael, remembering the manor of Mallilie, gifted to the abbey in return for the means of life to the giver. 'So they are safely in, are they? God give them joy of it! And you are the manservant who will carry their meals back and forth – yes, you'll need to find your way about the place. You've been to the abbot's kitchen?'

'Yes, master.'

'No man's master,' said Cadfael mildly, 'every man's brother, if you will. And what's your name, friend? For we shall be seeing something of each other in the days to come, we may as well be acquainted.'

'My name is Aelfric,' said the young man. He had come forward from the doorway, and stood looking round him with open interest. His eyes lingered with awe on the large bottle that held the oil of monk's-hood. 'Is that truly so deadly? Even a little of it can kill a man?'

'So can many things,' said Cadfael, 'used wrongly, or used in excess. Even wine, if you take enough of it. Even wholesome food, if you devour it beyond reason. And are your household content with their dwelling?'

'It's early yet to say,' said the young man guardedly.

What age would he be? Twenty-five years or so? Hardly more. He bristled like an urchin at a touch, alert against all the world. Unfree, thought Cadfael, sympathetic; and of quick and vulnerable mind. Servant to someone less feeling than himself? It might well be.

'How many are you in the house?'

'My master and mistress, and I. And a maid.' A maid! No more, and his long, mobile mouth shut fast even on that.

379

'Well, Aelfric, you're welcome to make your way here when you will, and what I can supply for your lady, that I will. What is it I can send her this time?'

'She asks for some sage, and some basil, if you have such. She brought a dish with her to warm for the evening,' said Aelfric, thawing a little, 'and has it on a hob there, but it wants for sage. She was out. It's a curious time, moving house here, she'll have left a mort of things behind.'

'What's in my way she may send here for, and welcome. Here you are, Aelfric, lad, here's a bunch of either. Is she a good mistress, your lady?'

'She's that!' said the youth, and closed upon it, as he had upon mention of the maid. He brooded, frowning into mixed and confused thoughts. 'She was a widow when she wed him.' He took the bunches of herbs, fingers gripping hard on the stems. On a throat? Whose, then, since he melted at mention of his mistress? 'I thank you kindly, brother.'

He drew back, lissome and silent. The door opening and closing took but a moment. Cadfael was left gazing after him very thoughtfully. There was still an hour before Vespers. He might well go over to the infirmary, and pour the sweet sound of Welsh into Brother Rhys's old, dulled ears, and dig the monk's-hood oil deep into his aching joints. It would be a decent deed.

But that wild young thing, caged with his grievances, hurts and hatreds, what was to be done for him? A villein, if Cadfael knew one when he saw one, with abilities above his station, and some private anguish, maybe more than one. He remembered that mention of the maid, bitten off jealously between set teeth.

Well, they were but newly come, all four of them. Let the time work for good. Cadfael washed his hands, with all the thoroughness he recommended to his patrons, reviewed his sleeping kingdom, and went to visit the infirmary.

Old Brother Rhys was sitting up beside his neatly made bed, not far from the fire, nodding his ancient, grey-tonsured head. He looked proudly complacent, as one who has got his due against all the odds, stubbly chin jutting, thick old eyebrows bristling in all directions, and the small, sharp eyes beneath almost colourless in their grey pallor, but triumphantly bright. For he had a young, vigorous, dark-haired fellow sitting on a stool beside him, waiting on him good-humouredly and pouring voluble Welsh into his ears like a mountain spring. The old man's gown was stripped down from his bony shoulders, and his attendant was busily massaging oil into the joints with probing fingers, drawing grunts of pleasure from his patient.

'I see I'm forestalled,' said Cadfael into Brother Edmund's ear, in the doorway.

'A kinsman,' said Brother Edmund as softly. 'Some young Welshman from up in the north of the shire, where Rhys comes from. It seems he came here today to help the new tenants move in at the house by the mill-pond. He's connected somehow – journeyman to the woman's son, I believe. And while he was here he thought to ask after the old man, which was a kind act. Rhys was complaining of his pains, and the young fellow offered, so I set him to work. Still, now you're here, have a word. They'll neither of them need to speak English for you.'

'You'll have warned him to wash his hands well, afterwards?'

'And shown him where, and where to stow the bottle away safely when he's done. He understands. I'd hardly let a man take risks with such a brew, after your lecture. I've told him what the stuff could do, misused.'

The young man ceased his ministrations momentarily when Brother Cadfael approached, and made to stand up respectfully, but Cadfael waved him down again. 'No, sit, lad, I won't disturb you. I'm here for a word with an old friend, but I see you've taken on my work for me, and doing it well, too.'

The young man, with cheerful practicality, took him at his word, and went on kneading the pungent oils into Brother Rhys's aged shoulders. He was perhaps twenty-four or twenty-five years old, sturdily built and strong; his square, good-natured face was brown and weathered, and plentifully supplied with bone, a Welsh face, smooth-shaven and decisive, his hair and brows thick, wiry and black. His manner towards Brother Rhys was smiling, merry, almost teasing, as it probably would have been towards a child; and that was engaging in him, and won Brother Cadfael's thoughtful approval, for Brother Rhys was indeed a child again. Livelier than usual today, however, the visitor had done him a deal of good.

'Well, now, Cadfael!' he piped, twitching a shoulder pleasurably at the young man's probing. 'You see my kinsmen remember me yet. Here's my niece Angharad's boy come to see me, my great-nephew Meurig. I mind the time he was born . . . Eh, I mind the time she was born, for that matter, my sister's little lass. It's many years since I've seen her – or you, boy, come to think of it, you could have come to see me earlier. But there's no family feeling in the young, these days.' But he was very complacent about it, enjoying handing out praise one moment and illogical reproof the next, a patriarch's privilege. 'And why didn't the girl come herself? Why didn't you bring your mother with you?'

'It's a long journey from the north of the shire,' said the young man Meurig, easily, 'and always more than enough to be done at home. But I'm nearer now, I work for a carpenter and carver in the town here, you'll be seeing more of me. I'll come and do this for you again – have you out on a hillside with the sheep yet, come spring.'

'My niece Angharad,' murmured the old man, benignly smiling, 'was the prettiest little thing in half the shire, and she grew up a beauty. What age would she be now? Five and forty, it may be, but I warrant she's still as beautiful as ever she was – don't you tell me different, I never yet saw the one to touch her . . .'

'Her son's not likely to tell you any different,' agreed Meurig comfortably. Are not all one's lost nieces beautiful? And the weather of the summers when they were children always radiant, and the wild fruit they gathered then sweeter than any that grows now? For some years Brother Rhys had been considered mildly senile, his wanderings timeless and disorganised; memory failed, fantasy burgeoned, he drew pictures that never had existed on sea or land. But somewhere else, perhaps? Now, with the stimulus of this youthful and vigorous presence and the knowledge of their shared blood, he quickened into sharp remembrance again. It might not last, but it was a princely gift while it lasted.

'Turn a little more to the fire – there, is that the spot?' Rhys wriggled and purred like a stroked cat, and the young man laughed, and plied deep into the flesh, smoothing out knots with a firmness that both hurt and gratified.

'This is no new skill with you,' said Brother Cadfael, observing with approval.

'I've worked mostly with horses, and they get their troubles with swellings and injuries, like men. You learn to see with your fingers, where to find what's bound, and loose it again.'

'But he's a carpenter now,' Brother Rhys said proudly, 'and working here in Shrewsbury.'

'And we're making a lectern for your Lady Chapel,' said Meurig, 'and when it's done – and it soon will be – I'll be bringing it down to the abbey myself. And I'll come and see you again while I'm here.'

'And rub my shoulder again? It gets winterly now, towards Christmas, the cold gets in my bones.'

'I will so. But that's enough for now, I'll be making you too sore. Have up your gown again, uncle – there, and keep the warmth in. Does it burn?'

'For a while it prickled like nettles, now there's a fine, easy glow. I don't feel any pain there now. But I'm tired . . .'

He would be, tired and drowsy after the manipulation of his flesh and the reviving of his ancient mind. 'That's right, that's well. Now you should lie down and have a sleep.' Meurig looked to Cadfael to support him. 'Isn't that best, brother?'

'The very best thing. That's hard exercise you've been taking, you should rest after it.'

Rhys was well content to be settled on his bed and left to the sleep that was already overtaking him. His drowsy fare-wells followed them towards the door, to fade into silence before they reached it. 'Take my greetings to your mother, Meurig. And ask her to come and see me . . . when they bring the wool to Shrewsbury market . . . I'm fain to see her again . . .'

'He set great store by your mother, it seems,' said Cadfael, watching as Meurig washed his hands where Brother Edmund had shown him, and making sure that he was thorough about it. 'Is there a hope that he may see her again?'

Meurig's face, seen in profile as he wrung and scrubbed at his hands, had a gravity and brooding thoughtfulness that belied the indulgent gaiety he had put on for the old man. After a moment he said: 'Not in this world.' He turned to reach for the coarse towel, and looked Cadfael in the eyes fully and steadily. 'My mother has been dead for eleven years this Michaelmas past. He knows it – or he knew it – as well as I. But if she's alive to him again in his dotage, why should I remind him? Let him keep that thought and any other that can pleasure him.'

They went out together in silence, into the chilly air of the great court, and there separated, Meurig striking across briskly towards the gatehouse, Cadfael making for the church, where the Vesper bell could be only a few minutes delayed.

'God speed!' said Cadfael in parting. 'You gave the old man back a piece of his youth today. The elders of your kinship, I think, are fortunate in their sons.'

'My kinship,' said Meurig, halting in mid-stride to stare back with great black eyes, 'is my mother's kinship, I go with my own. My father was not a Welshman.'

He went, lengthening a lusty stride, the square shape of his shoulders cleaving the dusk. And Cadfael wondered about him, as he had wondered about the villein Aelfric, as far as the porch of the church, and then abandoned him for a more immediate duty. These people were, after all, responsible for themselves, and none of his business.

Not yet!

Chapter Two

t was nearing mid-December before the dour man-servant Aelfric came again to the herb-gardens for kitchen herbs for his mistress. By that time he was a figure familiar enough to fade into the daily pattern of comings and goings about the great court, and among the multifarious noise and traffic his solitary silence remained generally unremarked. Cadfael had seen him in the mornings, passing through to the bakery and buttery for the day's loaves and measures of ale, always mute, always purposeful, quick of step and withdrawn of countenance, as though any delay on his part might bring penance, as perhaps, indeed, it might. Brother Mark, attracted to a soul seemingly as lonely and anxious as his own had once been, had made some attempt to engage the stranger in talk, and had little success.

'Though he does unfold a little,' said Mark thoughtfully, kicking his heels on the bench in Cadfael's workshop as he stirred a salve. 'I don't think he's an unfriendly soul at all, if he had not something on his mind. When I greet him he sometimes comes near to smiling, but he'll never linger and talk.'

'He has his work to do, and perhaps a master who's hard to please,' said Cadfael mildly.

'I heard he's out of sorts since they moved in,' said Mark. 'The master, I mean. Not really ill, but low and out of appetite.'

'So might I be,' opined Cadfael, 'if I had nothing to do but sit there and mope, and wonder if I'd done well to part with my

385

lands, even in old age. What seems an easy lie in contemplation can be hard enough when it comes to reality.'

'The girl,' said Mark judiciously, 'is pretty. Have you seen her?'

'I have not. And you, my lad, should be averting your eyes from contemplation of women. Pretty, is she?'

'Very pretty. Not very tall, round and fair, with a lot of yellow hair, and black eyes. It makes a great effect, yellow hair and black eyes. I saw her come to the stable with some message for Aelfric yesterday. He looked after her, when she went, in such a curious way. Perhaps *she* is his trouble.'

And that might well be, thought Cadfael, if he was a villein, and she a free woman, and unlikely to look so low as a serf, and they were rubbing shoulders about the household day after day, in closer quarters here than about the manor of Mallilie.

'She could as well be trouble for you, boy, if Brother Jerome or Prior Robert sees you conning her,' he said briskly. 'If you must admire a fine girl, let it be out of the corner of your eye. Don't forget we have a reforming rule here now.'

'Oh, I'm careful!' Mark was by no means in awe of Brother Cadfael now, and had adopted from him somewhat unorthodox notions of what was and was not permissible. In any case, this boy's vocation was no longer in doubt or danger. If the times had been troublesome he might well have sought leave to go and study in Oxford, but even without that opportunity, Cadfael was reasonably certain he would end by taking orders, and become a priest, and a good priest, too, one aware that women existed in the world, and respectful towards their presence and their worth. Mark had come unwillingly and resisting into the cloister, but he had found his rightful place. Not everyone was so fortunate.

Aelfric came to the hut in the afternoon of a cloudy day, to ask for some dried mint. 'My mistress wants to brew a mint cordial for my master.'

'I hear he's somewhat out of humour and health,' said Cadfael, rustling the linen bags that gave forth such rich, heady scents upon the air. The young man's nostril quivered and widened with pleasure, inhaling close sweetness. In the soft light within, his wary face eased a little.

'There's not much ails him, more of the mind than the body. He'll be well enough when he plucks up heart. He's out of sorts with his kin most of all,' said Aelfric, growing unexpectedly confiding.

'That's trying for you all, even the lady,' said Cadfael.

'And she does everything a woman could do for him, there's nothing he can reproach her with. But this upheaval has him out with everybody, even himself. He's been expecting his son to come running and eat humble pie before this, to try and get his inheritance back, and he's been disappointed, and that sours him.'

Cadfael turned a surprised face at this. 'You mean he's cut off a son, to give his inheritance to the abbey? To spite the young man? That he couldn't, in law. No house would think of accepting such a bargain, without the consent of the heir.'

'It's not his own son.' Aelfric shrugged, shaking his head. 'It's his wife's son by a former marriage, so the lad has no legal claims on him. It's true he'd made a will naming him as his heir, but the abbey charter wipes that out – or will when it's sealed and witnessed. He has no remedy in law. They fell out, and he's lost his promised manor, and that's all there is to it.'

'For what fault could he deserve such treatment?' Cadfael wondered.

Aelfric hoisted deprecating shoulders, lean shoulders but broad and straight, as Cadfael observed. 'He's young and wayward, and my lord is old and irritable, not used to being crossed. Neither was the boy used to it, and he fought hard when he found his liberty curbed.'

'And what's become of him now? For I recall you said you were but four in the house.'

'He has a neck as stiff as my lord's, he's taken himself off to live with his married sister and her family, and learn a trade. He was expected back with his tail between his legs before now, my lord was counting on it, but never a sign, and I doubt if there will be.'

It sounded, Cadfael reflected ruefully, a troublous situation for the disinherited boy's mother, who must be torn two ways in this dissension. Certainly it accounted for an act of spleen which the old man was probably already regretting. He handed over the bunch of mint stems, their oval leaves still well formed and whole, for they had dried in honest summer heat, and had even a good shade of green left. 'She'll need to rub it herself, but it keeps its flavour better so. If she wants more, and you let me know, I'll crumble it fine for her, but this time we'll not keep her waiting. I hope it may go someway towards sweetening him, for his own sake and hers. And yours, too,' said Cadfael, and clapped him lightly on the shoulder.

Aelfric's gaunt features were convulsed for a moment by what might almost have been a smile, but of a bitter, resigned sort. 'Villeins are there to be scapegoats,' he said with soft, sudden violence, and left the hut hurriedly, with only a hasty, belated murmur of thanks.

With the approach of Christmas it was quite usual for many of the merchants of Shrewsbury, and the lords of many small manors close by, to give a guilty thought to the welfare of their souls, and their standing as devout and ostentatious Christians, and to seek small ways of acquiring merit, preferably as economically as possible. The conventual fare of pulse, beans, fish and occasional and meagre meat, benefited by sudden gifts of flesh and fowl to provide treats for the monks of St Peter's. Honey-baked cakes appeared, and dried fruits, and chickens, and even, sometimes, a haunch of venison, all devoted to the pittances that turned a devotional sacrament into a rare indulgence, a holy day into a holiday.

Some, of course, were selective in their giving, and made sure that their alms reached abbot or prior, on the assumption that his prayers might avail them more than those of the humbler brothers. There was a knight of south Shropshire who was quite unaware that Abbot Heribert had been summoned to London to be disciplined, and sent for his delectation a plump partridge, in splendid condition after a fat season. Naturally it arrived at the abbot's lodging to be greeted with pleasure by Prior Robert, who sent it down to the kitchen, to Brother Petrus, to be prepared for the midday meal in fitting style.

Brother Petrus, who seethed with resentment against him for Abbot Heribert's sake, glowered at the beautiful bird, and seriously considered spoiling it in some way, by burning it, or drying it with over-roasting, or serving it with a sauce that would ruin its perfection. But he was a cook of pride and honour, and he could not do it. The worst he could do was prepare it in an elaborate way which he himself greatly loved, with red wine and a highly spiced, aromatic sauce, cooked long and slow, and hope that Prior Robert would not be able to stomach it.

The prior was in high content with himself, with his present eminence, with the assured prospect of elevation to the abbacy in the near future, and with the manor of Mallilie, which he had been studying from the steward's reports and found a surprisingly lavish gift. Gervase Bonel had surely let his spite run away with his reason, to barter such a property for the simple necessities of life, when he was already turned sixty years, and could hardly expect to enjoy his retirement very long. A few extra attentions could be accorded him at little cost. Brother Jerome, always primed with the news within and without the pale, had reported that Master Bonel was slightly under the weather, with a jaded appetite. He might appreciate the small personal compliment of a dish from the abbot's table. And there was enough, a partridge being a bird of ample flesh.

Brother Petrus was basting the plump little carcase lovingly with his rich wine sauce, tasting delicately, adding a pinch of rosemary and a mere hint of rue, when Prior Robert swept into the kitchen, imperially tall and papally austere, and stood over the pot, his alabaster nostrils twitching to the tantalising scent, and his cool eyes studying the appearance of the dish, which was as alluring as its savour. Brother Petrus stooped to hide his face, which was sour as gall, and basted industriously, hoping his best efforts might meet with an uninformed palate, and disgust where they should delight. Small hope, Robert had such pleasure in the aroma that he almost considered abandoning his generous plan to share the satisfaction. Almost, but not quite. Mallilie was indeed a desirable property.

'I have heard,' said the prior, 'that our guest at the house by the mill-pond is in poor health, and lacks appetite. Set aside a single portion of this dish, Brother Petrus, and send it to the invalid with my compliments, as an intermissum after the main dish for the day. Bone it, and serve it in one of my own bowls. It should tempt him, if he is out of taste with other foods, and he will appreciate the attention.' He condescended, all too genuinely, to add: 'It smells excellent.'

'I do my best,' grated Brother Petrus, almost wishing his best undone.

'So do we all,' acknowledged Robert austerely, 'and so we ought.' And he swept out as he had swept in, highly content with himself, his circumstances, and the state of his soul. And Brother Petrus gazed after him from under lowering brows, and snarled at his two lay scullions, who knew better than to meddle too close while he was cooking, but kept to the corners of the kitchen, and jumped to obey orders.

Even for Brother Petrus, orders were orders. He did as he had been instructed, but after his own fashion, seeing to it that the portion he set aside for the unoffending guest was the choicest part of the flesh, and laced with the richest helping of the sauce.

389

'Lost his appetite, has he?' he said, after a final tasting, and unable to suppress his satisfaction in his own skills. 'That should tempt a man on his death-bed to finish it to the last drop.'

Brother Cadfael on his way to the refectory saw Aelfric crossing the great court from the abbot's kitchen, heading quickly for the gatehouse, bearing before him a high-rimmed wooden tray laden with covered dishes. Guests enjoyed a more relaxed diet than the brothers, though it did not differ greatly except in the amount of meat, and at this time of year that would already be salt beef. To judge by the aroma that wafted from the tray as it passed, beef boiled with onions, and served with a dish of beans. The small covered bowl balanced on top had a much more appetising smell. Evidently the newcomer was to enjoy an intermissum today before coming to the apples from the orchard. Aelfric carried his burden, which must be quite heavy, with a careful concentration, bent on getting it safely and quickly to the house by the pond. It was not a long journey, out at the gatehouse, a short step to the left, to the limits of the monastery wall, then pass the mill-pond on the left, and the first house beyond was Aelfric's destination. Beyond, again, came the bridge over the Severn, and the wall and gate of Shrewsbury. Not far, but far enough in December for food to get cold. No doubt the household, though relieved of the need to do much cooking, had its own fire and hob, and pans and dishes enough, and the fuel was a part of the price of Bonel's manor.

Cadfael went on to the refectory, and his own dinner, which turned out to be boiled beef and beans, as he had foreseen. No savoury intermissum here. Brother Richard, the sub-prior, presided; Prior Robert ate privately in the lodging he already thought of as his own. The partridge was excellent.

They had reached the grace after meat, and were rising from table, when the door flew open almost in Brother Richard's face, and a lay brother from the porter's lodge burst in, babbling incoherently for Brother Edmund, but too short of breath from running to explain the need.

'Master Bonel – his serving-maid has come running for help . . .' He gulped breath deep, and suppressed his panting long enough to get out clearly: 'He's taken terribly ill, she said he looks at death's door . . . the mistress begs someone to come to him quickly!'

390

Brother Edmund gripped him by the arm. 'What ails him? Is it a stroke? A convulsion?'

'No, from what the girl said, not that. He ate his dinner, and seemed well and well content, and not a quarter of an hour after he was taken with tingling of the mouth and throat, and then willed to vomit, but could not, and lips and neck are grown stiff and hard. . . . So she said!'

By the sound of it, she was a good witness, too, thought Cadfael, already making for the door and his workshop at a purposeful trot. 'Go before, Edmund. I'll join you as fast as I may. I'll bring what may be needed.'

He ran, and Edmund ran, and behind Brother Edmund the messenger scuttled breathlessly towards the gatehouse, and the agitated girl waiting there. Prickling of the lips, mouth and throat, Cadfael was reckoning as he ran, tingling and then rigidity, and urgent need, but little ability, to rid himself of whatever it was he had consumed. And a quarter of an hour since he got it down, more by now, if it was in the dinner he had eaten. It might be late to give him the mustard that would make him sick, but it must be tried. Though surely this was merely an attack of illness from some normal disagreement between an indisposed man and his perfectly wholesome food, nothing else was possible. But then, that prickling of the flesh of mouth and throat, and the stiffness following . . . that sounded all too like at least one violent illness he had witnessed, which had almost proved fatal; and the cause of that he knew. Hurriedly, he snatched from the shelves the preparation he wanted, and ran for the gatehouse.

For all the chill of the December day, the door of the first house beyond the mill-pond stood wide, and for all the awed quietness that hung about it, a quivering of agitation and confusion seemed to well out at the doorway to meet him, an almost silent panic of fluttering movements and hushed voices. A good house, with three rooms and the kitchen, and a small garden behind, running down to the pond; he knew it well enough, having visited a previous inmate upon less desperate business. The kitchen door faced away from the pond, towards the prospect of Shrewsbury beyond the river, and the north light at this time of day and year made the interior dim, although the window that looked out southwards stood unshuttered to let in light and air upon the brazier that did duty as all the cooking facilities such pensioners needed. He caught the grey gleam of a reflection from the water, as the wind ruffled it; the strip of garden was narrow here, though the house stood well above the water level.

By the open inner door through which the murmur of frightened voices emerged, stood a woman, obviously watching for him, her hands gripped tightly together under her breast, and quivering with tension. She started eagerly towards him as he came in, and then he saw her more clearly; a woman of his own years and his own height, very neat and quiet in her dress, her dark hair laced with silver and braided high on her head, her oval face almost unlined except for the agreeable grooves of good-nature and humour that wrinkled the corners of her dark-brown eyes, and made her full mouth merry and attractive. The merriment was quenched now, she wrung her hands and fawned on him; but attractive she was, even beautiful. She had held her own against the years, all forty-two of them that had come between.

He knew her at once. He had not seen her since they were both seventeen, and affianced, though nobody knew it but themselves, and probably her family would have made short work of the agreement if they had known it. But he had taken the Cross and sailed for the Holy Land, and for all his vows to return to claim her, with his honours thick upon him, he had forgotten everything in the fever and glamour and peril of a life divided impartially between soldier and sailor, and delayed his coming far too long; and she, for all her pledges to wait for him, had tired at last and succumbed to her parents' urgings, and married a more stable character, and small blame to her. And he hoped she had been happy. But never, never had he expected to see her here. It was no Bonel, no lord of a northern manor, she had married, but an honest craftsman of Shrewsbury. There was no accounting for her, and no time to wonder.

Yet he knew her at once. Forty-two years between, and he knew her! He had not, it seemed, forgotten very much. The eager way she leaned to him now, the turn of her head, the very way she coiled her hair; and the eyes, above all, large, direct, clear as light for all their darkness.

At this moment she did not, thank God, know him. Why should she? He must be far more changed than she; half a world, alien to her, had marked, manipulated, adapted him, changed his very shape of body and mind. All she saw was the monk who knew his herbs and remedies, and had run to fetch aids for her stricken man.

'Through here, brother . . . he is in here. The infirmarer has got him to bed. Oh, please help him!'

'If I may, and God willing,' said Cadfael, and went by her into the next room. She pressed after him, urging and ushering. The main room was furnished with table and benches, and chaotically spread with the remains of a meal surely interrupted by something more than one man's sudden illness. In any case, he was said to have eaten his meal and seemed well; yet there were broken dishes lying, shards on both table and floor. But she drew him anxiously on, into the bedchamber.

Brother Edmund rose from beside the bed, wide and dismayed of eye. He had got the invalid as near rest as he could, wrapped up here on top of the covers, but there was little more he could do. Cadfael drew near, and looked down at Gervase Bonel. A big, fleshy man, thickly capped in greying brown hair, with a short beard now beaded with saliva that ran from both corners of a rigid, half-open mouth. His face was leaden blue, the pupils of his eyes dilated and staring. Fine, strong features were congealed now into a livid mask. The pulse for which Cadfael reached was faint, slow and uneven, the man's breathing shallow, long and laboured. The lines of jaw and throat stood fixed as stone.

'Bring a bowl,' said Cadfael, kneeling, 'and beat a couple of egg-whites into some milk. We'll try to get it out of him, but I doubt it's late, it may do as much damage coming up as going down.' He did not turn his head to see who ran to do his bidding, though certainly someone did; he was hardly aware, as yet, that there were three other people present in the house, in addition to Brother Edmund and Mistress Bonel and the sick man. Aelfric and the maid, no doubt, but he recognised the third only when someone stooped to slide a wooden bowl close to the patient's face, and tilt the livid head to lean over it. Cadfael glanced up briefly, the silent and swift movement pleasing him, and looked into the intent and horrified face of the young Welshman, Meurig, Brother Rhys's great-nephew.

'Good! Lift his head on your hand, Edmund, and hold his brow steady.' It was easy enough to trickle the emetic mixture of mustard into the half-open mouth, but the stiff throat laboured frightfully at swallowing, and much of the liquid ran out again into his beard and the bowl. Brother Edmund's hands quivered, supporting the tormented head. Meurig held the bowl, himself shivering. The following sickness convulsed the big body, weakened the feeble pulse yet further, and produced only a painfully inadequate result. It was indeed late for Gervase Bonel. Cadfael

393

gave up, and let the paroxysms subside, for fear of killing him out of hand.

'Give me the milk and eggs.' This he fed very slowly into the open mouth, letting it slide of itself down the stiff throat, in such small quantities that it could not threaten the patient with choking. Too late to prevent whatever the poison had done to the flesh of Bonel's gullet, it might still be possible to lay a soothing film over the damaged parts, and ease their condition. He spooned patient drop after drop, and dead silence hung all round him, the watchers hardly breathing.

The big body seemed to have shrunk and subsided into the bed, the pulse fluttered ever more feebly, the stare of the eyes filmed over. He lay collapsed. The muscles of his throat no longer made any effort at swallowing, but stood corded and rigid. The end came abruptly, with no more turmoil than the cessation of breathing and pulse.

Brother Cadfael laid the spoon in the little bowl of milk, and sat back on his heels. He looked up at the circle of shocked, bewildered faces; and for the first time saw them all clearly: Meurig, the bowl with its horrid contents shaking in his hands, Aelfric, grim-eyed and pale, hovering at Brother Edmund's shoulder and staring at the bed, the girl – Brother Mark had not exaggerated, she was very pretty, with her yellow hair and black eyes – standing frozen, too shocked for tears, both small fists pressed hard against her mouth; and the widow, Mistress Bonel, who had once been Richildis Vaughan, gazing with marble face and slowly gathering tears at what remained of her husband.

'We can do no more for him,' said Brother Cadfael. 'He's gone.'

They all stirred briefly, as though a sudden wind had shaken them. The widow's tears spilled over and ran down her motionless face, as though she were still too bemused to understand what caused them. Brother Edmund touched her arm, and said gently: 'You will need helpers. I am very sorry, so are we all. You shall be relieved of such duties as we can lift from you. He shall lie in our chapel until all can be arranged.I will order it . . .'

'No,' said Cadfael, clambering stiffly to his feet, 'that can't be done yet, Edmund. This is no ordinary death. He is dead of poison, taken with the food he has recently eaten. It's a matter for the sheriff, and we must disturb nothing here and remove nothing until his officers have examined all.'

After a blank silence Aelfric spoke up hoarsely: 'But how can that be? It can't be so! We have all eaten the same, every one of us here. If there was anything amiss with the food, it would have struck at us all.'

'That is truth!' said the widow shakily, and sobbed aloud.

'All but the little dish,' the maid pointed out, in a small, frightened but determined voice, and flushed at having drawn attention to herself, but went on firmly: 'The one the prior sent to him.'

'But that was part of the prior's own dinner,' said Aelfric, aghast. 'Brother Petrus told me he had orders to take a portion from it and send it to my master with his compliments, to tempt his appetite.'

Brother Edmund shot a terrified look at Brother Cadfael, and saw his own appalling thought reflected back to him. Hastily he said: 'I'll go to the prior. Pray Heaven no harm has come to him! I'll send also to the sheriff, or please God! Prior Robert shall do as much on his own account. Brother, do you stay here until I return, and see that nothing is touched.'

'That,' said Cadfael grimly, 'I will certainly do.'

As soon as the agitated slapping of Brother Edmund's sandals had dwindled along the road, Cadfael shooed his stunned companions into the outer room, away from the horrid air of the bedchamber, tainted with the foul odours of sickness, sweat and death. Yes, and of something else, faint but persistent even against that powerful combination of odours; something he felt he could place, if he could give it a moment's undisturbed thought.

'No help for this,' he said sympathetically. 'We may do nothing now without authority, there's a death to account for. But no need to stand here and add to the distress. Come away and sit down quietly. If there's wine or ale in that pitcher, child, get your mistress a drink, and do as much for yourself, and sit down and take what comfort you can. The abbey has taken you in, and will stand by you now, to the best if may.'

In dazed silence they did as he bade. Only Aelfric looked helplessly round at the debris of broken dishes and the littered table, and mindful of his usual menial role, perhaps, asked quaveringly: 'Should I not clear this disorder away?'

'No, touch nothing yet. Sit down and be as easy as you can, lad. The sheriff's officer must see what's to be seen, before we remedy any part of it.'

He left them for a moment, and went back into the bed-chamber, closing the door between. The curious, aromatic

395

smell was almost imperceptible now, overborne by the enclosed stench of vomit, but he leaned down to the dead man's drawn-back lips, and caught the hint of it again, and more strongly. Cadfael's nose might be blunt, battered and brown to view, but it was as sharp and accurate in performance as a hart's.

There was nothing more in this death-chamber to tell him anything. He went back to his forlorn company in the next room. The widow was sitting with hands wrung tightly together in her lap, shaking her head still in disbelief, and murmuring to herself over and over. 'But how could it happen? How could it happen?' The girl, tearless throughout, and now jealously protective, sat with an arm about her mistress's shoulders; clearly there was more than a servant's affection there. The two young men shifted glumly and uneasily from place to place, unable to keep still. Cadfael stood back from them in the shadows, and ran a shrewd eye over the laden table. Three places laid, three beakers, one of them, in the master's place where a chair replaced the backless benches, overturned in a pool of ale, probably when Bonel suffered the first throes and blundered up from his seat. The large dish that had held the main meal was there in the centre, the congealing remains still in it. The food on one trencher was hardly touched, on the others it had been finished decently. Five people – no, apparently six – had eaten of that dish, and all but one were whole and unharmed. There was also the small bowl which he recognised as one of Abbot Heribert's, the same he had seen on Aelfric's tray as he passed through the court. Only the smallest traces of sauce remained in it; Prior Robert's gift to the invalid had clearly been much appreciated.

'None of you but Master Bonel took any of this dish?' asked Cadfael, bending to sniff at the rim carefully and long.

'No,' said the widow tremulously. 'It was sent as a special favour to my husband – a kind attention.'

And he had eaten it all. With dire results.

'And you three – Meurig, Aelfric – and you, child, I don't yet know your name . . .'

'It's Aldith,' said the girl.

'Aldith! And you three ate in the kitchen?'

'Yes. I had to keep the extra dish hot there until the other was eaten, and to see to the serving. And Aelfric always eats there. And Meurig, when he visits . . .' She paused for only a second, a faint flush mantling in her cheeks: '. . . he keeps me company.'

So that was the way the wind blew. Well, no wonder, she was indeed a very pretty creature.

Cadfael went into the kitchen. She had her pots and pans in neat order and well polished, she was handy and able as well as pretty. The brazier had an iron frame built high on two sides, to support an iron hob above the heat, and there, no doubt, the little bowl had rested until Bonel was ready for it. Two benches were ranged against the wall, out of the way, but close to the warmth. Three wooden platters, all used, lay on the shelf under the open window.

In the room at his back the silence was oppressive and fearful, heavy with foreboding. Cadfael went out at the open kitchen door, and looked along the road.

Thank God there was to be no second and even more dismaying death to cope with: Prior Robert, far too dignified to run, but furnished with such long legs that Brother Edmund had to trot to keep up with his rapid strides, was advancing along the highroad in august consternation and displeasure, his habit billowing behind him.

'I have sent a lay brother into Shrewsbury,' said the prior, addressing the assembled household, 'to inform the sheriff of what has happened, as I am told this death – madam, I grieve for your loss! – is from no natural cause, but brought about by poison. This terrible thing, though clearly reflecting upon our house, has taken place outside the walls, and outside the jurisdiction of our abbey court.' He was grateful for that, at least, and well he might be! 'Only the secular authorities can deal with this. But we must give them whatever help we can, it is our duty.'

His manner throughout, however gracefully he inclined towards the widow, and however well chosen his words of commiseration and promise of help and support in the sad obligations of burial, had been one of outrage. How dared such a thing happen in his cure, in his newly acquired abbacy, and through the instrument of his gift? His hope was to soothe the bereaved with a sufficiently ceremonious funeral, perhaps a very obscure place in the actual church precincts if one could be found, bundle the legal responsibility into the sheriff's arms, where it belonged, and hush the whole affair into forgetfulness as quickly as possible. He had baulked in revulsion and disgust in the doorway of the bedchamber, giving the dead only a brief and appalled reverence and a hasty murmur of prayer, and

397

quickly shut the door upon him again. In a sense he blamed every person there for imposing this ordeal and inconvenience upon him; but most of all he resented Cadfael's blunt assertion that this was a case of poison. That committed the abbey to examine the circumstances, at least. Moreover, there was the problem of the as yet unsealed agreement, and the alarming vision of Mallilie possibly slipping out of his hands. With Bonel dead before the charter was fully legal, to whom did that fat property now belong? And could it still be secured by a rapid approach to the hypothetical heir, before he had time to consider fully what he was signing away?

'Brother,' said Robert, looking down his long, fastidious nose at Cadfael, who was a head shorter, 'You have asserted that poison has been used here. Before so horrid a suggestion is put to the sheriff's officers, rather than the possibility of accidental use, or indeed, a sudden fatal illness – for such can happen even to men apparently in good health! – I should like to hear your reasons for making so positive a statement. How do you know? By what signs?'

'By the nature of his illness,' said Cadfael. 'he suffered with prickling and tingling of lips, mouth and throat, and afterwards with rigidity in those parts, so that he could not swallow, or breathe freely, followed by stiffness of his whole body, and great weakness of his heart-beat. His eyes were greatly dilated. All this I have seen once before, and then I knew what the man had swallowed, for he had the bottle in his hand. You may remember it, some years ago. A drunken carter during the fair, who broke into my store and thought he had found strong liquor. In that case I was able to recover him, since he had but newly drunk the poison. Too much time had gone by before I reached Master Bonel. But I recognised all the signs, and I know the poison that was used. I can detect it by smell on his lips, and on the remains of the dish he ate, the dish you sent him.'

If Prior Robert's face paled at the thought of what that might all too easily have meant, the change was not detectable, for his complexion was always of unflawed ivory. To do him justice, he was not a timorous man. He demanded squarely: 'What is this poison, if you are so sure of your judgement?'

'It is an oil that I make for rubbing aching joints, and it must have come either from the store I keep in my workshop, or from some smaller quantity taken from it, and I know of but one place where that could be found, and that is our own infirmary. The poison is monk's-hood – they call it so from the shape of the flowers, though it is also known as wolfsbane. Its root makes an excellent rub to remove pain, but it is very potent poison if swallowed.'

'If you can make medicines from this plant,' said Prior Robert, with chill dislike, 'so surely, may others, and this may have come from some very different source, and not from any store of ours,'

'That I doubt,' said Cadfael sturdily, 'since I know the odour of my own specific so well, and can detect here mustard and houseleek as well as monk's-hood. I have seen its effects, once taken, I know them again. I am in no doubt, and so I shall tell the sheriff.'

'It is well,' said Robert, no less frigidly, 'that a man should know his own work. You may then, remain here, and do what you can to provide my lord Prestcote or his deputies with whatever truth you can furnish. I will speak with them first, I am responsible now for the peace and good order of our house. Then I will send them here. When they are satisfied that they have gathered all the facts that can be gathered, send word to Brother Infirmarer, and he will have the body made seemly and brought to the chapel. Madam,' he said in quite different tones, turning to the widow, 'you need have no fear that your tenure here will be disturbed. We will not add to your distresses, we deplore them heartily. If you are in any need, send your man to me.' And to Brother Edmund, who hovered unhappily: 'Come with me! I wish to see where these medicaments are kept, and how accessible they may be to unauthorised people. Brother Cadfael will remain here.'

He departed as superbly as he had come, and at the same speed, the infirmarer scurrying at his heels. Cadfael looked after him with tolerant comprehension: this was certainly a disastrous thing to happen when Robert was new in his eminence, and the prior would do everything he could to smooth it away as a most unfortunate but perfectly natural death, the result of some sudden seizure. In view of the unconcluded charter, it would present him with problems enough, even so, but he would exert himself to the utmost to remove the scandalous suspicion of murder, or, if it must come to that, to see it ebb away into an unsolved mystery, attributed comfortably to some unidentified rogue outside the abbey enclave. Cadfael could not blame him for that; but the work of his own hands, meant to alleviate pain, had been used to destroy a man, and that was something he could not let pass.

He turned back with a sigh to the doleful household within, and was brought up short to find the widow's dark eyes, tearless and bright, fixed upon him with so significant and starry a glance that she seemed in an instant to have shed twenty years from her age and a great load from her shoulders. He had already come to the conclusion that, though undoubtedly shocked, she was not heartbroken by her loss; but this was something different. Now she was unmistakably the Richildis he had left behind at seventeen. Faint colour rose in her cheeks, the hesitant shadow of a smile caused her lips to quiver, she gazed at him as if they shared a knowledge closed to everyone else, and only the presence of others in the room with them kept her from utterance.

The truth dawned on him only after a moment's blank incomprehension, and struck him as the most inconvenient and entangling thing that could possibly have happened at this moment. Prior Robert in departing had called him by his name, no usual name in these parts, and reminder enough to one who had, perhaps, already been pondering half-remembered tricks of voice and movement, and trying to run them to earth.

His impartiality and detachment in this affair would be under siege from this moment. Richildis not only knew him, she was sending him urgent, silent signals of her gratitude and dependence, and her supreme assurance that she could rely on his companionship, to what end he hardly dared speculate.

Chapter Three

ILBERT PRESTCOTE, sheriff of Shropshire since the town fell into King Stephen's hands during the past summer, had his residence in Shrewsbury castle, which he held fortified for the king, and managed his now pacified shire from that headquarters. Had his deputy been in Shrewsbury when Prior Robert's message reached the castle, Prestcote would probably have sent him to answer the call, which would have been a relief to Brother Cadfael, who had considerable faith in Hugh Beringar's shrewd sense; but that young man was away on his own manor, and it was a sergeant, with a couple of men-at-arms as escort, who finally arrived at the house by the mill-pond.

The sergeant was a big man, bearded and deep-voiced, in the sheriff's full confidence, and able and willing to act with authority in his name. He looked first to Cadfael, as belonging to the abbey, whence the summons had come, and it was Cadfael who recounted the course of events from the time he had been sent for. The sergeant had already spoken with Prior Robert, who would certainly have told him that the suspected dish had come from his own kitchen and at his own orders.

'And you swear to the poison? It was in this and no other food that he swallowed it?'

'Yes,' said Cadfael, 'I can swear to it. The traces left are small, but even so minute a smear of the sauce, if you put it to your lips, would bring out a hot prickling some minutes later. I have confirmed it for myself. There is no doubt.'

'And Prior Robert, who ate the remainder of the bird, is live and well, God be praised. Therefore somewhere between the abbot's kitchen and yonder table, poison was added to the dish. It is not a great distance, or a great time. You, fellow, you fetch the meals from the kitchen to this house? And did so today? Did you halt anywhere by the way? Speak to any? Set down your tray anywhere?'

'I did not,' said Aelfric defensively. 'If I delay, or the food is cold, I have to answer for it. I do to the letter what I am supposed to do, and so I did today.'

'And here? What did you do with the dishes when you came in?'

'He delivered them to me,' said Aldith, so quickly and firmly that Cadfael looked at her with new interest. 'He put down the tray on the bench by the brazier, and I myself set the small dish on the hob to keep warm, while we two served the main dish to our lord and lady. He told me the prior had kindly sent it for the master. When I had served them within, we sat down in the kitchen to eat our own meal.'

'And none of you noticed anything wrong with the partridge? In odour or appearance?'

'It was a very rich, spiced sauce, it had a fine smell. No, there was nothing to notice. The master ate it and found nothing wrong until his mouth began to prick and burn, and that was afterwards.'

'Both scent and savour,' confirmed Cadfael, consulted with a rapid glance, 'could well be covered by such a sauce. And the amount needed would not be so great.'

'And you . . .' The sergeant turned to Meurig. 'You were also here? You belong to the household?'

'Not now,' said Meurig readily. 'I come from Master Bonel's manor, but I'm working now for the master-carpenter Martin Bellecote, in the town. I came here today to visit an old great-uncle of mine in the infirmary, as Brother Infirmarer will tell you, and being about the abbey I came to visit here also. I came into the kitchen just when Aldith and Aelfric were about to share out their own meal, and they bade me join them, and I did.'

'There was enough,' said Aldith. 'The abbot's cook is generous-handed.'

'So you were three eating here together. And giving the little dish a stir now and then? And within . . .' He passed through the doorway and looked a second time about the debris of the table. 'Master Bonel and the lady, naturally.' No, he was not a stupid man, he could count, and he had noted the absence of one person both from the house and from their talk, as if they were all united to smooth the sixth trencherman out of sight. 'Here are three places laid. Who was the third?'

There was no help for it, someone had to answer. Richildis made the best of it. With apparently ingenuous readiness, rather as though surprised at the introduction of an irrelevancy, she said: 'My son. But he left well before my husband was taken ill.'

'Without finishing his dinner! If this was his place?'

'It was,' she said with dignity, and volunteered nothing more.

'I think, madam,' said the sergeant, with a darkly patient smile, 'you had better sit down and tell me more about this son of yours. As I have heard from Prior Robert, your husband was by way of granting his lands to the abbey in return for this house and guest status for the rest of his life and yours. After what has happened here, that agreement would seem to be forcibly in abeyance, since it is not yet sealed. Now, it would be greatly to the advantage of an heir to those lands, supposing such to be living, to have your husband removed from this world before the charter was ratified. Yet if there was a son of your marriage, his consent would have been required before any such agreement could have been drawn up. Read me this riddle. How did he succeed in disinheriting his son?'

Plainly she did not want to volunteer anything more than she must, but she was wise enough to know that too stubborn reticence would only arouse suspicion. Resignedly she replied: 'Edwin is my son by my first marriage. Gervase had no paternal obligation to him. He could dispose of his lands as he wished.' There was more, and if she left it to be ferreted out through others it would sound far worse. 'Though he had previously made a will making Edwin his heir, there was nothing to prevent him from changing his mind.'

'Ah! So there was, it seems, an heir who was being dispossessed by this charter, and had much to regain by rendering it void. And limited time for the business – only a few days or weeks, until a new abbot is appointed. Oh, don't mistake me, my mind is open. Every man's death may be convenient to

403

someone, often to more than one. There could be others with something to gain. But you'll grant me, your son is certainly one such.'

She bit her lip, which was unsteady, and took a moment to compose herself before she said gallantly: 'I don't quarrel with your reasoning. I do know that my son, however much he may have wanted his manor, would never have wanted it at this price. He is learning a trade, and resolved to be independent and make his own future.'

'But he was here today. And departed, it appears, in some haste. When did he come?'

Meurig said readily: 'He came with me. He's apprenticed himself to Martin Bellecote, who is his sister's husband and my master. We came here together this morning, and he came with me, as he has once before, to see my old uncle in the infirmary.'

'Then you arrived at this house together? You were together throughout that time? A while ago you said *you* came into the kitchen – "I", you said, not "we".'

'He came before me. He was restive after a while . . . he's young, he grew tired of standing by the old man's bed while we spoke only Welsh together. And his mother was here waiting to see him. So he went ahead. He was in at the table when I got here.'

'And left the table almost dinnerless,' said the sergeant very thoughtfully. 'Why? Can that have been a very comfortable dinner-table, a young man come to eat with the man who disinherited him? Was this the first time they had so met, since the abbey supplanted him?'

He had his nose well down on a strong trail now, and small blame to him, it reeked enough to lure the rawest pup, and this man was far from being that. What would I have said to such a strong set of circumstances, Cadfael wondered, had I been in his shoes? A young man with the most urgent need to put a stop to this charter, while he had time, and into the bargain, here on the scene just prior to the disaster, and fresh from the infirmary, which he had visited before, and where the means to the end was to be found. And here was Richildis, between holding the sheriff's sergeant fast with huge, challenging eyes, shooting desperate glances in Cadfael's direction, crying out to him silently that he must help her, or her darling was deep in the mire! Silently, in turn he willed her to spill out at once everything that could count against her son, leave nothing untold,

404

for only so could she counter much of what might otherwise be alleged against him.

'It was the first time,' said Richildis. 'And it was a most uneasy meeting, but it was for my sake Edwin sought it. Not because he hoped to change my husband's mind, only to bring about peace for me. Meurig, here, has been trying to persuade him to visit us, and today he prevailed, and I'm grateful to him for his efforts. But my husband met the boy with illwill, and taunted him with coming courting for his promised manor – for it *was* promised! – when Edwin intended no such matter. Yes, there was a quarrel! They were two hasty people, and they ended with high words. And Edwin flung out, and my husband threw that platter after him – you see the shards there against the wall. That's the whole truth of it, ask my servants. Ask Meurig, he knows. My son ran out of the house and back into Shrewsbury, I am sure, to where he now feels his home to be, with his sister and her family.'

'Let me understand you clearly,' said the sergeant, a thought too smoothly and reasonably. 'Ran out of the house through the kitchen, you say? – where you three were sitting?' The turn of his head towards Aldith and the young men was sharp and intent, not smooth at all. 'So you saw him leave the house, without pause on the way?'

All three hesitated a brief instant, each casting uncertain glances aside at the others, and that was a mistake. Aldith said for them all, resignedly: 'When they began to shout and throw things, we all three ran in there, to try and calm the master down . . . or at least to . . .'

'To be there with me, and some comfort,' said Richildis.

'And there you remained after the boy had gone.' He was content with his guess, their faces confirmed it, however unwillingly. 'So I thought. It takes time to placate a very angry man. So none of you saw whether this young fellow paused in the kitchen, none of you can say he did not stop to take his revenge by dosing the dish of partridge. He had been in the infirmary that morning, as he had once before, he may well have known where to find this oil, and what its powers could be. He may have come to this dinner prepared either for peace or war, and failed of getting peace.'

Richildis shook her head vigorously. 'You don't know him! It was *my* peace he wanted to secure. And besides, it was no more than a few minutes before Aelfric ran out after him, to

405

try to bring him back, and though he followed almost to the bridge, he could not overtake him.'

'It's true,' said Aelfric. 'He surely had no time to check at all. I ran like a hare and called after him, but he would not turn back.'

The sergeant was unconvinced. 'How long does it take to empty a small vial into an open dish? One twirl of the spoon, and who was to know? And when your master was calm again, no doubt the prior's gift made a very handy and welcome sop to his pride, and he ate it gladly.'

'But did this boy even know,' asked Cadfael, intervening very gingerly, 'that the dish left in the kitchen was meant solely for Master Bonel? He would hardly risk harm to his mother.'

The sergeant was by that time too certain of his quarry to be impressed by any such argument. He eyed Aldith hard, and for all her resolution she paled a little.

'With such a strange gathering to wait on, was it likely the girl would miss the chance of a pleasant distraction for her master? When you went in to serve him his meat, did you not tell him of the prior's kind attention, and make the most of the compliment to him, and the treat in store?'

She cast down her eyes and pleated the corner of her apron. 'I thought it might sweeten him,' she said despairingly.

The sergeant had all he needed, or so he thought, to lay his hands promptly upon the murderer. He gave a final look round the shattered household, and said: 'Well, I think you may put things in order here, I've seen all there is to be seen. Brother Infirmarer is prepared to help you take care of your dead. Should I need to question you further, I must be sure of finding you here.'

'Where else should we be?' asked Richildis bleakly. 'What is it you mean to do? Will you at least let me know what happens, if you . . . if you should . . .' She could not put it into words. She stiffened her still straight and lissome back, and said with dignity: 'My son has no part in this villainy, and so you will find. He is not yet fifteen years old, a mere child!'

'The shop of Martin Bellecote, you said.'

'I know it,' said one of the men-at-arms.

'Good! Show the way, and we'll see what this lad has to say for himself.' And they turned confidently to the door and the highway.

Brother Cadfael saw fit to toss one disturbing ripple, at least, into the pool of their complacency. 'There is the matter of a container for this oil. Whoever purloined it, whether from my store or from the infirmary, must have brought a vial to put it in. Meurig, did you see any sign of such about Edwin this morning? You came from the shop with him. In a pocket, or a pouch of cloth, even a small vial would hang in a noticeable way.'

'Never a sign of anything such,' said Meurig stoutly.

'And further, even well stoppered and tied down, such an oil is very penetrating, and can leave both a stain and an odour where even a drop seeps through or is left on the lip. Pay attention to the clothing of any man you think suspect in this matter.'

'Are you teaching me my business, brother?' enquired the sergeant with a tolerant grin.

'I am mentioning certain peculiarities about *my* business, which may be of help to you and keep you from error,' said Cadfael placidly.

'By your leave,' said the sergeant over his shoulder, from the doorway, 'I think we'll first lay hands on the culprit. I doubt if we shall need your learned advice, once we have him.' And he was off along the short path to the roadway where the horses were tethered, and his two men after him.

The sergeant and his men came to Martin Bellecote's shop on the Wyle late in the afternoon. The carpenter, a big, comely fellow in his late thirties, looked up cheerfully enough from his work, and enquired their business without wonder or alarm. He had done work for Prestcote's garrison once or twice, and the appearance of one of the sheriff's officers in his workshop held no menace to him. A brown-haired, handsome wife looked out curiously from the house-door beyond, and three children erupted one by one from that quarter to examine the customers fearlessly and frankly. A grave girl of about eleven, very housewifely and prim, a small, square boy of eight or so, and an elfin miss no more than four, with a wooden doll under her arm. All of them gazed and listened. The door to the house remained open, and the sergeant had a loud, peremptory voice.

'You have an apprentice here by the name of Edwin. My business is with him.'

'I have,' agreed Martin mildly, rising and dusting the resin of polish from his hands. 'Edwin Gurney, my wife's young brother. He's not yet home. He went down to see his mother in the Foregate. He should have been back before this, but I daresay she's wanted to keep him longer. What's your will with him?' He was still quite serene; he knew of nothing amiss.

'He left his mother's house above two hours since,' said the sergeant flatly. 'We are come from there. No offence, friend, if you say he's not here, but it's my duty to search for him. You'll give us leave to go through your house and yard?'

Martin's placidity had vanished in an instant, his brows drew into a heavy frown. His wife's beech-brown head appeared again in the doorway beyond, her fair, contented face suddenly alert and chill, dark eyes intent. The children stared unwaveringly. The little one, voice of natural justice in opposition to law, stated firmly: 'Bad man!' and nobody hushed her.

'When I say he is not here,' said Martin levelly, 'you may be assured it is true. But you may also assure yourselves. House, workshop and yard have nothing to hide. Now what are you hiding? This boy is my brother, through my wife, and my apprentice by his own will, and dear to me either way. Now, why are you seeking him?'

'In the house in the Foregate where he visited this morning,' said the sergeant deliberately, 'Master Gervase Bonel, his step-father, who promised him he should succeed to the manor of Mallilie and then changed his mind, is lying dead at this moment, murdered. It is on suspicion of his murder that I want this young man Edwin. Is that enough for you?'

It was more than enough for the eldest son of this hitherto happy household, whose ears were stretched from the inner room to catch this awful and inexplicable news. The law nose-down on Edwin's trail, and Edwin should have been back long ago if everything had gone reasonably well! Edwy had been uneasy for some time, and was alert for disaster where his elders took it for granted all must be well. He let himself out in haste by the back window on to the yard, before the officers could make their way into the house, clambered up the stacked timber and over the wall like a squirrel, and was away at a light, silent run towards the slope that dived riverwards, and one of the tight little posterns through the town wall, open now in time of peace, that gave on to the steep bank, not far from the abbot's vineyard. Several of the businesses in town that needed bulky stores had fenced premises here for their stock, and among them was Martin Bellecote's wood-yard where he seasoned his timber. It was an old refuge when either or both of the boys happened to be in trouble, and it was the place Edwin would make for if . . . oh, no, not if he had killed, because that was ridiculous! . . . but if he had been rejected, affronted, made miserably unhappy and madly angry. Angry almost to murder, but never, never quite! It was not in him.

Edwy ran, confident of not being followed, and fell breathless through the wicket of his father's enclosure, and headlong over the splayed feet of a sullen, furious, tear-stained and utterly vulnerable Edwin.

Edwin, perhaps because of the tear-stains, immediately clouted Edwy as soon as he had regained his feet, and was clouted in his turn just as indignantly. The first thing they did, at all times of stress, was to fight. It meant nothing, except that both were armed and on guard, and whoever meddled with them in the matter afterwards had better be very careful, for their practice on each other would be perfected on him. Within minutes Edwy was pounding his message home into bewildered, unreceptive, and finally convinced and dismayed ears. They sat down cheek by jowl to do some frantic planning.

Aelfric appeared in the herb-gardens an hour before Vespers. Cadfael had been back in his solitude no more than half an hour then, after seeing the body cleansed, made seemly, and borne away into the mortuary chapel, the bereaved house restored to order, the distracted members of the household at least set free to wander and wonder and grieve as was best for them. Meurig was gone, back to the shop in the town, to tell the carpenter and his family word for word what had befallen, for what comfort or warning that might give them. By this time, for all Cadfael knew, the sheriff's men had seized young Edwin . . . Dear God, he had even forgotten the name of the man Richildis had married, and Bellecote was only her son-in-law.

'Mistress Bonel asks,' said Aelfric earnestly, 'that you'll come and speak with her privately. She entreats you for old friendship, to stand her friend now.'

It came as no surprise. Cadfael was aware that he stood on somewhat perilous ground, even after forty years. He would have been happier if the lamentable death of her husband had turned out to be no mystery, her son in no danger, and her future none of his business, but there was no help for it. His youth, a sturdy part of the recollections that made him the man he was, stood in her debt, and now that she was in need he had no choice but to make generous repayment.

'I'll come,' he said. 'You go on before, and I'll be with her within a quarter of an hour.'

When he knocked at the door of the house by the mill-pond, it was opened by Richildis herself. There was no sign either of Aelfric or Aldith, she had taken good care that the two of them should be able to talk in absolute privacy. In the inner room all was bare and neat, the morning's chaos smoothed away, the trestle table folded aside. Richildis sat down in the great chair which had been her husband's, and drew Cadfael down on the bench beside her. It was dim within the room, only one small rush-light burning; the only other brightness came from her eyes, the dark, lustrous brightness he was remembering more clearly with every moment.

'Cadfael . . .' she said haltingly, and was silent again for some moments. 'To think it should really be you! I never got word of you, after I heard you were back home. I thought you would have married, and been a grandsire by this. As often as I looked at you, this morning, I was searching my mind, why I should be so sure I ought to know you . . . And just when I was in despair, to hear your name spoken!'

'And you,' said Cadfael, 'you came as unexpectedly to me. I never knew you'd been widowed from Eward Gurney – I remember now that was his name! – much less that you'd wed again.'

'Three years ago,' she said, and heaved a sigh that might have been of regret or relief at the abrupt ending of this second match. 'I mustn't make you think ill of him, he was not a bad man, Gervase, only elderly and set in his ways, and used to being obeyed. A widower he was, many years wifeless, and without any children, leastways none by the marriage. He courted me a long time, and I was lonely, and then he promised, you see . . . Not having a legitimate heir, he promised if I'd have him he'd make Edwin his heir. His overlord sanctioned it. I ought to tell you about my family. I had a daughter, Sibil, only a year after I married Eward, and then, I don't know why, time went on and on, and there were no more. You'll remember, maybe, Eward had his business in Shrewsbury as a master-carpenter and carver. A good workman he was, a good master and a good husband.'

'You were happy?' said Cadfael, grateful at hearing it in her voice. Time and distance had done well by the pair of them, and led them to their proper places, after all.

'Very happy! I couldn't have had a better man. But there were no more children then. And when Sibil was seventeen she married Eward's journeyman, Martin Bellecote, and a good lad

410

he is, too, and she's as happy in her match as I was in mine, thank God! Well, then in two years the girl was with child, and it was like being young again myself – the first grandchild! – it's always so. I was so joyful, looking after her and making plans for the birth, and Eward was as proud as I was, and what with one thing and another, you'd have thought we old folk were young newly-weds again ourselves. And I don't know how it happens, but when Sibil was four months gone, what should I find but I was carrying, too! After all those years! And in my forty-fourth year – it was like a miracle! And the upshot is, she and I both brought forth boys, and though there's the four months between them, they might as well be twins as uncle and nephew – and the uncle the younger, at that! They even look very like, both taking after my man. And from the time they were first on their feet they've been as close as any brothers, and closer than most, and both as wild as fox-cubs. So that's my son Edwin and my grandson Edwy. Not yet turned fifteen, either of them. It's for Edwin I'm praying your help, Cadfael. For I swear to you he never did nor even could do such wicked harm, but the sheriff's man has it fixed fast in his head that it was Edwin who put poison in the dish. If you knew him, Cadfael, if only you knew him, you'd know it's madness.'

And so it sounded when her fond, maternal voice spoke of it, yet sons no older than fourteen had been known to remove their fathers to clear their own paths, as Cadfael knew well enough. And this was not Edwin's own father, and little love lost between them.

'Tell me,' he said, 'about this second marriage, and the bargain you struck.'

'Why, Eward died when Edwin was nine years old, and Martin took over his shop, and runs it as Eward did before him, and as Eward taught him. We all lived together until Gervase came ordering some panelling for his house, and took a strong fancy to me. And he was a fine figure of a man, too, and in good health, and very attentive . . . . He promised if I would have him he'd make Edwin his heir, and leave Mallilie to him. And Martin and Sibil had three more children to provide for by then, so with all those mouths to feed he needed what the business can bring in, and I thought to see Edwin set up for life.'

'But it was not a success,' said Cadfael, 'understandably. A man who had never had children, and getting on in years, and a lusty lad busy growing up – they were bound to cross swords.'

'It was ten of one and half a score of the other,' she owned, sighing. 'Edwin had been indulged, I fear, he was used to his freedom and to having his own way, and he was for ever running off with Edwy, as he'd always been used to do. And Gervase held it against him that he ran with simple folk and craftsmen – he thought that low company, beneath a young man with a manor to inherit, and that was bound to anger Edwin, who loves his kin. Not to claim that he had not some less respectable friends, too! They rubbed each other the wrong way daily. When Gervase beat him, Edwin ran away to Martin's shop and stayed for days. And when Gervase locked him up, he'd either make his way out all the same, or else take his revenge in other ways. In the end Gervase said as the brat's tastes obviously ran to mere trade, and running loose with all the scallywags of the town, he might as well go and apprentice himself in good earnest, it was all he was fit for. And Edwin, though he knew better, pretended to take that, word for word, as well meant, and went and did that very thing, which made Gervase more furious than ever. That was when he vowed he'd hand over his manor by charter to the abbey, and live here retired. "He cares nothing for the lands I meant to leave him," he said, "why should I go on nursing them for such an ingrate?" And he did it, there and then, while he was hot, he had this agreement drawn up, and made ready to move here before Christmas.'

'And what did the boy say to that? For I suppose he never realised what was intended?'

'He did not! He came with a rush, penitent but indignant, too. He swore he does love Mallilie, he never meant to scorn it, and he would take good care of it if it came to him. But my husband would not give way, though we all pleaded with him. And Edwin was bitter, too, for he had been promised, and a promise should be kept. But it was done, and nobody could make my lord undo it. Not being his own son, Edwin's consent was never asked nor needed – it would never have been given! He went flying back to Martin and Sibil with his raging grievance, and I haven't seen him again until this day, and I wish he'd never come near us today. But he did, and now see how the sheriff's man is hunting him as a villain who would kill his own mother's husband! Such a thought could never enter that child's head, I swear to you,

412

Cadfael, but if they take him . . . Oh, I can't bear to think of it!'

'You've had no word since they left here? News travels this highroad fast. I think it would have reached us before now if they had found him at home.'

'Not a word yet. But where else would he go? He knew no reason why he should hide. He ran from here knowing nothing of what was to happen after his going, he was simply sore about his bitter welcome.'

'Then he might not wish to take such a mood home with him, not until he'd come to terms with it. Hurt things hide until the fright and pain wears off. Tell me all that happened at this dinner. It seems Meurig has been a go-between for you, and tried to bring him to make peace. Some mention was made of a former visit . . .'

'Not to me,' said Richildis sadly. 'The two of them came to bring down the lectern Martin has been making for the Lady Chapel, and Meurig took my boy with him to see the old brother, his kinsman. He tried to persuade Edwin then to come and see me, but he would not. Meurig is a good fellow, he's done his best. Today he did prevail on Edwin to come, but see what came of it! Gervase was in high glee about it, and monstrously unfair – he taunted my boy with coming like a beggar to plead to be restored, and get his inheritance back, which was never Edwin's intent. He'd die sooner! Tamed at last, are you, says Gervase! Well, if you go down on your knees, he says, and beg pardon for your frowardness, who knows, I might relent yet. Crawl, then, he says, and beg for your manor! And so it went, until Edwin blazed out that he was not and never would be tamed by a wicked, tyrannical, vicious old monster – which I grant you,' she sighed hopelessly, 'Gervase was not, only a stubborn and ill-tempered one. Oh, I can't tell you all they yelled at each other! But I do say this, it took a lot of goading today to get Edwin to blaze, and that's credit to him. For my sake he would have borne it, but it was too much for him. So he said what he had to say, very loudly, and Gervase flung the platter at him, and a beaker, too, and then Aldith and Aelfric and Meurig came rushing in to try and help me calm him down. And Edwin stamped out – and that was all.'

Cadfael was silent for a moment, ruminating on these other members of the household. A hot-tempered, proud, affronted boy seemed to him a possible suspect had Bonel been struck down with fist or even dagger, but a very unlikely poisoner.

True, the lad had been twice with Meurig in the infirmary, and probably seen where the medicines were kept, he had a reason for action, he had the opportunity; but the temperament for a poisoner, secret, dark and bitter, surely that was an impossibility to such a youngster, by all his breeding and training open, confident, with a fine conceit of himself. There were, after all, these others, equally present.

'The girl, Aldith – you've had her long?'

'She's distant kin to me,' said Richildis, almost startled into a smile. 'I've known her from a child, and took her when she was left orphan, two years ago. She's like my own girl.'

It was what he had supposed, seeing Aldith so protective while they waited for the law. 'And Meurig? I hear he was also of Master Bonel's household once, before he went to work for your son-in-law.'

'Meurig – ah, well, you see, it's this way with Meurig. His mother was a Welsh maidservant at Mallilie, and like so many such, bore her master a by-blow. Yes, he's Gervase's natural son. My lord's first wife must have been barren, for Meurig is the only child he ever fathered, unless there are one or two we don't know of, somewhere about the shire there. He maintained Angharad decently until she died, and he had Meurig taken care of, and gave him employment on the manor. I was not easy about him,' she admitted, 'when we married. Such a good, willing, sensible young man, and with no claims on any part of what was his father's, it seemed hard. Not that he ever complained! But I asked him if he would not be glad to have a trade of his own, that would last him for life, and he said he would. So I persuaded Gervase to let Martin take him, to teach him all he knew. And I did ask him,' said Richildis, with a quaver in her voice, 'to keep a watch on Edwin, after he ran from us, and try to bring him to make terms with Gervase. I never expected my son to give way, for he's able, too, and he could make his own road. I just wanted to have him back. There was a time when he blamed me – as having to choose between them, and choosing my husband. But I'd married him . . . and I was sorry for him . . . .' Her voice snapped off short, and she was silent a moment. 'I've been glad of Meurig, he has stood friend to us both.'

'He got on well enough with your husband, did he? There was no bad blood between them?'

'Why, no, none in the world!' She was astonished at the question. 'They rubbed along together quietly, and never any sparks. Gervase was generous to him, you know, though he never paid him much attention. And he makes him a decent living allowance – that is, he did . . . . Oh, how will he fare now, if that ends? I shall have to have advice, law is a tangle to me . . . .'

Nothing there to raise a brow, it seemed, even if Meurig knew as well as anyone how to lay hands on poison. So did Aelfric, who had been in the workshop and seen it dispensed. And whoever gained by Bonel's death, it seemed, Meurig stood only to lose. Manorial bastards were thick on the ground everywhere, the lord who had but one had been modest and abstemious indeed, and the by-blow who was set up with an expanding trade and an allowance to provide for him was fortunate, and had no cause for complaint. Good cause, in fact, to lament his father's passing.

'And Aelfric?'

The darkness outside had made the light of the little lamp seem brighter; her face, oval and grave, shone in the pallid radiance, and her eyes were round as moons. 'Aelfric is a hard case. You must not think my husband was worse than his kind, or ever knowingly took more than was his by law. But the law limps, sometimes. Aelfric's father was born free as you or I, but younger son in a holding that was none too large even for one, and rather than have it split, when *his* father died, he left it whole for his brother, and took a villein yard-land that had fallen without heirs, on my husband's manor. He took it on villein tenure, to do the customary duties for it, but never doubting to keep his status as a free man, doing villein service of his own undertaking. And Aelfric in his turn was a younger son, and foolishly accepted service in the manor household when his elder had family enough to run his yard-land without him. So when the manor was to be surrendered, and we were ready to come here, Gervase chose him to be his manservant, for he was the neatest-handed and best we had. And when Aelfric chose rather to go elsewhere and find employment, Gervase brought suit that he was villein, both his brother and his father having done customary service for the land they held. And the court found that it was so, and he was bound, however free-born his father had been. He takes it hard,' said Richildis ruefully. 'He never felt himself villein before, he was a free man doing work for pay. Many and many a one has found himself in the same case, never having dreamed of losing his freedom until it was lost.'

415

Cadfael's silence pricked her. He was reflecting that here was another who had a burning grudge, knew where to find the means, and of all people had the opportunity; but her mind was on the painful picture she had just drawn, and she mistook his brooding for disapproval of her dead husband, censure he was unwilling to express to her. Valiantly she sought to do justice, at least, if there was no affection left.

'You are wrong if you think the fault was all on one side. Gervase believed he was doing no more than his right, and the law agreed with him. I've never known him wilfully cheat any man, but he did stand fast on his own dues. And Aelfric makes his own situation worse. Gervase never used to harry or press him, for he worked well by nature, but now he's unfree he sticks stubbornly in every last extreme of servile labour, purposely, drives home his villein condition at every turn . . . It is not servility, but arrogance, he deliberately rattles his chains. He did give offence by it, and truly I think they grew to hate each other. And then, there's Aldith . . . . Oh, Aelfric never says word of it to her, but I know! He looks after her as if his heart's being drawn out of him. But what has he to offer a free girl like her? Even if Meurig wasn't casting an eye in that direction, too, and he so much more lively company. Oh, I tell you, Cadfael, I've had such trouble and grief with all this household of mine. And now this! Do help me! Who else will, if not you? Help my boy! I do believe you can, if you will.'

'I can promise you,' said Cadfael after scrupulous thought, 'that I'll do everything I can to find out the murderer of your husband. That I must, whoever he may be. Will that content you?'

She said: 'Yes! I *know* Edwin is guiltless. You don't, yet. But you will!'

'Good girl!' said Cadfael heartily. 'That's how I remember you from when time was. And even now, before your knowledge becomes my knowledge also, I can promise you one thing more. Yes, I will help your son to the utmost I may, guilty or innocent, though not by hiding the truth. Will that do?'

'She nodded, for the moment unable to speak. The stresses not only of this disastrous day, but of many days before, showed suddenly in her face.

'I fear,' said Cadfael gently, 'you went too far aside from your own kind, Richildis, in marrying the lord of a manor.'

'I did so!' she said, and incontinently burst into tears at last, and wept, alarmingly, on his shoulder.

Chapter Four

ROTHER DENIS the hospitaller, who always had all the news of the town from the wayfarers who came to the guest-hall, reported on the way to Vespers that the story of Bonel's death and the hunt for his stepson was all over Shrewsbury, and the sheriff's sergeant had drawn a blank at Martin Bellecote's shop. A thorough search of the premises had turned up no trace of the boy, and the sergeant was having him cried through the streets; but if the populace joined in the hunt with no more than their usual zeal for the sheriff's law, it was likely the crier would be wasting his breath. A boy not yet fifteen, and known to a great many in the town, and with nothing against him but a bit of riotous mischief now and then . . . no, they were not likely to give up their night's sleep to help in his capture.

The first necessity, it seemed to Cadfael no less than to the sergeant, was to find the boy. Mothers are partial, especially towards only sons, late sons conceived after hope of a son has faded. Cadfael felt a strong desire to see and hear and judge for himself before he made any other move in the matter.

Richildis, relieved by her fit of weeping, had told him where to find her son-in-law's shop and house, and it fell blessedly at the near end of the town. A short walk past the mill-pond, over the bridge, in through the town gates, which would be open until after Compline, and it was but a couple of minutes up the steep, curving Wyle to Bellecote's premises. Half an hour to go and return. After supper, and a quick supper at that, he would slip away, cutting out Collations – safe enough, for Prior Robert would absent himself on principle, standing on his privacy as abbot-designate, and leaving the mundane direction of the house to Brother Richard, who certainly would not meddle where it might cost him effort.

Supper was salt fish and pulse, and Cadfael disposed of it with scant attention, and made off across the great court in haste, and out at the gates. The air was chill, but as yet barely on the edge of frost, and there had been no snow at all so far. All the same, he had muffled his sandalled feet in well-wound strips of wool, and drawn his hood close.

The town porters saluted him respectfully and cheerfully, knowing him well. The right-hand curve of the Wyle drew him upward, and he turned off, again to the right, into the open yard under the eaves of Bellecote's house. After his knock at the closed door there was a longish silence, and that he could well understand, and forbore from knocking again. Clamour would only have alarmed them. Patience might reassure.

The door opened cautiously on a demure young person of about eleven years, erect and splendidly on guard for a troubled household at her back; all of whom, surely, were stretching sharp ears somewhere there beyond. She was bright, well primed and vulnerable; she saw the black Benedictine habit, drew deep breath, and smiled.

'I'm come from Mistress Bonel,' said Cadfael, 'with a word to your father, child, if he'll admit me. There's none else here, never fear.'

She opened the door with a matron's dignity, and let him in. The eight-year-old Thomas and the four-year-old Diota, naturally the most fearless creatures in the house, erupted round her skirts to examine him with round, candid eyes, even before Martin Bellecote himself appeared from a half-lit doorway within, and drew the younger children one either side of him, his hands spread protectively round their shoulders. A pleasant, square-built, large-handed man with a wide, wholesome face, and a deep reserve in his eyes, which Cadfael was glad to see. Too much trust is folly, in an imperfect world.

'Step in, brother,' said Martin, 'and, Alys, do you close and bar the door.'

'Forgive me if I'm brisk,' said Cadfael as the door was closed behind him, 'but time's short. They came looking for a lad here today, and I'm told they did not find him.'

'That's truth,' said Martin. 'He never came home.'

'I don't ask you where he is. Tell me nothing. But I do ask you, who know him, is it possible he can have done what they are urging against him?'

Bellecote's wife came through from the inner room, a candle in her hand. A woman like enough to be known for her mother's daughter, but softer and rounder and fairer in colouring, though with the same honest eyes. She said with indignant conviction: 'Rankly impossible! If ever there was a creature in the world who made his feelings known, and did all his deeds in the day-light, that's my brother. From an imp just crawling, if he had a grievance everyone within a mile round knew it, but grudges he never bore. And my lad's just such another.'

Yes, of course, there was the as yet unseen Edwy, to match the elusive Edwin. No sign of either of them here.

'You must be Sibil,' said Cadfael. 'I've been lately with your mother. And for my credentials – did ever you hear her speak of one Cadfael, whom she used to know when she was a girl?'

The light from the candle was reflected pleasingly in eyes suddenly grown round and bright with astonishment and can-did curiosity. '*You* are Cadfael? Yes, many a time she talked of you, and wondered . . .' She viewed his black habit and cowl, and her smile faded into a look of delicate sympathy. Of course! She was reflecting, woman-like, that he must have been heart-broken at coming home from the holy wars to find his old love married, or he would never have taken these bleak vows. No use telling her that vocations strike from heaven like random arrows of God, by no means all because of unrequited love. 'Oh, it must be comfort to her,' said Sibil warmly, 'to find you near her again, at this terrible pass. You she would trust!'

'I hope she does,' said Cadfael, gravely enough. 'I know she may. I came only to let you know that I am there to be used, as she already knows. The specific that was used to kill was of my making, and that is something that involves me in this matter. Therefore I am friend to any who may fall suspect unjustly. I will do what I can to uncover the guilty. Should you, or anyone, have reason to speak with me, anything to tell me, anything to ask of me, I am usually to be found between offices in the workshop in the herb-gardens, where I shall be tonight until I go to Matins at midnight. Your journeyman Meurig knows the abbey grounds, if he has not been to my hut. He is here?'

'He is,' said Martin. 'He sleeps in the loft across the yard. He has told us what passed there at the abbey. But I give you my word, neither he nor we have set eyes on the boy since he ran from his mother's house. What we know, past doubt, is that he is no murderer, and never could be.'

'Then sleep easy,' said Cadfael, 'for God is awake. And now let me out again softly, Alys, and bar the door after me, for I must hurry back for Compline.'

The young girl, great-eyed, drew back the bolt and held the door. The little ones stood with spread feet, sturdily staring him out of the house, but without fear or hostility. The parents said never a word but their still: 'Good night!' but he knew, as he hastened down the Wyle, that his message had been heard and understood, and that it was welcome, here in this beleaguered household.

'Even if you are desperate to have a fresh brew of cough syrup boiled up before tomorrow,' said Brother Mark reasonably, coming out from Compline at Cadfael's side, 'is there any reason why I should not do it for you? Is there any need for you, after the day you've had, to be stravaiging around the gardens all night, into the bargain? Or do you think I've forgotten where we keep mullein, and sweet cicely, and rue, and rosemary, and hedge mustard?' The recital of ingredients was part of the argument. This young man was developing a somewhat possessive sense of responsibility for his elder.

'You're young,' said Brother Cadfael, 'and need your sleep.'

'I forbear,' said Brother Mark cautiously, 'from making the obvious rejoinder.'

'I think you'd better. Very well, then, you have signs of a cold, and should go to your bed.'

'I have not,' Brother Mark disagreed firmly. 'But if you mean that you have some work on hand that you'd rather I did not know about, very well, I'll go to the warming-room like a sensible fellow, and then to bed.'

'What you know nothing about can't be charged against you,' said Brother Cadfael, conciliatory.

'Well, then, is there anything I can be doing for you in blessed ignorance? I was bidden to be obedient to you, when they sent me to work under you in the garden.'

'Yes,' said Cadfael. 'You can secure me a habit much your own size, and slip it into my cell and out of sight under my bed before you sleep. It may not be needed, but . . .'

'Enough!' Brother Mark was cheerful and unquestioning, though that did not prove he was not doing some hard and accurate thinking. 'Will you be needing a scissor for the tonsure, too?'

'You are growing remarkably saucy,' observed Cadfael, but with approval rather than disapproval. 'No, I doubt that would be welcomed, we'll rely on the cowl, and a chilly morning. Go away, boy, go and get your half-hour of warmth, and go to bed.'

The concoction of a syrup, boiled up lengthily and steadily with dried herbs and honey, made the use of the brazier necessary; should a guest have to spend the night in the workshop, he would be snug enough until morning. In no haste, Cadfael ground his herbs to a finer powder, and began to stir the honeyed brew on the hob over his brazier. There was no certainty that the bait he had laid would be taken, but beyond doubt young Edwin Gurney was in urgent need of a friend and protector to help him out of the morass into which he had fallen. There was no certainty, even, that the Bellecote household knew where to find him, but Cadfael had a shrewd inkling that the eleven-year-old Alys of the matronly dignity and the maidenly silence, even if she were not in her own brother's confidence, would be very well acquainted with what he probably considered his secrets. Where Edwy was, there would Edwin be, if Richildis had reported them truly. When trouble threatened the one, the other would be by his side. It was a virtue Cadfael strongly approved.

The night was very still, there would be sharp frost by dawn. Only the gentle bubbling of his brew and the occasional rustling of his own sleeve as he stirred punctured the silence. He had begun to think that the fish had refused the bait, when he caught, past ten o'clock, and in the blackest of the darkness, the faint, slow sound of the door-latch being carefully raised. A breath of cold air came in as the door opened a hair's-breadth. He sat still and gave no sign; the frightened wild thing might be easily alarmed. After a moment a very light, young, wary voice outside uttered just above a whisper: 'Brother Cadfael . . .?'

'I'm here,' said Cadfael quietly. 'Come in and welcome.'

'You're alone?' breathed the voice.

'I am. Come in and close the door.'

The boy stole in fearfully, and pushed the door to at his back, but Cadfael noticed that he did not latch it. 'I got word . . .' He was not going to say through whom. 'They told me you spoke with my sister and brother this evening, and said you would be

421

here. I do need a friend . . . You said you knew my gr – my mother, years ago, you are the Cadfael she used to speak about so often, the one who went to the Crusade . . . I swear I had no part in my stepfather's death! I never knew any harm had come to him, till I was told the sheriff's men were hunting for me as a murderer. You said my mother knows you for a good friend, and can rely on your help, so I've come to you. There's no one else I can turn to. Help me! Please help me!'

'Come to the fire,' said Cadfael mildly, 'and sit down here. Draw breath and answer me one thing truly and solemnly, and then we can talk. On your soul, mind! Did you strike the blow that laid Gervase Bonel dead in his blood?'

The boy had perched himself gingerly on the edge of the bench, almost but not quite within touch. The light from the brazier, cast upwards over his face and form, showed a rangy, agile youngster, lightly built but tall for his years, in the long hose and short cotte of the country lads, with capuchon dangling at his back, and a tangled mop of curling hair uncovered. By this reddish light it looked chestnut-brown, by daylight it might well be the softer mid-brown of seasoned oak. His face was still childishly rounded of cheek and chin, but fine bones were beginning to give it a man's potential. At this moment half the face was two huge, wary eyes staring unwaveringly at Brother Cadfael.

Most earnestly and vehemently the boy said: 'I never raised hand against him. He insulted me in front of my mother, and I hated him then, but I did not strike him. I swear it on my soul!'

Even the young, when bright in the wits and very much afraid, may exercise all manner of guile to protect themselves, but Cadfael was prepared to swear there was no deceit here. The boy really did not know how Bonel had been killed; that could not have been reported to his family or cried in the streets, and murder, most often, means the quick blow with steel in anger. He had accepted that probability without question.

'Very well! Now tell me your own story of what happened there today, and be sure I'm listening.'

The boy licked his lips and began. What he had to tell agreed with the account Richildis had given; he had gone with Meurig, at his well-intentioned urging, to make his peace with Bonel for his mother's sake. Yes, he had felt very bitter and angry about being cheated out of his promised heritage, for he loved

422

Mallilie and had good friends there, and would have done his best to run it well and fairly when it came to him; but also he was doing well enough at learning his craft, and pride would not let him covet what he could not have, or give satisfaction to the man who had taken back what he had pledged. But he did care about his mother. So he went with Meurig.

'And went with him first to the infirmary,' Cadfael mentioned helpfully, 'to see his old kinsman Rhys.'

The boy was brought up short in surprise and uncertainty. It was then that Cadfael got up, very gently and casually, from his seat by the brazier, and began to prowl the workshop. The door, just ajar, did not noticeably draw him, but he was well aware of the sliver of darkness and cold lancing in there.

'Yes . . . I . . .'

'And you had been there with him, had you not, once before, when you helped Meurig bring down the lectern for our Lady Chapel.'

He brightened, but his brow remained anxiously knotted. 'Yes, the – yes, we did bring that down together. But what has that . . .'

Cadfael in his prowling had reached the door, and laid a hand to the latch, hunching his shoulders, as though to close and fasten it, but as sharply plucked it wide open on the night, and reached his free hand through, to fasten on a fistful of thick, springy hair. A muted squeal of indignant outrage rewarded him, and the creature without, abruptly scorning the flight shock had suggested to him, reared upright and followed the fist into the workshop. It was, in its way, a magnificent entrance, erect, with jutted jaw and blazing eyes, superbly ignoring Cadfael's clenched hold on his curls, which must have been painful.

A slender, athletic, affronted young person the image of the first, only, perhaps, somewhat darker and fiercer, because more frightened, and more outraged by his fear.

'Master Edwin Gurney?' enquired Cadfael gently, and released the topknot of rich brown hair with a gesture almost caressing. 'I've been expecting you.' He closed the door, thoroughly this time; there was no one now left outside there to listen, and take warning by what he heard, like a small, hunted animal crouching in the night where the hunters stirred. 'Well, now that you're here, sit down with your twin – is it uncle or nephew? I shall never get used to sorting you! – and put yourself at ease. It's warmer here than outside, and you are two, and I have just been reminded gently that I am not as young as once I was. I don't propose to send for help to deal with you, and you have no need of help to deal with me. Why should we not put together our versions of the truth, and see what we have?'

The second boy was cloakless like the first, and shivering lightly with cold. He came to the bench by the brazier gladly, rubbing numbed hands, and sat down submissively beside his fellow. Thus cheek to cheek they were seen to share a very strong family likeness, in which Cadfael could trace subtle recollections of the young Richildis, but they were not so like as to give rise to any confusion when seen together. To encounter one alone might present a problem of identification, however.

'So, as I thought,' observed Cadfael, 'Edwy has been playing Edwin for my benefit, so that Edwin could stay out of the trap, if trap it turned out to be, and not reveal himself until he was certain I had no intention of making him prisoner and handing him over to the sheriff. And Edwy was well primed, too . . .'

'And still made a hash of it,' commented Edwin, with candid and tolerant scorn.

'I did not!' retorted Edwy heatedly. 'You never told me more than half a tale. What was I supposed to answer when Brother Cadfael asked me about going to the infirmary this morning? Never a word you said about that.'

'Why should I? I never gave it a thought, what difference could it make? And you *did* make a hash of it. I heard you start to say grandmother instead of mother – yes, and they instead of we. And so did Brother Cadfael, or how did he guess I was listening outside?'

'He heard you, of course! Blowing like a wheezy old man – and shivering,' added Edwy for good measure.

There was no ill-will whatever in these exchanges, they were the normal endearments current between these two, who would certainly have championed each other to the death against any outside threat. There was no malice in it when Edwin punched his nephew neatly and painfully in the muscles of the upper arm, and Edwy as promptly plucked Edwin round by the shoulder while he was less securely balanced, and spilled him on to the floor. Cadfael took them both by the scruff of the neck, a fistful of capuchon in either hand, and plumped them back firmly on to the bench, a yard apart this time, rather in defence of his softly bubbling syrup than in any very serious exasperation. The brief scuffle had warmed them, and shaken

424

fear away to a magical distance; they sat grinning, only slightly abashed.

'Will you sit still a minute, and let me get the measure of you? You, Edwin, are the uncle, and the younger . . . yes, I could know you apart. You're darker, and sturdier in the build, and I think your eyes must be brown. And Edwy's . . .'

'Hazel,' said Edwin helpfully.

'And you have a small scar by your ear, close to the cheek-bone. A small white crescent.'

'He fell out of a tree, three years ago,' Edwy informed him. 'He never could climb.'

'Now, enough of that! Master Edwin, now that you are here, and I know which one you are, let me ask you the same question I asked your proxy here a while ago. On your soul and honour, did you strike the blow that killed Master Bonel?'

The boy looked back at him with great eyes suddenly solemn enough, and said firmly: 'I did not. I carry no weapon, and even if I did, why should I try to harm him? I know what they must be saying of me, that I grudged it that he broke his word, for so he did. But I was not born to a manor, but to trade, and I can make my way in trade, I would be ashamed if I could not. No, whoever wounded him to the death – but how could it happen, so suddenly? – it was not I. On my soul!'

Cadfael was in very little doubt of him by then, but he gave no sign yet. 'Tell me what did happen.'

'I left Meurig in the infirmary with the old man, and went on to my mother's house alone. But I don't understand about the infirmary. Is that important?'

'Never mind that now, go on. How were you welcomed?'

'My mother was pleased,' said the boy. 'But my stepfather crowed over me like a cock that's won its bout. I answered him as little as I might, and bore it for my mother's sake, and that angered him more, so that he *would* find some way to sting me. We were three sitting at table, and Aldith had served the meat, and she told him the prior had paid him the compliment of sending a dish for him from his own table. My mother tried to talk about that, and flatter him with the distinction of it, but he wanted me to burn and smart at all costs, and he wouldn't be put off. He said I'd come, as he knew I would, my tail between my legs, like a whipped hound, to beg him to change his mind and restore me my inheritance, and he said if I wanted it, I should kneel and beg him, and he might take pity on me. And I lost my temper, for all I could do, and shouted back at him that

I'd see him dead before I'd so much as once ask him a favour, let alone crawl on my knees. I don't know now all I said, but he began throwing things, and . . . and my mother was crying, and I rushed out, and straight back over the bridge and into the town.'

'But not to Master Bellecote's house. And did you hear Aelfric calling after you as far as the bridge, to fetch you back?'

'Yes, but what would have been the use? It would only have made things worse.'

'But you did not go home.'

'I was not fit. And I was ashamed.'

'He went to brood in Father's wood-store by the river,' said Edwy helpfully. 'He always does when he's out of sorts with the world. Or if we're in trouble, we hide there until it's blown over, or at least past the worst. That's where I found him. When the sheriff's sergeant came to the shop, and said they wanted him, and his stepfather was murdered, I knew where to look for him. Not that I ever supposed he'd done any wrong,' stated Edwy firmly, 'though he can make a great fool of himself sometimes. But I knew something bad must have happened to him. So I went to warn him, and of course he knew nothing whatever about the murder, he'd left the man alive and well, only in a rage.'

'And you've both been hiding since then? You've not been home?'

'*He* couldn't, could he? They'll be watching for him. And I had to stay with him. We had to leave the wood-yard, we knew they'd come there. But there are places we know of. And then Alys came and told us about you.'

'And that's the whole truth,' said Edwin. 'And now what are we to do?'

'First,' said Cadfael, 'let me get this brew of mine off the fire, and stand it to cool before I bottle it. There! You got in here, I suppose, by the parish door of the church, and through the cloisters?' The west door of the abbey church was outside the walls, and never closed except during the bad days of the siege of the town, that part of the church being parochial. 'And followed your noses, I daresay, once you were in the gardens. This syrup-boiling gives off a powerful odour.'

'It smells good,' said Edwy, and his respectful stare ranged the workshop, and the bunches and bags of dried herbs stirring and rustling gently in the rising heat from the brazier.

'Not all my medicines smell so appetising. Though myself I would not call even this unpleasant. Powerful, certainly, but a fine, clean smell.' He unstoppered the great jar of anointing oil of monk's-hood, and tilted the neck beneath Edwin's inquisitive nose. The boy blinked at the sharp scent, drew back his head, and sneezed. He looked up at Cadfael with an open face, and laughed at his own pricked tears. Then he leaned cautiously and inhaled again, and frowned thoughtfully.

'It smells like that stuff Meurig was using to rub the old man's shoulder. Not this morning, the last time I came with him. There was a flask of it in the infirmary cupboard. Is it the same?'

'It is,' said Cadfael, and hoisted the jar back to its shelf. The boy's face was quite serene, the odour meant nothing more to him than a memory blessedly removed from any connection with tragedy and guilt. For Edwin, Gervase Bonel had died, inexplicably suddenly, of some armed attack, and the only guilt he felt was because he had lost his temper, infringed his own youthful dignity, and made his mother cry. Cadfael no longer had any doubts at all. The child was honest as the day, and caught in a deadly situation, and above all, badly in need of friends.

He was also very quick and alert of mind. The diversion began to trouble him just as it was over. 'Brother Cadfael . . .' he began hesitantly, the name new and almost reverent on his lips, not for this elderly and ordinary monk, but for the crusader Cadfael he had once been, fondly remembered even by a happy and fulfilled wife and mother, who had certainly much exaggerated his good looks, gallantry and daring. 'You knew about my going to the infirmary with Meurig . . . you asked Edwy about it. I couldn't understand why. Is it important? Has it something to do with my stepfather's death? I can't see how.'

'That you can't see how, child,' said Brother Cadfael, 'is your proof of an innocence we may have difficulty in proving to others, though I accept it absolutely. Sit down again by your nephew – dear God, shall I ever get these relationships straight? – and refrain from fighting him for a little while, till I explain to you what isn't yet public knowledge outside these walls. Yes, your two visits to the infirmary are truly of great importance, and so is this oil you have seen used there, though I must say that many others know of it, and are better acquainted than you with its properties, both bad and good. You must forgive me if I gave you to understand that Master Bonel was hacked down

427

in his blood with dagger or sword. And forgive me you should, since in accepting that tale you quite delivered yourselves from any guilt, at least to my satisfaction. It was not so, boys. Master Bonel died of poison, given in the dish the prior sent him, and the poison was this same oil of monk's-hood. Whoever added it to the partridge drew it either from this workshop or from the flask in the infirmary, and all who knew of either source, and knew the peril if it was swallowed, are in suspicion.'

The pair of them, soiled and tired and harried as they were, stared in horrified understanding at last, and drew together on the bench as threatened litters of young in burrow and nest huddle for comfort. Years bordering on manhood dropped from them; they were children indeed, frightened and hunted. Edwy said strenuously: 'He didn't know! All they said was, dead, murdered. But so quickly! He ran out, and there was nobody there but those of the house. He never even saw any dish waiting . . .'

'I did know,' said Edwin, 'about the dish. She told us, I knew it was there. But what did it matter to me? I only wanted to go home . . .'

'Hush, now, hush!' said Cadfael chidingly. 'You speak to a man convinced. I've made my own tests, all I need. Now sit quiet, and trouble your minds no more about me, I know you have nothing to repent.' That was much, perhaps, to say of any man, but at least these two had nothing on their souls but the ordinary misdemeanours of the energetic young. And now that he had leisure to look at them without looking for prevarication or deceit, he was able to notice other things. 'You must give me a little while for thought, but the time need not be wasted. Tell me, has either of you eaten, all these hours? The one of you, I know, made a very poor dinner.'

They had been far too preoccupied with worse problems, until then, to notice hunger, but now that they had an ally, however limited in power, and shelter, however temporary, they were suddenly and instantly ravenous.

'I've some oat-cakes here of my own baking, and a morsel of cheese, and some apples. Fill up the hollows, while I think what's best to be done. You, Edwy, had best make your way home as soon as the town gates open in the morning, slip in somehow without being noticed, and make as though you've never been away but on some common errand. Keep a shut mouth except with those you're sure of.' And that would be the whole united family, embattled in defence of their own. 'But for you, my friend – you're a very different matter.'

'You'll not give him up?' blurted Edwy round a mouthful of oat-cake, instantly alarmed.

'That I certainly will not do.' Yet he might well have urged the boy to give himself up, stand fast on his innocence, and trust in justice, if he had had complete trust himself in the law as being infallibly just. But he had not. The law required a culprit, and the sergeant was comfortably convinced that he was in pursuit of the right quarry, and would not easily be persuaded to look further. Cadfael's proofs he had not witnessed, and would shrug off contemptuously as an old fool fondly believing a cunning young liar.

'I can't go home,' said Edwin, the solemnity of his face in no way marred by one cheek distended with apple, and a greenish smudge from some branch soiling the other. 'And I can't go to my mother's. I should only be bringing worse trouble on her.'

'For tonight you can stay here, the pair of you, and keep my little brazier fed. There are clean sacks under the bench, and you'll be warm and safe enough. But in the day there's coming and going here from time to time, we must have you out early, the one of you for home, the other. . . . Well, we'll hope you need stay hidden only a matter of a few days. As well close here at the abbey as anywhere, they'll hardly look for you here.' He considered, long and thoughtfully. The lofts over the stables were always warmed from the hay, and the bodies of the horses below, but too many people came and went there, and with travellers on the roads before the festival, there might well be servants required to sleep there above their beasts. But outside the enclave, at one corner of the open space used for the horse-fairs and the abbey's summer fair, there was a barn where beasts brought to market could be folded before sale, and the loft held fodder for them. The barn belonged to the abbey, but was open to all travelling merchants. At this time of year its visitors would be few or none, and the loft well filled with good hay and straw, a comfortable enough bed for a few nights. Moreover, should some unforseen accident threaten danger to the fugitive, escape from outside the walls would be easier than from within. Though God forbid it should come to that!

'Yes, I know a place that will serve, we'll get you to it early in the morning, and see you well stocked with food and ale for the day. You'll need patience, I know, to lie by, but that you must endure.'

'Better,' said Edwin fervently, 'than falling into the sheriff's clutches, and I do thank you. But . . . how am I bettered by this, in the end? I can't lie hidden for ever.'

'There's but one way,' said Cadfael emphatically, 'that you can be bettered in this affair, lad, and that's by uncovering the man who did the thing you're charged with doing. And since you can hardly undertake that yourself, you must leave the attempt to me. What I can do, I'll do, for my own honour as well as yours. Now I must leave you and go to Matins. In the morning before Prime I'll come and see you safely out of here.'

Brother Mark had done his part, the habit was there, rolled up beneath Brother Cadfael's bed. He wore it under his own, when he rose an hour before the bell for Prime, and left the dortoir by the night stairs and the church. Winter dawns come very late, and this night had been moonless and overcast; the darkness as he crossed the court from cloister to gardens was profound, and there was no one else stirring. There was perfect cover for Edwy to withdraw unobserved through the church and the parish door, as he had come, and make his chilly way to the bridge, to cross into Shrewsbury as soon as the gate was opened. Doubtless he knew his own town well enough to reach his home by ways devious enough to baffle detection by the authorities, even if they were watching the shop.

As for Edwin, he made a demure young novice, once inside the black habit and the sheltering cowl. Cadfael was reminded of Brother Mark, when he was new, wary and expecting nothing but the worst of his enforced vocation; the springy, defensive gait, the too tightly folded hands in the wide sleeves, the flickering side-glances, wild and alert for trouble. But there was something in this young thing's performance that suggested a perverse enjoyment, too; for all the danger to himself, and his keen appreciation of it, he could not help finding pleasure in this adventure. And whether he would manage to behave himself discreetly in hiding, and bear the inactive hours, or be tempted to wander and take risks, was something Cadfael preferred not to contemplate.

Through cloister and church, and out at the west door, outside the walls, they went side by side, and turned right, away from the gatehouse. It was still fully dark.

'This road leads in the end to London, doesn't it?' whispered Edwin from within his raised cowl.

'It does so. But don't try leaving that way, even if you should have to run, which God forbid, for they'll have a check on the road out at St Giles. You be sensible and lie still, and give me a few days, at least, to find out what I may.'

The wide triangle of the horse-fair ground gleamed faintly pallid with light frost. The abbey barn loomed at one corner, close to the enclave wall. The main door was closed and fastened, but at the rear there was an outside staircase to the loft, and a small door at the top of it. Early traffic was already abroad, though thin at this dark hour, and no one paid attention to two monks of St Peter's mounting to their own loft. The door was locked, but Cadfael had brought the key, and let them in to a dry, hay-scented darkness.

'The key I can't leave you, I must restore it, but neither will I leave you locked in. The door must stay unfastened for you until you may come forth freely. Here you have a loaf, and beans, and curd, and a few apples, and here's a flask of small ale. Keep the gown, you may need it for warmth in the night, but the hay makes a kindly bed. And when I come to you, as I will, you may know me at the door by this knock. . . . Though no one else is likely to come. Should anyone appear without my knock, you have hay enough to hide in.'

The boy stood, suddenly grave and a little forlorn. Cadfael reached a hand, and put back the cowl from the shock-head of curls, and there was just filtering dawn-light enough to show him the shape of the solemn oval face, all steady, dilated, confronting eyes.

'You have not slept much. If I were you, I'd burrow deep and warm, and sleep the day out. I won't desert you.'

'I know,' said Edwin firmly. He knew that even together they might avail nothing, but at least he knew he was not alone. He had a loyal family, with Edwy as link, and he had an ally within the enclave. And he had one other thinking of him and agonising about him. He said in a voice that lost its firmness only for one perilous instant, and stubbornly recovered: 'Tell my mother I did not ever do him or wish him harm.'

'Fool child,' said Cadfael comfortably, 'I've been assured of that already, and who do you suppose told me, if not your mother?' The very faint light was magically soft, and the boy stood at that stage between childhood and maturity when his face, forming but not yet formed, might have been that of boy or girl, woman or man. 'You're very like her,' said Cadfael, remembering a girl not much older than this sprig, embraced

431

and kissed by just such a clandestine light, her parents believing her abed and asleep in virginal solitude. At this pass he had momentarily forgotten all the women he had known between, east and west, none of them, he hoped and believed, left feeling wronged. 'I'll be with you before night,' he said, and withdrew to the safety of the winter air outside.

Good God, he thought with all reverence, making his way back by the parish door in good time for Prime, that fine piece of young flesh, as raw and wild and faulty as he is, he might have been mine! He and the other, too, a son and a grandson both! It was the first and only time that ever he questioned his vocation, much less regretted it, and the regret was not long. But he did wonder if somewhere in the world, by the grace of Arianna, or Bianca, or Mariam, or – were there one or two others as well loved here and there, now forgotten? – he had left printings of himself as beautiful and formidable as this boy of Richildis's bearing and another's getting.

Chapter Five

T WAS now imperative to find the murderer, otherwise the boy could not emerge from hiding and take up his disrupted life. And that meant tracing in detail the passage of the ill-fated dish of partridge from the abbot's kitchen to Gervase Bonel's belly. Who had handled it? Who could have tampered with it? Since Prior Robert, in his lofty eminence within the abbot's lodging, had eaten, appreciated and digested the rest of it without harm, clearly it had been delivered to him in goodwill and in good condition. And he, certainly without meddling, had delivered it in the same condition to his cook.

Before High Mass, Cadfael went to the abbot's kitchen. He was one of a dozen or so people within these walls who were not afraid of Brother Petrus. Fanatics are always frightening, and Brother Petrus was a fanatic, not for his religion or his vocation, those he took for granted, but for his art. His dedicated fire tinted black hair and black eyes, scorching both with a fiery red. His northern blood boiled like his own cauldron. His temper, barbarian from the borders, was as hot as his own oven. And as hotly as he loved Abbot Heribert, for the same reasons he detested Prior Robert.

When Cadfael walked in upon him, he was merely surveying the day's battlefield, and mustering his army of pans, pots, spits and dishes, with less satisfaction than the exercise should have provided, because it was Robert, and not Heribert, who would consume the result of his labours. But for all that, he could not relax his hold on perfection.

'That partridge!' said Petrus darkly, questioned on the day's events. 'As fine a bird as ever I saw, not the biggest, but the best-fed and plumpest, and could I have dressed it for my abbot, I would have made him a masterwork. Yes, this prior comes in and bids me set aside a portion – for one only, mark! – to be sent to the guest at the house by the mill-pond, with his compliments. And I did it. I made it the best portion, in one of Abbot Heribert's own dishes. *My* dishes, says Robert! Did anyone else here touch it? I tell you, Cadfael, the two I have here know me, they do what I say, and let all else ride. Robert? He came in to give his orders and sniff at my pan, but it was all in one pan then, it was only after he left my kitchen I set aside the dish for Master Bonel. No, take it as certain, none but myself touched that dish until it left here, and that was close on the dinner hour, when the manservant – Aelfric, is it? – brought his tray.'

'How do you find this man Aelfric?' asked Cadfael. 'You're seeing him daily.'

'A surly fellow, or at least a mute one,' said Petrus without animosity, 'but keeps exact time, and is orderly and careful.'

So Richildis had said, perhaps even to excess, and with intent to aggrieve his master.

'I saw him crossing the court with his load that day. The dishes were covered, he has but two hands, and certainly he did not halt this side the gatehouse, for I saw him go out.' But once through the gate there was a bench set in an alcove in the wall, where a tray could easily be put down for a moment, on pretence of adjusting to a better balance. And Aelfric knew his way to the workshop in the garden, and had seen the oil dispensed. And Aelfric was a soured man on two counts. A man of infinite potential, since he let so little of himself be known to any.

'Ah, well, it's certain nothing was added to the food here.'

'Nothing but wholesome wine and spices. Now if it had been the rest of the bird that was poisoned,' said Petrus darkly, 'I'd give you leave to look sideways at me, for you'd have reason. But if ever I did go so far as to prepare a monk's-hood stew for that one, be sure I'd make no mistake about which bowl went to which belly.'

No need, thought Cadfael, crossing the court to Mass, to take Brother Petrus's fulminations too seriously. For all his ferocity he was a man of words rather than actions. Or ought it, after all, to be considered as worth pondering? The idea that a mistake had been made, and the dish intended for Robert sent instead to Bonel, had never entered Cadfael's head until now, but clearly Petrus had credited him with just such a notion, and made haste to hammer it into absurdity before it was uttered. A shade too much haste? Murderous hatreds had been known to arise between those who were sworn to brotherhood, before this, and surely would so arise again. Brother Petrus might have started the very suspicion he had set out to scotch. Not, perhaps, a very likely murderer. But bear it in mind!

The few weeks before the main festivals of the year always saw an increase in the parochial attendance at Mass, the season pricking the easy consciences of those who took their spiritual duties lightly all the rest of the year. There were a creditable number of local people in the church that morning, and it was no great surprise to Cadfael to discover among them the white coif and abundant yellow hair of the girl Aldith. When the service ended he noticed that she did not go out by the west door, like the rest, but passed through the south door into the cloister, and so out into the great court. There she drew her cloak around her, and sat down on a stone bench against the refectory wall.

Cadfael followed, and saluted her gravely, asking after her mistress. The girl raised to him a fair, composed face whose soft lines seemed to him to be belied by the level dark force of her eyes. She was, he reflected, as mysterious in her way as Aelfric, and what she did not choose to reveal of herself it would be hard to discover unaided.

'She's well enough in body,' she said thoughtfully, 'but distressed in mind for Edwin, naturally. But there's been no word of his being taken, and I'm sure we should have heard if he had been. That's some comfort. Poor lady, she's in need of comfort.'

He could have sent her some reassurance by this messenger, but he did not. Richildis had taken care to speak with him alone, he should respect that preference. In so tight and closed a situation, where only the handful of people involved in one household seemed to be at risk, how could Richildis be absolutely sure even of her young kinswoman, even of her stepson or her manservant? And could he, in the end, even be sure of Richildis? Mothers may be driven to do terrible things in defence of the rights of their children. Gervase Bonel had made a bargain with her, and broken it.

'If you'll permit, I'll sit with you a little while. You're not in haste to return?'

'Aelfric will be coming for the dinner soon,' she said. 'I thought I would wait for him, and help him carry everything. He'll have the ale and the bread as well.' And she added, as Cadfael sat down beside her: 'It's ill for him, having to do that same office daily, after what fell on us yesterday. To think that people may be eyeing him and wondering. Even you, brother. Isn't it true?'

'No help for that,' said Cadfael simply, 'until we know the truth. The sheriff's sergeant believes he knows it already. Do you agree with him?'

'No!' She was mildly scornful, it even raised the ghost of a smile. 'It isn't the wild, noisy, boisterous boys, the ones who let the world all round know their grievances and their tantrums and their pleasures, who use poison. But what avails my telling you this, saying I believe or I don't believe, when I'm deep in the same coil myself? As you know I am! When Aelfric came into my kitchen with the tray, and told me about the prior's gift, it was I who set the dish to keep hot on the hob, while Aelfric carried the large dish into the room, and I followed with the platters and the jug of ale. The three of them were in there at table, they knew nothing about the partridge until I told them . . . thinking to please the master, for in there the air was so chill you could hardly breathe. I think I was back in the kitchen first of the two of us, and I sat by the hob to eat my meal, and I stirred the bowl when it simmered. More than once, and moved it aside from the heat, too. What use my saying I added nothing? Of course that is what I, or any other in my shoes would say, it carries no weight until there's proof, one way or the other.'

'You are very sensible and very just,' said Cadfael. 'And Meurig, you say, was just coming in at the door when you returned to the kitchen. So he was not alone with the dish . . . even supposing he had known what it was, and for whom it was intended.'

Her dark brows rose, wonderfully arched and vivid and striking under the pale brow and light-gold hair. 'The door was wide open, that I recall, and Meurig was just scraping the dirt from his shoes before coming in. But what reason could Meurig have, in any case, to wish his father dead? He was not lavish with him, but he was of more value to him alive than dead. He had no hope of inheriting anything, and knew it, but he had a modest competence to lose.'

That was simple truth. Not even the church would argue a bastard's right to inherit, while the state would deny it even where marriage of the parents, every way legal, followed the birth. And this had been a commonplace affair with one of his own maidservants. No, Meurig had no possible stake in this death. Whereas Edwin had a manor to regain, and Richildis, her adored son's future. And Aelfric?

She had reared her head, gazing towards the gatehouse, where Aelfric had just appeared, the high-rimmed wooden tray under his arm, a bag for the loaves slung on his shoulder. She gathered her cloak and rose.

'Tell me,' said Cadfael, mild-voiced beside her, 'now that Master Bonel is dead, to whom does Aelfric belong? Does he go with the manor, to the abbey or some other lord? Or was he excluded from the agreement, conceded to Master Bonel as manservant in villeinage for life?'

She looked back sharply in the act of going to meet Aelfric. 'He was excluded. Granted to be my lord's villein personally.'

'Then whatever happens to the manor now, he will go to whoever inherits the personal effects . . . . to widow or son, granted the son escapes a criminal charge. And Aldith, you know Mistress Bonel's mind, would you not say that she would at once give Aelfric his freedom, with a glad heart? And would the boy do any other?'

All she gave him by way of answer was a brief, blinding flash of the black, intelligent eyes, and the sudden, veiling swoop of large lids and long dark lashes. Then she went to cross Aelfric's path, and fall in beside him on his way to the abbot's lodging. Her step was light and easy, her greeting indifferent, her manner dutiful. Aelfric trudged by her side stiff and mute, and would not let her take the bag from his shoulder. Cadfael sat looking after them for a long moment, observing and wondering, though after a while the wonder subsided into mild surprise, and by the time he set off to wash his hands before dinner in the refectory, even surprise had settled into conviction and reassessment.

It was mid-afternoon, and Cadfael was picking over the stored trays of apples and pears in the loft of the abbot's barn, discarding the few decayed specimens before they could infect their neighbours, when Brother Mark came hallooing for him from below.

'The sheriff's man is back,' he reported, when Cadfael peered down the ladder at him and demanded what the noise was about, 'and asking for you. And they've not captured their man – if it's any news I'm telling you.'

'It's no good news that I should be wanted,' admitted Cadfael, descending the ladder backwards, as nimbly as a boy. 'What's his will? Or his humour, at least?'

'No menace to you, I think,' said Mark, considering. 'Vexed at not laying his hands on the boy, naturally, but I think his mind's on small things like the level of that rubbing oil in your store. He asked me if I could tell if any had been removed from there, but I'm a slipshod hand who notices nothing, as you'll bear witness. He thinks you'll know to the last drop.'

'Then he's the fool. It takes a mere mouthful or two of that to kill, and in a container too wide to get the fingers of both hands round, and tall as a stool, who's to know if ten times that amount has been purloined? But let's as least pick his brains of what he's about now, and how far he thinks he has his case proven.'

In the workshop the sheriff's sergeant was poking his bushy beard and hawk's beak into all Cadfael's sacks and jars and pots in somewhat wary curiosity. If he had brought an escort with him this time, he must have left them in the great court or at the gatehouse.

'You may yet be able to help us, brother,' he said as Cadfael entered. 'It would be a gain to know from which supply of this oil of yours the poison was taken, but the young brother here can't say if any is missing from this store. Can you be more forthcoming?'

'On that point,' said Cadfael bluntly, 'no, the amount needed would be very small, and my stock, as you see, is large. No one could pretend to say with certainty whether any had been taken out unlawfully. This I can tell you, I examined the neck and stopper of this bottle yesterday, and there is no trace of oil at the lip. I doubt if a thief in haste would stop to wipe the lip clean before stoppering it, as I do.'

The sergeant nodded, partially satisfied that this accorded with what he believed. 'It's more likely it was taken from the infirmary, then. And that's a smaller flask by much than this, but I've been there, and they can none of them hazard an opinion. Among the old the oil is in favoured use now, who can guess if it was used one more time without lawful reason?'

'You've made little progress, I fear,' said Brother Cadfael.

'We have not caught our man, yet. No knowing where Edwin Gurney is hiding, but there's been no trace of him round Bellecote's shop, and the carpenter's horse is in its stable. I'd wager the boy is still somewhere within the town. We're watching the shop and the gates, and keeping an eye on his mother's house. It is but a matter of time before we take him.'

Cadfael sat back on his bench and spread his hands on his knees. 'You're very sure of him. Yet there are at least four others who were there in the house, and any number more who, for one reason or another, know the use and abuse of this preparation. Oh, I know the weight of the case you can make against this boy. I could make as good a case against one or two more, but that I won't do. I'd rather by far consider those factors that might provide, not suspicion, but proof, and not against one chosen quarry, but against the person, whoever he may be, towards whom the facts point. The time concerned is tight, half an hour at most. I myself saw the manservant fetch the dishes from the abbot's kitchen, and carry them out at the gate. Unless we are to look seriously at those who serve the abbot's kitchen, the dish was still harmless when it left our enclave. I don't say,' he added blandly, 'that you should, because we wear the cowl, write off any man of us as exempt from suspicion, myself included.'

The sergeant was indulgent, though not impressed. 'Then what limiting factors, what firm facts, do you refer to, brother?'

'I mentioned to you yesterday, and if you care to sniff at that bottle, and try a drop of it on your sleeve, you'll note for yourself, that it makes itself apparent both to the nose and the eye. You would not easily wash out the greasy mark from cloth, nor get rid of the smell. It is not the wolfsbane that smells so sharp and acrid, there's also mustard and other herbs. Whoever you seize upon, you must examine his clothing for these signs. I don't say it's proof of innocence if no such signs are found, but it does weaken the evidence of guilt.'

'You are interesting, brother,' said the sergeant, 'but not convincing.'

'Then consider this. Whoever had used that poison would be in haste to get rid of the bottle as soon as possible, and as cleanly. If he lingered, he would have to hide it about him, and risk marking himself, or even having it discovered

439

on him. You will conduct your business as you see fit. But I, were I in your shoes, would be looking very carefully for a small vial, anywhere within a modest distance of that house, for when you find it, the place where it was discarded will tell a great deal about the person who could have cast it there.' And with certainty he added: 'You'll be in no doubt of it being the right vial.'

He did not at all like the expression of indulgent complacency that was creeping over the sergeant's weathered countenance, as though he enjoyed a joke that presently, when he chose to divulge it, would quite take the wind out of Cadfael's sails. He himself admitted he had not captured his man, but there was certainly some other secret satisfaction he was hugging to his leather bosom.

'You have not found it already?' said Cadfael cautiously.

'Not found it, no. Nor looked for it very hard. But for all that, I know where it is. Small use looking now, and in any case, no need.' And now he was openly grinning.

'I take exception to that,' said Cadfael firmly. 'If you have not found it, you cannot *know* where it is, you can only surmise, which is not the same thing.'

'It's as near the same thing as we're likely to get,' said the sergeant, pleased with his advantage. 'For your little vial has gone floating down the Severn, and may never be seen again, but we know it was tossed in there, and we know who tossed it. We've not been idle since we left here yesterday, I can tell you, and we've done more than simply pursue a young fox and lose his trail a while. We've taken witness from any we could find who were moving about the bridge and the Foregate around the dinner hour, and saw Bonel's manservant running after the boy. We found a carter who was crossing the bridge just at that time. Such a chase, he pulled up his cart, thinking there was a hue and cry after a thief, but when the boy had run past him he saw the pursuer give up the chase, short of the bridge, for he had no chance of overtaking his quarry. The one shrugged and turned back, and when the carter turned to look after the other he saw him slow in his running for a moment, and hurl some small thing over the downstream parapet into the water. It was young Gurney, and no other, who had something to dispose of, as soon as possible after he'd tipped its contents into the dish for his stepfather, given the spoon a whirl or two, and rushed away with the bottle in his hand. And what do you say to that, my friend?'

440

What, indeed? The shock was severe, for not one word had Edwin said about this incident, and for a moment Cadfael did seriously consider that he might have been hoodwinked for once by a cunning little dissembler. Yet cunning was the last thing he would ever have found in that bold, pugnacious face. He rallied rapidly, and without betraying his disquiet.

'I say that "some small thing" is not necessarily a vial. Did you put it to your carter that it might have been that?'

'I did, and he would not say yes or no, only that whatever it was was small enough to hold in the closed hand, and flashed in the light as it flew. He would not give it a shape or a character more than that.'

'You had an honest witness. Now can you tell me two things more from his testimony. At exactly what point on the bridge was the boy when he threw it? And did the manservant also see it thrown?'

'My man says the fellow running after had halted and turned back, and only then did he look round and catch the other one in the act. The servant could not have seen. And as for where the lad was at that moment, he said barely halfway across the drawbridge.'

That meant that Edwin had hurled away whatever it was as soon as he felt sure he was above the water, clear of the bank and the shore, for it was the outer section of the bridge that could be raised. And at that, he might have miscalculated and been in too big a hurry. The bushes and shelving slope under the abutments ran well out below the first arch. There was still a chance that whatever had been discarded could be recovered, if it had fallen short of the current. It seemed, also, that Aelfric had not concealed this detail, for he had not witnessed it.

'Well,' said Cadfael, 'by your own tale the boy had just gone running past a halted cart, with a driver already staring at him, and no doubt, at that hour, several other people within view, and made no secret of getting rid of whatever it was he threw. Nothing furtive about that. Hardly the way a murderer would go about disposing of the means, to my way of thinking. What do you say?'

The sergeant hitched at his belt and laughed aloud. 'I say you make as good a devil's advocate as ever I've heard. But lads in a panic after a desperate deed don't stop to think. And if it was not the vial he heaved into the Severn, you tell me, brother, what was it?' And he strode out into the chill of the early evening air, and left Cadfael to brood on the same question.

441

Brother Mark, who had made himself inconspicuous in a corner all this time, but with eyes and ears wide and sharp for every word and look, kept a respectful silence until Cadfael stirred at length, and moodily thumped his knees with clenched fists. Then he said, carefully avoiding questions: 'There's still an hour or so of daylight left before Vespers. If you think it's worth having a look below the bridge there?'

Brother Cadfael had almost forgotten the young man was present, and turned a surprised and appreciative eye on him. 'So there is! And your eyes are younger than mine. The two of us might at least cover the available ground. Yes, come, for better or worse we'll venture.'

Brother Mark followed eagerly across the court, out at the gatehouse, and along the highroad towards the bridge and the town. A flat, leaden gleam lay over the mill-pond on their left, and the house beyond it showed only a closed and shuttered face. Brother Mark stared at it curiously as they passed. He had never seen Mistress Bonel, and knew nothing of the old ties that linked her with Cadfael, but he knew when his mentor and friend was particularly exercised on someone else's behalf, and his own loyalty and partisan fervour, after his church, belonged all to Cadfael. He was busy thinking out everything he had heard in the workshop, and making practical sense of it. As they turned aside to the right, down the sheltered path that led to the riverside and the main gardens of the abbey, ranged along the rich Severn meadows, he said thoughtfully:

'I take it, brother, that what we are looking for must be small, and able to take the light, but had better *not* be a bottle?'

'You may take it,' said Cadfael, sighing, 'that whether it is or not, we must try our best to find it. But I would very much rather find something else, something as innocent as the day.'

Just beneath the abutments of the bridge, where it was not worth while clearing the ground for cultivation, bushes grew thickly, and coarse grass sloped down gradually to the lip of the water. They combed the tufted turf along the edge, where a filming of ice prolonged the ground by a few inches, until the light failed them and it was time to hurry back for Vespers; but they found nothing small, relatively heavy, and capable of reflecting a flash of light as it was thrown, nothing that could have been the mysterious something tossed away by Edwin in his flight.

*

Cadfael slipped away after supper, absenting himself from the readings in the chapter-house, helped himself to the end of a loaf and a hunk of cheese, and a flask of small ale for his fugitive, and made his way discreetly to the loft over the abbey barn in the horse-fair. The night was clear overhead but dark, for there was no moon as yet. By morning the ground would be silvered over, and the shore of Severn extended by a new fringe of ice.

His signal knock at the door at the head of the stairs produced only a profound silence, which he approved. He opened the door and went in, closing it silently behind him. In the darkness within nothing existed visibly, but the warm, fresh scent of the clean hay stirred in a faint wave, and an equally quiet rustling showed him where the boy had emerged from his nest to meet him. He moved a step towards the sound. 'Be easy, it's Cadfael.'

'I knew,' said Edwin's voice very softly. 'I knew you'd come.'

'Was it a long day?'

'I slept most of it.'

'That's my stout heart! Where are you . . . ? Ah!' They moved together, uniting two faint warmths that made a better warmth between them; Cadfael touched a sleeve, found a welcoming hand. 'Now let's sit down and be blunt and brief, for time's short. But we may as well be comfortable with what we have. And here's food and drink for you.' Young hands, invisible, clasped his offerings gladly. They felt their way to a snug place in the hay, side by side.

'Is there any better news for me?' asked Edwin anxiously.

'Not yet. What I have for you, young man, is a question. Why did you leave out half the tale?'

Edwin sat up sharply beside him, in the act of biting heartily into a crust of bread. 'But I didn't! I told you the truth. Why should I keep anything from you, when I came asking for your help?'

'Why, indeed! Yet the sheriff's men have had speech with a certain carter who was crossing the bridge from Shrewsbury when you went haring away from your mother's house, and he testifies that he saw you heave something over the parapet into the river. Is that true?'

Without hesitation the boy said: 'Yes!' his voice a curious blend of bewilderment, embarrassment and anxiety. Cadfael had the impression that he was even blushing in the darkness,

443

and yet obviously with no sense of guilt at having left the incident unmentioned, rather as though a purely private folly of his own had been accidentally uncovered.

'Why did you not tell me that yesterday? I might have had a better chance of helping you if I'd known.'

'I don't see why.' He was a little sullen and on his dignity now, but wavering and wondering. 'It didn't seem to have anything to do with what happened . . . and I wanted to forget it. But I'll tell you now, if it does matter. It isn't anything bad.'

'It matters very much, though you couldn't have known that when you threw it away.' Better tell him the reason now, and show that by this examiner, at least, he was not doubted. 'For what you sent over the parapet, my lad, is being interpreted by the sheriff's man as the bottle that held the poison, newly emptied by you before you ran out of the house, and disposed of in the river. So now, I think, you had better tell me what it really was, and I'll try to convince the law they are on the wrong scent, over that and everything else.'

The boy sat very still, not stunned by this blow, which was only one more in a beating which had already done its worst and left him still resilient. He was very quick in mind, he saw the implications, for himself and for Brother Cadfael. Slowly he said: 'And you don't need first to *be* convinced?'

'No. For a moment I may have been shaken, but no longer. Now tell me!'

'I didn't know! How could I know what was going to happen?' He drew breath deeply, and some of the tension left the arm and shoulder that leaned confidingly into Cadfael's side, 'No one else knew about it, I hadn't said a word to Meurig, and I never got so far as to show it even to my mother – I never had the chance. You know I'm learning to work in wood, and in fine metals, too, a little, and I had to show that I meant to be good at what I did. I made a present for my stepfather. Not because I liked him,' he made haste to add, with haughty honesty, 'I didn't! But my mother was unhappy about our quarrel, and it had made him hard and ill-tempered even to her – he never used to be, he was fond of her, I know. So I made a present as a peace offering . . . and to show I should make a craftsman, too, and be able to earn my living without him. He had a relic he valued greatly, he bought it in Walsingham when he went on pilgrimage, a long time ago. It's supposed to be a piece of Our Lady's mantle, from the hem, but I don't believe it's true. But *he* believed it. It's a slip of blue cloth as long as my little finger,

444

with a gold thread in the edge, and it's wrapped in a bit of cloth of gold. He paid a lot of money for it, I know. So I thought I would make him a little reliquary just the right size for it, a little box with a hinge. I made it from pear-wood, and jointed and polished it well, and inlaid the lid with a little picture of Our Lady in nacre and silver, and blue stone for the mantle. I think it was not bad.' The light ache in his voice touched Brother Cadfael's relieved heart; he had loved his work and destroyed it, he was entitled to grieve.

'And you took it with you to give to him yesterday?' he asked gently.

'Yes.' He bit that off short. Cadfael remembered how he had been received, according to Richildis, when he made his difficult, courageous appearance at their table, his gift secreted somewhere upon him.

'And you had it in your hand when he drove you out of the house with his malice. I see how it could happen.'

The boy burst out bitterly, shivering with resentment still: 'He said I'd come to crawl to him for my manor . . . he taunted me, said if I kneeled to him . . . How could I offer him a gift, after that? He would have taken it as proof positive . . . I couldn't bear that! It was meant to be a gift, without any asking.'

'I should have done what you did, boy, kept it clutched in my hand, and run from there without a word more.'

'But not thrown it in the river, perhaps,' sighed Edwin ruefully. 'Why? I don't know . . . Only it had been meant for him, and I had it in my hand, and Aelfric was running after me and calling, and I couldn't go back . . . It wasn't his, and it wasn't any more mine, and I threw it over to be rid of it . . .'

So that was why neither Richildis nor anyone else had mentioned Edwin's peace offering. Peace or war, for that matter? It had been meant to assert both his forgiveness and his independence, neither very pleasing to an elderly autocrat. But well-meant, for all that, an achievement, considering the lad was not yet fifteen years old. But no one had known of it. No one but the maker had ever had the chance to admire – as Richildis would have done most dotingly! – the nice dove-tailing of the joints of his little box, or the fine setting of the slips of silver and pearl and lapis which had flashed just once in the light as they hurtled into the river.

'Tell me, this was a well-fitted lid, and closed when you threw it over?'

445

'Yes.' He was very fairly visible now, and all startled eyes. He did not understand the question, but he was sure of his work. 'Is that important, too? I wish now I hadn't done it, I see I've made everything worse. But how was I to know? There wasn't any hue and cry for me then, there wasn't any murder, I knew I hadn't done anything wrong.'

'A small wooden box, tightly closed, will float gallantly where the river carries it, and there are men who live by the river traffic and fishing, yes, and poaching, too, and they'll know every bend and beach from here to Atcham where things fetch up on the current. Keep your heart up, lad, you may yet see your work again if I can get the sheriff to listen to me, and put out the word to the watermen to keep a watch. If I give them a description of what was thrown away – oh, be easy, I'll not reveal how I got it! – and somewhere downstream that very thing is discovered, that's a strong point in your favour, and I may even be able to get them to look elsewhere for the bottle, somewhere where Edwin Gurney was not, and therefore could not have left it. You bide yet a day or two here in quiet, if you can bear it, and if need be, I'll get you away to some more distant place, where you can wait the time out in better comfort.'

'I can bear it,' said Edwin sturdily. And added ruefully: 'But I wish it may not be long!'

The brothers were filing out at the end of Compline when it dawned upon Cadfael that there was one important question which he and everyone else had neglected to ask, and the only person he could think of who might conceivably be able to answer it was Richildis. There was still time to ask it before night, if he gave up his final half-hour in the warming-room. Not, perhaps, a tactful time to visit, but everything connected with this business was urgent, and Richildis could at least sleep a little more easily for the knowledge that Edwin was, thus far at least, safe and provided for. Cadfael drew up his cowl, and made purposefully for the gates.

It was bad luck that Brother Jerome should be coming across the court towards the porter's lodge at the same time, probably with some officious orders for the morrow, or some sanctimonious complaint of irregularities today. Brother Jerome already felt himself to be in the exalted position of clerk to the abbot-elect, and was exerting himself to represent adequately his master Robert, now that that worthy man had availed himself of the abbot's privilege and privacy. Authority delegated to Brother Richard, and sedulously avoided by him wherever possible, would be greedily taken up by Brother Jerome. Some of the novices and boy pupils had already had cause to lament his zeal.

'You have a errand of mercy at so late an hour, brother?' smiled Jerome odiously. 'Can it not wait until morning?'

'At the risk of further harm,' snapped Cadfael, 'it might.' And he made no further halt, but proceeded on his way, well aware of the narrowed eyes following his departure. He had, within reason, authority to come and go as he thought fit, even to absent himself from services if his aid was required elsewhere, and he was certainly not going to explain himself, either truthfully or mendaciously, to Brother Jerome, however others less bold might conform for the sake of staying out of Robert's displeasure. It was unfortunate, but he had nothing ill to conceal, and to turn back would have suggested the contrary.

There was still a small light burning in the kitchen of the house beyond the mill-pond, he could see it through a tiny chink in the shutter as he approached. Yes, now, *there* was something he had failed to take into account: the kitchen window overlooked the pond, and close, at that, closer than from the road, and yesterday it had been open because of the brazier standing under it, an outlet for the smoke. An outlet, too, for a small vial hurled out there as soon as emptied, to be lost for ever in the mud at the bottom of the pond? What could be more convenient? No odour on clothing, no stain, no dread of being discovered with the proof.

Tomorrow, thought Cadfael, elated, I'll search from that window down to the water. Who knows but this time the thing thrown may really have fallen short, and be lying somewhere in the grass by the water's edge for me to find? That would be something gained! Even if it cannot prove who threw it there, it may still tell me something.

He knocked softly at the door, expecting Aldith to answer, or Aelfric, but it was the voice of Richildis herself that called out quietly from within: 'Who's there?'

'Cadfael! Open to me for a few minutes.'

His name had been enough, she opened eagerly, and reached a hand to draw him into the kitchen. 'Hush, softly! Aldith is asleep in my bed, and Aelfric within, in the room. I could not sleep yet, I was sitting late, thinking about my boy. Oh,

Cadfael, can you give me no comfort? You will stand his friend if you can?'

'He is well, and still free,' said Cadfael, sitting down beside her on the bench against the wall. 'But mark me, you know nothing, should any ask. You may truly say he has not been here, and you don't know where he is. Better so!'

'But you do know!' The tiny, steady light of the rush-candle showed him her face smoothed of its ageing lines and softly bright, very comely. He did not answer; she might read that for herself, and could still say truly that she knew nothing.

'And that's all you can give me?' She breathed.

'No, I can give you my solemn word that he never harmed his stepfather. That I know. And truth must come out. That you must believe.'

'Oh, I will, I do, if you'll help to uncover it. Oh, Cadfael, if you were not here I should despair. And such constant vexations, pin-pricks, when I can think of nothing but Edwin. And Gervase not in his grave until tomorrow! Now that he's gone, I no longer have a claim to livery for his horse, and with so many travellers coming now before the feast, they want his stable-room, and I must move him elsewhere, or else sell him . . . But Edwin will want him, if . . .' She shook her head distractedly, and would not complete that doubt. 'They told me they'll find him a stall and feed somewhere until I can arrange for him to be stabled elsewhere. Perhaps Martin could house him . . .'

They might, Cadfael thought indignantly, have spared her such small annoyances, at least for a few days. She had moved a little closer to him, her shoulder against his. Their whispering voices in the dimly lit room, and the lingering warmth from a brazier now mostly ash, took him back many years, to a stolen meeting in her father's outhouse. Better not linger, to be drawn deeper still!

'Richildis, there's something I came to ask you. Did your husband ever actually draw up and seal the deed that made Edwin his heir?'

'Yes, he did.' She was surprised by the question, 'It was quite legal and binding, but naturally this agreement with the abbey has a later date, and makes the will void now. Or it did . . .' She was brought back sharply to the realisation that the second agreement, too, had been superseded, more roughly even than the first. 'Of course, that's of no validity now. So the grant to Edwin stands. It must, our man of law drew it properly, and I have it in writing.'

'So all that stands between Edwin and his manor, now, is the threat of arrest for murder, which we know he did not do. But tell me this, Richildis, if you know it: supposing the worst happened – which it must not and will not – and he was convicted of killing your husband – then what becomes of Mallilie? The abbey cannot claim it, Edwin could not then inherit it. Who becomes the heir?'

She managed to gaze resolutely beyond the possibility of the worst, and considered what sense law would make of what was left.

'I suppose I should get my dower, as the widow. But the manor could only revert to the overlord, and that's the Earl of Chester, for there's no other legitimate heir. He could bestow it where he pleased, to his best advantage. It might go to any man he favoured in these parts. Sheriff Prestcote, as like as not, or one of his officers.'

It was true, and it robbed all others here, except Edwin, of any prospect of gaining by Bonel's death; or at least, of any material gain. An enemy sufficiently consumed by hate might find the death in itself gain enough, yet that seemed an excessive reaction to a man no way extreme, however difficult Edwin had found him.

'You're sure? There's no nephew, or cousin of his somewhere about the shire?

'No, no one, or he would never have promised me Mallilie for Edwin. He set great store by his own blood.'

What had been going through Cadfael's mind was the possibility that someone with his own fortune in view might have planned to remove at one stroke both Bonel and Edwin, by ensuring the boy's arrest for the man's murder. But evidently that was far from the mark. No one could have calculated with any certainty on securing for himself what the house of Bonel forfeited.

By way of comfort and encouragement, Cadfael laid his broad, gnarled hand on her slender one, and marked in the slanting light, with roused tenderness, its enlarged knuckles and tracery of violet veins, more touching than any girlish smoothness could ever have been. Her face was beautiful, too, even in its ageing, lined, now that he saw it almost at peace, with good-humour and the long experience of happiness, which this brief ordeal of exasperation, disruption and pain could do little now to deflower. It was his youth he was lamenting, not any waste of Richildis. She had married the right man and been blessed, and a late mistake with the wrong man was over without irreparable damage, provided her darling could be extricated from his present danger. That, and only that, Cadfael thought gratefully, is my task.

The warm hand under his turned and closed, holding him fast. The still beguiling face turned to gaze at him closely and earnestly, with limpid, sympathetic eyes and a mouth with delicate, self-congratulatory guilt. 'Oh, Cadfael, did you take it so hard? Did it have to be the cloister? I wondered about you so often, and so long, but I never knew I had done you such an injury. And you have forgiven me that broken promise?'

'The whole fault was mine,' said Cadfael, with somewhat over-hearty fervour. 'I've wished you well always, as I do now.' And he made to rise from the bench, but she kept her hold on his hand and rose with him. A sweet woman, but dangerous, like all her innocent kind.

'Do you remember,' she was saying, in the hushed whisper the hour demanded, but with something even more secret in its intimacy, 'the night we pledged our troth? That was December, too. I've been thinking of it ever since I knew you were here – a Benedictine monk! Who would ever have dreamed it would end so! But you stayed away so long!'

It was certainly time to go. Cadfael retrieved his hand gently, made her a soothing good night, and discreetly withdrew, before worse could befall him. Let her by all means attribute his vocation to the loss of her own delightful person, for the conviction would stand by her well until her world was restored in safety. But as for him, he had no regrets whatever. The cowl both fitted and became him.

He let himself out and returned enlarged through the chill and sparkle of the frosty night, to the place he had chosen, and still and for ever now preferred.

Behind him, as he neared the gatehouse, a meagre shadow detached itself from the shelter of the eaves of Richildis's house, and slid contentedly along the road after him, keeping well to the side in case he looked back. But Brother Cadfael did not look back. He had just had a lesson in the perils of that equivocal exercise and in any case, it was not his way.

Chapter Six

HAPTER NEXT morning promised to be as dull as usual, once Brother Andrew's readings were done, and the business of the house reached; but Cadfael, dozing gently behind his pillar, remained alert enough to prick his ears, when Brother Matthew the cellarer announced that the guest-hall was full to capacity, and more stabling space was needed for still more expected gentlefolk, so that it would be necessary to transfer some of the horses and mules belonging to the abbey to some other housing, to accommodate the travellers' beasts within the walls. Late merchants, taking advantage of the clement autumn after the summer of siege and disorder, were now on the roads making for home for the feast, and nobles with manors in the country were seeking their own retired firesides, to celebrate Christmas away from the burden of arms and the stress of faction in the south. It was manifestly true that the stables were overcrowded, and the great court daily brighter and busier with arrivals and departures.

'There is also the matter of the horse that belonged to Master Gervase Bonel,' said Brother Matthew, 'who is to be buried today. Our responsibility to provide stabling and feed is now at an end, though I know the case is in suspense until the matter of the man's death and the disposal of his property is cleared up. But the widow as survivor is certainly not entitled to livery for a horse. She has a daughter married in the town, and doubtless will be able to make provision for the beast, and of course we

451

must house it until she so disposes, but it need not occupy a stall in our main stables. Have I your approval to move it out with our own working beasts to the stabling under our barn in the horse-fair ground?'

Most certainly he had not Cadfael's approval! He sat stiff with alarm and exasperation, fuming at his own unfortunate choice of hiding-place rather than Matthew's practical dispositions. Yet how could he have foreseen this? Very seldom had it been necessary to make use of the stalls at the barn, apart from its actual purpose as temporary accommodation at the horse-fairs and St Peter's fair. And now how was he to get to Edwin in time to remove him from the peril of discovery? In broad daylight, and with the inescapable spiritual duties of the day confining his movements?

'That should certainly provide adequate stabling,' agreed Prior Robert. 'It would be well to make the transfer at once.'

'I will give instructions to the grooms. And you agree also, Father, to the Widow Bonel's horse being removed with them?'

'By all means!' Robert no longer had quite the same interest in the Bonel family, now that it seemed doubtful he would ever lay his hands on the manor of Mallilie, though he did not intend to give up without a struggle. The unnatural death and its consequences irked him like a thorn in his flesh, and he would gladly have removed not merely the horse but the whole household, could he have done so with propriety. He did not want murder associated with his convent, he did not want the sheriff's officers probing among his guests, or the whiff of notoriety hanging round the monastery buildings like a bad odour. 'It will be necessary to go into the legal complications on the vexed question of the charter, which inevitably lapses now unless a new lord chooses to endorse and complete it. But until after Master Bonel's burial, of course, nothing should be done. The horse, however, can well be moved. I doubt if the widow will now have any use for a mount, but that is not yet our problem.'

He is already regretting, thought Cadfael, that in the first flush of sympathy and concern he authorised a grave for Bonel in the transept. But his dignity will not let him withdraw the concession now. God be thanked, Richildis will have whatever comfort there is in a solemn and dignified funeral, since all that Robert does must be done with grandeur. Gervase has lain in state in the mortuary chapel of the abbey, and will lie in abbey ground by nightfall. She would be soothed and calmed by that.

452

She felt, he was sure, a kind of guilt towards the dead man. Whenever she was solitary she would be playing the ageless, debilitating game of: If only . . . If only I'd never accepted him . . . if only I had managed affairs between him and Edwin better . . . if only – then he might have been alive and hale today!

Cadfael closed his ears to the desultory discussion of a possible purchase of land to enlarge the graveyard, and gave his mind to the consideration of his own more pressing problem. It would not be impossible to find himself an errand along the Foregate when the grooms were stabling the horses in their new quarters, and the lay brothers would not question any movements of his. He could as well bring Edwin out of his retreat in a benedictine habit as lead him into it, provided he took care to time the exit properly. And once out, then where? Certainly not towards the gatehouse. There were people in one or two houses along the highroad towards St Giles who had had dealings with him when sick, some whose children he had attended in fever. They might give shelter to a young man at his recommendation, though he did not much like the idea of involving them. Or there was, at the end of this stretch of road, the leper hospital of St Giles, where young brothers often served a part of their novitiate in attendance on those less fortunate. Something, surely, might be arranged to hide one hunted boy.

Incredulously, Cadfael heard his own name spoken, and was jerked sharply out of his planning. Across the chapter-house, in his stall as close as possible to Prior Robert, Brother Jerome had risen, and was in full spate, his meagre figure deceptively humble in stance, his sharp eyes half-hooded in holy meekness. And he had just uttered Brother Cadfael's name, with odious concern and affection!

'. . . I do not say, Father, that there has been any impropriety in our dearly valued brother's conduct. I do but appeal for aid and guidance for his soul's sake, for he stands in peril. Father, it has come to my knowledge that many years since, before his call to this blessed vocation, Brother Cadfael was in a relationship of worldly affection with the lady who is now Mistress Bonel, and a guest of this house. By reason of the death of her husband he was drawn back into contact with her, by no fault of his, oh, no, I do not speak of blame, for he was called to help a dying man. But consider, Father, how severe a test may be imposed upon a brother's sincere devotion, when he is again brought unexpectedly into so close touch with a long-forgotten attachment according to this world!'

To judge by Prior Robert's loftily erected head and stretched neck, which enabled him to look from an even greater height down his nose at the imperilled brother, he was indeed considering it. So was Cadfael, with astonished indignation that congealed rapidly into cool, inimical comprehension. He had underestimated Brother Jerome's audacity, no less than his venom. That large, sinewy ear must have been pressed lovingly to the large keyhole of Richildis's door, to have gathered so much.

'Do you allege,' demanded Robert incredulously, 'that Brother Cadfael has been in unlawful conversation with this woman? On what occasion? We ourselves know well that he attended Master Bonel's death-bed, and did his best for the unfortunate, and that the unhappy wife was then present. We have no reproach to make upon that count, it was his duty to go where he was needed.'

Brother Cadfael, as yet unaddressed, sat grimly silent, and let them proceed, for obviously this attack came as unexpectedly to Robert as to him.

'Oh, no man of us can question that,' agreed Jerome obligingly. 'It was his Christian duty to give aid according to his skills, and so he did. But as I have learned, our brother has again visited the widower and spoken with her, only last night. Doubtless for purposes of comfort and blessing to the bereaved. But what dangers may lurk in such a meeting, Father, I need not try to express. God forbid it should ever enter any mind, that a man once betrothed, and having lost his affianced wife to another, should succumb to jealousy in his late years, after abandoning the world, when he once again encounters the former object of his affections. No, that we may not even consider. But would it not be better if our beloved brother should be removed utterly even from the temptations of memory? I speak as one having his wellbeing and spiritual health at heart.'

You speak, thought Cadfael, grinding his teeth, as one at last provided with a weapon against a man you've hated for years with little effect. And, God forgive me, if I could wring your scrawny neck now, I would do it and rejoice.

He rose and stood forth from his retired place to be seen. 'I am here, Father Prior, examine me of my actions as you wish. Brother Jerome is somewhat over-tender of my vocation, which is in no danger.' And that, at least, was heartfelt.

454

Prior Robert continued to look down at him all too thought-fully for Cadfael's liking. He would certainly fight any suggestion of misconduct among his flock, and defend them to the world for his own sake, but he might also welcome an opportunity of curbing the independent activities of a man who always caused him slight discomfort, as though he found in Cadfael's blunt, practical, tolerant self-sufficiency a hidden vein of satire and amusement. He was no fool, and could hardly have failed to notice that he was being obliquely invited to believe that Cadfael might, when confronted with his old sweetheart married to another, have so far succumbed to jealousy as to remove his rival from the world with his own hands. Who, after all, knew the properties of herbs and plants better, or the proportions in which they could be used for good or ill? God forbid it should enter any mind, Jerome had said piously, neatly planting the notion as he deplored it. Doubtful if Robert would seriously entertain any such thought, but neither would he censure it in Jerome, who was unfailingly useful and obsequious to him. Nor could it be argued that the thing was altogether impossible. Cadfael had made the monk's-hood oil, and knew what could be done with it. He had not even to procure it secretly, he had it in his own charge; and if he had been sent for in haste to a man already sick to death, who was to say he had not first administered the poison he feigned to combat? And I watched Aelfric cross the court, thought Cadfael, and might easily have stopped him for a word, lifted the lid in curiosity at the savoury smell, been told for whom it was sent, and added another savour of my own making? A moment's distraction, and it could have been done. How easy it is to bring on oneself a suspicion there's no disproving!

'Is it indeed truth, brother,' asked Robert weightily, 'that Mistress Bonel was intimately known to you in your youth, before you took vows?'

'It is,' said Cadfael directly, 'if by intimately you mean only well and closely, on terms of affection. Before I took the Cross we held ourselves to be affianced, though no one else knew of it. That was more than forty years ago, and I had not seen her since. She married in my absence, and I, after my return, took the cowl.' The fewer words here, the better.

'Why did you never say word of this, when they came to our house?'

'I did not know who Mistress Bonel was, until I saw her. The name meant nothing to me, I knew only of her first marriage.

455

I was called to the house, as you know, and went in good faith.'

'That I acknowledge,' conceded Robert. 'I did not observe anything untoward in your conduct there.'

'I do not suggest, Father Prior,' Jerome made haste to assure him, 'that Brother Cadfael has done anything deserving of blame . . .' The lingering ending added silently: '. . . *as yet!*' but he did not go so far as to utter it. 'I am concerned only for his protection from the snares of temptation. The devil can betray even through a Christian affection.'

Prior Robert was continuing his heavy and intent study of Cadfael, and if he was not expressing condemnation, there was no mistaking the disapproval in his elevated eyebrows and distended nostrils. No inmate of his convent should even admit to noticing a woman, unless by way of Christian ministry or hard-headed business. 'In attending a sick man, certainly you did only right, Brother Cadfael. But is it also true that you visited this woman last night? Why should that be? If she was in need of spiritual comfort, there is here also a parish priest. Two days ago you had a right and proper reason for going there, last night you surely had none.'

'I went there,' said Cadfael patiently, since there was no help in impatience, and nothing could mortify Brother Jerome so much as to be treated with detached forbearance, 'to ask certain questions which may bear upon her husband's death – a matter which you, Father Prior, and I, and all here, must devoutly wish to be cleared up as quickly as possible, so that this house may be in peace.'

'That is the business of the sheriff and his sergeants,' said Robert curtly, 'and none of yours. As I understand it, there is no doubt whose is the guilt, and it is only a matter of laying hands upon the youth who did so vile a thing. I do not like your excuse, Brother Cadfael.'

'In due obedience,' said Cadfael. 'I bow to your judgement, but also must not despise my own. I think there *is* doubt, and the truth will not be easily uncovered. And my *reason* was not an excuse; it was for that purpose I went to the house. It was my own preparation, meant to bring comfort and relief from pain, that was used to bring death, and neither this house nor I, as a brother herein, can be at peace until the truth is known.'

'In saying so, you show lack of faith in those who uphold the law, and whose business justice is, as yours it is not. It is an arrogant attitude, and I deplore it.' What he meant was that he wished to distance the Benedictine house of St Peter and St Paul from the ugly thing that had happened just outside its walls, and he would find a means of preventing the effective working of a conscience so inconvenient to his aims. 'In my judgment, Brother Jerome is right, and it is our duty to ensure that you are not allowed, by your own folly, to stray into spiritual danger. You will have no further contact with Mistress Bonel. Until her future movements are decided, and she leaves her present house, you will confine yourself to the enclave, and your energies to your proper function of work and worship within our walls only.'

There was no help for it. Vows of obedience, voluntarily taken, cannot be discarded whenever they become inconvenient. Cadfael inclined his head — bowed would have been the wrong word, it was more like a small, solid and formidable bull lowering its armed brow for combat! – and said grimly: 'I shall observe the order laid upon me, as in duty bound.'

'But you, young man,' he was saying to Brother Mark in the garden workshop, a quarter of an hour later, with the door shut fast to contain the fumes of frustration and revolt, rather Mark's than his own, 'you have no such order to observe.'

'That,' said Brother Mark, taking heart, 'is what I was thinking. But I was afraid you were not.'

'I would not involve you in my sins, God knows,' sighed Cadfael, 'if this was not urgent. And perhaps I should not . . . Perhaps he must be left to fend for himself, but with so much against him . . .'

'He!' said Brother Mark thoughtfully, swinging his thin ankles from the bench. 'The he whose *something*, that was not a vial, we did not find? From all I gather, he's barely out of childhood. The Gospels are insistent we should take care of the children.'

Cadfael cast him a mild, measuring and affectionate look. This child was some four years older than the other, and his childhood, since his mother's death when he was three years old, no one had cared for, beyond throwing food and grudged shelter his way. The other had been loved, indulged and admired all his life, until these past months of conflict, and the present altogether more desperate danger.

'He is a spirited and able child, Mark, but he relies on me. I took charge of him and gave him orders. Had he been left on his own, I think he would have managed.'

'Tell me only where I must go, and what I must do,' said Mark, quite restored to cheerfulness, 'and I will do it.'

Cadfael told him. 'But not until after High Mass. You must not be absent, or any way put your own repute in peril. And should there be trouble, you'll hold aloof and be safe – you hear?'

'I hear,' said Brother Mark, and smiled.

By ten o'clock of that morning, when High Mass began, Edwin was heartily sick of obedience and virtue. He had never been so inactive for so long since he had first climbed mutinously out of his cradle and crawled into the yard, to be retrieved from among the wagon wheels by a furious Richildis. Still, he owed it to Brother Cadfael to wait in patience, as he had promised, and only in the darkest middle of the night had he ventured out to stretch his legs and explore the alleys and lanes about the horse-fair, and the silent and empty stretch of the Foregate, the great street that set out purposefully for London. He had taken care to be back in his loft well before the east began to lighten, and here he was, seated on an abandoned barrel, kicking his heels and eating one of Cadfael's apples, and wishing something would happen. From the slit air-vents enough light entered the loft to make a close, dim, straw-tinted day.

If wishes are prayers, Edwin's was answered with almost crude alacrity. He was used to hearing horses passing in the Foregate, and the occasional voices of people on foot, so he thought nothing of the leisurely hoof-beats and monosyllabic voices that approached from the town. But suddenly the great double doors below were hurled open, their solid weight crashing back to the wall, and the hoof-beats, by the sound of them of horses being walked on leading reins, clashed inward from the cobbles of the apron and thudded dully on the beaten earth floor within.

Edwin sat up, braced and still, listening with pricked ears. One horse . . . two . . . more of them, lighter in weight and step, small, neat hooves – mules, perhaps? And at least two grooms with them, probably three or four. He froze, afraid to stir, weary of even the crunching of his apple. Now if they were only meaning to stall these beasts during the day, all might yet be well, and all he had to do was keep quiet and sit out the time in hiding.

There was a heavy trapdoor in the cleared space of flooring, so that at need grooms could gain access to the loft without having to go outside, or carry the other key with them. Edwin slid from his barrel and went to stretch himself cautiously on the floor, and apply an ear to the crack.

A young voice chirruped soothingly to a restive horse, and Edwin heard a hand patting neck and shoulder. 'Easy there, now, my beauty! A very fine fellow you are, too. The old man knew his horse-flesh, I'll say that for him. He's spoiled for want of work. It's shame to see him wasted.'

'Get him into a stall,' ordered a gruff voice shortly, 'and come and lend a hand with these mules.'

There was a steady to-ing and fro-ing about settling the beasts. Edwin got up quietly, and put on his Benedictine habit over his own clothes, for if by ill-luck he was seen around this building, it would be the best cover he could have. Though it seemed that everything would probably pass off safely. He went back to his listening station just in time to hear a third voice say: 'Fill up the hay-racks. If there's not fodder enough down here, there's plenty above.'

They were going to invade his refuge, after all! There was already a foot grating on the rungs of the ladder below. Edwin scrambled up in haste, no longer troubling to be silent, and rolled his heavy barrel on its rim to settle solidly over the trapdoor, for the bolts must be on the underside. The sound of someone wrestling them back from stiff sockets covered the noise of the barrel landing, and Edwin perched on top of his barricade, and wished himself three times as heavy. But it is very difficult to thrust a weight upwards over one's head, and it seemed that even his slight bulk was enough. The trap heaved a little under him, but nothing worse.

'It's fast,' called a vexed voice from below. 'Some fool's bolted it on top.'

'There are no bolts on top. Use your brawn, man, you're no such weed as all that.'

'Then they've dumped something heavy over the trap. I tell you it won't budge.' And he rattled it again irritably to demonstrate.

'Oh, come down, and let a man try his arm,' said he of the gruff voice disgustedly. There was an alarming scrambling of heavier feet on the rungs, and the ladder creaked. Edwin held his breath and willed himself to grow heavier by virtue of every braced muscle. The trap shook, but lifted not an inch, and the struggling groom below panted and swore.

'What did I tell you, Will?' crowed his fellow, with satisfaction.

'We'll have to go round to the other door. Lucky I brought both keys. Wat, come and help me shift whatever's blocking the trap, and fork some hay down.'

Had he but known it, he needed no key, for the door was unlocked. The voice receded rapidly down the ladder, and footsteps stamped out at the stable-door. Two of them gone from below, but only a matter of moments before he would be discovered; not even time to burrow deep into the hay, even if that had been a safe strategem when they came with forks. If they were only three in all, why not attempt the one instead of the two? Edwin as hastily rolled his barrel back to jam it against the door, and then flung himself upon the trap, hoisting mightily. It rose so readily that he was almost spilled backwards, but he recovered, and lowered himself hastily through. No time to waste in closing the trap again, all his attention was centred on the perils below.

They were four, not three! Two of them were still here among the horses, and though one of them had his back squarely turned, and was forking hay into a manger at the far end of the long stable, the other, a lean, wiry fellow with shaggy grey hair, was only a few feet from the foot of the lader, and just striding out from one of the stalls.

It was too late to think of any change of plan, and Edwin never hesitated. He scrambled clear of the trap, and launched himself in a flying leap upon the groom. The man had just caught the sudden movement and raised his head sharply to stare at its source, when Edwin descended upon him a cloud of overlarge black skirts, and brought him to the ground, momentarily winded. Whatever advantage the habit might have been to the boy was certainly lost after that assault. The other youth, turning at his companion's startled yell, was baffled only briefly at the sight of what appeared to be a Benedictine brother, bounding up from the floor with gown gathered in one hand, and the other reaching for the pikel his victim had dropped. No monk the groom had ever yet seen behaved in this fashion. He took heart and began an indignant rush which halted just as abruptly when the pikel was flourished capably in the direction of his middle. But by then the felled man was also clambering to his feet, and between the fugitive and the wide open doorway.

There was only one way to go, and Edwin went that way, pikel in hand, backing into the stall nearest him. Only then did he take note, with what attention he had to spare from his adversaries, of the horse beside him, the one which had been so restive, according to the young groom, spoiling for want of work and shamefully wasted. A tall, high-spirited chestnut beast with a paler mane and tail, and a white blaze, stamping in excitement at the confusion, but reaching a nuzzling lip to Edwin's hair, and whinnying in his ear. He had turned from his manger to face the fray, and the way was open before him. Edwin cast an arm over his neck with a shout of recognition and joy.

'Rufus . . . oh, Rufus!'

He dropped his pikel, knotted a fist in the flowing mane, and leaped and scrambled astride the lofty back. What did it matter that he had neither saddle nor bridle, when he had ridden this mount bareback more times than he could remember, in the days before he fell utterly out of favour with the owner? He dug in his heels and pressed with his knees, and urged an all too willing accomplice into headlong flight.

If the grooms had been ready to tackle Edwin, once they realised his vocation was counterfeit, they were less eager to stand in the way of Rufus. He shot out of his stall like a cross-bow bolt, and they leaped apart before him in such haste that the older one fell backwards over a truss of hay, and measured his length on the floor a second time. Edwin lay low on the rippling shoulders, his fists in the light mane, whispering incoherent gratitude and encouragement into the laid-back ears. They clattered out on to the triangle of the horse-fair, and by instinct Edwin used knee and heel to turn the horse away from the town and out along the Foregate.

The two who had mounted by the rear staircase, and had difficulty in getting the door open, not to mention finding it inexplicably unlocked in the first place, heard the stampede and rushed to stare out along the road.

'God save us!' gasped Wat, round-eyed. 'It's one of the brothers! What can he be at in such a hurry?'

At that moment the light wind filled Edwin's cowl and blew it back on to his shoulders, uncovering the bright tangle of hair and the boyish face. Will let out a wild yell, and began to scurry down the stairs. 'You see that? That's no tonsure, and no

461

brother, either! That's the lad the sheriff's hunting. Who else would be hiding in our barn?'

But Edwin was already away, nor was there a horse left in the stable of equal quality, to pursue him. The young groom had spoken the truth, Rufus was baulked and frustrated for want of exercise, and now, let loose, he was ready to gallop to his heart's content. There was now only one obstacle to freedom. Too late Edwin remembered Cadfael's warning not, in any circumstances to take the London road, for there was certainly a patrol out at St Giles, where the town suburbs ended, to check on all passing traffic in search of him. He recalled it only when he saw in the distance before him a party of four riders spread well across the road and approaching at a relaxed amble. The guard had just been relieved, and here was the off-duty party making its way back to the castle.

He could not possibly burst a way through that serried line, and the black gown would not deceive them for a moment, on a rider proceeding at this desperate speed. Edwin did the only thing possible. With pleading voice and urged knees he checked and wheeled his displeased mount, and set off back the way he had come, at the same headlong gallop. And well behind him he heard a gleeful shout that told him he was now pursued by a posse of determined men-at-arms, fully persuaded they were on the heels of a miscreant, even if they were not yet certain of his identity.

Brother Mark, hurrying along the horse-fair after High Mass, primed with his part to enter the loft unobserved, so that no one should be able afterwards to swear that only one went in where two came out, arrived close to the barn just in time to hear the commotion of a hue and cry, and see Edwin on his elated war-horse come hurtling back along the Foregate, cowl and skirts streaming, head stooped low to the flying mane. He had never before set eyes on Edwin Gurney, but there was no doubt as to who this careering desperado must be; nor, alas, any doubt that Mark's own errand came much too late. The quarry was flushed from cover, though not yet taken. But there was nothing, nothing at all, Brother Mark could do to help him.

The head groom Will, a stout-hearted man, had hastily hauled out the best of the remaining horses in his care, and prepared to pursue the fugitive, but he had no more than heaved himself into the saddle when he beheld the chestnut thundering back again in the opposite direction. He spurred forward

462

to try and intercept it, though the prospect was daunting; but his mount's courage failed of matching his, and it baulked and swerved aside before Rufus's stretched neck, laid-back ears and rolling eye. One of the undergrooms hurled a pikel towards the pounding hooves, but if truth be told, rather half-heartedly, and Rufus merely made a startled side-wise bound, without checking speed, and was past and away towards the town.

Will might well have followed, though with small hope of keeping that yellow, billowing tail in sight; but by then the clamour of the pursuers was approaching along the Foregate, and he was only too glad to surrender the task to them. It was, after all, their business to apprehend malefactors, and whatever else this pseudo-monk had done, he had certainly stolen a horse belonging to the Widow Bonel, and in the abbey's care. Obviously the theft should be reported at once. He rode into the path of the galloping guards, waving a delaying hand, and all three of his colleagues closed in to give their versions of what had happened.

There was a substantial audience by then. Passers-by had happily declined to pass by such a promising mêlée, and people had darted out from nearby houses to discover what all the hard riding meant. During the pause to exchange information, several of the children had drawn close to listen and stare, and that in itself somewhat slowed the resumption of the chase. Mothers retrieved children, and managed to keep the way blocked a full minute more. But there seemed no reasonable explanation for the fact that at the last moment, when they were virtually launched, the horse under the captain of the guard suddenly shrieked indignantly, reared, and almost spilled his rider, who was not expecting any such disturbance, and had to spend some minutes mastering the affronted horse, before he could muster his men and gallop away after the fugitive.

Brother Mark, craning and peering with the rest of the curious, watched the guards stream away towards the town, secure that the chestnut horse had had time to get clean out of sight. The rest was up to Edwin Gurney. Mark folded his hands in his wide sleeves, drew his cowl well forward to shadow a modest face, and turned back towards the gatehouse of the abbey, with very mixed news. On the way he discarded the second pebble he had picked up by the barn. On his uncle's manor he had been set to work for his meagre keep at four years old, following the plough with a small sack full of stones, to scare off the birds that took the seed. It had taken him two years to discover that he sympathised with the hungry birds, and did not really want to harm them; but by then he was already a dead shot, and he had not lost his skills.

'And you followed as far as the bridge?' Cadfael questioned anxiously. 'And the bridge-keepers had not so much as seen him? And the sheriff's men had lost him?'

'Clean vanished,' Brother Mark reported with pleasure. 'He never crossed into the town, at least, not that way. If you ask me, he can't have turned from the road by any of the alleys short of the bridge, he wouldn't be sure he was out of sight. I think he must have dived down along the Gaye, the shoreward side where the orchard trees give some cover. But what he would do after that I can't guess. But they haven't taken him, that's certain. They'll be hounding his kin within the town, but they'll find nothing there.' He beamed earnestly into Cadfael's troubled face, and urged: 'You know you'll prove he has nothing to answer for. Why do you worry?'

It was more than enough worry to have someone depending so absolutely on the victory of truth, and the credit with heaven of Brother Cadfael, but it seemed that this morning's events had cast no shadow upon young Mark, and that was matter for gratitude.

'Come to dinner,' said Cadfael thankfully, 'and then take your ease, for with such a faith as yours you can. I do believe when you come to cast a pebble with intent, it must hit the mark. Whoever named you foresaw your future. And since it arises, what is your own mark? A bishopric?'

'Pope or cardinal,' said Brother Mark happily. 'Nothing less.'

'Oh, no,' said Brother Cadfael seriously. 'Beyond bishop, and a pastoral cure, I think you would be wasted.'

All that day the sheriff's men hunted Edwin Gurney through the town, where they reckoned he must have sought help, somehow evading notice in crossing the bridge. Finding no trace there, they sent out patrols to cover all the major roads out of the peninsula. In a close loop of the Severn, Shrewsbury had only two bridges, one towards the abbey and London, by which he was thought to have entered, one towards Wales, with a fan of roads branching out westwards.

They were convinced that the fugitive would make for Wales, that being his quickest way out of their jurisdiction, though his

464

future there might well be hazardous. So it came as a surprise when a party patrolling the abbey side of the river, where they had little expectation of picking up the trail, was accosted by an excited young person of about eleven, who ran to them through the fields to demand breathlessly if it was true the man they were looking for was in monk's gown, and riding a bright-brown horse with primrose mane and tail. Yes, she had seen him, and only a short time since, breaking cautiously out of that copse and trotting away eastwards, as if he wanted to cross the next loop of the river and move round to join the highroad to London, some way past St Giles. Since he had first set out in that direction, and found the way blocked at the rim of the town, her report made sense. Evidently he had managed to find cover and lie up for a while, in the hope that the hunt would take the opposite direction, and now he felt secure in moving again. The girl said he might be making for the ford at Uffington.

They thanked her heartily, sent back one man to report the trail hot again and bring reinforcements after, and set off briskly for the ford. And Alys, having watched them out of sight, made her way back as briskly to the highroad and the bridge. No one was on the watch for eleven-year-old girls going in and out.

Beyond the ford at Uffington the hunters got their first glimpse of the quarry, jogging along almost sedately on the narrow road towards Upton. From the moment he turned and saw them, he flashed away at speed; the colour and the gait of the horse were unmistakable, and the pursuers could not but wonder why the rider had retained his purloined habit, which was now more liability than asset, for everyone in the country-side must be looking out for it.

It was then mid-afternoon, and the light beginning to dim. The chase went on for hours. The boy seemed to know every byway and every covert, and managed to lose them several times, and lead them into some unexpected and perilous places, often leaving the roads for marchy meadows where one stout man-at-arms was thrown into odorous bog, or broken places where it was soon impossible to see the easiest passage, and one horse picked up a stone and went lame. Through Atcham, Cound and Cressage he held them off, and from time to time lost them, until Rufus tired and stumbled in the woods beyond Acton, and they were on him and round him, grasping at gown and cowl and pinioning him fast. They pulled him down and tied his hands, and for the chase he had led them they gave him some rough handling, which he bore philosophically and

465

in silence. All he asked was that the miles they had to go back to Shrewsbury should be taken at an easy pace, for the horse's sake.

At some stage he had rigged a serviceable bridle from the rope girdle of his habit. They borrowed that back to secure him behind the lightest weight among them, for fear he should leap clear even with bound hands, and make off into the darkening woods on foot. Thus they brought their prisoner back the lengthy journey to Shrewsbury, and turned in at the abbey gatehouse late in the evening. The stolen horse might as well be returned at once where he belonged; and since that was, at present, the only crime that stood manifestly proven against the culprit, his proper place, until further examination had been made of his deeds, was in the abbey prison. There he could safely be left to kick his heels until the law was ready to proceed against him on graver charges of acts committed outside the pale, and therefore within the sheriff's juridiction.

Prior Robert, courteously informed that the wanted youth was brought in captive, and must remain in abbey keeping at least overnight, was torn between satisfaction at the prospect of getting rid of the criminal implications of Master Bonel's death, in order to be able to deal more skilfully with the legal ones, and the vexation of having temporarily to accommodate the criminal within his own domain. Still, an arrest for the murder must follow in the morning, the inconvenience was not so great.

'You have this youth in the gatehouse now?' he asked the man-at-arms who had brought the news to his lodging.

'We have, Father. Two of your abbey sergeants are with him there, and if you please to give orders that they hold him in charge until tomorrow, the sheriff will certainly take him off your hands on the graver count. Would it please you to come and examine him for yourself on the matter of the horse? If you see fit, there could be charges of assault against your grooms, a serious matter even without the theft.'

Prior Robert was not immune to human curiosity, and was not averse to taking a look at this youthful demon who had poisoned his own stepfather and led the sheriff's men a dance over half the shire. 'I will come,' he said. 'The church must not turn its back upon the sinner, but only deplore the sin.'

In the porter's room at the gatehouse the boy sat stolidly on a bench opposite the welcome fire, hunched defensively against the world, but looking far from cowed, for all his bruises and

466

wariness. The abbey sergeant and the sheriff's patrol circled him with brooding eyes and hectoring questions, which he answered only when he chose to do so, and then briefly. Several of them were soiled and mud-stained from the hunt, one or two had scratches and bruises of their own to show. The boy's bright eyes flickered from one to another, and it even seemed that his lips twitched with the effort to suppress a smile when he contemplated the one who had gone head over heels in the meadows near Cound. They had stripped his borrowed habit from him and restored it to the porter's care; the boy showed now slender and light-haired, smooth and fair of skin, with ingenuous-seeming hazel eyes. Prior Robert was somewhat taken aback by his youth and comeliness; truly the devil can assume fair shapes!

'So young and so marred!' he said aloud. The boy was not meant to hear that, it was uttered in the doorway as Robert entered, but at fourteen the hearing is keen. 'So, boy,' said the prior, drawing near, 'you are the troubler of our peace. You have much upon your conscience, and I fear it is even late to pray that you may have time to amend. I shall so pray. You know, for you are old enough to know, that murder is mortal sin.'

The boy looked him in the eye, and said with emphatic composure: 'I am not a murderer.'

'Oh child, is it now of any avail to deny what is known? You might as well say that you did not steal a horse from our barn this morning, when four of our servants and many other people saw the act committed.'

'I did not *steal* Rufus,' the boy reported promptly and firmly. 'He is mine. He was my stepfather's property, and I am my stepfather's heir, for his agreement with the abbey has never been ratified, and the will that made me his heir is sound as gold. What belongs to me how could I steal? From whom?'

'Wretched child,' protested the prior, bristling at such bold defiance, and even more at a dawning suspicion that this imp, in spite of his dire situation, was daring to enjoy himself, 'think what you say! You should rather be repenting while you have time. Have you not yet realised that the murderer cannot live to inherit from his victim?'

'I have said, and say again, I am not a murderer. I deny, on my soul, on the altar, on whatever you wish, that ever I did my stepfather harm. Therefore Rufus *is* mine. Or when the will is proven, and my overlord gives his consent as he promised, Rufus and Mallilie and all *will* be mine. I have committed no crime, and nothing you can do or say can make me admit to any. And nothing you can do,' he added, his eyes suddenly flashing, 'can ever make me guilty of any.'

'You waste your goodwill, Father Prior,' growled the sheriff's sergeant, 'he's an obdurate young wretch meant for the gallows, and his come-uppance will be short.' But under Robert's august eye he refrained from clouting the impudent brat round the ears, as otherwise he might well have done. 'Think no more of him, but let your servants clap him into safe hold in your cell here, and put him out of your mind as worth no more pains. The law will take care of him.'

'See that he has food,' said Robert, not altogether without compassion, and remembering that this child had been in the saddle and in hiding all the day, 'and let his bed be hard, but dry and warm enough. And should he relent and ask . . . Boy, listen to me, and give a thought to your soul's welfare. Will you have one of the brothers come and reason and pray with you before you sleep?'

The boy looked up with a sudden sparkle in his eye that might have been penitent hope, but looked more like mischief, and said with deceptive meekness: 'Yes, and gratefully, if you could be so kind as to send for Brother Cadfael.' It was time, after all, to take thought for his own situation, he had surely done enough now.

He expected the name to raise a frown, and so it did, but Robert had offered a grace, and could not now withdraw it or set conditions upon it. With dignity he turned to the porter, who hovered at the door. 'Ask Brother Cadfael to come here to us at once. You may tell him it is to give counsel and guidance to a prisoner.'

The porter departed. It was almost the hour for retirement, and most of the brothers would certainly be in the warming-room, but Cadfael was not there, nor was Brother Mark. The porter found them in the workshop in the garden, not even compounding mysteries, either, but sitting somewhat glumly, talking in low and anxious tones. The news of the capture had not yet gone round; by day it would have been known every-where within minutes. It was common knowledge, of course how the sheriff's men had spent their day, but it was not yet common knowledge with what an achievement they had crowned it.

'Brother Cadfael, you're wanted at the gatehouse,' announced the porter, leaning in at the doorway. And as Cadfael looked up at him in surprise: 'There's a young fellow there asks for you as his spiritual adviser, though if you want my view, he's very much in command of his own spirit, and has let Prior Robert know it, too. A company of the sheriff's men rode in towards the end of Compline with a prisoner. Yes, they've taken young Gurney at last.'

So that was how it had ended, after all Mark's effort and prayers, after all his own ineffective reasonings and seekings and faith. Cadfael got up in grieving haste. 'I'll come to him. With all my heart I'll come. Now we have the whole battle on our hands, and little time left. The poor lad! But why have they not taken him straight into the town?' Though of that one small mercy he was glad, seeing he himself was confined within the abbey walls, and only this odd chance provided him with a brief meeting.

'Why, the only thing they can charge him with, and nobody can question, is stealing the horse he rode off on this morning, and that was from our premises and our care, the abbey court has rights in it. In the morn they'll fetch him away on the count of murder.

Brother Mark fell in at their heels and followed to the gatehouse, altogether cast down and out of comfort, unable to find a hopeful word to say. He felt in his heart that that was sin, the sin of despair; not despair for himself, but despair of truth and justice and right, and the future of wretched mankind. Nobody had bidden him attend, but he went, all the same, a soul committed to a cause about which, in fact, he knew very little, except the youth of the protagonist, and the absolute nature of Cadfael's faith in him, and that was enough.

Cadfael entered the porter's room with a heavy heart but not in despair; it was a luxury he could not afford. All eyes turned upon him, understandably, since he entered upon a heavy silence. Robert had abandoned his kindly meant but patronising exhortations, and the men of law had given up the attempt to get any admissions out of their captive, and were content to see him safely under lock and key, and get to their beds in the castle. A ring of large, well-equipped men on guard round a willowy lad in country homespun, bare-headed and cloakless on a frosty night, who sat braced and neat and alert on a bench by the wall, pleasantly flushed now from the fire, and looking, incredibly, almost complacent. His eyes met Brother Cadfael's eyes, and danced; clear, dark-fringed, greenish eyes. His hair was light brown, like seasoned oak. He was lightly built but tall for his years. He was tired, sleepy, bruised and dirty, and behind the wary eyes and solemn face he was undoubtedly laughing.

Brother Cadfael looked long, and understood much, enough at that moment to have no great worries about what as yet he did not understand. He looked round the attentive circle, looked last and longest at Prior Robert.

'Father Prior, I am grateful that you sent for me, and I welcome the duty laid on me, to do what may be done for the prisoner. But I must tell you that these gentlemen are in some error. I cast no doubt on what they may have to report of how this boy was taken, but I do advise them to make enquiry how and where he spent this morning's hours, when he is said to have escaped from the abbey barn on the horse belonging to Mistress Bonel. Gentlemen,' he informed the sheriff's bewildered patrol very gravely, 'this is not Edwin Gurney you have captured, but his nephew, Edwy Bellecote.'

Chapter Seven

HE ABBEY prison was two little cells attached to
the rear of the gatehouse, very clean, furnished with
bench-beds no worse than the novices endured, and
very rarely occupied. The summer period of Saint
Peter's fair was the chief populator of the cells, since it could
be relied upon to provide two happy drunken servants or lay
brothers nightly, who slept off their excesses and accepted their
modest fines and penances without rancour, thinking the game
well worth the candle. From time to time some more serious
disturbance might cast up an inmate, some ill-balanced brother
who nursed a cloistered hate long enough to attempt violence,
or lay a servant who stole, or a novice who offended too grossly
against the imposed code. The abbey court was not a busy
one.

In one of the two cells Brother Cadfael and Edwy sat side
by side, warmly and companionably. There was a grille in the
door, but it was most improbable that anyone was paying attention to anything that could be heard through it. The brother
who held the keys was sleepy, and in any case indifferent to
the cause that had brought him a prisoner. The difficulty would
probably be to batter loudly enough to wake him when Cadfael
wanted to leave.

'It wasn't so hard,' said Edwy, sitting back with a grateful
sigh after demolishing the bowl of porridge a tolerant cook
had provided him, 'there's a cousin of father's lives along the

riverside, just beyond your property of the Gaye, he had an orchard there, and a shed for the donkey and cart, big enough to hide Rufus. His boy brought word into the town to us, and I took father's horse and came out to meet Edwin there. Nobody was looking for a bony old piebald like our Japhet, I never got a second glance as I crossed the bridge, and I didn't hurry. Alys came with me pillion, and kept watch in case they got close. Then we changed clothes and horses, and Edwin made off towards – '

'Don't tell me!' said Cadfael quickly.

'No, you can truly say you don't know. Plainly not the way I went. They were slow sighting me,' said Edwy scornfully, 'even with Alys helping them. But once they had me in view it was a matter of how long I could keep them busy, to give him time to get well away. I could have taken them still further, but Rufus was tiring, so I let them have me. I had to, in the end, it kept them happy several more hours, and they sent one man ahead to call off the hunt. Edwin's had a clear run. Now what do you think they'll do with me?'

'If you hadn't already been in abbey charge, and the prior by, at that,' said Cadfael frankly, 'they'd have had the hide off you for leading them such a dance and making such fools of them. I wouldn't say Prior Robert himself wouldn't have liked to do as much, but dignity forbids, and authority forbids letting the secular arm skin you on his behalf. Though I fancy,' he said with sympathy, viewing the blue bruises that were beginning to show on Edwyn's jaw and cheekbone, 'they've already paid you part of your dues.'

The boy shrugged disdainfully. 'I can't complain. And it wasn't all one way. You should have seen the sergeant flop belly-down into the bog . . . and heard him when he got up. It was good sport, and we got Edwin away. And I've never had such a horse under me before, it was well worth it. But now what's to happen? They can't accuse *me* of murder, or of stealing Rufus, or even the gown, because I was never near the barn this morning, and there are plenty of witnesses to where I was, about the shop and the yard.'

'I doubt if you've broken any law,' agreed Cadfael, but you have made the law look very foolish, and no man in authority and office enjoys that. They could well keep you in close hold in the castle for a while, for helping a wanted man to escape. They may even threaten you in the hope of fetching Edwin back to get you out of trouble.'

Edwy shook his head vigorously. 'He need take no notice of that, he knows in the end there's nothing criminal they can lay against me. And I can sit out threats better than he. He loses his temper. He's getting better, but he has far to go yet.' Was he as buoyant about his prospects as he made out? Cadfael could not be quite sure, but certainly this elder of the pair had turned his four months seniority into a solid advantage, perhaps by reason of feeling responsible for his improbable uncle from the cradle. 'I can keep my mouth shut and wait,' said Edwy serenely.

'Well, since Prior Robert has so firmly demanded that the sheriff come in person tomorrow to remove you,' sighed Cadfael, 'I will at least make sure of being present, and try what can be got for you. The prior has given me a spiritual charge, and I'll stand fast on it. And now you'd better get your rest. I am supposed to be here to exhort you to an amended life, but to tell the truth, boy, I find your life no more in need of amendment than mine, and I think it would be presumption in me to meddle. But if you'll join your voice to mine in the night prayers, I think God may be listening.'

'Willingly,' said Edwy blithely, and plumped to his knees like a cheerful child, with reverently folded hands and closed eyes. In the middle of the prayers before sleeping his lips fluttered in a brief smile; perhaps he was remembering the extremely secular language of the sergeant rising dripping from the bog.

Cadfael was up before Prime, alert in case the prisoner's escort should come early. Prior Robert had been extremely angry at last night's comedy, but grasped readily at the plain fact that it gave him full justification for demanding that the sheriff should at once relieve him of an offender who had turned out to be no concern of his at all. This was not the boy who had taken away a Benedictine habit and a horse in Benedictine care, he was merely the mischievous brat who had worn the one and ridden the other to the ludicrous discomfiture of several gullible law officers. They could have him, and welcome; but the prior considered that it was due to his dignity – in this mood fully abbatial – that the senior officer then in charge, sheriff or deputy, should come in person to make amends for the inconvenience to which the abbey had been subjected, and remove the troublesome element. Robert wanted a public demonstration that henceforth all responsibility lay with the secular arm, and none within his sacred walls.

Brother Mark hovered close at Cadfael's elbow as the escort rode in, about half past eight in the morning, before the second Mass. Four mounted men-at-arms, and a spruce, dark, lightly built young nobleman on a tall, gaunt and self-willed horse, dappled from cream to almost black. Mark heard Brother Cadfael heave a great, grateful sigh at the sight of him, and felt his own heart rise hopefully at the omen.

'The sheriff must have gone south to keep the feast with the king,' said Cadfael with immense satisfaction. 'God is looking our way at last. That is not Gilbert Prestcote, but his deputy, Hugh Beringar of Maesbury.'

'Now,' said Beringar briskly, a quarter of an hour later, 'I have placated the prior, promised him deliverance from the presence of this desperate bravo, sent him off to Mass and chapter in tolerable content, and retrieved you, my friend, from having to accompany him, on the grounds that you have questions to answer.' He closed the door of the room in the gatehouse from which all his men-at-arms had been dismissed to wait his pleasure, and came and sat down opposite Cadfael at the table. 'And so you have, though not, perhaps, quite as he supposes. So now, before we go and pick this small crab out of his shell, tell me everything you know about this curious business. I know you must know more of it than any other man, however confidently my sergeant sets out his case. Such a break in the monastic monotony could never occur, and you not get wind of it and be there in the thick of it. Tell me everything.'

And now that it was Beringar in the seat of authority, while Prestcote attended dutifully at his sovereign lord's festal table, Cadfael saw no reason for reserve, at least so far as his own part was concerned. And all, or virtually all, was what he told.

'He came to you, and you hid him,' mused Beringar.

'I did. So I would again, in the same circumstances.'

'Cadfael, you must know as well as I the strength of the case against this boy. Who else has anything to gain? Yet I know you, and where you have doubts, I shall certainly not be without them.'

'I have no doubts,' said Cadfael firmly. 'The boy is innocent even of the thought of murder. And poison is so far out of his scope, he never would or could conceive the idea. I tested them both, when they came, and they neither of them even knew how the man had died, they believed me when I said he had been cut down in his blood. I stuck the means of murder under the

474

child's nose, and he never paled. All it meant to him was a mild memory of sniffing the same sharp smell while Brother Rhys was having his shoulders rubbed in the infirmary.'

'I take your word for all that,' said Beringar, 'and it is good evidence, but it is not in itself proof. How if we should both of us underestimate the cunning of the young, simply because they *are* young?'

'True,' agreed Cadfael with a wry grin, 'you are none so old yourself, and of your cunning, as I know, the limit has not yet been found. But trust me, these two are not of the same make as you. I have known them, you have not; agreed? I have my duty to do, according to such lights as I see. So have you your duty to do, according to your office and commission. I don't quarrel with that. But at this moment. Hugh, I don't know and have no means of guessing where Edwin Gurney is, or I might well urge him to give himself up to you and rely on your integrity. You will not need me to tell you that this loyal nephew of his, who has taken some sharp knocks for him, does know where he is, or at least knows where he set out to go. You may ask him, but of course he won't tell you. Neither for your style of questioning nor Prestcote's.'

Hugh drummed his fingers on the table, and pondered in silence for a moment. 'Cadfael, I must tell you I shall pursue the hunt for the boy to the limit, and not spare any tricks in the doing, so look to your own movements.'

'That's fair dealing,' said Cadfael simply. 'You and I have been rivals in trickery before, and ended as allies. But as for my movements, you'll find them monstrously dull. Did Prior Robert not tell you? I'm confined within the abbey walls, I may not go beyond.'

Hugh's agile black brows shot up to meet his hair. 'Good God, for what cloistered crime?' His eyes danced. 'What have you been about, to incur such a ban?'

'I spent too long in talk with the widow, and a stretched ear gathered that we had known each other very well, years ago, when we were young.' That was one thing he had not thought necessary to tell, but there was no reason to withhold it from Hugh. 'You asked me, once, how it came I had never married, and I told you I once had some idea of the kind, before I went to the Holy Land.'

'I do remember! You even mentioned a name. By now, you said, she must have children and grandchildren . . . Is it really so, Cadfael? This lady is your Richildis?'

'This lady,' said Cadfael with emphasis, 'is indeed Richildis, but mine she is *not*. Two husbands ago I had a passing claim on her, and that's all.'

'I must see her! The charmer who caught your eye must be worth cultivating. If you were any other man I should say this greatly weakens the force of your championship of her son, but knowing you, I think any scamp of his age in trouble would have you by the nose. I will see her, however, she may need advice or help, for it seems there's a legal tangle there that will take some unravelling.'

'There's another thing you can do, that may help to prove to you what I can only urge. I told you the boy says he threw into the river an inlaid wooden box, quite small.' Cadfael described it minutely. 'If that could come to light, it would greatly strengthen his story, which I, for one, believe. I cannot go out and contact the fishermen and watermen of Severn, and ask them to keep watch for such a small thing in the places they'll know of, where things afloat do wash up. But you can, Hugh. You can have it announced in Shrewsbury and downstream. It's worth the attempt.'

'That I'll certainly do,' said Beringar readily. 'There's a man whose grim business it is, when some poor soul drowns in Severn, to know exactly where the body will come ashore. Whether small things follow the same eddies is more than I know, but *he*'ll know. I'll have him take this hunt in charge. And now, if we've said all, we'd better go and see this twin imp of yours. Lucky for him you knew him, they'd hardly have believed it if he'd told them himself that he was the wrong boy. Are they really so like?'

'No, no more than a general family look about them if you know them, or see them side by side. But apart, a man might be in doubt, unless he did know them well. And your men were after the rider of that horse, and sure who it must be. Come and see!'

He was still in doubt, as they went together to the cell where Edwy waited, by this time in some trepidation, exactly what Beringar meant to do with his prisoner, though he had no fear that any harm would come to the boy. Whatever Hugh might think about Edwin's guilt or innocence, he was not the man to lean too heavily upon Edwy's staunch solidarity with his kinsman.

'Come forth, Edwy, into the daylight,' said Beringar, holding the cell door wide, 'and let me look at you. I want to be in no doubt which of you I have on my hands, the next time you change places.' And when Edwy obediently rose and stepped warily out into the court, after one nervous side-glance to make sure Brother Cadfael was there, the deputy sheriff took him by the chin and raised his face gently enough, and studied it attentively. The bruises were purple this morning, but the hazel eyes were bright. 'I'll know you again,' said Hugh confidently. 'Now, young sir! You have cost us a great deal of time and trouble, but I don't propose to waste even more by taking it out of your skin. I'll ask you but once: Where is Edwin Gurney?'

The phrasing of the question and the cut of the dark face left in doubt what was to happen if he got no answer; in spite of the mild tone, the potentialities were infinite. Edwy moistened dry lips, and said in the most conciliatory and respectful tone Cadfael had heard from him: 'Sir, Edwin is my kin and my friend, and if I had been willing to tell where he is, I should not have gone to such pains to help him get there. I think you must see that I can't and won't betray him.'

Beringar looked at Brother Cadfael, and kept his face grave but for the sparkle in his eyes. 'Well, Edwy, I expected no other, to tell the truth. Nobody does ill to keep faith. But I want you where I may lay hand on you whenever I need to, and be sure you are not stravaiging off on another wild rescue.'

Edwy foresaw a cell in Shrewsbury castle, and stiffened a stoical face to meet the worst.

'Give me your parole not to leave your father's house and shop,' said Beringar, 'until I give you your freedom, and you may go home. Why should we feed you at public expense over the Christmas feast, when I fancy your word, once given, will be your bond? What do you say?'

'Oh, I do give you my word!' gasped Edwy, startled and radiant with relief. 'I won't leave the yard until you give me leave. And I thank you!'

'Good! And I take your word, as you may take mine. My task, Edwy, is not to convict your uncle, or any man, of murder at all costs, it is to discover truly who did commit murder, and that I mean to do. Now come, I'll take you home myself, a word with your parents may not come amiss.'

They were gone before High Mass at ten, Beringar with Edwy pillion behind him, the raw-boned dapple being capable of carrying double his master's light weight, the men-at-arms of the escort two by two behind. Only in the middle of Mass, when his mind should have been on higher things, did Cadfael recall vexedly two more concessions he might have gained if he had thought of them in time. Martin Bellecote, for certain, was now without a horse, and the abbey was willing to part with Rufus, while Richildis would surely be glad to have him settled with her son-in-law, and no longer be beholden to the abbey for his keep. It would probably have tickled Beringar's humour to restore the carpenter a horse, on the pretext of relieving the abbey of an incubus. But the other thing was more important. He had meant to go searching the shores of the pond for the poison vial the previous day, and instead had found himself confined within the walls. Why had he not remembered to ask Beringar to follow up that tenuous but important line of inquiry while he was asking him to have the watermen watch for the pear-wood reliquary? Now it was too late, and he could not follow Beringar into the town to remedy the omission. Vexed with himself, he even snapped at Brother Mark, when that devoted young man questioned him about the outcome of the morning's events. Undeterred, Mark followed him, after dinner, to his sanctuary in the garden.

'I am an old fool,' said Cadfael, emerging from his depression, 'and have lost a fine chance of getting my work done for me, in places where I can no longer go myself. But that's no fault of yours, and I'm sorry I took it out on you.'

'If it's something you want done outside the walls,' said Mark reasonably, 'why should I be of less use today than I was yesterday?'

'True, but I've involved you enough already. And if I had had good sense I could have got the law to do it, which would have been far better. Though this is not at all dangerous or blameworthy,' he reminded himself, taking heart, 'it is only to search once again for a bottle . . .'

'Last time,' said Mark thoughtfully, 'we were looking for something we hoped would *not* be a bottle. Pity we did not find it.'

'True, but this time it *should* be a bottle, if the omen of Beringar's coming instead of Prestcote means anything. And I'll tell you where.' And so he did, pointing the significance of a window open to the south, even in light frost, on a bright day.

'I'm gone,' said Brother Mark. 'And you may sleep the noon away with a good conscience. My eyes are younger than yours.'

'Mind, take a napkin, and if you find it, wrap it loosely, and touch only as you must. I need to see how the oil has run and dried.'

It was when the afternoon light was dimming that Brother Mark came back. There was half an hour yet before Vespers, but from this time on any search for a small thing in a narrow slope of grass would have been a blind and hopeless quest. Winter days begin so late and end so early, like the dwindling span of life past three score.

Cadfael had taken Brother Mark at his word, and dozed the afternoon away. There was nowhere he could go, nothing he could do here, no work needing his efforts. But suddenly he started out of a doze, and there was Brother Mark, a meagre but erect and austere figure, standing over him with a benign smile on the ageless, priestly face Cadfael had seen in him ever since his scared, resentful, childish entry within these walls. The voice, soft, significant, delighted, rolled the years back; he was still eighteen, and a young eighteen at that.

'Wake up! I have something for you!'

Like a child coming on a father's birthday: 'Look! I made it for you myself!'

The carefully folded white napkin was lowered gently into Cadfael's lap. Brother Mark delicately turned back the folds, and exposed the contents with a gesture of such shy triumph that the analogy was complete. There it lay to be seen, a small, slightly misshapen vial of greenish glass, coloured somewhat differently all down one side, where yellowish brown coated the green, from a residue of liquid that still moved very sluggishly within.

'Light me that lamp!' said Cadfael, gathering the napkin in both hands to raise the prize nearer his eyes. Brother Mark laboured industriously with flint and tinder, and struck a spark into the wick of the little oil-lamp in its clay saucer, but the conflict of light, within and without, hardly bettered the view. There was a stopper made of a small plug of wood wrapped in a twist of wool cloth. Cadfael sniffed eagerly at the cloth on the side that was coloured brown. The odour was there, faint but unmistakable, his nose knew it well. Frost had dulled but still retained it. There was a long trail of thin, crusted oil, long dried, down the outside of the vial.

'Is it right? Have I brought what you wanted?' Brother Mark hovered, pleased and anxious.

'Lad, you have indeed! This little thing carried death in it, and, see, it can be hidden within a man's hand. It lay thus, on its side, as you found it? Where the residue has gathered and dried the length of the vial within? And without, too . . . It was stoppered and thrust out of sight in haste, surely about someone's person, and if he has not the mark of it somewhere about him still, this long ooze of oil from the leaking neck is a great deceiver. Now sit down here and tell me where and how you found it, for much depends on that. And can you find the exact spot again, without fail?'

'I can, for I marked it.' Flushed with pleasure at having pleased, Brother Mark sat down, leaning eagerly against Cadfael's sleeve. 'You know the houses there have a strip of garden going down almost to the water, there is only a narrow footpath along the edge of the pond below. I did not quite like to invent a reason for entering the gardens, and besides, they are narrow and steep. It would not be difficult to throw something of any weight from the house right to the edge of the water, and beyond – even for a woman, or a man in a hurry. So I went first along the path, the whole stretch of it that falls within reach from the kitchen window, the one you said was open that day. But it was not there I found it.'

'It was not?'

'No, but beyond. There's a fringe of ice round the edge of the pond now, but the current from the mill-race keeps all the middle clear. I found the bottle on my way back, after I'd searched all the grass and bushes there, and thought to look on the other side the path, along the rim of the water. And it was there, on its side half under the ice, held fast. I've driven a hazel twig into the ground opposite the place, and the hole I prised it from will stay unless we have a thaw. I think the bottle was thrown clear of whatever ice there may have been then, but not far enough out to be taken away by the mill current, and because the stopper was in it, it floated, and drifted back to be caught in the next frost. But, Cadfael, it couldn't have been thrown from the kitchen window, it was too far along the path.'

'You're sure of that? Then where? Is it the distance that seems too great?'

'No, but the direction. It's much too far to the right, and there's a bank of bushes between. The ground lies wrong for it. If a man threw it from the kitchen window it would not go where I found it, it could not. But from the window of the other room it well could. Do you remember, Cadfael, was that window unshuttered, too? The room where they were dining?'

Cadfael thought back to the scene within the house, when Richildis met him and ushered him desperately through to the bedchamber, past the disordered table laid with three trenchers. 'It was, it was! – the shutter was set open, for the midday sun came in there.' From that room Edwin had rushed in indignant offence, and out through the kitchen, where he was thought to have committed his crime and rid himself of the evidence later. But not for a moment had he been alone in that inner room; only in his precipitate flight had he been out of sight of all the household.

'You see, Mark, what this means? From what you say, this vial was either thrown from the window of the inner room, or else someone walked along that path and threw it into the pond. And neither of those things could Edwin have done. He might, as they suppose, have halted for a moment in the kitchen, but he certainly did not go along the path by the pond before making for the bridge, or Aelfric would have overtaken him. No, he would have been ahead of him, or met him at the gate! Nor did he have the opportunity, at any time afterwards, to dispose of the vial there. He hid with his bitter mood until Edwy found him, and from then on they were both in hiding until they came to me. This small thing, Mark, is proof that Edwin is as clear of guilt as you or I.'

'But it does not prove who the guilty man is,' said Mark.

'It does not. But if the bottle was indeed thrown from the window of that inner room, then it was done long after the death, for I doubt if anyone was alone in there for a moment until after the sergeant had come and gone. And if the one responsible carried this somewhere on him all that time, as ill-stoppered as it is now, then the marks of it will be on him. He might try to scrub the stain away, but it will not be easily removed. And who can afford to discard cotte or gown? No, the signs will be there to be found.'

'But what if it was someone else, not of the household, who did the deed, and flung the vial in from the pathway? Once you did wonder, about the cook and the scullions . . .'

'I won't say it's impossible. But is it likely? From the path a man could make very sure the vial went into the mid-current and the deep of the pool, and even if it did not sink – though he would have had time in that case to ensure that it did! – it would be carried away back to the brook and the river. But you see it fell short, and lay for us to find.'

'What must we do now?' asked Brother Mark, roused and ready.

'We must go to Vespers, my son, or we shall be late. And tomorrow we must get you, and this witness with you, to Hugh Beringar in Shrewsbury.'

The lay contingent at Vespers was always thin, but never quite absent. That evening Martin Bellecote had come down out of the town to give a word of hearty thanks first to God, and then to Cadfael, for his son's safe return. After the service ended he waited in the cloister for the brothers to emerge, and came to meet Cadfael at the south door.

'Brother, it's to you we owe it that the lad's home again, if it is with a flea in his ear, and not lying in some den in the castle for his pains.'

'Not to me, for I could not free him. It was Hugh Beringar who saw fit to send him home. And take my word, in all that may happen you can rely on Beringar for a decent, fair-minded man who'll not tolerate injustice. In any encounter with him, tell him the truth.'

Bellecote smiled, but wryly. 'Truth, but not all the truth, even to him – though he showed generous indeed to my boy, I grant you. But until the other one's as safe as Edwy, I keep my own counsel on where he is. But to you, brother . . .'

'No,' said Cadfael quickly, 'not to me, either, though soon, I hope, there may be no reason left for hiding him. But that time's not yet. Is all well, then, with your own family? And Edwy none the worse?'

'Never a whit the worse. Without a bruise or two he'd have valued his adventure less. It was all his own devising. But it's caused him to draw in his horns for a while. I never knew him so biddable before, and that's no bad thing. He's working with more zeal than he commonly shows. Not that we're overburdened with work, this close to the feast, but wanting Edwin, and now Meurig's gone to keep Christmas with his kin, I've enough on hand to keep my scamp busy.'

'So Meurig goes to his own people, does he?'

'Regularly for Christmas and Easter. He had cousins and an uncle or so up in the borders. He'll be back before the year ends. He sets store by his own folk, does Meurig.'

Yes, so he had said on the day Cadfael first encountered him. 'My kinship is my mother's kinship, I go with my own.

482

My father was not a Welshman.' Naturally he would want to go home for the feast.

'May we all be at peace for the Lord's nativity!' said Cadfael, with heartier optimism since the discovery of the small witness now lying on a shelf in his workshop.

'Amen to that, brother! And I and my household thank you for your stout aid, and if ever you need ours, you have but to say.'

Martin Bellecote went back to his shop with duty done, and Brother Cadfael and Brother Mark went to supper with duty still to be done.

'I'll go early into the town,' said Brother Mark, earnestly whispering in Cadfael's ear in a corner of the chapter-house, during some very lame readings in the Latin by Brother Francis, after the meal. 'I'll absent myself from Prime, what does it matter if I incur penance?'

'You will not,' Brother Cadfael whispered back firmly. 'You'll wait until after dinner, when you are freed to your own work, as this will truly be legitimate work for you, the best you could be about. I will not have you flout any part of the rule.'

'As you would not dream of doing, of course!' breathed Mark, and his plain, diffident face brightened beautifully into a grin he might have borrowed from Edwin or Edwy.

'For no reason but matter of life and death. And owning my fault! And you are not me, and should not be copying my sins. It will be all the same, after dinner or before,' he said reassuringly. 'You'll ask for Hugh Beringar – no one else, mind, I would not be sure of any other as I am of him. Take him and show him where you found the vial, and I think Edwin's family will soon be able to call him home again.'

Their planning was largely vain. The next morning's chapter undid such arrangements as they had made, and changed everything.

Brother Richard the sub-prior rose, before the minor matters of business were dealt with, to say that he had an item of some urgency, for which he begged the prior's attention.

'Brother Cellarer has received a messenger from our sheep-fold near Rhydycroesau, by Oswestry. Lay Brother Barnabas is fallen ill with a bad chest, and is in fever, and Brother Simon is left to take care of all the flock there alone. But more than this, he is doubtful of his skill to tend the sick brother successfully, and asks, if it's possible, that someone of more knowledge should come to help him for a while.'

'I have always thought,' said Prior Robert, frowning, 'that we should have more than two men there. We run two hundred sheep on those hills, and it is a remote place. But how did Brother Simon manage to send word, since he is the only able man left there?'

'Why, he took advantage of the fortunate circumstance that our steward is now in charge at the manor of Mallilie. It seems it is only a few miles from Rhydycroesau. Brother Simon rode there and asked that word be sent, and a groom was despatched at once. No time has been lost, if we can send a helper today.'

The mention of Mallilie had caused the prior to prick up his ears. It had also made Cadfael start out of his own preoccupations, since this so clearly had a bearing on the very problems he was pondering. So Mallilie was but a few short miles from the abbey sheepfolds near Oswestry! He had never stopped to consider that the exact location of the manor might have any significance, and this abrupt enlightenment started a number of mental hares out of their forms in bewildering flight.

'Clearly we must do so,' said Robert, and almost visibly reminded himself that the errand could with propriety be laid upon the abbey's most skilled herbalist and apothecary, which would effectively remove him not only from all contact with the Widow Bonel, but also from his meddlesome insistence on probing the unfortunate events which had made her a widow. The prior turned his silver, stately head and looked directly at Brother Cadfael, something he normally preferred not to do. The same considerations had dawned upon Cadfael, with the same pleasing effect. If I had devised this myself, he was thinking, it could not have been more apposite. Now young Mark can leave the errand to me, and remain here blameless.

'Brother Cadfael, it would seem this is a duty for you, who are accomplished in medicine. Can you at once put together all such preparations as may be needed for our sick brother?'

'I can and will, Father,' said Cadfael, so heartily that for a moment Prior Robert recoiled into doubt of his own wisdom and penetration. Why should the man be so happy at the prospect of a long winter ride, and hard work being both doctor and shepherd at the end of it? When he had been so assiduously poking his nose into the affairs of the Bonel household here? But the distance remained a guarantee; from Rhydycroesau he would be in no position to meddle further.

'I trust it may not be for very long. We shall say prayers for Brother Barnabas, that he may rally and thrive. You can again send word by the grooms at Mallilie, should there be need. And is your novice Mark well grounded enough for minor ailments in your absence? In cases of serious illness we may call on the physician.'

'Brother Mark is devoted and able,' said Cadfael, with almost paternal pride, 'and can be trusted absolutely, for if he feels himself in need of better counsel he will say so with modesty. And he has a good supply of all those remedies that may most be needed at this season. We have taken pains to provide against an ill winter.'

'That's very well. Then in view of the need, you may leave chapter and make ready. Take a good mule from the stables, and have food with you for the way, and make sure you're well provided for such an illness as Brother Barnabas seems to have contracted. If there is any case in the infirmary you feel you should visit before leaving, do so. Brother Mark shall be sent to you, you may have advice for him before you go.'

Brother Cadfael went out from the chapter-house and left them to their routine affairs. God is still looking our way, he thought, bustling blithely into his workshop and raking the shelves for all that he needed. Medicines for throat, chest, head, an unguent for rubbing into the chest, goose-grease and strong herbs. The rest was warmth and care and proper food. They had hens at Rhydycroesau, and their own good milch-cow, fed through the winter. And last, a thing he need take only into Shrewsbury, the little green glass vial, still wrapped in its napkin.

Brother Mark came with a rush and out of breath, sent from his Latin studies under Brother Paul. 'They say you're going away, and I'm to be custodian here. Oh. Cadfael, how shall I manage without you? And what of Hugh Beringar, and this proof we have for him?'

'Leave that to me now,' said Cadfael. 'To go to Rhydycroesau one must go through the town, I'll bear it to the castle myself. You pay attention only to what you've learned from me, for I know how well it's been learned, and I shall be here with you in spirit every moment. Imagine that you ask me, and you'll find the answer.' He had a jar of unguent in one hand, he reached the other with absent affection and patted the young, smooth tonsure ringed by rough, thick, spiky straw-coloured hair. 'It's only for a short while, we'll have Brother Barnabas on his feet in no time. And listen, child dear, the manor of Mallilie, I find, is but a short way from where I shall be, and it seems to me that the answer to what we need to know may be there, and not here.'

'Do you think so?' said Brother Mark hopefully, forgetting his own anxieties.

'I do, and I have a thought – no more than the gleam of an idea, that they loosed in me at chapter . . . Now make yourself useful! Go and bespeak me a good mule at the stables, and see all these thing into the saddle-bags for me. I have an errand to the infirmary before I leave.'

Brother Rhys was in his privileged place by the fire, hunched in his chair in a contented half-doze, but awake enough to open one eye pretty sharply at every movement and word around him. He was in the mood to welcome a visitor, and brightened into something approaching animation when Cadfael told him that he was bound for the north-west of the country, to the sheepfolds of Rhydycroesau.

'Your own countryside, brother! Shall I carry your greetings to the borderland? You'll still have kinsfolk there, surely, three generations of them.'

'I have so!' Brother Rhys bared toothless gums in a dreamy smile. 'If you should happen to meet with my cousin Cynfrith ap Rhys, or his brother Owain, give them my blessings. Ay, there's a mort of my people in those parts. Ask after my niece Angharad, my sister Marared's girl – my youngest sister, that is, the one who married Ifor ap Morgan. I doubt Ifor's dead before this, but if you should hear of him living, say I remember, and give him my good word. The girl ought to come and visit me, now her lad's working here in the town. I remember her as a little lass no higher than a daisy, and that pretty . . .'

'Angharad was the girl who went as maidservant in the house of Bonel of Mallilie?' said Cadfael, gently prompting.

'She did, a pity it was! But they've been there many years now, the Saxons. You get used to foreigner families, in time. They never got further, though. Mallilie's nothing but a thorn stuck in the side of Cynllaith. Stuck far in – nigh broken off, as some day it may be yet! It touches Saxon land barely at all, only by a claw . . .'

'Is that truth!' said Cadfael. 'Then properly speaking Mallilie, for all it was held by an Englishman, and has been three generations now, is rightly within Wales?'

'As Welsh as Snowdon,' said Brother Rhys, harking back to catch once again a spark of his old patriotic fire. 'And all the neighbours Welsh, and most of the tenants. I was born just to the west of it, nearby the church of Llansilin, which is the centre of the commote of Cynllaith. Welsh land from the beginning of the world!'

Welsh land! That could not be changed, merely because a Bonel in William Rufus's reign had pushed his way in and got a hold on some acres of it, and maintained his grasp under the patronage of the Earl of Chester ever since. Why did I never think, wondered Cadfael, to enquire earlier where this troublous manor lay? 'And Cynllaith has properly appointed Welsh judges? Competent to deal according to the code of Hywel Dda, not of Norman England?'

'Surely it has! A sound commote court as there is in Wales! The Bonels in their time have pleaded boundary cases, and suchlike, by whichever law best suited their own purposes, Welsh or English, what matter, provided it brought them gain? But the people like their Welsh code best, and the witness of neighbours, the proper way to settle a dispute. The just way!' said Brother Rhys righteously, and wagged his old head at Cadfael. 'What's all this of law, brother? Are you thinking of bringing suit yourself?' And he fell into a moist, pink-gummed giggling at the thought.

'Not I,' said Cadfael, rising, 'but I fancy one that I know of may be thinking of it.'

He went out very thoughtfully, and in the great court the low winter sun came out suddenly and flashed in his eyes, dazzling him for the second time. Paradoxically, in this momentary blindness he could see his way clearly at last.

Chapter Eight

E WOULD have liked to turn aside from the Wyle to have a word with Martin Bellecote and see for himself that the family were not being hounded, but he did not do it, partly because he had a more urgent errand on his mind, partly because he did not want to call attention to the house or the household. Hugh Beringar was one man, of independent mind and a strong attachment to justice, but the officers of the sheriffry of Shropshire were a very different matter, looking for their lead rather to Gilbert Prestcote, understandably enough, since Prestcote was King Stephen's official representative in these parts; and Prestcote's justice would be sharper, shorter-sighted, content with a brisk and tidy ending. Prestcote might be away in Westminster, Beringar might be nominally in charge, but the sergeants and their men would still be proceeding on their usual summary course, making for the most obvious quarry. It there was a watch set on Bellecote's shop, Cadfael had no intention of giving it any provocation. If there was not, so much the better, Hugh's orders had prevailed.

So Cadfael paced demurely up the Wyle and past the Bellecote yard without a glance, and on through the town. His way to the north-west lay over the bridge that led towards Wales, but he passed that, too, and climbed the hill to the High Cross; from that point the road descended slightly, to mount again into the castle gatehouse.

King Stephen's garrison was in full possession since the summer siege, and the watch, though vigilant, was assured and easy. Cadfael lighted down at the approach, and led his mule up the causeway and into the shadow of the gate. The guard waited for him placidly.

'Goodmorrow, brother! What's your will?'

'A word with Hugh Beringar of Maesbury,' said Cadfael. 'Tell him Brother Cadfael, and I think he'll spare me a short while of his time.'

'You're out of luck, brother, for the present while. Hugh Beringar is not here, and likely won't be till the light fails, for he's off on some search down the river with Madog of the Dead-boat.' That was news that heartened Cadfael as suddenly as the news of Hugh's absence had disheartened and dismayed him. He might have done better, after all, to leave the vial with Brother Mark, who could have paid a second visit after the first one missed its mask. Of all but Beringar here, Cadfael had his doubts, but now he was caught in a situation he should have foreseen. Hugh had lost no time in setting the hunt in motion after Edwin's reliquary, and better still, was pursuing it himself instead of leaving it to underlings. But long delay here to wait for him was impossible; Brother Barnabas lay ill, and Cadfael had undertaken to go and care for him, and the sooner he reached him the better. He pondered whether to entrust his precious evidence to another, or keep it until he could deliver it to Beringar in person. Edwin, after all, was somewhere at liberty yet, no immediate ill could befall him.

'If it's the matter of the poisoning you're here about,' said the guard helpfully, 'speak a word to the sergeant who's left in charge here. I hear there's been strange goings-on down at the abbey. You'll be glad when you're left in quiet again, and the rascal taken. Step in, brother, and I'll tether your mule and send to let William Warden know you're here.'

Well, no harm, at any rate, in taking a look at the law's surrogate and judging accordingly. Cadfael waited in a stony anteroom within the gatehouse, and let the object of his visit lie hidden in his scrip until he made up his mind. But the first glimpse of the sergeant as he entered rendered it virtually certain that the vial would remain in hiding. The same officer who had first answered the prior's summons to Bonel's house, bearded, brawny, hawk-beaked, self-assured and impatient of caution once his nose had found an obvious trail. He knew

Cadfael again just as promptly; large white teeth flashed in a scornful grin in the bushy beard.

'You again, brother? And still finding a dozen reasons why young Gurney must be blameless, when all that's wanting is a witness who stood by and watched him do the deed? Come to throw some more dust in our eyes, I suppose, while the guilty make off into Wales?'

'I came,' said Brother Cadfael, not strictly truthfully, 'to enquire whether anything had yet come to light, concerning what I reported to Hugh Beringar yesterday.'

'Nothing has and nothing will. So it was you who set him off on this fool's errand down the river! I might have guessed it! A glib young rogue tells you a tall tale like that, and you swallow it, and infect your betters into the bargain! Wasteful nonsense! to spare men to row up and down Severn in the cold, after a reliquary that never was! You have much to answer for, brother.'

'No doubt I have,' agreed Cadfael equably. 'So have we all, even you. But to exert himself for truth and justice is Beringar's duty, and so it is yours and mine, and I do it as best I may, and forbear from snatching at what offers first and easiest, and shutting my eyes to everything else in order to be rid of the labour, and at ease again. Well, it seems I've troubled you for nothing. But let Hugh Beringar know that I was here asking for him.'

He eyed the sergeant closely at that, and doubted whether even that message would be delivered. No, grave evidence that pointed the wrong way could not be left with this man, who was so sure of his rightness he might bend even circumstances and facts to match his opinions. No help for it, the vial would have to go on to Rhydycroesau and wait its time, when Brother Barnabas was restored, and back among his sheep.

'You mean well, brother,' said William generously, 'but you are far out of your cloister in matters like these. Best leave them to those who have experience.'

Cadfael took his leave without further protest, mounted his mule, and rode back through the town to the foot of the hill, where the street turning off to the right led him to the westward bridge. At least nothing was lost, and Beringar was following up the lead he had given. It was time now to keep his mind on the journey before him, and put aside the affairs of Richildis and her son until he had done his best for Brother Barnabas.

The road from Shrewsbury to Oswestry was one of the main highroads of the region, and fairly well maintained. The old people, the Romans, had laid it long ago when they ruled in Britain, and the same road ran south-eastward right to the city of London, where King Stephen was now preparing to keep Christmas among his lords, and Cardinal-bishop Alberic of Ostia was busy holding his legatine council for the reform of the church, to the probable discomfiture of Abbot Heribert. But here, riding in the opposite direction, the road ran straight and wide, only a little overgrown with grass here and there, and encroached upon by the wild verges, through fat farming country and woods to the town of Oswestry, a distance of no more than eighteen miles. Cadfael took it at a brisk but steady pace, to keep the mule content. Beyond the town it was but four miles to the sheepfolds. In the distance, as he rode due west in the dimming light, the hills of Wales rose blue and noble, the great rolling ridge of Berwyn melting into a faintly misted sky.

He came to the small, bare grange in a fold of the hills before dark. A low, solid wooden hut housed the brothers, and beyond lay the much larger byres and stables, where the sheep could be brought in from ice and snow, and beyond again, climbing the gentle slopes, the long, complex grey-stone walls of the field enclosures, where they grazed in this relatively mild beginning of winter, and were fed roots and grain if ever stubble and grass failed them. The hardiest were still out at liberty in the hills. Brother Simon's dog began to bark, pricking his ears to the neat hooves that hardly made a sound in the thin turf of the ride.

Cadfael lighted down at the door, and Simon came eagerly out to welcome him, a thin, wiry, dishevelled brother, some forty years old but still distrait as a child when anything went wrong with other than sheep. Sheep he knew as mothers know their babes, but Brother Barnabas's illness had utterly undone him. He clasped Cadfael's hands in his, and shook them and himself in his gratitude at no longer being alone with his patient.

'He has it hard, Cadfael, you hear the leaves of his heart rustling as he breathes, like a man's feet in the woods in autumn. I cannot break it with a sweat, I've tried . . .'

'We'll try again,' said Cadfael comfortably and went into the dark, timber-scented hut before him. Within it was blessedly warm and dry; wood is the best of armours against weather, where there's small fear of fire, as in this solitude there was none. A bare minimum of furnishing, yet enough; and within, in the inner room Brother Barbanas lay in his bed neither asleep nor awake, only uneasily in between, rustling at every breath as

Simon had said, his forehead hot, and dry, his eyes half-open and vacant. A big, massive man, all muscle and bone, with reserves of fight in him that needed only a little guidance.

'You go look to whatever you should be doing,' said Cadfael, unbuckling his scrip and opening it on the foot of the bed, 'and leave him to me.'

'Is there anything you will need?' asked Simon anxiously.

'A pan of water on the fire, out there, and a cloth, and a beaker ready, and that's all. If I want for more, I'll find it.'

Blessedly, he was taken at his word; Brother Simon had a childlike faith in all who practised peculiar mysteries. Cadfael worked upon Brother Barnabas without haste all the evening, by a single candle that Simon brought as the light died. A hot stone wrapped in Welsh flannel for the sick man's feet, a long and vigorous rub for chest and throat and ribs, down to the waist, with an ointment of goose-grease impregnated with mustard and other heat-giving herbs, and chest and throat then swathed in a strip of the same flannel, cool cloths on the dry forehead, and a hot draught of wine mulled with spices and borage and other febrifuge herbs. The potion went down patiently and steadily, with eased breathing and relaxing sinews. The patient slept fitfully and uneasily; but in the middle of the night the sweat broke like a storm of rain, drenching the bed. The two attentive nurses lifted the patient, when the worst was past, drew the blanket from under him and laid a fresh one, rolled him close in another, and covered him warmly again.

'Go and sleep,' said Cadfael, content, 'for he does very well. By dawn he'll be wake and hungry.'

In that he was out by some hours, for Brother Barnabas, once fallen into a deep and untroubled sleep, slept until almost noon of the following day, when he awoke clear-eyed and with quiet breathing, but weak as a new lamb.

'Never trouble for that,' said Cadfael cheerfully. 'Even if you were on your feet, we should hardly let you out of here for a couple of days, or longer. You have time in plenty, enjoy being idle. Two of us are enough to look after your flock for you.'

Brother Barnabas, again at ease in his body, was content to take him at his word, and luxuriate in his convalescence. He ate, at first doubtfully, for savour had left him in his fever, then, rediscovering the pleasures of taste, his appetite sharpened into fierce hunger.

'The best sign we could have,' said Cadfael. 'A man who eats heartily and with enjoyment is on his way back to health.'

And they left the patient to sleep again as thoroughly as he had eaten, and went out to the sheep, and the chickens and the cow, and all the rest of the denizens of the fold.

'An easy year so far,' said Brother Simon, viewing his leggy, tough hill-sheep with satisfaction. Sheep as Welsh as Brother Cadfael gazed towards the south–west, where the long ridge Berwyn in the distance; long, haughty, inscrutable faces, and sharp ears, and knowing yellow eyes that could outstare a saint. 'Plenty of good grazing still, what with the grass growing so late, and the good pickings they had in the stubble after harvest. And we have beet-tops, they make good fodder, too. There'll be better fleeces than most years, when next they're shorn, unless the winter turns cruel later on.'

From the crest of the hill above the walled folds Brother Cadfael gazed towards the south–west, where the long ridge dipped towards lower land, between the hills. 'This manor of Mallilie will be somewhere in the sheltered land there, as I judge.'

'It is. Three miles round by the easy track, the manor-house drawn back between the slopes, and the lands open to the south-east. Good land for these parts. And main glad I was to know we had a steward there, when I needed a messenger. Have you an errand there, brother?'

'There's something I must see to, when Brother Barnabas is safely on the way to health again, and I can be spared.' He turned and looked back towards the east. 'Even here we must be a good mile or more the Welsh side of the old boundary dyke. I never was here before, not being a sheep man. I'm from Gwynedd myself, from the far side of Conwy. But even these hills look like home to me.'

Gervase Bonel's manor must lie somewhat further advanced into Welsh land even than these high pastures. The Benedictines had very little hold in Wales, Welshmen preferred their own ancient Celtic Christianity, the solitary hermitage of the self-exiled saint and the homely little college of Celtic monks rather than the shrewd and vigorous foundations that looked to Rome. In the south, secular Norman adventurers had penetrated more deeply, but here Mallilie must, indeed, as Brother Rhys had said, be lodged like a single thorn deep in the flesh of Wales.

'It does not take long to ride to Mallilie,' said Brother Simon, anxiously helpful. 'Our horse here is elderly, but strong, and gets little enough work as a rule. I could very well manage now, if you want to go tomorrow.'

'First let's see,' said Cadfael, 'how Brother Barnabas progresses by tomorrow.'

Brother Barnabas progressed very well once he had the fever out of him. Before nightfall he was sick of lying in his bed, and insisted on rising and trying his enfeebled legs about the room. His own natural strength and stout heart were all he needed now to set him up again, though he swallowed tolerantly whatever medicines Cadfael pressed upon him, and consented to have his chest and throat anointed once again with the salve.

'No need to trouble yourself for me now,' he said. 'I shall be hale as a hound pup in no time. And if I can't take to the hills again for a day or two – though I very well could, if you would but let me! – I can see to the house here, and the hens and the cow, for that matter.'

The next morning he rose to join them for Prime, and would not return to his bed, though when they both harried him he agreed to sit snugly by the fire, and exert himself no further than in baking bread and preparing dinner.

'Then I will go,' said Cadfael, 'if you can manage alone for the day, Simon. If I leave now I shall have the best of the daylight, and be back with you in time for the evening work.'

Brother Simon went out with him to where the track branched, and gave him directions. After the hamlet of Croesau Bach he would come to a cross roads, and turn right, and from that point he would see how the hills were cleft ahead of him, and making straight for that cleft he would come to Mallilie, beyond which the track continued westward to Llansilin, the central seat of the commote of Cynllaith.

The morning was faintly misty, but with the sun bright through the mist, and the turf wet and sparkling with the hint of rime already melting. He had chosen to ride the horse from the grange rather than his mule, since the mule had had lengthy exercise on the way north, and was entitled to a rest. The horse was an ungainly bay, of homely appearance but amiable disposition and stout heart, willing and ready for work. It was pleasant to be riding here alone in a fine winter morning on cushioned turf, between hills that took him back to his youth, with no routine duties and no need for talk, beyond the occasional greeting for a woman splitting kindling in her yard, or a man moving sheep to a new pasture, and even that was a special pleasure because he found himself instinctively calling his good-day in Welsh. The holdings here were scattered and few until he came through Croesau into lower and richer ground, where the patterns of ordered tillage told him he was already entering Mallilie land. A brook sprang into life on his right hand, and accompanied him towards the cleft where the hill-slopes on either side drew close together. Within a mile it was a little river, providing level meadows on either bank, and the dark selions of ploughed land beyond. Trees clothed the upper slopes, the valley faced south-east into the morning sun; a good place, its tenant holdings sheltered and well found. Well into the defile, drawn back into a fold of the slope on his right, and half-circled with arms of woodland, he came to the manor-house.

A timber stockade surrounded it, massive and high, but the house stood on rising ground, and showed tall above it. Built of local stone, granite grey, with a great long roof of slates, gleaming like fish-scales in the sun as the frost on them turned to dew. When he had crossed the river by a plank-bridge and ridden in at the open gate of the stockade, the whole length of the house lay before him, a tall stone stair leading up to the main door of the living floor at the left-hand end. At ground level three separate doors, wide enough to take in country carts, led into what was evidently a vaulted undercroft, with storage room enough for a siege. Judging by the windows in the gable end, there was yet another small room above the kitchen. The windows of hall and solar were stone-mullioned and generous. Round the inner side of the stockade there were ample outhouses, stables, mews and stores. Norman lordlings, promised heirs, Benedictine abbeys might well covet such a property. Richildis had indeed married out of her kind.

The servants here would be Bonel's servants, continuing their functions under a new rule. A groom came to take Cadfael's bridle, feeling no need to question one who arrived in a Benedictine habit. There were few people moving about the court, but those few assured in their passage; and impressive though the house was, it could never have needed a very numerous body to run it. All local people, surely, and that meant Welsh people, like the serving-maid who had warmed her lord's bed and borne him a disregarded son. It happened! Bonel might even have been an attractive man then, and given her pleasure, as well as a child; and at least he had kept her thereafter, and the child with her, though as mere indulged dependents, not members of his family, not his kin. A man who did not take more than he felt to be legally his, but would not forgo any item of what fell within that net. A man who let an unclaimed villein holding go to a hungry younger son from a free family, on terms of customary service, and then, with the law firmly behind him, claimed that questionable tenant as villein by reason of the dues rendered between them, and his progeny as unfree by the same code.

In this disputed borderland of soil and law, Cadfael found his heart and mind utterly Welsh, but could not deny that the Englishman had just as passionately held by his own law, and been sure that he was justified. He had not been an evil man, only a child of his time and place, and his death had been murder.

Properly speaking, Cadfael had no business at this house but to observe, as now he had observed. But he went in, nevertheless, up the outdoor stair and into the passage screened off from the hall. A boy emerging from the kitchen louted to him and passed, accepted him as one of the breed, who would know his way here. The hall was lofty and strongly beamed. Cadfael passed through it to the solar. This must be where Bonel had intended to install the panelling commissioned from Martin Bellecote, the transaction which had first caused him to set eyes and heart on Richildis Gurney, who had once been Richildis Vaughan, daughter of an honest, unpretentious tradesman.

Martin had done good work, and fitted it into place here with skill and love. The solar was narrower than the hall, there being a garderobe off it, and a tiny chapel. It glowed and was scented with the polished and sparely carved oak panelling, the suave silvery grain glinting in the light from the wide window. Edwin had a good brother and a good master. He need not repine if he missed the illusory heritage.

'Your pardon, brother!' said a respectful voice at Cadfael's back. 'No one told me there was a messenger here from Shrewsbury.'

Cadfael turned, startled, to take a look at the abbey's steward here; a layman, a lawman, young enough to be deferential to his employers, mature enough to be in command of his own province.

'It's I who should ask your pardon,' said Cadfael, 'for walking in upon you without ceremony. Truth to tell, I have no errand here, but being in the neighbourhood I was curious to see our new manor.'

'If it is indeed ours,' said the steward ruefully, and looked about him with a shrewd eye, assessing what the abbey might

496

well be losing. 'It seems to be in doubt at the moment, though that makes no difference to my commission here, to maintain it in good order, however the lot falls in the end. The place has been run well and profitably. But if you are not sent to join us here, brother, where is your domicile? As long as we hold the manor, we can well offer you lodging, if it please you to stay.'

'That I can't,' said Cadfael. 'I was sent from Shrewsbury to take care of an ailing brother, a shepherd at the folds by Rhydycroesau, and until he's restored I must take on his duties there.'

'Your patient is mending, I trust?'

'So well that I thought I might use a few hours to come and see what manner of property may be slipping through our fingers here. But have you any immediate reason for feeling that our tenure may be threatened? More than the obvious difficulty of the charter not being sealed in time?'

The steward frowned, chewing a dubious lip. 'The situation is strange enough, for if both the secular heir and the abbey lose their claim, the future of Mallilie is a very open question. The Earl of Chester is the overlord, and may bestow it as he pleases, and in troublous times like these I doubt if he'll want to leave it in monastic hands. We could appeal to him, true, but not until Shrewsbury has an abbot again, with full powers. All we can do in the meantime is manage this land until there's a legal decision. Will you take your dinner here with me, brother? Or at least a cup of wine?'

Cadfael declined the offer of a midday meal; it was yet early, and he had a use for the remaining hours of daylight. But he accepted the wine with pleasure. They sat down together in the panelled solar, and the dark Welsh kitchen-boy brought them a flagon and two horns.

'You've had no trouble with the Welsh to west of you?' asked Cadfael.

'None. They've been used to the Bonels as neighbours for fifty years now, and no bad blood on either side. Though I've had little contact except with our own Welsh tenants. You know yourself, brother, both sides of the border here there are both Welsh and English living cheek by jowl, and most of those one side have kin on the other.'

'One of our oldest brothers,' said Cadfael, 'came from this very region, from a village between here and Llansilin. He was talking of his old kinship when he knew I was coming to Rhydycroesau. I'd be glad to carry his greetings, if I can find

497

his people. Two cousins he mentioned, Cynfrith and Owain ap Rhys. You haven't encountered either? And a brother by marriage, one Ifor ap Morgan . . . though it must be many years since he had any contact with any of them, and for ought I know this Ifor ap Morgan may be dead long ago. He must be round about Rhys's own age, and few of us last so long.'

The steward shook his head doubtfully. 'Cynfrith ap Rhys I've heard spoken of, he has a holding half a mile or so west of here. Ifor ap Morgan . . . no, I know nothing of him. But I tell you what, if he's living the boy will know, he's from Llansilin himself. Question him when you leave, and do it in Welsh, for all he knows English well enough. You'll get more out of him in Welsh . . . and all the more readily,' he added with a wry grin, 'if I'm not with you. They're none of them ill-disposed, but they keep their own counsel, and it's wonderful how they fail to understand English when it suits them to shut the alien out.'

'I'll try it,' said Cadfael, 'and my thanks for the good advice.'

'Then you'll forgive me if I don't accompany you to the gate and give you God-speed. You'll do better alone.'

Cadfael took the hint and his leave, there in the solar, and went out through the hall and by the screened way into the kitchen. The boy was there, backing red-faced from the oven with a tray of new loaves. He looked round warily as he set down his burden on the clay top to cool gradually. It was neither fear nor distrust, but the wariness of a wild creature alert and responsive to every living thing, curious and ready to be friendly, sceptical and ready to vanish.

'God save you, son!' said Cadfael in Welsh. 'If you bread's all out now, do a Christian deed, come out to the gate with me, and show a stranger the way to the holding of Cynfrith ap Rhys or his brother Owain.'

The boy gazed, eyes brightening into interest at being addressed placidly in his own tongue. 'You are from Shrewsbury abbey, sir? A monk?'

'I am.'

'But Welsh?'

'As Welsh as you, lad, but not from these parts. The vale of Conwy is my native place, near by Trefriw.'

'What's your will with Cynfrith ap Rhys?' asked the boy directly.

Now I know I'm in Wales, thought Cadfael. An English servant, if he ventured to challenge your proceedings at all, would do it roundabout and obsequiously, for fear of getting his ears clipped, but your Welsh lad speaks his mind to princes.

'In our abbey,' he said obligingly, 'there's an old brother who used to be known in these parts as Rhys ap Griffith, and he's cousin to these other sons of Rhys. When I left Shrewsbury I said I'd take his greetings to his kin, and so I will if I can find them. And while we're about it there's one more name he gave me, and you may at least be able to tell me if the man's alive or dead, for he must be old. Rhys had a sister Marared, who married one Ifor ap Morgan, and they had a daughter Angharad, though I'm told she's dead years ago. But if Ifor is still living I'll speak the good word to him, also.'

Under this rain of Welsh names the boy thawed into smiles. 'Sir, Ifor ap Morgan is still alive. He lives a fair way beyond, nearly to Llansilin. I'll come out with you and show you the way.'

He skipped down the stone staircase lightly, ahead of Cadfael, and trotted before him to the gate. Cadfael followed, leading his horse, and looked where the boy pointed, westward between the hills.

'To the house of Cynfrith ap Rhys it is but half a mile, and it lies close by the track, on your right hand, with the wattle fence round the yard. You'll see his white goats in the little paddock. For Ifor ap Morgan you must go further. Keep to the same track again until you're through the hills, and looking down into the valley, then take the path to the right, that fords our river before it joins the Cynllaith. Half a mile on, look to your right again, just within the trees, and you'll see a little wooden house, and that's where Ifor lives. He's very old now, but he lives alone still.'

Cadfael thanked him and mounted.

'And for the other brother, Owain,' said the boy cheerfully, willing enough now to tell all he knew that might be helpful, 'if you're in these parts two more days you may catch him in Llansilin the day after tomorrow, when the commote court meets, for he has a dispute that was put off from the last sitting, along with some others. The judges have been viewing the impleaded lands, and the day after tomorrow they're to give judgement. They never like to let bad blood continue at the Christmas feast. Owain's holding is well beyond the town, but you'll find him at Llansilin church, sure enough. One of his neighbours moved his boundary stone, or so he claims.'

He had said more than he realised, but he was serenely innocent of the impression he had made on Brother Cadfael. One question, perhaps the most vital of all, had been answered without ever having to be asked.

Cynfrith ap Rhys – the kinship seemed to be so full of Rhyses that in some cases it was necessary to list three generations back in order to distinguish them – was easily found, and very willing to pass the time of day even with a Benedictine monk, seeing that the monk spoke Welsh. He invited Cadfael in heartily, and the invitation was accepted with pleasure. The house was one room and a cupboard of a kitchen, a solitary man's domain, and there was no sign of any other creature here but Cynfrith and his goats and hens. A solid, thickset, prominent-boned Welshman was Cynfrith, with wiry black hair now greying round the edges and balding on the crown, and quick, twinkling eyes set in the webs of good-humoured creases common to outdoor men. Twenty years at least younger than his cousin in the infirmary at Shrewsbury. He offered bread and goat's-milk cheese, and wrinkled, sweet apples.

'The good old soul, so he's still living! Many a time I've wondered. He's my mother's cousin in the first degree, not mine, but time was I knew him well. He'll be nearing four-score now, I suppose. And still comfortable in his cloister? I'll send him a small flask of the right liquor, brother, if you'll be so kind as to carry it. I distil it myself, it will stand him in good stead through the winter, a drop in season is good for the heart, and does the memory no harm, either. Well, well, and to think he still remembers us all! My brother? Oh, be sure I'll pass on the word to Owain when I see him. He has a good wife, and grown sons, tell the old man, the elder, Elis, is to marry in the spring. The day after tomorrow I shall be seeing my brother, he has a judgment coming up at the commote court at Llansilin.'

'So they told me at Mallilie,' said Cadfael. 'I wish him good speed with it.'

'Ah, well, he claims Hywel Fychan, who lives next him, shifted one of his boundary stones, and I daresay he did, but I wouldn't say but what Owain has done the like by Hywel in his time. It's an old sport with us . . . But I needn't tell you, you being of the people yourself. They'll make it up as the court rules, they always do until the next time, and no hard feelings. They'll drink together this Christmas.'

'So should we all,' said Cadfael, somewhat sententiously.

He took his leave as soon but as graciously as he well might, truthfully claiming another errand and the shortness of the daylight, and rode on his way by the little river, both heartened and chastened by contact with open and fearless goodwill. The little flask of powerful home-distilled spirit swung in his scrip; he was glad he had left the other, the poisoned one, behind at the sheepfold.

He came through the defile, and saw the valley of the Cynllaith open before him, and the track to the right weaving a neat line through rising grass to ford the little tributary. Half a mile beyond, woodland clothed the slope of the ridge, and in the full leaf of summer it might have been difficult to detect the low wooden house within the trees; but now, with all the leaves fallen, it stood clear behind the bare branches like a contented domestic hen in a coop. There was clear grass almost to its fence, and on one side continuing behind it, the veil of trees drawn halfway round like a curtain. Cadfael turned in towards it, and circled with the skirt of grass, seeing no door in the side that faced the track. A horse on a long tether came ambling round the gable end, placidly grazing; a horse as tall and rakish and unbeautiful as the one he rode, though probably some years older. At sight of it he pulled up short, and sat at gaze for a moment, before lighting down into the coarse grass.

There must, of course, be many horses that would answer to the description given: a bony old piebald. This one was certainly that, very strikingly black and white in improbable patterns. But they could not all, surely, be called by the same name?

Cadfael dropped his bridle and went softly forward towards the serenely feeding beast, which paid him no attention whatever after a single glance. He chirruped to it, and called quietly: 'Japhet!'

The piebald pricked long ears and lifted a gaunt, amiable head, stretching out a questing muzzle and dilated nostrils towards the familiar sound, and having made up his mind he was not mistaken, advanced confidently and briskly to the hand Cadfael extended. He ran caressing fingers up the tall forehead, and along the stretched, inquisitive neck. 'Japhet, Japhet, my friend, what are you doing here?'

The rustle of feet in the dry grass, while all four feet of this mild creature were still, caused Cadfael to look up sharply towards the corner of the house. A venerable old man stood looking at him steadily and silently; a tall old man, white-haired and white-bearded, but still with brows black and thick as gorse-bushes, and eyes as starkly blue as a winter sky beneath them. His dress was the common homespun of the countryman, but his carriage and height turned it into purple.

'As I think,' said Cadfael, turning towards him with one hand still on Japhet's leaning neck, 'you must be Ifor ap Morgan. My name is Cadfael, sometime Cadfael ap Meilyr ap Dafydd of Trefriw. I have an errand to you from Rhys ap Griffith, your wife's brother, who is now Brother Rhys of the abbey of Shrewsbury.

The voice that emerged from the long, austere, dry lips was deep and sonorous, a surprising music. 'Are you sure your errand is not to a guest of mine, brother?'

'It was not,' said Cadfael, 'it was to you. Now it is to both. And the first thing I would say is, keep this beast out of sight, for if I can know him again from a mere description, so can others.'

The old man gave him a lengthy, piercing blue stare. 'Come into the house,' he said, and turned on his heel and led the way. But Cadfael took time to lead Japhet well behind the house and shorten his tether to keep him there, before he followed.

In the dimness within, smoky and wood-scented, the old man stood with a hand protectively on Edwin's shoulder; and Edwin, with the impressionable generosity of youth, had somehow gathered to himself a virgin semblance of the old man's dignity and grace, and stood like him, erect and quiet within his untried body as was Ifor ap Morgan in his old and experienced one, copied the carriage of his head and the high serenity of his regard.

'The boy tells me,' said Ifor, 'that you are a friend. His friends are welcome.'

'Brother Cadfael has been good to me,' said Edwin, 'and to my nephew, Edwy, also, as Meurig told us. I have been well blessed in my friends. But how did you find me?'

'By not looking for you,' said Cadfael. 'Indeed, I've been at some pains *not* to know where you had taken yourself, and certainly I never rode this way to find you. I came with a harmless errand to Ifor ap Morgan here, from that same old brother you visited with Meurig in our infirmary. Your wife's brother, friend, Rhys ap Griffith, is still living, and for his age hale, too, in our convent, and when he heard that I was bound into these parts he charged me to bring his kinsmen his greetings and prayers. He has not forgotten his kin, though it's long since he came among you, and I doubt he'll come no more. I have been with Cynfrith ap Rhys, and sent the same word by him to his brother Owain, and if there are any others of his generation left, or who would remember him, be kind enough to give them word, when chance offers, that he remembers his blood and his own soil yet, and all those whose roots are in it.'

'So he would,' said Ifor, melting suddenly into a warm smile. 'He was always a loyal kinsman, and fond of my child and all the other young in our clan, having none of his own. He lost his wife early, or he'd have been here among us yet. Sit down a while, brother, and tell me how he does, and if you'll take my blessings back to him, I'll be grateful.'

'Meurig will have told you much of what I can tell,' and Cadfael, settling beside him on a bench at the rough table, 'when he brought you Edwin to shelter. Is he not here with you?'

'My grandson is away making the round of all kins and neighbours,' said the old man, 'for he comes home rarely now. He'll be here again in a few days, I daresay. He did tell me he'd been to see the old man, along with the boy here, but he stayed only an hour or so before making off about his visiting. There'll be time to talk when he comes back.'

It was in Cadfael's mind that he ought to cut short his own stay, for though it had never entered his mind that the officers of the law might find it worth while to keep a watch on him when he left Shrewsbury, the too easy discovery of Edwin in this house had shaken his assurance. It was true that he had neither expected nor wished to trace the boy as yet, but even Hugh Beringar, let alone his underlings, might well have considered the contrary as a possibility, and set a discreet hound on his trail. But he could not flatly deliver his message and go, while the old man clearly took pleasure in polishing up old memories. He was rambling away happily about the time when his wife was with him, and his daughter a fair and lively child. Now all that remained to him was a single grandson, and his own dignity and integrity.

Exile and refuge in this remote place and this impressive company had had a strong effect on Edwin. He withdrew into the shadows to leave his elders undisturbed, making no plea, asking no question yet concerning his own troubled affairs. Quietly he went and brought beakers and a pitcher of mead, and served them unobtrusively and neatly, all dignity and humility, and again absented himself, until Ifor turned to reach a long arm and draw him to the table.

'Young man, you must have things to ask of Brother Cadfael, and things to tell him.'

The boy had not lost his tongue, after all, once invited he could talk as volubly and vehemently as ever. First he asked after Edwy, with an anxiety he would never have revealed to the object of it, and was greatly eased to hear how that adventure had ended better than it had threatened. 'And Hugh Beringar was so fair and generous? And he listened to you, and is looking for my box? Now if he could but find it . . .! I was not happy leaving Edwy to play that part for me, but he would have it so. And then I took Japhet a roundabout way to a place we used to play sometimes, a copse by the river, and Meurig met me there, and gave me a token to carry to his grandfather here, and told me how to find the place. And the next day he came, too, as he said he would.'

'And what,' asked Cadfael gently, 'had you planned to do, if truth never did come out? If you could not go back? Though God forbid it should end so, and God granting, I'll see that it does not.'

The boy's face was solemn but clear; he had thought much, here in his haven, and spent so much time contemplating the noble face of his patron that a kind of shining likeness had arisen between them. 'I'm strong, I can work, I could earn my keep in Wales, if need be, even if it must be as an outlander. Other men have had to leave their homes because of unjust accusations, and have made their way in the world, and so could I. But I'd rather go back. I don't want to leave my mother, now that she's alone, and her affairs in such disorder. And I don't want to be remembered as the man who poisoned his stepfather and ran away, when I know I never did him harm or wished him any.'

'That shall not happen,' said Cadfael firmly. 'You lie close in cover a few days more, and put your trust in God, and I believe we shall get to the truth, and you can go home openly and proudly.'

'Do you believe that? Or is it just to hearten me?'

'I believe it. Your heart is not in want of bolstering up with false cheer. And I would not lie to you, even for good cause.' Yet there were lies, or at least unspoken truths, hanging heavy on his mind in this house, and he had better make his farewells and go, the passing of time and daylight giving him a sound excuse. 'I must get back to Rhydycroesau,' he said, making to rise from the table, 'for I've left Brother Simon to do all the work alone, and Brother Barnabas still shaky on his legs yet. Did I tell you I was sent there to get a sick man well again, and to supply his place while he was mending?'

'You'll come again if there's news?' said Edwin, and if his voice was resolutely steady, his eyes were anxious.

'I'll come again *when* there's news.'

'You'll be in Rhydycroesau some days yet?' asked Ifor ap Morgan. 'Then we shall see you again at more leisure, I trust.'

He was leading the way to the door to speed his guest, his hand again possessive on Edwin's shoulder, when he halted suddenly, stiffening, and with the other hand, outstretched with spread fingers, halted them, too, and enjoined silence. Age had not dulled those ancient ears; he was the first to catch the muted sound of voices. Not muted by distance, close and deliberately quiet. The dry grass rustled. In the edge of the trees one of the tethered horses whinnied enquiringly, giving notice of other horses approaching.

'Not Welsh!' said Ifor in a soundless whisper. 'English! Edwin, go into the other room.'

The boy obeyed instantly and silently; but in a moment he was back, shadowy in the doorway. 'They're there – two, outside the window. In leather, armed . . .'

The voices had drawn nearer, outside the house-door, their whispers grew louder, satisfied, abandoning stealth.

'That's the pied beast . . . no mistaking it!'

'What did I tell you? I said if we found the one we'd find the other.'

Someone laughed, low and contentedly. Then abruptly a fist thudded at the door, and the same voice called aloud, peremptorily: 'Open to the law!' The formality was followed up immediately by a strong thrust, hurling the door inwards to the wall, and the doorway was filled by the burly figure of the bearded sergeant from Shrewsbury, with two men-at-arms at his back. Brother Cadfael and William Warden confronted each other at a distance of a couple of feet; mutual recognition made the one bristle and the other grin.

'Well met, Brother Cadfael! And sorry I am I have no writ for you, but my business is with the young man behind you. I'm addressed to Edwin Gurney. And you, I think, my lad, are he?'

Edwin came forward a step from the inner doorway, pale as his shirt and huge-eyed, but with a chin jutting valiantly, and a stare like a levelled lance. He had learned a great deal in his few days here. 'That is my name,' he said.

'Then I arrest you on suspicion of the murder of Gervase Bonel by poison, and I'm here to take you back in custody to answer the charge in Shrewsbury.'

Chapter Nine

FOR AP Morgan drew himself up in a single long breath, seeming to grow half a head in the process, and stood forth to face his unexpected visitor.

'Fellow,' he said in his deep voice, in itself a weapon, 'I am the master of this house, and you have not, as yet, addressed yourself to me. There are visitors I invite, there are some I welcome, unexpected. You I do not know and have not invited, and you I do not welcome. Have the courtesy to make yourself known to me, if you have business with me or with others under my roof. Otherwise, leave this house.'

It could not be said that the sergeant was abashed, since he was protected by his office from any personal humiliation; but he did make a shrewd appraisal of this venerable person, and abate what would otherwise have been a boldly abrasive manner. 'I understand that you are Ifor ap Morgan. I am William Warden, a sergeant serving under Gilbert Prestcote, the sheriff of Shropshire, and I am in pursuit of Edwin Gurney on suspicion of murder. My commission is to bring him by whatever means to Shrewsbury, where the charge stands, and that I shall do, as I am bound. You also, as an elder of this region, are bound by law.'

'But not by English law,' said Ifor simply.

'By law! Knowing murder for murder, by whatever law. Murder by poison, grandsire!'

507

Brother Cadfael glanced once at Edwin, who stood motionless and pale, one hand advanced to take the old man pleadingly and comfortingly by the arm, but too much in awe and love of him to complete the gesture. Cadfael did it for him, laying a hand gently on the lean old wrist. For whatever was done and said now, they would take the boy with them. If there were three of them there, and two guarding the rear of the house, who was to stop them? And this was a self-assured, arrogant man, who might take petty revenges for past impudent reverses, but who would also have full regard for his own skin when dealing with a deputy sheriff of Beringar's measure, who might unaccountably have strict scruples about the handling of prisoners. Better not alienate Warden unnecessarily, when a little sweet reasonableness might do more to protect Edwin.

'Sergeant, you know me, and know I do not believe this boy has any guilt to answer for. But I know you, too, and know you have your duty to do. You must obey your orders, and we cannot stand in your way. Tell me, was it Hugh Beringar sent you here to look for me? For I'm sure I was not followed from Shrewsbury. What brought you to this house?'

The sergeant was by no means averse to detailing his own cleverness. 'No, we never thought to have you followed, brother, after you left us, for we thought you were bound back to your abbey. But when Hugh Beringar came back empty-handed from his follies down the river, and heard you'd been asking for him, he went down to the abbey after you, only to find you were gone north to Rhydycroesau. I bethought me then how close Bonel's manor was, and took it upon me to bring a party up here to enquire what you were up to. The steward at the manor never questioned it when an officer from Shrewsbury came asking for Brother Cadfael. Why should he? Or his servants, either? They told us you'd been asking directions to a couple of houses this side the hills, and here at the second we've overtaken you. Where the one casts up, I said, the other won't be far.'

So no one had wittingly informed on the fugitive; that would be some compensatory good news for Ifor ap Morgan, who would have felt himself shamed and dishonoured for ever if one of his kin had betrayed the guest in his house. It was news of no less vital importance to Cadfael.

'Then Hugh Beringar did not send you on this quest? "*I took it upon me*," you said. What's he about, while you're doing his work for him?'

'He's off on some more tomfoolery down the river. Madog of the Dead-boat sent up to him early this morning to come down to Atcham, and off he went as hopeful as ever, though nothing will come of it. So I took the chance of following my own notions, and a fine surprise he'll get by this evening, when he comes back with nothing to show for his day, and finds I've brought him his prisoner.'

That was reassuring, since he was clearly looking forward to the presentation of his prize, and pleased with his own success, therefore the less likely to find satisfaction in rough-handling the boy.

'Edwin,' said Cadfael, 'will you be guided now by me?'

'I will,' said Edwin steadily.

'Then go with them peaceably, and make no trouble. You know you have done no wrong, therefore you cannot be proven guilty, and on that you must take your stand. When you are delivered into the hand of Hugh Beringar, answer freely whatever he may ask of you, and tell him all the truth. I promise you, you will not be long in prison.' And God stand by me, he thought, and help me make that good! 'If the boy gives you his pledge to go with you of his own will, sergeant, and attempt no escape, you surely need not bind him. It's a long ride, and you'll be pressing before the dark comes.'

'He may have the use of his hands, and welcome,' said Warden indifferently, 'seeing the two men I have outside are archers, and masters of their craft. If he tried to evade us he would not get many yards.'

'I shall not try,' said Edwin firmly. 'I give you my word. I'm ready!' He went to Ifor ap Morgan, and bent the knee to him reverently. 'Grandfather, thank you for all your goodness. I know I'm not truly of your kinship – I wish I were! – but will you give me your kiss?'

The old man took him by the shoulders, and stooped to kiss his cheek. 'Go with God! And come again free!'

Edwin took up his saddle and bridle from the corner where they were stowed, and marched out with his head up and his chin jutting, his attendants closing in on either side. In a few minutes the two left behind, gazing through the open door, saw the little cortège form and move off, the sergeant ahead, the boy between two men-at-arms riding close, the archers behind. The day was already chilling, though the light had not yet dimmed. They would not reach Shrewsbury until after dark; a drear journey, and a stony cell in Shrewsbury castle at the end of it. But please God, not for long. Two or three days, if all went well. But well for whom?

'What am I to tell my grandson Meurig,' said the old man sadly, 'when he returns, and finds I have let his guest be taken?'

Cadfael closed the door upon the last glimpse of Edwin's brown head and slight figure; well grown as he was, he looked very small and young between his brawny guards.

'Tell Meurig,' he said after heavy thought, 'that he need have no fears for Edwin, for in the end truth will out, and the truth will deliver him.'

He had one day of inactivity left to live through now, and since there was nothing he could do of use to Edwin's cause in that time, it behoved him at least to try to turn the waiting time into a day of grace by some other means. Brother Barnabas, heartily convalescent, could at least be persuaded to forbear from the heavier work and keep the warmth of the house for a little longer. Brother Simon could take his own day of rest, all the more since on the morrow Cadfael would again be absent. Moreover, they could observe together all the main offices of the day, as if they had been home in the abbey of St Peter. The patient recital of the proper forms must surely in itself be regarded as prayer.

There was time for thought all that day, while he scattered grain for the hens, milked the cow, groomed the old bay horse, and moved the sheep to a fresh hill-pasture. Edwin was lodged in his prison by now, though only, Cadfael hoped, after a long and calming interview with Hugh Beringar. Had Martin Bellecote yet heard that he was taken? Did Edwy know that his decoy ride had been all for nothing? And Richildis . . . Had Beringar seen it as his duty to visit her and tell her of her son's capture? It would be done as courteously and kindly as possible, but there was no way of allaying the pain and dread she would feel.

But Cadfael was even more exercised in mind for the old man Ifor ap Morgan, left alone now after his brief experience of being trusted and revered by a creature fresh and young, like a vision of his own youth returning. The unruly vigour which had made Edwin rebel and wage war against Gervase Bonel had all been charmed and tamed into willing duty and service by Ifor ap Morgan. We are all both the victims and the heirs of our fellow-men.

'Tomorrow,' said Cadfael at supper, round the brazier hissing with resiny logs and giving forth a blue, weaving smoke as aromatic as his workshop at Shrewsbury, 'I must set out very early.' The commote court would sit as soon as there was daylight, and hope to adjourn in time for all present to reach their homes before night. 'I'll try to be back to fold the sheep in the evening. You have not asked me where I go this time.'

'No, brother,' agreed Simon mildly. 'We've seen that you have much on your mind, and would not trouble you yet with questions. When you wish it, you will tell us what we need to know.'

But it was a long story, of which they, here in this solitude and with their own tranquil world undisturbed, knew not even the beginnings. Better say nothing.

He rose before dawn and saddled the horse, taking the same track he had ridden two days previously as far as the ford, when he had turned aside to cross the tributary and make his way to Ifor's house. This time he did not turn aside, but rode on into the valley of the Cynllaith, and crossed by a wooden bridge. From there it was little more than a mile into Llansilin, and the sun was up, veiled but bright. The village was wide awake, and full of people, converging on the timber church. Every house in the neighbourhood must have given shelter overnight to friends and kin from other parts of the commote, for the normal population of this hamlet could be no more than a tenth part of those met here on this day. Cadfael turned his horse into the paddock by the churchyard, where there was a stone water-trough and peaceful grazing, and joined the leisurely procession of men entering the church. Out in the roadway he was conspicuous in his black Benedictine habit, the species being so rare here, but within, he could be well hidden in a retired corner. He had no wish to be noticed too soon.

He was glad that Ifor ap Morgan did not appear among the elders who came to see justice done, the duty of neighbours who knew the land and the people involved. Better by far the testimony of these familiar and respected men than the legal arguments of professional lawmen, though these, too, would be here in plenty. Nor did he see Cynfrith ap Rhys until after the bench of three judges had taken their places, and the first adjourned case was called. Then, when the plaintiff was asked to stand forth with his guarantors on

511

one side, Cadfael recognised Cynfrith among his brother's backers. Owain was the younger of the two, but very like his brother. Hywel Fychan, the defendant, was a wiry, dark man of belligerent aspect, with his own little cluster of witnesses at his back.

The presiding judge gave the verdict of the bench. They had viewed the two disputed holdings on the spot, and taken measurements to match with old charters. Their judgment was that Hywel Fychan had indeed moved the corner boundary stone in such a way as to filch some yards of his neighbour's land. But they had also found that Owain ap Rhys, more discreetly, and admittedly after he had discovered the defendant's fraud, had countered by shifting a whole length of fencing between them by a cautious yard, adequately repaying himself for his loss. They therefore decreed that both marks should be restored to their former positions, and amerced both parties by a negligible fine. Predictably, Owain and Hywel clasped hands amicably enough in acceptance of the verdict; and probably they would be drinking away together, later in the day, the excess of their expected fines over those imposed. The game would be resumed next year. Cadfael was familiar with the national sport.

There were two more boundary disputes which had been awaiting a judgment arrived at on the disputed land, the one settled amicably, the other accepted with some bitterness by the losing party, but none the less accepted. There was a widow who claimed a patch of land against her husband's kin, and won her claim by the testimony of no less than seven neighbours. The morning wore away, and Cadfael, constantly looking over his shoulder towards the door, began to wonder if he had been utterly mistaken in his reading of the probabilities. How if he had interpreted all the signs wrongly? Then he had all to do again, and Edwin was in genuine peril, and his only resort was Hugh Beringar, whose rule would end when Gilbert Prestcote returned from the king's Christmas.

The grateful widow was withdrawing with her witnesses, flushed and happy, when the door of the church opened wide. The light of day flowed across the crowded assembly, and so remained for some minutes, as a numerous group entered the nave. Cadfael looked round, as half those met there were also doing, and saw Meurig advance into the open aisle, and there take his stand, with seven grave elders at his back.

512

He was wearing, Cadfael noted, the same cotte and hose in which he had always seen him, no doubt his best, worn to the commote court as they were worn to visit the abbey at Shrewsbury. His only other garments would be those he wore at work. And the linen scrip hanging by its leather thongs from his belt was the same Cadfael had seen on him at the infirmary, where he had laboured, certainly out of kindliness and with nothing to gain, to coax the aches and pains out of an old man's rusty joints. Such scrips cost money, and are durable for many years. Doubtful if he even owned another such.

An ordinary enough figure, this square, sturdy, black-avised young fellow, anybody's son or brother; but not ordinary now. He stood in the middle of the open aisle, feet spread, arms down at his sides but braced, as if either hand had a weapon within reach, though he surely had not so much as a hunting-knife on him, here in a place doubly sacred as church and court. He was shaven and bathed clean, and the subdued light within the nave found and plucked into relief every bony line of his powerful face, the outline of a skull drawn white and taut, shadowy dark flesh clothing it sparely. His eyes were like burning lamps sunk into cavernous hollows; he looked both piteously young and age-old, and hungry to starving.

'With the court's leave,' he said, and his voice was high and clear, 'I have a plea that will not wait.'

'We were about to declare this sitting at an end,' said the presiding judge mildly. 'But we are here to serve. Declare yourself and your business.'

'My name is Meurig, son of Angharad, daughter of Ifor ap Morgan, who is known to all men here. By this same Angharad I am the son of Gervase Bonel, who held the manor of Mallilie while he lived. I am here to advance my claim to that manor, by reason of my birth, as the son, and the only child, of Gervase Bonel. I am here to introduce testimony that that same land is Welsh land, and subject to Welsh law, and that I am that man's son, and the only child he ever engendered. And by Welsh law I lay claim to Mallilie, for by Welsh law a son is a son, whether born in or out of wedlock, provided only that his father has acknowledged him.' He drew breath, and the pale, drawn lines of his face sharpened yet further with tension. 'Will the court hear me?'

The shudder and murmur that rippled through the church caused even the dark timber walls to quiver. The three on the bench stirred and peered, but kept their more than human balance and calm. The president said with the same restraint: 'We must and will hear whoever comes with an urgent plea, however proffered, with or without legal advice, but the cause may involve adjournment for proper procedure. On that consideration, you may speak.'

'Then first, as to the land of Mallilie, here with me are four respected men, known to all here, who hold land bordering the manor, and their boundaries between them encircle nine-tenths of the manor lands. Only the remaining tenth touches English soil. And all is on the Welsh side of the dyke, as all men know, I ask my witnesses to speak for me.'

The oldest said simply: 'The manor of Mallilie is within the land of Wales, and causes within it and concerning it have been tried by Welsh law within my lifetime, on two occasions, even though the manor was in English hands. True it is that some cases have also been heard in English court and by English law, but Gervase Bonel himself twice preferred to plead in this court and by Welsh law. I hold that Welsh law has never lost its right in any part of that land, for whatever its ownership, it is part of the commote of Cynllaith.'

'And we hold the same opinion,' said the second of the elders.

'That is the view of you all?' asked the judge.

'It is.'

'Is there any present here who wishes to refute that opinion?'

There were several, on the contrary, who spoke up in confirmation of it, one indeed who recalled that he had been the party in dispute with Bonel on the last occasion, over a matter of cattle straying, and had had his case heard in this court, by a bench on which one of the present judges had sat with two others. As doubtless the judge in question recalled without need of reminders.

'The bench is in agreement with the witness of neighbours,' said the president, having consulted his colleagues with hardly more than a glance and a nod. 'There is no question that the land involved is within Wales, and any plaintiff advancing a claim on it is entitled to Welsh law if he desires it. Proceed!'

'As to the second matter of substance,' said Meurig, moistening lips dry with tension, 'I declare that I am the son of Gervase Bonel, his only son, his only child. And I ask these who have known me from birth to testify to my parentage, and any

514

here who may also know the truth to speak up in support of me.'

This time there were many in the body of the church who rose in turn to confirm the declaration of the elders: Meurig, son of Angharad, daughter of Ifor ap Morgan, had been born on the manor of Mallilie, where his mother was a maidservant, and it had been known to everyone before his birth that she was with child by her lord. It had never been any secret, and Bonel had housed and fed the boy.

'There is a difficulty here,' said the presiding judge. 'It is not enough that the common opinion should be that a certain man is father, for common opinion could be mistaken. Even the acceptance of the duty of providing for a child is not in itself proof of acknowledgement. It must be shown that the father has himself acknowledged the child as his. That is the validation the kinship requires for the admittance of a young man into full rights, and that is the validation necessary before property can be inherited.'

'It is no difficulty,' said Meurig proudly, and drew out from the bosom of his cotte a rolled parchment. 'If the court will examine this, they will see that in this indenture, when I took up a trade, Gervase Bonel himself called me his son, and set his seal to it.' He came forward and handed up the parchment to the judges' clerk, who unrolled and studied it.

'It is as he says. This is an agreement between Martin Belle-cote, master-carpenter, of Shrewsbury, and Gervase Bonel, for the young man Meurig to be taken and taught the whole craft of the carpenter and carver. A payment was made with him, and a small allowance made to him for his keep. The seal is in order, the young man is described as "my son". There is no doubt in the matter. He was acknowledged.'

Meurig drew breath deep, and stood waiting. The bench conferred in low and earnest tones.

'We are agreed,' said the president, 'that the proof is irrefu-table, that you are what you purport to be, and have the right to make claim upon the land. But it's known that there was an agreement, never completed, to hand over the manor to the abbey of Shrewsbury, and on that ground, before the man's unfortunate death, the abbey placed a steward in the house to administer the estate. A claim by a son, in these circumstances, must be overwhelmingly strong, but in view of the complica-tions it should be advanced through the channels of law. There is an English overlord to be taken into account, as well as such claims as the abbey may advance, by virtue of Bonel's having shown his intent even in an uncompleted agreement. You will have to bring formal suit for possession, and we would advise that you brief a man of law at once.'

'With respect,' said Meurig, paler and brighter than ever, and with hands cupped and curled at his sides, as if he had already filled them with the desired and coveted soil, 'there is a provision in Welsh law by which I may take possession even now, before the case is tried. Only the son may do so, but I am the son of this man who is dead. I claim the right of *dadanhudd,* the right to uncover my father's hearth. Give me the sanction of this court, and I will go, with these elders who uphold my claim, and enter the house which is mine by right.'

Brother Cadfael was so caught into the intensity of this consuming passion that he almost let the just moment slip by him. All his Welsh blood rose in helpless sympathy with so strong a hunger and love for the land, which Meurig's blood would have granted him, but by Norman-English law his birth had denied him. There was almost a nobility about him in this hour, and the bleak force of his longing carried with him judges, witnesses, even Cadfael.

'It is the court's judgment that your claim is justified,' said the president gravely, 'and your right to enter the house cannot be denied you. For form's sake we must put it to this assembly, since no notice has been given beforehand. If there is any here who has anything to raise in objection, let him stand forward now, and speak.'

'Yes,' said Cadfael, wrenching himself out of his daze with a great effort. 'Here is one who has somewhat to say before this sanction is granted. There is an impediment.'

Every head turned to peer and crane and stare. The judges ranged the ranks looking for the source of the voice, for Cadfael was no taller than the majority of his fellow-country-men, and even his tonsure could be matched by many here conferred by time rather than a cloistered order. Meurig's head had turned with a wild start, his face suddenly fixed and bloodless, his eyes blank. The voice had pierced him like a knife, but he did not recognise it, and for the moment was too blind to be able to mark even the undulation of movement as Cadfael pushed his way clear of the crowd to be seen.

'You are of the Benedictine order?' said the presiding judge, bewildered, as the sturdy, habited figure emerged and stood in

516

the aisle. 'A monk of Shrewsbury? Are you here to speak on behalf of your abbey?'

'No,' said Brother Cadfael. He stood no more than two yards from Meurig now, and the mist of shock and unbelief had cleared from the black, brilliant eyes; they recognised him all too well. 'No, I am here to speak on behalf of Gervase Bonel.'

By the brief, contorted struggle of Meurig's throat, he made an attempt to speak, but could not.

'I do not understand you, brother,' said the judge patiently. 'Explain yourself. You spoke of an impediment.'

'I am a Welshman,' said Cadfael. 'I endorse and approve the law of Wales, that says a son is a son, in or out of marriage, and has the same rights though English law may call him a bastard. Yes, a son born out of wedlock may inherit – but not a son who has murdered his father, as this man has.'

He expected uproar, and instead there was such a silence as he had seldom known. The three judges sat rigid and staring, as though turned to stone, and every breath in the church seemed to be held in suspense. By the time they all stirred out of their daze, and turned almost stealthily, almost fearfully, to look at Meurig, he had regained his colour and his hardihood, though at a price. Forehead and high cheekbones had a wet sheen of sweat, and the muscles of his neck were drawn like bow-strings, but he had himself in hand again, he could look his accuser in the face, refrain from hurling himself upon him, even turn from him with dignity and calm to look at the judges, in eloquent protest against a charge he disdained to deny except by silent contempt. And probably, Cadfael reflected ruefully, there are some here who will take for granted that I am an agent sent by my order to prevent, or at least delay, the surrender of Mallilie to its rightful owner. By any means, however base, even by accusing a decent man of murder.

'This is a most grave charge,' said the presiding judge, formidably frowning. 'If you are in earnest, you must now stand to it, and make good what you have said, or withdraw.'

'That I will do. My name is Cadfael, a brother of Shrewsbury, and the herbalist who made the oil with which Gervase Bonel was poisoned. My honour is involved. The means of comfort and healing must not be used to kill. I was called to attend the dying man, and I am here now to demand justice for him. Allow me, if you will, to tell you how this death befell.'

517

He told the story very baldly, the narrow circle of those present, of whom one, the stepson, seemed then to be the only one with anything to gain from the death.

'Meurig, as it seemed to us, had nothing to gain, but you and I have now seen how much, indeed, was at stake for him. The agreement with my abbey had not been completed, and by Welsh law, which we had not understood could be invoked in the matter, he is the heir. Let me tell you his story as I see it. Ever since he grew a man he has been well aware that by Welsh law his position as heir was unassailable, and he was well content to wait for his father's death, like any other son, before claiming his inheritance. Even the will Gervase Bonel made, after his second marriage, making his stepson his heir, did not trouble Meurig, for how could such a claim stand against his right as a true son of the man's blood? But it was a different case when his father granted his manor away to the abbey of Shrewsbury in return for housing, food and comfort for life, after the usual fashion of such retirements. I do believe that if that agreement had been completed and sealed at once, all would have been over, and this man would have grown reconciled to his loss and never become a murderer. But because my abbot was summoned away to London, with good reason to think that another may be appointed in his place, he would not complete the charter, and that respite caused Meurig to hope again, and to look about him desperately for the means to prevent it ever being completed. For, see, if the abbey ever established its legal right by final ratification, his position at law would have been hopeless. How could he fight Shrewsbury abbey? They have influence enough to ensure that any suit should be tried in an English court and by English law, and by English law, I acknowledge it with regret and shame, such children as Meurig are deprived, and cannot inherit. I say it was mere chance, and that resulting from an act of kindness, that showed him where to find the means to kill, and tempted him to use it. And great pity it is, for he was never meant to be a murderer. But here he stands in his guilt, and must not and cannot enter into possession of the fruit of his crime.'

The presiding judge sat back with a heavy and troubled sigh, and looked at Meurig, who had heard all this with a motionless face and a still body. 'You have heard and understood what is charged against you. Do you wish now to answer?'

'I have nothing to answer,' said Meurig, wise in his desperation. 'This is nothing but words. There is no substance. Yes, I

518

was there in the house, and as he has told you, with my father's wife, the boy her son, and the two servants. But that is all. Yes, by chance I have been in the infirmary, and did know of this oil he speaks of. But where is there any thread to link me with the act? I could as well put forward the same story against any of those in that household that day, and with as little proof, but I will not. The sheriff's officers have held from the beginning that my father's stepson did this thing. I don't say that is true. I say only that there is no proof to entangle me rather than any other.'

'Yes,' said Cadfael, 'there is such proof. There is one small matter that makes this crime all the more grievous, for it is the only proof that it was not all impulsive, done in an angry instant and regretted after. For whoever took away a portion of my monk's-hood oil from our infirmary must have brought with him a bottle in which to put it. And that bottle he had to conceal afterwards, as long as he was observed, but dispose of as soon as he privately might. And the place will show that it could not have been put there by the boy Edwin Gurney, Bonel's stepson. By any other of the household, yes, but not by him. His movements are known. He ran straight from the house to the bridge and the town, as there are witnesses to declare.'

'We have still nothing but words, and deceptive words, too, said Meurig, gaining a little confidence. 'For this bottle has *not* been found, or we should have known it from the sheriff's men. This is a whole-cloth tale compounded for this court alone.'

For of course he did not know; not even Edwin knew, not even Hugh Beringar, only Cadfael and Brother Mark. Thank God for Brother Mark, who had done the finding and marked the place, and was in no suspicion of being anyone's corrupted agent.

Cadfael reached into his pouch, and brought forth the vial of flawed green glass, unwrapping it carefully from the napkin in which it was rolled. 'Yes, it has been found. Here it is!' And he held it out sharply at the full stretch of his arm into Meurig's appalled face.

The instant of sick disintegration passed valiantly, but Cadfael had witnessed it, and now there was no shadow of doubt left, none. And it was a piercing grief to him, for he had liked this young man.

'This,' said Cadfael, whirling to face the bench, 'was found, not by me, but by an innocent novice who knew little of the case, and has nothing to gain by lying. And it was found – the

519

place is recorded – in the ice of the mill-pond, under the window of the inner room of that house. In that room the boy Edwin Gurney was never for one moment alone, and could not have thrown this out from that window. Inspect it, if you will. But carefully, for the marks of the oil are there in a dried stream down one outer side of the vial, and the dregs are still easily identifiable within.'

Meurig watched the small, dreadful thing being passed among the three in its napkin, and said with arduous calm: 'Even granted this – for we have not the finder here to speak for himself! – there were four of us there who could well have gone in and out of that inner room the rest of the day. Indeed, I was the only one to leave, for I went back to my master's shop in the town. They remained there, living in the house.'

Nevertheless, it had become a trial. Even with his admirable and terrible gallantry, he could not entirely prevent the entry of a note of defence. And he knew it, and was afraid, not for himself, for the object of his absorbing love, the land on which he had been born. Brother Cadfael was torn in a measure he had hardly expected. It was time to end it, with one fatal cast that might produce success or failure, for he could not bear this partition of his mind much longer, and Edwin was in a prison cell, something even Meurig did not yet know, something that might have reassured him if he had been aware of it, but no less might have moved and dismayed him. Never once, in that long afternoon of questioning, had Meurig sought to turn suspicion upon Edwin, even when the sergeant pointed the way.

'Draw out the stopper,' said Cadfael to the three judges, almost strident now in his urgency. 'Note the odour, it is still strong enough to be recognised again. You must take my word for it that it was the means of death. And you see how it has run down the vial. It was stoppered in haste after the act, for all was then done in haste. Yet some creature carried this vial on his person for a considerable while after, until the sheriff's officers had come and gone. In this condition, oiled without as well as within. It would leave a greasy stain not easy to remove, and a strong smell – yes, I see you detect the smell.' He swung upon Meurig, pointing to the coarse linen scrip that hung at his belt. 'This, as I recall, you wore that day. Let the judges themselves examine, with the vial in their hands, and see whether it lay within there an hour, two hours or more, and left its mark and its odour. Come, Meurig, unbuckle and give up your scrip.'

Meurig indeed dropped a hand to the buckles, as though stunned into obedience. And after this while, Cadfael knew, there might be nothing to find, even though he no longer had any doubts that the vial had indeed lain within there all that prolonged and agonising afternoon of Bonel's death. It needed only a little hardihood and a face of brass, and the single fragile witness against Meurig might burst like a bubble, and leave nothing but the scattered dew of suspicion, like the moisture a bubble leaves on the hand. But he could not be sure! He could not be sure! And to examine the scrip and find nothing would not be to exonerate him completely, but to examine it and find the seam stained with oil, and still with the penetrating scent clinging, would be to condemn him utterly. The fingers that had almost withdrawn the first thong suddenly closed into a clenched fist denying access.

'No!' he said hoarsely. 'Why should I submit to this indignity? He is the abbey's man sent to besmirch my claim.'

'It is a reasonable requirement,' said the presiding judge austerely. 'There is no question of your surrendering it to anyone but this court. There can be no suspicion that we have anything to gain by discrediting you. The bench requires you to hand it over to the clerk.'

The clerk, accustomed to having the court's orders respected without demur, advanced trustingly, extending a hand. Meurig dared not take the risk. Suddenly he whirled and sprang for the open door, scattering the old men who had come to back his claim. In a moment he was out into the wintry light of the morning, running like a deer. Behind him uproar broke out, and half of those in the church poured out after the fugitive, though their pursuit was half-hearted after the first instinctive rush. They saw Meurig vault the stone wall of the churchyard and head for the fringes of woodland that clothed the hillside behind. In a moment he was lost to view among the trees.

In the half-deserted church a heavy silence fell. The old men looked at one another helplessly, and made no move to join the hunt. The three judges conferred in low and anxious tones. Cadfael stood drooping in a weariness that seemed temporarily to have deprived him of energy or thought, until at last he drew breath long and deeply, and looked up.

'It is not a confession, nor has there been a formal charge, or any suit as yet brought against him. But it is evidence for a boy who is now in prison at Shrewsbury on suspicion of this crime. Let me say what can and should be said for Meurig:

521

he did not know Edwin Gurney had been taken, of that I am sure.'

'We have now no choice but to pursue him,' said the presiding judge, 'and it will be done. But certainly the record of this court must be sent, out of courtesy, to the sheriff at Shrewsbury, and at once. Will that content you?'

'It's all I ask. Send also, if you will, the vial, concerning which a novice by the name of Mark will testify, for it was he who found it. Send all to Hugh Beringar, the sheriff's deputy, who is in charge, and deliver the report only to him, of your kindness. I wish I might go, but I have still work to do here.'

'It will take some hours for our clerks to make the necessary copies and have them certified. But by tomorrow evening, at latest, the report shall be delivered. I think your prisoner will have nothing more to fear.'

Brother Cadfael uttered his thanks, and went out from the church into a village thronging with agitated, head-shaking neighbours. The tale of the morning's events was on the wing by now, surely already being carried over the hills throughout the commote of Cynllaith, but even rumour had not flown so fast as Meurig, for nothing was seen of him all that day. Cadfael led his horse from the paddock, and mounted and rode. The weariness that had fallen upon him when the need for effort ended so suddenly was subsiding slowly into a desperate sadness, and that again into a drear but grateful calm. He took the journey back very slowly, for he needed time to think, and above all, time for another to do some even more urgent thinking. He passed by the manor-house of Mallilie with only a rueful glance. The ending would not be there.

He was very well aware that it was not yet over.

'You are back in good time, brother,' said Simon, stoking the brazier with fresh fuel for the evening. 'Whatever your business, I trust God prospered it.'

'He did,' said Cadfael. 'And now it must be your turn to rest, and leave the remaining work to me. I've stabled and groomed and fed the horse, he's not overdone for I took things gently with him. After supper there'll be time for shutting the hen-house and seeing to the cow, and light enough still to bring down the ewes in lamb to the barn, for I think there may be harder frost in the night. Curious how the light lies in these hills a good half-hour longer than in the town.'

'Your Welsh eyes, brother, are only just regaining their proper vision. There are few nights here that a man could not travel safely even among the upland bogs, knowing the ground at all well. Only in the woods is it ever truly dark. I talked with a wandering brother from the north once, a rough red-haired man with a tongue I could barely understand, a Scot. He said in his far country there were nights when the sun barely set before it rose again on the other side, and you could see your way in an endless afterglow. But I do not know,' said Brother Simon wistfully, 'if he was romancing. I have never been further than Chester.'

Brother Cadfael forbore from citing his own travels, remembered now with the astonished contentment of a man at rest. To tell the truth, he had enjoyed the storms no less than he now enjoyed the calm, if this was indeed calm: but each had its own time and place.

'I've been glad of this stay with you,' he said, and that at least was true. 'It smells like Gwynedd here. And the folk hereabouts have me speaking Welsh to them, and that's gain, for I use it little enough in Shrewsbury.'

Brother Barnabas came with the supper, his own good bread, barley gruel, ewe's-milk cheese and dried apples. He breathed without labour, and strode round the house unwearied and energetic. 'You see I'm ready and able for work, brother, thanks to your skills. I could fold the ewes myself tonight.'

'You will not,' said Cadfael firmly, 'for I've taken that task for myself, having been truant all day. You be content to see us devouring this baking of yours, for that's one art I have not, and at least I have the grace to know it, and be thankful for the skills of other men.'

They ate early at Rhydycroesau, having normally laboured out of doors from early morning. There was still a muted half-light, the east a clear, deep blueness, the west a pallid glow, when Cadfael went out to climb to the nearer crest and bring down the ewes already heavy with lamb. They were few but precious, once in a while they even dropped twins, and with care both survived. Cadfael discerned a deep and tranquil satisfaction in the shepherd's life. The children of his solicitude were seldom killed, unless disease, injury or decrepitude threatened, or in time of desperation the flock could not all be fed through the winter. Their wool and milk were of more value than their meat, and their precious skins could be garnered only once, and better when for distress they had to be slaughtered. So they remained through their natural lives, growing into familiarity and affection, trusting and being understood, even acquiring names. Shepherds had a community of their own, peopled with gentle, obstinate, quiet companions, who did no murder or theft or banditry, broke no laws, made no complaints, fuelled no rebellions.

All the same, he thought, climbing the hill in long, easy strides, I could not be a shepherd for long. I should miss all the things I deplore, the range and grasp of man for good and evil. And instantly he was back with the struggles and victories and victims of the day.

On the crest of the ridge he stood to contemplate the coming night, aware that he must be seen from a good distance around. The sky above was immense and very lofty, a very deep blue, with a faint dappling of stars so new and fine that they were visible only when seen from the corner of the eye, and a direct stare immediately put them out. He looked down at the cluster of walled folds and the snug dark huddle of buildings, and could not be quite sure whether he had not seen a mere quiver of movement at the corner of the barn. The ewes, accustomed to extra pampering, were gathering about him of their own will, ready to go down into the steamy, wool-scented warmth of the barn for the night. Their rounded sides and bellies swayed contentedly as they walked. By this light only an occasional gleam showed the disconcerting yellow stare of their eyes.

When at last he stirred, and began slowly to descend the hill, they followed daintily on their little, agile feet, crowding close, jostling one another, the mild, warm, greasy smell of their fleeces making a flowing cloud about them. He counted, called softly back to one or two stragglers, young ones in their first lamb, and irresponsible, though they came hurrying at his call. Now he had them all.

Apart from himself and his little flock, the night was empty and still, unless that was the momentary intrusion and instant withdrawal of some live thing he had caught between the buildings below. Blessedly, Brother Simon and Brother Barnabas had taken him at his word, and remained contentedly in the warmth of the house, by this time probably nodding over the brazier.

He brought his charges to the large barn, half of which was cleared by now for their housing at night until they gave birth. The wide doors opened inwards, he thrust them open before him and ushered his flock within, where there was a rack filled for their use, and a trough of water. These needed no light to find their way. The interior of the barn was still peopled with vague, bulky shadows, but otherwise dark, and smelled of dried grass and clover and the fat scent of fleeces. The mountain sheep had not the long, curly wool of the lowlands, but they brought a very thick, short fleece that carried almost as much wool of a somewhat less valuable kind, and they converted handsomely the pasture their spoiled lowland cousins could not make use of. Their cheeses alone were worth their keep.

Cadfael chided the last and most unbiddable of his charges into the barn, and passed in after her, advancing into the dimness that left him temporarily blind. He felt the sudden presence behind him, and stood, every muscle stilled. The blade that was laid cold and sudden against the skin of his throat started no movement; he had had knives at his throat before, he was not such a fool as to provoke them into malice or fright, especially when he approached them forewarned.

An arm encircled him from behind, pinning both arms fast to his body, and he made no move to recoil or resist. 'And did you think when you destroyed me, brother,' panted a suffocating voice in his ear, 'that I would go into the dark alone?'

'I have been expecting you, Meurig,' said Brother Cadfael quietly. 'Close the door! You may safely. I shall not move. You and I have no need now of witnesses.'

Chapter Ten

O,' SAID the voice in his ear, low and savagely, 'no need of witnesses. My business is with you alone, monk, and brief enough.' But the arms withdrew from him, and in a moment the heavy doors closed with a hollow sound upon the glimpse of sky in which, from this walled darkness within, the stars showed doubly large and bright.

Cadfael stood motionless, and heard the soft brushing of cloth as Meurig leaned back against the closed door, arms spread, drawing deep breaths to savour the moment of arrival, and anticipate the last vengeful achievement. There was no other way out, and he knew his quarry had not moved by so much as a step.

'You have branded me murderer, why should I draw back now from murder? You have ruined me, shamed me, made me a reproach to my own kin, taken from me my birthright, my land, my good name, everything that made my existence worth calling a life and I will have your life in recompense. I cannot live now, I cannot even die, until I have been your death, Brother Cadfael.'

Strange how the simple act of giving his victim a name changed everything, even this blind relationship, like the first gleam of light. Further light could only assist the change.

'Hanging behind the door, where you are,' said Cadfael practically, 'you'll find a lantern, and on another nail there a leather bag with flint and steel and tinder in it. We may as well see each other. Take care with the sparks, you've nothing against our sheep, and fire would bring people running. 'There's a shelf where the lantern will stand.'

'And you will make your bid to keep your forfeit life . . . I know!'

'I shall not move hand or foot,' said Cadfael patiently. 'Why do you suppose I have made so certain the last work tonight should fall to me? Did I not say I was expecting you? I have no weapon, and if I had I would not use it. I finished with arms many years ago.'

There was a long pause, during which, though he felt that more was expected of him, he added nothing more. Then he heard the creek of the lantern as Meurig's questing hand found it, the grating noise of the horn shutter being opened, the groping of fingers to find the shelf, and the sound of the lantern being set down there. Flint and steel tapped sharply several times, sparks flashed and vanished, and then a corner of charred cloth caught and held the tiny fire and Meurig's face hung ghostlike over it, blowing until the wick caught in its turn, and sent up a lengthening flame. Dim yellow light brought into being the feeding-rack, the trough, the forest of shadows in the network of beams above, and the placid, incurious ewes; and Cadfael and Meurig stood looking intently at each other.

'Now,' said Cadfael, 'you can at least see to take what you came for.' And he sat down and settled himself solidly on a corner of the feeding-rack.

Meurig came towards him with long, deliberate strides through the straw-dust and chaff of the floor. His face was fixed and grey, his eyes sunken deep into his head and burning with frenzy and pain. So close that their knees touched, he advanced the knife slowly until the point pricked Cadfael's throat; along eight inches of steel they eyed each other steadily.

'Are you not afraid of death?' asked Meurig, barely above a whisper.

'I've brushed elbows with him before. We respect each other. In any case there's no evading him for ever, we all come to it, Meurig. Gervase Bonel . . . you . . . I. We have to die, every one of us, soon or late. But we do not *have* to kill. You and I both made a choice, you only a week or so ago, I when I lived by the sword. Here am I, as you willed it. Now take what you want of me.'

He did not take his eyes from Meurig's eyes, but he saw at the edge of vision the tightening of the strong brown fingers and the bracing of the muscles in the wrist to strike home. But there was no other movement. All Meurig's body seemed suddenly to writhe in an anguished attempt to thrust, and still he could not. He wrenched himself backward, and a muted animal moan came from his throat. He cast the knife out of his hand to whine and stick quivering in the beaten earth of the floor, and flung up both arms to clasp his head, as though all his strength of body and will could not contain or suppress the pain that filled him to overflowing. Then his knees gave under him, and he was crouched in a heap at Cadfael's feet, his face buried in his arms against the hay-rack. Round yellow eyes, above placidly chewing muzzles, looked on in detached surprise at the strangeness of men.

Broken sounds came from Meurig's buried mouth, muffled and sick with despair: 'Oh, God, that I could so face my death . . . for I owe it, I owe it, and dare not pay! If I were clean . . . if I were only clean again . . . ' And in a great groan he said: 'Oh Mallilie . . . '

'Yes,' said Cadfael softly. 'A very fair place. Yet there is a world outside it.'

'Not for me, not for me . . . I am forfeit. Give me up! Help me . . . help me to be fit to die . . . ' He raised himself suddenly, and looked up at Cadfael, clutching with one hand at the skirts of his habit. 'Brother, those things you said of me . . . never meant to be a murderer, you said . . . '

'Have I not proved it?' said Cadfael. 'I live, and it was not fear that stayed your hand.'

'Mere chance that led me, you said, and that because of an act of simple kindness. . . . Great pity it is, you said! Pity . . . Did you mean all those things, brother? Is there pity?'

'I mean them,' said Cadfael, 'every word. Pity, indeed, that ever you went so far aside from your own nature, and poisoned yourself as surely as you poisoned your father. Tell me, Meurig, in these last days you have not been back to your grandfather's house, or had any word from him?'

'No,' said Meurig, very low, and shuddered at the thought of the upright old man now utterly bereft.

'Then you do not know that Edwin was fetched away from there by the sheriff's men, and is now in prison in Shrewsbury.'

No, he had not known. He looked up aghast, seeing the implication, and shook with the fervour of his denial: 'No, that

528

I swear I did not do. I was tempted. . . . I could not prevent that they cast the blame on him, but I did not betray him . . . I sent him here. I would have seen that he got clear . . . . I know it was not enough, but oh, this at least don't lay to my charge! God knows I liked the boy well.'

'I also know it,' said Cadfael, 'and know it was not you who sent them to take him. No one wittingly betrayed him. None the less, he was taken. Tomorrow will see him free again. Take that for one thing set right, where many are past righting.'

Meurig laid his clasped hands, white-knuckled with tension, on Cadfael's knees, and lifted a tormented face into the soft light of the lantern. 'Brother, you have been conscience to other men in your time, for God's sake do as much by me for I am sick, I am maimed, I am not my own. You said . . . great pity! Hear me all my evil!'

'Child,' said Cadfael, shaken, and laid his own hand over the stony fists that felt chill as ice, 'I am not a priest, I cannot give absolution, I cannot appoint penance . . .'

'Ah, but you can, you can, none but you, who found out the worst of me! Hear me my confession, and I shall be better prepared, and then deliver me to my penalty, and I will not complain.'

'Speak, then, if it gives you ease,' said Cadfael heavily, and kept his hand closed over Meurig's as the story spilled out in broken gouts of words, like blood from a wound: how he had gone to the infirmary with no ill thought, to pleasure an old man, and learned by pure chance of the properties of the oil he was using for its true purpose, and how it could be put to a very different use. Only then had the seed been planted in his mind. He had a few weeks, perhaps, of grace before Mallilie was lost to him for ever, and here was a means of preventing the loss.

'And it grew in me, the thought that it would not be a hard thing to do . . . and the second time I went there I took the vial with me, and filled it. But it was still only a mad dream . . . Yet I carried it with me, that last day, and I told myself it would be easy to put it in his mead, or mull wine for him . . . . I might never have done it, only willed, it, thought that is sin enough. But when I came to the house, they were all in the inner room together, and I heard Aldith saying how the prior had sent a dish from his own table, a dainty to please my father. It was there simmering on the hob, a spoon in it . . . The thing was done almost before I knew I meant to do it . . . And then I heard Aelfric and Aldith coming back from the table, and I had

529

no time for more than to step quickly outside the door again, as if I had just opened, it and I was scraping my shoes clean to come in when they came into the kitchen. . . . What could they think but that I had only just come? A score of times in the next hour, God knows how wildly, I wished it undone, but such things cannot be undone, and I am damned . . . . What could I do but go forward, when there was no going back?'

What, indeed, short of what he was doing now, and this had been forced on him. Yet it was not to kill that he had flown like a homing bird to this meeting, whatever he himself had believed.

'So I went on. I fought for the fruit of my sin, for Mallilie, as best I could. I never truly hated my father, but Mallilie I truly loved, and it was mine, mine . . . if only I could have come by it cleanly! But there is justice, and I have lost, and I make no complaint. Now deliver me up, and let me pay for his death with mine, as is due. I will go with you willingly, if you will wish me peace.'

He laid his head on Cadfael's steadying hand with a great sigh, and fell silent; and after a long moment Cadfael laid his other hand on the thick dark hair, and held him so. Priest he might not be, and absolution he could not give, yet here he was in the awful situation of being both judge and confessor. Poison is the meanest of killings, the steel he could respect. And yet . . . Was not Meurig also a man gravely wronged? Nature had meant him to be amiable, kindly, unembittered, circumstances had so deformed him that he turned against his nature once, and fatally, and he was all too well aware of his mortal sickness. Surely one death was enough, what profit in a second? God knew other ways of balancing the scale.

'You asked your penance of me,' said Cadfael at last. 'Do you still ask it? And will you bear it and keep faith, no matter how terrible it may be?'

The heavy head stirred on his knee. 'I will,' said Meurig in a whisper, 'and be grateful.'

'You want no easy penalty?'

'I want all my due. How else can I find peace?'

'Very well, you have pledged yourself. Meurig, you came for my life, but when it came to the stroke, you could not take it. Now you lay your life in my hands, and I find that I cannot take it, either, that I should be wrong to take it. What benefit to the world would your blood be? But your hands, your strength, your will, that virtue you still have within you, these may yet be of the greatest profit. You want to pay in full. Pay, then! Yours is a lifelong penance, Meurig, I rule that you shall live out your life and may it be long! and pay back all your debts by having regard to those who inhabit this world with you. The tale of your good may yet outweigh a thousand times the tale of your evil. This is the penance I lay on you.'

Meurig stirred slowly, and raised a dazed and wondering face, neither relieved nor glad, only utterly bewildered. 'You mean it? This is what I must do?'

'This is what you must do. Live, amend, in your dealings with sinners remember your own frailty, and in your dealings with the innocence, respect and use your own strength in their service. Do as well as you can, and leave the rest to God, and how much more can saints do?'

'They will be hunting for me,' said Meurig, still doubting and marvelling. 'You will not hold that I've failed you if they take and hang me?'

'They will not take you. By tomorrow you will be well away from here. There is a horse in the stable next to this barn, the horse I rode today. Horses in these parts can very easily be stolen, it's an old Welsh game, as I know. But this one will not be stolen. I give it, and I will be answerable. There is a whole world to reach on horseback, where a true penitent can make his way step by step through a long life towards grace. Were I you, I should cross the hills as far west as you may before daylight, and then bear north into Gwynedd, where you are not known. But you know these hills better than I.'

'I know them well,' said Meurig, and now his face had lost its anguish in open and childlike wonder. 'And this is all? All you ask of me?'

'You will find it heavy enough,' said Brother Cadfael. 'But yes, there is one thing more. When you are well clear, make your confession to a priest, ask him to write it down and have it sent to the sheriff at Shrewsbury. What has passed today in Llansilin will release Edwin, but I would not have any doubt or shadow left upon him when you are gone.'

'Neither would I,' said Meurig. 'It shall be done.'

'Come, then, you have a long pilgrimage to go. Take up your knife again.' And he smiled. 'You will need it to cut your bread and hunt your meat.'

It was ending strangely. Meurig rose like one in a dream, both spent and renewed, as though some rainfall from heaven has washed him out of his agony and out of his wits, to revive, a man half-drowned and wholly transformed. Cadfael had to lead him by the hand, once they had put out the lantern. Outside, the night was very still and starlit, on the edge of frost. In the stable Cadfael himself saddled the horse.

'Rest him when you safely may. He's carried me today, but that was no great journey. I'd give you the mule, for he's fresh, but he'd be slower, and more questionable under a Welshman. There, mount and go. Go with God!'

Meurig shivered at that, but the pale, fixed brightness of his face did not change. With a foot already in the stirrup, he said with sudden inexpressibly grave and burdened humility: 'Give me your blessing! For I am bound by you while I live.'

He was gone, up the slope above the folds, by ways he knew better than did the man who had set him free to ride them, back into the world of the living. Cadfael looked after him for only a moment, before turning down towards the house. He thought as he went: Well, if I have loosed you on the world unchanged and perilous, if this cleansing wears off once you are safe, then on me be the guilt. But he found he could not feel greatly afraid; the more he reviewed the course he had taken, the more profound became his soul's tranquillity.

'You were a long time, brother,' said Simon, welcoming him with pleasure into the evening warmth within the house. We were wondering about you.'

'I was tempted to stay and meditate among the ewes,' said Brother Cadfael. 'They are so calming. And it is a beautiful night.'

Chapter Eleven

T WAS a good Christmas; he had never known one more firelit and serene. The simple outdoor labour was bliss after stress, he would not have exchanged it for the ceremonial and comparative luxury of the abbey. The news that came in from the town, before the first snow discouraged travel, made a kind of shrill overtone to the homely Christmas music they made between them, with three willing but unskilled voices and three contented and fulfilled hearts. Hugh Beringar sent word, not only that he had received the record of the Llansilin court, but also that Edwin's well-meant conciliatory gift had been cast up in the shallows near Atcham, in considerable disarray, but still recognisable. The boy was restored to his doting mother, and the Bonel household could breathe freely again, now that the culprit was known. The apologetic report that the horse belonging to the Rhydycroesau sheepfolds had gone missing, due to Brother Cadfael's reprehensible failure to bar the stable door securely, had been noted with appropriate displeasure by the chapter of the abbey, and repayment in some form awaited him on his return.

As for the fugitive Meurig, cried through Powys for murder, the hunt had never set eyes on him since, and the trail was growing cold. Even the report of his voluntary confession, sent by a priest from a hermitage in Penllyn, did not revive the scent, for the man was long gone, and no one knew where. Nor was

Owain Gwynedd likely to welcome incursions on his territory in pursuit of criminals against whom he had no complaint, and who should never have been allowed to slip through authority's fingers in the first place.

In fact, all was very well. Cadfael was entirely happy among the sheep, turning a deaf ear to the outer world. He felt he had earned a while of retreat. His only regret was that the first deep snow prevented him from riding to visit Ifor ap Morgan, to whom he owed what consolation there was to be found for him. Frail though it might seem, Cadfael found it worth cherishing, and so would Ifor; and the very old are very durable.

They had no less than three Christmas morning lambs, a single and twins. They brought them all, with their dams, into the house and made much of them, for these innocents shared their stars with the Christ-child. Brother Barnabas, wholly restored, nursed the infants in his great hands and capacious lap, and was as proud as if he had produced them of his own substance. They were very merry together, in a quiet celebration, before Brother Cadfael left them to return to Shrewsbury. His patient was by this time the most vigorous force within twenty miles round, and there was no more need for a physician here at Rhydycroesau.

The snow had abated in a temporary thaw, when Cadfael mounted his mule, three days after the feast, and set out southwards for Shrewsbury.

He made a long day of it because he did not take the direct road to Oswestry, but went round to pay his delayed visit on Ifor ap Morgan before cutting due east from Croesau Bach to strike the main road well south of the town. What he had to say to Ifor, and what Ifor replied to him, neither of them ever confided to a third. Certainly when Cadfael mounted again, it was in better heart that he set out, and in better heart that Ifor remained alone.

By reason of this detour it was already almost dusk when Cadfael's mule padded over the Welsh bridge into Shrewsbury, and through the hilly streets alive with people and business again after the holiday. No time now to turn aside from the Wyle for the pleasure of being let in by the shrewd little housewife Alys, and viewing the jubilation of the Bellecote family; that would have to keep for another day. No doubt Edwy was long since released from his pledge to keep to home, and off with his inseparable uncle on whatever work, play or mischief offered. The future of Mallilie still lay in the balance; it was to be hoped that the lawmen would not manage to take the heart out of it in their fees, before anyone got acknowledged possession.

And here round the curve of the Wyle the arc of the river showed before him, the waning day regaining half its light as he stepped on to the open span and passed through the gates on to the draw-bridge. Here Edwin checked in his indignant flight to hurl away his despised offering. And here beyond was the level road opening before him, and on his right the house where Richildis must still be living, and the mill-pond, a dull silver plane in the twilight; then the wall of the abbey enclosure, the west front and the parish door of the great church looming before him, and on his right hand the gatehouse.

He turned in and checked in astonishment at the bustle and noise that met him. The porter was out at his door, brushed and flushed and important as though for a bishop's visitation, and the great court was full of brothers and lay brothers and officials running to and fro busily, or gathered in excited groups, conversing in raised voices, and looking round eagerly at every creature who entered at the gate. Cadfael's coming caused one such stir, which subsided with unflattering promptness when he was recognised. Even the schoolboys were out whispering and chirruping together under the wall of the gatehouse, and travellers crowded into the doorway of the guest-hall. Brother Jerome stood perched on the mounting-block by the hall, his attention divided between giving orders left and right, and watching every moment at the gate. In Cadfael's absence he seemed, if anything, to have grown more self-important and officious than ever.

Cadfael lighted down, prepared to stable his own beast, but unsure whether the mules might still be housed in the barn on the horse-fair; and out of the weaving excitement around him Brother Mark came darting with a whoop of pleasure.

'Oh Cadfael, what joy to see you! Such happenings! And I thought you would be missing everything, and all the while you were in the thick of it. We've heard about the court at Llansilin . . . Oh, you're so welcome home again!'

'So I see,' said Cadfael, 'if this reception is for me.'

'*Mine* is!' said Brother Mark fervently. 'But this . . . Of course, you won't have heard yet. We're all waiting for Abbot Heribert. One of the carters was out to St Giles a while ago, and he saw them, they've made a stop at the hospital there. He came to give the word. Brother Jerome is waiting to run and tell Prior Robert as soon as they come in at the gate. They'll be here any moment.'

'And no news until they come? Will it still be *Abbot* Heribert, I wonder?' said Cadfael ruefully.

'We don't know. But everybody's afraid . . . Brother Petrus is muttering awful things into his ovens, and vowing he'll quit the order. And Jerome is *unbearable!*'

He turned to glare, so far as his mild, plain face was capable of glaring, at the incubus of whom he spoke, and behold, Brother Jerome had vanished from his mounting-block, and was scurrying head-down for the abbot's lodging.

'Oh, they must be coming! Look – the prior!'

Robert sailed forth from his appropriated lodging, immaculately robed, majestically tall, visible above all the peering heads. His face was composed into otherworldly serenity, benevolence and piety, ready to welcome his old superior with hypocritical reverence, and assume his office with hypocritical humility; all of which he would do very beautifully, and with noble dignity.

And in at the gate ambled Heribert, a small, rotund, gentle elderly man of unimpressive appearance, who rode like a sack on his white mule, and had the grime and mud and weariness of the journey upon him. He wore, at sight, the print of demotion and retirement in his face and bearing, yet he looked pleasantly content, like a man who has just laid by a heavy burden, and straightened up to draw breath. Humble by nature, Heribert was uncrushable. His own clerk and grooms followed a respectful few yards behind; but at his elbow rode a tall, spare, sinewy Benedictine with weathered features and shrewd blue eyes, who kept pace with him in close attendance, and eyed him, Cadfael thought, with something of restrained affection. A new brother for the house, perhaps.

Prior Robert sailed through the jostling, whispering brothers like a fair ship through disorderly breakers, and extended both hands to Heribert as soon as his foot touched ground. 'Father, you are most heartily welcome home! There is no one here but rejoices to see you back among us, and I trust blessed and confirmed in office, our superior as before.'

To do him justice, thought Cadfael critically, it was not often he lied as blatantly as that, and certainly he did not realise even now that he was lying. And to be honest, what could he or any man say in this situation, however covetously he exulted in the promotion he foresaw for himself? You can hardly tell a man to his face that you've been waiting for him to go, and he should have done it long ago.

'Indeed, Robert, I'm happy to be back with you,' said Heribert, beaming. 'But no, I must inform all here that I am no longer their abbot, only their brother. It has been judged best that another should have charge, and I bow to that judgement, and am come home to serve loyally as a simple brother under you.'

'Oh, no!' whispered Brother Mark, dismayed. 'Oh, Cadfael, look, he grows taller!'

And indeed it seemed that Robert's silver head was suddenly even loftier, as if by the acquisition of a mitre. But equally suddenly there was another head as lofty as his; the stranger had dismounted at leisure, almost unremarked, and stood at Heribert's side. The ring of thick, straight dark hair round his tonsure was hardly touched with grey, yet he was probably at least as old as Robert, and his intelligent hatchet of a face was just as incisive, if less beautiful.

'Here I present to you all,' said Heribert almost fondly, 'Father Radulfus, appointed by the legatine council to have rule here in our abbey as from this day. Receive your new abbot and reverence him, as I, Brother Heribert of this house, have already learned to do.'

There was a profound hush, and then a great stir and sigh and smile that ran like a quiet wave all through the assembly in the great court. Brother Mark clutched Cadfael's arm and buried what might otherwise have been a howl of delight in his shoulder. Brother Jerome visibly collapsed, like a pricked bladder, and turned the identical wrinkled mud-colour. Somewhere at the rear there was a definite crow, like a game-cock celebrating a kill, though it was instantly suppressed, and no one could trace its origin. It may well have been Brother Petrus, preparing to rush back into his kitchen and whip all his pots and pans into devoted service for the newcomer who had disjointed Prior Robert's nose in the moment of its most superb elevation.

As for the prior himself, he had not the figure or the bearing to succumb to deflation like his clerk, nor the kind of complexion that could be said to blench. His reaction was variously reported afterwards. Brother Denis the hospitaller claimed that Robert had rocked back on his heels so alarmingly that it was a wonder he did not fall flat on his back. The porter alleged that he blinked violently, and remained glassy-eyed for

537

minutes afterwards. The novices, after comparing notes, agreed that if looks could have killed, they would have had a sudden death in their midst, and the victim would not have been the new abbot, but the old, who by so ingenuously acknowledging his future subordination to Robert as prior had led him to believe in his expected promotion to the abbacy, only to shatter the illusion next moment. Brother Mark, very fairly, said that only a momentary marble stillness, and the subsequent violent agitation of the prior's Adam's-apple as he swallowed gall, had betrayed his emotions. Certainly he had been forced to a heroic effort at recovery, for Heribert had proceeded benignly:

'And to you, Father Abbot, I make known Brother Robert Pennant, who has been an exemplary support to me as prior, and I am sure will serve you with the same selfless devotion.'

'It was *beautiful!*' said Brother Mark later, in the garden workshop where he had submitted somewhat selfconsciously to having his stewardship reviewed, and been relieved and happy at being commended. 'But I feel ashamed now. It was wicked of me to feel such pleasure in someone else's downfall.'

'Oh, come, now!' said Cadfael absently, busy unpacking his scrip and replacing the jars and bottles he had brought back with him. 'Don't reach for your halo too soon. You have plenty of time to enjoy yourself, even a little maliciously sometimes, before you settle down to being a saint. It *was* beautiful, and almost every soul there rejoiced in it. Let's have no hypocrisy.'

Brother Mark let go of his scruples, and had the grace to grin. 'But all the same, when Father Heribert could meet him with no malice at all, and such affection . . . '

'Brother Heribert! And you do yourself less than justice,' said Cadfael fondly. 'You're still endearingly green, it seems. Did you think all those well-chosen words were hit upon by accident? "A simple brother *under* you . . . " He could as well have said among you, since he was speaking to us all a moment before. And "with the same selfless devotion", indeed! Yes, the very same! And by the look of our new abbot, Robert will be waiting a long, long time before there's another vacancy there.'

Brother Mark dangled his legs from the bench by the wall, and gaped in startled consternation. 'Do you mean he did it all *on purpose?*'

'He could have sent one of the grooms a day ahead, couldn't he, if he'd wished to give warning? He could at least have sent one on from St Giles to break the news gently. And privately! A long-suffering soul, but he took a small revenge today.' He was touched by Brother Mark's stricken face. 'Don't look so shocked! You'll never get to be a saint if you deny the bit of the devil in you. And think of the benefit he's conferred on Prior Robert's soul!'

'In showing the vanity of ambition?' hazarded Mark doubtfully.

'In teaching him not to count his chickens. There, now be off to the warming-room, and get me all the gossip, and I'll join you in a little while, after I've had a word or two with Hugh Beringar.'

'Well, it's over, and as cleanly as we could have hoped,' said Beringar, comfortable beside the brazier with a beaker of mulled wine from Cadfael's store in his hand. 'Documented and done with, and the cost might well have been higher. A very fine woman, by the way, your Richildis, it was a pleasure to hand her boy back to her. I've no doubt he'll be in here after you as soon as he hears you're back, as he soon will, for I'll call at the house on my way into the town.'

There had been few direct questions asked, and a few but oblique answers. Their conversation was often as devious as their relationship was easy and secure, but they understood each other.

'I hear you lost a horse while you were up on the borders,' said Beringar.

'*Mea culpa!*' owned Cadfael. 'I left the stable unlocked.'

'About the same time as the Llansilin court lost a man,' observed Hugh.

'Well, you're surely not blaming me for that. I found him for them, and then they couldn't keep their hold on him.'

'I suppose they'll have the price of the horse out of you, one way or the other?'

'No doubt it will come up at chapter tomorrow. No matter,' said Brother Cadfael placidly, 'as long as no one here can dun me for the price of the man.'

'That can only be charged at another chapter. But it could come high.' But Hugh's sharp, dark face behind the quivering vapour from the brazier was smiling. 'I've been saving a piece of news for you, Cadfael, my friend. Every few days a new wonder out of Wales! Only yesterday I got word from Chester that a rider who gave no name came into one of the granges of the monastery of Beddgelert, and left there his horse, asking that the brothers would give it stable-room until it could be returned to the Benedictine brothers at the sheepfolds of Rhydycroesau, whence it had been borrowed. They don't yet know of it at Rhydycroesau, for they had their first snow before us, up there in Arfon, and there was no chance of getting a messenger through overland, and I gather is none even yet. But the horse is there, and safe. Whoever the stranger was,' said Hugh innocently, 'he must have left it there no more than two days after our own vanished malefactor made his confession in Penllyn. The word came by way of Bangor, when they could reach it, and by sea to Chester with one of the coastal boats. So it seems you'll get a shorter penance than you bargained for.'

'Beddgelert, eh!' said Cadfael, pondering. 'And left there on foot, it seems. Where do you suppose he was bound, Hugh? Clynnog or Caergybi, and oversea to Ireland?'

'Why not into the cells of the *clas* at Beddgelert?' Hugh suggested, smiling into his wine. 'After all your buffeting around the world, you came into a like harbour.'

Cadfael stroked his cheeks thoughtfully. 'No, not that. Not yet! He would not think he had paid enough for that, yet.'

Hugh gave a brisk bark of laughter, set down his cup, and got to his feet, clapping Cadfael heartily on the shoulder. 'I'd better be off. Every time I come near you I find myself compounding a felony.'

'But it may end like that, some day,' said Cadfael seriously.

'In a felony?' Hugh looked back from the doorway, still smiling.

'In a vocation. More than one has gone from the one to the other, Hugh, and been profitable to the world in between.'

It was in the afternoon of the following day that Edwy and Edwin presented themselves at the door of the workshop, in their best, very well brushed and trimmed, and both looking slightly shocked into unusually discreet behaviour, at least at first. This subdued demeanour rendered them so alike that Cadfael had to look closely for the brown eyes and the hazel to be certain which of them was which. Their thanks were cheerfully and heartily expressed, their contentment had made total peace between them for the time being.

'This ceremonial finery,' said Cadfael, eyeing the pair of them with cautious benevolence, 'can hardly be for me.'

'The lord abbot sent for me,' explained Edwin, his eyes rounding in awe at the recollection. 'My mother made me put on my best. *He* only came with me out of curiosity, he wasn't invited.'

'And *he* fell over his feet in the doorway,' Edwy countered promptly, 'and blushed red as a cardinal's hat.'

'I did not!'

'You did! You're doing it now.' And indeed he was; the very suggestion produced the flooding crimson.

'So Abbot Radulfus sent for you,' said Cadfael. Clearing up unfinished business, he thought, and briskly, too. 'And what did you think of our new abbot?'

Neither of these two was going to own to being impressed. They exchanged a considering glance, and Edwy said: 'He was very fair. But I'm not sure I'd want to be a novice here.'

'He said,' reported Edwin, 'that it would be matter for discussion with my mother, and with the lawmen, but clearly the manor can't belong to the abbey, the agreement is void, and if the will is proven, and the Earl of Chester confirms his assent as overlord, Mallilie will be mine, and until I'm of age the abbey will leave a steward there to manage it, and the lord abbot himself will be my guardian.'

'And what did you say to that?'

'I thanked him and said yes, very heartily. What else? Who knows better how to run a manor? I can learn all the art from them. And we are to return there, my mother and I, as soon as we wish, and that will be very soon, if we don't get more snows.' Edwin's eager brightness, though not dimmed, nevertheless grew very solemn. 'Brother Cadfael, it was a terrible thing about Meurig. Hard to understand . . .'

Yes, for the young very hard, and almost impossible to forgive. But where there had been liking and trust there still remained a residue of unquenchable warmth, incompatible with the revulsion and horror he felt for a poisoner.

'I wouldn't have let him have Mallilie without a fight,' said Edwin, dourly intent on absolute honesty. 'But if he'd won, I don't think I'd have grudged it to him. And if I'd won . . . I don't know! *He* would never have shared it, would he? But I'm glad he got away! If that's wicked, I can't help it. I am glad!'

If it was wicked, he had company in his fault, but Cadfael said nothing of that.

'Brother Cadfael . . . As soon as we're home again in Mallilie, I mean to go and visit Ifor ap Morgan. He did give me the kiss when I asked him. I can be a kind of grandson.'

'Thank God I didn't make the mistake of suggesting it to him, thought Cadfael devoutly. There's nothing the young hate and resent so much as to be urged to a good act, when they've already made the virtuous resolve on their own account.

'That's very well thought of,' he said warmly. 'He'll be glad of you. If you take Edwy with you to his house, better teach him how to tell you apart, his eyes may not be quite so sharp as mine.'

They both grinned at that. Edwy said: '*He* still owes me for the buffeting I got on his account, and the night I spent in prison here. I mean to have a foot in the door of Mallilie as often as I please on the strength of that.'

'I had *two* nights of it,' objected Edwin smartly, 'and in a much worse place.'

'*You*? Never a bruise on you, and in clover there with Hugh Beringar looking after you!'

And thereupon Edwin jabbed Edwy smartly in the middle with a stiff forefinger, and Edwy hooked a knee under Edwin's, and spilled him to the floor, both laughing. Cadfael looked on tolerantly for a while, and then grasped two separate handfuls of thick, curling hair, and plucked them apart. They rolled clear and came obligingly to their feet, grinning broadly, and looking much less immaculate than before.

'You are a pestilential pair, and I wish Ifor ap Morgan joy of you,' said Cadfael, but very complacently. 'You're the lord of a manor now, young Edwin, or will be when you're of age. Then you'd better be studying your responsibilities. Is that the kind of example uncle should set before nephew?'

Edwin stopped shaking and dusting himself into order with abrupt gravity, and stood erect, large-eyed. 'I have been thinking of my duties, truly. There's much I don't yet know, and have to learn, but I told the lord abbot . . . I don't like it, I never liked it, that my stepfather entered suit against Aelfric, and made him villein, when he thought himself born free, as his fathers had been before him. I asked him if I could free a man, or if I had to wait until I was of age, and got seisin myself. And he said certainly it could be done at will, and he would be sponsor for me. I am going to see Aelfric a free man. And I think . . . that is, he and Aldith . . . '

'*I* told him,' said Edwy, giving himself a brief shake, like a dog, and settling back at ease on the bench, 'that Aldith likes Aelfric, and once he's free they will certainly marry, and Aelfric is lettered, and knows Mallilie, and will make a splendid steward, when the abbey hands over the manor.

'*You told me*! I knew very well she liked him, only he wouldn't say how much he liked her. And what do you know about manors and stewards, you prentice carpenter?'

'More than you'll ever know about wood, and carving, and craftsmanship, you practice baron!'

They were at it again, locked in a bear's hug, propped in the corner of the bench, Edwy with a grip on Edwin's russet thatch, Edwin with fingers braced into Edwy's ribs, tickling him into convulsions of laughter. Cadfael hoisted the pair of them in his arms, and heaved them towards the door.

'Out! Take your cantrips off these premises, where they hardly belong. There, go and find a bear-pit!' Even to himself he sounded foolishly proud and proprietary.

At the door they fell apart with bewildering ease and neatness, and both turned to beam at him. Edwin remembered to plead, in penitent haste: 'Brother Cadfael, will you please come and see my mother before we leave? She begs you!'

'I will,' said Cadfael, helpless to say otherwise, 'I will, surely!'

He watched them go, out towards the great court and the gatehouse, again wrangling amiably, arms round each other in ambiguous embrace and assault. Strange creatures at this age, capable of heroic loyalty and gallantry under pressure, earnest in pursuing serious ends, and reverting to the battle-play of pups from one litter when all was serene in their world.

Cadfael turned back into his workshop, and barred the door against all the rest of the world, even Brother Mark. It was very quiet in there, and very dim with the darkness of the timber walls and the faint blue smoke from the brazier. A home within a home to him now, and all he wanted. It was well over, as Hugh Beringar had said, with no more waste than was inevitable. Edwin would have his manor, Aelfric would have his freedom, a secure future, good ground for loosening his tongue and declaring himself to Aldith; and no doubt, if he proved obstinate about it, she would find the means of prompting him. Brother Rhys would have a long gossip about his king, and his little flask of the right spirit, and hazy memory would film over the gap left by a lost great-nephew. Ifor ap Morgan would have

543

a grief of his own, never mentioned, but a hope of his own, too, and a substitute grandchild only a short ride away. And Meurig, somewhere at large in the world, had the long penance before him, and good need of other men's prayers. He would not want for Cadfael's.

He settled himself at ease on the bench where the boys had wrestled and laughed, and put up his feet comfortably. He wondered if he could legitimately plead that he was still confined within the enclave until Richildis left for Mallilie, and decided that that would be cowardly only after he had decided that in any case he had no intention of doing it.

She was, after all, a very attractive woman, even now, and her gratitude would be a very pleasant indulgence; there was even a decided lure in the thought of a conversation that must inevitably begin to have: 'Do you remember. . . .?' as its constant refrain. Yes, he would go. It was not often he was able to enjoy an orgy of shared remembrances.

In a week or two, after all, the entire household would be removing to Mallilie, all those safe miles away. He was not likely to see much of Richildis after that. Brother Cadfael heaved a deep sigh that might have been of regret, but might equally well have been of relief.

Ah, well! Perhaps it was all for the best!